WILD FOREST ROSE

Wild Forest Rose

A Novel

Ken Fulmer

Treerise Press

First published in 2025 by Treerise Press

Wild Forest Rose Copyright © 2025 by Ken Fulmer All rights reserved

Scripture quotations are taken from the *Holy Bible*, New Living Translation, copyright ©1996, 2004, 2015 by Tyndale House Foundation. Used by permission of Tyndale House Publishers, Carol Stream, Illinois 60188. All rights reserved.

www.kenfulmer.com

Publisher's Note:

This is a work of fiction. Names, characters, places, and incidents either are the products of the author's imagination or are used fictitiously, and any resemblance to actual persons, living or dead, business establishments, events, or locales is entirely coincidental.

Manufactured in the United States of America

The Library of Congress has cataloged the hardcover edition as follows: Fulmer, Ken, 1969—

Wild Forest Rose : A Novel / Ken Fulmer

Library of Congress Control Number: TXU002445999

ISBN: 978-1-955323-12-3 (hardcover)

ISBN: 978-1-955323-13-0 (trade paperback)

ISBN: 978-1-955323-14-7 (ebook)

ISBN: 978-1-955323-15-4 (audio)

Without limiting the rights under copyright reserved above, no part of this publication may be reproduced, stored in or introduced into a retrieval system, or transmitted, in any form or by any means (electronic, mechanical, photocopying, recording, or otherwise), without the prior written permission of both the copyright owner and the above publisher of the book.

Wild Forest Rose

A Novel

Ken Fulmer

Treerise Press

First published in 2025 by Treerise Press

Wild Forest Rose Copyright © 2025 by Ken Fulmer All rights reserved

Scripture quotations are taken from the *Holy Bible*, New Living Translation, copyright ©1996, 2004, 2015 by Tyndale House Foundation. Used by permission of Tyndale House Publishers, Carol Stream, Illinois 60188. All rights reserved.

www.kenfulmer.com

Publisher's Note:

This is a work of fiction. Names, characters, places, and incidents either are the products of the author's imagination or are used fictitiously, and any resemblance to actual persons, living or dead, business establishments, events, or locales is entirely coincidental.

Manufactured in the United States of America

The Library of Congress has cataloged the hardcover edition as follows: Fulmer, Ken, 1969—

Wild Forest Rose : A Novel / Ken Fulmer

Library of Congress Control Number: TXU002445999

ISBN: 978-1-955323-12-3 (hardcover)

ISBN: 978-1-955323-13-0 (trade paperback)

ISBN: 978-1-955323-14-7 (ebook)

ISBN: 978-1-955323-15-4 (audio)

Without limiting the rights under copyright reserved above, no part of this publication may be reproduced, stored in or introduced into a retrieval system, or transmitted, in any form or by any means (electronic, mechanical, photocopying, recording, or otherwise), without the prior written permission of both the copyright owner and the above publisher of the book.

For my Family

We are Seven

—A simple Child,
That lightly draws its breath,
And feels its life in every limb,
What should it know of death?

—William Wordsworth

ONE

Psalm 1:1
Oh, the joys of those who do not
follow the advice of the wicked,
or stand around with sinners,
or join in with mockers.

July 1893

Nathan Marsh sat alone on a green upholstered bench, his dour bones rattling in time with the dismal locomotive. His cares hid in the country scenes outside his window, where shaded valleys sloped lonely from thicket to thicket, winding away from the haunts of men. As he slumped into the contours of the bench, his thoughts tumbled backward to an era long gone, when his spirit was fresh and lovely, and his boyish strength grew with each threshold crossed. He pulled back from his recollections, and his eyes rose to meet the celestial city where he once hoped to dwell. Passing clouds mesmerized him; their woven strands pulled apart and shrank into unfeigned nothingness, exposing a great despair.

His city pure had vanished, its light put out by worldly hands.

The porter's feet kicked at the floor as he shuffled down the aisle, and his stony face demanded tickets from each weary passenger. He paused, noting the lateness of the hour, and his eyes fell over Nathan. In furious angst, he whispered *hurry*. Nathan's hand grasped through his pockets frantically, took hold of the ticket, and thrust it outward. The porter studied it and pulled it close to his abdomen. He continued to the next row.

A rosy-faced man appeared from the rear of the train and tapped Nathan on the shoulder. "I hate to be a bother, sir." Nathan caught a tilt of desperation in his voice. "Are you Dr. Marsh of St. Louis?"

"Who makes the inquiry?"

The man swayed in the railcar's half-light. "My ribs have ached for the last hundred miles. Would you mind if I rest?" He hesitated. "My delightful wife counsels me never to sit at a piano uninvited."

Nathan pointed to the empty seat across the aisle. "I suppose you'll ask for a free consultation. I must warn you, the level of effort you'll receive will be commensurate with your payment."

The swaying man's rotund body plopped onto the adjacent bench, and he fell into a friendly talk. "Leland Prentiss is the name, and I write for the Globe-Democrat." Nathan exchanged a glance with a woman sitting behind him; when she saw him look at her, she smiled. "If you would be so kind, please describe your formative years and your marriage to Catherine Belmont. From all accounts, your union was front page news."

"Our season has long ago faded," said Nathan with a faint smile. "These days, I live as a besotted relic. I am hardly interesting."

The locomotive gave a cursing whistle. A gruff town approached.

New passengers replaced old, diverting Nathan's attention.

The train surged, and sweet clover filled the air. "Our readers yearn for a romantic tale," said Leland, unwilling to give up his position. "You don't yet understand this keen insight, but our thoughts must elevate to a higher plane, where we remember things past and imagine things yet to come."

"Dare I ask, what are the things to come?"

"We are all orphans in one sense or another, and we wander like deer through life's meadows rich with corn, we climb green-walled hills, and we wind down into pleasant dales, solitary in our endeavors. Rarely do we encounter a worthy companion. Our hearts search here and there and call out for a romance more glorious than the glistering sun. Love often eludes us mortals, but for you and Catherine, it dropped from the sky."

"You may wax poetic, sir, but my life has not been one of wild worship. The sun has beat fierce upon my head since boyhood."

An unbroken silence fell over the railcar as the train reached the immense and stifling outer limits of New York. Leland pressed Catherine's eventual desertion, threading the needle, obliged to thread it again and again, his editor unwilling to let the events of 1883 rest undisturbed.

The evening sun sunk low. Along the aisle, the tread of feet lulled.

A wide-shouldered man appeared from nowhere and shoved Leland's corpulent face into a window, and his large-handed partner grabbed Nathan by his coat lapels and jerked him to a standing position. Something hard walloped the back of Nathan's head as he called for the authorities.

His mind fell to dizziness. His legs and knees wobbled.

The men dragged him down the aisle and onto the platform.

The group thudded down several steps and marched around the station to a waiting cab. Nathan attempted to call out again, but the words would no longer form in his throat. Wide-shouldered man shoved him into a black Quinby carriage; his partner climbed aboard and slammed the door. The carriage retched forward as the driver whipped his team of trembling horses. Thrown backward against the plush leather cushion, Nathan succumbed to unconsciousness, once more lost to a dreamland of boyhood innocence.

An hour later, the tips of his shoes dragged along planks of a narrow walkway, as barefaced moonlight sparkled on the water, reflecting brazenly against a few desolate sloops tied to wooden pilings, their ropes creaking as they loosened and pulled taut again. Wind yanked at Nathan's hair as they approached a steamship which had parked itself alongside the dock.

A shadowy, stern-faced man puffed on a cigarette.

Large-handed man shoved Nathan and guided his arms as they marched. Stern-faced man flicked his cigarette against the iron hull; it plunged into the murky waters of the Long Island Sound. "I am Special Agent Fremont Lacy with the Secret Service." He waltzed up the gangplank and halted, looking back at Nathan. "Won't you join us in the salon?" Without waiting for a reply, Agent Lacy led upward to the crew deck, along the gangway of the 200-foot *Oneida*, and then downward to the lower decks.

Agent Lacy opened the salon door and beckoned his prisoner to enter the nebulous domain. Nathan discarded any notion of retreat.

A butler announced his entry. "Doc-tor Nathan Marsh of St. Louis."

Covered in oak and fine tapestries, the stylish salon stretched across *Oneida's* twenty-four-foot breadth. Distinguished members of the White House staff and the presidential cabinet filled the smoky thickness with sack jackets and Van Dyke mustaches. Servants awaited their command.

"I knew your father," said a temperate but jaded voice. The crowd halved to reveal the president of the United States, who peered from behind a cherry desk. "He helped me untangle a scandalous knot in the early '80s."

The president blinked across the tight space.

"Her name was Maria Halpin." Nathan realized at last who had summoned him. "And you are Grover Cleveland."

"You have an avid memory and a canny perception. I have long owed Samuel an immeasurable debt, which I would like to recompense."

"Your stooges dumped Maria into an asylum." Nathan spoke to the president with a gathering indignation. "A child blessed your brief accord. His name was Oscar Cleveland until he was adopted by another family."

A pall fell over the room.

Even the footmen gasped at such impertinence.

"Like you, she was an alcoholic. Maria had it out for me in the worst way after our relationship ended. It was all I knew to do. I'm not proud of that period in my life, as I'm sure the last decade has not gratified you."

"Point taken," Nathan said.

"Since then, I've returned to my father's Presbyterian roots, and the Good Lord has selected me to become a modern version of King David. With the help of the men in this room, I will navigate our people through uncharted economic waters. A great recession descends upon us like a howling tempest, the likes of which our nation has never known. War is inevitable if we cannot repeal the Sherman Act and avoid a depression."

"Politicians promise the moon, but deliver hot air."

A high-pitched voice flung itself from the corner, seeking to embarrass.

"This man knows nothing about leadership." John Belmont was a noted cotton press magnate from St. Louis, a benefactor to the president, and worst of all, Catherine's father. "Brothels shield a man from harsh realities."

The president looked coarsely at Belmont and turned toward Nathan with a renewed zeal. "An unyielding animosity exits between the two of you. We cannot hope to repair your relationship during this meeting."

"Our feud goes back to my teenage years, Mr. President. I doubt even a man of your stature could solve it."

Cleveland's voice shallowed. "You strike me as a man who unravels complex problems. Am I correct?" Nathan nodded his agreement. "I don't share your scientific prowess, but I've observed you over the past twenty years, both your rise to prominence in your field and your decline after tragedy. You've lost sight of the Lord and who you are, Dr. Marsh. It's understandable. Your grief must have been unbearable."

A proper reply eluded Nathan. "I'm no longer a believer."

"So I've gathered."

Dark circles gave Cleveland's eyes a cavernous appearance. His hand movements were lethargic, his posture bent and saggy.

"Let's get to the point," Nathan said. "Why am I here?"

"To remove a tumor from my mouth. This will be a private procedure."

"Why me? You have well-trained surgeons."

Cleveland's eyes rose to meet the man standing to his right. "This is Dr. Joseph Bryant, my personal physician and a good friend. He diagnosed the tumor as cancerous." His eyebrows arched. "What did you call it?"

"I said it was an unruly tenant, worthy of immediate eviction."

The president's lips drew apart into a forced smile. "As it causes me to walk the floor at night, I would agree with my doctor's assessment. Few in Washington know about this activity. Most believe this to be a four-day fishing trip, a relaxing vacation before the floor fight begins."

"It's a risky surgery, and you'll lose a few front teeth."

Cleveland's hand flashed to his mouth and then fell slack. He gestured his understanding and his commitment. "I've been so advised."

"You could lose your life as well."

The president got himself up and moved toward Nathan.

"Regain your childlike trust in the Lord, the reverent understanding of His presence and authority in heaven and also in this earthly realm. You must perform the surgery as a first step in your reclamation."

"If the surgery fails and you pass away, what happens to me?"

Nathan's belly quailed at the question.

"I'm an optimistic man by nature, Dr. Marsh, and I am aware of the task the Lord has set before me. My work is not yet complete, so I will not pass away, but I will survive your operation and continue my fight."

"I'll ask again. If you expire, what happens to me?"

Cleveland's eyes opened wide, and he grinned.

Nathan held his breath. An inner voice begged to go.

The president nodded to Agent Lacy, who stood guarding the single exit. "This man will feed your body to the fishes in the windswept Atlantic." Nathan had a gruesome vision of his own demise. The open sea would provide no escape. "Further, you'll be responsible for the death of Leland Prentiss, the good-natured newspaperman who you met on the train. He has a family, you know. Although his children are grown, his wife has an undisclosed health problem which is bound to occupy his time in the coming months. Please don't deprive her of his close attention."

"I wouldn't dream of it."

"I hope my words convey the urgency of this matter. Failure will not be a consideration." He smiled. "Do we understand one another?"

Nathan looked in all directions, and his feet instinctively moved toward the door. Agent Lacy blocked his path. He turned Nathan's body around and shoved him toward the president of the United States.

"I see why you wouldn't burden your private physician with this task."

"He and I go back many years." The president's hand dropped onto Nathan's shoulder. "You are at the end of your rope, and one more mistake will end your life. Might as well end it here."

Nathan had appreciated the world and everything in it as a boy. Now he was fuzzy, distracted, an inebriated daydreamer. He glanced at John Belmont, who fiddled with his hat. "What do you think?"

Belmont peeked at President Cleveland and then spoke. "First, you have nothing to lose. As with soldiers in battle, consider yourself a dead man standing; the Reaper approaches us all with grim intentions, as they say. However, if you proceed with the surgery and succeed, you may resume your life, such as it is. I'm sure our brothels will celebrate."

"My soul blazed whenever your daughter entered a room." Nathan looked about him as if the past were once again within reach.

"Every suitor did likewise."

"I sought to make her proud of me. Everything marriage may apportion, we achieved, including finances, material possessions, and children." Nathan's voice intonated his heartbreak. "You were against our pairing from the start and made no bones about it."

Belmont took off his bowler, studied it, and put it back on.

"Losing Catherine ended all my aspirations for this life. For your wicked efforts to break us apart, I hope you have repented."

"I make no claim as the source of your debauchery," Belmont said. "Your choices have been your own."

The president's face softened. "I notice your quivering hands, Dr. Marsh. You've been consuming alcohol for days as you rode the Central line, and now delirium tremens have set in. Is my layman's diagnosis correct?"

"Yes," said Nathan, licking his parched lips. "Billy Bones or John Raffles. I'll let you choose which scoundrel you like best."

Cleveland's butler delivered a glass which held two fingers of whiskey. Nathan downed the contents, toasting Cleveland's infallible principles and his unfortunate character. The butler delivered a second glass and a look of pity. Nathan rubbed his nose and downed its contents, slipping listlessly into his usual routine. He handed the empty glass to the butler.

"I'll need another."

Belmont fumed. "Will you allow him to become intoxicated?"

The president's eyes fell on his wealthy patron. "As with all of God's devout servants, my constant endeavor is to make progress in the study of His law. I know God is favorable only to those who devote themselves to divine truth. As corruption prevails in the world, I separate myself from the ungodly while still maintaining my position as leader of this nation. It's a fine line for me to tread as formidable and feeble men alike willingly and thoughtlessly throw themselves into the snares of Satan."

His tone carried a fierce resolve.

Belmont's fingertips skimmed along his jawline. "You are a man of moral conduct, and your tireless labors are legendary."

Nathan consumed the contents of a third glass.

Cleveland's voice lowered an octave. "As such, I believe I understand the good doctor. The potential for greatness remains locked inside him, untapped and ready for release on the Lord's timeline, a chronology we often misunderstand. If today he requires an entire bottle to perform this daring operation, then I will not judge. For tomorrow his soul may cry out for Jesus and once cleansed, he may serve the Lord as I do."

Several men gasped in unison. Collective voices rose to a fever pitch.

Nathan set the glass on a tray without affectation. He remained silent for several minutes, growing his confidence. The pathway through the mouth was fraught with treachery; a dose of ether would give him just under two hours to work a miracle.

The president resumed his position behind the desk. "You must take risks in order to reach your destiny, Dr. Marsh. Let others be jealous. We possess a stronger constitution than other men might imagine." A pause followed his remark. "You'll perform the surgery, and I'll survive it. On this, you have my word as a gentleman."

Suddenly, medicine seemed like a despicable occupation. Nathan called for another drink and then yet another until he wore a bright, joyful smile.

"What's it going to be, you drunken fool?" asked Belmont violently.

Nathan finished his fifth drink before responding, holding up a finger to ward off Belmont's intrusions. Spotless bliss had not yet found him.

At long last, President Cleveland cut in. "Have you made your choice?"

Nathan handed the glass to the butler, who smirked and spun around.

"Give me one more drink, and I'll consider your offer."

Two

Psalm 2:1
Why are the nations so angry?
Why do they waste their time with futile plans?

Daisy Lawrence dug through her bag and retrieved a photograph. Her sore back pressed against the wooden bench, and her lonely fingers rubbed along each scar of the oak frame which scarcely held together. She would have been less blue if the smooth faced girl stared at her from within the oval, cream-colored boundary. Instead, the girl forever peered over the side of a cliff at the rocks seventy feet below. Her expressionless face and timeworn eyes conveyed a forbidden and merciless intention, one which would be remembered and reconsidered for time immemorial. The phantom in the photograph had crossed the icy Atlantic to Liverpool, and she both comforted and provoked during freshman year in Paris. The girl later rode the train to Vienna inside a handbag, sharing a sleeper and the trying ordeals to follow. Since her own repatriation, Daisy maintained her distance from other Americans, withdrawing from thorny conversations, preferring to search the girl's pensive eyes for answers rather than ask for help. The complex maze created by her mistakes begged for her attention, and effigies ran through her mind in the darkness, interrupting her sleep. A curative must soon find Daisy, or the exquisite rocks below the cliff would call her home. The penalty for such rebellion would be a second death.

Perhaps she might finally see her sister, Rose, if only for a moment.

Daisy said a silent prayer and received a word in her spirit.

Cry out to Jesus in your agony, and He will hear you.

She deposited the picture frame into her bag and retrieved a button hook, recalling her mother's admonition never to bend while wearing a corset, as it could deform the front busk. Patrice would never know of the flexibility, the curviness, or the silky texture of the Leoty corset, a popular fashion statement Daisy had adopted while in Paris. The eight o'clock engine had arrived thirty minutes ago, spilling its passengers across the Union Depot platform and onto the grass surrounding her bench. With watery eyes, she watched their loving embraces and careless demonstrations of a flowing joy she had never known. The station since cleared of travelers, and she was once again alone, save for the cabs aligned at the curb. Daisy threw a look at the drivers, calculating the likelihood of a confrontation. Satisfied with the distance and their lack of interest, she removed her boots and placed them beside her feet on the turf. She brushed her skirt, removing bits of grass. The warm breeze carried a whisper of rain.

A bearded stranger sat on an adjacent bench. He offered her a wide smile as she fanned herself, and then burst into uproarious laughter, pressing his palms to his cheeks and oscillating with mirth. Every so often, he repeated the line, half under his breath and half out loud. "I cannot believe it happened." He looked her in the eye. "You won't believe it happened." His hand slammed the armrest. "No one in the world will believe it happened!"

Her eyes searched for help before returning to him.

"Are you quite mad, sir?"

"No, but I'll need extra training to handle the stench emanating from your feet, madam." He grabbed a flask from his inside coat pocket, opened the cap, and took a swig. "No offense intended, of course."

His sudden breach of decorum took her by surprise. Daisy gave a small yelp and put a hand over her mouth as she burst into unexpected laughter.

"I suppose you've got me there. I walked from the park."

"Which one? Forest?"

Her ankles ached from the three-mile hike. "Tower Grove."

"Why not take a trolley? Surely one must have been available."

Her hand rubbed sweat from the back of her neck. "I'm far too exhausted to recite the details of my reasoning." She forced a smile and clutched her fawn-colored gloves tensely, still unconvinced of her welfare.

He held out his right hand, watching it tremble, and let it fall to his lap. "I departed the eight o'clock train some time ago, and sat inside the station in dutiful introspection, meditating on my next move. After getting nowhere, I ventured outside, hoping the fresh air would induce action. So far, the night's humidity and your pleasant company have kept me here."

His quandary intrigued her. "What is at issue?"

He leaned toward her and held up a thumb. "Number one. Whether I have enough fortitude to visit my favorite brothel. Sheila is wonderful, I might add." He extended an index finger. "Number two. I could end this spree and chase nightmares in my bed." He leaned into the bench and sighed. "I must admit, my journey has left me bone-tired."

"Select the latter option." Daisy's body tingled. "You look like Dorian Gray's ghastly portrait, if you don't mind my impertinence." She hesitated. "A drunkard never prospers, and the Lake of Fire burns eternally."

He took another gulp from his flask and tested his right hand once more. "Quite right, madam." He twisted the cap shut. "On that glum note, I must make a romantic inquiry. It seems you'll answer honestly."

Had he found an article about her in the Globe-Democrat? Perhaps her name had resurfaced in a Chicago or New York paper.

"Sir, my virtue remains intact." Her voice dropped low and shy. "Despite what you may have read, an unsullied woman sits before you."

"I have no doubts about your character."

Perhaps he would dredge her past. "Are you a journalist?"

His eyebrows arched. "It's a curious question. I met a newspaperman on the Central line, but I am not employed in such a capacity."

"Did this newspaperman mention a woman's name?"

He sighed. "She was from *my* past, not yours."

"A lady must take care when discussing such topics." She looked about the yard and detected no journalists nearby. "As the matter is now settled between us, I will allow *one* question. Please choose wisely."

"What sort of fellow might strike your fancy?"

She was relieved to have a worthy answer.

"In school, our teachers taught us to petition God for the well-being of our future husbands and counseled us to keep our purity of innocence. I took their advice to heart, but sadly, a husband has not manifested."

Union Depot's gleaming lights put a flame on Daisy's every move, making her feel like a vaudeville performer, but they also shined on the man beside her. For a mature gentleman, his face was handsome and his bodily features were pleasing. She found herself drawn to his free spirited manner, so she recited Psalm 2:2-3. "The kings of the earth prepare for battle; the rulers plot together against the Lord and against his anointed one. 'Let us break their chains,' they cry, 'and free ourselves from slavery to God.'"

He shifted heavily on his bench. "You appreciate men of power and influence, the type with war in their heart."

"My husband must be strong and vigilant and compassionate," she said, her eyes narrowing. "The ungodly are not so, but seek to break their chains, freeing themselves from subservience to the Lord."

"Might I hear another verse?"

Her voice sang as she recited Psalm 2:10-12. "Now then, you kings, act wisely! Be warned, you rulers of the earth! Serve the Lord with reverent fear and rejoice with trembling. Submit to God's royal son, or he will become angry, and you will be destroyed in the midst of all your activities—for his anger flares up in an instant. But what joy for all who take refuge in him!"

"I must ransack my attic at once," the man said. "Several moth-eaten Bibles lie there in wait, ready to pounce on unsuspecting travelers."

She laughed and blushed. "You misquote proverbs, sir, but I give you ample credit for inventiveness." Forgetting herself, she confided in him. "My father owns a winery, and I have recently agreed to become his storefront manager." A wave of melancholy went over her. "After ten years in Europe, it seems the last fraction of my childhood has come and gone." Daisy fixed her attention on the cab drivers, drawing confidence from them. She smoothed her blonde curls with her hand and gently settled her sleeves, her movements effortless and graceful in the style of a lady.

"Boredom makes fools of us all, madam."

"We were never idle in Paris," she said with haste. "After university, I assisted a small group of neurologists whose work has advanced the field of experimental psychology. I accompanied one of those gentlemen to Vienna."

"You respect the man you followed."

"Oh, I do," she said, beaming with delight. "I first worked at a rather large hospital in Paris, which has become an asylum. It's called La Salpêtrière. My mentor, Jean-Martin Charcot, is one of the finest men I've ever known, but the administrators were another matter entirely. I grew tired of their bureaucracy, so I left to further Sigmund Freud's burgeoning practice in Vienna. With my help, he's had brilliant success with hysteria patients, alleviating many of their symptoms through hypnosis."

"I don't believe you," said the stranger after a moment.

"Concerning what matter?"

"The reason for your homecoming." He looked around with concealed annoyance. "Your face gleamed like these electric lights when speaking about Freud and your asylum patients, but mere mention of your father's winery caused your voice to hesitate and your limbs to slacken."

He read her well. "How shall I explain myself?"

"I find sincerity the best avenue."

"Alright, I'll say it this way." She tapped the wood with her fingers. "Complications arose, influencing my sudden withdrawal."

"There is a different man in the picture, another Dorian Gray," he said with a profound air. "Your use of language masks a heartbreak."

"It's a sordid business, a story for less public surroundings."

"I find you ironic, but I doubt you'll see it as I do."

He gave her a reticent look, which piqued her interest.

"I put little faith in a stranger's discovery, but you are a different sort, and I will allow for the rare possibility of surprise." She looked at him in silence, preparing for his moral indictment. Who was this man to see anything in her at all? Others found her fervent and indelicate. They took great amusement at her expense, implying she had gone feral like a cat in heat, when her only crime had been a naïve interest in saving a wretched man from himself. She had since paid dearly for her efforts.

"Hysteria patients often suffer paralysis. Is this not correct?"

She nodded.

"Here is my summation. While helping your hysterics in Vienna, you engaged in a relationship with some dastardly fellow who drove you away from your European calling, leaving those poor souls abandoned."

"With full regret, I must agree." Her heart froze and then pounded. "Departing from them filled me with a shame I cannot conquer."

"I see."

What else did he see? She signaled her curiosity.

"You work in your father's winery, greeting trustful Johns, some of them former hysteria patients, no doubt. I'll bet they arrange transport across the frigid Atlantic for the honor and privilege of partaking of your boozy concoctions. Nothing better than self-imposed paralysis, I say." He took a swig. "What would Mr. Freud say about that bit of sadistic irony?"

"He'd ask about my childhood, which I refuse to discuss with anyone."

Their eyes met, and he smiled. "Judging by your diminutive stature, your cares are likely to melt away after two glasses of wine."

"My sorrows run deeper than the bottom of a bottle."

"Ah, yes, some days, it takes three glasses. No hypnosis needed."

Her thoughts detached as her eyes searched the station. Finding no other hopeful beloved, she returned to him. "I drink no alcohol."

"The irony never ceases with you." His eyes widened. "How marvelous."

His candor gave her pause. A gentleman should not take such liberties. "Our customers know what they're being served, and why they need it."

The oppressive heat had consumed Daisy and soaked her chemise with sweat. As was her custom, she withdrew from their conversation and turned her gaze to the sweltering darkness above the road, regarding it intently. A cool bath and a soft bed awaited her at the Laclede Hotel.

"Melancholics to the awful end, are they?" he asked, unwilling to let her spirit wander. "In that case, I must hop on a fast-moving train and partake of your products. I'm always good for a laugh and a crippling evening."

Her back pressed onto the bench as she chuckled. Such a mischievous and gifted man had entered her life in Paris. "What is your name, sir?"

"Nathan Marsh, a surgeon to the downtrodden and a drunkard of the highest order." His voice died away, and she heard the beating of her heart.

At some moment in her youth, his name had made itself known to her, but the *when* and the *where* hid from her recollection.

"Glad to make your acquaintance," she said.

He pretended to tip his hat and grinned. "Same to you, madam."

Although he filled his speech with a gracious and worldly intelligence, his witty banter masked a sadness and a pain which was both remarkable and unmistakable. He was much like the man who taught her to love on the banks of the Seine. Daisy raised her eyes to meet the twinkling stars, wistful for lost weekends spent on a cozy blanket in the shade. It was there she had first experienced life in all its fullness, and the great joy of living had fled from her soon afterward. If she could only go back to the spot and reunite with her abiding youth, all would be made right, and regret would fall from grace. She must know more about Nathan Marsh.

"So, kind sir, what is the nature of your arrival this evening?"

"I operated on the president of the United States."

"You mock me, and I would beg you to cease at once."

"Madam, I remain at your service," he said, feigning indignation.

His roguish wit would go unpunished on one condition. To regain his favor, he must tell her the outrageous tale, including every particular.

After his eyes whirled about in obvious remembrance, he regained his composure and removed his bowler. He tapped his hat against the wooden bench to shake off the dust and then took another swig, musing for a moment. "Happy to, madam, but first I'll need your name."

"Daisy Lawrence."

"Should I hail you a cab, Miss Lawrence?"

"My father will be along any minute."

A sound like gunshots startled her, and she leapt from her seat. Rockets rose above Tower Grove's treetops and momentarily burned luminous, glowing into patterns which danced across the heavens.

"They're just fireworks. It's the Fourth of July."

Her cheeks flushed red. "The explosions frighten me."

He changed the subject before she could speak again. "Your mixed accent is intriguing, but I cannot rightly place it." As she sat down, he rested the underside of his sleeve on the back of the bench. "I detect some French in your voice, but I also hear a faint hint of German and some tiny bits of English or Scottish. Are you American by birth?"

His interrogative question required a lengthy explanation. She was born and raised in Pollard, a lifeless village on the banks of the Missouri river. Her parents, Pierre and Patrice, had emigrated from Paris just after their wedding. When Daisy came of age, Pierre expected her to attend college in their native city as a matter of family honor. Their surname was Lorens before their arrival in Philadelphia, but the couple desired to blend in, so Pierre changed the name to sound more English. Both Lawrence and Lorens originated from the root Latin word, *Laurentius*, which meant "the man from Laurentum." She breathlessly fell silent.

He nodded his understanding.

"You don't sound like a Frenchman's daughter."

"Dare I ask whom I sound like?"

He pondered his response for a few moments.

"Please don't keep me in suspense, Dr. Marsh."

"Your voice is reminiscent of a carnival barker I knew in New York. She could scream paint off the side of a house."

Daisy snorted and pressed a hand against her chest. "Lewis and Clark should have brought me on their landmark expedition to the Pacific," she said excitedly. "My gruff utterances would have scared away the grizzlies."

"Clever women are so refreshing," he said in startled surprise.

Feeling lightheaded, Daisy begged him to continue his story, as she was sure there would be many embellishments. He recounted his heroic feat of bravery, and she voiced her wonderment, unable to comprehend how a disheveled and whiskey-soaked man could perform under such pressure. He must have been terrified by the surety of a savorless death.

"The writer I met on the train to New York," he said. "Leland was an affable fellow, and I hoped to visit with him again on the return trip, but it was not to be. They offered him a better position in Chicago, and he moved there. It's what I was told when the agent dropped me at Union Station. I took another train from Chicago and ended up on this bench."

"I sense you'll soon broaden your practice." She stood and whisked her skirt from side to side, creating a slight breeze through her petticoat. "Word spreads of such things, and talented men stand apart."

She pressed her toes into the grass.

"They assured me no one would ever know about the surgery, as it was to remain a secret for the ages." He hesitated. "And if any expansion is to occur in my medical practice, it won't be soon. My assistant quit two weeks ago, claiming my sporadic payments would send her to the poorhouse on Arsenal Road. Jane's performance was substandard, so the loss is minimal." He smiled. "In my estimation, she belongs in the building next door."

"Another poorhouse?"

He shook his head. "The city asylum."

Nathan eyed Daisy, looking her up and down.

Did he think her mad along with Jane? Perhaps Daisy crossed a line by shaking her skirt, but the night was hot, and she had walked so far. The good doctor must grant her license to ease her suffering.

"You might be a suitable replacement," he said.

Relief washed over her. "Where is your office?"

"When not visiting patients on rounds, I work from my residence in the Central West End. My ex-wife and I shared the house before our divorce." Nathan cleared his throat and looked at the ground in front of their benches. "As you said, a story for another day."

They smiled at one another.

A mule-drawn trolley appeared at the corner and lumbered to a stop in front of Union Depot. Pierre disembarked as Daisy buttoned her boots. "This is my father," she said, her eyes turning toward Nathan. "Like you, he's a bit of a disaster." Daisy's knee bounced as Pierre approached.

She grasped the wooden bench with her fingers and stared straight ahead. "Father, I am a grown woman. I will do what I please."

"Your selfishness forced me to watch the fireworks alone."

"The threat of murder compelled my departure."

"Nonsense, *ma chéri*."

"You cannot see inside my mind, nor understand my feelings."

He waved his hand dismissively and blew a sharp breath. "Although you often fancy yourself a victim, you were never in danger."

Pierre must listen for the sake of her dignity. "Your festive rejoicing made you weary, and you sacked out on a blanket. How could you know what transpired?" Before he could answer, her hand made a slicing motion. "The monster's bullet whizzed by the woman's neck, brushing her collar." Daisy turned and threw both hands into the air. "It continued over *my* head and embedded itself into an inch of hickory."

Nathan's mood seemed to uplift. "Did something happen at the park?"

Daisy's eyes fell lightly on him. "Nearby in the crowd, a woman had soothed her worried daughter and promised reunification with her papa. Without warning, a crazed lunatic burst into the open and pointed a pistol at his wife, freezing us all in time and space. His dark and serious eyes pleaded with her, asking for tender words he might need to hear. The mother yanked her child close, her posture bent and tight as the husband squeezed the trigger, his own form now tall and loose." Daisy's hand rubbed her sore calves. "Men wrestled the would-be killer to the ground. He writhed and shook as they held him in place. It was a hideous scene."

"Well, my dear, you are an instinctive storyteller." Nathan slapped his knee. "Your tale competes with my own for ingenuity and originality. Congratulations on such a fine achievement on this balmy evening."

Daisy smiled at Nathan and then looked up at Pierre.

Her father's countenance fell over her. What had transpired in Vienna was intolerable in his eyes. He placed a fist over his mouth, inhaling and exhaling through his nose, implying wretchedness abounded within her.

She said a silent prayer. *Lord, you have overcome the afflictions of this world. I will grow closer to you each day, seeking comfort in your magnificent healing presence. You will restore my sorrowful heart to happiness.*

With fresh enthusiasm, she resumed the conversation. "I followed the woman and her daughter to ensure their safety, and once outside the gate, finding you in such an enormous crowd was an impossibility. Therefore, I escorted the pair to the police station and helped the mother file a report. The amiable night clerk provided captivating details about the modern court system. Apparently, Judge Welkin is more likely to incarcerate the madman in the city asylum than send him to the hangman's gallows."

Nathan smiled as he pointed southwest. "You know the path to Arsenal Road, having walked from the park in air as thick as soup." His exuberance gathered pace. "I think you would make a proper match for the pistol waving madman, and if you speak to Jane upon your admittance, please wish her a speedy recovery. Like yourself, she possesses a singular charm."

Daisy relaxed for the first time in weeks. A prominent person recognized her weakening grip on reality and was willing to joke about it.

"We could have reunited without incident." Pierre stared at the brick building, avoiding eye contact. "It's not only today I am talking about."

Her father refused her an ounce of credit.

"I had to help the woman and her child, didn't I?"

"You were interested in the criminal, just as you were curious about Frank Kaneski. You simply *must* learn to leave well enough alone."

"Frank never fired a pistol in my direction, but he did other things which were equally vile. I had hoped to retrieve his soul from everlasting damnation and return him to the Lord. We can agree he was a wicked man in the final accounting, but was I so wrong to try?"

Pierre glared at her. "More reclamation schemes. You are unbendable."

His voice intended paternal shelter, but his words were empty and weak, and his pleading face burned an image in her mind which would forever remain, pushing her once again to search for a replacement. "Your worries on my behalf are groundless. I hazarded forth in the dark and asked the streetlamps to guide my path. Electric lights dazzled across the great distance, promising sanctuary. That's when I met this gentleman."

She pointed.

"Alright, you win. I will drop the subject." Pierre eyed the bearded man. "So, who is this scruffy character?"

She smiled. "He is Dr. Nathan Marsh, a surgeon who practices medicine in the county, but dwells in the city near Forest Park."

There was a faint flow of thunder from across the river. Nathan's eyes met the approaching sound. "I never mentioned where my patients live," he said over his shoulder.

Somehow, Nathan's voice put things right. "One thing is certain," said Daisy steadily. "Vandeventer Place is off limits to men in your condition."

He turned, and his eyes fell on her. "I'll admit to treating farmers in the county, but I also see a few regulars within the city limits."

"I'd wager they are getting on in years."

He stood and shook Pierre's hand. "Your daughter has a mind like a steel trap; even minor details must run for their lives."

Pierre emitted a quick, high-pitched laugh at the notion and said she would try her hand at fixing Nathan as she did everyone else. Pierre slapped him on the back and told him to keep up his chin. This, too, would pass.

Nathan forced a chuckle and winked a *good night* at Daisy.

She gave him a penniless look. "Were you serious about your offer?"

"Which would that be, madam? I make so many."

Her heart pounded. She turned her face.

He took a final swig from his flask. Emptying the last few drops onto the ground, he shook Pierre's hand once more and tipped his hat to the lady. "Miss Lawrence, it was a pleasure to make your acquaintance. With your permission, I shall take my leave."

"We may discuss my employment tomorrow morning," she said in a resolute voice. "I will knock on your door at an early hour."

"Your arrival will be most welcome, but I predict you will recant after more consideration." His hard gaze made her uneasy.

At the street, he passed between two cabs and trudged along the road as it approached oblivion. She grew afraid he might vanish.

Daisy called out to him in desperation. "Never forget, Doctor Nathan Marsh! You operated on the president of the United States!"

He paused for a moment and then plodded into the night.

Pierre spoke with a voice drained of adornment. "I'll hail a cab to take us to the hotel. A suitable rest will fix everything."

"Laclede's kitchen will be closed."
"No matter," he said. "I'm not hungry."
"Me either. All I want is to be alone."
"On this, we agree."

THREE

Psalm 3:5
I lay down and slept, yet I woke up in safety,
for the LORD was watching over me.

Nathan ascended a creaky staircase in an early morning dream and trudged down a gloomy corridor toward Sheila's bedroom. Rays of cheerful sunlight curved around the edges of her door, beaconing safe harbor. They turned the handle and opened the door, revealing an open window and a well-made bed. His eyes flashed about the room in search of Sheila, but she was not there. Three words scrawled across the wall: *You Have Sinned.* An aggregate of rays pushed Nathan back several steps, and her door shut in his face. Once more surrounded by a sunless gloom, his knees fell into weakness, and his desperate throat closed tight. The dream next took him to his parents' farm, where his father screamed obscenities at his caste-like mother. When the boy tried to intervene, June slapped him across the face and sent him outside. Storm clouds gathered on the hilled horizon. They rolled and tumbled toward the unkempt yard.

The dream let Nathan go. He startled awake.

His bedroom was soured overnight by a mixture of ethanol and sweat. Sneaks of light prowled around the curtained window and attacked his withdrawn face. His hand raised to block the offensive light. Nathan's throat was horribly parched, and his body ached. He faced the shadowy wall.

A knock from downstairs jolted him out of bed.

On his way out, a wadded robe and upturned slippers tripped his feet, sending his body crashing. Nathan quickly stood and threw the robe against his dresser, where it languidly thumped and dropped to the floor. Tired of the fight, he jammed his feet into the slippers and plunged his arms into the sleeves of his robe, wrapping it around him in a soft embrace.

He stood quietly, glad for small satisfactions.

The knock grew louder and more resentful.

His hands slowly fastened the sash on his robe as he descended the stairs.

In the foyer, he took a brief glance at the door to the kitchen. He could go for a glass of water. He turned toward his desk. There was whiskey in a drawer which might ease more than his mighty thirst.

The intruder knocked a third time.

He wiped sleep from his eyes and opened the front door. "Yes?"

An attractive woman tilted her head to one side and arched her eyebrows. For the life of him, he couldn't remember her name.

"Would you be so kind as to allow my entrance, sir?"

Samuel climbed the steps behind her. "Who do we have here?"

Nathan flung open the door. "Did you two plan this encounter?"

The woman wore a confused expression. "I do not know this man."

"I am his father, Dr. Samuel Marsh." He smiled warmly.

"Some father," said Nathan with contempt.

He moved into the parlor and paced across a dusty oval rug, trying his best to untangle his thoughts and see through a throbbing blur. The pair on the stoop stepped into the foyer, where each gave Nathan a concerned look.

He stretched himself in a sharp motion and frowned at his father. "I suppose you have a legitimate reason to be here?"

"What would you say if I informed you of a golden opportunity, one that would solve all your money woes?"

"You answered my question with another question," Nathan said. "What comes next must be a doozy."

"Nonsense. You haven't heard my proposal."

The woman distributed herself near the bay window in the parlor, watching them earnestly. She waited as if expecting an apology.

Nathan gave the woman a fractious look and pointed at the couch.

"Why don't you take a seat while I speak with my father?"

She peeked underneath a cloth which covered the couch and folded the material bottom up, laying it gently underneath the window, and then sat at one end of the couch, where she attempted to make herself plainly snug. Satisfied, she retrieved a newspaper from her bag and opened it wide, perusing both large and small articles. Every so often, she cleared her throat.

Samuel turned from his brief study of the woman. "We must meet at once so you can seize competitive advantage. Others will be in the mix."

"Must we cover the same tired ground?"

"I would like a chance to win your faith, Nathan. As I'm now retired, I recommended you for the position when it was first offered to me. You can thank me later." There was a touch of obligation in Samuel's bearing.

"I'm not going anywhere with you. Today or any other day."

The woman looked up from her paper, intent on shifting the balance of power in the room. She tightened her grasp on the edges of the pages. "Please move your conversation along, gentlemen." When Nathan hesitated, she huffed in an awkward voice. "I offered to replace your assistant, Jane, the one who demanded a regular paycheck. Was I so forgettable?"

He had consumed whiskey for a week and scantly recollected meeting this woman, but her mention of Jane's name embarrassed him. They had a brief affair, which ended with her departure. It was not love but something to pass the time while waiting for love, and Sheila made herself available at all hours, day and night, thankful he was her only customer. His eyes turned toward the bookcase and a worn picture of Catherine. Jane had left for the same reason all women left him. He clung to the memory of a ghost.

"I hoped you would at least remember my first name." She laid the paper aside and stood, extending a hand. "I am Daisy Lawrence."

A detail emerged in his memory: she had studied in Paris.

"Glad to make your acquaintance once more, Miss Lawrence."

Daisy sat and snapped open the paper. Nathan glanced at the front page and then snatched the paper from her hands.

"How rude, sir!"

"Where did you get this?"

"Laclede's front desk." Her face flushed crimson. "I did not steal it, if that's what you're implying."

He sat at the far end of the couch, anxious as he read the bold headline.

"Thomas Hannah Named Suspect in Bakery Murder Investigation."

Nathan's eyes rose to Samuel. "Did you know he was back in town?"

"The investigator I hired said the trail went cold in Arizona, but he mentioned Thomas having family here in St. Louis, so I'm not surprised." Samuel's sigh indicated his own grief. "Mike shared his information with our local police department, but of course, they never followed up. He grew tired of sparring with them and moved to greener pastures in Chicago."

"Why didn't I know any of this?"

"These aren't details to share with a child. You had already seen and heard enough, Nathan. I didn't want to burden you any further."

"So instead you became a monstrous drunkard. How did that help me?"

Samuel took a deep breath and exhaled. "I've had my share of painful experiences, and they exploded within me all at once."

Nathan returned to the article. "It's no excuse."

"Do you mind if I look around?" Daisy's eyes shifted toward the rear of the house, and her voice seemed curious. "I promise to be considerate."

Nathan nodded while reading down the page.

She marched through the kitchen, and the door to the backyard opened and closed. He looked up, his mind visualizing her reaction upon the discovery of his chaos. The dilapidated shed at the back of the property had imploded and should be condemned by the city. Most of his yard tools had since fallen victim to rust or theft by midnight vandals. She would likewise appreciate the overgrown lawn and the weeds sticking through the fence.

Her boots trudged through the kitchen.

She eased by the two men and moved toward the staircase.

The paper fell to his lap. "What do you think you're doing?"

"I must gauge the fathoms if I am to sink to your depth." Daisy glanced momentarily at the stairs. "If you have no further objections." Her narrow shoulders drooped, and she frowned. "It will only take a few minutes."

His hand waved, and he shifted in his seat, unable to get comfortable. His gaze darted to Samuel, who offered a forced smile. Nathan looked away, unwilling to give his father any measure of satisfaction.

Nathan placed the folded paper on a chair and tried to forget the sudden reappearance of Thomas Hannah. A trial was likely, and they might once again seek his testimony. He was only seven at the time of her murder, and taking the witness stand had been too much for him to endure.

His mother's voice called to him from across the decades. Whatever the circumstance, he should have avenged her death. Perhaps there was still time.

Twenty minutes later, the heel of Daisy's boots thudded with each step as she descended the staircase. She sat opposite Nathan in a rocking chair, studying him as a scientist might observe a test subject.

"Did the former homeowner have children?"

Nathan remained silent.

"A swing hangs by a fraying rope in the backyard, and upstairs in the attic, children's toys heap in the corner."

Nathan's eyes squinted. His breathing shallowed.

Daisy's fingers played with her necklace. "Were children here?"

"Yes," he said faintly.

Samuel turned to Daisy. "You are a delightful young woman."

She smiled. "I met your son last night at Union Depot."

"Had you also traveled from New York?"

"No, sir. I was with my father at Tower Grove Park, preparing to watch the fireworks display. A deranged man from the crowd raised a pistol and opened fire on his wife and daughter. In the melee, I almost got shot."

"My word," Samuel said. "What a changing world we inhabit."

A piercing sun infiltrated through the uncovered bay window.

"I wasn't prepared for the morning headline," Nathan said.

He went over to the window and pulled the curtains closed.

"What's done is done, boy. Leave the past where it belongs."

Nathan turned toward Daisy. "No matter how much time passes or how much I try, the harsh memories and the terrible nightmares will not leave me alone. Without whiskey and beer, I'm a rudderless ship."

He looked watchfully at her, inviting more insight.

She moved from her chair to the rear corner of the room where papers had strewn themselves across his desk. Each hand sorted the papers into neat piles, aided by some method of inventory which Nathan would never comprehend. She spoke absently over her shoulder and without a hint of jealousy. "Don't exclude your woman at the brothel. Her name is Sheila."

Daisy was fresh air from the garden. Her presence lightened his spirit.

"Yes, her, too." He retreated once more into his misery. "I cannot deny myself simple pleasures, for without them, what's the point of living?"

"You sound more like a pirate than a physician," said Samuel, his formerly benign countenance stirred. "This is not the boy I raised."

"You raised nothing but a bottle and a hand to strike."

"Yes, and like you, I was ready to end my vile existence. One unsavory morning, I hiked Johnson's Mill Road with a loaded pistol in my right hand and a bottle in my left, talking to God, screaming at Him in furious anger. I could no longer stand in such a drunken state, so I hit my knees right beside the corn at that fateful spot, where I poured out the bottle and my heart to Jesus." He slowly wiped tears from his eyes, uncaring if anyone saw him. "The Lord has since healed me in ways I never imagined possible, helping me to carry my burdens when I couldn't sustain them alone."

His father's incessant preaching was too much to bear. Nathan went to his desk, where he shoved Daisy out of the way and fished through a drawer. He located a flask and gulped the contents. Samuel rushed over to him and knocked the flask out of his hand, spilling whiskey on Daisy's dress.

Samuel dipped backward two steps. "My earnest apologies, Miss Lawrence. It was clumsy of me, but I can no longer watch my son destroy himself. Nathan is a much better man than he realizes."

He paced the oval rug as Nathan had done earlier.

"I suffered no permanent damage." There was a pause before she took a step to meet him. "Stains come out in the wash."

He stopped pacing. "Some blemishes need heavenly intervention."

Daisy nodded. Her eyes fell to the floor.

Samuel kicked at a newly formed rise in the rug and squatted. He lifted the end with his hands and flipped it upward, allowing fresh air to flow underneath. The rug floated back to the floor, and he rose again, offering her a brief recitation from Psalm 3. "But you, O Lord, are a shield around me; you are my glory, the one who holds my head high. I cried out to the Lord, and he answered me from his holy mountain." His voice grew solemn, as if beset by the past. "God's assurance stills my raging soul, bringing me contentment on arduous nights. He fills me with a divine ambition."

Nathan stood near the desk, intoning unkind things.

"You should take heart," Daisy said. "Your father is a wise man."

"If you had known him as a child, your opinion would differ."

Samuel stepped forward, and his hand squeezed Nathan's shoulder. "Son, stop fleeing from Jesus and treating His light as a distant memory. It wasn't so long ago when you believed in Him."

Nathan touched the finger where his ring had rested, and his insides quivered. "I rode with June because of *you*. How can you now stand here and preach at me as if you've led a pastor's life?"

"You blame me," he said. "That much is obvious."

"Yes, for all of it." Nathan took a step back and freed himself.

Samuel pulled a chair beside Daisy and gave it to her.

She sat down with a devoted and meddlesome face.

He turned to Nathan. "Did I also murder Caesar?"

"Don't make light of the situation. Ones so lovely should have been afforded longer lives." Already exhausted, he wanted to lie down and sleep.

"Accompany me to a meeting tomorrow, Son."

Nathan returned to the far end of the couch and peered at Daisy. "Have you shed any tears over your skirmish at the park?"

"I tried last night and this morning, but so far, I've been unable." She hesitated. "It's not the first tragedy I've experienced."

"I assumed as much. The same holds true for me."

"We're two peas in a pod," she said, satisfied with herself.

"I suppose we are." He straightened his robe and kicked off his slippers. "You should allow yourself to cry. It will help."

"I'll keep trying. I'm sure you'll give me many reasons."

Father and son chuckled in unison, offering one another a fleeting grin.

"I've seen so much darkness in this world," she said after a moment. "I sometimes wonder if God's light has burned itself out."

A shadow lowered over Samuel as if her declaration bothered him exceedingly. "Surely you don't mean it. I sense you to be a woman of faith."

Daisy's face adopted a sullen look. "I used to feel God's presence all around me and within me, but now I feel corrupt and perverse and without form." She glanced upward as if she hoped the Lord had not forgotten her.

Samuel stood with a sudden restlessness and broke into a wide grin. "Miss Lawrence, I believe you'll be a beneficial influence on my son. On that note, I invite you to become his assistant. He'll need one in the days to come, and your honesty, bleak as it might be at present, will prove vital."

"Nathan, what do you think?" She picked up the newspaper and read several lines on the front page. "I don't know what this murder investigation means to you, but I'd like to help. We could visit the courthouse together."

His arms crossed in front of his chest. "What's in it for you?"

"There's very little privacy at my father's winery, and he imposes too many rules, forcing me to report my activities as if I'm a child."

"He cares," said Nathan, glancing at Daisy impatiently, "and desires to keep you safe." His tone clearly surprised her.

"I try to forgive his mistrust as Jesus commands, but bitterness often derails my spiritual walk." Her brow was grave, and the look in her eyes had grown severe. "I will not survive for much longer as his storefront manager. My father's manner is too severe, and my will too firm. I must resume the Lord's calling to help a physician with his medical practice. Nathan, I am an orderly bookkeeper, and although I may appear to be low and ill-bred, I'm quite good with people when I want to be." Her lips pursed. "As to the latter topic, my father caught me in a lie this morning and stormed away in a huff. He doesn't want me to stay here, but, exorbitant in my expectations or not, I won't allow him to further divert my progress."

"If my practice flourishes once again and you quit, the workload will destroy me. Finding a worthy replacement may prove impossible."

"I will remain loyal."

Nathan reflected on the murder investigation. If the case went to trial, the court would require him to split time between the proceedings and his patients. With her neurology background, Daisy might substitute for him on days when he must be absent. Her helpful presence could mean the difference between sustained growth and an outright collapse of his practice.

"Alright, you win," he said. "I recall Pierre saying the same last night."

Her eyebrows arched again. "So you remember?"

"It's coming back to me."

She smiled. "You may also recall my tenacious nature."

Seeing she might be later discouraged, he spoke plainly. "I'll hire you for one month. We'll each be on our own when the money runs out."

She looked at Samuel, then at Nathan. "Gentlemen, thank you for giving me this chance. I won't let either of you down."

"We'll see," Nathan said.

"What's my first assignment?"

He sank down to the couch and stuffed a small pillow under his neck, resting his head on the armrest. He was in no hurry to answer.

"Well, speak up," she said.

Samuel laughed. "I believe this one has you pinned, Son."

Nathan frowned and opened his eyes. He gestured at the room. "Clean up this dusty house. There are spiderwebs and animal tracks everywhere."

"I'm aware. I saw many in the attic."

Nathan shut his eyes. "All attics are the same."

"On this we disagree." Daisy waited for his response. "A field mouse ran beside my boots, and I jumped clear out of my skin. For the life of me, I can't understand why, since my father's land has many animals."

Nathan kept his eyes shut. "You're in a strange man's house."

He sensed her thoughts as they banged into one another inside her head. Soon she would shift from negotiating terms of employment to a battle for details from his background, abusing his confidence without remorse.

"Did your earlier conversation regard the folded wedding dress?"

He sat up, revolted. "You snooped inside a locked trunk?"

"I had to know its contents." She shrugged her shoulders and smiled in an amused way. "There was a key on top. I'm not a burglar."

Samuel grabbed his hat from the stand and put it on.

"You've made a good first impression, Miss Lawrence." His voice carried itself with greater authority. His sanction rose and widened as he spoke. "Let's not push the boy too hard. He has a long way to go."

Her smile quickly faded. "I apologize. I did not mean to upset."

After bidding Samuel farewell, she surveyed the room with a pitying look. "Why did you let this house fall into ruin?"

Her watchful eyes made Nathan uncomfortable, so he withheld a reply.

"I get the impression you are an adaptable man. Am I correct?"

"Life has forced my adaptation on many an occasion."

"Well, you're fortunate to have found me. I provide valuable care and attention to those in need." She hesitated. "Are you a man in need, Nathan?"

"Sometimes I ponder the question."

"We share a grand and awful despair." She chuckled under her breath and nodded at her growing awareness. "Yes, we are two peas in a pod." A thought occurred to her, and she stiffened. "Nathan, if you cannot shake your past, you must right whatever wrong has transpired."

He threw an annoyed look at her. "You're one to talk."

She sighed and went straight to work.

Nathan wandered into a dream. He stood wearily on a rocky shoreline, mesmerized by the sea. A fair maiden flailed about; her wan face and her luminous hair bobbed in between each crest and trough. A rowboat drifted beside her and ventured ever so close, a severed anchor line trailing behind it. Up and down the waves rolled, carrying the line further away from the fair maiden. Why did she not stretch out her arms and grab at the life-saving rope? Perhaps she feared this stormy realm beyond mere survival.

FOUR

Psalm 4:4
Don't sin by letting anger control you.
Think about it overnight and remain silent.

Father and son roamed east along Locust Street, drawing closer to the poise and bustle of downtown. Mule-drawn trolleys gave way to electric, and two brick structures arose from the concrete, the first advertising fine furnishings, the second field photography. Nearby, a billiard window reflected sunlight into Nathan's eyes, sending him thoughtlessly under the next awning. Once there, sweetly fragrant ladies with ivory teeth smiled while cool-rooted gentlemen nodded with a temperate sharpness, fanning their petulant noses as if the warm days of summer would never cease, and the corrupted air would forever fill with lower-class odor and street dust. The ladies affected a politeness and a concord, never speaking too loudly or too low but with a beautiful tone perfectly adjusted to the ear of their companion. The gentlemen were forward and bold as they conversed in a loud and unruly timbre, careful to select words which conveyed the delicate accuracy of their meaning while ceaselessly bragging of success in business and battle, fierce warriors from the fields of Ivy.

"I'm displeased with our agreement," said Nathan, watching.

"You've made your feelings clear," Samuel said.

"My responsibilities will swell to an untenable level."

"It's why we hired Miss Lawrence. I'm already impressed with her skills. She will make a fine manager. Your practice has never been one for order."

The billiard parlor promised beer at half price.

Nathan held out a trembling hand. "We could share a quick pitcher."

"We'll miss our consultation." Samuel glanced at his pocket watch.

"Would it be so insufferable? I'm a lost cause, and you know it."

"Answer me when I call to you, O God, who declares me innocent. Free me from my troubles. Have mercy on me and hear my prayer."

Nathan's chest pulled taut, and a heavy weight dropped into his belly. His eyes followed the tarnished road, and the angled sidewalk beyond the far intersection, where the yellow sun met the celestial sphere.

"Why quote it to me? I'm not interested."

"The psalms capture your spirit through repeated exposure, and their poetic parallelism is unmatched in literature."

"Faith isn't for me, Pop. I'm a scientist."

"You think I'm not? I was once revered in these parts."

"You still are," Nathan said. "It's why they offered *you* the job."

Samuel made a pretense of being exasperated. "All the same, I will quote the Lord's Word to my heart's content, if you don't mind."

"I mind. That's my point."

South on Broadway, horse-drawn carriages aligned with the domed courthouse. As he passed the columned entrance, Nathan yearned to storm the bastille, seize control of the inner apparatus, and remove those who would dare abuse their power.

"I sense what you're planning," Samuel said. "So does the Lord."

"I've done nothing wrong."

"You've done nothing right, either. The Lord knows all."

"Cease your moralizing, Pop. You aren't the man for the job."

At Broadway and Walnut, Nathan gazed at the three-story theater building which sat contented and weather-beaten. "Maybe I should try vaudeville," he said. "It might suit a washed up drunkard."

Samuel stopped walking. "The Olympic hasn't done vaudeville in years. You would know if you ever ventured outside of Sheila's boudoir."

Nathan's eyes turned toward the drugstore entrance. "We should soak your head in a tub of turpentine. I hear Michelson sells all the ingredients in one convenient package."

"Colorful," said Samuel, grimacing. "Perhaps another time."

They continued toward the tunnel entrance on Spruce Street, peering over the side, captivated as rail cars poured underground in a graceful line.

"The spectacle excites me, although I'm not sure why," Samuel said. "I suppose it's a mixture of sight and sound and the sheer magnificence of our engineering achievements."

In the distance, trains entered and exited the rail yard behind the Union Depot building. Sets of tracks with gravel between them circulated in contrary directions, and one lingering platform reposed beside the closest track. Passengers surged from the four o'clock train and gathered socially on the platform, rested and restless, as hurried porters unloaded their luggage.

Nathan tugged his father's coat sleeve, and the pair continued to the depot's front entrance, where a newly shaded bench greeted them. The sky was angelic blue and cloudless, the sun's march toward midnight resolute.

Nathan craned his neck. "Why are you leading me in a circle?"

"Mournful thoughts have overwhelmed you lately. I thought a stroll past the courthouse might restore your stoic sense of reflection."

"You think I'm headed for the gallows?"

"If you miscalculate. The legal process must run its course."

Nathan nodded, surprised at his acceptance. "It's been a long time coming, and I'm ready for the trial."

Samuel turned his head slowly, raising his eyes to meet the observant clock which clung to the station tower. A thought occurred to him, and he stiffened. "We have time to speak with the police, if you're sure of yourself."

"I am." Nathan quickly stood. "My questions demand answers."

"Please try to behave in an agreeable manner."

Samuel's steadfast patience eroded as they marched northeast.

His mood matched the soreness which smoldered over the entire police station. In the lobby, narrow benches congested a mass of guests who fumed to their neighbors about their misfortune and others who accepted their fates and cradled their faces in tearful hands. Officers dragged barking perps through the side door and flung them deep into a hollow corridor. Dense cigarette smoke coursed effortlessly about the ceiling to an elongated front counter, where it fell in batches on a sallow clerk. As his hand stamped an assortment of papers and scattered them among several wicker baskets, he seemed destined for a happier calling, perhaps something warm and tropical.

Samuel stepped forward. "Might we have a moment of your time?"

The clerk glanced searchingly between the two men.

Nathan elbowed past Samuel. "We need to speak to the detective assigned to the June Marsh murder case. It directly correlates to the bakery murder investigation which is underway."

"Are you members of the Marsh family?"

"We are." He raised a thumb toward his father. "He was her husband."

"And you?"

"The son."

"I see." The clerk tapped his papers on the counter and curtly shoved them into a drawer. "I'll let him know you're here." His shape ducked around a partition and into the corridor, twisting a ball of smoke in his wake. Leather shoes scuffed loudly against the tile and faded to a complete stop. Midway down, a door creaked open and voices rose to an angry pitch. As a door slammed, the echoing sound bounced off rattled glass and stale wood, bending and shaping and spreading all the way to the front desk.

A few minutes later, they entered Detective Kincaid's office.

Kincaid pointed at two wooden chairs. "Please sit."

Nathan wished with all his might to leap backward across the decades and right the incalculable harm. Others thought him morose and irrational to dwell on the matter. Her hand had struck him the night before, sending him to the barn, where he slept overnight with the horses.

June had been imperfect, often cold.

Kincaid opened the case file and flipped through the papers, listing each fact surrounding the shadowy incident. "From these notes, seems Dr.

Samuel Marsh was the prime suspect. The Marsh couple had recurrent marital difficulties, and two separate neighbors said they heard male and female shouts most every night. Words were exchanged, but the behavior continued. Over time, each neighbor learned to tune out the sounds." The detective's brow wrinkled, and his head tilted as if weighing the evidence. "Then June began riding the fence line with the farm hand, Thomas Hannah, while Dr. Marsh left for his rounds. That's when each neighbor became sure the doctor would murder his wife, and when her death occurred, they were not surprised. They believed Samuel had also murdered Mr. Hannah, although the body was never discovered."

He paused and looked at Nathan.

"There's more if you'd like to hear it. Notes from after the murder."

"Please continue," Nathan said.

"While riding their fence line, neighbors often spotted Dr. Marsh sleeping under trees with an empty whiskey bottle beside him. Each time they found him in such a condition, they wondered if he was dead." Kincaid rustled the paper as he sighed. "Then Dr. Marsh would breathe heavy or roll over, giving them permission to leave him to his vices."

Samuel leaned forward, his skin flush and his jaw set. "Sir, is it your intention to manipulate me today?"

"In my experience, men who ask such questions have something to hide," said Kincaid with a weak smile.

Nathan had asked for fairness and justice without sneers or derision. The detective viewed Samuel as a drunken abuser whose wife had resolved to leave home, the implication clear. Samuel fixed his eyes on a shirt button and twisted. Kincaid tapped his fingers together and studied Samuel.

Nathan's fists clenched as he leaned forward. "Leave this track, detective, or I will inform your captain." He pushed backward with wide eyes.

"From what I gather, you've obsessed over this case for many years," said Kincaid flatly. "When we closed it for lack of concrete evidence or credible suspects other than your father, you threatened to write the governor."

"I wrote him several letters. Whether he received them, I cannot be sure." Nathan looked at Samuel for encouragement, but found none.

"Now the threats begin anew. I will spend minimal time with you today, gentlemen. We have Thomas Hannah in custody for the bakery murder, as you know, and we plan to investigate the matter to the fullest extent."

"We must leave, Son. Let the man work his case."

Samuel got to his feet.

As the pair exited the station, Nathan's heart pounded. He stopped to catch his breath. Samuel continued to the street and wheeled.

"I'm not going anywhere until you make a full confession."

Samuel's cheeks went ashen. "Oh?"

"Who scheduled this appointment?"

"John Belmont." Samuel wore a look of relief.

"I knew something strange was afoot. You've been unusually giddy with excitement since this morning," Nathan said. "Where are we going?"

Samuel eyed a mule-drawn trolley. "Evening approaches with each fleeting minute. We must hop aboard."

"Let me translate. You're feeling guilty for dragging me into a ridiculous scheme, and you want to make up for it by paying my fare on a slow trolley rather than a more expensive electric, which further means you are hot and will do anything necessary to get yourself out of the oppressive sun."

Samuel's hand waved, dismissing the snide observation.

He started for the trolley.

After they took the rear seats, he nudged Nathan, and his voice struggled against the humidity and the heat. "You long for a simpler time, but those days were merely a foundation for the ordeals of adulthood. We must move through each stage of life with enthusiasm for the lessons God teaches us. If brooding becomes a habit, we will sink into the abyss."

"You would know, Pop."

"Yes, I would," said Samuel, his face calm and patient. "You're no better than me, spending the last decade wallowing in self-pity."

Nathan's thoughts burned fervently for the balance of the journey, but he kept silent, focusing on the world outside himself. On Washington Avenue, oblivious patrons laughed and spoke to one another without restraint, while worried bankers wore strained looks on their faces. A lanky trumpeter stared at lumbering trolleys and rickety carriages from a bench while he played "The Royal March of the Lion" and waved heartily to anyone who passed. Some stopped to listen and to throw change into his hat. All wore a bemused smile and clapped in time to the high and lows which accompanied each footstep of the marching lion. Further down, a cacophony of hammers banged in unison as an old structure was torn down and a stronger, taller building was erected in its place. Women from a nearby brothel strolled along the avenue, receiving catcalls from each carpenter, their rough bouncer turned chaperone eyeing each man, returning him to the captivity of his body and mind. The clip clop of hooves mesmerized.

Nathan turned away from the avenue's good welcome, and his thoughts fell on Daisy. Although her body maintained an alarming rigidity in keeping with her nature, she was a kind and productive woman, and most likely she had remained hard at work, even during his afternoon absence.

His lungs breathed full and exhaled.

She may prove a rare find.

The midtown trolley dropped the men onto a brilliant sidewalk at Vandeventer Place. Father and son straightened attire and entered through the wrought iron east gate. Their feet pushed along a grassy median for fifty yards until grass begat a bricked enclosure, and a murmuring water fountain greeted their stroll. They watched the pure water surge and rill for a few moments, but the oblique sun turned them right along the curvilinear street to John Belmont's grand manor, where a colossal oak provided shade.

Nathan took position near a perimeter wall, enthralled by the garrulous lawn, the manicured hedges, the elegant main building partially covered in ivy. Its castle-like turret called to him and urged him to flee, to hide, to never show his face in this or any other private place, and for the first time since boyhood, he entertained the notion of traveling out west, where outlaws had free rein. He gauged his father's sentiment, guessing it matched his own.

Samuel heaved a sigh and looked at the vacant street.

"I will cede the point," Nathan said, breaking the awkwardness between them. "Catherine's desertion blighted my will to live."

"You were the architect of your own demise, Son. Your grief and your indignation weighed more than any crown." Samuel's pupils flashed in an unsettling way. "While we're on the subject, what do you think of the delightful and dutiful Miss Lawrence? For a potential relationship, I mean."

"I like her and find her physically appealing, but we are from dissimilar worlds, and our ages are rather far apart."

"When I came back mid-afternoon, you reposed on the couch, still as the calmest sea. Daisy was hard at work in the kitchen, so I ventured to the table and sat down, watching her for a few minutes. Her disposition faltered in my presence, as if older men tend to judge her actions harshly. I redirected my attention to internal thoughts for a time until she felt more comfortable. It was then we conversed in greater detail about her background, and she willingly shared her age with me. Just so you know, I didn't ask for it."

"Oh, yes, you did. It was probably your first question."

Samuel smiled complacently. "Regardless of who said what to whom, a separation of fourteen years is not insurmountable in my estimation, and at twenty-seven, she remains a relatively young woman." Samuel hesitated. "I detect a spark between you, which I never shared with your mother."

"Do not bring June into this conversation. Not when they have her killer in custody."

Samuel stepped into the sunlight, and his shadow threw itself at the house. He retreated into the cool darkness. "Her name will be much repeated over the next few weeks. You can count on it."

"Well, regarding your question, I have no time for a bookish girl like Daisy Lawrence. She's the sort of woman who enjoys correcting a man's grammar more than cooking him a fine breakfast."

Samuel crossed his arms. "Did Catherine cook for you?"

Nathan's belly knotted. "She never once prepared a meal. I'm not sure she understood how, being raised in a household filled with servants."

"That is exactly my point. You might be surprised by our Miss Lawrence. She is a woman of character and substance." He removed his pocket watch, noting the time. "We must go inside."

Through double doors and a Corinthian columned hallway, the butler led them into the silk-covered library. Nathan sat at a square table and admired the mahogany woodwork in the mantle, the Medieval inspired bookcases, and the sutured ceiling. The butler wheeled, leaving as promptly as he'd arrived. Aimless bits of powder wafted through the air.

"I'll soon need more money from you."

"What on earth for?" Samuel's eyes rose toward a bookcase.

"I must install locks on my windows and doors."

"This ought to be entertaining." Samuel slid back his chair and perused a series of books on a shelf. "Let's hear your odious tale of woe."

"You mock, but I am serious. Thomas Hannah had friends who may visit me during the trial."

Samuel's hand calmed Nathan's alarmed voice. "This is a perfect example of a man leaning on his own understanding. You should trust God in all things." He allowed Nathan a moment of reflection. "It's all I intend to say on the matter. Nothing further will come from my lips."

"Thank the Lord for small favors."

Belmont entered the library. "I see you two still bicker like schoolboys."

"We have you to thank for it," Nathan said.

"I take no joy from your quarrels," said Belmont, his eyes ferociously aglow. "Nor will I accept your childish premise."

Nathan grew annoyed. "Why are we here?"

Belmont went to a window and spread open a curtain. He stared at his yard and his gate and the street beyond his perimeter wall.

Nathan and Samuel exchanged glances.

Belmont at last turned toward father and son, his eyes reticent.

"I suppose there's no use in beating around the bush. Catherine has unceremoniously resurfaced across the river in Illinois. They found her beaten and unconscious, lying naked on Main Street in Dealey. The Sheriff is a former admirer of Catherine, and a trusted friend of our family. He wired me at once, and we had her transported here." Belmont's words hung in the air like locusts. "I could barely recognize her."

The admission seemed to take his wind.

Nathan's hands clapped over his ears. He pictured his mortal body as it crumpled to the floor and dissolved between the slats. He would melt into the rocky soil and into the city's celebrated underground springs, ride the turbulent waters into the majestic Mississippi river, and flow southward toward the deep blue sea. A mile out, he would exchange grief and isolation for the welcome void of nothingness. A quiet peace waited there.

Belmont's nostrils flared. "Did you hear what I said?"

"You speak of your own desires without consideration for anyone else. It's all I've ever heard from you."

"She is your wife, and you will tend to her with all your residual strength." Belmont allowed Nathan a moment to process the circumstance. "I had her placed in a Chicago hospital where the doctors have proven utterly helpless. They say she's in a coma and likely has suffered brain damage. She may never wake up."

"I'm sorry, Son." Samuel's hand dropped onto Nathan's shoulder. "You know I always cared for Catherine."

"Yes. You two were thick as thieves when the children were alive."

"She kindly gave me a fresh start. I enjoyed my time as a grandfather."

"See what you can do with her," Belmont said.

Nathan had a high pain tolerance, but this was beyond measure. His legs weakened, and his eyes formed black spots. He sat on the couch, spent, ready for a full bottle and Sheila's Irish embrace. "What's in it for me?"

"Is greed all you know?"

"It's a tall summit, Son, but you are man enough to climb it."

"Why should I try?"

"I sensed you would resort to bribery. Fine, have it your way. Against my better judgement, I am prepared to place you in charge of my new hospital. It has sixteen beds and all the latest equipment. Once it performs well enough, I will expand."

"Is it a going concern?"

"It's been open for months, but you won't like the current clientele."

"Try me."

"We have a handful of bothersome hysterics. They sleepwalk, prance around at all hours, and cry out in unholy torment. For now, my hospital operates as an overflow facility for the city asylum. After you take over, I expect you to make certain improvements."

"Jolly good times."

Belmont smiled. "I see on this point we agree. I'll leave it up to you to get rid of them and to convince members of the community to trust our hospital. You have an existing patient list, correct?"

"They're an aging, peculiar bunch."

Samuel's eyes looked warmly at Belmont. "They are lovely people once you get past their eccentricities."

Nathan nodded.

"Since pop's retirement," he said, "I've inherited the list."

"You'll probe them for additional prospects. If that fails, you'll knock on every door in town. Restore Catherine to respectability and supervise my hospital with even a modicum of success, and I will place you in charge permanently. Fail and I will drag your name through the press as a drunken quack. Do I make myself clear?"

Nathan avoided his eyes. He looked at a tapestry on the wall.

"I will ask again. Do I make myself perfectly clear?"

"Crystal," said Nathan, making direct eye contact.

Belmont handed him a wad of cash. "It will get you through the next few weeks. I maintain a healthy account for the hospital at Rhodes Bank. Soon I will grant you access so you can withdraw what you please."

"I feel guilty for allowing Catherine to run off with another man and for not bringing her home."

"As you should."

Samuel rose from the chair. "I've had just about enough of your folly, Belmont. I recommended Nathan for this task because it may avert his ruination, not for your rude enjoyment. Do I make myself clear, sir?"

Belmont squeezed his eyes shut as if imagining Catherine in the grime and among the refuse. "She's my little girl, Samuel. He destroyed her."

"Whatever transpired between them was their own doing. Let's give them some quiet and allow them to sort the pieces, shall we?"

Portraits from a long ago wedding reception flashed relentlessly through Nathan's mind. The mid-November afternoon had grown cheerful and expectant as children played, hopped, and held hands in glee. Belmont's palatial backyard shimmered and belled with the post fervor of the cathedral wedding, the elegant reception now before them, and the night of nuptials yet to be realized. Round tables covered in pristine tablecloths and centered with gushing floral arrangements hosted succulent meals for guests who scraped silverware across dinner plates and spoke in raised voices as they struggled to hear one another over the din. Forks tapped against glasses.

Couples with radiant smiles encouraged the blessing of an impressive kiss. Graceful and charming lips happily obliged, their blooming love as free as the songs of birds, their joy sweeping the ground, scooping all for the ride.

The hush of a moment took their love and tossed it to the wind.

Belmont had been standing in front of a wide and sturdy bookcase. He stepped toward a thin mahogany table, and Annie's curly brown hair revealed itself inside a picture frame on a shelf. Anxiety, guilt, and shame overwhelmed Nathan. Within a five-minute span, he had received news of Catherine's return and seen his darling daughter's face, each a reminder of his inability to function in a world which seemed ordinary and easy for others. He had failed Catherine as a husband; he had failed his children as a father. Regret overflowed, and he rushed to the hallway and the double doors, held onto a handle for dear life, and pushed himself against the sturdy wood. He hadn't allowed himself to cry since the fateful July morning ten years prior, the worst moment in recorded history.

Tears coursed down his bearded cheeks.

Samuel approached.

"Don't sin by letting anger control you. Think about it overnight and remain silent. Offer sacrifices in the right spirit, and trust the Lord."

No matter how hard he gripped the handle or pressed himself against the door, Annie's smiling face would not leave his thoughts. She was forever gone to another planet, another realm, or merely a hole in the ground. "More quotes from the Bible? The psalms must have all your answers."

"They do, Son, and one fine day, you'll see I'm right." Samuel drew closer. "For now, I am content to remain steadfast by your side."

"I read of Thomas Hannah's capture in the paper." Belmont fell in behind the men slowly, with caution, and spoke in a soft voice. "Nathan, this is your father's fight, as he was June's husband. Your wife has returned to the fold, blessing you once more with her presence. As a result, you must avoid involving yourself in the trial proceedings, which could last weeks, if not months. Nothing must interfere with your evaluation of my daughter or interrupt her care. I simply won't stand for it."

Nathan's hand waved, and he nodded his pained understanding. As the instigator of this foul circumstance, Belmont deserved no additional time or consideration. Nathan flung open the door and marched toward the street. Samuel followed closely behind, fast stepping to catch his son.

Belmont called after the men. "You there! Stop!"

Nathan's feet paused. He considered over his shoulder.

"Your days of drinking and sleeping your way around this city have reached an end. For years, you've used the pursuit of pleasure as a means to cope, but I will no longer tolerate your weakness."

"I'll never forgive you for separating us." Nathan wheeled and glared sharply at Belmont. "It produced a gulf we could not overcome."

"I'm aware. You'd be a liar to say otherwise."

"For our children's sake, especially my beloved Annie, I will weigh your offer." He wiped tears from his face. "It's the best I can do."

His back turned on the shameful tyrant, and his feet continued their journey toward home. The double doors slammed behind him. A shrill thwack echoed against the sinuous perimeter wall, leaving only the birds and the bustle beyond the gate and the grasping call from yesteryear.

FIVE

Psalm 5:8

Lead me in the right path, O Lord,
or my enemies will conquer me.
Make your way plain for me to follow.

August 1867

Fifteen-year-old Nathan hid from his father under a droopy willow, reading a medical book from a bygone prison on Gratiot Street. He had perused the worn pages since the sun's early crest, disquieting himself and a nearby herd of Quarter Horses. Bays and chestnuts pawed at the ground as they watched the boy with breathy displeasure, uncertain if they should suffer the inescapable quarrel or risk flight to a more settled land. A well-groomed poodle ran into the shade and sat on its haunches, panting with delight. Nathan wobbled on his unsteady stump and growled affably as a pretend threat, but the dog's playful and lawless smile melted all but the coldest of hearts. In a now extinct war, the boy and the dog were friends. They had explored Gratiot and found the medical book together.

Samuel climbed the hill from the dirt road.

He cursed sourly as he approached, awakening the drowsy pasture from its peaceful slumber. Kindling was not cut, nor logs for the wood stove.

"Just what I need," he said, pointing. "Get that mutt out of here."

"Pippy is Aunt Joy's poodle."

"I don't care if he belongs to the mayor. I want him out of this field."

Nathan wished to agree with his father and avoid another beating, but he longed to see his mother's sister. Her love had once been real to him.

"You should forget any foolish notions," Samuel said. "Joy was done with you two years ago." He stuck his hands deep into his pockets. "When I collected you, she was glad to be rid of your useless hide."

Pippy's tail wagged as he chased a butterfly in circles.

"Aunt Joy said she loved me." Nathan struggled to make sense of his father's words. "She cried when I left. Even Edward said he would miss me."

"William had recently passed, and she was overly sentimental for a time, which is most unlike Joy. Since then, she's fully recovered her pompous ways and does as she pleases. I hear she recently moved into a new private street near Lafayette Square; from what folks say, she dotes on her spoiled son and demands he enter high society or what passes for it in these parts. In usual Joy fashion, she expects to see Edward well married by Christmas."

"I could ask her if it's true."

"Her servants won't let you near the house, much less through her front door." Samuel scowled at Pippy. "Her ugly dog has fared little better."

The breeze shifted, alerting Major to the threat of danger. He raised his head as a signal to Ruby and the rest of the horses. One second later, he led the charge toward the far end of the pasture, and the herd's hooves rumbled behind him in unison. Nathan's eyes tracked Ruby's dutiful bond with Major, the same she had shared with her former owner. Since June's murder, Ruby seemed uneasy in Nathan's presence and kept her distance. He could chase her down and break the bad pasture habit, but Ruby's perceptive and honest eyes made him nervous. Her empathic spirit knew, as did his own.

Samuel turned toward the horses and then back to his son.

"Ruby wants nothing to do with you, either."

"She knows I should have done more to stop him."

Samuel's eyes flickered. "You ran like anyone would."

"Not *you*."

"You're a stubborn fool." Samuel wore a callous smile.

He marched down the hill to the dirt road, where his form diminished and eventually shrank from sight. Nathan stuck out his tongue in defiance.

His childish act harkened to a simpler time.

The ever sweeping countryside beckoned Nathan and Pippy once more to adventure. As they hiked northeast toward Lafayette Square, Pippy hopped and circled and zigzagged. He was happy to lead his maturing pal home, and Nathan was relieved his good friend knew the way.

Inside the private gates of Benton Place, Nathan climbed Aunt Joy's granite front steps and positioned himself on her stoop. His arms clutched Pippy to his chest as he rang her bell. Footsteps pounded in the foyer and then grew louder. Nathan's mouth went bitter, and his hands trembled.

The door opened.

Randolph's eyes fell on him with disdain.

"Yes?"

"May I see my aunt?"

"She has not mentioned your arrival. It is most unexpected."

A faint voice groveled from the hallway. "Do I have a caller?"

The butler turned toward her, easing the door shut in Nathan's face.

In a moment, the door reopened, revealing Aunt Joy.

"What is this?" She looked at Nathan with disbelieving eyes.

His own eyes stared at her with an equal measure of surprise and shock. Pippy rested peacefully. He panted with a glad face.

She broke into a wide smile. "You, sir, are my hero!"

Aunt Joy took the poodle from Nathan and ran her shaky fingers over Pippy's fur. She hugged him close and kissed him and told him kind and loving things. Pippy dropped to the stoop and wandered into the grass.

"You go round to the kitchen, Pippy. My cook will give you a treat."

Pippy heard the word *treat* and pepped up, most willing to comply.

Aunt Joy turned toward Nathan and hugged him with a sainted mercy. Her warmth eased his worried soul and scattered his restive thoughts.

"Please come inside this instant."

In the drawing room, Joy's hand patted Nathan's knee.

"I haven't seen you since the war ended. Where have you kept yourself?"

"I live with pop at the farm. He said you never loved me."

"For a year, I attempted to visit you and to have you visit my house, but Samuel steadily instructed me to stay out of your lives. Another year passed, and I assumed you felt the same." She hesitated. "I never meant to offend, but it seems all I am capable of these days. Even my servants are disloyal."

Nathan's hand clutched a small pillow in his lap as his eyes glanced about the room. Within the confines of her gentility, he stuck out like a pig at a funeral. He took a deep breath and exhaled; perhaps he should try.

"I've always loved you."

"The same holds for me," she said in quick fashion.

"Since I left you, things have been awful." His hands dropped the pillow, and his fists clenched. "My father drinks every day." His voice lifted with excitement. "Pop says his patients demand too much of him."

"I believe there's more to it," she said, patting his hand to calm him down. "He's enjoyed the spirits since we were adolescents."

Nathan nodded his understanding. "Pop wails in his sleep most nights. Sometimes he wakes up, sometimes not."

"Do you know what distresses him so?"

"Things he saw in the war."

Her hand rose to his shoulder. "It's a mark of uncommon faith when filled with alarm to make your complaint openly to God. Casting upon Him all the cares which burden us is the only remedy for our apprehensions. Men like your father refuse to grasp this basic tenet of faith."

Nathan picked up a book from the end table and opened the cover. Near the title page, there was an inscription from Psalm 5:1-2. "O Lord, hear me as I pray; pay attention to my groaning. Listen to my cry for help, my King and my God, for I pray to no one but you."

He muttered a curse and tossed the book onto the floor. After so many lies and so many broken promises, he had no use for meaningless words.

Aunt Joy retrieved the book and placed it in her lap. Her eyes closed, and she sat still, as if in exalted contemplation. She lowered her head and silently whispered a prayer. A slant of sun crawled across her sullen face.

Her eyes opened and fell on Nathan. "Rather than remain in this house and allow me to guide his path, my son, Edward, has gone east for college. Whether he will actually attend an institution, I cannot say, but he's asked for a monthly stipend all the same. William's passing was hard on Edward; that much I know." She hesitated. "However, I am fuzzy on why he's so angry with me, the adoring mother who loved him through his grief."

She paced in front of the couch, her face set upon by dread. Her hand shielded her eyes from the sun, but she paid the nuisance little attention.

"Unlike your good-hearted mother, I was once a haughty woman. Life has since stripped away my youthful vainglories, and as a comfortless widow, I no longer possess the slightest residue of pride." Her eyes fastened on him, and she smiled. "Would you agree to visit me again? You could play with Pippy. He loves you, as do I." She took his hand, and her voice carried a desperate tone. "Please say you will. I cannot bear the loneliness."

Nathan's thoughts ticked in thunderous time with the grandfather clock as it cuffed the air, its loud beats ringing and rolling from the foyer to the drawing room, pushing Nathan further inside himself. His aunt lied about her love as everyone had lied. There was never any truth in their words or their promises, only wrath in their behavior. She had left him with a father who screamed and struggled through each day, never comforting.

"Please talk to me, honey."

He blurted the words. "Pop beats me."

"What?"

"Although I try hard, I cannot please him."

"Why on earth?"

"He blames me."

"For the war?"

"For everything."

She nodded, taking his meaning. "You must come to live with me."

"What about Edward? He might come home."

"He is bent on martyrdom and wants nothing to do with me."

She paused.

"I fear word of his demise will soon reach my door."

"Will you be sad?"

She looked surprised by the question. "Why, yes, I will."

"Would you be sad if I died?"

"Since my Edward left me alone, I have been morbidly depressed, losing all desire for life. I prayed to the Lord for rescue yesterday, and today you arrived at my doorstep, a blessing sent from heaven above."

"You didn't answer my question."

"Honey, you are all I have left in the world, and if you withdraw from me once more, a wretched corpse will greet my morning maid."

Nathan had waited an entire life to hear those words.

She needed him as much as he needed her.

He hugged Joy goodbye. "I'll ask pop."

At home, his father's whiskey soaked body slept on the living room floor, and the neck of an empty bottle pointed toward the road. Nathan wiped vomit from Samuel's face and put him to rest on the couch. Tears coursed down his cheeks as he sat at the kitchen table. He kept still and silenced his fear of the unknown; he was young and must think of the future. Although his life had been filled with angry shouts and hard punches, he had become tougher than most other kids.

He left a note on the table. A shaving mirror held it in place.

"When you awake and find me absent, do not pursue. I have gone to live with Aunt Joy. I take only my medical book. You may keep the balance."

Blood drained from Nathan's cheeks as Aunt Joy knocked on his bedroom door. She meant to cultivate his education with a classical course of study, a punishment he'd avoided since leaving his father's farm. Her plans included a private school run by Jesuit priests called The Academy of the Christian Brothers. It was a most impressive name, and one he knew well.

His lungs constricted as he summoned her entry.

"The headmaster is awaiting our arrival." She opened his door all the way. "Hurry now, Nathan. We must make haste."

"Why can't I attend Central High School like a normal student?"

She looked at him with soft eyes and infinite compassion.

"They've moved the building further west from its original location on Fifteenth. I have no means to get you to such a remote destination."

"I could walk."

"The academy serves the children of the Big Cinch, and I want you climbing social ladders, not learning subversion in a public school. If you are to become a member of the St. Louis elite, your journey begins today."

It was an illogical opinion. "They will hate me."

"You should read the psalms, my dear. They soothe the soul."

He sent her a pained look. "I want nothing to do with Bible poems."

"Listen to my voice in the morning, Lord. Each morning I bring my requests to you and wait expectantly." She allowed her words to register. "O God, you take no pleasure in wickedness; you cannot tolerate the sins of the wicked." Her shrill voice rose unfairly, buoyed by his distaste. "Therefore, the proud may not stand in your presence, for you hate all who do evil."

"I'm not going, no matter what you say."

"David was alone like you," she said. "He never allowed adversity or scorn to prevent him from addressing God."

"I'm not him."

At the academy, Aunt Joy stood with Nathan at the front of his class, shimmering like the sunset. She announced his presence and asked the group to greet him with grace and fraternal affection. He had once been a pupil but left upon Samuel's return from uncivil southern battlefields. Nathan surveyed the squalor of boys, noting their position in society, measuring each against his own. One by one, their contemptuous faces confirmed his inferior status and the harassment which was sure to follow.

"It's alright." He took a step backward to increase his distance from the others. "They know my name."

"That's right, dear." Good tidings emanated from her. "Soon your friendships will be renewed and all will be made right with the world."

The first debutante ball of the season arrived faster than Nathan had expected, rousing Aunt Joy and sapping him. Nathan's stiff formal attire slackened his mouth and widened his eyes. His classmates, in their tailored outfits, danced and giggled and swapped partners as it suited them. Careless adults sipped and then gulped expensive champagne. They merely tiptoed with the music at first, but over many glasses, they cascaded into a frenzied and dizzied and tortured frolic, their configuration resembling a laughing pirouette. Every so often, a couple bounced near Nathan in tarnished glee.

"Won't you mix with them?"

Nathan kept silent.

"Stop folding your arms." Aunt Joy pulled at his wrists while she made firm eye contact with the alluring daughter of a glass manufacturer. With the wealthy man's recent passing, the young woman was now a lonely heiress in search of a husband. "These people will assume you are without class."

"They would be correct."

"Rubbish," she said indignantly. "An enterprising young man must improve himself at every turn, if not through marriage, then by education."

Jason Jeffries stepped forward and whispered in Nathan's ear. "Orphans with one foot in the grave shouldn't concern themselves with grandiose attachments or interfere with those who will architect the future."

Nathan pretended to have misheard.

"You recognize the truth of my statement."

"I have a father."

"Yes, of course." Jason feigned disbelief. "A drunken fool who is as likely to murder his patients as to save them."

Confused and wary, Nathan stormed outside and walked a quarter mile, sensing danger in every dark spot along the private lane. Past the west gate, he trusted his instincts and retraced his path back to the ball. At the entrance, Nathan flung open the polished front door and marched forward like a committed soldier, his footsteps thundering against the lustrous marble floor. Without uttering a syllable, he punched Jason Jeffries in the nose and moved away, covered in the boy's blood. The violinist's graceful bow ceased, and the piano player removed his delicate fingers from the ivory. Nathan looked about the ballroom in all directions, defying mortified eyes with a fiery glare, allowing himself one last act of insolence.

Tomorrow, Benton Place would no more be his home.

At first light, Aunt Joy scolded Nathan for tearing up his good clothes and for ruining the reputation she'd wanted to build for him.

"If you are to bring a measure of light to earth's abounding darkness, you must learn to control your impulses." She hesitated. "I realize you have lingering sentiments which threaten your rise, but a portion of my wealth has been set aside for your college, and unlike Edward's painful reminder of my failures as a mother, you will attend. Let others sell their wisdom for the freedom of momentary violence while you focus entirely on education and stability. It's a fenceless world for the learned man."

"I assumed you would ask me to leave."

"Nonsense, Nathan. I would die to protect you."

He had underestimated Aunt Joy as he had misjudged his mother.

"On that happier note, I will introduce you to a beautiful young woman who also requires a tutor. I taught for twenty years, but my failing eyesight has forced me to hire a scholarly replacement."

Two days later, Catherine Belmont dropped by to discuss the matter of her tutoring. Upon agreement of terms, she sat beside Nathan on the couch, her green eyes narrowed, and her reddish lips pursed. Catherine's brown, curly hair flowed past her shoulders, making her the spitting image of June Marsh. Nathan's brow furrowed as he gazed at her splendor. Memories and emotions threatened to overwhelm his senses. He stared at the antique rug.

"Would you not speak to me, sir?"

Aunt Joy took a seat opposite the couple. "Why have you done poorly in school, my dear? I assume your window opens for a summer night's breeze and your furnace operates in the cold and blustery wintertime. Are there any lesser known obstacles in your path or any physical maladies of concern?"

Catherine smiled and spoke softly. "Like your Pippy, I prefer to be in the meadows with the butterflies and the bees. They calm my wary soul."

"I see."

Aunt Joy encouraged Nathan and Catherine to wander the length of Benton Place and afterward to sit on her porch rockers.

As they strolled, Catherine asked about Nathan's parents.

"There's not much to say."

She took his hand. "You were strong to defend your father's honor at the ball, and I remain impressed."

"It's all I know."

She nodded, understanding his hurt. "I miss my mother."

"What happened to her?"

Catherine's hand covered her throat. "She died in childbirth."

Like him, Catherine dredged the past to understand her present.

He stopped and pondered the darkening sky, noting the sudden rush of wind and a line of rain across the horizon. "I feel broken inside."

She pressed her tender lips to his fist, each plush and delicate and wet against his knuckles. The breeze quickened around them, tossing strands of hair and yanking bits of clothing. Nathan looked into Catherine's emerald eyes, ceasing his search. She saw clear to his hardened soul, and for her, there never had been another man. He was the dream she had conjured and the outlaw on which she waited. No other was worthy and never would be.

Catherine was forever paired with him on earth and in the celestial.

"There's so much death around us," she said, kissing his fingers.

"I have noticed the curse," he said. "Still, we must persevere."

His hand pulled away from her lips. It was too much, too soon.

Nathan packed his clothes into a leather satchel. He backed away from his dresser and stared at his reflection in the mirror. His indignant mind implored him to leave. His long and lonely heart petitioned him to stay.

Aunt Joy blocked his path in the foyer. She asked where he would go.

"San Francisco."

Her face tightened. "Son, you'll get two miles outside of town and learn death approaches at great speed and with fierce resolve."

"Jason mocked me at school. The entire class laughed."

"I have a remedy. Please allow my plan to unfold."

Catherine's boots ascended the steps, and she opened the front door, taken aback by the hostilities. "What is this commotion?"

Nathan's belly quivered. "I will no longer play the court jester."

She noted his bag with a hesitating nod. "If you are to become a western outlaw, I must go with you."

He dropped the bag onto the wood floor and plunged his hands deep into his pockets. "You wouldn't last a week."

Aunt Joy's arms crossed. She smirked at him.

His eyes turned away from her.

"You cannot leave me alone with my disapproving father." Catherine drew a sharp breath and released it. "I love you, Nathan, but your uncaring abandonment will send me to an early grave. Mark my words, for children will play in the green grass above my head. My fate depends upon you."

His ears pounded as stirred blood rushed throughout his body, sweeping in waves against his cheeks. "You don't know me. How can you be in love?"

Catherine's nostrils flared. "I know you well enough, Nathan Marsh. You are the love of my life. It is impossible for me to love another."

"I don't believe you."

She sighed. "Despite what you may believe, I speak the truth."

"I don't know how to love you back."

She gave him an amused smile. "Then you had better learn."

Three days later, Aunt Joy introduced a tutor from New York. The lanky, spectacled academic made stern eye contact when shaking hands. "Because of health concerns, I've taken a sabbatical for the school year. My wife and two children are tending to my home while I'm away."

"Tell them your name," Aunt Joy said.

"Oh, yes. Where are my manners?" His rigid posture relaxed and his voice softened. "I'm Professor Roy Collins."

He extended a hand to Nathan, who refused to shake it.

At the kitchen table, Roy mentioned his excitement at being presented with this splendid opportunity. He grinned at Nathan like a sociable bird.

Nathan shifted in his chair. "What opportunity?"

Roy's breath quickened. "We'll travel to New York in a year, and you'll want to be ready. Hudson Medical College can be a rigorous environment for the unprepared." He spoke as if relaying a heavenly vision.

Nathan's eyes flashed. "You wish to send me away?"

"It's in your best interest, dear. Unlike Edward, you'll work diligently and return as the conquering hero. I'll be so proud and happy to have you home again." Aunt Joy seemed taken with the notion, but also agitated.

"Yes, and while you're in school, you'll live with my family. My wife, Colleen, is a kind and devoted woman. You two will become fast friends."

If Nathan's conversation with Professor Collins continued, he might be tempted to punch his wiry face. The nearer and more familiar the man became, the less Nathan liked him. He looked at Roy and shook his head.

"We'll see."

Catherine visited the house each weekday to work on her dyslexia, and her condition improved steadily. She asked Nathan to join her sessions with the professor, but he refused, claiming an inability to concentrate in her presence. She gave him a coy look. "What's the *real* reason?"

Nathan cracked his knuckles, hoping to intimidate everyone around him. "A snotty college back east will be worse than the academy."

Catherine wrinkled her brow. "You are tempted by the southwest."

"Why not? At least I could shoot my way out of trouble instead of eating contempt for breakfast, lunch, and dinner."

In the afternoon, he and Catherine strolled along the private lane. He made excuses for his lack of participation and reassured her of his loyalty.

"I should consider Chicago for college," she said. "Father believes in travel before marriage." She looked up at the sky.

"I'm not going back east."

Her eyes fell on him. "Oh?"

Catherine's mounting desire was barely concealed.

He ran a hand through his hair. "After graduating high school, I'll head to San Francisco where a hardy schooner will take me across the globe."

He did not wish to exhibit a trace of weakness in her presence.

"Will you ever return?" The question pouted her lips.

"Yes, but only after I've lived in Australia and Japan for several years. I must know their perilous climes as well as I've known my own."

"Nathan, you are a romantic at heart." Her voice carried a tint of rosy adulation. "In my estimation, your plan will provide you with many noble adventures, but it's also quite precarious for our love, as I will be tested in your absence. A belle of my caliber rarely meets such trials."

She paused.

"I hope you recognize the strain your excess puts upon my brow."

"Excess is all I know, with romance or any other endeavor."

Catherine wiped a tear and pulled his body closer.

"We're both the same, Nathan. We originate from unhappy homes."

"Yes," he said, nodding.

"We must help one another survive in this fallen realm. If you must travel the globe in search of your elaborate destiny, then I will wait. You have awakened a love in me which had lain dormant since birth, but you are not disposed to help me cope. Please tell me you feel a deep and abiding love."

"I love you, Catherine." Nothing could have been more true.

She retrieved a piece of paper and unfolded it.

"Where did you get this?"

"The professor," she said. "Will you listen to the words? They might help you someday, while you're crisscrossing the oceans."

"For you, anything."

She read Psalm 5:6-7. "You will destroy those who tell lies. The Lord detests murderers and deceivers. Because of your unfailing love, I can enter your house; I will worship at your temple with deepest awe. Lead me in the right path, O Lord, or my enemies will conquer me. Make your way plain for me to follow."

"What does it mean?"

"It means I love you, Nathan. That's exactly what it means."

"I hope you will remain true."

She whispered into his ear. "Never leave my side."

He pulled back from her. "What if I do?"

Catherine smiled. "It will end badly for all."

Six

Psalm 6:2

Have compassion on me, LORD, for I am weak.
Heal me, LORD, for my bones are in agony.

Nathan detected an empty liquor bottle near the alley entrance. He plopped onto a water-stained crate and listened as crickets chirped from the filthy and wet abyss. They sang songs of renewal and happiness, having retreated from the sparkle and fury of fallen creation. A gust of wind scraped trash into a far corner, and about half-way down, a little dog rooted through garbage, clanging a tin can against the alley's brick floor. Nathan's back ached from proceeding so often about town since Daisy and Catherine's arrival, the two women touching one another as knifelike cohorts without speaking a word. The vile netherworld of the alley called to him, beckoning his entry, offering a gentle spot to lie down. It was his due, his fatal calling, a return to earthly perdition.

The two women would be there with the crickets, waiting for blood.

"There's nothing in there but death," Samuel said. "Take another course." His voice carried a bored and disdainful tone.

"Stop pushing me."

Samuel leaned against the brick wall. "You need to face facts."

"Which are?"

"Your patients are loyal, but they won't be around for much longer."

"It doesn't matter," Nathan said. "The younger generation won't go near my roster. Their road to gold is paved elsewhere."

"It matters plenty. Some have turned to that fool, Pierce. He still believes in bleeding away their ailments." Samuel hesitated. "Pierce isn't the only one bleeding them dry. Mrs. Parson's older son, Charles, has convinced her to pass her wealth to him before she dies. For all I know, she's of sound mind and body, but her reasoning remains a mystery."

"Never underestimate an imploring son's persistence."

"Oh, trust me, I know all about it." Samuel's hand nudged Nathan. "You must reach out and grab the next generation before it's too late."

Nathan kicked over the crate. Each brick echoed its thwack toward the end of the alley. The startled little dog yelped and ran past them, his tail firmly stuck between his legs. He bobbed between those out for a stroll.

"Do you remember what Catherine did to me?"

"You can win her back," said Samuel politely.

"I don't want her, and from the sound of it, no one else does either."

"You underestimate her appeal."

Nathan gave his father a quizzical look. "I don't think I do."

"She was once the Caroline Astor of St. Louis."

Nathan winced at the impressionistic portrait. His mind quickly conceived four counter suppositions, each one a simile as silly and worthless as Catherine's former triumphs. The elite of St. Louis had once thought her cheerful as roomy sunshine, fresh as a bath after the dust and heat of travel, right as a fan upon the table in summer, and cozy as a good fire in winter. In their eyes, she was the very picture of noble fineness and delicate grace. Nathan knew her better than anyone, even her father. She had thrown her wild hands to the heavens and claimed war was lovely, leaving him for the arms of a genuine outlaw, a man who gambled and lurched through the southwest and beat her senseless on multiple occasions. He had tossed her onto the street with the horse droppings and the crawling insects and the slithering snakes. Those who passed by her wretched form ridiculed her with scornful rebukes. She was the daughter of Satan, tempted by the ruby apple.

Oh, how the mighty had fallen.

Nathan shook the woeful images. "That was ten years ago, Pop."

"It wasn't so long ago. Take advantage of her reappearance."

"Do you imagine I yearn for the Big Cinch's endorsement?"

"Your medical practice requires financial support." Samuel went on in a convinced way. "Newly minted millionaires are stretching our fair city ever westward, one development after another." He squeezed Nathan's arm. "The money in your account is dwindling, and soon you'll be on the street begging for change while you desperately roam from one part of town to another. You cannot survive as a beaten down drunkard forever."

"I can live on your farm," Nathan said. "I know how to pick corn."

"No, Son, you'll never live with me. I'm old and set in my ways, and I don't want a bored layabout pinching pennies at my expense."

Nathan sighed. "I see you aren't one for sentimentalities."

"Neither are you, Son."

Nathan stared in silence. Moths pranced above the city lamps.

Samuel watched him, waiting for his response.

"It helps to know she's worse off than me."

Samuel arched his eyebrows. "No one has found you naked on Main Street." His voice carried an ominous tone.

"Don't count me out."

"I'll unload my pistol into your hide on that day."

Nathan sized up his father. "You'd do it."

"Yes, I would. Ten years is enough penance."

Nathan steadied himself on Samuel's shoulder. "I should have saved them, Pop." Tears coursed down his bearded cheeks. "I let them all down, Catherine, our two boys, and our darling Annie."

"You were a man who could not defy our Lord and Savior, Jesus Christ." Samuel pulled away from Nathan's attempted hug. "Get a hold of yourself before the entire town sees you fall apart right here on Locust Street."

Nathan took a step backward and swiped the tears from his eyes. "I knew there was a reason I didn't like you."

"I failed you as a father then and now," said Samuel, nodding. "But it's not about me and you. It's about a helpless woman who needs your empathy and your compassion. She'll die without you, Nathan."

A gentler portrait of Catherine formed. She was a terribly damaged woman who had lost everything, including her will to live.

For years, Nathan had longed to think of nothing but her betrayal.

"After we buried the kids, she went back to Martin, the husband I didn't know existed. Her desertion shattered my pride and corrupted my honor. There was no room for ordinary thoughts once our fairy tale ended."

"Based on her bruises, Martin worked her over regularly. The Dealey sheriff said it looked like a powerful man tried to break her in half." Samuel looked at Nathan with concern. "She woke up today, you know."

A flutter formed in Nathan's belly. "I hadn't heard."

He paced several yards up the sidewalk, turned, and retraced his steps.

"It appears she has aphasia," Samuel said. "She can't understand what anyone around her is saying and can't speak or write a word."

"I guess some people have it coming."

"Maybe so, but you're the only one who can save her."

Nathan stepped into the street. The breeze tickled his face and neck while the stars twinkled accusations from the heavens. Across the corner, the grand architecture of the Methodist church caught his attention and refused to let go. The magnificent building hosted funerals for well-loved priests and city dignitaries and soldiers lost in the War Between the States. Holy battle cries had gone out many times during Nathan's childhood.

Christ has died!

Christ is risen!

Christ will return in the clouds with a shout!

He pointed. "Mom loved her church."

"She sure did." Samuel's eyes moistened at the recollection.

Nathan took a deep breath. His hands had become sweaty in the humid night air. He slipped them into his pockets. "You carry her legacy."

"Our Most High God provides answers to the innermost uncertainties in the hearts of men and women, if they will only ask for His guidance."

There were times when Samuel seemed naïve and innocent. Had he not seen death and destruction? Did he not remember the war which had torn his family and the once bonded nation asunder? Over six hundred thousand souls had lost their lives. Heroes died gallant deaths on the field while cowards with greedy intentions made it home. They ran for office and started businesses and claimed their rightful place as moral pillars of the community. The cost for families and towns over the next century would be unfathomable, and America would likely become a nation unrecognizable.

John Belmont had been one of those covetous men who returned untouched by war, and as such, he preserved an equally childish sense of right and wrong. He was Catherine's father and would do anything to restore her physical body first and her reputation for polite excellence a more important second. Those superficial pursuits deemed superior, recovery of her starless soul was never under consideration, just as bravery in the face of an enemy had been deemed trivial by his ambition. Once recovered, Catherine would likely rule St. Louis society, the same in the future as in the past, and as before, Nathan wanted no part of her vain undertakings.

He shallowed his breaths and tried to forget Belmont's proposition.

"Your religious views originate from an obsolete book written thousands of years ago in a forsaken desert plain." Nathan hesitated. "Did a loving mother instill a sentimental attachment to your backward notions?"

"There is truth to your assertion. My mother and father were religious people, as were most in their generation. It was when I left their home and ventured into the streets that I first witnessed hideous things. Many I have never shared with you and probably never will. To some degree, I was already a hardened veteran when I entered the war, but the horrors there were unimaginable to all of us, and they marked us for life. Since then, I've observed a downward trend in our culture, and I believe the war was the cause. Many towns, especially in the south, were completely obliterated by invading troops or marauders who murdered and pillaged." Samuel tapped his heel on the sidewalk. "Our looming financial crisis stems from the resulting moral decline, and only through a revival of faith can we make a successful transition into the next century. I see gradual change even in the church, and it concerns me. If we lose our relationship with Jesus Christ, we'll become a barren void, and I shudder to think how we will fill the gap."

"You filled it nicely in New York. I was sent into a lion's den with only my skill as a surgeon to keep me alive. Why would you do such a thing to your only son?" Nathan stared at the church building and recalled sermons from his youth. Would this version of Samuel meet with June's approval?

"John Belmont informed me of Catherine's return a few weeks ago," said Samuel, his disposition sinking into melancholy. "She was on the brink of death in a Chicago hospital, and her floundering condition spurred me to action. I could no longer bear to see you destroy yourself by holding onto her memory, and I knew what would happen if she died."

"So you sent me to die in her place?"

"No, Son. I sent you to *live*."

Nathan stared at the church building once more.

Perhaps his mother would approve. "I suppose it's worth a try."

"That's the spirit." Samuel bounced on his toes. "You'll snatch poor Catherine from the dusty grave, and our newspapers will hail the return of Antony and Cleopatra."

"It didn't end so well for them," said Nathan, smirking. "I should scramble out of St. Louis tonight."

"Leave here and become an orphan again?" Samuel shook his head. "You wouldn't last five minutes in the wilderness."

"I'm more resourceful than you think."

"You need this community," said Samuel, smiling. "Most of all, you need her love. Catherine's flesh and blood are once more in your presence."

Nathan chuckled at his father's transgression. "You forgot to say I need God above anyone else. What would He have to say about that?"

"You fell from His grace long ago." Samuel's eyes rose to the heavenly firmament. "You'll come back to Him one of these days. He's assured me you won't stay lost indefinitely."

Nathan and Daisy observed Catherine from their position near the cherry tree front door. A thickness in Nathan's throat threatened an onset of tears and diverted his desirous gaze, wiping all expression from his face.

Daisy put her hand on his shoulder and squeezed, soothing him.

He brushed off her touch. "Catherine's general state of cognition has been affected, causing difficulties with sustainment of focus and memory." He pointed. "It appears she has Bell's paralysis." His hand dropped to his side. "She also has a combination of amnesia and ataxia aphasia."

"*Femme pauvre*," Daisy said.

Nathan withheld a response.

He caught her inquisitive look from the corner of his eye.

"It means poor woman," she said. "I feel sorry for her."

Catherine flailed about in the bed. A nurse calmly applied restraints.

Daisy gestured. "That's Nurse Pratt. She's very attentive to Catherine's needs, and she works well with the other patients. I am most impressed."

"It's her job."

"It wasn't always so in Europe." They both stared at Catherine for several minutes. "Does it bother you to see her in distress?"

Nathan shrugged.

"How would you treat her condition?"

"I'd review her physical symptoms, give her a tonic, and then get roaring drunk at the brothel. It's been my way for a decade."

"You will not be that man anymore."

His eyes rolled.

Someone cried out from a bed halfway up the line. The voice was a flash which caught Daisy's interest. She turned toward the sound.

"They should force her to write dictation," Nathan said, "and keep the pages for reference, noting what words have been obliterated or confused and her ability to pronounce consonants. Catherine has a long road ahead."

"If you were her doctor, you could see to it."

Daisy strolled up the aisle. She spoke with Nurse Pratt while gesturing toward Nathan. When he didn't move, she summoned him to Catherine's bedside. He was content to keep his distance and disliked the idea of close contact with anyone, especially when it involved diagnosing and treating the woman who had abandoned him. If he were to be honest, he'd rather march over to Catherine, place his hands around her throat, and squeeze. It would only take a few minutes, and she deserved it.

Nurse Pratt approached and stood beside him, surveying the room.

"Mr. Belmont has built an impressive hospital."

Nathan crossed his arms over his chest.

"Catherine has mostly slept since her arrival," said the nurse, her speech careful and ordered. "When conscious, she's very nervous."

"Sleep is the best thing for her ailments. The brain often heals itself."

Nurse Pratt nodded.

A German man moaned and flailed his arms, as if copying Catherine.

"Excuse me, sir. I must take my leave."

Nurse Pratt marched directly toward the distraught man, appeasing him with mellow talk while softly referring to him as Heinrich. She sat in a chair beside Heinrich's bed, took his trembling hand, and offered kind solace.

Daisy gently tapped the nurse's shoulder and traded places with her.

"My name is Daisy Lawrence, and I'm here to help."

Nathan opened a folder and removed a piece of paper which diagrammed the bed assignments and provided the patients' names, their psychological maladies, and a summary of their background.

Scanning the entries, Nathan had a discomforting thought.

My father is right about one thing.

Malevolence is the default human condition.

On each side of the main hall, there was a line of eight beds, and in the middle, a wide walkway for staff observation and patient transport.

At the far left end, Heinrich Besseler sat up and leaned against his metal headboard, wailing as if at the gallows. There were three beds between him and the next patient, John Hutchinson, who said no words, but chose only to stare at the ceiling and move his hands as if conducting an orchestra.

Opposite Heinrich at the far right end, Catherine laid in a twisted ball, her body battered into a grim presentation by a man who deserved death.

The adjacent bed was empty, but the next was occupied by John's wife,

Susanna Hutchinson. Rather than stay in bed like her husband, Susanna preferred to elegantly but dangerously dance around the room. Nurses asked her to return to her bed, but she refused in such a deranged manner and with such fierce and wide eyes, it frightened even the orderlies.

Next in line, twelve-year-old Ida Barnes blinked in rapid fashion as if sending encoded messages across a clouded field, and her head bobbed like a flexible owl. When in motion, her riotous little spirit ran about the room and bashed into everything it touched, until, momentarily winded, she plopped onto a rocking chair and observed both lines of beds like a general.

Her nervous feet bounced and slid against the glazed oak floor.

Nathan was relieved to find notes in the background section for Shirley Fletcher, a woman who reposed two beds up from Ida. While on her way to work at a brewery, an assailant had jumped from a nearby alley and strangled Shirley almost to death. Other men quickly appeared and stopped the fiendish adversary before he killed her. Since the event, her mind could not shake the feeling of being choked, and she had been left disabled. Shirley slept throughout the day, but awakened periodically and inspected the room for safety before she fell asleep again. She was convinced an apparition would return at night and commit an unspeakable act against only her.

Down the line, Catherine's fragile vulnerability beckoned Nathan closer. He scanned the page, and another thought manifested.

Only the toughest survive this cruel world.

On cue, Belmont descended the stairs. His boot heels thumped the wood, and his iron eyes glowed scarlet from a forge of hatred.

He gave a curt nod. "Are you *afraid* of these patients?"

"This is a tour." Nathan's muscles tightened in readiness for battle. He was born to fight, and so he would. "Go your way and let me be."

Belmont fumed for a few moments, but he let the comment go.

The two men surveyed the room.

When Heinrich refused consolation, Daisy leaned forward with merciful eyes. She opened her Bible and recited Psalm 6:1-3. "O Lord, don't rebuke me in your anger or discipline me in your rage. Have compassion on me, Lord, for I am weak. Heal me, Lord, for my bones are in agony. I am sick at heart. How long, O Lord, until you restore me?"

Heinrich swiped at his tears and then clutched his hands together.

"What right do you have to preach Bible verses to me, Miss Lawrence?"

"Right, sir? Whatever do you mean?"

"I am still a man, although a pitiful one who has known sorrow and regret." He looked about the hall and turned to her. "Where is *your* pain?"

His question clearly confused her, and she looked about the hall as he had just done, her eyes noting the grim deportment of the other hysterics, the lines which carved themselves along their faces, cut by time and harsh experience. Their stares saw through her meager pretense of advantage.

Nathan almost went to her but thought it better to postpone.

"People close to me perished because I was envious and wrathful."

"You know nothing of what I have lost," Heinrich said.

Daisy wiped her tears, glared reproachfully at Nathan, and then stood.

She rushed by him and out of the front door. It slammed behind her.

Nathan traded a sad look with Heinrich, and his mind rolled backward to the fall of 1883. After the funerals, he had begged Catherine to remain his wife and promised to make things right, no matter the cost or the effort expended. If her depression worsened, and she needed to see an expert in the newly developing field of psychology, he would see to it she had the best available neurologist, and if necessary, they would travel to La Salpêtrière in Paris. As was Catherine's custom, she retreated into a fast carriage and left nothing in her wake but the ashes of a scorched marriage. Nathan rushed to a saloon for whiskey and beer and a corner bedroom on the second floor. For ten years, he courted Sheila Byrne, the grateful Irish lass from the old country without a penny to her name and a temperament wholly unsuited for prostitution. They at once struck a bargain. Probing questions were off limits, and she would see only him. His bank account held enough to tide them over for many years, assuming he kept his other expenses low. In this manner, her grateful and affectionate haven afforded him a motherly encampment and kept him alive. Thus it continued, one cheerless night after another, until Daisy's piercing arrival set the darkness ablaze.

Belmont's eyes narrowed. "My daughter needs you to become a man."

Daisy cracked the door and peeked into the room.

Nathan summoned her closer with a scowl, and she moved to his side.

"Do *not* run away again."

She spoke in a monotone voice. "I cannot work in this hospital."

"What?"

Daisy spun around and marched to the front door. She opened and closed it, waning from his life as quickly as she had appeared.

Nathan and Belmont exchanged glances.

"Catherine requires your full attention. Do not discard her."

"As I mentioned, I'll consider your offer."

Belmont sneered bitterly and trudged upstairs to his office.

Empty and numb, Daisy walked to Fountain Park and sat underneath a gazebo where she considered her dwindling options. She could be Nathan's housekeeper instead of his physician's assistant. It might be enough.

Her father was probably right. She should move back to the winery.

A nearby squirrel taunted a young dog who passed through, prompting Daisy to pray. *Father, I put my trust in you. Many question my sanity, but I know you are real. You shine such a bright light upon me, Lord, and sometimes I cannot withstand it. Please cover me with your grace and mercy, so I might feel safe once again, and I ask you to send me a sign, so I might know your will.*

Nathan sat down beside her on the bench and took a long swig from his flask. He made idle conversation about the weather. When she asked him to leave, he demanded she work for him at the hospital.

"Heinrich invaded my privacy, and the rest will do the same."

"We'll find you an office." Nathan removed his hat.

"I don't believe you."

"You may not, and that is certainly your right, but I don't believe your concern for privacy or your belief in my sincerity is your problem," he said. "You see me as nothing but a drunkard, and it disgusts you."

"I formed a positive opinion at Union Depot."

"You thought me an amusement. It was nothing more."

"Your personal habits, odd as they are, both fascinate and concern me."

She took a deep breath and exhaled, filled with self doubt. "I will only align myself with a man of character. You know that by now."

"I remain unconvinced of your honesty, Miss Lawrence."

"I can share one story from my past which might illuminate the current state of my feelings." She wished to retire from a rising argument.

"Please do." He took another sip.

Her posture straightened as she prepared for the inevitable flood of emotion. "As I mentioned the night we met, I attended the University of Paris. It was a wonderful atmosphere, and I enjoyed friendship with a group of carefree students. We spent time together along the Seine on warm and lovely afternoons, drinking wine and swimming in the cool water. After one such excursion, my best friend, Adrienne, left early to study in the library, drawing jeers from the rest of us who were intent on having fun. Not long afterward, a father and son were arrested for running over my friend as she attempted to cross the street. The two men had been drinking in a corner cafe, and they started their horse at a gait dangerous for pedestrians. Their wagon dragged Adrienne forty or fifty feet over the hard pavement on account of her dress becoming fastened on the wheels. The men were arrested and fined five dollars in an appalling miscarriage of justice."

"Should they have hanged?"

She flipped her hair in annoyance. "I don't know."

"Then why hold on to the memory?"

"Adrienne's sweet, smiling face haunts my dreams. I could not save her when it was my job to do so. I'm an abominable mess, and I wouldn't be any good for your patients. They need someone with a clear conscience."

"She was not your family." He stiffened. "I don't understand."

Daisy paced in front of him. "I cannot help you, Nathan."

"The hospital will not work without your tenacious spirit."

"How can you say that?" She placed a hand over her mouth, then dropped it to her side. "You are the physician, the engine turning the gears."

"You will become the heart of the machine." He hesitated. "Join me for rounds in the morning. I'll show you my true nature, and you can reveal yourself to me in return." He held out his hand. "It's all I ask."

Her eyes darted left and right. Unsure of what else to do, she raced to

Enright and waved her hand. She pleaded her case to a carriage driver who took pity on her and stopped. The sun beat down upon her neck.

She stepped inside.

Nathan approached. He asked her again.

Daisy shook her head. "It's too difficult."

She tried to close the carriage door, but he held it open.

"It's obvious we have feelings for one another, Daisy."

"I would rather avoid love than lose it."

"I know you don't believe such a morbid statement," he said softly. "It's out of character for you."

"You don't know me well enough to say such a thing." She tugged on the door. "I would only distract from your actual battle, choosing between Catherine Belmont and the lovely Sheila."

His hands gripped the door with brute strength. Tears coursed down her tender cheeks, and she pulled again. He released his grip on the handle, and she slammed the door shut.

"How could a bookish girl ever hope to compete with such women?"

He leaned closer to the window. "What do you mean?"

"Samuel was kind enough to share your unfavorable comments about my nature. It hurt me at first, but then I realized you were right to say them. We come from different backgrounds, Nathan. You do not know what pain I've suffered or what horrors I've seen."

"We just met. Don't wander out of my life so soon."

"Step back, sir!"

He obliged, pushing away from the cab.

As the carriage shifted forward, and Nathan Marsh faded into the distance, he became yet another blank face from her past. Daisy closed her eyes, knowing full well she would always be alone, a sullen and withdrawn caretaker of love, watching it unfold for others from afar, never to know it deep within her own marrow. The vastness of her life was meant for *one*.

SEVEN

Psalm 7:14

The wicked conceive evil;
they are pregnant with trouble
and give birth to lies.

July 1891

Attendants shoved programs in Daisy's face as she wandered through the crowded lobby. She spotted the door on the far side and rushed forward, continuing up the stairs to the private dining area. A smiling usher led her to a designated theater box, taking her gloved hand, steadying her frame as she rested on an embroidered seat, careful to avoid wrinkling her bell-shaped skirt. He returned a few minutes later with a glass of champagne and stood behind her, waiting for instruction. Below Daisy, lower-level audience members read gaudy brochures and prattled with neighbors. Muffled footsteps on the carpeted stairs interrupted her viewing, and she craned her neck to learn the identity of the offending party.

Lights dimmed. The sound passed as quickly as it had arrived.

Frank Kaneski strode onto the stage and stood at a podium, confident, radiant, filled with a depraved passion. Within minutes, his enraptured congregation leaned forward, eyes wide, imbibing his intoxicating rhetoric.

Sigmund had warned her about a relationship with such a man. Accord with the wrong people, those who guarantee progress but deliver genocide will lead a naïve soul to perdition. Daisy bristled at the attack on her gallant hero, and Sigmund placed his hands in his pockets, breaking off their conversation. Frank since traveled across Europe in promotion of his latest book, *Consciousness of Domination*, the fifth in a series of philosophical discourses. The strain in their relationship increased with the length and breadth of yet another tour, but Daisy clung to Frank as her fiancé and her God chosen companion, a man of honor who pined away his sleepless nights alone as he awaited reunification with his one true love. The fantasy of a grand wedding and a blissful life together had kept her alive after Frank's departure, and she had since waited patiently for news of his return. When none came, she took matters into her own hands. She would see for herself what Frank Kaneski did while alone in his hotel room.

Once his speech concluded, admirers surrounded their hero and tugged him in different directions, forcing Daisy to loiter alone. A stunning woman, Rosemarie Bello, parted the crowd and whispered in Frank's ear. His reaction to her fiery presence struck Daisy with terror. Was he infatuated with this woman? Could he be in love? Daisy's legs weakened as she steadied herself against a doorframe and grasped at the wood with unsteady fingers.

Rosemarie led Frank toward the stairs. Her lips blazed red.

A thousand generations of evil minions stabbed at Daisy, made ghastly accusations, and called her vicious names. The chorus washed over her.

She marched to her room, where she adorned herself with a new outfit and a new outlook. One glance at her, and Frank would reaffirm their bond.

The door to his hotel room was unlocked. Noises emanated from the other side. She turned the knob, hoping against all hope.

The door pushed open. It revealed a desperate truth.

Naked bodies made furious love in his bed.

Daisy picked up a vase and threw it at Frank.

It crashed against the wall beside him.

Rosemarie's voice was light. "So happy to see you, darling. Won't you join us?" She enjoyed playing the cruelest of games.

Daisy glimpsed the Danube River through the open window. Her feet were restless as tiny boats rafted past the hotel, faintly calling to her.

She could leap.

Daisy recited Psalm 7:1-2. "I come to you for protection, O Lord my God. Save me from my persecutors—rescue me! If you don't, they will maul me like a lion, tearing me to pieces with no one to rescue me."

The couple laughed at her girlish outburst.

"You are far too innocent to remain in this world." Frank sat up and leaned against the headboard. His sneer ran into every recess of her body.

"You were once like me," said Daisy, still convinced of his goodness.

He lit a cigarette. "I've since accepted the realities of life." He took a long puff and exhaled. "Lucifer is now my god."

"It's not too late for us, Frank. If you get on your knees in humble surrender and offer Jesus sincere repentance, He will hear your cries."

Frank stuffed his cigarette into an ashtray. "Lucifer calls you home to him, Daisy, where you most belong. His appetite for you knows no bounds, and he is a most expectant lover."

"Would you have me run a dagger through my heart?"

He gave her a tender smile. "No, my dear. Rosemarie and I are here to help. We offer you a gentle and painless exit."

"You are not this man. I know the real man inside, the one who wished to change things for the better."

"You don't know the first thing about him or how to appreciate his theories," Rosemarie said with a casual authority. "His latest book has become all the rage, and soon Frank will lead a cultural revolution, replacing your antiquated norms with a stateless anarchy. In the next century, our long awaited Utopia will emerge, and we will be free at last."

"Free to do what?"

Rosemarie smiled. "To do as we wilt."

"God won't stand for it."

Rosemarie reveled in her nakedness, laughing as she strolled past Daisy.

In the corner, she dressed and stepped out.

Her eyes fell on Frank, who remained in the bed. He watched her with a lustful admiration. "We'll have dinner tonight with beastly men who have the funds and the influence to place you well. They despise tardiness, so we mustn't be late. I want maximum satisfaction from our meeting."

He sat up straight at her command. "Will they control me?"

Rosemarie gave him an intense look. "Completely."

Daisy asked God for the right words. The Lord delivered them.

He is selling his soul for thirty pieces of silver. Remind him of the cost.

"Frank, your soul is worth more than a momentary gain in popularity. Those who spread your theories will leave you at the first opportunity, and in the end, you will die broken and penniless, a shell of your former self. You say I am to leave this realm as a young woman, but it is you who will die before old age. Mark my words, the Lord will not be mocked."

Rosemarie lit a cigarette and sat down. "Little girls have no place in a modern Europe. After I write letters to our controllers, your reputation will be dragged through the mud, and no one will hire you to clean floors, much less tend patients. You mark *my words*, little one, your days here are over."

Daisy's eyes filled with tears. "What happened to you, Frank? All I ever wanted was to love you and to make a home together in Vienna."

Rosemarie blew a sensual kiss in his direction.

He stiffened, and his wrathful eyes sought Daisy. "I am a man of power and influence, and nothing you say will alter my course."

"You're repeating Rosemarie's thoughts."

He threw her a look of contempt. "The world repeats my ideas, so it's a fair trade." He was intent on denying their relationship to the last.

"Then I bid you farewell."

Rosemarie's slender hand waved in grand fashion. "*Arrivederci*, young Daisy. May you venture forth to the next life sooner than later."

"We were supposed to wed." Daisy's eyes bored through her nemesis. "The Lord will judge your works, and you will be found wanting."

"So be it," said Rosemarie indifferently. "Some of us want to burn."

"You'll get your wish." Daisy's teeth bared. She wanted to rip out the woman's foul heart. "The second death awaits your dreadful soul."

Rosemarie disrobed and climbed back into bed with Frank.

He gave her a surprised look. "I thought we had to meet *beastly* men for dinner." He pulled her bright, willowy body close.

"Another time, *amore*. This one has excited my flesh." She grinned at Daisy and patted the sheet which covered Frank's leg. "Won't you join us, little girl? We have so much to teach the young ones."

A wild anger flooded Daisy's body and overwhelmed her senses. She would gladly and fiercely pound Rosemarie's face until no teeth remained.

"Yes, that's it." Rosemarie closed her eyes. "I sense the rage within you. It boils your blood and fills me with an inexpressible delight." Her eyes rose to meet Frank's. "This one might be easier to entice than you were."

He placed a strand of hair behind her ear. "Do your best."

Rosemarie kneeled on the bed and curled her finger, summoning.

"Come here, little one, join our group of diviners. Our fangs sink deep, drawing forth the purest among you. We have lived behind the scenes for generations, hiding our powers from the light of day, waiting for the time spoken of in prophecy. Many an unsuspecting fool has entered our evening lair and succumbed to our penetrating charms, your fiancé among them. Like Circe with Odysseus, I have shown Frank an enlightened path, and with his intellectual prowess, we will blend in with your population and take over all aspects of culture and government, piece by piece."

Daisy's hand, which was affixed to the door handle in a death grip, relaxed. Her flesh desired the passionate couple, their strength, their beauty, their lustful pursuits. She could reach out, take Rosemarie's hand.

It would be so easy.

The dank smell of freshly spilled blood wafted through the air. Patrice stood in her kitchen near the sink. Her hand held a knife. Even many years later, the gruesome memory haunted Daisy. Today, it might actually save her soul. Daisy backed into the door. She fumbled with the handle.

"Where are you going?" Rosemarie slid from the bed and stood.

She quickly ushered Frank beside her and whispered into his ear.

Her eyes fell on Daisy. "Frank will show you the love you seek, little one." She caressed him, as if placing him under a spell. "Kill her, Frank. We will throw her bloodless body into the Danube. Her death will energize us for the meeting, and our controllers will be most proud of our work."

As Rosemarie pushed him toward Daisy, her fangs appeared.

Daisy's eyes widened in sheer terror.

"This is the part I most enjoy," Rosemarie said. "The look in their eyes before their blood spills." She moved forward, pushing Frank and speaking in a soothing tone. "Don't fight us, little one. We only seek to help."

"You want me dead." Daisy was frozen in place by her own desire.

"Oh, yes. It is most definitely what I want."

Saliva dripped from Rosemarie's fangs as she eased past Frank and drew close to Daisy's neck. The enervating moisture fell lightly onto Daisy's skin, preparing and marking it. "We will soon have our way with the world, little one, but for now, we will have our way with *you*." Rosemarie pulled away slightly and looked into Daisy's eyes. "I will relish the taste of your blood."

Daisy was paralyzed by a web of her own transgressions.

The only way through the maze was surrender and deliverance.

She recited the Lord's Prayer from Matthew 6:9-13. "Our Father in heaven, may your name be kept holy. May your Kingdom come soon. May your will be done on earth, as it is in heaven. Give us today the food we need, and forgive us our sins, as we have forgiven those who sin against us. And don't let us yield to temptation, but rescue us from the evil one."

A strong wind swept into the room. It pushed Daisy against the door and threw Rosemarie and Frank onto the bed, pressing their naked bodies flat against the sheets and pulling their eyes wide in astonished horror.

As the wind subsided, Daisy yanked on the handle and rushed through the doorway. She ran down the hall to the stairs, fled to the first floor, and then to the street. On a sidewalk bench, she fanned herself and caught her breath, trying to extricate the images and the words from her mind.

In her hotel room, Daisy holed up in a corner. She pressed her back into the wall, dropped to the floor, and slid her legs outward. There, she stared at her empty palms through glassy eyes, and considered following Patrice.

To calm her wild and lawless mood, she focused on Romans 12:2. "Don't copy the behavior and customs of this world, but let God transform you into a new person by changing the way you think. Then you will learn to know God's will for you, which is good and pleasing and perfect."

Daisy called out to God in repentance for her wickedness.

She asked Jesus to forgive her and begged Him to remain her eternal Savior. She received a word from the Most High.

Rest easy, my dear. You comported yourself well in the face of an ancient evil. The demon inside Rosemarie has hunted men and women alike since the Great Flood, and many have fallen to ruin in its presence. Keep your focus on my Word, which overrules all temptations in your heart and inspires you to live for me. Remember, Daisy, I have many plans for you which will unfold over the course of your life. You must visit Paris before returning to America.

"Why, Lord? There is nothing for me there."

Encouragement awaits your arrival.

Daisy closed her eyes. "Yes, Lord."

She rode the train from Vienna to Paris. Her belly hardened and dropped with each manifestation of dread. Rosemarie's words pecked at her soul from a distance, relentless in their pursuit, tempting in their intention.

An older man offered timely advice. With kind eyes, he recounted his younger years spent in California, where he panned for gold. It was a fool's errand, but he had once possessed a need for wealth and adventure.

The train made its next stop. Passengers made their way to the exits.

He readied himself for departure. "Your adventure is waiting just over the heavenly horizon, and your riches are stored in love, not Mammon."

The man tipped his hat and hauled his bag down the aisle.

She smiled at his fading form, thankful for the kind words.

Daisy prepared to battle for her good standing. Although her heart trembled at the prospect, she would not leave Charcot and Paris without a fight. At La Salpêtrière, she discovered the latest gossip which circulated the halls and even took root among the patients. Frank had told everyone in the neurology community Daisy was a woman of ill repute, and Rosemarie made good on her promise to leverage her controllers. Newspaper articles followed. They ripped apart Daisy's reputation like Anne Hutchinson in the Massachusetts Bay Colony, and like Anne, Daisy would be forever banished.

Charcot embraced her with a grave countenance. "Walter was in love with you, and he would have loved you for the rest of your life."

"Our personalities clashed, Jean-Martin."

"What is clashing, but lovers having a spat which can be overcome?"

He took a step back, his hands still gripping Daisy's arms. "None of it matters now. If Walter pursued a relationship with you, his medical career at La Salpêtrière would end. Our asylum patients would suffer."

She leaned forward and whispered farewell. "Please tell Walter I will miss him. He was a better man than I understood." Daisy hugged him tight, her voice strained. "As are you, Jean-Martin."

"You will be long remembered, Miss Lawrence."

He sat down, winded.

"Are you alright?"

He smiled up at her. "You are like a lost daughter I never knew. I fear this will be our final meeting together. My health is not what it once was, and you will have no reason to return here again." He wiped a tear. "I will never forget your intelligence, nor your kind heart, nor your wonderful spirit."

She hugged him once more. "I love you, Jean-Martin."

"As do I, Miss Lawrence." He hesitated. "I wish you a most happy life."

She turned to leave and then stopped. Her eyes fell on him again.

"Things I've seen cause me to question my sanity."

He nodded.

"You cannot escape such questioning throughout the entirety of your life, but if you give up all hope, there can be no better tomorrow."

Daisy braved the crowds to board an ocean liner, *Majestic*, operated by the White Star line. It made its record setting run across the Atlantic in 1891, leaving from Liverpool on July 30th and reaching New York on August 5th. She rode in a cheaper cabin below decks and fought seasickness, vowing never to step foot on a ship again.

She spent a solitary year in New York as a French woman and most of another in Chicago as an Austrian maid before coming home to her father's winery. Daisy told no one of her travails in Europe and received no letters.

Eventually, the malicious newspaper articles ceased.

After returning home, she wandered the winery shop and grounds, unable to concentrate. Her father employed her in a minor capacity, and she kept the peace, working while depressed, making mistakes and receiving a scolding. She no longer cared about anyone or anything.

EIGHT

Psalm 8:1

O Lord, our Lord, your majestic name fills the earth!
Your glory is higher than the heavens.

Daisy navigated the east gate at Westmoreland Place, known to residents as the *good end*, and passed between impervious worlds. At Number Five, she climbed granite steps, wandered through a massive doorway, and entered the main hall. She removed her fawn-colored gloves and arranged herself at the center, a careful defense against sisterly attacks. The ponderous brass chandelier twinkled its acknowledgement and gave quiet attention while it brightened her and the English mosaic tile. A curved stairway rose to the second and third floors as its polished balusters and profane tapestries promised to reveal innermost secrets. Daisy resolutely followed Brenda's butler, Jeffrey, into the drawing room, where Dan's irksome cigar smoke lingered, and the vigorous smell of a man lightened even her darkest moods and revived her will to live, if only for another hour.

"Miss Daisy Lawrence, madam. Will there be anything else?"

"That will be all, Jeffrey. Please leave us."

"Yes, madam."

The door closed with a thud, sealing sisters into a common space.

"Where are the kids?"

"Dan took them to his law office this morning." Brenda hovered uneasily about the room. "He said I need a break."

"It was nice of him."

"His trial lasted several weeks, and he's making amends. To further elevate my spirit, he's proposed an odyssey to the World's Fair in Chicago."

"I doubt you'll leave the hotel," said Daisy after a moment. She stared at her boots, withholding a giggle.

"You'd be wise to counsel him on the matter. If he cannot restore my good humor, I'll throw him out of the window."

"A philistine stands before me. This woman who claims to be my sister, I do not recognize."

Brenda's arms crossed. "Is that so?"

"It is."

"You'll feel the same when your wild heart has been married for a decade." Brenda's comment seemed to reassure her. She stood confidently.

Daisy inventoried the drawing room and noted its embellishments; if she were Dan Harper's wife, her problems would evaporate in an instant. She flipped back her hair and went to the window, where she opened a curtain to the street. Further commentary would only result in a tongue lashing. Daisy had been a fool to abandon her family and lurk inside the behemoth La Salpêtrière with a man old enough to be her grandfather and later to share an apartment with a married Austrian and his entire family. She had done nothing improper in either situation, but letters to Pierre and Parisian news articles had said otherwise, forcing her home.

Daisy spoke over her shoulder. "Don't refer to me as wild, Brenda. You know how it pains me."

"Please sit." Brenda's hand motioned toward the couch.

Daisy stared at the street, unmoving.

Brenda's voice lowered. "I will not ask you again."

Daisy sat. Her palm raised to keep her sister at bay.

"If you must hear something positive, I toured Belmont Hospital this morning. It's quite impressive. They even have a small kitchen in the rear."

"Was Catherine Belmont in a tragic state?"

"She thrashed about in her bed, and I thought she might land on the floor," Daisy said. "There were other patients as well."

"Of what kind?"

Daisy's shoulders dropped. "Hysterics."

"You must have felt right at home." Brenda's voice carried a touch of contempt. She was a limited person who viewed others as moveable pawns.

"On the contrary. I was mortified."

"Brave the challenge, my dear. Those patients need your help."

Daisy was no neurologist, nor had she acquired the level of knowledge necessary to practice experimental psychology. Brenda would suggest Nathan's paternal guidance, a thought which made Daisy laugh out loud. The esteemed physician could not suffer through one day without emptying a bottle of whiskey. How could Daisy invest herself in such a man? She sniffed the air and rested her hands on her knees. "You have not persuaded your husband to cease smoking in here."

"We must make allowances. Men cannot be tamed to our liking."

"Which is why we love them."

"I suppose," said Brenda, rather uncharitable about her admission. She sat beside Daisy. "Tell me about your plans. Will you sort out the ignoble hysterics, or will you return to our father's winery as his kept spinster?" She laughed and patted her sister's leg. "I hear there's an opening."

"There are suitable men in Pollard," Daisy said. "Don't sell me short."

"Those farmers and shopkeepers would never satisfy your passions. You need a sophisticated man, and you know it."

"Well, I was invited to go with Dr. Marsh on his rounds."

Brenda straightened her posture. "When?"

"Tomorrow."

Brenda fanned herself. "The memories flood my brain at the mere mention of his name."

"Why do you favor him? Dan Harper is twice the gentleman."

"You should have seen Nathan and Catherine Marsh ten years ago, when they were the talk of the town. They had three children then, and the family ate Sunday brunch at the Regency Arms." She shook her head in sorrowful remembrance. "Such a shame. Each child gone within thirty days."

Daisy gasped. "It cannot be true."

"There are many layers to people who've experienced loss. You've only scratched the surface of this man."

On Daisy's first visit to Nathan's home, clues to his past had presented themselves. A neglected swing greeted her in the backyard, lamenting its lack of use and begging for one more chance to delight. As she stepped between boxes in the attic, her path was blocked by children's toys, some large and well used and others small and brand new. An elegant wedding dress inside a locked trunk produced a scornful glare and a deep sigh; upon hearing of its reopening, Nathan thrust himself backward and closed his eyes while doing his level best to forget her bothersome presence.

Brenda's eyes dropped to the oak floor. "My mind travels further back in time to the summer of 1878, five years before the death of their children. Nathan Marsh was a handsome rogue, and Catherine was his regal bride. He was an up-and-coming physician, and she was the daughter of the cotton press magnate, John Belmont. You were with me on one occasion." Brenda raised her eyes to the ceiling, ordering her memories. "Let's see, you must have been twelve. We were eating breakfast at the Regency, and in they strolled, a perfect resemblance of the ill-fated pair, Louis and Marie."

"He's nothing much to look at now, and he smells like the vats in our winery," Daisy said. "If he showed up at our father's lobby in his current condition, Pierre would beat him back with a broom handle."

Brenda laughed out loud. "I believe he would. What a sight it would be." She took Daisy's arm, squeezing hard. "Their nobility will live on forever in my mind. We must accept his invitation."

Daisy grimaced and yanked herself free. "I won't be sardined into a carriage with a sweaty lush."

"Then you'll miss out on a grand adventure, I'm sure."

"You'll travel alone with him? The city will gossip."

"What others assert matters little to me, and it should be of no concern to you, either." Brenda surprised Daisy by opening her form like the tiny and nimble sundew. "You'll sit in your room all alone while we explore the countryside. I'm told tomorrow's weather will be divine."

Daisy's hand stroked her throat. "I'll go on your foolish excursion, if only to prove you wrong. Honestly, I cannot wait to see the motley cast of characters this man treats, and once he's proven to be an unworthy choice, he'll be out of our lives forever."

Brenda's eyes fell on the rosewood table to her right. "When I open the secret door to my past, it's difficult to close. I was once younger, unmarried, and infatuated with a man of charm, gallantry, and intelligence. Much has changed in all our lives over the years." She studied her reflection in a mirror. "Today, this face is cracked, and it sags in all the wrong places. My countless corset enlargements have turned Dan Harper to stone." She gave Daisy a forced smile. "I might as well be Medusa."

"You've had children. It's natural."

Brenda paced the room, and her eyes flashed about restlessly. "Divorce is not a choice for a woman in my position. Where would I go? What would I do for money?" She glared at Daisy, demanding her full attention. "You knew all along I was making a mistake with Dan Harper, but still you said nothing. I believe you felt superior in Europe and also isolated from life's intricacies, as if the rules somehow did not apply to you there."

Daisy returned to the window and spread the curtain.

"Are you listening?"

"I am."

"You must probe further before shunning Nathan, for in my estimation, he presents your last opportunity for happiness. If you cannot seize the initiative, another will occupy your rightful station, and you may end up a spinster, or worse."

Daisy snorted. "What could be worse than spinsterhood?"

"Being cast into the role of wife and mother with no consideration for your needs or your desires, and being unable to scream or to flee or to change anything for the better, your gleeful acceptance of the unfolding tragedy, your only recourse."

"Brenda, your flair for the melodramatic is unsurpassed. You have a marvelous life here with Dan and the kids. You should accept your blessings and allow yourself to be happy." Daisy sat in a chair and opened the Bible to Psalm 8:2-5, reading aloud. "You have taught children and infants to tell of your strength, silencing your enemies and all who oppose you. When I look at the night sky and see the work of your fingers—the moon and the stars you set in place—what are mere mortals that you should think about them, human beings that you should care for them? Yet you made them only a little lower than God and crowned them with glory and honor."

Brenda's eyes flashed defiantly. "You should become a patient in John Belmont's asylum." She laughed at Daisy with a tasteful disdain.

The taunt had achieved its cold purpose. Daisy's subconscious dread returned, sending her spinning into an expanding abyss of worthlessness.

She closed the book with an impatient huff. "Your unwillingness to hear me tears at my heart. My deliverance must soon come, for I fear my nature."

"As do we all."

Daisy's chest tingled and her breathing became restricted; she pulled at her collar, seeking relief, fighting against urgent alarm. "Even the Lord cannot reach me, and it seems Nathan, the foul smelling drunkard, might be the only one left with enough fortitude to divert me from the inevitable."

"You once said the same about Frank Kaneski, and you used that belief to begin your reclamation project, one which failed, I might add, worsening your depression and pushing your resolve past the breaking point. I was so worried about you, Daisy. I slept little for months, and until I saw your return with my own eyes, I feared your death had already occurred."

"My reclamation depends on love. Nothing less will suffice."

"What about God? You just recited verses which declare His grandeur."

"Grandeur is not what I need. My soul is ready to depart."

Brenda rubbed her sister's back. She whispered into Daisy's ear. "You call me melodramatic, but I pale compared to your spectacle."

"So you've said many times." Daisy sprang from the chair.

Brenda stood, stroking her sister's arms. "Join me tomorrow."

"You were right to mention Frank. Like him, Nathan will depress my senses, and I will be the poorer for my trouble."

"We shall go together." Brenda hummed a cheerful tune, moving Daisy's arms up and down. "Your mood will improve." She leaned over to the table, still holding Daisy's arm with her left hand. With the right, she rang a bell.

Jeffrey entered the room. "Yes, madam?"

"My sister is just leaving."

"Yes, of course, madam." He gestured toward the main hall.

Brenda followed Daisy out, stopping in the drawing room's doorway. "Do you want love or not?" Her voice carried a pleading tone.

"I cannot endure another heartbreak."

"I will watch over you as Patrice should have done."

Daisy followed Jeffrey to the front door.

Brenda called out. "Be here at six o'clock, sharp!"

"Yes, *Mother*," said Daisy, her eyes rolling.

She exited her sister's house.

Brenda's boots bounded down her granite steps as she smiled and savored the Saturday morning. Daisy followed and presented Nathan with a look of pious disfavor. When asked for her hand, she held it close to her side, leaving little doubt as to her moral superiority and her frosty intentions. Nathan regretted how their encounter at Fountain Park had ended, but his immoral lifestyle and her changeable behavior gave each reason for pause.

The day would try them both.

Nathan helped the women into the wagon and took middle position.

Brenda offered him a wide smile, her voice singing. "Strange sightings have been reported across the county, especially in the outer regions. Should we meet charismatic elves or magical sorcerers, I will require a full measure of valor. What say you, sir?"

He throttled the reins, and the wagon surged forward. "We'll be safe enough. The only upsetting creatures on this trip are us."

Daisy looked admiringly at him. When he noticed, she turned and sat quietly beside him for a time. She kept so still, he assumed she'd fallen asleep.

Near Lafayette Square, Nathan winced as they passed the entrance to Benton Place. He turned, and his glance carried across the road to the field of knee-high alfalfa which grew there. Yellow canola flowers lived on the shoulder. They swayed in the wind as it feathered through the dry grass.

He sipped whiskey and considered.

Daisy tapped him on the shoulder. "You shouldn't imbibe during work, sir. It will dull your medical senses." She held her sides as if pained.

He took another sip and presented a sly grin.

She withheld comment for half a mile and pretended to be aloof. The warm breeze blew into bursting gusts and then retreated. It strengthened the heat and her need for an answer.

"What does Benton Place mean to you, Nathan?"

"Years ago, an old woman gave me aid when I most needed it."

"What was her name?"

"I knew her as Aunt Joy, and she was filled with it."

Daisy pressed her shoulder into him. "Pity there's no *joy* in your life."

"Your banter can take a rest."

"Sorry," said Daisy, blushing.

Nathan stopped first at Anderson's Hardware Store on Broadway near the river and spoke to a young man, Zackary Hill, who was slightly sick from using lead paint on a backroom wall. Nathan encouraged Zackary to marry his sweetheart, Gloria Baker, and become a laborer for Harold Whitlock, a pig farmer who was overwhelmed with work, his ham in high demand by the city asylum. Harold had been treated for trichinosis, as he enjoyed eating his own raw ham, a practice Nathan counseled him to cease at once.

They traveled north to Locust Street and visited with Reverend Charles Lindsay at the First Methodist Church, where builders had embedded a stained glass cross in the brick behind the pulpit. The sights and sounds of Reverend Lindsay's preaching bored Nathan as a boy, and he resorted to counting the glass pieces on the cross. He squirmed against a polished wooden bench as he chastised the minister for pushing his voice past its limits. Reverend Lindsay appreciated Nathan's concern over his strained vocal cords, but there was little time left for him in the pulpit, and he must make the most of every day. Before he let the group leave, the reverend reflected on June's enduring love for her Lord, her church, and her son.

"My clearest memory is of the back of her hand," Nathan said.

"When your heart is ready, you'll remember more."

Nathan bid the reverend farewell and led the group to the next stop, where he hoped to treat a young girl, Julie Paxton, for stomatitis, or oral sores. Her parents had dumped Julie onto an elderly caretaker, Florence Malone, while they traveled throughout Europe over the summer. After a careful examination, he concluded nothing much could be done, as Florence had lost much of her vision and could barely keep up with the child. She couldn't control what Julie consumed, giving the girl free rein to do as she pleased. The situation was further worsened by itinerant servants who visited the home twice each week. They presented Julie with treats as a reward for her absence from their workspace, and she happily complied.

An hour later, the wagon ventured beyond the far edge of Central West End and stopped near the east entrance to Portland Place. It was home to David Francis, the former mayor of St. Louis and the current governor of the State of Missouri. His entry into the community offered great prestige.

Daisy raised her chin. "Who will you see here?"

"I received a telegram a few days ago, asking if I would add the address to my rounds." He shrugged. "It must not be a crisis."

Nathan led Daisy and Brenda through a heavy gate and along a sidewalk to a well-appointed estate. Leafy trees gave way to manicured hedges and a colorful flower garden. The main building had rooftop sitting areas, a rectangular balcony overlooking their approach, and an expansive entryway.

Sarah Robinson greeted them without a knock. "Hello, Dr. Marsh. Won't you follow me into the parlor?"

She sat in a chair, and Nathan moved her hand up and down, testing wrist flexion and extension. He took a step back. "Can you perform the same movements on your own?"

"I can," said Sarah lightly.

Her superficial malady aroused suspicion. "May I ask, do you compose many letters?"

"Oh, yes. Every day." She adopted a languid pose and dropped her hand to her side. "My husband owns the Globe-Democrat, where he employs me as an editor. I'm the secret ingredient which makes his operation a success."

"How splendid," Brenda said. "Women have made such magnificent progress since the end of Reconstruction."

"Dr. Marsh, I wish you would make yourself more comfortable." Sarah glanced at Nathan impatiently and gestured toward several chairs. "Please humor me and sit." She pointed to a stack of newspapers on the floor to her left. "You might appreciate today's headline."

Brenda's eyes sparkled. "You're welcome beside me."

Nathan picked up a newspaper and sat in a chair opposite Brenda.

She frowned. "We've had such a good morning. Have I displeased you?"

"I'm afraid she's smitten," said Daisy with a tense buoyancy.

The headline read: "Grand Jury to Convene."

"I remember Brenda from my youth," he said with an expression of thoughtful sadness. "She was a most determined admirer."

"As I should have been. You and Catherine were a striking match."

Sarah moved heavily in her chair. "If I may interrupt the festivities, we have items to discuss."

"By all means."

Nathan tossed the paper to the floor.

"You may have guessed I have other motives for bringing you here."

"I gathered as much."

"Before he left our paper, Leland Prentiss joined your expedition to New York for one purpose—to collect the many missing pieces from your background." She allowed him to digest her words. "There is to be a spread in the Sunday edition. It will launch our coverage of the Thomas Hannah murder trial, and I must warn you, we are relentless in our pursuits."

"Is there enough evidence to begin the proceedings?"

She pursed her lips. "You tell me."

"I have no bearing on the murder investigation."

"Don't you?"

"Let's not play games. I came to your home in good faith."

"Your secret will not stay hidden for much longer." Sarah waited for his reaction, but found none. "The public deserves the truth, Nathan. Did your father kill June, or did *you*?"

Nathan steeled himself. "You should pray for health and a long life. Some have theirs cut short."

"We know the full story, and it's quite savage. Once the world learns what happened, you'll have a date with the hangman." She went on, sure of herself. "Your day of reckoning is long overdue."

Nathan's fury at Thomas Hannah resurfaced, and he glanced around the parlor, hoping his sudden discomfort remained unnoticed. He tightened his hands into a fist and then loosened them, trying to slow his breathing and restore serenity. A mounting sense of foreboding overwhelmed him, an unshakeable sense something was terribly wrong. Without understanding why, he rose to leave, making his way to the front door, moving fast, unwilling to be corralled in such a horrible atmosphere.

Daisy caught up with him.

Her hand grabbed his arm. "Is Sarah telling the truth?"

He turned toward her, his voice filled with anger. "You cannot believe this woman's lies. She hopes to sell newspapers. Nothing more."

"You are no gentleman, Nathan. How can I believe anything you say?"

She rushed outside and climbed onto the wagon.

Brenda approached. "Daisy is a temperamental woman, but she's worth every sacrifice. Please give her a chance to win your heart."

He glanced helplessly at Sarah. She gave him a smirk.

His eyes fell on Brenda. "Do you believe what was alleged here today?"

"I do not. You would never do such a thing."

His shoulders drooped. "Well, I have no desire for Catherine, if that's what you're implying. She is my past."

Brenda shook her head. "Catherine may yet prove formidable, but she's not at issue today."

"What is?"

"Who is your present, Nathan?"

"I spend time with a woman named Sheila Byrne."

"Dan says you have a longstanding friendship with the madam who runs the brothel, a lonely woman who talks to herself at night in her room."

"Her name is Joanna Sinclair." Sarah had moved close behind them. She raised her voice, reinforcing who held the upper hand.

Brenda widened her eyes and glared at Sarah, who looked away.

Her attention returned to Nathan. "Joanna has given you freedom to do as you wish with Sheila. Dan says no other man ever gets a turn, and you two might as well be a couple. Is that how it goes?"

"Your husband paints the right portrait," said Nathan intently. "I'm not one to share a woman."

"What happens when you must share, Nathan?" Sarah crossed her arms, confident in her line of questioning. "Does your jealousy know no bounds?"

Nathan and Brenda shouted at Sarah in unison. "Be quiet!"

Sarah dropped her arms to her sides and sulked in place.

Brenda touched his coat. "Sheila is a lovely Irish lass from all accounts."

"She's a human being who does what she must."

"Are you willing to forgo the uncomplicated and try the real?"

"Daisy and I have quarreled since the night we met at Union Depot. I have no such problems with Sheila."

"Then we shall align your dispositions. It's why we joined you today."

"You are a confidant woman, Brenda Harper."

"And you are a better man than you know."

Nathan scowled at Sarah and then gave Brenda a kind smile.

"The day grows hot, and we have many more stops." He grabbed his hat from the post near the front door. "Shall we take our leave?"

Brenda placed her hand in his. "Please, sir, lead me forth as you must."

At Seymore Hagen's home in Vandeventer Place, Nathan listened with a stethoscope down the left edge of Seymour's sternum near the ensiform cartilage, hearing it also at the apex. He moved the stethoscope, placing it against the carotid artery, noticing a systolic murmur created by the pressure of the scope. The apex beat was around the seventh left interspace, and it was forcible, indicating a hypertrophic heart.

Nathan took his friend's pulse.

It rose like a water hammer and soon collapsed.

Seymore's exploits during the cholera outbreak of 1849 were legendary. The death rate had reached two-hundred-fifty per day out of a population of forty thousand. It inundated local physicians with cases and restricted their ability to tend the entire community. Seymore went to the worst afflicted areas at his own expense and cared for the sick the best he could. He made a powerful impact, having studied medicine for a time before he became an attorney. There was no other reward but the knowledge of helping others, and it was undertaken at significant risk to his own life. Although his heart was weakened by the ordeal, he had never once complained about his affliction, and his smile always reached his eyes.

Nathan swiped at his tears. He withdrew to the window and observed the private street. "There are no carriages at this time of day."

"Far too hot," Seymore said. "The younger people have work. I'm just a retired codger with nothing useful to occupy my hours."

"You've accomplished more in one lifetime than three normal men. You should be proud." Nathan tapped his fist against the window pane.

Daisy walked over to him. "May I help?"

He whispered into her ear. "My friend's condition is most grave. There's a see-saw murmur where the diastolic grows louder than the systolic."

They both observed the passing clouds, sharing a bit of calm.

"I'm not sure how to interpret your words."

"I can do nothing more for him."

"You could try."

"He has days," Nathan said. "Weeks if he's lucky."

"I have been telling you for years to get married," said Seymore eagerly. "You must settle down before it's too late." He looked at Nathan. "My example lies before you, and my folly must not become your destiny."

Nathan nudged Daisy. "My lovely colleague appreciates your romantic encouragement." She blushed and nudged Nathan with a sheepish smile.

"I'm sure she does, but you must shape up, sir, if you are to meet her lofty standards. This one has ideas for what merits a husband."

They practiced in unrelated disciplines and were of different ages, but Seymore had always approved of Nathan, and sought his acceptance in return. As he lacked a son or daughter of his own, he viewed himself as a moral failure. Seymore's opinion of himself was not shared by his doctor.

Nathan sat in a chair. "We should discuss your condition."

"I'm aware there's not much time."

"Does it frighten you?"

Seymore shook his head and gave a sad smile. "It's been a good life, and now I look forward to eternity with the Lord. The prospect gives me peace."

"I wish I shared your faith," said Nathan, honestly surprised by his own statement. He took a deep breath and exhaled.

"Proverbs 9:10 says it best."

Nathan's hand raised. "Please, no recitations."

"Fear of the Lord is the foundation of wisdom. Knowledge of the Holy One results in good judgment."

"God doesn't need a worthless wretch like me. I disappoint people."

"He has inscribed you on His palms. So says the prophet, Isaiah."

Nathan paced near the bookcase. He stopped to peruse a title.

"If you see anything you like, take it home with you."

Nathan's voice carried over his shoulder. "Don't give your possessions away, Seymore. It's not yet time to meet the Reaper."

"I cannot take them with me, now can I?"

Nathan wheeled. "How do you stay so calm?"

"I keep my focus on what is set before me." Seymore looked at his chest. "Soon this body will die, and mortal men will place it six feet under the grass. Upon the glorious return of Jesus Christ, the dead in Christ shall rise first, and we will meet Him in the sky. Because my name is recorded in the Book of Life, I will be given a heavenly and eternal body." He smiled at Nathan. "I look forward to being thirty-three once again."

Daisy leaned forward. "Why thirty-three?"

"We will be the same age as Jesus at the time of His crucifixion."

"Some of us aren't sure what we believe," Nathan said. "I'm not one to deny science, as it has provided mankind with many benefits, and will continue to do so in the next century."

"Human industry is impressive, I grant you, but it will melt with fervent heat when Christ returns. Don't be fearful, Nathan. Jesus has called you by name, and you are His forever."

An hour later, they said goodbye to Seymore and settled into the carriage. Nathan understood it to be their last visit.

"You care a great deal about him," Daisy said.

Nathan's eyes filled with tears. "He's the best man I've ever known."

Daisy nudged him with her shoulder. "I'm glad we met Seymore."

At the last stop, Nathan eased the reins and told the horses, "Whoa."

"Mind yourself." He helped Daisy exit the wagon. "The child has a necrotic femur. It may prove an unpleasant experience."

Daisy surveyed the farm buildings and the hills. She remained silent.

"Did you hear what I said?"

"Your medical jargon confuses me."

Nathan grew annoyed. "What did you study in Paris?"

"English was my primary course. All the talented authors were placed under the microscope. Novelists, poets, playwrights. We left no stone unturned in our quest to determine what makes great literary art."

"Wouldn't a medical course of study and experience in neurology be a prerequisite for your line of work?"

"It was the Lord's doing." She shifted her weight from one foot to another. "More to the point, my force of will prevailed on Charcot's assistant, Walter Resnick. He became infatuated with me and allowed me into La Salpêtrière, where I made the rest happen. Monsieur Charcot was quite taken with me from the start."

"How wonderful," said Nathan after a moment. "You might have mentioned this when you applied for the job. I assumed you were qualified."

"I agreed to become an assistant in your medical practice. Clean your home. Keep your records. Give a pleasant attitude to your patients. Those would have been my responsibilities." Daisy put her hands on her hips. "You've since enlisted me in a position beyond my skill level."

"It's too late to turn back now. I'm stuck with you."

He took Brenda's hand.

She accepted with a smile and displayed a wry grin to her sister. "Yes, this has turned into a grand afternoon." Brenda gave Nathan a flirtatious look. "Shall we repair to this man's home together?"

He led her to the front door and tapped on the wood.

Daisy followed.

She muttered unkind words as she approached the house.

Inside, they sat at the kitchen table. Nathan waited for the man to speak.

"My name is Ed Wilson. I lost my wife six months ago, and it's been a tremendous difficulty keeping up the place without her by my side. Our son, Ronnie, had just turned twelve when Alva got sick with the cancer, and I sent him to town most days. Didn't want him here, listening to her cry out."

"That was most sensible," Brenda said.

"He played croquet with some other boys, and one dared him to make an athletic shot." Ed's voice softened. "Ronnie twisted his left leg hard in an outward direction." Ed's arms made a forceful movement as he emulated the action. "A few hours afterward, the thigh became stiff, and it hurt him to walk. We passed it off as a sprained hip, especially since it swelled around the top of the leg, but it continued swollen and painful until about a month later, when it diminished under an iodine tincture from the doctor. Come to find out, there were three tumors in Ronnie's leg. We had them removed, and the doctor swore the last operation would make our boy whole again." Ed stood, shoving his chair backward. "Please, doctor, you've got to help us. Before her death, Alva made me swear to protect our son. The last week or two, the swelling has returned, making it hard for Ronnie to get about the house. He's been in so much pain, and I don't know where else to turn."

Ed paced the kitchen floor.

"I worked the railroad before I got married to Alva, and we started this farm. Sometimes we had a tough year, and I worked as a section hand for extra money." He picked up a picture frame and studied it. "Alva was worried about my health, and she didn't like my travels." He grunted. "Ironic, isn't it?"

"I agree, Ed. You were dealt a poor hand."

In the bedroom, Nathan noted Ronnie's waxen and clammy skin. "The upper third of the left thigh presents a cylindrical swelling along the anterior and inner aspect. It is not connected with the bone but fluctuates in front, hard beneath, non-pulsating, and tender."

"Yes, I see," said Daisy.

In the kitchen, Nathan settled into the chair and rubbed the table's surface. "Now Ed, I know you promised Alva, and I further know you don't want him to leave the farm." He stiffened his posture. "Am I right?"

"With you here, Ronnie has everything he needs."

"I know you think so, and, in your position, I would think the same." He kept silent for several moments and then flung his arm over the back of the chair. "We have all the modern tools at our hospital, and he would have a private bed, all to himself."

Ed looked dumbfounded. "This is our home."

"I understand, believe me, but there might come a time over the next week when we're forced to operate. The cancer may have returned along with all the swelling, and I want our best shot at success."

Ed gazed at the front door, lost in thought.

"It's the best facility around," Nathan said. "I promise."

"When you talk to us, does it make you anxious?" asked Daisy kindly.

"Nightmares have destroyed my sleep, and I'm a nervous wreck."

Daisy pointed at a tool in the corner. "What's that?"

"It's a railroad fork. Why do you ask?"

Her cheeks reddened. "No reason."

"Everything alright?" asked Nathan, frowning.

"Yes, fine."

"This is not the time for your theatrics."

"I have worked with his type before," she said. "I see the signs."

"You've explained your lack of qualifications in great detail. Let's not complicate Ronnie's predicament with tales of heroic victories in Paris."

"You may disbelieve, but I was most helpful there."

Ed dropped to the floor, where he flopped like a fish.

Nathan sprang from the chair, tending to Ed as best he could. "It seems like epilepsy, but he said nothing about such a condition."

After several minutes, Ed laid still and quiet.

Daisy kneeled beside Nathan. "Is he dead?"

"Of course not."

Brenda peered over the edge of the table. "What should we do?"

"There doesn't seem to be anything wrong with him medically. He responds to stimuli, and I don't think he's unconscious."

Daisy gave him a displeased look. "What does that *mean*, Nathan?"

"It's not epilepsy. Beyond that, who knows?" He scratched his head.

Ed stirred.

He tried to stand. "Hand me my cane, please. My left side is numb."

Nathan found his cane which leaned the corner.

He helped him to the table.

Ed poked his left arm and leg. He tried to awaken his extremities.

"The seizures only happen when a doctor examines Ronnie, and since we haven't seen one for a while, I'd forgotten about them."

"Your speech is slurred," Daisy said. "Have you had trouble eating?"

"It's hard to chew on the left side of my mouth. My whole left side feels numb and cold, especially when I'm tired." Ed held up his cane. "It's why I need this. As long as the ground is smooth and level, I get around alright."

"We need to take you both to our hospital," Nathan said. "You can have your own bed, right beside Ronnie."

Ed's unhappy eyes fell on his wife's photograph. He seemed a most extraordinary portrait of human misery.

"It's what needs to happen." Nathan glanced about with concealed annoyance. A patient's hesitancy had always confounded him.

Ed nodded his understanding. "We'll travel in our own wagon, if it's all the same to you. That way, if we don't like what we find inside your chamber of horrors, we can return here to die in peace."

Daisy called Nathan closer and whispered in his ear. "He has displayed the classic symptoms of hysteria. It's most curious."

"Are you sure?"

She nodded and pushed him away. "Ed, did you sit with Alva during her last week?"

Nathan shot Daisy a harsh look. "Remember what we discussed."

Ed offered her a humble smile. "Life has been a blur since last year."

"You've blocked out the painful memories," said Daisy, fanning herself.

"There are so many."

"Yes, for me as well."

She considered for several moments.

Daisy leaned forward. "Please allow us to help you. It's all we ask."

"He's so thin." Ed choked back tears. "I'm exhausted."

"Dr. Marsh operated on the president of the United States. He's the perfect surgeon for Ronnie."

Ed eyed Nathan and then cradled his face in his hands. He spoke in a muffled tone. "Alright, Miss Lawrence. You have convinced me."

At the hospital, Ed became more fearful and tried to club Nathan with his cane. "You will not go near my boy!"

Nathan deepened his voice. "Please lie down, Ed."

"You will murder my boy!"

"Ed, you might have another seizure. Please lie down."

After he failed to calm Ed's unpredictable behavior, Nathan summoned orderlies for physical help. With watery eyes, Ed avoided them. He wandered about the room with his cane. He laid on beds, got up, looked out of the windows and then withdrew from the light.

"I already lost my wife, Dr. Marsh. You must save my son!" He leaned close to Nathan's face. "If Ronnie dies, you will have killed me, too."

"I'm doing my best." Nathan shoved Ed onto the adjacent mattress. "Please sit down and let me work!"

Monday morning, Nathan sat alone in his office and stared through the window at the street below and its many passing carriages. He hadn't had a drink since Saturday, and he wanted to be left alone. Before climbing the stairs, he examined Ronnie Wilson and noted the skin over his swelling had become tense and glossy. The boy's temperature ranged from 100 to 101 degrees and his pulse from 110 to 120 beats per minute. Nathan would soon be compelled to operate, and he feared the worst.

Samuel entered, his manner determined. "Now that Ronnie and Ed Wilson are here, will you wean off the booze?"

"I plan to do what I said."

"Which is?"

"Stop for all time."

Samuel sat in a chair which faced Nathan. "How is your progress?"

Nathan's head fell to the desk, and he moaned. "The cravings wear on me. Yesterday, I couldn't stop shaking." He held up his trembling hand and then grabbed it, shoving it out of view.

"We both know the shakes will pass," Samuel said. "Your emotional attachment to alcohol is what most troubles me."

"I have the same concern." Nathan looked at his father. "How did you deal with withdrawal symptoms?"

Samuel's eyes brightened. "I walked often and spoke to the Lord in prayer." He rose and gripped his hat. "A trolley ride and a stroll through downtown are what you need. I will explain the basic tenets of Christianity as we go. They can be quite an excitement to those with an open mind."

Nathan's head lowered. "Go away."

"It will do you good to leave this dreary place."

The trolley ambled east along Locust Street and passed the First Methodist church. It dropped father and son at Broadway Avenue.

Samuel quoted Romans 8:25-27 as they walked due south. "But if we look forward to something we don't yet have, we must wait patiently and confidently. And the Holy Spirit helps us in our weakness. For example, we don't know what God wants us to pray for. But the Holy Spirit prays for us with groanings that cannot be expressed in words. And the Father who knows all hearts knows what the Spirit is saying, for the Spirit pleads for us believers in harmony with God's own will." After a quarter of a mile, Nathan stopped in front of the Laclede Hotel and gazed at the six-story building from across Chestnut Street. People entered and exited continually.

"She may not see us," said Samuel with hesitation.

"We won't know unless we ask."

Inside, Nathan approached the attendant at the front desk. Although it sported electrified elevators and steam heating in every room, there was a peculiar quality of oppressiveness in the form and the nature of Laclede. The attendant sent a messenger to Daisy's room, and soon she appeared.

"May we sit and discuss our arrangement?"

"It won't be necessary."

"The patients need your keen intellect and your stubbornness." Samuel smiled with a pleasant confidence. "Won't you reconsider a partnership?"

"You resent them," she said, facing Nathan. "I see it in your eyes."

Her disfavor perplexed him. "Whom do I resent?"

"Your patients. When you mention them, it becomes all too visible. Ed senses it, too, and it strengthens his hysteria."

"I was trained in one of the finest medical colleges in America."

"Do you deny my observation?"

Nathan rubbed his hand against his heart and sighed. "I admit to a certain bitterness for all but Seymore Hagen. He is a most honorable man."

"Alright, there's progress. What will you do about it?"

"Work the problem until a solution arises. It's all I know." He gave Daisy a stern look. "You must make good on your promise and your bold claims. I will not tolerate a hypocrite or a deceiver. I feel the latter most deeply."

"The murder investigation will take precedence over all else," she said.

"It has waited thirty years, and it will wait longer." He pinched the brim of his bowler. "I have been without a drink since Saturday."

"I am a woman who knows her own mind."

He glanced quickly at Samuel and then back at her. "No one has implied otherwise." He hesitated. "Are you well?"

"Do you know yours, sir?"

"I believe so," said Nathan in a resigned manner. "For many years, I was saddened by the death of my children and by my wife's desertion."

"Now that Catherine has returned, what will you do with her?"

"Restore her to health."

"What then? Will the rightful king and queen retake the throne?"

He smiled. "I have no more wish for prominence."

"My association with you will further damage my reputation," she said without gratitude. "Have you entertained Sheila in your house?"

"I restrict our liaisons to Joanna's brothel. Sheila's room is small, but the bed is adequate for her occupation."

"I am the only woman who visits your home?"

"Yes."

"I have one more question. Will your present comportment hold?" Her eyes went over him, every square inch under scrutiny.

"With you by my side, there can be optimism."

"Then I agree to your terms. I will be there tomorrow."

Nathan and Samuel left the Laclede and caught a trolley north to Eads Bridge, where they stared at the muddy river and shared a kinship with Ronnie and Ed Wilson. After so many years apart and so many missed opportunities, each was unsure how to help anyone, including himself.

NINE

Psalm 9:6

The enemy is finished, in endless ruins;
the cities you uprooted are now forgotten.

November 1872

Nathan would study in his dormitory room over the newly approved Thanksgiving break. On the first morning, he mostly avoided thoughts about his past and those who had wronged him in every manner a person may be wronged in this life. His lips pressed together as he read his medical handbook, and his hand rubbed the back of his neck. Many deemed him without merit and antagonized him at each step of his afflicted journey. His acceptance of their faults with patience and a cordial good will had long ago grown tiresome. In his current state of mind, he would rather call out their savage brutality and provide means for a sincere recompense. Otherwise, he would become the worst of them.

Thomas Hannah.

Nathan put down the book. It was no use.

Later in the afternoon, he left the room to clear his head and endure the insufferable cold of the campus quad. Professors with thicker coats and lesser ambitions brushed past him with spectacled, beady eyes. They were just like the Jesuits at the academy, sure of themselves and their place in the world, and equally sure of Nathan's inferior status. He refused to affirm their presence and made his way back to the sanctuary of his room.

Nathan's only friend awaited there: his medical book.

Roy knocked three times. There was no answer.

He invited himself into the room.

"Will you speak to me?"

Nathan kept still and quiet.

"I've been sent on a mission of the utmost import," said Roy with a mischievous grin. "You must attend our Thanksgiving dinner."

"No, thanks."

"From what your professors tell me, you're doing well in each of your classes. You should use this break for merriment and relaxation."

"I'm better alone. It's always been my way."

Roy shifted his weight to another foot. "Look, you must come to our home today, or I'll be in serious trouble. Colleen can be quite persistent, as you know, and she loves you more than anyone."

Nathan smiled at the notion. "I'm known for my unreliability."

Roy sent an incredulous look. "You'd hurt her on purpose?"

Nathan shrugged. Too many had already hurt him.

The professor recovered his senses. "It's no way to travel through life."

"As I mentioned, Roy, it's always been my way."

"There must be another reason."

Nathan looked up and sighed. "I don't fit into your world."

"You might if you would only try, Nathan. We've known you for years."

"Your three girls are young, but one day they'll be just like the kids at the academy, and I'll be judged harshly by them. I'm a different sort."

"Don't you think we know that?" He hesitated. "It's what we like most about you." He gripped his hat and looked about the small room. "Nathan, you must respond to those who show you kindness, especially my wife."

"She's a beautiful woman. You're a lucky man."

"Spend the holiday with us," said Roy emphatically. "It's all I ask."

"Will you fail me if I decline?"

Roy smiled, his countenance calmed. "It's a distinct possibility."

"Alright, you win."

Nathan wandered through town and to their front stoop.

He debated whether to knock or to rush back to the safety of his room.

Colleen opened the door with a big smile and ushered him inside. In the parlor, she sat down and quickly broached the subject of June's early death, a mounting breach of etiquette he had dreaded for weeks. Since his arrival at fifteen, he had enjoyed a friendly rapport with Colleen and the girls, and he believed this present visit would be tolerable, assuming she didn't probe deeper and threaten his balance. When Colleen did just that during dinner, he kept silent. Roy tapped a dinner glass with his fork and threw her a harsh look. He asked her to cease her line of questioning.

Undeterred, she invited Nathan to help her clean the dishes, and for several minutes they worked side by side in awkward silence.

Colleen turned toward him. "Do you think I'm pretty?"

Taken aback, Nathan did his best to reply honestly. "Yes."

"How old do you think I am?"

"I don't know."

"I'm thirty-nine." Her lips trembled slightly. "I will be forty soon."

"You're not old, Colleen, if that's what's bothering you."

He washed a dish in the sink and felt her eyes on him.

"I've known you for several years, but you never reveal yourself to me, honey." She hesitated. "You're twenty now, and I want to know who you really are, the genuine man behind the facade of mystery."

"Roy was there for some of it. I'm sure he's told you a few things."

"Not enough. I must know about your childhood."

He sat on a stool near the icebox and told her about quarrels with his father, why he later moved in with Aunt Joy, and how she had influenced him in small ways each day. He recounted academy attendance and how he met Catherine Belmont, the green-eyed beauty who taught him what it meant to love. It had been hard to leave her, but she willingly let him go.

He had never opened up to anyone, and it felt good.

"I'm speechless." Colleen's hand rose to her chest. "Why would you desert a young woman who needs you? Surely, she's lost with you gone."

"Her father would never allow us to marry, so I began a new life here in New York. It's doubtful we will ever see one another again."

He went back to the sink and resumed his work.

"All the more reason to let me guide your path," said Colleen with passion. "There are plenty of suitable young women here in New York, and as soon as we get your sorted, they'll see your many charms, as *I* do."

There were elements of both Catherine and Aunt Joy in Colleen's demeanor, and he found it impossible to cease fidgeting in her presence. Her shimmering warmth radiated into him, even from across the kitchen. She noticed his discomfort and removed the distance between them; her body stood so close he felt her breath on his neck. Colleen raked her fingers through his hair; it felt both good and peculiar at the same time. He kept an air of stoic forbearance, unsure about her feminine intentions.

At daybreak, Colleen shook Nathan from a sound sleep. He was angry, so she placed her cool hand over his mouth, which silenced his outburst. Her hand pulled away, and she shuffled in front of his bed in edgy unrest.

The floor creaked beneath her slender feet. She summoned him outside.

A wooden swing under the leafless birch hung by two thick ropes. She turned in several circles until the ropes twisted and tightened, and then released all tautness, allowing her jet black hair to hover with the quick unwind of her light and attractive frame. When the swing stopped its motion, she shivered in her nightclothes. Nathan rubbed sleep from his eyes and wondered how long she would continue this unnecessary and childish display. The eastern sun broke through a gap in the far trees. Nathan wanted to utter a shrill scream and wake the entire town. Colleen knew exactly what she was doing to him, and she liked it. He considered Roy and the children.

Her brown eyes glistened in the crisp morning air.

Her breath blew misty smoke as she smiled.

Her full lips were meant for a kiss.

"We can just talk," she said. "It's alright."

"Why would you do this to Roy? He loves you."

"And I love *him*, but it's not the same as what I feel for you, Nathan."

"Tell me how you feel."

"I love you like a son, and I believe you need me."

She confused him. "The way you're behaving, it seems you want more."

Colleen smiled and shook her head. "You never really had a mother."

His arms crossed. "I'm aware."

She frowned. "I imagine June was a sensual woman like me."

"I suppose," he said. "The man who killed her thought so."

She nodded.

"It's a pity you never formed romantic feelings for her as you matured. If she had lived, June's inviting looks and her fervent passion would have forced you to work through strange and new feelings, and once on the other side of adolescence, you would be a man who knows his own mind. I believe your relationships with young women would have benefited as a result."

Colleen paused.

"Since June is no longer here, the burden falls on me. I want to help you through this moment in your life and calm the turmoil which churns inside of you. Don't worry, I love my husband and will remain true to him in *every* sense of the word. You are mistaken if you think otherwise."

"You only want a son?"

"I see your trauma, Nathan. I really do." Her eyes met his. "I knew my share of it as a girl, and I'd like to help you."

His chin jutted. "I'm doing just fine on my own."

"Won't you please talk to me? I am a woman you can trust."

His emotions swirled around him and through him, pushing his body toward her with all their might. He wanted to take her into his arms and kiss her. She might cry out. Where would he be then?

"I don't trust anyone, not even *you*."

"Fine, honey. We'll talk when you're ready."

She sent him back to bed as abruptly as she'd awakened him. There was a touch of panic in her voice, as if the number of days to accomplish a great and lamentable task would soon reach their end and the penalty for missing the deadline would be a swift and painful death. The strain wore on her face.

The next morning, she repeated her previous performance. When Nathan asked her to stop, she moved close to him and hugged his neck. His breath quickened and his blood rushed to scandalous places in his body.

"You should stay here and become our son," she said.

He pulled back from her warm embrace. "Roy is a good man, and he doesn't deserve this betrayal."

"There is no disloyalty. I love my husband."

Nathan looked about the yard, sizing up the area and the house.

He nodded at the street. "I should go."

"You're growing into manhood, Nathan. Once you've completed medical school and gained work experience, you can live with anyone you want, wherever you want. The world in all its fullness will be open to you."

"Meaning?"

"Stop thinking about St. Louis. Make your life here with us."

He sat on a bench. "I'm sorry, Colleen, but I can't."

She shared bits of her backstory, hoping to convince him.

"In 1846, my mother shot her eighteen-year-old son, Tommy, an inch below his right eye with a revolver she thought to be unloaded. Those Colts were still somewhat new at the time, and she wasn't sure how to use it. The situation was made worse by my younger brother, David, who had loaded a cartridge the day before without informing anyone. Tommy lived, and surgery was not attempted because of the dangers of dislocation."

"Where was your father?"

"He'd gone to Albany to be treated for wounds suffered during the Chesapeake Campaign. When he got home and found out about the bizarre event, he beat my mother to a pulp, which forced a visit from Doc Adams. David became distraught by his mistake and ran away, never to come home. To this day, Nathan, I do not know his whereabouts." The pained look returned. "I would like to see him, to know he's alright. I hope he no longer blames himself." She looked toward the woods. "People do the oddest things, like leave the ones who love them the most. It's something I'll never understand, no matter how many years I take residence on this planet."

"Did your family recover?"

She shook her head. "I married Roy a year later, at fifteen. He was an older man and more experienced. Roy gave me the strength and support I needed. There was nothing left for me in that house."

Dim clouds grayed the brilliant sunlight, bringing back the chill.

"Your wandering eyes remind me of David." Her body stopped the swing, and her mouth grinned in a sad playfulness. "Please don't run. It hurts everyone around you and the pain is forever."

He patted her hand. "It's all I know."

"We all feel overwhelmed, Nathan. It's called *life*."

Colleen returned to the swing and swayed in a circular motion.

Desirous and possessive thoughts spread across Nathan's mind.

Normal civility seemed to have passed away, along with consideration of a future with Catherine Belmont. He saw only Colleen, a shadowy figure in the dark mine of his appetite. The chilly air became fresh and warm in his burning lungs. He wanted to lean over and help Colleen out of the swing.

He would pull her form close to his for a momentous kiss.

All would change in a flash, and suddenly *he* would be the man of this house. There would be no more Roy and no more children. He paused, understanding the horror and the power of his own desire. If she continued to arouse his passion, he would soon become another Thomas Hannah.

He moved toward her on the swing. He must possess her body.

Her eyes met his, and she took his hand. She squeezed it tightly.

She placed the other hand against his beating heart. His arousal brought a crash of blood against her cheeks, and her breath quickened.

"You do things to me, Nathan, but I must resist."

"I cannot," he said.

"You must. Both our lives depend on it."

Her awareness of his capacity for evil had grown to match his own.

"I don't want to hurt you or your family, but I *will*."

She smiled faintly and pushed against his chest. He took a step back.

"This is exactly how my mother died," he said. "Be careful."

Colleen nodded her understanding. "It's a dangerous game she played."

"So don't play it with me. I don't want to follow in his footsteps."

"It's precisely why I'm playing it with you. In Revelation, Jesus instructs us to rise above persecution and temptation. We must be overcomers."

"I've always been a mistake," he said. "God doesn't want me."

"We are all fallen, but none are a mistake in His eyes."

Colleen left the swing and moved closer. She hugged his neck and blew warm whispers against his trembling skin. His muscles quivered.

"Nathan, you are already a part of our family, but we need to make it official. Our world presents many heartaches and a few brief moments of happiness. If you stay with us, my joy will finally outweigh my grief. It's been a long time since I could say such a thing."

She took a step back from him.

Nathan clenched his jaw. "Trust me. You don't want this."

"Oh, but I do." She looked at the sky. "You'll be the son I never had."

"More like the brother you lost."

Her eyes met his, and she smiled. "Yes, that, too."

"Please, Colleen."

She gave him a relaxed smile. "You think we are different, but our souls are connected, and our thoughts are the same. Join us and believe the Lord has rescued you from the Lake of Fire. It burns eternally and there is no escape for the damned. Remember that whenever you feel like Thomas."

Stimulated by anger, Nathan's cheeks flushed red. How dare this deranged woman impose her own disappointment and stifled expectations on him? There was a gleam in her eyes, a dangerous inner light.

When she smiled at him, her dark eyebrows arched in such a frolicsome manner, his male passion for her could not be quieted.

Colleen toyed with his emotions and his body.

Roy and the girls deserved better.

Nathan started toward the house, and she called after him, hurt by his refusal. Her mood flustered, and she called out to Nathan to please come back to her. At the porch, he faced her, noting the tears which coursed down her cheeks. There was a break in the clouds, and a burst of punishing sunlight overwhelmed him. The wind carried accusations from far away.

She spoke one last time. "The Lord will provide if you trust in Him."

Nathan held still for a moment, unsure, and then went back to bed.

Nathan wandered the streets of New York City, where he studied the flow of crowds and tried to remove Colleen Collins from his thoughts. Tired of fighting her provocative memory, he visited art museums and cheap theatrical plays and an entertaining but primitive picture show.

At the edge of Central Park, he dreamed of residence on Fifth Avenue and routine dalliances with the Astors and the Delanos and the Vanderbilts.

He stretched himself along the length of a bench and shut his eyes.

Even now, he felt a strong desire for Colleen and knew it was wrong.

Perhaps she had meant well and spoke the truth about her moral resolve.

She was correct about one thing. He never really had a mother.

Did June's murder ruin me for women?

A policeman approached, boots stomping.

Nathan sat up straight.

The officer waved a baton and pressed his lips into a fine line. "Why are you asleep on the bench? You'd better think twice before you rob anyone in the park, or you'll get clubbed on the head for your trouble."

Nathan made a motion with his hands and tried to speak, but he was unsure what to say. After some additional thought, he rose from the bench and assured the police officer he was a medical student with good prospects.

"Medicine? Mere quackery."

"We save people's lives. You club them over the head."

A burst of anger came upon the officer, and he lifted Nathan by his coat like a sack of potatoes. The young man tried to struggle, but the officer was much too strong. His thick arms shoved Nathan down the sidewalk, where he tripped and rolled a few feet before he hopped to his feet.

"Get along with the likes of you!"

Nathan threw a mean look at the officer and trotted like a horse.

Manhattan was not a kind place, nor a suitable spot to build his life.

Further down, Nathan sat on another iron bench and planned his next series of moves. St. Louis might prove the better home. It was the fourth largest city in the nation, and was still the hub to the west, especially the southwestern corner. Much prosperity awaited a man with the right skills, a nobler nature, and a determination to succeed.

His hand slapped his knee. The matter was settled.

There would be no more blush of shame, and he would tolerate no more unbalanced women. He had grown tired of the chaos they carried. Once back home in St. Louis, he would find a proper lady, and together they would construct the perfect family. Doors would fly open for him, or his two hands and two feet would force them open.

Nathan wandered out of the park and blended into the crowd, a mass of strangers who provided the most comfort. It was a bright and cloudless November afternoon. Nathan stood still, hands clasped in full attention to life's many mysteries. A child presented a flower to his young mother. She embraced him with a loving smile which warmed his heart.

The police officer approached once more. Nathan took his leave.

TEN

Psalm 10:4

The wicked are too proud to seek God.
They seem to think that God is dead.

Tuesday morning, Daisy's feet scuffed hard at the ground as she fought to make her way through the hospital entrance. The heavy railroad fork she carried banged against the wooden door and left a scrape in the wood. She looked up, hoping no one had seen. The long, rectangular main hall was abuzz with activity as orderlies and nurses moved from bed to bed, attempting to corral unruly patients or tend to their cries for help. Daisy's gaze and her feet wandered to a corner, where she placed the fork for safe storage. She turned, and her eyes moved to Ed, who slept soundly on his cot. If his hysteria symptoms worsened, he might be sent to the city asylum for permanent residence. Daisy had retrieved the tool from his farm and now hoped it might prove a useful aid in his treatment.

Nathan grinned. "What do you plan to do with *that*?"

"Hypnosis may help Ed avoid Arsenal Road," she said softly. "The mind affects the body in ways we are yet to understand."

"Have you mentioned your plan to Belmont?"

She shook her head. "Why would I?"

"He'll never allow mesmerism in his hospital." Nathan walked down the line of beds. He paused halfway and reviewed Catherine's chart. "I'm not sure I like it much either," he said over his shoulder.

Daisy sat in a rocker near the front entrance.

"Fine," she said defensively.

He gave her an amused look and returned to Catherine.

The faint sound of a voice caught Daisy's attention. Her back unbent, and she listened intently. A word made itself known to her ever so subtle and low—almost imperceptible. *Nathan.* She went outside to the stoop, where her eyes and ears scanned her surroundings. At the far intersection, a brown-haired woman called Nathan's name and stared at the hospital. Daisy stepped down to the curb, but the brown-haired woman turned away. Might she be a friend of Catherine's, perhaps a former classmate? If so, she didn't seem comfortable in her dress, as if it was new or didn't quite fit. Sunlight reflected from a different angle as the obscure woman turned, and her hair color changed from brown to red, revealing her identity with perfect clarity. *Sheila Byrne.* Something about her seemed strange, as she was without escort and wore no hat. Daisy tried to put herself in Sheila's place, knowing how desperately she must need to see Nathan and to believe he still cared for her. Sheila must have borrowed the dress, but then couldn't bring herself to enter an upper crust hospital on such an unforgiving side of town. Daisy's palm raised as a symbol of solidarity. *There is no threat here.* Sheila frowned, and her feet marched to Fountain Park, where she disappeared into a thick grove of trees. From the south, a carriage rumbled through the open intersection without stopping and continued out of sight to the north. Daisy looked at the park and waited for another appearance, but Sheila did not show herself again. What a terrible effect Nathan had on women.

Daisy grew tired of the wait and went back inside, determined to probe for more detail on the sunny Irish lass. Nathan stood at the end of Ronnie's bed, his eyes affixed to the boy's chart. She approached with caution.

Before she could speak, he hung the chart on the bedrail and blurted, "I had hoped for the best, but this boy's leg simply won't cooperate with me."

His face took on the appearance of a hurt child. He needed her.

She tried to forget Sheila. "And now?"

"I believe there's a massive tumor in the boy's leg."

"Can we ease his pain until you know for sure?"

"Soon, there won't be enough painkillers or sedatives to help Ronnie. That's when we'll have to go." He hesitated. "I'm not looking forward to such an arduous surgery." He sat down on a bed. "It might kill the boy."

"Ed will run wild if it does."

"So will Belmont."

As the day progressed, Ronnie's pain worsened beyond measure.

Nathan assembled a team in a small storage room on the left side of the hospital. Two orderlies carried Ronnie to the table, where they gently stretched him out lengthwise. Ronnie's tremoring hand grabbed Nathan's arm, and he led the group in a brief prayer. He shut his eyes, and through a choked voice, he instructed Nathan to do his best. Nurse Pratt administered ether through an air mask as nervousness filled the air. Soon, it took effect.

Nathan made an incision on the anterior surface of the tumor two inches long. His finger inserted inside the wound, and he felt a soft, friable mass which spread in every direction. A substance resembling disintegrated blood clot, some of which seemed to have a laminated structure, escaped in significant quantities. His scalpel made a second incision which lengthened the opening from two to four inches, exposing more of the mass. Nathan's hands scooped large quantities of clots and soft disintegrating tissue, after which he worked his finger beneath Poupart's ligament. After a tense breath, he disarticulated the limb and covered the wound with lateral skin flaps. The adductor group of muscles, clear to their point of origin, presented a dark gelatinous appearance, the result of beginning infiltration, and they were removed as thoroughly as possible with scissors. Hemorrhage was almost nil, but the shock was so great that during the latter part of the operation, Ronnie's pulse rose to 180. Daisy assisted Nathan, injecting, at his request, twenty ounces of normal salt solution into the median cephalic vein on the right side. Ronnie's pulse fell to 150, allowing the operation to conclude.

While Nathan wrapped Ronnie's leg in a blanket, Ed woke up and beat severely against the locked door. Daisy tried to soothe him with kind and gentle words, but he flailed himself against the dense wood until he fell into a heap and convulsed with abandon. The orderlies unlocked the door and pushed it open, exposing Ronnie's now deformed shape. Angered but also resigned, Nathan requested the storage room door be left open, as whatever damage might occur had already been done. He resumed his work while the orderlies dragged Ed to his cot and covered his now limp body with a sheet.

He fell into a deep slumber, and a quiet peace fell over the hall.

After the orderlies placed Ronnie beside his father, Nathan went upstairs to his office. In his absence, Heinrich shouted for his wife and two children who had heartbreakingly died in a Boston fire. Daisy sat beside him with her Bible in hand and recited the first few verses from Psalm 10. It was such a resplendent and timely message. She continued through the entire psalm, contented by the grace and mercy of the Lord. Whenever she mentioned what the wicked do to the meek, Heinrich's fingers dug into his ankle, which caused several minor lacerations. She scolded Heinrich, but he could not stop himself from wantonness any more than she could cease her holy recitation. Tragedy had left him destitute and without restraint.

Her frustration level increased with each moment.

Someone appeared from nowhere and tugged at Daisy's skirt, making her start, and she quickly got to her feet. Ida asked how long things would be chaotic as the yells and the cries for help made her ears throb with pain. Daisy affably took her hand and led her to the bed. She sat the girl down and then retrieved a chart from the bedrail, noting potential damage to the acoustic nerve. As her hand raised for a brief examination of the ear, Ida bared her teeth and bit into Daisy's arm. The girl's brazen eyes flickered with delight, and her little face bore a faint resemblance to Rosemarie.

Daisy yanked her arm away and rubbed it. "Ouch, you devil!"

Ida sneered. Her puny arms crossed in villainous satisfaction.

Nathan flung open the stairwell door and grunted loudly. "I'm exhausted and need repose. You must keep the room under control."

"I'm trying, but the patients aren't making things easy."

Shirley Fletcher had stretched herself into a prostrate position.

She stared at the ceiling, stiff as a cadaver. Her eyes did not blink.

Daisy grew scared and went to Shirley's bedside.

"Are you alright?"

Unable to speak, Shirley placed her hands over her throat as if she were choking. Daisy pried her mouth open but discovered no obstructions.

She called out to Nathan. "There's nothing here."

He gave her a sidelong glance. "There must be some impediment in the larynx." He pointed at Shirley. "Can't you hear the stridor in her breathing and observe her paroxysms?"

"You must define those words for me. I am not a physician!"

His voice lowered. "Paroxysms are sudden outbursts or spasms."

Daisy stood back and studied Shirley. "There's nothing to find in her throat." She looked about the room. "It's the same for all the rest."

"Belmont said some were somatic." Nathan's cheeks went colorless at a growing realization. "I assumed he exaggerated the facts." He pointed at the beds. "Surely you can find a portion with genuine physical symptoms."

"I thought you already knew," she said simply. "Excluding Ronnie, every one of these patients is a hysteric." Her voice trailed.

"You forgot about Catherine," he said.

He saw only what he wanted to see. Daisy must be cautious in her response. "If Catherine functioned normally, she wouldn't be here."

A nurse directed him to a washing bowl on another table, where he cleaned his hands. He looked confused and shaken as he studied the floor.

Daisy placed her hands on her hips. "Did you hear what I said?"

"I did." Nathan frowned while drying his hands on a towel. "Belmont also said we're receiving overflow from the city asylum." He surveyed the room. "It seems lunatics comprise our entire roster."

Daisy's imagination retrieved a long buried portrait, and her hand grabbed a bedrail. A young girl was face down on a pile of bloodstained rocks. Daisy's eyes closed for a moment and then reopened.

"They may have once been overflow, but they are now our concern." A strong conviction filled her voice. "We cannot abandon them."

"As you did in Paris and Vienna."

"Yes." Her eyes moistened.

"I didn't sign up for this carnival," he said contemptuously.

"You have Ronnie. He is real."

Orderlies examined the boy's bandages while Ed slept on top of the covers beside his son, snoring. Nathan and Daisy stood nearby.

She nudged Nathan. "Ed's not so bad when he's asleep."

Nathan's eyes fell on her. "Ronnie won't appreciate losing a leg. We may see two peas in a pod once they awaken."

Her shoulders shrugged. "Like us, then."

***

Over the next few days, Ronnie regained strength of body, if not spirit. His temperature, which rose to 102 degrees earlier in the week, fell to normal by Friday afternoon. As Nathan predicted, a surge of anxiety and shame ran through the boy when Daisy roused him. He first wept, and then his right side went limp in alignment with his father's somatic symptoms. Daisy had assisted with a similar case at La Salpêtrière and another while working with Sigmund in Vienna. She retrieved the railroad fork from the corner and dragged it to Ronnie's bedside. Much had happened to her since leaving Freud and Charcot, and she struggled to recall how to use the tool.

Nathan approached her with a scowl. "Can you use this thing or not?"

"It's been two years."

He moved to the base of the stairs and scrutinized her rudely. Her hand waved him off, but he continued. She huffed impatiently and threw Nathan a helpless but determined look. He grunted and stomped up the stairs to the second level. She was thankful for his exit.

During her first tour through Belmont Hospital, she had soothed an inconsolable Heinrich. It only frightened him and brought up a wellspring of emotions in her. She left Nathan and ran to Fountain Park to hide in the trees like Sheila. He found Daisy and somehow brought her back into his life, but now her troubled mind could not shake the portrait of a desperate and panic-stricken prostitute at the intersection. It had taken a wagon load of courage for Sheila to venture from her brothel in borrowed clothes. Daisy took a deep breath and exhaled. The disaster in Vienna hung heavily over her soul. It haunted her nights and fostered daily insecurities. She must not make the same mistake twice. Another Frank Kaneski would kill her.

Nurse Pratt sat at a desk outside the bed line, where she entered patient information into numbered forms. The city demanded a proper accounting of each diagnosis, and batches of forms were to be delivered to government officials by the end of each week. Too many mistakes in the documentation, and the hospital could be shut down. Susanna danced around the line of beds in a circle. She brushed by Nurse Pratt, bumping into her chair without apology, and resumed circumnavigation. Nurse Pratt dropped the pencil and craned her neck to scold Susanna. Her eyes fell on Daisy.

She approached and took a seat in an adjacent rocker.

Daisy had only said a few words to the woman until this moment.

Nurse Pratt smiled and patted Daisy's hand like a mother. "Is everything alright, dear? You seem a bit shaken." Her eyes moved from right to left across the room, and her chair creaked in a soft cadence as she rocked.

Daisy's mind was elsewhere, stuck in a land of romantic worries and dreadful self-loathing. She did her best to focus on Ed Wilson. He should go home to his farm, where he was needed. She stopped rocking and adopted a serious tone. "I fear if we release him, he will do something regrettable to himself." She listened, caught acutely by the many noises of the main hall.

Nurse Pratt thought for a few moments. "You're kind to worry about him, but I think Ed is far too meek to end it all." She sighed. "He would merely sit at his kitchen table, weeping over his wife and son, same as he's doing here. Pity. They had such a powerful family bond only a year ago. Ronnie had learned so much and was apt to take over the farm soon. It was beneficial for Ed, who had never really taken to farming. In his youth, his dream was to live his life on the railroad. He's the type to seek adventure."

The last sentence captured Daisy's attention. "You said he was meek."

Nurse Pratt smiled. "No man shrinks from exploration and adventure. Best you remember what I said." Her eyes glanced toward the stairs.

Daisy took her meaning. "It would seem we have received all the hysterics in St. Louis." She surveyed the room. "How will we cure them all?"

"That, my dear, is for *you* to say." She stood and patted Daisy's hand again. "Please call me Dora. Nurse Pratt is too formal for my liking."

Daisy smiled as Dora returned to her desk.

It had been a long time since she'd made a new friend.

As the afternoon wore on, patients responded to her kind affections and her biblical recitations. She gained a hope of turning a psychological corner, but she'd seen the same immediate rebound in Europe, and it never lasted.

Nathan pulled her into his office in the evening. He sat in his office chair and studied her for several minutes. It made her self-conscious, and she squirmed in her own chair as she faced him. He wrote something.

"I want you to sign this paper," he said, handing it to her.

Her eyes swept the page.

"What's this?"

"It's a letter which outlines your expanded duties. I've watched you with the patients all afternoon, and in my estimation, your methods have merit. Because of your background with those men in Europe, you have gained a great deal of knowledge of experimental psychology. I must admit to very little understanding of the topic, and my eagerness to learn is limited, being naturally more oriented toward the human body and all its many wonders. You, on the other hand, have a delightful rapport with the hysterics, and I now believe you may have what it takes to cure these people." He pointed at the paper. "Please sign so we can make it official."

"Please tell me this isn't a source of amusement at my expense."

His head pushed backward, and his eyebrows arched in surprise. "My life may be in shambles, madam, but I take my medical career seriously." He hesitated. "My outward appearance notwithstanding, in my heart, I remain a gentleman." His eyes rose to the door. "Those poor souls need your help."

"Am I to cure Catherine of whatever ailments brought her back to you?"

"Those wounds were physical. She was beaten gravely."

He sees what he wants to see.

Daisy forced a smile. "As I previously mentioned, once her outward wounds heal, she will prove most abnormal on the inside. I would wager the former Caroline Astor of St. Louis will become queen of our hysterics."

"Better her than you," he said lightly.

She chuckled. "You have a valid point."

"Will you take the position?"

She beamed. "I will."

"Very good. I have already mentioned our need and your qualifications to Belmont, and he approved your promotion."

She appreciated Nathan's mounting confidence, but she had cured no one yet, most especially John and Susanna Hutchinson. Their chart was left curiously blank the last time Daisy reviewed it, and she needed answers.

John Belmont passed Nathan's office.

She rose from her chair and leaned through the doorway.

"John, please join our conversation."

He wheeled and entered the office with arched eyebrows. "Yes?"

"I need to know more about the Hutchinsons."

"Why?"

"Treating hysterics requires knowledge of their past traumas."

"Have you asked *them*?"

"The Hutchinsons aren't very talkative." As before, her voice trailed.

Belmont smirked at her weakness and pointed to Nathan. "According to this unkempt charlatan who apparently has better things to do than treat his patients, you are my resident psychologist. Leave me out of it."

"Fine," she said, taking a deep, calming breath.

He moved toward the door and stopped. His voice grew sinister. "I'll tell you the same thing I told him. Fail me once, and I'll ruin your tiny and inconsequential existence. I tolerate no excuses and accept only excellence. "

She had been promoted and threatened in the breadth of one afternoon.

Daisy and Nathan returned downstairs to the main hall.

They strolled out to the floor and approached the Hutchinson's beds. Susanna flitted about like a ballerina. Nathan asked her to stop, but she refused. John laid on his bed and stared at Daisy with a flat expression. She stared back at him with wide eyes, hoping to stimulate a vocal response.

He sneered and sat up in his bed. "You are not my wife!"

Daisy shifted to another foot. "I know, John."

"You know nothing."

"May we get you a cold drink? The ice man delivered this morning."

"Get me a locker of food and place it beside my bed." He waved his hands like an orchestra conductor. "I must prepare for what's coming."

Nathan interjected. "What's coming, John?"

"Moon travelers watch us with a firm resolve. Soon they will arrive."

Nathan suppressed a laugh.

Daisy's hand poked him. "For what reason, John?"

"They seek those who pursue enlightenment, for they wish to enhance our bodies and further evolve our spirits to a godlike form."

Nathan elbowed Daisy and gave her an amused smile.

"Another worthy candidate for your railroad fork."

"The others are hysterics," she said. "He likely has schizophrenia."

John flopped onto his back and stared at the ceiling. "You think me a madman, but I have great insight into your future. It would be wise to pay detailed attention. Notes will be a source of exam material."

His words and sentences fell to disjointed mutterings.

At the front, Nathan and Daisy sat in rockers, observing John.

"Any idea what brought it on?"

Daisy's shoulders shrugged. "Some believe it's the inescapable result of occult activity. Others claim unchecked depression."

"I'm asking for your expert opinion. What do *you* think?"

Expert? She liked the sound of it.

They rocked back and forth, watching the room, thankful for calm.

"All this time, I've only considered the battle between medicine and psychology, the flesh and the mind. It's why you and I stay at odds."

"You are avoiding my question," he said.

"Now I see the truth." She stopped rocking. "Our actual struggle is between the corrupt soul of man and the holiness of the Lord."

Nathan looked around, peeking high and low. "I don't see angels saving these patients, or my hide." He pointed toward the fork. "If that thing works, then get busy using it. We have little time to waste."

He stood and surveyed the line of beds with a calculating disposition.

His agitated eyes fell on her. "I've given you the opportunity to prove your intelligence and your capabilities. Don't let me down."

He left her to contemplate his words.

What did he expect, a miracle?

She considered Jean-Martin and Sigmund's use of hypnosis.

Was she immoral to try such a modality?

Once again, she read Psalm 10, this time from start to finish.

"O Lord, why do you stand so far away? Why do you hide when I am in trouble? The wicked arrogantly hunt down the poor. Let them be caught in the evil they plan for others. For they brag about their evil desires; they praise the greedy and curse the Lord. The wicked are too proud to seek God. They seem to think that God is dead. Yet they succeed in everything they do. They do not see your punishment awaiting them. They sneer at all their enemies. They think, 'Nothing bad will ever happen to us! We will be free of trouble forever!' Their mouths are full of cursing, lies, and threats. Trouble and evil are on the tips of their tongues. They lurk in ambush in the villages, waiting to murder innocent people. They are always searching for helpless victims. Like lions crouched in hiding, they wait to pounce on the helpless. Like hunters, they capture the helpless and drag them away in nets. Their helpless victims are crushed; they fall beneath the strength of the wicked. The wicked think, 'God isn't watching us! He has closed his eyes and won't even see what we do!' Arise, O Lord! Punish the wicked, O God! Do not ignore the helpless! Why do the wicked get away with despising God? They think, 'God will never call us to account.' But you see the trouble and grief they cause. You take note of it and punish them. The helpless put their trust in you. You defend the orphans. Break the arms of these wicked, evil people! Go after them until the last one is destroyed. The Lord is king forever and ever! The godless nations will vanish from the land. Lord, you know the hopes of the helpless. Surely you will hear their cries and comfort them. You will bring justice to the orphans and the oppressed, so mere people can no longer terrify them."

She gracefully shut her Bible and released a long, inaudible sigh.

Although her newfound responsibility gave her reason for trepidation, she no longer required the approval of those who favored Babylon and its mammon. Daisy had found herself in the center of Sodom while in Vienna, where the ancient face of evil stole the love of her life and then tried to possess her soul. Daisy overcame Rosemarie in Vienna and removed herself to the wilderness of Missouri, where lesser wolves of desire prowled.

America was a shining city upon a hill, but its light had faded.

It would take men and women of God to reclaim the land.

Many had faltered since the war, its toll immeasurable.

She watched as the hysterics laid in their beds or floated inaccessible about the main hall. They needed someone special to save them, a fighter who had overcome the demons within and without, and it was no matter if the survivor proved a flawed mentor in the final accounting. Daisy's endurance in Europe and her bold moves since meeting Nathan Marsh had paid dividends, as she was now the psychologist on duty at the illustrious Belmont Hospital. Once the hysterics rediscovered their love of God and learned by His perfect example to conquer the Rosemarie of their own pasts, their lives would again be their own. Daisy looked forward to such a day.

For the first time in years, she felt alive.

ELEVEN

Psalm 11:4

But the Lord is in his holy Temple;
the Lord still rules from heaven.
He watches everyone closely,
examining every person on earth.

December 1868

Nathan read at the servant's table while the cooks in the kitchen traded petty insults. A footman stuck his head inside the door and asked when the room would be free. Nathan's eyes remained affixed. He was behind in his schedule and hoped to get through the nervous system before supper. The footman gave him warm encouragement and an ephemeral smile as Catherine slid past him. When she sat down, the footman apologized for his presence and closed the door, giving them the room. She gazed at Nathan, and her breaths grew heavy and loud. Her green eyes pierced his concentration and demanded his attention.

He must give it to her at this very moment. If not, she would scream.

"Mr. Stewart bites, you know." Nathan flipped a page. "If he catches you at this table, I'll never hear the end."

"Let the butler say what he wants." She slapped a hand against the table. "You may *not* shut me out."

Nathan frowned. "This is my study time, Catherine. We talked about my responsibilities and my plan for the future, remember?"

"I have needs. You've read that dour book more times than I can count."

"It's how I will make my living."

"I thought you would move west and become an outlaw."

"Am I not grand enough for you?"

"You once were."

"No longer?"

"You've become my father's lackey, a kept man, and you'll work for him as a paid stooge." She allowed her words to have their effect. "Medicine has its share of yes men, and you'll be one of them, ceding to his every demand."

Nathan closed the book. "Aunt Joy and my mother wanted me to attend school in the east, and I must honor their wishes."

"You would leave me for the east when all you want is to travel west and live as a gunslinger?"

He gave her a smirk. "Those were boyish dreams from a penny novel. I've grown since then, and I no longer care for adventure."

"What then?"

"I care for meaning, purpose, a life that matters. I can have it in New York among the Fifth Avenue elite."

"We have a medical college here in St. Louis," she said softly.

Her beauty overwhelmed him, especially when she pouted in her girlish way. Real or contrived, her vulnerability was potent. He walked around the table and kneeled in front of her. His fingers gently stroked her brown curls.

Nathan placed a strand behind her ear.

"You know I love you," he said. "I always will."

"Then kiss me before I die of a broken heart."

His firm hand cupped her neck, and his lips pressed against hers. The moment grew tender. He hoped it might last a lifetime.

The door creaked open. "What are you doing to my daughter?"

Nathan arose and took a step backward. "Apologies, sir."

It was all he knew to say.

Belmont's hot and fuming eyes searched viciously about the room. He grabbed an iron poker from the fireplace and slouched forward.

Nathan had often stirred the fire, and although he understood the poker was the property of John Belmont, he imagined the tool didn't want to be there anymore than he did, and together they would make the best of their time in this fallen realm. It was a useful notion which helped Nathan cope.

"Father, please. You're a gentleman!"

Belmont's eyes landed on her like a hammer. "*You* are no lady."

He pointed the treasonous poker at Nathan's chest.

"Sir, we are in love. You cannot blame us for a stolen kiss."

Belmont stopped. "Blame you?" His eyes were engulfed by flames. "I am going to kill you today, you ungrateful brat!" He yelled and rushed forward.

Nathan brushed the friendly weapon to one side. Belmont's momentum carried him forward, and he stumbled into the wall.

Catherine burst into laughter. "It's what you deserve, Father, for your display of madness. We are mere children, not criminals marked for the gallows." Her voice carried a mixture of admiration and hatred.

Belmont steadied himself against the wall. "You are a reckless fool."

"Perhaps, but if you hurt him, I will no longer remain on this earth. Of that, you have my word."

He dusted off his pants for a moment and then straightened.

His eyes softened. "Your tone causes me to believe you are serious."

"This world is sinister, and men like you excel in it. If I cannot have Nathan Marsh, then I will not tolerate one more minute." She hesitated. "There are many ways to end one's life, you know. I've learned a thing or two from his medical book when he was busy with chores. You won't stop me once my mind is made up." She pointed at her father. "Choose your next steps with care or they will mark the end of your daughter's life."

Belmont would not give up so easily, as his mind was now bent on war. He had become a mindful knight, charging forth to save a lady in distress, and he would not stop until his foe was a bloody, tottering thing.

Nathan rushed through the door and ascended the stairs.

At the top, he paused, hoping his benefactor would calm down and come to his senses. Belmont thudded up the stairs with a knife from the kitchen. He swore a murderous oath and kept a rapid pace.

Nathan stood motionless and grave. "Please be reasonable, John."

"You will get out of this house and out of Catherine's life forever!"

Nathan's hand raised. "Put away the knife, and I'll leave."

"Do it *now*."

A few minutes later, Nathan had packed his things. His legs felt heavy, and he wanted to lie down in an earthly hole. He searched his mind for answers, but found only turbulent thoughts. Catherine pleaded with him to stop his flight to the wild green forest and become the man she had foreseen, a gallant hero for the ages like Mr. Rochester. Once her father saw the real man inside a boy's youthful body, he would be forced to accept their love.

If Nathan could only hold on for one hour, or even one second, this would become a laughable anecdote for their children and grandchildren.

Nathan closed the drawer.

He sat on his bed and took her hand. "Speak to him."

"I will," she said helplessly.

Her eyes rose to the doorway.

Belmont stood glaring at Nathan. "Why have you stopped?"

"Ask your daughter, sir."

Catherine appealed for a change of heart.

Belmont stared at her for a few moments, as if calculating the depth of her love and her willingness to carry through with her threats.

He turned toward Nathan. "I want you out."

"You're making a big mistake, Father."

Belmont loudly and boldly recited Psalm 11:1-3. "I trust in the Lord for protection. So why do you say to me, 'Fly like a bird to the mountains for safety! The wicked are stringing their bows and fitting their arrows on the bowstrings. They shoot from the shadows at those whose hearts are right. The foundations of law and order have collapsed. What can the righteous do?' Boy, you'll want to pay close attention to this last part."

Nathan sat still.

"The Lord examines both the righteous and the wicked. He hates those who love violence. He will rain down blazing coals and burning sulfur on the wicked, punishing them with scorching winds. For the righteous Lord loves justice. The virtuous will see his face."

"Am I the bird in your parable?"

Belmont nodded.

"You must fly to the mountains."

"What am I supposed to do on the mountain, eat bark from the trees?"

"You must seek the Lord in all things, Nathan, because now is your time to be tested. He purifies us through water and fire and sometimes, yes, we must eat bark from the trees. However, if you turn to Him now, perhaps there is still hope for the rest of your life."

If anyone deserved righteous judgement, it was John Belmont.

Nathan would gladly beat the tyrant into submission, but committing an act of violence would only land him in prison or place him at the end of a taught rope. He grabbed his bag and moved to the doorway. Belmont tensed and prepared for battle, but Nathan passed the smaller man without another word between them. He would rather speak to the blameless stars.

Downstairs, he hopped from the porch to the grass and said goodbye over his shoulder. Catherine sat on a bench near the door.

"I will use poison, Nathan. Your book has taught me well."

She seemed far away, as if already at home in another land.

He spun around and stepped within, containing his rage. "You may say those words to your father out of spite, but do not use them around me."

"I cannot live without you."

"Catherine, to you I'm a hero from one of your gothic novels, and you love the portrait your mind has conceived more than you love the real man who stands before you, human and imperfect." He hesitated. "You should know I'll never become an outlaw. They die young and mean."

"Nonsense. I won't listen."

"Before we kissed, I was a dullard who would sacrifice his dreams."

"Those were only playful words. I toyed with your heart."

"Now?"

"I am as serious as death, Nathan."

His hand waved her off, and he cursed.

"Find a real gunslinger, someone who sanctions your rashness and your headstrong desire." He turned toward the woods.

"Nathan, wait."

"I am not the man for you, Catherine," he said over his shoulder.

Nathan reached the edge of the yard.

"I will always love you! My fragile soul waits for your return!"

He spun around once more, and his eyes met hers across the distance.

"I will make a new start somewhere else. You will love another and create a family to call your own." He looked at the passing clouds, squinting his eyes. "Do better by them. Don't let them leave as I am doing now."

"Will you be alright, Nathan? I fear for your safety without my care."

"Samuel's many drunken rages have taught me to live outside our house." His hand clutched the handle of his suitcase. "I'm at peace as long as I have my medical book." He wondered how long he might survive.

"Promise me something?"

"Anything."

"Become a famous surgeon and make this world a better place." She sat down and then stood again. "One more thing?"

He sighed. "*Yes?*"

"Know you were once loved by a woman with a true heart."

He nodded and threw Catherine a rebuking look.

"Her name was June Marsh."

As he headed into the woods, the front door slammed.

June's last words reverberated through the treetops.

Run, Nathan. Oh God, please make him run away!

Just after the frost covered dawn, Nathan dreamed of life with Catherine. Their manicured house contained many cozy fireplaces and three mindful children and a pedigreed dog who loved the family and would protect it at any cost. Three crows landed in a tree. Their cawing startled Nathan awake. Professor Collins approached through the oaks and the hickories. His awkward stomps awakened every species of bird in the vicinity.

"There you are! Thought I'd never find you."

Nathan propped his weight on his elbows. "Why are you here?"

"When I learned of Belmont's tirade, I pleaded with him to reconsider his stance against you. He refused, and I resigned in protest."

"What does it mean for you?"

Roy's eyes narrowed, as if in confusion. "It means, dear boy, I will become your new legal guardian. You'll live with my family in New York until you graduate from college. After commencement, you'll work as a physician in the city, learning from the best surgeons in the nation."

Nathan wanted to argue with the professor, saying he didn't need charity and had plans of his own out west, but June would have wanted better for him. In his moment of weakness, and with no other options, he accepted the professor's offer and muttered an inarticulate *thanks*.

Colleen Collins greeted them with a *Merry Christmas* at the front door, her smile tender and her face beautiful. She ushered Nathan inside and showed him to his room, where he placed his leather bag in a corner. On a small table, she had placed writing materials in case he wanted to write home about his safe journey. Perhaps the season would inspire positive thoughts.

"That won't be necessary," he said with a melancholy smile.

"I pity your situation, honey. Not to worry, because I have drawn you a warm bath, and there's a hearty meal waiting for you downstairs."

He almost shared details from his early childhood, but decided against it, as their home was still unfamiliar. Instead, he made a joke at her expense.

"For a pretty woman, you're rather large in the belly."

"I'm pregnant, Nathan. Due in four months."

His insult had rattled her. If he kept going, she might allow him to leave.

"How *old* are you?"

"I'm thirty-four."

His eyes rolled.

Colleen stiffened, and her resolve steeled. "We all have chores around here," she said. "Roy teaches, and I tend the house. You can help with our two girls when you're not in school."

"I'm not a reclamation project."

"In God's eyes, you are worthy."

Nathan's palm raised. "Trust me, Colleen. Your children are too precious, and you don't want them around me." He looked at her tummy. "When the baby comes, do you expect me to help with the cleaning and the cooking, or am I to change its little diapers? Perhaps I can feed it stew."

She glanced at her oldest daughter, who now stared at the floor.

"Roy won't be much help, what with his academic routine taking up his time. It will be nice to have a strong young man around here."

Nathan sat on his bed and rubbed the blanket. "Stop judging me."

"No one here wants to do that. Only God judges us right or wrong."

"I see it in your eyes. I'm not Christian enough for you." He took a deep breath and exhaled. "I'll tell you right now, I stopped believing in some old man in the sky a long time ago, so don't be thinking I'm going to church."

Elizabeth gasped. Colleen gave her a kind look and sent her to the parlor to sit with Roy and Rebecca. Little boots thudded down the stairs.

Colleen sat beside him and thought for several moments.

"What are you afraid of, Nathan?"

She paused.

"What frightens you, deep down in your core?"

He withheld a reply.

Colleen stood and exhaled. "Think on my question."

She went to the door and turned around. "I'll soon require an answer."

After the family went to bed, Nathan went outside to the front porch and sat in a rocker. He could leave. New York would present a new cast of characters and a fresh set of experiences. Colleen and Roy were friendly people, but they would smother him with kindness and affection and expect him to embrace them as replacement parents. It was too much, too soon, and he must escape from their clutches. Eventually, he would do something or say something or be something which was not to their liking, and they would expel him from their perfect lives. It was as sure as snow in the winter or blistering heat in the summer. If he were to make it to adulthood without losing his sanity, Nathan would operate alone and on his own terms. He peeked in the window, noting a calm stillness, and then took a deep breath and exhaled, knowing what must be done. Nathan huddled in the chair and gazed at the stars. He counted them until he fell asleep.

Nathan stared at the small chalkboard, unsure how to determine the correct number of ounces in a gallon. Roy grew impatient with Nathan's struggles and snatched the tablet from his hands. He wrote the conversion chart as he'd done several times. One cup equaled eight ounces. Two cups equaled a pint. Two pints equaled a quart. And four quarts equaled a gallon.

"How many ounces are in a cup?"

"Eight?"

"Are you asking or telling?"

"It's eight," Nathan said, nodding.

Colleen shooed them away so she could set the table.

Roy took a seat in the parlor and gestured for Nathan to do likewise. "So how many ounces in a gallon?"

Nathan's eyes fell to the oval rug.

Colleen stuck her head into the room and curled her finger. "Honey, won't you come help me serve dinner?"

"I'm working with the boy, Colleen. I'll be in there soon."

Her eyebrows arched. "I was talking to *him*."

Roy chuckled. "Fine then. Off with you both."

In the kitchen, Nathan wrapped his hands around a serving bowl to steady it while Colleen ladled gravy over mashed potatoes. He'd helped his mother in the same manner.

"May we talk some more?"

"About what?"

"You know, the usual fare, like what happened to your mother, or why you left Catherine behind. Was it because her father is a stubborn fool?"

"I don't know what you want me to say."

"It's alright, Nathan. You don't have to talk if you don't want to."

"Good."

"Please understand something." She looked deep into his eyes. "If you suppress your painful feelings now, you'll go numb, and when *that* happens, you can't feel anything at all. Trust me. I know all about it." She hesitated. "There's a bigger problem. When you get older, like around my age, those feelings won't stay buried. They'll come roaring to the surface, and you'll become a furious person who doesn't know how to be with people." Her words hung in the air. "You would like a family, right?"

"Someday."

"You'll want to have the best family around, and by that, I mean everyone in the household gets along and loves one another. No one screams or fights or leaves home for good, never to return."

He nodded his understanding. "Sometimes I think about hurting people." He picked up a knife. "I want to become a surgeon who cuts people open to save their lives, but I could also use my knife to cut people open who hurt me. I try to put those thoughts out of my mind."

She gave him a concerned look. "All men are capable of such things, Nathan, and it takes less than you think to bring out their sadistic side." She smiled. "Us women have to learn early to manipulate you men. Otherwise, we might get cut up with a knife just like the one in your hand."

Nathan put it down and felt ashamed. He was nothing like his father, or at least he didn't want to be like Samuel. "I've had enough cruelty for one life, if that's what you're trying to say." He thought about Thomas Hannah.

She sat down at the small table and placed her chin in her palms. She stared at him. He sat opposite her, feeling uncomfortable at her refusal to look away. Tears formed in her eyes.

"What's wrong, Colleen?"

"Do you trust us?"

His eyes fell to the tabletop. "I guess."

"Then won't you share what happened?" Her hand squeezed his. "I want to help, Nathan. Please don't shut me out."

"I can't."

"How come?"

"It would destroy me."

"It will destroy you if you don't, honey." She hesitated. "It's time."

Nathan left her in the kitchen and sat at the dinner table with his arms crossed. They ate dinner in silence. Around ten o'clock, Nathan stared at the ceiling in his bedroom, unable to sleep. He'd wanted to express his pain to Colleen, but couldn't bring himself to trust her. She and Roy were just another set of people who would betray him. There was only one person still alive who he could trust, and her name was Catherine Belmont. He missed her and hoped she thought about him.

Someone knocked on the bedroom door.

"Yes?"

Roy stuck his head inside the bedroom. "Colleen mentioned you had trouble discussing your past with her. I just wanted you to know she means well and has your best interest at heart."

"She's very nice, but I can't handle the pressure she puts on me."

"There's no weakness in feeling sad, Nathan. You've been through a lot for a young man. It's why she wants to help you."

Nathan sat up in bed. "I want to be part of the family, but living here makes me uncomfortable. Can I stay somewhere else?"

Roy sat in a chair. "I suppose we could arrange a room in the dormitory at my college campus. You could live there while you finish your studies."

"Will they mind if I'm still in high school?"

"Our medical college has taken on orphans with bright prospects in past years, so it shouldn't pose a problem. I'll speak with the dean tomorrow."

Relief washed over Nathan.

Roy gave him a pained look. "Is it what you need?"

"I have to be on my own."

Two days later, Roy and Colleen took Nathan to the men's dormitory at Hudson Medical College. With tears in her eyes, Colleen hugged his neck.

"I'm sorry, honey. All I wanted to do was love you like a mother."

"I had a mother, but she's gone, and I'll never get her back."

After Roy and Colleen left, he watched through the window as they walked through the grass and hailed a cab. He would miss their cheerful home, but it was not the place for him. Nathan was an orphan, and his mission was clear. He would graduate high school and medical college, and then he would secure his status as an excellent surgeon. A heavenly beauty waited for him somewhere in New York, and Nathan would find her.

Failure was not a consideration. He couldn't afford to be hurt again.

Twelve

Therefore, Lord, we know you will protect the oppressed,
preserving them forever from this lying generation,
even though the wicked strut about,
and evil is praised throughout the land.

The following Monday morning, Daisy observed Catherine while Nathan tended to her improving condition. As a measure against Bell's paralysis, he applied electrodes to Catherine's ear and to the limp side of her face. She lightly grabbed his hand and gave a half smile, aware of his presence for the first time. Nathan patted her leg for comfort, but said nothing to her. His duty was to mend her physical ailments and be respectful of her emotional state of mind, but his stated happiness ended at approaching her station. For Daisy, it most was interesting to see Catherine in such a moneyless condition, as, according to Nathan, she had so often ridiculed the weak and the poor, her devotion keenly allied with privilege.

Even so, his coldness was off-putting. Physicians must never be aloof. "Your bedside manner could use improvement."

He looked up at her. "I suppose you would do better?"

"I would at least *try*."

"For you, she's a deserving sister in need. For me, she's a monster."

"She's the mother of your children, Nathan."

His eyes widened, showing the whites, and his voice went cold.

"You should ward off the spirits which distort her face and impede her speech with a verse from your well-worn book of myths. I'm sure a word from our resident faith healer will exceed my proven scientific techniques."

For several moments, there was silence between them. Their romantic relationship hadn't materialized to meet her expectations, and she felt herself slip into a far off country, her current land suddenly returning to its former strange and unfriendly condition. She longed for and would enjoy a kind and affectionate talk with him, but it would be easier to converse with the howling winds which swirled over the great river or the blinking stars which populated the firmament above, as his manner in romance was as detached and clinical as his bedside manner in their hospital. She was a bystander to his selfishness, and he was a learned fool. It would be less cumbersome to break a stick over his head, and she would feel her life much improved for her trouble. He might later thank her for the worthy deed.

"There's no need for acrimony," she said. "Toward me or Catherine."

Detective Kincaid entered the front door and spoke with Nurse Pratt, who directed him toward Nathan and Daisy. He marched at a brisk pace.

"Can we talk?"

Nathan's eyes remained on Catherine as he adjusted an electrode.

"Right now?"

"It's about the bakery murder." Kincaid stood without a hint or a trace of self-consciousness and spoke impatiently, as if Nathan took up his most valuable time. "The deceased's name was Chester Langley. Ring any bells?"

"Why would it? My attention is here with these patients."

"I've got another patient for you. He's a material witness to the murder, and he initially agreed to testify in open court. Two days later, he panicked and started talking about Armageddon. We held him for a while, then took him to the city asylum for observation and evaluation. Since they were three deep in the hallways, we brought him here." Kincaid's mouth broke into a wide grin, and he chuckled. "Funny how things go sometimes."

"The world is a dangerous and unpredictable place."

Kincaid's curious eyes fell on Catherine. "This your wife?"

Nathan took a deep breath and exhaled. "Ex-wife." He sat up straight and placed the electrodes in Catherine's lap.

Her listless eyes lagged as they followed his movements.

Nathan carefully rearranged her pillow. "Does this feel better?"

Catherine relaxed into the soft texture. Her eyes closed.

Kincaid chuckled a second time. "I see you two have a fine relationship."

Nathan grimaced, and his face made it clear he could take no more sarcasm or suggestions for improvement. He wheeled and left the detective without offering a reply. At the far side of the hall, he swung open the heavy stairwell door and trudged hard up the stairs. Daisy and the officer exchanged momentary glances and then followed the good doctor to the second floor. Her boots and Kincaid's shoes thudded on each wooden step. The sound reverberated off the oak walls, forming a temporary but unpleasant chamber of competing sounds which hurt her ears and made her wary. At the top, Daisy wondered if she would ever be made whole again.

Inside Nathan's office, she shut the door. Nathan motioned for her to sit in a chair beside his desk. The room was plain but neatly ordered.

Kincaid looked annoyed as he sat. "Does she need to be here?"

"Daisy Lawrence is our psychologist and my administrative assistant. What I know, she knows."

"Have it your way."

The detective flipped through his notebook.

"Are you blaming me for what happened to Catherine Belmont? If so, I can assure you there's been a mistake."

Kincaid sighed. "Like father, like son."

Nathan kicked his chair against the wall, frightening Daisy. She uttered a small yelp and rose to a standing position, unsure of her next move.

Nathan's cheeks reddened. "What do you think you're doing?"

"Leaving this room," she said. "I'm not sure what else."

"You are ungrateful."

"How can you say such a thing? I've cleaned your home until my fingers bled, and I've sorted your medical paperwork, which you'll never get around to doing in a thousand years, and I've done my best to reach those rueful patients on the floor. What else do you want from me?"

"I want your loyalty, something you seem unwilling to give."

"I have been loyal to a fault, which was the reason for my struggles in the past, but now I must take infinite care when choosing the beneficiary of my allegiance." Her breath calmed, but her wish for independence drove her across a line. "Right now, I'm not sure that man is *you*."

"Have you given thought to my offer?"

"To take a room in your home?"

He nodded.

She glanced at Kincaid and remained silent.

"Or you could move into the hospital." Nathan seemed intent on persuasion. "We can convert one of these offices into a bedroom."

His first request would define her primarily as his housekeeper, a role unlikely to produce love in a man of letters, and the crucible would lead to arguments born of proximity and temperament, the latter a towering obstacle neither of them knew how to surmount. "I would prefer a room here, if you can maintain your stature as a gentleman." Another thought entered her mind: If she moved into his home, he would soon grow tired of her presence, and she might find him disagreeable in his sobriety.

Kincaid slapped his knee, unwilling to lose the advantage he'd worked to attain. "You two are quite the pair. Why not get married so you can really have it out? My wife and I wake the neighbors some nights."

Nathan's fits clenched tightly. "Get out of my hospital."

Kincaid's palm raised in feigned alarm. "Alright, sir, no need for a quick temper. I wouldn't be doing my job if I didn't probe a bit."

His hand gestured toward Nathan's chair. "You'll be doing me a favor."

"Alright," Nathan said, sitting. "You'd better make this quick. We have a hall full of very sick patients."

"I only need to ask you one question."

Nathan shifted heavily. "Which is?"

"Why did Samuel frame Thomas Hannah for property theft?"

Daisy eyed the investigator.

Kincaid seemed interested in holding his evidence close to the vest.

Nathan leaned forward. "Someone said this?"

Kincaid nodded.

"Then I suppose you know more than me." Nathan glanced at Daisy with sheepish eyes and then realigned his posture curiously.

Kincaid stood and opened the office door.

He stopped and closed it, waiting for the clicking sound, then turned and faced Nathan, wearing a sly grin. "There's just one more thing." He put a finger over his lips. "I need more information about the relationship between Thomas Hannah and June Marsh."

"I do not take your meaning," Nathan said. "It is obvious Thomas murdered her."

"Would you agree the couple knew one another well?"

"You're calling them a *couple*?"

"Slip of the tongue," Kincaid said. "They were well acquainted?"

"I suppose."

"Hannah trained horses at your father's farm." Kincaid made a clucking sound with his tongue and tapped his finger on his lips. "I hear she liked to ride a chestnut mare." He retrieved his notebook and flipped through the pages. "Let's see. What was her horse's name?"

"Ruby," Nathan said. "Her mare's name was Ruby."

"That's the one." Kincaid thumped the page. "If my facts are correct, a Mr. Thomas Hannah trained the horse."

"Once again, I see no connection to my mother's murder."

"Were they in love?"

"Ridiculous." Nathan's hands signaled his frenzied disapproval and the upsetting portrait in his mind. "The man was a laborer with delusions of grandeur. Since my father was busy with a full roster of patients, he unknowingly enabled Hannah's psychosis by hiring him to train our horses. It was a fatal mistake, and one I'm sure he regrets, but the fact remains, Thomas was fired for stealing. He left in bitterness and took his rage out on my unsuspecting mother, forcing me to watch her agonizing death."

"Nathan, I'm so sorry that happened to her." Daisy wiped tears from her eyes. "And to you."

"It was a long time ago," he said. "Thank you."

Daisy closed her eyes and prayed Psalm 12:1 aloud while stroking Nathan's arm. "Help, O Lord, for the godly are fast disappearing! The faithful have vanished from the earth!"

She squeezed Nathan's arm more tightly.

Kincaid flipped through the pages of his notebook several times. "You watched June die?"

Nathan pulled away from Daisy. He gave the detective a blank look.

"Our records show you fled the scene and could not confirm Hannah as the murderer." Kincaid stared at Nathan, waiting for a response.

"I was seven, and Thomas haunted my dreams. My father explained I would have to testify in open court. What would you have done?"

"It's not for me to say, Nathan." Kincaid's tone made him seem honestly surprised. "I seek the truth, no matter how long it's been buried."

"It's about time someone gave the matter serious consideration."

Kincaid scribbled something in his notebook. "For the record, you are one hundred percent sure Thomas Hannah murdered June Marsh?"

"Who else could have done it?"

"An accomplice, or a hundred different people. Anyone could have had their way after Hannah exited the scene. As you know, she was in a most vulnerable position." At his last utterance, Kincaid glanced at Daisy.

Nathan pushed his chair backward and went to the window; he spread the thin curtain and gazed absently at the street. "The papers stated you have him in custody for the bakery murder, but he's not talking."

"He's had plenty to say about you and Samuel."

Nathan turned toward Kincaid. "Such as?"

"Samuel kept a valuable sword from the war."

"Thomas Hannah stole it. It's why my father fired him."

"There's one problem, Nathan." Kincaid closed his notebook and rested his hands on his lap. "Last August, there was a soldier's reunion at the Drummond's farm. From what I recall, there was a parade in town and a big dinner where drunken ex-soldiers told whoppers about their gallantry and their exploits. A waste of time and money, if you ask me."

"I take it you never served," Nathan said. "Your mockery might be diminished if you knew what those men suffered."

The detective's expression changed from sand to stone.

"I'm sure you're correct, but it doesn't alter the facts of this case. Your father was wearing the stolen sword in the commemorative photograph. He must be getting senile in his old age. It was an unfortunate blunder."

Daisy gasped.

The room fell silent.

Friday, Nathan sat with Catherine at her bedside. Her facial paralysis had cleared, and she was ambulatory, although written words remained mostly undecipherable, and she could not speak. Nathan tried to focus on her remaining symptoms, but his mind struggled to concentrate. Daisy stood near the window and spoke with James Clifton, who studied the pane and muttered to himself. The lack of breakthroughs in the Clifton case further escalated the tension between doctor and psychologist, as the hospital's reputation was on the line, and both Kincaid and Belmont expected efficient results. She hugged James and squeezed his hand before she made her way down the line of beds. James moaned at the window, and Daisy looked back at him with sincere concern. A flood of jealousy sloshed over Nathan.

Ever since Kincaid had paid a call, she avoided his company.

Should he go to her and start a conversation?

Perhaps he should moan like James. Nathan laughed silently.

Daisy drew close to his location. "Would you like to trade? There are other patients in the hall besides Catherine."

Nathan's fingers ran along his jaw. "It would be a relief."

Daisy grabbed a chair from beside the adjacent bed and sat. "You look tired. Have you slept?" Her voice carried pangs of distrust and contempt.

"Too many nightmares," he said automatically.

"What brings them about?"

"The wrong person was taken when my mother died," he said. "I'm merely a drunken quack who will soon be destitute."

Daisy's eyes closed, and she prayed Psalm 12:5-6 aloud. "The Lord replies, 'I have seen violence done to the helpless, and I have heard the groans of the poor. Now I will rise up to rescue them, as they have longed for me to do.' The Lord's promises are pure, like silver refined in a furnace, purified seven times over."

"Is that necessary?"

"I think so, yes."

"Well, I think not."

Her eyes widened. "You remind me of the man I almost married. He thought religious instruction was equivalent to child abuse. Much of Europe now feels the same, and I fear it will spread to America in the next century." She ran her hand across the cotton sheet on the adjacent bed. "A fierce battle awaits us, and I'm not sure we are ready as a nation."

He stared crossly at her for several moments and made little attempt to conceal his displeasure. "No one wants to live in a theocracy or have someone else's morality imposed on them. We may lose our ever dwindling frontier, but we haven't yet lost our freedom to choose our own path."

"It's the same absurd argument in Europe," she said. "Jesus didn't come to enslave mankind, but to free us from the bondage of our own sin."

"I like my sin. Thank you very much."

Undeterred, Daisy continued. "The Lord is not a hostile enemy, and He does not force himself on us, Nathan. He advances His will through love."

Nathan changed the subject. "What did James say to you earlier?"

She adopted a sullen look. "A stray dog has been roaming up and down the street all morning, and he wants to bring it inside and feed it lunch. He claims a grateful and lovesome dog will help him recover more quickly."

"He would cover us all with fleas."

Her eyebrows arched. "Why do you assume the dog is a male?"

"In my experience, men wander more often than women."

"James claims she's a female." She hesitated. "He says she's pregnant."

"Terrific."

He turned his focus toward the ever tiresome Heinrich Besseler and noted aloud how much the patient's facial tic had worsened. Heinrich believed June bugs bit him and everyone else in the room throughout the day. He sometimes called out from his bed and warned others in his vicinity.

Nathan's legs kicked out in front of him, and his heels thudded on the wooden floor. "Are we making any progress at all?"

"I sometimes wonder," she said, standing.

Daisy looked about the hall like an unhappy child. The atmosphere of her mood had changed upon the mention of yet another sad specimen.

"Ed Wilson went home, which is a good thing." Nathan's eyes raised to meet hers. "My father and several other men traded turns as they tended to his land and livestock. It was an arduous task, and I have not envied them."

"I grew up on a farm, Nathan. You don't have to tell me about hard work." She straightened the covers on the adjacent bed, displeased with their appearance. Her arms and hands moved gruffly.

Her indignation confused him. "I never said otherwise."

Daisy stopped her work and glared at him. "Don't be insensitive to a man's shock at losing his beloved wife." Her nostrils flared. "Then a whiskey drenched doctor cut off his son's leg at the hip, which has forever rendered the boy useless as a three-legged mule." She hesitated. "As the ragged scoundrel who did such a horrid thing, I would expect a certain empathy from you, sir." Her voice raised. "Or is *that* too much for a big city doctor?" She looked about the hall again. "Are we merely your loyal subjects?"

Daisy had lost what remained of her fragile sanity. "If you believe Ronnie is of no more use, perhaps *you* are the one lacking in sensitivity."

"I only meant for farm work, and you know it." Daisy's hands splayed out wide to stretch and then relaxed. Her voice calmed. "I hope Ed learns to deal with what happened to his son. Ronnie will need his father's stability."

"Ed found the courage to leave here and resume farming." He shrugged and hoped he could scoot away if she grabbed a scalpel. "It's *something*."

She glared at him again. "You expressed the same notion a few moments ago, Nathan. Must you repeat yourself?"

He had grown tired of her arbitrary outbursts and so he spoke to her in a strained voice. "I'm glad to see the return of Ed's backbone, and yes, both he and Ronnie must be strong to face the years ahead. We all must."

Her furious hands picked up a pillow and pounded it before they placed it on an empty bed. "I think you have a deeper problem than a belief in God. You feel tremendous guilt over failing to save your children." She moved to the next bed, where she grabbed another pillow and pounded on it.

His lips pursed. "Yes."

She nodded.

"Do you feel the same about failing Catherine as a husband?"

He gave her a coarse look. "You should leave the room."

She released the pillow and put her hands on her hips. "Yes. I should. Otherwise, I'm liable to say some nasty words to you, Nathan."

She marched into the storage room and slammed the door.

You already have, Daisy.

He sat for a moment, curiously inanimate, as her perfume lingered. He looked about the main hall, expecting an embarrassing basket of jaundiced expressions, but found only busy activity. Nathan returned to his study of the storage room door, finding himself in a peculiar position, hoping it would open, and she would rush over to him and reveal her endless love.

If only my life could ever go right, I would be a better man.

Nathan hugged Catherine and kissed her cheek, wafting a desolate chill across the breadth of the main hall. Daisy had been pacing the line of beds, but she stopped and gave him an involuntary look of surprise and shock. He glanced uneasily in her direction, and Daisy forced a weak grin. Nathan returned a quick nod and a smile, which did not reach his eyes, providing clear indication of the depth of his feelings for his ex-wife and the mother of his children, whether he was willing to plainly admit their existence or not. Catherine had pushed on a wall already bent, and she clearly planned to mingle Nathan among the finished ruin of her own life and marriage.

Daisy spun around and hastened toward the entrance, her mind fixated once again on escape to Fountain Park. Catherine would prove yet another Rosemarie, merely the latest in Daisy's long line of female adversaries, and like the others, Catherine would steal her chance at attachment and security.

At the cherry tree front door, a dark and barren shape jiggled the handle in a rough manner. There was a tilt of panic in the movements.

Daisy grabbed her side and tried to turn. "Please let go."

The other party complied, and Daisy flung open the paneled door.

Sheila Byrne sauntered past Daisy and down the line of beds.

Daisy called out to her. "May I help you?"

Sheila said nothing as her feet sped toward Nathan. Her lips smiled broadly, and her hand covered a bloody cut on one arm. Dora offered to look at the wound, but Sheila waved off her attempt. Blood rushed from Nathan's cheeks as he stood before his new patient, the one he had discarded to the cupidity of her ancestral ties and the rage of a harsh landlord.

Daisy walked close enough to overhear.

"Joanna did this," said Sheila helplessly.

"She cut you?"

"Joanna paid a man to do it. She hates me with a fiery passion."

"We have to get you out of there. It's not a safe environment."

She leaned close to him. "It never was, my love."

The moniker *my love* stung Daisy more than she would have predicted. She held her ground and exchanged a brief but knowing glance with Dora.

Nathan led Sheila past Daisy to a group of empty beds near the entrance. They rushed close beside her, and she whirled fast enough to catch the look of pained concern in both of their eyes. A junior nurse tended Sheila's frightful lesion. Her naïve eyes met Daisy's from afar as Nathan and Sheila exchanged lovely words of mistake and shed tears of connection.

He looked like a lost puppy whose mother had found him.

A train of thoughts cascaded through Daisy's mind. Why did he avoid Sheila after his success in New York? Was he capable of love with anyone? Had Catherine realized the truth of his failings and left him to the brothels, the only worthy realm for him? If so, Sheila clearly proved herself an anomaly among such women, giving him affection and warmth for ten years, never asking for anything of substance in return. After so much time and intimacy and money exchanged, was there no spark of love in his soul for her? Could he be that cold-hearted? Surely the adoring lass did nothing to deserve such misery. A final thought made itself known to Daisy, the worst of them all. Although their bond was undeniable and most painful to watch from a helpless distance, it was clear from both of their dispositions, he never expected to see Sheila again and, although he wanted her safe and well, she would soon be asked to leave this hospital, never to return.

Would he someday do the same to Daisy?

She turned, and her eyes fell on Catherine, who observed quietly and studiously from her bed. For the first time since her arrival, there was clear and undeniable activity behind those lethargic eyes, and in this particular moment, she might have well been one of those newfangled Comptograph adding machines which were all the rave in New York and Chicago.

Daisy's attention was recaptured by Sheila's soothing tone, the type a mother provides her hopeful child, the form most obviously withheld from Nathan as a small boy by a mother without the capacity and gone too soon.

It was no wonder he sought a replacement. Daisy had done the same.

She spun around and caught the look on his face. The love which she had assumed was dead inside him was suddenly resurrected. It shone like a glittering diamond in his eyes. He leaned over and gave Sheila a warm hug.

"Why haven't you come to see me, Nathan? I hope you're not angry."

"It's nothing like that." His hand gestured across the room. "As you can see, we have our hands full here. We barely keep the chaos in check from hour to hour, and I haven't had the time."

Dora cleaned the wound and wrapped the gauze bandage around it.

"There," she said. "You'd better get along before Mr. Belmont discovers you in here. He'll have a blooming fit."

"She's right, Sheila. He's not the understanding type."

"Then you'll come see me soon? I can't bear our forced separation."

Nathan nodded his willingness. "Real soon."

"Alright then." Sheila stood and kissed him on the cheek. She lingered, and her slender fingers squeezed his arm. "I need someone to need me, Nathan. Please allow me into your world. I won't bite."

Nathan chuckled.

Her red lips trembled. "What's so funny?"

He pointed to Ida, who sat in the rocking chair, unable to keep still. "We have one of those, too."

Sheila smiled. "Someone who bites?"

He nodded.

"This hospital has become a madhouse."

"Joanna's brothel has become much the same in your absence." She held up her arm. "My madhouse has brutal men who cut."

She walked to the front door and opened it.

Her fearful eyes fell on Nathan. "Joanna is jealous. She believes I stole you from her ten years ago, and without your powerful protection, my life isn't worth a Liberty Head Nickel." There was something unearthly in the reality of her words. "Oh, Nathan, don't you know the depth of my soul?"

Nathan stood and spoke with sincerity. "I'll visit you soon."

"Please do, my love. I won't last much longer."

After Sheila left, Nathan stomped upstairs to his office.

Daisy debated whether she should follow him. She tried to take her mind off the idea, but failed. What did she want from life, a home with a picket fence, a flourishing career, or perhaps a new adventure on a foreign continent? Frank had celebrity-like status in Europe, and the press had publicized his every movement. Freud and Charcot had shunned her, forcing her back to America. Could she live the rest of her days as a spinster in Pollard, Missouri? Could she surrender once again to an overbearing father, a man who treated her like a helpless child? She sat in a chair and clutched at her chest, and her mind went to a bleak and lonely place, a high ledge above a bloodstained pile of rocks, the setting for her photograph.

She prayed for rescue. *Please, Lord, break the arm of the corrupt, help the fatherless, and seek out my wickedness until no more remains. You are the Most High, and I await your heavenly return with a waning endurance.*

Daisy knocked on Nathan's office door and heard no answer.

She opened it and was surprised to find him organizing papers on his desk, completely engrossed in his work. Daisy sat in front of him and stared with a joyless intention, but she could not capture his regard. She wondered about his emotions. Did he doubt her unraveled and weakened heart as much as she feared the strength and thickness of his? Did the very idea of love enrapture him and also make him want to run for the tallest peak? Did he carry the omnipotent burden of anxiety, the omnipresent yoke of guilt, and the omniscient cross of shame? As before, recriminations threatened to derail her senses. Rather than ponder his devouring mysteries and worsen her deepening turmoil, she spoke to him about the intricacies of medical care. In her estimation, the brain was more important than the body, but it rarely received the same level of scrutiny or lofty acclaim.

"What say you?"

His eyes arched as they continued their perusal. "You are a strange bird, Miss Lawrence." His bearing shimmered with faint astonishment.

"I'm aware, but you have dodged my question."

His eyes met hers. "Alright, I'll play your game. The body is the most vital because it contains and fuels the brain. Without the various systems of the body, the brain would be relegated to life in a jar on the shelf."

"The brain allows us to feel and to ponder, to connect with our Lord and Savior, Jesus Christ. The animals with lower cognitive abilities have no such link to the divine. Their souls have been given over to wickedness."

"From my experience, human beings are every ounce as malevolent." He stuffed the papers into his folder and then placed the folder in a desk drawer. "I see you are intent on furthering our spiritual disagreement."

"I want to find common ground."

"Is that all?"

Daisy gave him a pleading look. "You must tell me about Sheila."

"I wouldn't claim to know much about her. She's a passionate Irish lass of about thirty, and from what I've gathered, Sheila came here looking for the proverbial pot of gold, but she only found poverty and hardship, even worse than the old country, which apparently was bad enough to force her across the Atlantic. She made her way from Philadelphia to Chicago and then down to St. Louis. I met her ten years ago after Catherine's desertion."

He paused.

"You know her occupation and the nature of our carnal relationship."

"I left Europe to escape from scandal, and you've brought it once again to my doorstep," she said sarcastically. "You, sir, are to be congratulated."

His back pressed into his chair. "My intentions remain pure, madam."

Daisy nodded her agreement. "I will cede the point. You mentioned Sheila the night we met, which now feels like a long time ago."

He sighed. "It certainly does."

"You know nothing else about her?"

He shook his head. "We don't talk about our pasts."

"Or much of anything."

"Point ceded to your side."

"This isn't lawn tennis," she said. "Despite your attempt at rivalry."

He grinned. "I merely agreed with your assessment."

Daisy diverted him elsewhere. He must explain his motivation.

"Men are the strange ones. You want women to be ladies in public, yet you consort with prostitutes in private. It's confusing to me."

"I suppose it's how we maintain order."

"Do you care for her?"

He clasped his hands together. "I'm sorting through a variety of feelings right now, and to be honest, I'm not sure about anything."

"Do you care about *anyone*, even Catherine?"

"Now there's a sore subject," he said flatly. "I take it you think I've done something offensive to your blend of American and Parisian sensibilities?"

She smiled. "Would you like to know what I most want?"

"This ought to be good. Let's have it."

"I want you to treat Catherine as a human being, not as a corpse."

He snorted. "Why do you care about a woman who betrayed me ten years ago? A loyal assistant would despise her on my behalf."

"Nathan, she's a woman who wants to live again, if you'll only allow it."

"How am I stopping her?"

"Your hatred of her, of yourself, of God is blocking your progress, and hers. Catherine could have an honest chance if we worked together."

"I hugged her earlier," he said. "You saw our embrace."

Daisy nodded.

"Her heart was engaged in full, but yours was absent any semblance of intimacy. A woman watches and a woman knows."

"How do you know Catherine wants to live without our children? There are many days when I don't want to live without them."

"You aren't the only one to lose someone, Nathan."

She paused.

"My past haunts me, especially at night when the room is still and dark and my mind races. In those moments, I cry myself to sleep."

"I'm done with crying," he said.

"Now that you've ceased living a debauched life, perhaps you'll cry again. It's something to hope for, don't you think?"

He stared through Daisy. "Maybe it's what Catherine needs."

August 1893

A week passed for Catherine with little improvement. Nathan felt helpless and alone in the world, even though he was surrounded by active people, and he wondered if his hysteria patients were much the same. Daisy had claimed superior knowledge of experimental psychology and of the proper modalities for hysteria, but her flimsy methods had yet to flourish. His initial faith in her had turned to suspicion, and he hoped he hadn't hired an inept person for the job. If her success rate didn't improve soon, he might be forced to admit defeat and make a change, and he worried over the ordeal to follow. Mostly, he dreaded the loss of Daisy's company on a daily basis.

Without her to steady his course, his ship may run aground.

Kincaid entered the front door with feverish, over-bright eyes. "Any progress? It's been two weeks, and the judge is getting irritated."

Nathan shook his head. "Not much has changed. James stands in front of the window, studying each pane for the smallest pits. That's about it."

Kincaid's cheeks flushed crimson. "I'm not sure you understand our situation. We're holding Thomas Hannah without evidence out of the good graces of Judge Winfield. If he changes his mind, Hannah will walk out the front door, never to be seen or heard from again."

"That's your problem."

"Don't you care about solving a murder?"

Nathan gave the man a baleful sneer. "Her name was June Marsh." His voice rose an octave. "We've told each detective who's been assigned to her case Thomas Hannah murdered her. They never once listened to us."

"Thomas and June were romantically involved. I'm sorry to have to say it, Nathan, but it's true. You should face the facts."

"Whatever their relationship might have been, it was temporary, and it changes nothing. The man murdered her out of spite and vindictiveness. He's a monster, and I want him to hang."

"Then testify as you should have done years ago."

"It's your job to hang the man, not mine."

Kincaid's fist slammed into the desktop. "There's no talking to you!" He opened the office door, slammed it shut, and stormed out the building.

Daisy stuck her head into the office. "Everything alright in here? He seemed furious." Her eyebrows arched. "Nathan, what did you do?"

"I asked him to right a horrible wrong from my past."

"If you can't fix it, you'll just have to move on with your life."

"You're a fine one to talk about such things."

She blushed.

"Allow me to say a brief prayer from Psalm 12:7-8." Before he could answer, her eyes closed. "Therefore, Lord, we know you will protect the oppressed, preserving them forever from this lying generation, even though the wicked strut about, and evil is praised throughout the land."

Nathan's mind drew a portrait of his mother as she writhed on the ground. He stood and shoved his hands into his pockets and paced the room, desperately trying to rid his imagination of the emotional moment.

"I need something positive today. Bring Ida Barnes to my office."

"Alright, but why?"

"She's young, and the human brain is malleable at her age. Maybe we can help her recover. I must know it's possible to help these people."

Daisy summoned orderlies up the stairs and requested Ida.

When asked to sit in a chair, the child's legs and feet shook as if Nathan's abominable disposition scared her half to death. She removed her shoes and gave him a dour look while she unbuttoned and buttoned her overcoat.

She wandered aimlessly about the small office.

"What are you looking for?"

"A centerpiece for my table." Her swaying reminded Nathan of Colleen.

"Will you clarify your statement?"

"If I was Stephen Foster, I wouldn't be here."

"The composer?"

"My mother loved 'Beautiful Dreamer.' It was her favorite."

Ida hummed as she moved in ever-widening and shrinking circles.

"Another parlor song?"

"We also sang 'Jeanie with the Light Brown Hair.' My father loved that one." Her eyes prowled every nook and cranny as she spoke.

"Your parents sure knew their music," Nathan said. "Did your father pass before your mother?"

"I don't know."

He asked her to sit down again. She complied.

Ida wobbled in her chair, unable to sit still.

"What's happening to you now?"

"Is it Monday or Thursday?"

"What do you think?"

"I do not know." Her chin jutted outward. "Clocks are tragic."

"What are you afraid of, Ida?"

"My mother said to always fear improper verb conjugation."

He asked for clarification, but she provided none. She went to a window and studied the light on her arm. She fumbled with the curtain and then sat down after grabbing a small picture of a sunflower from Nathan's shelf. He asked her what it was. She said a sunflower, but it looked like an eclipse or a tempest. Ida should have hidden it so she wouldn't be there. She fanned her face while she bounced her feet against the floor and rocked in place. He asked if she was too warm, and she scratched her leg. Her sharp and pointy fingernails cut into the flesh until Nathan forced her to cease. Ida paced about the room for several minutes and then sat on his desk. She kicked her legs against the side like a loathsome fiend under house arrest.

"Please stop at once," he said emphatically.

Ida screamed at him. "We've got to contact someone important! I'll compose a letter right now!" She stood and searched in his drawers for a few moments before she gave up. "Paper matters naught."

Nathan escorted Ida downstairs to the main hall. Daisy walked beside him and the girl. She supported the child's frail body as necessary.

He blew out a quick breath. "Her anxiety is impossible to withstand. She's like a ghastly creature from a gothic novel, and if left with her for too lengthy an interval, she will drive me to Arsenal Road."

"We're already there," said Daisy, smiling.

He gave her a reproachful look and addressed a nurse. "Please return Ida to her bed and offer her something to calm her nerves."

"Yes, doctor. Right away."

In his office, he slammed his papers onto the floor near his desk. He placed his head in his hands and tried to cry, but no tears would flow.

As she walked the bed line Monday morning, Daisy checked on Ronnie. The inner part of his stump had become red, hard, cedematous, and painful over the weekend. She petitioned Nathan to confirm the grave development.

"It's nice to know I can depend on you," he said. "For a moment, I had my doubts about your work ethic. You've since proven me wrong."

"I felt your ferocious eyes on me. You placed me under your microscope and scrutinized my every move. I thought I had returned to Pierre's house."

When Ed Wilson arrived and Nathan informed him about Ronnie's leg, he became inconsolable. Nathan ordered Dora to attend to Ronnie while he tried to calm Ed's wild anger, but as was his custom, Ed became hysterical and fell into a seizure, flopping about the shiny oak floor. Nathan issued Ed his earlier cot beside Ronnie and then sat in a chair beside Ronnie's bed.

His eyes rose to Daisy. "I wonder if the boy will make it to Friday."

She gasped. "Don't say such things in his presence."

Ronnie smiled at her. "It's alright, Miss Lawrence. I know the situation has turned grim." His voice was surprisingly light.

"How do you know?" asked Nathan.

"The Lord gave me a word in my spirit," Ronnie said. "It's almost time to come home, and to be honest, I'm growing more ready by the day."

"As a boy, I dreamed of escape to the west," Nathan said. "Once again, it sounds like a splendid notion. I like to fight my way out of trouble."

Ronnie gave Nathan a soft smile.

"You need to search the scriptures for God's holy purity. It does you no good to follow a soiled and bloody map to King Solomon's mines, where moth and dust corrupt. Your answers lie above in the Lord's twinkling firmament, not below in the dank and the dust of lowly darkness. My body may soon go into the ground, but my soul will rise upon the return of Jesus in the first resurrection. I hope to see you there."

Upstairs in Nathan's office, Daisy grew concerned.

"Will the police detective blame you if Ronnie passes?"

Nathan nodded.

"My arrest might be justified, as I missed the tumor's return." He sighed. "The whole stump is likely infiltrated by the same broken-down material we found in his leg. I fear the disease has extended around to his buttocks and now involves the gluteal muscles."

"This cannot stand, Nathan. You must work a miracle as you did with the president. Ronnie is so young and so filled with the breath of life."

"Even if we removed all possible signs, a strong recurrence is likely within weeks. I'm afraid this tumor has the upper hand."

"Then you'll go after the mass again and as many times as it takes."

"Angio-sarcoma is an aggressive, fast-moving cancer, one which likely took Ronnie's mother, Alva. You should prepare yourself for his passing."

"It's so sad for Ed. He's lost them both in quick succession."

Although Nathan's heart ached with every beat, his tears hid themselves. He surveyed the room. "My nerves long for a drink of whiskey."

Daisy quoted Romans 15:13. "I pray that God, the source of hope, will fill you completely with joy and peace because you trust in him. Then you will overflow with confident hope through the power of the Holy Spirit."

"It's a nice sentiment, but not very helpful."

"I'm sorry for questioning your opinion of Ed Wilson. It seems he's a weak man." She hesitated. "I appreciate your strength of will."

Nathan's eyes dulled. "As you mentioned, Ed has endured substantial loss since last year, and it takes its toll on anyone. I coped for a decade with large amounts of whiskey and beer, but Ed is not a drinking man."

"Which will serve him well in the end, if he can find a fresh path."

"Perhaps."

To take Nathan's mind off Ronnie and Ed, she asked for his honest assessment of Shirley Fletcher. She had hardly moved since her arrival.

"Shirley fears strangulation by anyone and everyone, and her terror has caused partial paralysis. As we discussed the night we met, a complete loss of ambulation seems to be a common symptom of hysteria."

"When we cannot reach them through emotional or psychological means, their bodies shut down," Daisy said, nodding. "The mind remains an unknown territory, ripe for exploration. Even our most prominent scientists have much to learn, and as I work with these patients, I help expand the base of their knowledge." Her eyes flickered. "Perhaps I should publish."

"If you achieve something here, I will publish my own book on making medicines right alongside yours. We'll be two peas in a pod once again."

"First, we must focus on Shirley Fletcher. She is most distressed."

"Like me, she tosses and turns in her bed all night." Nathan sighed and then smiled at Daisy. "I think we all need a stiff drink."

Daisy returned his smile. "It's what Pierre would say."

Catherine's physical symptoms slowly healed, which allowed Nathan and Daisy to walk her inside the hospital for two weeks. In the third week, they led her around the block for one loop. Like Nathan and Daisy and the other hysterics, Catherine had long buried her emotional trauma, most especially the loss of her three children—Annie, Peter, and Ely. To climb out of her self-imposed abyss, she needed to face their deaths and perhaps cry over them. Nathan and Daisy took her to a cemetery in the Central West End.

As they boarded the trolley, Daisy noticed a man who leered at them from the opposite side of the street. She waited for him to do something unexpected, like to draw a pistol and point it at the passengers. Although her mind became afraid, Daisy tried to avoid breaking into little pieces beside her mending archenemy. It would be most unfortunate to trade places with her so fast, although based on Catherine's astute observation of Nathan and Sheila, she likely had plans for retaking her throne sooner than later. Theirs would be a historic battle for land and resources, with flaming arrows poised at daybreak, bent on immobilizing destruction and control over the castle.

She drew close to Nathan. "Do you know *him*?"

Nathan placed Catherine and sat beside her. "Whom?"

Daisy pointed.

"Cannot say that I do."

The trolley surged forward, jolting their bodies. Daisy sat beside Nathan, and her eyes scanned the area. The peculiar man was gone.

At the cemetery, Daisy and Catherine sat on a stone bench. Nathan stood before them and recounted the death of their children. As he spoke of the past, tears streamed down Catherine's face. Her frail body trembled.

"Nathan, I believe the stone markers have raised her memories."

He looked away.

"Please hold her."

He sat on a nearby bench and refused Daisy's request.

"Why, Nathan?"

"If I touch her, I won't be able to stop my own tears."

He paused.

"I've worked very hard to keep them inside."

"Maybe you should let them out."

"I'm afraid of losing my children forever."

"They're gone, Nathan. You must let them go."

"Once again, I'm afraid."

"As am I."

He smiled. "Of your feelings for me, I take it."

She gave him an understanding smile. "You see what you want to see."

"Do you deny it?"

Daisy stood and showed her back to him. She tended to Catherine.

"I asked you a question."

She turned and leaned close to him and squeezed his hand.

"You are not as alone as you might imagine."

"Face it, Daisy, your God has left us to fend for ourselves in this cruel world." He hesitated. "I didn't ask to be here, and neither did you."

"Do you remember what Jesus said before He ascended?"

"Why would I? He abandoned me in a cornfield."

Daisy quoted Jesus's comments in John 14:2-3. "There is more than enough room in my Father's home. If this were not so, would I have told you that I am going to prepare a place for you? When everything is ready, I will come and get you, so that you will always be with me where I am."

"My mother was a praying woman like yourself."

"You may see her again, Nathan. The knowledge should comfort."

"She died alone on a bloodstained patch of trail where the crows pecked at her body before it was even cold. What does she get in heaven for her trouble, a fancy house? Allow your imagination to wander and tell me about the golden streets and the pearly gates. I'll wager the colors are more vivid there and the mountains are taller and the days are filled with an abiding love that is patient and kind. If His love never gives up, nor loses hope, and if it endures through every circumstance, then where is my mother?"

His eyes flashed about with rage.

"Your fairy tales are for children."

"You're angry, Nathan, and it's understandable."

He drew close and grabbed her shoulders.

"Don't avoid the question, Daisy. What is my mother's reward for suffering at the hand of Thomas Hannah, her boy hiding in the corn, staring in wide-eyed disbelief?" He shook her violently. "Tell me!"

Daisy maintained her composure as best she could.

"Please take your hands off of me, Nathan."

He released her. "You have fewer answers than Kincaid."

Daisy sat on her bench and stared at the ground. "I sometimes fear you will hurt me. Do you want to become like the wicked man who took June from you?" Her eyes met his. "Don't throw away all your achievements."

"Now *you're* the one who sees what she wants to see. I've had to live with hurt for a lifetime, something you know nothing about."

"We all hurt, Nathan."

"I'll ask you once again, what is my mother's reward?"

"Nathan, she'll have Jesus. He is enough reward for us all."

Catherine placed her hand over Daisy's. Her face was frozen into a smile.

Daisy turned to Nathan.

"Help me understand her better. Does this mean she approves of my comment, or does she think me a fool who belongs on Arsenal Road?"

"Why don't you ask her for yourself?"

Daisy took Catherine's hand and lightly squeezed it. She looked into the eyes of her nemesis, pondering the depth of her cognitive abilities and the speed of her cunning will. She had meant *something* by her gesture; that much was obvious. Catherine gazed into Daisy's eyes as only a mesmerist could, piercing the tenuous veil of her normality, delving deeper and more stridently into the shadows and the blood and the marrow. There was an entity alive within Catherine, and it probed Daisy just as Rosemarie had done in Vienna, seeing the threat she posed, not only to her immediate concerns but to her plans for ownership. Daisy tried to pull away but could not break their connection. A fight loomed for life itself, and the entity wanted Daisy uncertain and humiliated and terrified of the awful truth.

She had been born a *mistake* and would forever remain so.

Nathan gently took Catherine's hand and led her to the wagon.

A woeful tempest consumed Daisy as she stared at the greenery above the graves of Nathan's three children. They were naïve and innocent like her, but their little bodies were dead and their souls rested in a peace which defied all human understanding. A curse had befallen them, which took them from this fleshly world within the span of one month. What had Daisy done to deserve her own childhood curse, and why did she survive when others perished? Whatever sin might have brought about the monster, it had encircled her for a lifetime, diving and surfacing, showing its dorsal and its array of teeth. She took a deep breath and grabbed the stone surface with her fingers. There was a fast approaching point of no return. Once reached, Daisy would be at her wit's end, and it would be time to leave.

"Are you coming or not?" Nathan gave her an annoyed look.

"In a moment."

THIRTEEN

Psalm 13:4

Don't let my enemies gloat, saying, "We have defeated him!"
Don't let them rejoice at my downfall.

September 1868

On his sixteenth birthday, Nathan sat under the shade of an oak tree in murky remorse while he completed the work assigned by Professor Collins. He gave his heel to a thin stick which had pestered him all morning from its nearby spot on the ground. Nathan wanted to feel like a member of Aunt Joy's family, but he seemed a paying guest who had neglected to offer any compensation other than casual words of disgust or meager appreciation when she did something uniquely wonderful. He resolved to do better in the future. She had taken him into her good care under no obligation to June or Samuel. Her pious charity overspread with angelic wings and her ever patient love pierced with the density of iron. She was a gracious port in a fervent storm.

As if summoned by his unquiet thoughts, Aunt Joy opened the front door and stepped gingerly down the granite front steps. She walked toward him in a creaky manner, no doubt pained by his lack of gratitude and general sour disposition. She presented him with a fresh glass of water from the well and sat on a wooden bench. Her grave countenance lurched in his direction like the unavoidable pitch of night, and her dimpled voice rang hollow like the bottomless eddies in the river. Nathan sensed a bridge would soon be crossed, but he knew not how many steps it might take to reach the other side. At present, Aunt Joy seemed monotone and misaligned, as if she made urgent preparations for departure, and the fast passage of time was now their enemy. She must have foreseen a narrow road ahead because she stiffened at the profound disruption which sculptured itself clearly across her face, taking service against her humble and drowsy demeanor. Nathan wondered when and where they might travel. The dusty southwest forever called to him, but she would never last there. His brief existence was one thoughtless roam after another, and he hoped to settle in this makeshift family, which softened his anger and seized him with compassion. She had brought him out of the wet and the cold, lightening him with her newfound timidity and beseeching him with the goodness of her nature, and without the rigid masks of their former bravado, each would be a downright fool to leave the city. He straightened his posture and steeled himself for the worst.

Aunt Joy plunged headlong into the conversation.

"How are your studies progressing?"

His eyes fell to the stick on the ground.

"June would be so proud of you, Nathan." She wiped a tear. "You have become such a fine young man. I'm thrilled you came to live with me."

He looked up and smiled. "Me, too."

"There are things you don't know about her, and it's time I told them to you." Aunt Joy hesitated. "My sister almost married another man before your father. His name was Aldrich Berry, and I kidded her endlessly, as only a younger sister could about taking such an entertaining last name. I enjoyed taunting her with the moniker, 'June Berry is just so *very*', which invariably produced a fiery anger in her and indebted me with a mutinous pleasure."

"I suppose sisters give each other a hard time."

She beamed. "Oh, yes. June relished paying me back years later when I married William Stagg. She would say, 'Don't brag, you're merely a *stag*.' It wasn't a clever response to my earlier taunt, but it gave her such enormous exultation, which I now remember most distinctly." She shifted on the bench. "Aldrich was a fine man of deep religious conviction, and he had made quite the name for himself in the burgeoning Philadelphia insurance industry. He and his brother, Warren, were planning to open an investment house, which would have made them two of the wealthiest men on the eastern seaboard." She sighed. "Such a pity about Aldrich's death." Her sorrowful eyes met Nathan's. "He died in an accidental drowning not long after his proposal to June. They had set a date for the following May."

"I knew none of this."

Aunt Joy nodded sympathetically.

"June was once much like me, not in the haughty sense, but in her desires for you. She wanted you to go east for college and experience the world of refinement we each cherished in our youths. She was a most charming belle, and many estimable suitors catered to her every whim. I was two years younger and watched with both envy and amusement as our poor father worried himself half to death. It was a curious development when June married an unknown medical student who promptly moved her to St. Louis, made even more so when I followed her two years later after meeting William on a month-long visit. Philadelphia was awash with gossip."

She caught her breath, having said so much so quickly.

Nathan's hand scrubbed over his face. "You want me to recapture her former glory, but I'm not meant for those circles. I'm a farmer at heart, like Samuel." His eyes squinted slightly. "It's difficult to admit the latter."

Aunt Joy reminded Nathan how much his mother had loved Psalm 13:5-6. "But I trust in your unfailing love. I will rejoice because you have rescued me. I will sing to the Lord because he is good to me."

"What did it mean to her?"

"Mostly that Samuel had rescued her from a life of wealth and privilege which she despised. June longed for horses and rolling hills."

"They have those in Pennsylvania, don't they?"

She smiled at the quickness of his thinking.

"Yes, but those hills come at a very high cost."

He nodded his understanding. She must have felt like a traveler in a strange country while surrounded by those who thought differently than she did, and good sense prodded her to find a more modern land.

"They fought all the time, much of it in front of me."

"I'm well aware," said Aunt Joy with a gentle warmth. "It was a sore subject, one I often broached regretfully with her. June considered leaving Samuel for the shutterless world, but in the end, her love for him won out."

"She would have fared better in Philadelphia."

"The Lord wanted June and Samuel united. He is always a perfect matchmaker, even when temptation blinds in the early years of marriage. If the couple endures with patience, growth occurs, and the passion blooms into something more wonderful than the fallen heart can imagine."

"Are you saying my mother and father were good for each other?"

"Perhaps not when you were little, but the Lord had worked on both of their spirits, and they were each changing for the better. If she lived to complete her transformation, you would have seen the chasm between them fill with the fruit of His effect on their lives, and you would have rejoiced at the harmonious result. Sometimes June spoke of her wish for another child." Aunt Joy turned toward her nephew. "June was pregnant."

Nathan's eyebrows made a slight motion of bewilderment.

"When she died?"

Aunt Joy nodded.

Her eyes bore the weight of her meaning.

"With my father's baby?"

She gave him a pained look. "I certainly hope so."

Nathan stood and paced, his mournful reserve breaking into pieces.

"God didn't rescue my mother, even with her many affectations. Instead, He allowed that man to murder her. I wonder if her cold and aloof nature were too much for a resentful laborer with obsessions greater than his intellect. My father only displayed such fire when he drank whiskey."

"It seems so on the surface." Aunt Joy tapped his hand. "Like you, June sought a secure place of retreat from social circles both in Philadelphia and here in St. Louis. I tried to tell her seclusion in the country only lasts for so long, and eventually one must face up to their guilt."

Nathan pondered her comments for several moments. *Guilt.* It was a peculiar word to describe his mother, as she was the victim of a heinous crime, one she hadn't asked for or desired. Had she used Thomas Hannah to make her husband jealous? If so, it had gone too far and ruined many lives.

A heavy earthen smell wafted from the direction of the river.

"Why would she withdraw from the only life she knew?"

"As a young woman, June realized the world was filled with wickedness and delusions of grandeur, and she became sickened by it. Once seen, it could not be unseen." Her voice trailed. "Samuel was much the same."

"Were you likewise affected?"

Aunt Joy shook her head. "I loved attending the all-night balls. Even in January, when the carriage ride home threatened to bring pneumonia, I danced until the early morning light. My husband and I each fell ill from such a ball, which pained Edward deeply. William died, and my heart was weakened, but still I attended every one. It's why Edward left me alone."

"He wanted to hurt you as you had hurt him."

"I'm afraid so."

"Why would anyone want to hurt another person?"

"The question has been asked since Cain picked up a stone and cracked open the head of his brother. Some people hate for no apparent reason."

She took a sip of water. Her skin seemed blanched and clammy.

Nathan's eyes widened. "Are you alright?"

"Yes," she said, smiling. "The recent bout of heat has tired me."

She set her glass on a rickety and undersized metal table. "Thomas Hannah was one of those people. He roamed the countryside looking for victims, and he specialized in those who had previously retreated from the world. The reason for their escape didn't matter. Once he found June, however, he thought he'd met his imperfect soulmate, and he presumed they could meld for life, which, of course, he took from her in the end." She fell silent, enraptured by her memories. "Although Thomas was a murderer, he must have loved her in his own maniacal manner. It's not the love we expect from a normal mind, but in his psychotic state, he assumed he had freed her from an unfolding life of misery." She sighed. "Samuel's continual bouts of drunkenness wore on June's good nature, and she was tired of fighting battles with him. Although you interpreted her to be cold and aloof, in truth, she had grown contemptuous of Samuel's indifference to her primal fascination with savagery and her bashful need to hide from its mortal effects, both outside of her in everyday newspaper articles about this murder or that burglary and within, deep inside her own carnal essence. I honestly believe the latter curiosity, forbidden as it often is, even within the confines of the marriage bed, is what scared her most. June secretly feared her own ridiculous inexperience with the realities of human sensuality, mostly due to her youthful willingness to discard anyone and everyone who exhibited any aspect of it in the presence of a lady from polite society. When she no longer trembled in Thomas Hannah's presence, her fire was lit, and it could not be extinguished by civilized means." Aunt Joy hesitated. "Our father had provided each of us with a sizable inheritance, and she could have easily moved to Chicago, where few knew anyone in Philadelphia."

"With *him*?"

"Yes, if that had been her choice."

"You're implying she chose my father?"

"We'll never receive an answer to that question."

She paused.

"I like to think so."

Aunt Joy stood and steadied herself against the oak tree. "Your cake has been cooling in the window for a while, and it's time for me to cover it with icing. When your studies are done, come see me, and I'll cut you a slice."

"Yes, mam!"

Aunt Joy walked toward the house, and Nathan was filled with love for her. She looked back at him, smiling, and he smiled, too.

He finished his work and headed inside for dinner, where he discovered Aunt Joy dead on the floor. He shook her, but she didn't move.

A sharp flash of lightning on the forward edge of a gale had stabbed blindly at her guarded heart and shattered her huddled position.

After retrieving the doctor, Nathan sat under the oak and stared into the woods, contemplating why everyone he loved had abandoned him. His spirit wandered to faraway places, and the dust-filled breeze forced his dry throat nearly closed. He sat noiseless with his maddening thoughts, seeking violent retribution for the crimes of incessant betrayal, and, like Thomas Hannah, he wanted to travel across a figurative line to a place without redemption, the realm of murderers and pillagers. The knowledge of his own propensity for sin jolted Nathan, but also comforted. There was little distance between himself and the men who would take whatever they wanted and leave only crumbs for the meek and the poor. He understood what it took to navigate the twisting maze of ambition, and he would climb for the rest of his days.

An hour later, Catherine tried to comfort, but Nathan said little.

He had missed the signs of his aunt's failing condition, loftily consumed as he was with his own boastful affairs. He could have brought the doctor for a thorough examination and faithfully made her take the prescribed medicine. Perhaps they could have formed a bond which would have surpassed the deficit left by his mother, but now, because of his unending pride and negligence, Aunt Joy was gone in an instant, a worthy and loving replacement no more. She was a grand discovery found much too late.

Why had she chosen today to give more details about his mother?

She was a relatively young woman. Did she know her end was near?

The idea likely sprang from her daily conversations with the wandering and vindictive God who no one in two thousand years had claimed to see. She was a smart and capable woman, but Aunt Joy had unintelligently convinced herself the old man in the sky was real. Unfortunately for her, the ever merciful Lord issued a decree to end her life at thirty-six with a helpless boy in her care and no one to take up her mantle. How could a loving God commit such an act? Either way, Nathan would offer Him no special prayer of gratitude, and he would never darken the door of a church again.

Catherine paid his dour mood polite attention as she held his hand and hummed her favorite hymns. Finally, she asked where he planned to live.

"Oklahoma or possibly San Francisco."

John Belmont thudded down the front steps and stood looking at Nathan with a silent shriek of contempt. He most obviously wanted to spatter the boy's blood across the front lawn for all the neighbors to see.

"You should return home to your father's farm," Belmont said.

"It's an impossibility."

The notion sent Nathan into a soundless panic. His eyes fell low.

Catherine pleaded with her father to allow Nathan to live with them. Otherwise, he would likely starve to death in the woods.

Belmont reluctantly agreed.

After Nathan packed a suitcase, he rode with Catherine and John in a carriage to the Belmont estate in Lucas Place. Nathan stared out of the window, still shocked by Aunt Joy's abrupt exodus.

How could a healthy woman die so suddenly?

At the estate, Belmont addressed Mr. Stewart, the butler.

"Escort young Mr. Marsh to the servants' quarters. He'll drop his poor excuse for a suitcase and get fitted for a proper footman's uniform."

"Why, Father?"

"Don't expect me to accept him as a member of our family. I'll allow him to stay here as a servant and nothing more, at least until we move from this foundering area to our new home in Vandeventer. Julius Pitzman recently showed me his most current plans, and the new private place will be spectacular. After we move there, I want our lives to reflect our first class status in every possible manner. Thus, your relationship with Nathan will halt most judiciously, and he will be on his own. I won't be responsible for a miscreant who refuses his own father. Samuel may be a drunkard, but he is family, and a man doesn't walk away from his responsibilities, problematic or otherwise. Do I make myself perfectly clear?"

"Will you at least consider funding his college expenses?"

"Joy Stagg was a wealthy woman. She set aside money for his future in medicine and left the rest to her son. I have wired Edward the news."

Catherine paced in front of Nathan, who kept still and quiet.

"Isn't there something more we can do for him?"

Belmont sneered as he looked Nathan up and down.

"We are providing employment in a prestigious house. What more do you need?" Belmont listened intently, ready to draw a particular inference from her response. If Catherine gave her father what he wanted, he would rain fire on both her and Nathan. She used her charms to full effect.

"It's enough," she said with a coy grin. "I'll ensure the rest."

November 1868

As Nathan walked toward downtown, a corner of a lawn caught his eye, its edge extending past the shade of the darkening night and into the mothy glimmer of a gas streetlamp. It diffused all of his mounting concerns into a fine mist and affixed all his aspirations to the future. A strange apparition growled in the shadowy distance, and Nathan bounded forward, dazzled by the ferocity of life and the heaviness which closed itself upon him. He would no longer resist solitude, but embrace its dampness and desolation. His feet marched with purpose across an intersection, weary and unskilled at the art of pliable consent. He reached out for a person unseen and then retracted his hands, bringing them close to his sides. His fingers grasped clumsily through his pocket for his watch. He must record the lateness of the hour and the remaining time allowed for his companionless sojourn.

There was no one left to help him but himself.

An older teen who went by the name Stonecipher threw rocks at a train as it ambled in front of his position in the lane. Nathan stopped and stood beside the young man, saying no words. He picked up a large stone and threw it at a thunderous railcar, which squeaked and rattled and thumbed its nose at the quietude of the November night. The rock clanged against the steel wall of the car and landed on the ground with a thud, elaborating perfectly the nothingness Nathan felt in his soul, its enraged embers having gone out like a wan campfire at dawn's early rain. The flow of cars departed as quickly as they had arrived, leaving only the marvel of a lingering hope.

"Follow me," said Stonecipher with a toothy grin. "I've got a woman in town who might have a friend."

Nathan followed the young man to a boarding house on Broadway.

Stonecipher tossed a small pebble at the window, and a pretty young woman slid open the pane. "I told a policeman what you did to me," she said. "He wants to arrest you."

"I did nothing wrong. We were just fooling around, is all."

She threw an astonished look at him, and her voice reverberated off the bricks. "I got pregnant, and there's a name for what you did. It's called bastardy." Her fingers dug into the windowsill as she called down to him.

"You shouldn't have done that, Marsha." He looked up and down the street. "I'm on the run from the law in other parts."

"What for?"

"They said I killed a man, but I only meant to rob him."

He paused.

"Is it my fault if he fought back when all I wanted was his wallet?"

Nathan took a step backward. "You killed someone?"

"Good buddy, you don't know the half of what I've done. Of course, more was done to me first, and I'm just reacting to my sorry start in life."

"There's always a ready excuse," said Marsha impatiently. "You roped me into your wickedness, and now I've got to pay with a child."

Stonecipher's voice rose with a crisp vanity. "Listen, honey, if I'd struck it rich in the California mines, we'd get hitched tomorrow morning, but the universe has left me destitute and without an ounce of gold. My only worthy belongings are a handsome smile and a calamitous temper."

"Your big talk means nothing."

He offered her a wretched shrug. "I'm serious, honey. So why not rustle up a friend and come down here?" He pointed to Nathan. "I've got a new partner who could use cheering up before we hit the wintry trail."

A policeman rounded the corner and descended frightfully on their location. He yelled at them to freeze and pointed his revolver at Stonecipher. Nathan instinctively walked several paces in the opposite direction, but the law officer yelled for him to stop. More police arrived within minutes. They rounded both young men up and tossed them into a paddy wagon. The fiend, Stonecipher, said they were merely in the wrong place at the wrong time. The hands of fate were mostly unkind, and he often felt like a caged tiger with an unfortunate desire for death. Was it his fault he enjoyed killing?

Two hours later, Belmont bailed Nathan out of jail. He wore a stoic countenance, saying little to Nathan while in the station. The policeman behind the counter opined on the rebellious nature of today's youth.

Belmont nodded his agreement. "Our Lord looks away while the very foundations of law-and-order collapse around us. We are long overdue for a reckoning." He turned toward Nathan and arched his eyebrows.

"I remain hopeful," said the policeman, his bearing kinder than most.

Belmont tipped his hat. "On that favorable note, we'll take our leave."

As the pair rode home in Belmont's carriage, he told Nathan to shape up or leave his care. He must stop behaving like his drunkard father. "The covenant between us, which ought to have stability by being faithfully kept, has been shamefully violated by you, Nathan." He stared out of the window. "I try my best to be a pillar of the community, but you make me feel as if I'm on trial." He eyed Nathan like a despised adversary. "Buildings fall down and become a heap of ruins when their foundations are undermined."

"Justice is on my side, sir, although in your eyes, I am merely a destroyer of your happy home." Nathan's fists tightened. "I will ultimately prevail."

"You believe Catherine loves you enough to marry?"

"As the officer said, hope is on my side."

"Your optimism is only surpassed by your naivety." He sneered. "Once she realizes you're no outlaw, her affections for you will vanish."

"She can do better than an outlaw, sir."

Belmont's countenance grew earnest. "On this, we agree."

He paused.

"I aim to keep her contented with playthings like you until she realizes the same. Guiding children to maturity is no small task, something of which you have no knowledge or experience, but as in all matters, it is *I* who will triumph in the end. Mark my words, sir, your days are numbered."

As they stopped at the front door, Belmont exited the carriage.

"Use the servant's entrance around the back. It's where you belong."

As Nathan walked toward the corner of the house, Belmont called out with an order to stop. "Stonecipher is wanted for murder in Illinois and will be transported to Dealey to hang in a few days. See to it, you avoid a similar fate." Belmont wheeled and slammed the door behind him.

Nathan sat on the back steps and gazed at the friendly stars. The furious sounds of an argument between Catherine and her father made their way down to his abject ears; he was reassured to know she sincerely cared and would fight for her commitment. If he could somehow avoid the many temptations to leave her or to commit a bloodthirsty act on her behalf, perhaps there could be a future for them—the unnaturally bright and durable kind few would have suspected or allowed.

The night of Stonecipher's visit to the gallows, Nathan dreamed of his mother. He stood near the wagon and the edge of the cornfield, begging June not to leave. He grabbed at her form with panic-stricken hands, hoping to make up for his past mistakes, but there was little satisfaction to offer, no tender tribute which returned her to the realm of flowing gowns and January balls, or into the arms of a whiskey soaked husband, or even under the careful and watchful eye of a judgmental mare. She had broken his fragile heart, but then again, he had broken hers, having given his masculine ground to a heartless killer bent on her destruction. He was in love with her now as he should have been then, willing to die in her place if necessary.

And it *was*.

June pushed him away. "Release me!" She looked to the clouding sky. "How long must I struggle with anguish in my soul, with sorrow in my heart every day? How long will my enemy have the upper hand?" Thomas Hanna appeared from the far end of the road, and June stared at him with contempt. "Turn and answer me, O Lord my God! Restore the sparkle to my eyes, or I will die." Thomas stopped cold in his tracks with an uneasy countenance. Her eyes glowed red, and the wind blew through the tops of the corn, swaying them from right to left and then left to right.

June walked to the edge of the field and turned. "Someday, Nathan, I hope you find an everlasting peace." She disappeared into the row.

Nathan called after her but heard only a gentle breeze swirling above his head and a slight whistle which resounded from far in the distance.

The morning sun shone brightly, infiltrating his bedroom through an uncovered window. The whistle grew louder and more painful in his ears.

A voice reverberated, making itself heard above the approaching train, its momentum unrelenting, its forward motion unstoppable.

The Lord favors the righteous.

He does not forget, nor does He disregard.

Nathan awakened from his dream. Audible words filled his room.

Your anguish is but a moment.

Return to me and rejoice.

He sat up straight and peered through the tiny window, finding only the steely clink of coupled cars and the roar of churning wheels. The train passed through an outlying field near the property line on the way to a cotton warehouse near the river. Powerful men with families to feed awaited its arrival with anticipation. There was much work to be done and a brief interval for completion. Stores would soon clamor for their wares as an impatient public expected to be served on time and with a charming display of fervor, as if everything was just, and humanity was back in the garden, eating all but the forbidden fruit, unless the mood struck, and an unwise few decided the forbidden fruit should not be so forbidden after all.

Nathan went to the dresser and splashed water on his sweaty face. The awful truth was clear: He was born a *mistake* and would always be so. In this world and the next, Nathan would travel alone.

He laid on his bed and stared at the ceiling.

No one downstairs would miss him for a few more minutes.

As they had approached the awful location of her death, June had patted his hand, saying she'd always be there for him. Then Thomas Hannah appeared, and she was gone forever, forging her son's entry into the gloom.

Fourteen

Psalm 14:1

Only fools say in their hearts,
"There is no God."
They are corrupt, and their actions are evil;
not one of them does good!

September 1893

Ronnie Wilson's candle waned the previous afternoon, and now he drifted among the stars in the celestial. His character had proven exemplary through to the end, even with occasional bouts of hysteria which bounced his wits about with an untenable vigor. The somber funeral occurred Friday at one o'clock, and only a few hearty souls attended. Ronnie's death deflated an already weakened Ed and forced him to stay home during the ceremony. Because of her own tearful despair, Daisy left the hospital for parts unknown, and afterward, Kincaid rushed inside with a face expressive of the most resolute concern. Judge Wilkins was about to let

Thomas Hannah go free. In reckless desperation, Kincaid promised the judge firm evidence regarding the June Marsh murder of 1859.

"I hope you're happy now. You'll finally watch him hang."

Nathan's eyes toured the main hall as his turbulent thoughts ran wild.

A heavy pattern of light, which had shone brightly in the morning, now gave way to dusty shadow, isolating him in the past, appearing at first to understand his dreary reticence but then drawing nearer, insisting upon his consent to the wishes of the court system and the cries across the decades from a mother long ago placed in the earth with green grass over her head and three stately children playing nearby. The surreal portrait of their happy encirclement around his own grave made him want to swing his arms at the detective like a lunatic bent on fighting against the proportion of life which slipped away from him each day and sent him ever closer to the Reaper's embrace. The latter thought created a recognition of his ten year longing for death in the arms of an attentive prostitute in hopes of one more glimpse of a wife who was gone from his life in an instant, only to find her echoed back to him in the gutter. He calmed his neurotic reflections and forced his focus once more on the stoic detective, wishing to throw a bucket over his head.

He spoke in a flat tone. "I never said I would testify."

Kincaid's eyes fell reproachfully on him. "*What?*"

Nathan deepened his voice for effect. "I said you should do your job and collect evidence. You have Thomas for the bakery murder. I'm sure he's committed other serious crimes in his sixty years on this earth."

"You don't understand me, Nathan. This case is paper thin and you're all we've got. If you won't testify, he'll go free on Monday morning."

"I'll think over the matter. It's the best you'll get from me today."

"Don't take too much time. There's a great deal to be done." Kincaid's tight shoulders fell slack, and his tense breath exhaled. "I was sorry to hear about the boy's death. As a physician, I'm sure it was hard to accept."

"Thanks, but I'm surprised you don't blame me for it." He'd felt a similar dishonor when his aunt had abruptly perished. "I certainly do."

"You aren't God, and you won't win every fight, especially against cancer. Believe it or not, I am on your side, Nathan. I'm not your adversary, but your ally, at least in the pursuit of justice."

Nathan gestured impulsively, as he had done on the *Oneida*.

"If you're not here to arrest me, leave my hospital."

Kincaid walked to the door and turned. "Remember what I said."

He gave an annoyed smile and left the building.

Nathan knew where Daisy would go to mull over her life choices. He approached her at the park with caution, prudent to keep his distance while she enjoyed the soft breeze. A vendor passed who sold flowers, and Nathan selected a rose. He scolded the man for shouting and instructed him to cease at once, as the noise would likely muddle Daisy's thoughts and fill her with confusion. He took the long way round as he walked toward her bench in a surrendered and reverential silence. The wind shifted, and the brazen sun broke through the tops of the trees, highlighting the beauty of her face.

"Are you contented to sit alone?"

His appearance startled her, but she quickly recovered her senses.

"Why yes, Doctor Marsh. I believe I am."

"We're back to formalities?"

"For now, yes. Jesus provides me with all the peace a woman requires."

Her comment made Nathan uncomfortable. When he asked about it, her lips formed a smile and her eyes filled with amusement at his expense. He placed the rose in her hand, and she sniffed it; her vague pleasure skipped his heart a double beat. He hoped the moment might last forever, but the sunny warmth which flowed between them passed as fast as it had arrived.

Reticence returned, fading the prettiness from their connection, replacing it with something distant and broken, the magic in their banter which had presented so easily the night of their first meeting, at once thrilling and lovely, now difficult. Her manner had grown cold and blank.

Emotions swirled within Nathan, disrupting his desire for tranquility at all costs. The feelings stimulated a flood of good natured inspections.

Her attire kept with modern fashion, while simultaneously avoiding the slightest glimmer of ostentation. Nathan teased her about her fawn-colored gloves, worn and tired as they were, and her dainty hat and her compulsive devotion to an outdated religion, and then he mentally noted the shape and fullness of her mouth, realizing in a blink he liked everything about her.

Neither spoke for a few moments.

She broke the stillness. "The Lord looks down from heaven on the entire human race; he looks to see if anyone is truly wise, if anyone seeks God. But no, all have turned away; all have become corrupt. No one does good, not a single one!" She frowned at him, as if speaking to a hypocrite.

"Why do people insist on recitations of poetic nonsense?"

"So you recognize the opening to Psalm 14?"

"My mother said the psalms were a gateway to the Bible. She enjoyed some more than others. The verses you quoted were some of her favorites."

Daisy sucked in a quick breath and then paced under the gazebo.

When she spoke, she rambled nervously, which placed Nathan on firmer ground. She redirected their conversation to Ronnie and Ed and then told him the rose was very thoughtful. It was an odd comment, as no one had ever called him thoughtful, not even his mother. He told her to be careful in strange parks, as some demented man might take another shot at her. Daisy laughed and then caught herself while she straightened her posture.

It seemed she expected to be reprimanded for a general lack of empathy.

She sat beside him, and he grew more comfortable in his deportment.

"Your work at the hospital is progressing nicely," he said, "and I believe we will make solid progress with Catherine over the next several weeks."

Her gaze drifted. She struggled against some unseen force.

He squeezed her hand. "Won't you tell me what you're feeling?"

She remained silent, lost in a dark remembrance, unwilling to share.

Her countenance brightened after a few moments.

"Ronnie found Jesus before he passed. Did you know that?"

Her emotions must have clouded her memory.

"He talked about Jesus often," said Nathan, his mind having returned to his mother and the blowing corn tops. A portrait of Thomas Hannah swinging from the end of a rope flashed through his mind. It was both a just and ghastly sight. Nathan stood, unwilling to endure further torment.

"Where are you going?" Daisy looked up at him.

"I will leave you to your thoughts. For now, we are on contrary tracks, locomotives who each blow our whistle loudly as we pass one another in awe and attraction but continually move in opposite directions." His words carried a faded bearing of logic, but his once strong assurance lessened with each moment spent in her presence. He must take his leave soon or fall victim to the blush in her cheeks and the smooth parting of her lips.

"I had hoped our paths might converge," she said. "It's too much. I'm a simple girl with a fragile heart, and your intensity frightens me."

He tipped his hat and smiled. "Then I shall take my leave, madam."

She smiled in return. "Thank you, Nathan."

"For what, may I ask?"

"For your restoration of my faith in men. Not all are monsters."

<hr>

Monday morning, Daisy felt an inaudible flatness in her spirit, as if God's voice had become foreign and quiet. Fragments of her tireless working hours at La Salpêtrière and brief excursions to Nice continually clamored for her attention. Each scrap blew lightly or lounged indiscreetly while unkindly mentioning disagreeable and rigid facts. She was mortified and wished to silence her thoughts, unruly and vivid as they were at present. She rested motionless under her covers with half-open eyelids and daydreamed of the emerald greens and the royal blues of the elegant Mediterranean Sea. The water more than her experiences along the coastline would calm her spirit, carefree and alive as it was, teeming and bristling with a perfect clarity.

She offered a lengthy prayer beside her bed before leaving for work.

Dear Lord, I ask you to help the poor to overcome their oppression and the emotionally devastated to recover their stability. Your words are pure, and you keep them eternally, never faltering, never forsaking even across the many generations of the ungodly and the weak and the haughty. I try to forgive and to forget, Lord, but the memories are overwhelming, and I lose my way most unceasingly. Please help me grow stronger, for in Jesus, all things are possible. This I know in my mind, if not yet inside my damaged heart. My soul weeps for those of my youth and for the pains I've yet to endure. I cannot take much more, Lord, for I fear too much, and I wish only to hide under my covers.

She slammed her palm on the bed. "I must counter the exaltation of wicked men, Lord! I will do everything possible to heal someone today. Evil shall not prevail in our hospital."

Daisy marched briskly to work, her mission rejuvenated and clear.

She met Nathan at the front door with a cheerful smile.

He seemed morose and intent on setting her along his grim path.

"Hello," she said pleasantly.

"Leave me alone." His voice carried a tilt of boyish embarrassment.

He went inside and trudged up the stairs.

Undeterred, she followed him into his office and closed the door.

She hoped to decipher his mood. "Is everything alright today?"

Nathan was silent for a moment. "Kincaid can't hold Thomas Hannah much longer without concrete evidence. He is forcing my hand."

She kept her position near the door. "In what manner?"

"If I testify against Thomas in court, everyone will know what he did to my mother." There was a tremor in his voice which touched Daisy. "The event will be described in gruesome detail, partially by me on the stand."

She looked at him, and a thrill overcame her, passing narrowly through her veins, confirming the eagerness of her need to escape her own unbridled enthusiasm, felt most honestly when he spoke in such a needful manner.

"I'm sorry you have to endure such an ordeal."

He went to the window and stared at the street.

His dilemma strangely affected her in a most unshakeable way, and she particularly wondered if he speculated about the possibility of romance as she now did. The sudden inspiration toward love made her shiver with excitement and fear, as another risk might be too much. "I'm angry with you for keeping this from me. It must have weighed on you for some time."

"I've been preoccupied with Catherine, Ronnie, and the others."

"The world has hurt them." Her eyes fell low and bashful. "It has nearly destroyed me on many occasions, opening and closing my heart on a whim."

"I'd like to hear more about your time in Europe."

"There were many impressive sights and sounds and experiences, as you might imagine." Her eyes rose to meet his. "In the end, each left me hollow."

He looked confused. "Why?"

She sat in a chair opposite his desk. "There is a cultural transformation underway in Europe, an undercurrent of change at the core of each man and woman, and I suppose even the small children." She waited for his response.

"I'm listening."

"Europeans have rejected the idea of truth itself, and I'm astonished at their disorder and their carelessness. The continent may soon find itself in a ruined heap." She dared not show the depth or the breadth of her emotions. "I see a similar Nihilism in you, Nathan, and it concerns me."

"I've been through a great deal, more than you can imagine."

"You've shared some details with me which I appreciate, but it shouldn't negate absolute truth, for without it, Christianity becomes most offensive to the masses and something which must be discarded." She considered the perverse implications of her last statement. "By force if necessary."

"What has replaced absolute truth?"

"Tolerance." She inspected her blouse and smoothed her sleeves and stretched them to their proper length. "For anything and everything. If it feels good, do it. All ideas are equal under the guise of tolerance."

They each grew silent, waiting for the other to suggest a remedy.

A flurry of activity in the street threatened to absorb Nathan's attention. His expression was pleasant, but his mind was elsewhere.

"Will you speak to me?" asked Daisy devotedly.

He turned toward her, wearing a newly formed look of exasperation.

"You believe it will destroy Europe in the end?"

She shook her head. "It already has."

"I read the papers daily, and the last time I checked, the continent remains in one piece." He sat at his desk and stared blankly at her.

She smiled coyly, in her best imitation of a sought after belle. Her mind whispered accusations of fraudulent machinations, but she continued, uncaring of making herself out to be a fool in his eyes. "For now, but the next century will be fraught with disasters. There can be no other way."

"As always, your insecurities fuel my depression."

"It's not my intention, Nathan."

"I suppose you came by it honestly." He grinned as if desperate to clap her roughly on the back like a schoolmate. "Was your mother such a solemn woman?" The sarcasm in his voice flittered uncertainly between them.

Daisy tensed but said nothing. She went to a drawer in his desk and retrieved a Bible. Flipping it open, she pointed to Colossians 3:15.

She handed him the book. "Read this aloud, please."

His eyes met hers. "Why?"

"I asked you to read it. Shouldn't that be enough?"

He sighed deeply and focused on the page. "And let the peace that comes from Christ rule in your hearts. For as members of one body you are called to live in peace. And always be thankful."

His arms outstretched, and his hands presented the Bible to her like a bowl of poison. Daisy thought about the Lord's last supper, the agape love shared amongst the brethren as they sat about the table before the great and awful day, when the Lord gave Himself over to the inconceivable intensity of crucifixion and death, only to arise in glory and holiness three days later. The resurrected Jesus greeted His huddled disciples with a hospitable grace and a tender mercy, undeserved and unmatched in all of history. She must be on guard against the prospect of becoming unequally yoked, as she had done in Europe. She had seen for some time the resemblance this man presented with the former Frank Kaneski, but the similarity ended with a continual chipping away at the stone fortification around her heart which had not made itself known in Paris or Vienna or even Nice by the quavering sea, where gliding and restless urges prowled noiselessly along the shoreline, presenting themselves blindly and impatiently to her desirous and receptive heart. Nathan Marsh was by far a more dangerous and worthy man. He encompassed all the distress she had ever known or would likely know in the future in one masculine form, who sometimes sneered condescendingly at her in his own unique intelligence but who mostly endured the unending anxieties of life with the same level of patience and bewilderment as her. Each aspect of his character bonded them in a land of unjust verdicts and unlawful pronouncements, a nation in the midst of losing its faith and its hope and its ability to love, favoring the boldness of action and the pleasure of sin. If she kept in his presence, the brightness of her feelings might soon be overcome by the intolerable dimness of his despair, wearing down the last of her brittle edges, breaking her delicate surface into a thin, hot flame, and pushing her toward the sky and the sun and the hovering darkness.

As a countermeasure, she flipped to Philippians 4:6-7 and read aloud. "Don't worry about anything; instead, pray about everything. Tell God what you need, and thank him for all he has done. Then you will experience God's peace, which exceeds anything we can understand. His peace will guard your hearts and minds as you live in Christ Jesus."

She gently closed the book.

"How do those passages apply to me?"

"You will use them to endure the trial."

"As I tell everyone, I'll consider your offer."

Daisy returned the Bible to the drawer in his desk.

She went to the door and turned toward him, allowing her calm and speechless countenance to wash over him. She gave him a warm smile.

His lack of response troubled her further.

Still, she left him alone.

As her boots thudded down the oak stairs, the sound reverberated off the paneled walls and shook her back to her logical senses. Her adoration fell to a sudden realization as she entered the main hall and encountered the mountainous group of hysterics, whose shadowy forms milled about like the rise and fall of fish underneath a starlit lake. She could never marry a man who believed in nothing and no one but his own ability. Many others before Nathan had tried to live in rebellion and failed, their efforts thwarted by a mixture of mortal vanity and earthly incompetence. She sat in a rocker and surveyed the assembly, feeling for the first time the abominable weight of her perennial sacrifice. The need to avenge a fallen sister and a maimed mother made Daisy like Eve in the garden—unable to claw her way to freedom or to convince herself to love, the only remedy her own sinful death, knowing with certainty the wasteful whisper her life would become.

<hr>

Nathan and Daisy worked with Catherine all morning but made little progress with her. She often fell into impatience and abuse, her eyes glancing and darting, forcing them to give her and themselves a break.

"Have you seen the time?" asked Nurse Pratt, determinedly.

Daisy squeezed Nathan's arm. "We must go now or we'll be late."

While they rode a trolley, Sheila's brothel passed before them. The well traveled building fully encompassed the end of the block, its appeal an uneasy reality for Daisy who had never understood the male propensity for such things, coarse and transient as they were, their manifestations of sin most clear in a society bent on the daily sketch of moral pretense.

"I'm surprised you know about such carnal activity."

"Nothing gets past me, Nathan. Not anymore."

His armored serenity and lack of effort at courtship set the walls of her heart ablaze with wonder and excitement. She sought redress for the upheaval, which churned within her private and sensual soul. "Does Sheila hold a place in your heart? For a prostitute, she's quite alluring."

Like a watchful painter, he would allow no insight to go unnoticed. "She's beautiful. It doesn't matter if she's a prostitute or a lady-in-waiting."

Daisy's jealousy flared, flooding her cheeks with the hotness of her blood. "You're enchanted with her, then? It must be a privilege to have so many women at your disposal, but you seem indifferent, as if it's expected."

Shame might push him from Sheila's arms.

He frowned and stared at the buildings.

She longed for more words from him.

"I didn't have a mother in my life past a certain point." He hesitated as the trolley rocked slightly. "I suppose you could say I've never had a mother at all." There was the boy again who lacked a precise understanding.

"I'd like to hear more about it, Nathan."

"We'll talk at lunch. For now, I'll say one thing. I've been searching high and low for the perfect woman."

"You've turned over every rock, even those found in brothels."

"I wanted the perfect woman for me, not necessarily for everyone else."

"Have you found her?"

He gazed into Daisy's eyes, immediately piercing beyond her pupils to her excitable nerves and her sincere bones and her considerate marrow, seeing deeply into the four corners of her soul, and then just as quickly, looking away to a shallow and less troublesome unknown. Had he found something unacceptable at her core? Her cheerful and methodical thoughts fell out of order as her jaded memories resurfaced like a howling monster.

Flustered, she had to say something. "Well?"

She hoped her tone didn't sound cross.

His sharp grin and sarcastic voice marked a return to youthful defiance. "I'm not sure yet. Does *that* satisfy your curiosity, at least for the moment?"

"Yes."

She paused.

"On a related note, this was no coincidental lunch. Our very own Nurse Pratt scheduled the encounter to ensure we conversed over a meal."

He again looked surprised. "Pop pushed me into it as well." His eyebrows raised. "I wonder if something exists between them."

She shrugged.

"Anything is possible at this point."

"I suppose," he said.

While they ate, Daisy and Nathan talked with ease, and he shared details from his backstory, including how he and Catherine had met. From his description, he still loved his ex-wife, and her desertion remained a source of unending trauma. Compelled to share her own agonizing details, Daisy held off for as long as possible, believing she would be judged harshly by the accomplished doctor, a handsome man once married to the Caroline Astor of St. Louis. She couldn't stop herself from blurting the next thought which came to mind, no matter how dangerous or unwise its content.

She took a drink of water to steel herself.

He watched her movements with a mirthful interest.

"I almost married a man named Frank Kaneski in Vienna, and as the wedding date approached, he said if we made love, it would be alright with God." She took a deep breath and exhaled. "Frank didn't believe in Jesus or want anything to do with Him if he did, so there was nothing to stop him from tempting me in such a manner." Daisy blushed after she spoke, believing her current life to be comfortless and unenviable, and her past choices to be stupid and stubbornly foolish. She divulged another pertinent fact: her sister and mother had died during her adolescence, and it remained a source of her own injury. She had tried to heal hysterics in Europe as recompense.

He shifted in his seat. "Yes, indeed. We are two peas in a pod."

"Will your regard for me falter at my vulgar admission?"

"That depends on you, madam."

"No, Nathan." Daisy straightened, unable to abate correction. "It relies on your life decisions. If you know what you want, you may receive it. Just be sure it's what you need." Her thoughts screamed accusations as she gripped the edges of her table, hoping to calm them, but they kept at their quest. Her fingers released while her back pushed secretly into her chair.

Had her silly confession and her bossy nature ruined the romance which might have developed between them? She should learn the art of quietude.

He nodded his understanding.

"Knowing what we need is the real trick, isn't it?"

She picked up her fork and pointed at him. "It certainly is."

After lunch, they strolled along the city sidewalks, taking in the sights.

"I've read forty percent of total births in Vienna are illegitimate," Nathan said. "Could it be true?"

Europe had struck yet another blow against her.

"I would believe your statistic. As much as I am in awe of the great city, it is a hotbed of iniquity. Perhaps it's why we received so many hysterics."

"I doubt sin had much to do with it. Anxiety is the more likely culprit."

"The two are inextricably linked, Nathan."

He considered her comment. "Perhaps."

Unable to resist her melancholic nature, she pushed him to accept her faith. He must turn from his Canaanite ways and become a Christian man.

"Peter said it best in the New Testament."

She paused.

"Would you mind if I shared a quote?"

"By all means. I'm getting used to your ramblings."

She smiled. "I realize my pushy nature can be off-putting."

"Not to me, madam."

She hugged his arm as they walked, feeling his strength coursing through her blood, both heating and cooling it, at once hurrying her forward and holding her in place, reassuring her gently and scaring her intensely, the ride wild like Rose in the forest. "Please don't be cross with me."

"I wouldn't dream of it."

"Stay alert! Watch out for your great enemy, the devil. He prowls around like a roaring lion, looking for someone to devour. Stand firm against him, and be strong in your faith. Remember that your family of believers all over the world is going through the same kind of suffering you are."

He pulled her arm and body close and then stopped. "Am I to surmise life won't get any better for us, since the world suffers the pangs of a lion?"

"Sometimes I wonder," she said. "It would be nice to stop feeling like an orphan. I have often considered myself a mistake in this bustling realm."

"The same goes for me," he said. "We were never meant to be born."

"Are you angry about the imposition?"

His eyes scanned their surroundings, and he stood quiet for a moment.

"It causes a furious debate to rage within me, which I dare not suggest."

"Murder?"

"Yes."

"I have a similar urge, but my wrath is aimed only at myself."

FIFTEEN

Psalm 15:1

Who may worship in your sanctuary, Lord?
Who may enter your presence on your holy hill?

Daisy sat beside Catherine, troubled by her lack of improvement and the unnecessary delays caused by John's new operational processes. Her eyes raised to the main hall, and she observed the various spots of commotion, where tangles of patients nestled close to one another, some fully dressed as if going to work, others in their usual attire of bedclothes and bare feet, all mourning with astonishment their lack of place in the world and their anguished desire to live anywhere but Belmont Hospital. A man arrived with a small parcel in his hand, and Dora accepted it without uttering a word. The man took one look at the hall and a vivid color rose to his cheeks. He quickly left, inspiring Daisy to question what reputation the hospital had formed throughout the many corridors of their fine city. Whatever people thought of the place, their regard likely wasn't positive. She directed her attention to Catherine once more.

Overnight, a voice had set itself inside Daisy's mind, insulting her and pleading with her to end her life. The mysterious horrors of schizophrenia were known to her, and she wondered if the malady could somehow be caught, since John and Susanna Hutchinson suffered so terribly, the origin of their illness still yet to be determined. The voice seemed withered and bruised, as if jaded from centuries spent in misery. It sought restitution from her through the affliction of pain on those who already were mired in it—namely the hysterics who populated her hospital. The longer she lingered at Catherine's bedside, the louder and more ghastly the voice became, grasping and clambering and resolving itself against her, pushing her busily through a dark haze of confusion and anger and shame. It instructed Daisy to take hold of Catherine's hand—which she did as a matter of congenial obedience —and it surprised her with the coldness of a corpse marked for burial. Catherine smiled at Daisy in her formerly strange and appalling way, pushing Daisy's back against her chair in sudden fright.

If Daisy mentioned a word about an entity in their midst, especially if she blamed Catherine's recent ascension from her comatose abyss for its sudden appearance, Nathan would think her a fool and a child. Catherine's skull-like eyes followed movements in the main hall with a stealthy interest, as though a cunning predator was hard at work inside her mind, making plans and preparations, seeking those it may wish to devour. Daisy sighed. She had seen more than Nathan, both in Europe and at home in Missouri, and she knew what horrors this fallen world could produce and how quickly things could change for the worse. Daisy considered the intensity of her mother's envy and how desperately she had desired status, only to be thwarted by a man whose primary ambition was to own a winery on the banks of the Missouri, crowning himself king of the small town drunkards. It had ended badly for Patrice and would likely end badly for Catherine, as Daisy was sure her desires had not waned in the slightest. If anything, her husband's unceremonious dumping of her broken body in the filth of Dealey's main street had likely buttressed her covetous aspirations. Once fully healed, she would do everything in her power to reclaim Nathan as her husband and retake her position as the Caroline Astor of St. Louis.

The notion made Daisy want to cry.

She had come so far since Vienna.

Surely the Lord would not leave her flat once again, the punchline of jokes in the press, a false Parisian in New York, a counterfeit Viennese in Chicago, a disappointment to her sister, a burden to her father.

Daisy's shoulders slumped, and she noiselessly wept in her chair.

Catherine gave Daisy a victorious smile, as if the battle was already won and the better woman had prevailed without firing a shot or landing a blow. The hot light glistening in Catherine's eyes made Daisy furious with anger. As in Vienna, she wanted to pound the teeth from Catherine's smug face and send her tumbling into the Mississippi River, its eddies swirling her writhing form down to the depths of hell, where she could endure the blazing scrutiny of the entity she had so unpleasantly introduced into Daisy's life. It was only fair, and two could play Catherine's game.

An eye for an eye, a tooth for a tooth.

Catherine detected Daisy's internal turmoil and struggled to sit up. Daisy should help her nemesis by shoving soft pillows against her headboard and easing her fragile torso against them, but at the moment, there was no way she would help such a fiend with anything but a carriage ride to nowhere. She fanned her face, hoping to calm the boiling nature of her blood. If Nathan recognized her deviation from professional decorum, he would suspend her or worse, send her packing—a fate unbearable.

In search of a remedy, she went to the storage room where Nathan had operated on Ronnie and sat in front of her locker. Daisy retrieved her bag and fumbled through her belongings for a few moments. At last, she located the threadbare photograph of Rose, who stood on a pile of rocks at the base of a tall cliff. She studied her sister's face and pondered her countenance. As an adolescent, Daisy had been too selfish to notice another's emotional pain, especially a dour younger sister with an itinerant intelligence and a rebellious stride and an inclination toward the eternal. A portrait of Catherine Belmont and the rest of the patients in the hall formed in Daisy's mind. After failing Rose in such a grand manner, what made her think she was qualified to help anyone else? Was she any less preoccupied at present?

Nathan opened the storage room door.

"Have you filled out the progress reports for the last three days? Belmont wants them for the file cabinet."

"I completed them last night," she said.

Nathan smiled. "Good." He rubbed his beard. "One less worry."

A man entered the hospital and asked for the administrator.

Daisy's eyes met Nathan's, and her heart swelled.

"It's probably the deliveryman with another package," he said.

Once more, she hoped against all hope.

Frank Kaneski's voice penetrated the vast expanse of time and space and entered the storage room with a blast force of a hundred explosions. It detained Daisy in her spot on the bench and clasped its bony fingers around her brow, gripping hard on her temples and poking against her frontal lobe.

"I need to speak with Dr. Nathan Marsh! The matter is most urgent!"

His booming voice made Daisy tremble. She forgot all else.

"What's wrong?"

"I hear the sound of evil."

Nathan turned toward the hall and then back to Daisy.

"Have you lost your sanity?"

A portrait of Frank and Rosemarie's laughing faces formed in Daisy's mind, and she felt a sensation of fangs dripping saliva onto her neck. She glanced down and was relieved to see no trace of a puncture wound.

Nathan grabbed her arm. "Answer me."

"It's the man I knew in Vienna, the one who robbed me of my dignity and my reputation." She wished to go back to sleep, but was jolted awake again by his wicked voice, the one which almost convinced her to surrender.

"Daisy, I know you are here. You must come to me now!"

She had gotten too close to the fervent entity who resided within Catherine, guarding its lair and its future princess, making cunning plans for domination, and now it had sent Frank to jealously guard its treasure. The entity had won both Catherine and Nathan into its clutches and it had no intention of letting go of its prey. Like Frank, the entity would hoard and brood and threaten destruction on all who dared interfere with its plans.

Nathan nodded.

"How may I help?"

Daisy recounted how Frank behaved abusively and then broke her heart by taking up with another woman. To make matters worse, Frank and the woman spread rumors in the press, implying Daisy was a woman of ill repute. She may have made a few mistakes, but Daisy didn't deserve to have her reputation ruined in the European psychological community, nor did she want to see the vile man ever again. She needed Nathan's help.

He sat beside her and held her hand. "I appreciate your trust and your honesty. It's about time you shared the details of your past with me."

"I do not wish to pull you into my morass of gloom. You are too good for me." Daisy looked away while she wiped her cheeks.

"Is there more to the story?"

"There is a deeper, more sinister subject, which I cannot discuss."

"Why?"

She swiped more tears. "It would break me into a thousand pieces."

He lightly ran his fingers underneath her chin, pulling it up so their eyes might meet. "Tell me."

Frank's voice rumbled against the storage room door.

His powerful body might soon follow.

Daisy wanted to fold into a ball on the floor. How could she have ever trusted such a man? He had left her fragile mind with nothing but doubt and disorder, flying into a rage at the smallest infraction, making himself— his strong arms and legs and broad shoulders and chest—the center of her existence, banging her about with his demands and his interests and his lusts, oppressing her with his hot breath against her skin, taking from her the one most valuable thing she could offer a future husband, her purity.

She squeezed Nathan's hand and offered him a pleading look.

"It's a story for another day."

"I'll accept your denial for now, but you will reveal yourself fully to me soon." He stared deeply into her eyes. "We will return to this conversation, and when I ask you to be honest, give me everything. Understand?"

He squeezed her arm for effect. She surrendered to his strength.

"Yes, sir." It was all she knew to say. Nathan was now her keeper, and he offered the only semblance of sanity remaining, and her crumbling psyche held onto him for dear life. If he accepted her as his property and then left her alone, it would signal the end for her already embittered soul.

She must help him. It was her only means of survival.

"May I change the subject?"

He pursed his lips. "By all means."

"John Belmont wants to unseat you and insert Frank Kaneski into your place. I'm sure he has heard about my earlier relationship with Frank, and he likely hopes to drive a wedge between you and me. It's the only explanation for Frank's appearance here today."

"His plan is working," said Nathan with a smirk. "I recognize the man from the president's yacht. He stood near Belmont, but I paid him little attention." He gave her another snide look, as if ready to collapse their affair.

"Most likely, he was present to confirm your mental stability."

"Is he qualified for such an endeavor?"

"Not in the clinical sense, but he has written extensively on social matters, and men like John have a high regard for Frank's opinion."

"I see." Nathan's eyebrows arched. "Who *is* this man?"

"He's from a wealthy Chicago family, and he absolutely detests every aspect of St. Louis." The voice boomed again, and Frank's derisive tone fell on her head like a stone. What if Rosemarie had accompanied him? Daisy gripped her chair with her fingers, holding on for dear life. She could not endure such an ordeal a second time, as the seduction towards Rose's eternal was already pulling on her like gravity. She closed her eyes and forced herself to continue. "Frank holds America in contempt. He prefers the finer cities of Europe, especially Vienna. He calls it the cultural capital of the world."

She opened her eyes, half expecting to see Nathan approaching with dripping fangs. Daisy almost cried exultantly when he appeared normal.

He stood and cracked open the door, peeking through the opening.

"Do you see anything?"

"He must have gone upstairs to my office."

Nathan closed the door gently, and his eyes fell on her.

"I grew up on a farm out in the county, so I wouldn't know about elite European cities. I spent my youth under shade trees with the horses."

"Don't forget stray dogs." She gave him a somewhat wasteful smile.

His countenance fell into unsteady repose. "Yes, those, too." He studied her for several moments. "So why would he want my lowly position?"

She sighed. "There's only one reason."

"Which is?"

"To be near me."

"To win your heart once again?"

She nodded.

"I'm afraid so."

Nathan grabbed her hand, and they ducked out of the hospital.

As the pair walked toward downtown, they spotted a man who abused a gorgeous bay Thoroughbred most viciously. They traded a glance and then marched over to the man, and each gave him a piece of their minds. The man told them to shove off and turned his back on the bay's hindquarters.

The horse kicked him hard, and the force knocked him unconscious.

Nathan examined the abuser, who regained consciousness after several minutes. He then asked the man to provide a selling price.

"I've never liked this one. You can have him for a song."

"What is his name?"

"The sellers called him Firefly. I didn't bother to change his name."

Nathan handed the man two dollars as a retainer.

"My father will be along in a few days with the rest of your money. No horse should be alone in this fallen world."

"Have it your way, mister."

Daisy proudly watched the man leave and then turned to Nathan with her eyebrows raised and her lips parted in a mischievous smile.

"You said *fallen*, as in the Garden of Eden. I thought you didn't believe in Adam and Eve." She hoped he would accept Christ for her benefit as much as his. It might help her overcome the unrelenting voice in her head.

"Perhaps I have evolved like the animals in the forest."

"It's called emotional growth, Nathan. The theory of evolution is a myth which was created by a man of iniquity."

Nathan waved her off. "It matters little," he said knowingly. "Darwin is dead, so he's no longer a threat to anyone. You can rest easy on this matter."

"Oh, he and Frank Kaneski will stay evil until the Lake of Fire consumes their warped souls." She hooked her arm under his and marched them forward. "Their teachings will inspire great malevolence and death in the new century." She took a deep breath and exhaled. "Of this, I am certain."

Friday morning, the front door rested momentarily ajar as Nathan stomped up the stairs, and wet spots lingered on the wood where his shoes had stepped. Thunder boomed in the distance and hammer-like rain blew the door wide open. Daisy grabbed the handle and shoved her body against the wooden frame, fighting with all her might against the wind. As the door was about to close all the way, she stopped. A man watched the entrance from a fixed location across the street. She waved worriedly, but he offered no reply. The wind blew water against her face, and she slammed the door shut, rattling the multi-colored glass. After she wiped the floor and the steps with a towel, Daisy made her way upstairs to Nathan's office.

"We have another watcher outside."

Rain pounded puddles in the street and pelted the glass in his office window. He gazed blankly at the indefinite gray, as if lost in thought.

"Did you hear me?"

He swiveled his chair to face her, and for a moment, kept still. "If anyone is foolish enough to stand in this gully washer, I say good for them. We have nothing to hide here, do we?" His words descended on her like an accusal.

She considered his comment. "I suppose not."

"Then let everyone in town stare until their heart is contented."

Daisy waved her hand toward the window. "Very well."

His eyebrows arched as he pondered. "Actually, it might be someone who wishes to become a patient. I should ask him to come inside for proper treatment. This could begin our transition to real medical cases."

"He did not seem like a prospective patient."

"What then?"

She sat in the chair opposite his desk.

"I don't know, honestly, but I fear something disastrous may happen."

He frowned. "Now, who's the one lacking faith?"

She smiled at him. "Point taken."

He examined her from head to toe, forcing her to change the subject.

"Can we discuss our current roster of patients?"

"If we must," he said impatiently.

"Heinrich needs our help to move forward."

"Ask God to fix him, since nothing we've done so far has worked."

When Nathan mocked her faith, it bruised her fragile ego. He brought up feelings inside her, which were stronger than any she'd ever known.

"On days like this, I need a shot of whiskey," he said with a dry smile.

"If you would only accept the love of Jesus in your heart, your desire for intoxicating poison would cease."

"As a boy, I asked God to return my mother, but He never answered my prayers. It's one of the many reasons I became a drunken sot."

A portrait of Nathan kneeling before the Lord formed in her mind.

"Would you like to pray now?"

"Not if my life depended on it."

"You know exactly what I'm about to say."

He nodded.

"That my life, in point of fact, does depend on it."

Her eyes raised to the ceiling. She silently requested a helpful message. *Please help me find the right words, Lord.*

"You have no more pithy comments?"

She waved him off and spoke her prayer aloud.

"Lord, please give me your word. This man needs to hear from you."

"What word?"

The Lord spoke to her in the spirit with the recitation Nathan needed to hear. Daisy returned her gaze to Nathan. "The Holy Spirit just shared Psalm 15 with me. It may offer you comfort in this moment."

Nathan frowned but gestured for her to continue.

"You should make this quick," he said.

She nodded and retrieved her Bible.

"Those who lead blameless lives and do what is right, speaking the truth from sincere hearts. Those who refuse to gossip or harm their neighbors or speak evil of their friends. Those who despise flagrant sinners, and honor the faithful followers of the Lord, and keep their promises even when it hurts. Those who lend money without charging interest, and who cannot be bribed to lie about the innocent. Such people will stand firm forever."

"It's a nice passage, but I'm nowhere close to standing firm." He waved his hand at some imaginary object in the distance or a name on the tip of his tongue he dare not speak. He looked at Daisy as if she failed to understand him as everyone else had in his past. It instantly broke her heart to imagine herself exactly like the rest. "From my vantage point, I'm at the precipice of the highest cliff, and a slight breeze will knock me over the edge."

"You still have a chance at redemption. Men such as Darwin have already fallen over the edge and into the fire." She considered Rose. "Others I once knew are no more, their lives having ended abruptly."

Shouts erupted from the first floor. Daisy and Nathan turned in unison to face the sound. Boots quickly thudded up the stairs and approached the office. Nurse Pratt knocked on the door and stuck her head inside the room.

"Would you ask the patients to keep the noise to an acceptable level?" asked Nathan. "I have a splitting headache this morning."

"You must come to the main hall at once."

"We're having a conversation."

"Sir, I regret to override your authority, and you can fire me if you see fit, but right now, I need you in the main hall."

Nathan's eyes rolled.

"This had better be worth the effort."

Dora seemed troubled, as if seized with apprehension. "Miss Catherine has emerged from her abyss. She once again resides among the living."

Daisy exchanged a glance with Nathan. "We have made little progress with her lately." She had not prayed for Catherine for some time, consumed as she was with Frank's unexpected visit and the possibility of another deathly encounter with Rosemarie. What could have brought her to life?

"Something you've done must have worked."

Nathan and Daisy rushed down the stairs and stood near the front entrance at the precise location of their first tour of the hospital. Catherine spoke to the nurses as if making preparations for an elegant wedding.

They approached her bed with a wary countenance.

"You two make a pleasant couple." Catherine studied Nathan and then Daisy. "You should hold hands. It's what couples do when in love."

Daisy fumbled for words. "We're merely colleagues, Catherine."

Catherine's countenance seemed pleasantly snobbish.

"My dear, I am no longer naked and face down in the gutter with the horse droppings and the crawling insects and the slithering snakes." She swept off her covers and staggered to her feet and plodded over to Daisy, grabbing her arms like Brenda had done in her drawing room. "My senses have returned, and I know exactly *who* and *what* lurks before me."

"We must focus on your continued recovery," Nathan said, maintaining an air of earnestness and patience. "You shouldn't become agitated."

Catherine turned toward him. "Please do not interrupt me."

He cleared his throat. "Alright."

She returned her attention to Daisy and squinted. "Now, Miss Lawrence, are you my worst adversary or my best friend?" She gave Daisy a tender smile, which sent adrenaline through every corner of her body. "Please consider your opinion carefully, young lady. I will be a most formidable aggressor, and your choppy little frame will be no match."

"It depends on you, Catherine. For now, I do not know."

Catherine gave a dismissive nod. "Flawless response, my darling. I'm certain your answers always carry the determined fury of perfection."

Daisy blushed. "My father would disagree."

"As would my own." Catherine returned her tired body to the bed and pulled the covers to her chin. She beamed. "It's our sisterly bond."

Sixteen

Psalm 16:1

Keep me safe, O God,
for I have come to you for refuge.

June 1890

Tuesday night at La Salpêtrière, Daisy used her railroad fork for an hour, but failed to mesmerize a hysteric patient. A deafening commotion filled the room, and the elderly man stared blankly into space as she swiped the tears from her cheeks, hiding her pain as best she could. Daisy couldn't speak to anyone about her lack of satisfactory progress or her inner torment. The psychiatric hospital was a political environment, and Daisy must be careful with what she said and to whom she said it. Her colleagues were atheists who ridiculed her beliefs with a heated intensity, seeing them as simple relics from a bygone era. Daisy had been raised primarily in isolation since birth, having spent most of her formative years in the woods near her father's winery, and she now existed without the neural pathways necessary for clever responses to sudden verbal lashes in which the sociopaths of modern society excelled. Her habitual inclination of late to be sullen and manipulative had not helped relationship matters in the slightest.

She prayed Psalm 16:5-6 aloud, hoping to brighten her sad disposition, while she simultaneously watched for those who might be angered by her public expression of Christian faith. "Lord, you alone are my inheritance, my cup of blessing. You guard all that is mine. The land you have given me is a pleasant land. What a wonderful inheritance!"

The elderly patient mouthed the words as she spoke. When she finished, he grinned and patted her hand. "*J'ai toujours aimé celui-là.*"

"I always liked that one, too," she said, smiling with delight.

He immediately fell into a blank stare. She snapped her fingers in front of his face, but his eyes glazed into an endless nothingness, and he did not twitch a muscle. She turned over the situation in her mind, warning herself not to get too excited. It was only one sentence and could happen to anyone.

She clutched the Bible in her pocket.

Had her recitation penetrated the man's hysteria?

Walter Resnick sat beside her. "Women should be in the home, not here messing about, worsening patient outcomes."

He sent the man back to his bed and told her to go home.

"I'll stay," she said. "It's obvious I need the practice."

Frank Kaneski stepped through the doorway and sent his charming voice on a mission of rescue. It reached out to her grateful ears.

"Why don't *you* go home, Walter? No one wants you here, least of all me." He grabbed a chair and spun it around. "Mind if I sit?"

Daisy gestured her approval, although Frank Kaneski did not require her permission. It was more his hospital than hers, and each of them knew it.

Walter gave Frank a fearful look and returned to his office in a huff.

Frank's eyes followed him with disgust. "The cowering fool."

"Why are you here?" She sat straight in her chair and brushed the blonde curls away from her blue eyes. "I thought everyone had left for the evening."

"Well, obviously not everyone, since you and Walter work late."

"Oh, he was merely spying on me, picking a fight, as usual." Her long practiced formality of speech fell low. "He doesn't like me very much."

"Walther's true feelings might surprise you."

Daisy suddenly felt self-conscious. She wondered if he meant to extract a promise from her, and if she had the means to satisfy his terms.

"You avoided my question, so I'll ask again. Why are you still here?"

"I enjoy the contemplation of my theories at night." He rubbed the metal legs of the chair. "This hospital offers a treasure trove of insights into the human psyche. It doesn't matter if the patient is lost to hysteria or in the middle of the fight of their lives for a continuance of sanity, as I see in *you*."

He stuck out his hand, and his finger lightly touched her forehead.

She smiled at him as only a smitten woman could.

"I'm not sure who is worse, you, Sigmund, or Jean-Martin."

His villainous eyes secretly removed her garments. One by one, he laid her naked before him as if her clothes had vanished into the night's oblivion. He pretended to catch himself in the act and paused. "How so?"

His soft and lustful excitement caught her off guard. She gave him a girlish laugh, and his skin took on a vague sheen. He wanted her in a private liaison where flesh may press against flesh in the heat of the act.

The storage room on the far side of the room called to her.

She pushed her consciousness back to the topic at hand.

"Each of you wants to be the first to map the mind like a modern day Captain Cook. You should understand it's not a competition or a race with a finish line. We are here to help these people recover from personal tragedy, the kind which sends an otherwise normal man or woman into the abyss of hysteria or, worse, schizophrenia, the latter a completely mysterious phenomenon which plagues a person for the rest of their life."

"I've spent time in German medical circles," Frank said conversationally. "There is a physician named Emil Kraepelin, who has studied neuropathology and experimental psychology extensively, having become a disciple of my friend Wilhelm Wundt."

His knowledge comforted and reassured her of his value.

"Jean-Martin and Sigmund respect Wilhelm immensely. They refer to him as the originator of the field."

"Yes, it's true, and Emil is Wilhelm's finest pupil, perhaps even with greater long-term potential than either of us."

She gave him another little laugh. "I doubt it very much. He would have much to achieve to unseat the three of you from your lofty thrones."

Frank pretended to tip his hat. "I'll take it as a compliment, madam."

She offered a spurious curtsy. "You are welcome, sir."

Frank slid his chair close to hers with a graceful move and a sly grin. She felt his breath on her neck as he whispered into her ears, inciting her soul toward a decision. "Emil was just this year appointed head of the Treatment and Nursing Institute in Dresden, where I interviewed him. For a man of thirty, he has fine ideas, and I predict his theories will become popular, although it may take twenty years before they catch fire." His body pulled away from her with an equal measure of force and determination, allowing her to relax into their conversation. He was an act of nature, bending her will like a rod made of bamboo, pulling her close and releasing on a whim.

She did her best to recover her senses and to speak logically.

"Why so long? If his work is sound, scholars will take notice."

He smiled and waved both of his hands. "You, of all people, know the difficulties of breaking through the bureaucratic morass."

She searched for a way to create a physical distance between them and then sat on the steps which led to the stage. "Yes, and sometimes I wonder if my work has any merit or has done any good at all."

"You look weary. Will you allow me to walk you home?"

Her back stiffened.

What had he meant by such an ill-timed remark?

"Never tell a morose woman she looks tired. It's a hangable offense."

He stared at her for several moments and then laughed. "For a moment, you had me going. Your deadpan delivery makes you sound serious."

His marvelous voice renewed her spirit. "I joke, but in all honesty, you have a crass air about you, sir, and I'm not sure what to make of it."

"Oh, you like me. There's no doubting it."

"What makes you certain, other than your dangerous overconfidence?"

"An opinionated woman would never show herself fully to a man of meek character. Only a man who offers security may win your trust."

Her blood stirred. "We've only just met, and you know me so well."

"Yes, I do," he said. "And I will now go with you to your dormitory."

Romance had found her for the first time. "We have a chaperone."

"An older woman, a spinster or a widow, no doubt."

He saw through her every defense. "She is the latter."

"Perfect, for I enjoy using my charms on lonely women who once knew a man's allure." He held out his hand. "Shall we take our leave?"

Her iron fortifications melted in his presence.

"You are no gentleman, sir."

"Regardless, you'll embrace me with all your vigor."

Daisy stood and placed her hand inside his. "You may walk me home and bid me goodnight at my door. That will end our engagement for the evening." She nodded as she spoke, hoping to follow through on her chaste and virtuous promise. She must not fold weakly into his arms like an absurd house made of cards. For the first time since her arrival in Paris, she was thankful for the supervision of the glaring and distrustful chaperone.

Frank's fearless smile hurried itself toward her. "It's enough."

At her entrance, Daisy stiffened once more, unsure of what to make of this handsome man. Psalm 16:7-8 helped her regain composure. "I will bless the Lord who guides me; even at night my heart instructs me. I know the Lord is always with me. I will not be shaken, for he is right beside me."

"Where does your quote originate?"

She distrusted the motives behind his question.

"It's from the Bible."

His eyes shone bright, as if inspired. "I believe superstition is for the feeble, but your verses resound through the corridors of my intellect."

"Does that mean I'm converting you?"

"Hardly," he said, smiling. "It merely means there is a lyrical quality to your faithful recitation." He gestured for Daisy to continue.

"Troubles multiply for those who chase after other gods. I will not take part in their sacrifices of blood or even speak the names of their gods."

"That's a harsh commentary on your colleagues, don't you think? I know Walter is a weasel, but he's there to further science, and we will need all the understanding we can muster in the next century."

She changed the subject, intent on probing his sincerity.

"Sigmund is taken with Jean-Martin's hypnosis techniques, and he plans to take them back to Vienna next year."

"Oh?"

She nodded.

"He's asked me to join him as he begins his psychiatric practice."

Frank seemed perplexed, as if his own fortifications had been cast down and arrayed in pieces along a shattered roadway. "I thought his primary pursuit was neurology. What has changed?"

"I don't know, honestly, but Sigmund understands the mind is more than a collection of cells and neurons, and, like Wilhelm, he wants to drill deeper into the human psyche than anyone else. It's an opportunity to make a genuine impact on the world, and I admire his dedication."

Frank smiled. "The reason is *you*, Daisy."

"What do you mean? If you're implying something scandalous, I'll have you know Sigmund is a happily married man."

She paused.

"I have no wish to disrupt a gentleman's family."

His breath shallowed, and his eyes narrowed. The energy in his voice could power a hundred electric stations. His intensity rang through her mind and rippled across her soul. It threatened to leave her tremulous and insane in some forlorn asylum on the outer reaches of human misery.

"Your fiery passion has inspired Sigmund. You have that effect on men."

"You take liberties, sir. We barely know one another."

The blue in his eyes chilled her into absolute submission.

"I can think of a remedy. Might I call on you for another walk?"

"It depends," she said. "Will you continue your work at the hospital?"

"Yes, for a time. When Sigmund leaves in January, I'll travel with him. I'm writing a new essay and I want his opinion on its merits."

Frank's coercive will prevailed over Daisy's efforts to thwart him. He kissed her for several minutes on the stoop, quieting her dark apprehensions, compelling her weak resolve to slink across the grass in a desperate crawl, replacing each reason for escape with a shouting desire which could only be quenched in a raw and unprotected form. Frank would soon take her to a private location, most likely an expensive hotel or a shady blanket beside the Seine. He would possess her like a farmer owns a strip of land, fully digging into her depths, planting his good seeds, growing her into a fruitful crop.

Her long stifled need for pleasure had overcome his own, and she would not allow him to recede like the low tide. He would lap against her shores, eroding her sandy embankments, removing the ground underneath her house of light, forcing reinforcements of sand and rock and hopeful love.

She blurted the end of the psalm in a morose but determined effort to calm her exploding desire, knowing with all her heart, she would relent. "No wonder my heart is glad, and I rejoice. My body rests in safety. For you will not leave my soul among the dead or allow your holy one to rot in the grave. You will show me the way of life, granting me the joy of your presence and the pleasures of living with you forever."

His laugh carried a hint of masculine triumph, as if they would always be beautiful and young. "Are the words about me or your God?"

She clutched his arm. "I cannot say."

"It's a good sign."

He stepped to the sidewalk and offered her a knowing wink and then strolled carelessly to the corner. Soon he was gone into the night.

Inside, Mrs. Coolidge cautioned Daisy to beware.

"I don't like him. He has evil eyes and impure intentions."

Daisy left the woman standing in the hallway and went to bed.

Daisy concealed her disappointment as she worked with a female patient named Zelia. Frank watched Daisy from a chair at the side of the room. She did her best to ignore his elaborately groomed manner and the maze of emotions which swirled within her. It was a vain and pitiful attempt to guard herself from his possessive charms. She gave him a restless glance, noting with unmistakable clarity the intention behind his bearded and bitter smile, one which threatened to both give her hope and remove it forever. It was discourteous and presumptuous to intrude upon her heart and then throw it merrily on the ground as a form of ungentlemanly adventure.

Daisy had thought about Mrs. Coolidge's comments until deep into the night, and she finally realized there was more to being a woman than lustful pleasures and the offer of weak but approachable comfort. She was tired of men who were devoted only in the mind's eye. She needed a vigorous man of actual flesh and blood, a husband who would stay the course in this life and the next—a friend and a lover and a fatherly replacement to guide her through the many layers of her sorrow and her despair.

Could Frank Kaneski become that sort of man?

Walter lumbered into the room. "I need to see your progress."

"I've made some," she said. "The paralysis is lessening."

Walter eyed Frank with a dimly shaped frown. "His presence is causing the patients to become alarmed. He must leave the hospital at once."

"He gives me insight into their internal struggle. Like Captain Cook, he has a layman's manner and a unique way of charting new territories." She grew flustered but hoped the eagerness in her tone might stimulate Walter's wan curiosity. There was a time when he had accepted her statements without the necessity of a confrontation. He was more likable then.

Walter shook his head gravely and retrieved his pocket watch. "Yes, and he may receive the same reward as the honorable captain if he's not careful."

"Which would be?"

He looked up from his watch. "Ambush and a burial at sea."

Frank slapped his leg. "Daisy, you must commend your meek little friend on his comedic talents. There are minstrel houses in dire need of entertainers. Mr. Resnick would be paid in bags of gold."

Jean-Martin entered the room. "What do have we here, another rash argument?" He looked at Frank. "Sir, you continually disrupt our days and our hard-fought progress. Perhaps your time would be better spent with Sigmund on the main floor."

"Jean-Martin, we work well together." Daisy patted the woman's drooped shoulder. "Zelia is fond of Frank, and she responds to treatment more favorably when he's near to her."

Charcot snorted his displeasure and then sneered at Frank.

"Sir, this isn't a social club for your amusement."

"Don't worry. I keep my distance from the beautiful women."

Frank grinned at Daisy. "All but *one*."

"He stays quiet most of the time," said Daisy, blushing.

Charcot surveyed the room. "Where are your notes, Miss Lawrence?"

In the previous week's chaos, she had forgotten to make a single journal entry. Her desire for Frank Kaneski had overwhelmed her senses and her ability to perform her duties. She must stop the back and forth with him.

Daisy sat on the steps. "Walter told you about my earlier failures?"

Charcot glanced at the younger man. "I have eyes and can see for myself what occurs in my hospital. Now, where are your weekly notes?"

Frank raised his hand and interjected.

"Listen, Jean-Martin, it was my fault. I shouldn't have distracted her."

Charcot's furious eyes fell on him. "You plan to take more than her attention." He turned toward Daisy. "You are much too young, still too naïve, and far too American for this sort of man. I fear he will break you."

Walter cleared his throat before he spoke. "He's right. You should be home tending kitchen pots instead of disrupting our activities."

Daisy's cheeks flushed red. "I'll have you know there is a bright future for the field of psychology, and women will eventually dominate it." She pointed toward Charcot. "I am no woman of ill repute, sir. My dignity and my honor remain intact. Please do not imply otherwise."

Charcot waved his hand dismissively. "One execrable day, you'll see I am correct. That is all I have to say on the matter."

Frank sat down again, sure of himself. "Then why not ask me to leave your hospital? You certainly have the authority."

"Because Sigmund wants you here, and I respect his wishes. Unlike yourself, he does not use people for his pleasure." Charcot turned toward Daisy and gave her a soft look. "When he has lost interest, he will move to another plaything, someone with greater prestige, most likely, and you'll be a dazed lump of coal who once might have become a diamond."

Daisy instinctively knew Jean-Martin's words to be true.

"Don't listen to him," Frank said. "I will marry you if given the chance."

Daisy stiffened, unsure what to make of the handsome man and his declarations of true love. In the past, she'd ruined relationships by refusing to trust, pushing a man past his irrevocable breaking point.

"I believe you, Frank." She put her hand over her heart, hoping she might gentle his brutal nature. "Please don't damage me further."

He winked at her. "I wouldn't dream of it, my dear."

Daisy's shame led to stomach issues and a lack of appetite. She tossed and turned at night, roiling the covers from side to side as stern rebukes and cheerless pleas dominated her sleep. Her fragmented emotions were strewn like pebbles in a creek bed, and her dreams alternated between sluggishly light and violently dark, the variation in intensity because of exhaustion and her proximity to their last liaison. As expected by everyone around her, he had proven a damaging influence in her life, but she could not deny herself the carnal bliss of his dominance. He owned her, and she was his property.

Frank got out of bed and put on his clothes. His motion startled her awake, and she rubbed her eyes. There was a long pause, and they each stared at one another. A flood of sunlight streamed into the window.

He lit a cigarette. "You had nightmares again. Am I so appalling?"

His walls were up again, protecting him from some infinitesimal speck in the distance. When he fell into a mood, he stretched his darkness across her form, as if painting her like an empty canvas meant merely for his vanity. "Please don't start, Frank. I cannot bear to argue with you this morning."

"We should discuss the situation, don't you think?"

She stared at the ceiling. "Yes, but I am bone-tired."

"You believe I have defiled you."

"You won't marry me as I'd hoped."

He waved his hands, sending puffs of smoke in circles about the room. "Who needs the institution? We have each other, which should be enough."

"I must make things right before God and the rest of society. No one knows what we're doing, Frank, but soon word will leak, and my career will end." There was a deafening boom from some far off location as to be of no consequence to their tawdry affair, but it startled her just the same.

"Good, let it drop. I'd like you to travel with me to Germany. You could become my assistant." He was evidently unwilling to give her more.

"You mean your private bedmate who maintains an alter ego as your spinster secretary?" Her eyebrows arched. "How appealing."

He became somewhat troubled, as if her words made him nervous.

His mounting anxiety fueled an inexhaustible rage, which scared her.

"I don't care what anyone says or what they think. My popularity only grows with each news headline. Soon, I will become untouchable, a man who controls the flow of world events, and I want you by my side."

When he spoke with such a fiery intensity, it seared her soul with the flames of hellfire. Daisy knew her name had been removed from the Book of Life, and the second death awaited her resurrected body. She only hoped to become an honest woman and to remove the scarlet letter from around her neck. She had worn it too long, and the misery had become intolerable.

She sat up, letting the covers fall beside her, fully exposing herself to the man she loved. "Then marry me, please. I beg you."

"I'll never give Him the satisfaction."

"Him?"

"That God of yours."

"I thought you hadn't succumbed to superstition like the rest of us."

"Oh, He and I are old enemies, and I will overcome Him someday. It has all been foreseen."

She smiled coyly. "Written in an ancient scroll?"

"Now you're making fun of me."

"Someone has to lighten the mood. You've grown far too serious."

"I won't marry you or anyone else." He puffed the cigarette. "If you want me, this is who you will get."

"No children either?"

"Oh, we can have a son, and his lineage will rule the world in the centuries to follow, but for now, my only solemn vow is to stand against God at all costs."

Daisy held her breath for a few moments.

"Are you serious?"

"I never joke about such matters."

Frank went downstairs to make breakfast.

Daisy stared at the ceiling again, alarmed at her predicament.

She tried to say a prayer, but her mind could not remember the words. Her mother and sister had sealed their fates in the Lake of Fire. Perhaps it was Daisy's time to join them. She could throw herself from a tall ledge.

It would be so easy.

SEVENTEEN

O Lord, hear my plea for justice.
Listen to my cry for help.
Pay attention to my prayer,
for it comes from honest lips.

Daisy pondered her life choices throughout Sunday afternoon and into the night, finally reaching an inescapable truth: she had grown exhausted from being alone. She marched from her bed to the water closet down the hall, where she sponged her face and hands as she noted the invariable boorishness and the bitter scratchiness and the demure reluctance of her ineffectual lips. She stared into the mirror at her rather shiny forehead and her imperfect nose and her faintly colored cheeks, unsparing in her examination of her every flaw, comparing herself faithlessly against the perennial elegance of Catherine Belmont, who, even in such a sorry state of affairs had the audacity to outclass her unworthy opponent.

Catherine would remain a firebrand to the end and the better element.

Daisy needed a counterbalance against her adversary, some vague thing to stabilize the situation. Her emotions raced, and her desire for Nathan grew more impassioned. A small melee of thoughts humbly and quietly swept through her mind, murmuring vivid rose-like pleasantries, squeezing themselves through every nuanced passageway, begging Daisy to lessen her confusion and her clotted remembrances in a quick and grateful retreat.

She trudged down the stairs Monday morning and plopped into her usual position at Catherine's bedside, waiting for her nemesis to awaken from her aristocratic slumber. Like clockwork, the voice which had set itself inside her head chattered incessantly about this or that, never seeming to tire, only to gain momentum like a speedy woman with a singular purpose. Daisy wondered how long it might take Catherine to snatch Nathan away from her, and if she could ever hope to call the older woman an ally. It would be one or the other, but not both, as she could never align herself with the thief of her last shred of hope, the one who sent her home.

An hour passed without movement.

Daisy fell into a semi-hypnotic repose, as those who moved about her and Catherine did so in a solemn and respectful manner, disliking the notion of yet another outburst at their expense. As her first her attempt at the resumption of life, Catherine was unpracticed in the art of the routine and therefore had blossomed into a handful, one moment showing doubt and tears, the next waving a beautiful smile in an accomplished manner.

Daisy told the staff Catherine's best days were ahead.

In private, she scarcely avoided a complete surrender to the daily torment of betrayal and abandonment, sure as she was of its predictable occurrence at the hands of a more experienced heart. To a man with a wandering eye, she was no sparkling diamond and could never compete with the lustful and easily managed deportment of Sheila Byrne or the poised displeasure of Catherine Belmont. Could Daisy's kindness and honor ever hope to gain the upper hand? Nathan so far had shown noble character and restraint, the very opposite of her former disastrous flirtation. Unlike the portrait which had formed in her mind the night of their meeting at Union Depot, he was a man of virtue and great decency at his core, and she was most glad to have met such a gentleman at least once in her troublesome life. She looked about the room, its drab freshness burning her eyes and dissolving her insecurities into a flushed panorama of lost fortunes.

Nathan entered through the cherry and glass door. He smiled warmly at Daisy as he moved in her direction. Catherine had awakened with a start only moments before his arrival, and she seemed jealous. Daisy rose to meet his approach, unwilling to let go of the man who had become a revelation to her. She returned his smile with grace and affection and then turned briefly toward Catherine. She gave her adversary a slight nod.

Catherine frowned and, surprisingly, turned away.

Tears streamed down her cheeks.

Daisy decided in the moment to withhold care and instead hooked her arm under Nathan's and led him toward the front entrance, where they sat in their familiar rocking chairs, surveying the room like a king and queen.

"I was sorry to see Ed brought in from his farm yesterday afternoon, and his appearance brought a deep melancholy to my spirit. I had hoped he would make it on his own after Ronnie's death." She hesitated. "Last night, he experienced another fainting spell and this morning before you arrived, he suffered temporary hearing loss." Nathan sat and offered no response, so she continued. "I was shocked to see Shirley walk over to his bed and sit down in a chair. Her presence seemed to enable his hearing. They talked for some time, and she even held his hand. It was remarkable."

Nathan's eyes glided about the room. "Sometimes, no matter what we do, they spontaneously improve. Other days, they regress into infancy."

She nodded.

"I see a legitimate connection between them and I think his fainting has allowed her to see not all men are cruel brutes who want to choke her to death. It seems his mild-mannered and vulnerable nature has broken her fatalistic silence. In her own fragile condition, he could do her some good."

"We'll move their beds next to one another this afternoon," Nathan said. "We can evaluate their progress over the next couple of weeks."

"On that note of encouragement, I will suggest we document our empirical theories and determine where there is agreement and overlap."

He gave her a look of tacit bafflement, which animated her stillness.

She continued, hoping to avoid his censure. "You give me your medical best practices, and I'll list mine for experimental psychology."

He paused a moment. "You know many people still question whether psychology is mere quackery or, even worse, sorcery."

"People have said the same about medicine for centuries."

"Yes, but you're playing with people's minds, their temperaments, their personalities. I mend bones when they break, which people can see with their own two eyes. Your field remains a mystery, even to me."

She settled into her chair. "Charcot made progress with mesmerism, but was ridiculed for the practice. Sigmund was taken with Charcot's hypnosis techniques at first, but then realized more could be gained by talking to the patient. I've seen both methods work, but after my hours spent with our group, I now lean toward the talking cure."

"You just lost me. Talking cure?"

"Yes, the term was coined in Europe by a patient of Josef Breuer. Her real name is Bertha Pappenheim, but she uses the alias, Anna O. Sigmund plans to include her case history in an upcoming book. For the first time, he will depict hysteria as a genuine disease worthy of scientific analysis."

She paused.

"Some people call the method Chimney Sweeping."

"How does it work?"

"When patients discuss the events surrounding the onset of their somatic symptoms and force themselves to relive the suppressed emotions, those symptoms often disappear as suddenly as they arrived."

"You make it sound so easy."

She smiled at his dig, knowing his skepticism was rooted in fear. "You're right, and I don't mean to make light of the process. Often it takes a long time, sometimes months before the patient finds permanent healing, and even in those situations, regression may occur for unknown reasons, sending the patient back to the clinic for more therapy over years."

"Doesn't sound much like a cure."

"Well, it's better than living with paralysis or all the other combinations of symptoms. Wouldn't you say?"

"I suppose."

"I understand your reticence," she said. "We've been counseled and warned since childhood not to discuss our traumas, to sweep them under the rug, but those traumas may manifest in physical ways down the road when a person least expects it."

"During times of stress?"

She nodded.

"The phenomenon is most commonly observed when a loved one is in jeopardy or one is attacked like Shirley Fletcher. The only way forward is to acknowledge what happened and to talk it out."

They collaborated all afternoon, theorizing how best to mix methods of treatment for both medical and psychological conditions. While they worked, Daisy took a break in the wash closet on the second floor, again fighting the urge to step through the last barrier into a world of utter complacency and the befuddlement of twiddled thumbs. There wasn't much chance the burgeoning field of psychology would ever compensate for her losses or offer a new guarantee of meaning and purpose in her life, as much as she had wanted to believe otherwise in Europe. Then came a long pause as she gazed at her reflection, seeing past the skin and the bones to the mind within, measuring the years of work which had gone into her misshapen and hastily formed vitality. She tried to make out if she was an agreeable woman who could someday overcome her fear of speaking in more than half-truths to the man she loved. Her head drooped, and she stared at her hands which gripped the sides of the sink basin, her knuckles bare with the force of her determination to believe she was no good.

Her reddish lips parted slightly with the gleam of a realization.

A new vision wasn't needed. Rather, she must turn to the same place she had always looked—the eternal. One of the greatest blessings which stemmed from one's relationship with the Lord was His life affirming message of faith, hope, and love, with the greatest being love. There was no other religion or view of the world which protected life and liberty like Christianity. The same omnipresent, omniscient, and omnipotent being who created living and non-living structures in the universe could provide answers to our most thought-provoking questions. Daisy must surrender to His will and lay her many problems at the foot of the cross.

That night, Daisy and Nathan showed the notebook—which contained their combined thoughts—to Samuel. He reminded them he was retired and not their desired audience. They should send them to President Cleveland, who was waging a great battle to restore a broken economy. The president would enjoy receiving something positive for a change.

Nathan and Daisy exchanged glances and smiles and dreamed of a pleasant visitation to the oval office with a buoyant flush across their cheeks.

"As soon as I die," said Samuel with a grin, "you'll beat down his door."

Tuesday evening, Nathan read a novel at home in hopes of a rare timbre of quiet, his thoughts both distant and undefinable, fading into the darkness of the night and then reappearing like golden apples in September. He had been called to testify against Thomas in the early blaze of morning and then dejectedly excused himself from work for the rest of the day, all the while fighting the urge to drink a bottle of whiskey. The act of recounting what had occurred so long ago made him feel more like an orphan than ever before, and he materialized a portrait of June in his mind with every hour's passage. Her lack of warmth notwithstanding, she possessed an inner light which no man could extinguish, and it simmered effervescent within Nathan each day. Now, as in his youth, he laid awake in deep contemplation of her delightful grandeur, subtle and farm laden as it was prior to her death. It was she who had shielded and muffled his vision, while simultaneously shoving him toward the world in all its fullness while she lived. Afterward, it was the steadfast and intelligent Aunt Joy who directed his immature and inexperienced eyes at the luminous vision who went by the name of Catherine Belmont, the same urchin whose candle nearly waned on the well-rehearsed streets of Dealey, Illinois, the known capital of chirping gossips and clodhopping catnips, a place where a naked wretch of previous renown became a sensation, her story captured merrily in the local paper and lustily talked about in church, their cares more physical than moral, their private intonations excessively inexpressible, their placid disapproval taken for granted, their honor bound to lost souls on their way to perdition.

What a fine mess Nathan and Catherine had made of this life.

He looked with jovial condescension about the room, which had attracted no attention from him since Daisy's first visit, a recollection which now made him laugh. She had mashed her way through his house and into his affairs with thick boots and muddy intentions. No aspect of his human existence had been the same since her impeccably timed arrival.

There was a knock at the front door.

He was surprised anyone would venture to his stoop at such a late hour. His hand dropped the book on the end table as he made his way to the door with a dour expression, which had aligned itself perfectly with his dull and practical mood. He was no stranger to embarrassment, but the activity which occupied his time earlier in the day left him humbled and ashamed.

Daisy stood nervously with members of the hospital staff.

He swung open the door.

She smiled at him. "Hello, Nathan."

He allowed her into the foyer, but left the others on his stoop. "You have work tomorrow at the hospital. It takes precedence over anything else."

"Right now, this is more important."

"*Daisy*."

She held up a palm. "Let me oversee the cleaning of your home."

"It's late, and I'm tired." He eyed the novel on the table, hoping the cover wouldn't fly open and the pages wouldn't flow forth with all his many contradictions, like an open door which no one could shut. Perhaps the blue dreariness in his countenance did all the talking, stark as it was at present.

She rubbed her gloved finger on the stair railing and held it up to him. "Your house hasn't had a thorough cleaning since I last did it."

Nathan peaked through the window, his eyes allowing no escape from a full and costly accounting. He was astounded his father had missed the opportunity to interrupt his nightly repose, intent as Samuel had been of late to meddle in matters unbecoming to a gentleman of letters and the accumulation of years. He would fiercely chide his father in the morning. "Where's Nurse Pratt? She would normally lead this miniature brigade."

Daisy put her hand on his arm and drew a long breath. "Someone has to maintain the hospital tonight. We cannot leave it unattended."

"We might have hysterics wandering the countryside like Frankenstein. What a ghastly sight it would be, rather like your Dorian Gray."

She blushed. "Stop, Nathan. You know half of them wouldn't make it out of bed, no matter what we did or didn't do for them."

"Quite right, madam, as usual."

"You're one to talk, *Mister I Know Everything.*"

His tone grew more serious, as she had crossed a line. "You should leave. It's been a trying day, and I cannot afford company at this late hour."

"Why didn't you tell me?"

"I'm not sure what you mean."

She flung herself verbally at him, unwilling to let the foul matter rest undisturbed. "You testified against the murderer, Thomas Hannah, today."

"Yes."

"When you excused yourself from the hospital after lunch, the staff thought you went to a pub. I assumed you visited Sheila at her brothel."

"It crossed my mind at several intervals."

Her eyes moistened. "Instead, you suffered through that painful ordeal from your childhood in open court and with no encouragement."

"My father was present this morning."

"All the more reason I should have been there to comfort you both."

Nathan sighed, fighting defeat at her hands.

She opened the door and allowed the group inside, ushering some into the parlor, others into the kitchen, the rest to the bedrooms on the second floor. At the moment, he felt a deep romantic affection for her.

Still, he knew what she had in store for him and resented her intrusion.

He called up the stairs. "Stay out of my attic, please."

A deep voice descended on him with a boom. "Will do, sir!"

Thirty minutes later, Daisy swept the parlor while others cleaned and straightened around her. Nathan attempted to read his novel, treating the voyage of his house cleaning as a solitary adventure. His thoughts were once again blanketed by the past, covered in rust and moss and green grass above a row of graves, each soul dealing with the great burden of glory.

"I'm here because you need me." She drew closer to his end of the couch. "You don't know what you believe, why you believe it, or why anything matters in this world. Well, you matter to me, and I will prove myself to you." She seemed blown full of life, as if he was her purpose.

He shut the book. "How can I practice a religion I don't understand?"

Daisy gave him a tremendous and unvisited smile, the type usually reserved for severe isolation in frozen tundras or the west side of a sunny lake. "You are like the Earth in its original state, void and without form. You need a sovereign Lord to shape you into a marvelous and irresistible man, but since you won't allow Him into your heart, your soul, or any other aspect of your trivial existence, I'll have to do."

He went to the bookcase and slid his book onto its shelf with a *whoosh*.

Nathan turned, and his eyes fell on her wonderful frame. He felt hollow and shapeless, as she had said, but still he wouldn't relent to her demands of religious conformity. His experiences had taught him more than her, and he would stand his ground in this and all other matters of tangible reason. If they were to have a future, it depended on their ability to reach a mutual understanding, as shared values were the central reason for a relationship's success over a lifetime. "I believe in science's power to heal the human body and to transform our society into something unfathomable, not some old man in the sky no one has ever legitimately seen or heard." There was a pause as he worked out how far he might go within the confines of this rough and reckless dialogue. "You know, I've always wondered, why doesn't your God make an appearance? He could pull up a chair and have a basic conversation. Would that be so terrible or so out of the norms of His polite society, our drawing rooms being unclean to His Holy Eminence?" He crossed his arms. "I'm merely asking a question which has been lingering on my mind since I reached the Age of Enlightenment, which was just about the time I could breathe the fresh air and feel the green grass under my bare feet, you know the stuff of life, which He seems all too willing to snuff out at an early age, leaving us with nothing but our false presumption of free will."

He had said his peace and meant it.

Work stopped, and the room fell silent.

"What did you say?"

He smirked.

"You heard me."

"You have no biblical literacy, just like most of the men in Europe." She pointed at him. "Quick to mock is quick to judgement."

His eyebrows arched. "Is that a real saying, or did you just make it up?"

"What if I did? Does it matter?"

"I suppose not, but you should learn to hold your tongue lest you become an annoyance." He sensed her beautiful spirit fade into the shadowy mist like a translucent apparition, seeking a place in this realm to call home and finding none. She wore an expression of surprise, as if he and this world continually shocked her. Daisy should learn to breathe and determine how others had learned to breathe, rather than continue to choke on the horrors of this life, sucking and holding her air like an underwater swimmer.

She whisked her broom toward him. It kicked up debris.

He sneezed.

"Serves you right," she said.

He playfully threw a pillow at her, and she dodged it.

"Stop that and let me ask you a question."

Nathan grabbed another pillow.

"Fine," he said, raising its fluffy form high in the air.

She pointed an accusing finger at him and arched her eyebrows.

"Don't you *dare*, Nathan."

He grinned as he prepared to throw.

She put her hands on her hips. "Do you believe in absolute truth?"

His smile faded, and he hurled the pillow at her. It hit her squarely in the face. Daisy's cheeks flushed red and her anger rose to a fever pitch.

She clenched her fists and yelled an unintelligible word.

Her outburst took him aback. "What kind of woman asks a man such a question, and in the middle of cleaning his house, I might add?"

Daisy's cheeks lost their reddish color, and her breathing calmed.

He had to admit; it was great fun getting under her skin.

She smiled as she studied him like a scientific specimen.

Daisy picked up the pillow and heaved it toward him. He allowed it to hit his chest while he stared at her with a fiery determination. He would always be more physical than her, and they both knew it was a powerful intoxicant which unlocked her feminine sensibilities and sent her sprawling into a state of arousal to be gingerly appreciated and touched upon. His breath would blow hot against her neck and his granite expression would carve her into submission and his inexhaustible flame would spread across her skin like a wildfire through the dry plains. His masculine command over her will stirred the fire within him, too, if he were inclined to be honest.

The pillow dropped harmlessly to the floor.

Daisy took a step forward and picked it up. She waited for his nod.

He complied with her need for submission, and she tossed the pillow onto the couch. There was a pause of silence between them, as they each recalibrated the flavor of the air and the glint in one another's eyes.

She occupied a portion of his space, if but for a moment. For Daisy as she stood with eyes affixed on him, it seemed to be enough, although each understood more would be required in the near approach of dawn, and he should give the matter over to reflection, for their combined lives were to hang in the balance until the verdict was uttered—to love and hold, or to betray and abandon. To give her a life or take it from her forever.

Daisy climbed the stone walls of his heart like a creeping ivy and rafted across the deep sea of his defiant intelligence with a wild abandon, sadly and outrageously unaware of the natural effect she had on him. The mystery of her sudden appearance led him to question the varying levels of his delusion and his capacity for derangement as if he were incarcerated in the asylum on Arsenal Road, a prisoner of the world within and also without, a detractor of the very idea of love, but a practitioner of its charms and embraces, unable to live beyond its means, enraptured by the feminine beauty of the woman who now stood menacingly before him. She would allow him to wander and to hide no more, as he had done for ten years in the arms of a woman who needed to be needed more than she longed for his recovery and resurgence into the immediate community, essential as he was in medical and family matters. Daisy enforced a kind but authoritative hold on his spirit, or what passed for a spirit within his warped and confused psyche, and she meant to take him all the way to the church altar and beyond, to a state of grace and sanctified existence under the watchful eyes of the Most High, the same deity who lounged and stared, but did nothing useful.

Her eyes fell on him with an attentive devotion. Clearly, she sensed the conflict within him because it was also swirling like a peculiar storm within her, roaming and inspecting, searching for signs or inscriptions. "You may find bliss in your ignorance and want," she said, "but it has crippled your life." He wished to move noiselessly across their divide and kiss her mouth.

His pride had other ideas. "It's my life to maim."

Her bearing carried a tilt of intimacy, which could almost pass for romantic love. It was a new sentiment for him, unfelt since his boyhood longings for Catherine as they had strolled along the lane in Benton Place, and for the first time in years, he was deathly afraid of a painful loss.

Daisy's voice fell low and hesitant. "Nathan, I sometimes think you are at a fork in the road, deciding which direction to take, the simple path toward Thomas Hannah's fate or the uphill trail leading to Christ. There's no in between, only a choice which must be made by us all."

"I'm no murderer." There was a pause, as he was unsure of the truth of his statement, and then a firm nod of his head, made with a full and lasting commitment, only just realized. "Of that fact, I can assure you."

She shook her head, unwilling to accept the sincerity of his intent, expressing with her eyes and her breath and her lips the urgency of her need, and the perpetual desire which searched for an outlet. "You have the heart of a murderer, Nathan. We all do, though we may not care to admit it."

Her words were more easily said inside than out, for in the light of the ferocious day, when bones cracked and screams were shouted above the whistle of a pounding locomotive, when blood spattered and then sunk lazily into the dirt, when corn and wolves and the footsteps of a killer flanked on all sides, it was a simple task to frame one's virtue like a landscape or to pretend each day was ripe and delicious, made for the picking.

"It's easy to say, my dear, when you haven't seen death up close."

She recited Psalm 17:9-12. "Protect me from wicked people who attack me, from murderous enemies who surround me. They are without pity. Listen to their boasting! They track me down and surround me, watching for the chance to throw me to the ground. They are like hungry lions, eager to tear me apart—like young lions hiding in ambush."

"More poetic hot air," he said, recalling his time on the *Oneida* amid the self-proclaimed pillars of society, each man filled with gas and dust, offering his most worthy of deferential protestations to a deafening wall of political bureaucracy bent on world domination but calling itself a meritocracy which cowered to the will of the voting public, as if that would ever pass muster in the halls of the elite and the seething radicals who with a grin and a handshake called themselves moral. "You should run for president."

He went to the stairs and sat down while Daisy barked at the workers.

Ten minutes passed.

A flurry of activity surrounded and encapsulated him, superb in the rashness of its dispatch, crude in its ability to create order from his chaos.

Daisy hugged his neck and then ordered him to read his book in his hospital office. "Someday, I hope we can share a language of love. It would mean so much to my withered soul, and I think it's also what you crave."

She lingered for a moment and then turned.

He surrendered to her enthusiasm and left her firmly in control of his home. As he walked along Locust Street, he considered how far they had come, both individually and collectively. Nathan was the principal force which bound them together, and Daisy was the obedient companion, loyal to a fault, never too tired to help the man of her dreams accomplish any task, be it mountainous or microscopic. There was no doubt about the intensity of their devouring lack, only the lengths each would trek to fill the gaps with a substance other than poison. Daisy Lawrence had captured his heart like no other, and he would fight to stand tall and strong in her forest of ever bending trees. The tiny path which led to her heart was narrow, but it led onward with an unyielding grace and a mercy undeserved, certainly by the likes of Nathan Marsh. He would hug the sides of her precipice like a timid traveler in a dangerous land. His fear was bold and wide, but her love was found in equal measure. Could his own dislodge from its hole in the soggy river bottom and match her ascent and sustain the dizzying heights?

There could be no repetition of his failure with Catherine Belmont.

This time, the fight was for life itself.

EIGHTEEN

After the patients fell asleep, Nathan and Daisy talked into the night, glad for a distraction from the circus called Belmont Hospital, the center of the all the world's tragedy under one bright canvas. They were each particular about their daily tasks and appreciated the chance to sit together for a pleasant dinner—made special by the cook—just the two of them alone at last, unbound from the plentiful supply of confusion which greeted them in the bitter folds of gloom, those moments of darkness when each struggled to escape the harm of their own pasts and put their focus on the present, flashes when each felt like a criminal who had stolen their credentials or faked their experiences and stowed away on a ship bound for nowhere, pirates who would soon walk the plank as felonious imposters.

These two partners in crime—otherwise known as practitioners of surgical medicine and experimental psychology—now sat in Nathan's office, well guarded from the burdensome millstone of day, calm in their repose, and happy in their affections, each flimsy in their conviction for freedom.

A slight noise from the main hall found their ears.

Nathan opened his office door and listened.

"Anything?"

He shook his head and then closed the door.

"I'm surprised you can stay so calm." Daisy gave him a wide smile.

He resumed his earlier position in his desk chair. "Why?"

She wished to unearth the stability of his mind at present and the mood which accompanied it, unwilling to allow his grumpy and callous exterior to paint the portrait, as this was his normal demeanor, and it was merely a cover for a far more sinister unknown. "It's not every day one attends a morning sentencing and then watches a man hang in the afternoon."

"Did I mention they allowed me to speak to Thomas before his death?"

Her posture stiffened. "Why would you do such a thing?"

"After all your preaching, I wondered if Thomas felt contrition."

"Well, did he?"

"I wouldn't call him remorseful."

"What then? You must relieve my suspense."

"He freely admitted his many heinous crimes. It lifted a burden from his spirit, and he fell into a giddy mood. As I stood with him, a priest arrived and offered last rites, but Thomas sneered and waved him off."

Daisy leaned forward, her eyes lit with quick excitement. "What did he say? I can't imagine shooing a priest away when I'm about to meet my maker." She held her position, awaiting his response.

"He said, 'I don't need your God.' That was all there was to it."

She shrugged. "Thomas sounds a bit like you."

"The notion occurred to me on the way home."

She gave him a look of concern. "You seem tired. Are you alright?"

"Yes," he said, nodding and smiling. "I too feel a weight has been lifted. Perhaps Thomas and I were two peas in a pod."

She threw a look at the window to relieve the anger which rose within her and then shallowed her breath. "That phrase must only apply to us, not to you and some madman who murdered innocents for sport."

A shout erupted from the main hall.

Nathan smirked at Daisy. She gave him a smirk in reply.

"What now?"

She slid her chair backward. "It must be Susanna, caught up in her nightly sleepwalk. It agitates Heinrich, and he calls out in distress. Our orderlies complain about it each morning as I come down for work."

"Let's go," said Nathan, standing.

Downstairs, Susanna raised her arms to each side and ran in circles. Nathan eased behind her and wrapped his arms gently about her waist, momentarily caught inside her annular frolic. He joined Susanna in a light rendition of some indiscernible tune, humming the brisk and cheerful melody which emanated from the blend of their twisted souls. She brought her fingers against his beard and stroked it with great fondness, as if she hadn't been touched by a man of profound strength for many years. Daisy took Susanna's hands and led the pair of skylarks toward her bed.

Once there, she tucked Susanna under the covers. "It's all better now," she said kindly. "Have a good night's sleep." Daisy smiled wistfully at the poor woman and felt a stir of regret. She sensed a faint prompting and a mutual ambition to love and to obey and to belong to someone worthy.

"I want to dance," said Susanna in a childlike voice.

Her arms fluttered about like carefree butterflies.

"You can dance every day, but for now, let's get our rest."

"Miss Daisy, you must promise to watch me dance in the morning." Susanna dropped her arms and frowned. "Please say you will."

"It will be my utmost pleasure."

Susanna pulled the sheet over her chin and used the child's voice again. "Would you pray a psalm for me?"

Daisy was taken aback. "I thought you wanted nothing to do with God. Has something changed your mind? I'd like to believe it's true."

"I used to read Psalm 18 to my newborn baby before she died."

Daisy gasped and traded a glance with Nathan. It was the first mention of Susanna's past trauma. "Did your daughter like the psalms?"

Susanna curled into a fetal position and placed her thumb inside her mouth. After a few seconds of sucking like a baby, she pulled it out and affixed her eyes to it. "I wanted to be a good mother once."

"I'll bet you loved your little girl."

Susana nodded.

"The verses soothed her and helped her decide."

"Decide?"

"To leave this world for a better place."

Tears coursed down Daisy's cheeks. "What was her name?"

"She didn't have one." Susanna slammed her hands onto the bedding and grabbed it hard with her fingers. She stared at the ceiling. "I wanted to call her Beth, but we never had a chance to give her the name."

Susanna's fingers released the clumps of bedding.

Daisy swiped at her tears, and her moist fingers retrieved her Bible.

"Beth, it is then."

The leather cover dried her fingers as she flipped to Psalm 18. "This one is very long, having fifty verses, and I would be honored to pray it aloud for you and for Beth. I hope it gives you both a sense of peace."

Susanna clutched the covers. "Me, too."

The poor woman drifted into a mellow slumber as Daisy completed her recitation. She surveyed the other patients who were sound asleep. "When I see them finally reach a state of serenity, it makes me smile." She settled into her chair and clutched her Bible to her chest. Unlike the others, she would work here without receipt of a single wage. They needed her desperately.

Nathan put his hand on her arm and squeezed.

"I've had enough of our mayhem for one night."

"You had a horrid experience with Thomas this afternoon."

"Yes."

"It's to be expected." She hesitated. "Will you sit with me for a bit longer? I'll go to my room soon, but for now, I want to watch them sleep."

He nodded.

A few minutes later Daisy stood and stretched, thankful for the return to quiet on the floor. She made rounds along the perimeter of the beds and discovered Ida asleep in the far corner of the hall. She approached the young girl and nudged her. Ida sprang to life and bit her hand.

Daisy yanked her arm away from the little terror.

"Ouch! Not again!"

The room grew loud with the calls from distressed patients who flailed about in their beds. They muttered accusations and cried out for help.

As Daisy nursed her wound, Nathan grabbed Ida by the back of the hair. He dragged her down the line and tossed the girl onto her bed.

Ida scrambled under the covers.

Daisy backed two steps away from him. "Never do that again."

He yelled in her direction, startling her.

"I'll do what I see fit in my hospital!"

Daisy stormed away in a huff, as she'd seen Walter do many times.

Frank was probably right. Her antagonistic but highly intelligent colleague at La Salpêtrière had romantic intentions for her, after all.

Nathan had once again hurt her feelings. Why was he such a brute?

She considered a return trip to Europe. She could make a new start.

Her eyes fell to the floor as she paced in her room.

Such nonsense was out of the question.

I burned those bridges. There is nowhere left but here.

At four in the morning, they drank coffee and disagreed over methods. When they had exhausted their momentum, they laughed at silly things, intoxicated by a lack of sleep and pleased to have worked through their earlier confrontation with such ease. They might yet make a lovely couple.

James Clifton called out from the main room.

They scrambled downstairs and observed him at the window.

His hand pointed toward the street. "The pregnant dog is back," he said. "She's very sick. You must check on her right now."

"I'm not that kind of doctor," Nathan said.

James shook his head. "You don't care about anyone but yourself."

Nathan sighed.

"That's not true, James. I've been trying to reach you for weeks."

"Then bring Sophie inside so we can make her feel better."

Daisy put her hand on James' shoulder, and he recoiled at her light touch. "I'm sorry, James, but I hoped to offer you a bit of affection."

"Sophie will give me all I need."

Nathan grew intrigued. "Why do you call the dog Sophie?"

"I had one just like her as a boy. It was her name."

"One what?"

"A German Shepherd."

"I see," Nathan said.

James shook his head once more. "You see only what you want to see."

Shirley cried out. "Someone bring me my blue blanket!"

Ed tried to console her, and when she wouldn't calm down, he cried.

She slammed her fists on the bed and thrashed about, mimicking the effects of being choked to death. Her eyes bulged into frightful shrieks which tormented those who dared look at her, and the muffled gurgles sent Ed onto the floor, where he fell into yet another gripping seizure.

Nathan sprinted up the stairs.

Daisy flung open the stairwell door and called after him.

"Where are you going? We have to deal with these patients!"

"I forgot my surprise!"

A few moments later, he returned with a blue blanket.

He handed it to Shirley, and she hugged it against her chest.

"That was nice of you," said Daisy, lost in the throes of admiration.

After Shirley drifted to sleep, Daisy ushered James to the rocking chairs for a conversation. She hoped he might disclose a few details from his hazy background and ease the magnitude of his misery.

He gave her a concerned look. "Will you search for Sophie?"

"Tomorrow." Nathan sat on the far side of Daisy. "I promise."

James rocked in his chair. "Alright."

"Please tell us about your past," Daisy said. "It might do you some good in the meantime." She hesitated. "We are here to listen."

James touched her arm and lowered his voice. "You are a most beautiful woman, Miss Lawrence, almost as pretty as Catherine Belmont."

Daisy stirred in her seat, unsure how to take the compliment.

Nathan's face contorted into a slight grimace. "Let's get on with it. There are other sick people in this room, and we don't have all day."

Daisy frowned at Nathan and then cast a reassuring smile at James. "Please tell us how you were placed at Belmont Hospital."

"Yes, mam." He looked at Nathan and then cleared his throat. "I was shot with a rifle while I raced for land in Oklahoma."

He stared at an unknown in the distance, recalling times and places. "The bullet dropped me from my horse, and I hit my head on a rock."

"Oh, my." Daisy placed a hand over her mouth.

"The gunshot wound was minor, but my head injury almost killed me."

"Why would anyone do such a thing?"

"The soldier who shot me was mired in avarice," James said. "He coveted the same parcel of land and would do anything to get it."

Catherine awakened and listened to James' story for several minutes. She seemed enthralled and amazed by his adventurous background, enjoying the warmth and smallness of his tale, while climbing like a rider into his mind, bound for the farthest reaches of his imagination and fathoming the purpose of his drive. "Before coming here, I toured Oklahoma with my husband, Martin," she said sincerely. "It's beautiful country, and on a clear day we could see for miles." Catherine's eyes shifted about nervously, as if she contemplated the vagrant breeze which she noted in James Clifton's countenance, his deportment laden with the need for open spaces and fragrant flowers, a tranquil and pleasurable land of repose, where only the bees took violent action against the senses, and the woodlands were alive with the butterflies of summer, whispering acres where birds sang without melancholy, the vague suggestion of death lost to a time forgotten.

"I wanted to build a new life out of the soft, rich earth," James said. "Once my farm prospered, I would take a wife."

"There's still time," said Catherine in a convinced way.

Nathan arched his eyebrows. "You seem frightened of the corrupt soldier who shot you, James, and also of the man who killed your friend from the bakery. Well, you can rest easy because Thomas Hannah was hanged yesterday afternoon." He sighed. "I watched the proceedings."

"There are other outlaws like Thomas. What about them?"

"My husband is like him," Catherine said. "Martin beat me daily, and then he left me for dead. I was naked on the street in the center of town, covered in my blood." She wiped tears from her cheeks. "I'm still here, and so are you." Catherine gave Nathan a wide smile and pointed at him. "I'm once again with the love of my life, and he fills me with a renewed hope."

Daisy tensed and looked toward the front door.

"Don't worry, my dear." Catherine gave her an innocent smile. "He's no longer in love with me, but the knowledge of his presence in this hospital gives me enough peace to continue living in this world, at least for now."

Nathan sat up straight. "What do you mean, Catherine?"

She reached over and squeezed James' hand. "I saw you do this, Daisy, and I wondered if it helped him. You have such a *womanly* touch."

"It did," said James after a moment.

"Does it help when I do it?"

"Even more."

"Then I shall squeeze your hand every day for the rest of my life."

James beamed for the first time since his arrival.

Daisy stood and poked Nathan. "We should take our leave."

Nathan smiled at the loudness and the brightness of her dismay. She knew he had enjoyed Catherine's playful banter, and he also rather liked to watch Daisy squirm. His ex-wife's arrival had blown off any remaining pretense between them, leaving a diffused magic in its wake, the glow of their wills dimming like a garden lantern at morning light. Soon the time for graciousness would evaporate, and what would be left was anyone's guess. Each possibility was predestined to be void of happiness if Catherine's will were to prevail upon Nathan. It was up to Daisy to thwart Catherine's every move, and she would exhaust the woman's mental faculties at every turn, the expanse of Daisy's intellect being broader and deeper than any fragile delights Catherine could hope to offer a man, her bodily strength having not yet returned and her looks not as fair after receipt of Martin's battery.

She gave Nathan a slight glare. He turned toward Catherine and James.

"We'll be upstairs in my office if you need anything."

"We'll be alright, my love."

"Stop saying those things," said Nathan, scowling. "It makes me crazy."

"Join the club, dear." She laughed. "I enjoy making you blush."

Nathan walked to the stairs and stopped. He wheeled and threw her a harsh look. "Good *night*, Catherine. You need to get some sleep."

She giggled like a schoolgirl.

"May I leave you with a word from the Lord?" asked Daisy.

Catherine's expression grew more serious. "If you must."

"Here goes. 'For our present troubles are small and won't last very long. Yet they produce for us a glory that vastly outweighs them and will last forever!' That's from 2 Corinthians 4:17."

"Should it mean something to me?"

"It meant something to you once, before the loss of your children and your husband. I read an inscription in one of your Bibles."

"Which husband, my dear? I have so many suitors." She flung her hand up in the air like a woman of nobility. "It's arduous to recall their names."

Daisy smiled. "Your aphasia is playing tricks with your memory, but in time you'll remember who was most important."

"Were you important once, Daisy?"

Catherine paused.

"To a*nyone*?"

"There was a sister, but I let her down."

"It seems you fail at everything you try." Catherine smiled with a soft tint which highlighted the polished cut of her features, her cheeks full of a rose-like color, the formerly severe lines receding, as if all annoyance or exhaustion had been driven into the night by an internal will stronger than iron. Daisy took a step backward, feeling her blonde curls turning a slight shade of gray. She thought of Patrice, how tired she had been near the end of her existence and how pleased she seemed at the notion of sweet surrender. Daisy resembled her mother in nature and now felt the same heaviness of spirit. As before, at the cemetery, Catherine looked deeply into the darkness of Daisy's eyes, noting her desire for the beautiful brilliance of dusk. As if feeding from Daisy's depleted store of energy, Catherine brightened. She gestured romantically toward the stairs, and Daisy heard a faint whisper. *He's mine, you know.* Catherine winked ferociously at her ex-husband, and then her eyes drifted up and down Daisy's frame. Catherine's entity took inventory of every blemish and imperfection, documenting them with glee. It was alive as much as Daisy was not, and it wanted what little was left of her crumbling soul. A wicked smile crept across Catherine's face. She waved dismissively, as if Daisy were a bug to be squashed. The world stopped on its axis as the entity spoke through Catherine in a voice only Daisy could hear.

Run along now and play with my little Nathan.

Around daybreak, Daisy had only a vague purpose. She felt a sudden and dire need to eat a decent meal, something conventional but yet impressive, the kind which helped a person greet the new day. She needed to assemble a firmer foundation, as her soul was worn and patched, and her high-laced ambitions, which seemed appropriate in Paris, were now tearing through her like a plague of locusts. Daisy gave the room a tentative look and smartly cleared her mind of any sight or sound. Still, her stomach howled in protest, her continual confrontations with Catherine having created the tiniest but worthiest of ulcers, which presently threatened to rupture, the portrait of which Daisy fought to keep from becoming a torturous reality.

Nathan tossed his notebook on his desk and frowned at her.

"We cannot leave these patients. We barely got them to sleep last night."

"I must eat something, Nathan, and we promised to look for Sophie."

A buoyant ray of light entered through the window behind his chair, scandalously accosting Daisy in her time of need. She had fallen madly in love with Nathan, but she had no power over him, at least none worth a mention, and he gladly accepted help from anyone but her, case in point being the eccentric woman who ran the boarding house nearby and who fashioned atrocious and largely inedible meals, mostly consisting of liver.

He looked at his office door as if he expected a visitor. "Miss Cecilia graciously cooks breakfast for the hospital. She'll be over soon with covered dishes." He hesitated. "We wouldn't want to be rude, would we?"

"Of course not, but I cannot stand her food."

"So you want me to fire her? We'll be on our own with no one to cook."

"I have a plan for our kitchen, and I need you to trust me."

He must listen to her need to console a persistent ulcer.

Nathan threw up his hands. "Terrific."

They walked to Miss Wallace's three streets over for breakfast, while scanning the alleyways for a pregnant German Shepherd.

There was no trace of Sophie or her litter of newborn puppies.

As they passed Miss Cecilia near the end of the block, Nathan pointed toward the hospital and told her to walk right in. Nurse Pratt would pay her for the food out of petty cash. His uncharacteristic kindness baffled Daisy.

They ate eggs, bacon, and biscuits, mostly in silence. It was a nice change of pace. Daisy appreciated an opportunity to sit with him without the forced necessity of shallow talk or, even worse, deep discussions of this or that, which usually highlighted their differences in temperament.

At the conclusion of breakfast, Daisy led Nathan to the front entrance of Sheila's brothel. She was unsure of her path forward and needed an ally.

"Why are we here?"

"Please take me to her room."

"Whose room?"

"Must we play these childish games? You're behaving like Susanna."

Nathan stood in mute protest for several minutes, but finally relented.

As they marched up the stairs, Daisy trembled, her senses keenly alerted to danger. She knocked once on the door and then invited herself inside.

"It's you," said Sheila sharply.

"Please don't be afraid." Daisy held up a palm. "I come in peace."

At the first sight of Nathan, Sheila leapt out of her chair.

She threw herself at him with every ounce of her constrained desire. "My love, you finally came to see me! I've been so sad in your absence."

Daisy looked about the room briefly and then inspected the prostitute's belongings, aware her actions made Nathan and Sheila feel awkward. She couldn't believe the corner she'd been pushed into or how she had become the primary obstacle to Nathan and Catherine's reconnection.

She asserted herself as best she could manage. "Your room makes for a private watering hole, a place away from the crowded barroom downstairs."

There was an uneasiness in Sheila's face. "What's it to you?"

Daisy's voice fell low. "I'll bet you learn a lot about men in here, what they think, who they like, how they intend to live out their lives."

"Judge me all you want. I don't care."

Daisy shook her head. "It's just the opposite. I'd like to help you."

Sheila crossed her arms. "I trust no one, especially your kind."

"Which is?"

"A preachy woman who's holier than thou."

Nathan laughed. "She's got you pegged."

Undeterred, Daisy continued. "May I quote scripture?"

"I knew you would."

Daisy looked anxiously at Nathan before she spoke. "Trust in the Lord with all your heart; do not depend on your own understanding."

Sheila shrugged. "So?"

"It's Proverbs 3:5."

"Your fancy words mean nothing to me."

Daisy sat down in a chair by the door.

Sheila arched her eyebrows. "Well, help yourself, lassie."

Daisy put her face in her hands as she realized the situation was useless. She had planned to use Sheila as a wedge between Catherine and Nathan, but there was no place in John Belmont's hospital for a former prostitute, stuck as he was on proper convention. It was a spur-of-the-moment decision to drop by Sheila's boudoir, and Daisy was most likely mistaken in her thinking, but she was losing patience with tedious people, and her world was now filled with them. She must find a remedy, some relevant flash of hope.

Sheila felt herself gain the upper hand. It showed brightly on her face.

"We are waiting. Has the cat got your tongue?"

An idea settled itself inside Daisy's mind, which carried the required bolt of logic. It was both pressing and concerning, and it just might work.

Daisy clasped her hands in her lap and beamed.

"I have an idea."

Shelia gave her a look of suspicion. "Oh?"

"You'll take my place as Nathan's housemaid. We recently discussed his move into in an empty office at the hospital. He spends most of his time there, anyway, so it makes sense. It's best if he remains in proximity to the patients, as they need him at all hours of the day and night."

Nathan nodded and pointed to Daisy.

"The same goes for her. There are moments when she's the only one who can help them." He smiled. "As much as it pains me to say it out loud."

"Then what will I do at your house? Read the newspaper?"

Daisy chuckled.

"No, dear. You will keep the place clean. I took care of it yesterday, and you'll do it in the future. Once you get his affairs in order, you can cook meals for the hospital. We're tired of eating Miss Cecelia's food."

Sheila crossed her arms again. "How do you know I can cook?"

"I don't, but I'm leaving it up to the Most High, who guides me in all things. He hasn't chastised me, so I must be doing something correctly."

Sheila seemed shaken. "Are you trying to get rid of me or push me into Nathan's arms? It must be one or the other. I'm not a stupid woman."

Daisy grinned. "You are very perceptive, but in this case, as I mentioned, I am placing the matter into the Lord's hands. I want you as close to this man as possible, so there's no ambiguity when his final choice is made."

Sheila sat on her bed and looked at the floor. "I see."

Nathan smiled at Daisy and spoke as if he understood her feminine motivation. "Keep your friends close and your enemies closer?"

Daisy smiled back at him. "Of course."

"I'm a strong Irish lass, and I can cook just fine."

Daisy slapped her knee. "Then it's settled. Shall we pack your things?"

Sheila looked at Nathan and then at Daisy. "I suppose it's worth a try."

She quickly pointed a finger at Daisy.

"Don't be thinking I will answer to the likes of you."

"You'll answer only to me." Nathan moved close to her and put his hand on her shoulder. His touch diffused her worry. "Understand?"

"That's better," said Sheila softly.

She squeezed his hand and stared at Daisy. "What do you really want from me?" Her voice fell low and humble. "I'm nothing, and no one on this earth cares about me. So you can cease with your moral pretension."

"I care." Nathan sat beside her. "Although I often cannot show it."

She gently bumped her shoulder against his.

"You don't love me, Nathan. You never did."

He sighed. "I'm a confused man who doesn't know what he wants. If you realized what I have suffered, you would understand."

"I came to America with plans for marriage and a family. Do you think for one second I wanted to become a prostitute who lives in a brothel?"

His face flushed red. "Honestly, it hadn't crossed my mind."

Nathan placed his hand on her thigh. Daisy stiffened at the sight.

"You have great potential," he said earnestly. "You're an intelligent and capable woman who has suffered misfortune and who needs to become whole again. Let us help you, for the sake of my sanity, if nothing else. I couldn't bear to see you end up in the hog pen." He hesitated, as if the words choked him. "I've lost so many people in my life and I don't think I could bear to lose you, too." He gazed into Sheila's eyes. "Please don't run from this chance at redemption." He turned toward Daisy and gave her an appreciative look. "Since we met at Union Depot on the Fourth of July, this woman has taught me to accept help and to seek my reclamation. It's a painful process, but a worthy one, and I know she can do likewise for you."

"You don't love me. Admit it."

His eyes sought permission from Daisy. Her nod gave it to him.

He leaned close to Sheila. They had shared a heartfelt intimacy, and it showed in their affectionate deportment. Even if it wasn't love, it was worthy of acceptance. They were like Adam and Eve after the fall, two children in adult bodies, who scavenged the burdensome landscape for food and shelter and escape from themselves, knowing with certainty the evil which lurked within their bones and their marrow, terrified of their perpetual propensity for wickedness, stooping to pick up their damaged egos while darting to a far corner in horrified alarm, the entirety of iniquity suddenly at their feet.

"As I mentioned, I hold you in high regard."

Daisy leaned forward. "Be honest with her, Nathan."

"I don't want to hurt her any further."

Sheila squeezed his hand. "The truth is difficult sometimes, but it's also necessary. If you don't love me, please allow me to move on from you." She lifted his hand and kissed it. "Perhaps another man might feel passionately for me, and we might have a life together."

"You certainly deserve it."

"You're making me furious," Daisy said. "*Tell her.*"

"Alright! Enough!"

Nathan took Sheila's hands in his own. "You are a wonderful woman, but I do not love you, at least not in the romantic sense."

Sheila pulled her hands away and looked at the floor. "Of course I knew it all along, but I always hoped you would open yourself to me someday."

"I'm sorry for causing you pain, Sheila. I never intended it."

She faced him and wiped tears from her eyes.

"Thank you for being sincere, Nathan."

"I value decency in others," he said, "so I should more often practice it."

Sheila reluctantly looked at Daisy. "I'm not your competition, you know. His ex-wife is much more dangerous to your battle plans."

"She was his past, and you were his present."

"You hope to be his future?"

"It's time for something good to happen, don't you think?"

"Prostitutes rarely have happy endings," said Sheila, glancing around with a concealed annoyance. "I had nearly given up hope."

Daisy was glad to have found a cohort. She stood in front of her new friend and extended her hand. "Then allow us to show you the love of Jesus. He will never forsake you, and He knows your pain all too well."

Sheila carried a bag as the group stepped into the hallway.

A tear coursed down her cheek. "I'll miss this place."

"You and Nathan bonded here," Daisy said.

Sheila gave her a painful nod. "Yes, and I'm grateful for his kinship."

She paused.

"There's more to it."

Daisy put her hand on Sheila's arm and gently squeezed.

"What then?"

"I was a naïve lass when I came to America, and now I'm a full-grown woman who knows her own mind." She rubbed the door. "This room kept me from certain death and taught me to stand up for myself."

Nathan spoke softly into her ear. "You'll make someone a fine wife."

Daisy took Sheila's bag. "And a mother to a lucky child."

Saturday evening, Daisy and Nathan set out in his wagon toward John Belmont's estate in Vandeventer Place. The moonless night set the lane into a bleak and desolate condition, where a gray mist settled into each hollow and onto each hedgerow, and shadows enlivened each formless tree. The roadway hilled upward as they moved west, away from the river. Noises to their right and to their left startled Daisy, and although her logical mind surmised their origin to be squirrel or rabbit or bird, her emotional heart grew frightened of the possibility of attack. Monsters of the night which gouged eyes and chewed flesh were of secondary import to the temptations which threatened her relevance and his resolve to leave the caverns of his past. Nathan's present life offered hope for a better tomorrow, but to him it seemed a burdensome ordeal, and he resisted Daisy's call to adventure.

Sheila drove Daisy to impatience as she moved into Nathan's home and cleaned it thoroughly on her first attempt. Worse, she cooked fine meals for the hospital, and the hysterics immediately took a shine to her nature. The lovely Irish lass was beautiful and captivating and energetic in her need to please Nathan in all things, keeping alive the dim hope of his love. For ten years, she had tempted him with whiskey and ease and the gratification only she could offer a man, and Nathan was lulled into neglect and ruin as he pursued his animal appetites, his will blunted and given over to indulgence.

An excursion was in order, made especially so by James Clifton's urgent pleas to search for Sophie, his imaginary childhood German Shepherd.

Their journey took them from the hospital near Forest Park through the countryside, and as their wagon dipped and wound, footsteps stirred behind them continually. Daisy told herself nothing was there, and she was a fool to look, but still she craned her neck to confirm the unfounded aspect of her fears. Her eyes fell on the road once more, and she grew satisfied with her safety for but a moment, as nebulous shapes on each side of the lane became fearsome lions ready to pounce. She leaned to her right and fathomed the bowels of a ditch, made deeper by the plunge of darkness, and she then peered behind Nathan's back at the murky bog to their left, which played host to any number of slithery creatures who made terrible sounds.

An oak up ahead was hollow, and a man was said to have been hung inside a gibbet cage from the overhang of a limb, a beastly practice thought to be extinct in the modern Industrial Age. She looked up as the wagon passed underneath and swore to keep her sanity, no matter what might befall her over the course of the evening, as she had seen madness up close in the form of her mother, and she vowed never to fall into the same trap. Steps thundered near the back of their wagon, and her head swiveled, her eyes hoping to catch the perpetrator as he made a criminal leap into their midst.

"Please stop your fidgeting," said Nathan with a scowl.

"This area looks different at night."

He snapped the reins. "I thought you grew up on a farm."

"Yes, and there were nights when I almost lost my grip."

He stopped the horses and turned to her. "What happened?"

Her nerves calmed as the breeze kissed her neck.

"Nothing of substance, really, but there were times when I heard the siren song of the nightingale, even during the light of day, when I strolled through the dark woods or sat atop my high ledge we called Big Rock. It seemed there was a spiritual battle which raged about me, each side vying for my allegiance, and each determined to best the other's advance."

He smirked. "Oh."

Her lips pinched. "You asked me what happened, and I told you."

"I should've known better."

There was a rustle to their right.

Daisy shifted in her seat and then poked Nathan, who jolted slightly as the man behind the tree spoke aloud. "Hello there, mister and miss big dealie. How's your evening fairing under such a moonless sky?"

He sniffed the air. "Mossy, if you ask me."

"Have you been following us?" asked Nathan indignantly.

"Why, yes, I believe I have done."

"For what purpose?"

"That one beside you helped my good wife file a report against me."

Daisy gasped. She peered through the gloom.

"Are you the man from the park?"

He gave her a generous smile. "That would be me, madam."

The clouds parted, and rays of moonlight set the man aglow.

He stepped from behind the tree, a pistol in hand.

Nathan sighed. "Whom do you plan to kill tonight?"

Daisy whispered to him. "This is the lunatic who almost shot me."

Nathan gave her a harsh look and turned to the man.

"I asked you a question, sir."

"You have essential commerce elsewhere?"

"Yes, with a party who expects a return on his investment."

The man waved his pistol as he approached the wagon. He surveyed the emptiness of the cargo bed and gave a low whistle. "Not much to rob."

"You'll get nothing from us, regardless. I have no time for highwaymen."

"I am without means since I left my former abode, my wife having sent me to Arsenal Road for my trouble and having taken our daughter to her parents in another portion of the state. You see my dilemma."

"I do, but I'd wager the asylum fed you well."

The lunatic nodded.

"They do serve a fine breakfast, three eggs and a slab of ham."

"Then why did you leave? The doctors might have helped you."

"Escape's more the word. They prodded me half to death, asking me questions with no meaningful answer, like why did you want to kill your wife, or what makes you an unhappy man, or would you do it again?"

"Was anyone hurt as you left?"

"Those who got in my way, but that's all. I'm naturally a peaceful sort."

Nathan considered.

"I see."

"Oh, don't you worry none, because you are not in my way, and if you were, then you would no longer be breathing this unpleasant night air."

"Alright then, I'll play along. Why have you detained us?"

Daisy squeezed Nathan's leg. "Please don't provoke him."

The lunatic's eyes flickered green as he glanced at her.

He smiled, and his irregular teeth glimmered in the moonlight.

"You two seem like the married type." He held his pistol up to Nathan. "Want to take a shot at her? It quelled the anger which had built itself inside my belly, and I would have sauntered out of the park without a care in the world if my brother hadn't tackled me to the ground. He's the one who has a day of reckoning running in his direction. You mark my words, sir."

"Get his weapon," said Daisy hurriedly.

"That won't be necessary."

"Why not?"

The lunatic chuckled. "The good doctor knows if I wanted the two of you dead, it would have already been done. Isn't that right, Nathan Marsh?"

"It is, but how might you know my name? Are you a former patient?"

"Can't say I am, since I don't cotton to besotted physicians, most likely because I am a drunkard on occasion, and I know the perils which often accompany the loss of good judgement and common sense in a man."

He tipped his maltreated hat.

"Or woman."

Nathan spoke to the two horses, soothing them.

"Will you let us pass? We are late for an appointment."

"Yes, I know, with a Mr. John Belmont, the leader of our order, and a cajoler of spirits. I used to manage one of his businesses, and he took me under his wing, brought me into the fold so to speak, back when I was eaten alive by unbridled ambition and was dutiful to impress my Christian wife."

"I've had my share of difficulties with Belmont," Nathan said.

"Oh, I'm fully aware. You have been a topic of discussion for many a day, let me assure you. There are fateful plans for such a man as yourself."

Nathan's countenance muddled. "Did John send you with a message?"

The lunatic turned to Daisy. "He wasn't the one who sent me, but the other one, the light bearer who will lead us from the underworld, so we might bring ourselves up from the abyss and build a home atop the surface of the earth. He will harness the power of the sun and the moon and the waters, and we will become spirits who float about in leisurely comfort."

Nathan laughed. "You are quite delusional."

He jerked the reins, and the horses broke forth in a flash.

Daisy watched over her shoulder as the lunatic faded into oblivion.

A pistol shot rang out, and a sliver of wood flew against her back.

Nathan stopped the wagon again and rubbed her torso for any sign of an entry wound, but found none. He leaned over and noticed a gash near the top of the side rail where the bullet must have landed. It was a close call, but Daisy had survived a second encounter with the pistol waving madman.

"That was a warning," she said with a blank face.

"From whom?"

"I wish I knew."

Nathan snapped tight the reins, and the wagon surged.

As they approached the imposing wrought-iron gate at the eastern edge of Vandeventer Place, Daisy cast weary glances at the stone wall which surrounded the private enclosure. Her mind fell to lonely distress as the sombre shadows formed jagged holes in her will, and the desire to flee sped up the flow of blood within her arteries and veins. Unclean spirits towered above the walls and the iron gate, summoning them onward and at the same time castigating their naivety for undertaking such a perilous journey.

Nathan drove the team through the gate while Daisy clutched his coat.

He parked the wagon in front of John's door and helped her down.

Daisy took a cleansing breath at the stoop and tried to muster a ladylike deportment as Brenda would demand and John would likely appreciate.

A butler led them up the stairs to the second floor.

He turned to Nathan. "Please wait inside the billiard room."

"Where's Belmont? We don't have all night."

"He's been delayed by the arrival of a new partner."

The butler paused.

"I expect you will soon meet her as well."

Nathan gestured his disapproval but relented.

Daisy could not bear the silent and monotonous wait for their host, so she drifted away from her protector, and a shadowy presence surrounded her, a colorless mist of depravity and outrage, entirely deviant in its form and most effective in its unholy persuasiveness. John entered the room, and a slight gush of air brushed through her curls. She was mortally paralyzed with an awful sense of guilt, as if every accusation which had ever been uttered in the malevolent history of mankind was tangled with one another into a fierce ball of hatred and hurled at her. Daisy leaned over, and her fingers gripped the cherry arms of a silk-covered chair for dear life.

"Have a drink with me while we play billiards," said John to Nathan.

Like a boy serving his superior, the lackey complied.

"I would like to place a wager on each game. Are you of means?"

Nathan nodded.

The presence invited her to sit in the chair, and she agreed, hoping to avoid a fainting spell. She stared at the elegant fireplace, where pictures of a girl and two boys adorned the mantle, and Daisy instantly knew they were Nathan's children. The daughter, Annie, possessed a generous face which argued for her incompleteness while it simultaneously believed her father completed her. Annie liked to accompany Nathan on his medical tours through the countryside, and she entertained him as they went, enchanting as she was with her unique personality, one similar to her late grandmother, June. The older son, Eli, would have been helpful magic to an army if allowed to bloom to adulthood. He was a born leader in every way, and his father knew he would become a rogue outlaw if not raised properly. Nathan was up front in the boy's development, taking charge, unrelenting in his drive to mold Eli into a field general, even in the boy's tender youth. The youngest son, Peter, was fearful of storms and would hide under the bed to escape them. He was a born architect, a builder of lasting structures, and he detected inconsistencies of speech at an early age. His ability to concentrate outshined anyone Nathan had ever met—man, woman, boy, or girl.

John stroked each ball like a lion who toyed with his prey. He sized up each move while he grinned with a villainous delight. Every so often, he glanced at Daisy, and with each knowing look from him, the layers of anxiety piled atop of her, pressing down, pushing against her skull. She would be responsible for the carnage which would arrive in the approaching days and weeks, but she did not know the nature of her actions or the reason for them. A tunnel stretched before her, providing a glimpse of the future, and the lineage of Nathan's offspring many years ahead, in the century after next, where people ran to and fro, and knowledge was greatly increased. A man of the last days arose who led the multitudes astray like the Pied Piper, whistling a merry tune as they followed him straight into the furnace of perdition. The ghastly sight of his name made her shudder. *Jeremy Marsh.*

The entity reminded Daisy of her previous connection with Frank Kaneski and his stated desire to have a son whose bloodline would rule the world. Soon Frank would reappear at the hospital, and she should prepare her soul for a sudden departure. She shook her head. There could be no love with him after what transpired in Vienna, and, even if she considered the idea, the vile demon, Rosemarie, would kill her the next time their paths crossed. Daisy could not expect God to intervene twice for the same offence.

A guileful voice explained why Nathan could never love again, unless his special someone was a childhood friend, a woman of darkness who shared a similar background—an orphan of God's kingdom like him. Daisy was a praying daughter of the backwoods and a Bible quoting woman of renown who could never meet this qualification. As a man who suffered no fools, he would soon recognize the invariable gulf which separated them and come back to his logical senses, and on that day, she would be tossed aside like yesterday's garbage, assigned eternally to the trash heap of his memory.

Her will faded as the mist whispered into her ear.

Please tell me there's a way. I'll do anything.

A woman like June could easily capture and keep his heart, especially if this woman shared his unruly taste for death. She must be wild and free, a woman who makes others blush in crimson but feels nothing for herself.

How might I become such a woman?

Daisy should retreat from Nathan's life and venture to the high ledge near her father's winery on the Missouri River. Frank would soon be along to shepherd her gracefully to the rocks below, which had bloodlessly awaited her return for many years, knowing as she did, it was her destiny. Frank had always been tapped to escort her to the other side, and Daisy should have allowed his will to prevail in Vienna. Rosemarie's pride had gotten in the way, and she was summarily punished for her grievous mistake.

What of my love for Nathan?

Once his earthly tasks have been completed, he would join her in a comfortable rest, where they would wait together for Lucifer, the archangel who defied a tyrannical God. It would be a most joyful reunion, and Nathan would have many tales of conquests to share with her. Daisy must rely on Lucifer who was born to satisfy her best interests and whom gives his love freely and without restriction, rules and traditions having no meaning for him, only the powerful odor of burnt flesh and cries for a satisfying relief.

She received a terrifying revelation.

Nathan's wicked medical legacy would far surpass anything Frank had accomplished in Europe. Daisy's death would end Nathan's desire for love and prepare him for the woman of darkness. Jeremy Marsh would later arise from their union to lead mankind's evolution to wondrous heights.

Daisy closed her eyes and clenched her fists. She stifled a scream.

Nathan's descent into hellfire was more than she could bear.

She recited the Lord's Prayer, hoping against all hope. "Our Father in heaven, may your name be kept holy. May your Kingdom come soon. May your will be done on earth, as it is in heaven. Give us today the food we need, and forgive us our sins, as we have forgiven those who sin against us. And don't let us yield to temptation, but rescue us from the evil one."

The torturous spirit released her.

She leapt from her chair as she'd seen Sheila do at the brothel and gulped a deep breath. She exhaled loudly, which interrupted their game.

"Everything alright?" asked Nathan.

"I'm fine," she said, hardly able to make a sound.

Daisy leaned against the mantle and stared into the eyes of Nathan's children, feeling a centered kinship with them, dead as each of them were, but secure in their relationship with the hereafter, lacking in the fear of life and the dread of death. They were little figures to the larger world, urchins to be discarded from memory, but for her at this moment, they were central to the mystery of a grass covered eternity, deep as they were within the peaceful soil and the deficient coldness and the somber repose.

He gave her a harsh look and then refocused his attention on John.

She was aware of Nathan's response when she misbehaved, but she hated this foul room, contained as it was within a sprawling and menacing structure, which looked down upon the lower houses in its surrounding vicinity with a clever and sarcastic sneer. Every ostentatious tapestry and every slight knock on the door by a subservient butler and every alarming tone of the grandfather clock screamed horrible obscenities in her direction. She would tolerate little more of this abuse, as her fear mounted with each passing moment and soon it would grow into the starkness of sheer terror. John and his staff of minions bustled with the trifles of prestige, stout with the knowledge of their combined brilliance, careless in their vanity and the attention paid to details of grandeur, as only peoples of violence might.

Daisy cleared her throat and jumped into the acidic water with both feet. "Can we have a professional discussion about the hysteric patients at our hospital, or will you two play immature games all evening?"

Belmont paused and stared at her for several moments.

"What do people get for all their hard work under the sun? Generations come and generations go, but the earth never changes."

"Ecclesiastes 1:3," she said, as if speaking to a child in need of correction. "Scripture can be used by even the most evil amongst us."

"This one is fiery." Belmont sneered at her, but his bearing reflected a hesitant esteem. "You'll do well to keep your mouth closed, madam."

"She's got a point, John." Nathan's dangerous curiosity had brought him into the conversation. "We need to discuss our patients."

"Fine, let's begin." He gave them both a contemptuous expression. "The first order of business is to remove those freaks from my hospital."

"What?"

He was prepared to confirm his iniquity. "The city asylum had a few recent transfers and deaths. Their staff now has room to accept the hysteria patients. We will not continue to allow them full roam in my care."

"You must be so proud of yourself," she said scornfully.

John gave Daisy a wry smile, as if he felt a kinship with her.

"It's time for my hospital to achieve its intended purpose."

"Which is?"

"I will serve the Big Cinch in a manner which befits their position."

She explained the unpredictable improvement they'd observed in each patient over the last few days, but it made no difference to his greedy plans. Paltry advances with the lesser classes served no interest for him.

"Will you transfer your daughter to the city asylum?"

His eyes flickered. "Of course not."

"Then why the others?"

"They are a soft cushion for you both and a foolish distraction. I want Catherine to receive Nathan's undivided attention. She is his wife."

"*Was*," said Daisy irreverently.

"Phrase it however you want, Miss Lawrence." He pointed at Nathan. "My daughter will always be the mother of his children."

"The other hysteric patients in the hall form a social club of sorts," Daisy said. "It provides an outlet for her pain and a comfort when she's sad. You won't benefit her by removing them."

He dropped the cue onto the felt surface. "What real benefit do they provide? Give me something tangible."

She grew lightheaded for a few moments, but continued.

"Sometimes we are like archaeologists who dig into a patient's past to uncover the origin of their trauma." Her mind whirled at the prospect of throwing the hysterics at John like bait in a pool of piranhas.

"Is that the only way? It seems a waste of time and money."

She searched for something, anything, to placate him.

Her guilt compounded with each ticking second.

The presence goaded her into submission. She must offer John a prize worthy of his status in society. She would give the patients over to him fully and completely and for all time. There could be no reward for them in the eternal, as their names would forever be removed from the Book of Life.

A much bolder and louder voice shouted into her ear.

You must do it now!

Daisy heard herself speak words aloud. She could not stop their flow.

"Neurologists in Europe have had success with hypnosis techniques."

John gave her a look of surprise. "Mesmerism? Surely, you jest."

Daisy was shocked at how easily she had abandoned her values, and the regret made her want to run into the unforgiving wilderness. "It's a topic of much controversy, to be sure, but the results speak for themselves."

He pondered her comment. "You train them to perform tricks on command? I read something about it in the paper a few years ago."

Time seemed to stop within the confines of the room.

Daisy was alone with a much more formidable entity, the leader of their monstrous pack. This presence seethed with a lust for raw power.

Tell him what he needs to know.

The Prince of St. Louis commands you!

She would pay a price for her actions. Daisy must stop providing John with ammunition for his ravenous weapon, whatever form it might take within his pathologic mind. If she refused to continue the conversation, perhaps time would remain at a standstill.

Do it now or I will destroy your precious Nathan!

The words confused her. Nathan could not be hurt, for he had been chosen to father a lineage which would span the centuries. She felt stronger now and would stand her ground against this loathsome enemy.

I can easily find another man. Can you say the same?

Vile laughter filled the background, terrifying her.

"You need both of us," she said, hoping it was true.

A colossal and enigmatic voice manifested, which seemed at once ancient and young, as if it searched for a world which had not yet become a reality. Daisy instantly knew its name to be Lucifer.

If he dies, you will die, both to God and to me. There will be no more chances for either of you, only an eternity of torture at my hands.

"We'll end up in the same place, regardless."

No, Daisy. You will be treated as royalty in my kingdom.

"It's what you said to Jesus."

I meant every word then and I mean every word now.

She shook her head, calling his bluff. "You won't kill Nathan."

I will have John murder him in front of you tonight.

A vision of Nathan's bloody death unfurled before her.

She must protect him at all costs, even if it meant harming the hysteric patients under her care. He was the love of her life, and she would gladly die the second death for him. The words which condemned her poured from her wicked lips with a rebellious wrath. It was too late to turn back now. The verdict was inescapable, and the awaiting punishment would be worse than Sodom or Gomorrah, where the elements melted with a fervent heat.

"Alright, you win."

Eve said the same to me in the garden. I always get what I want.

Time resumed, and Daisy began the walk toward her destiny.

"We want the patients to feel comfortable enough to describe their past and to reconnect with the associated emotional pain."

She paused.

"Yes, to your point, we can influence patient behavior."

"You've given me much to consider, Miss Lawrence." John placed the cue stick in its rack. "Now leave me to contemplate my next move."

Nathan took her hand.

"Let's go before you do any further damage."

John's eyes opened wide, and his nose flared. "Listen to him, Miss Lawrence. Ideas can be dangerous if not harnessed."

When they reached the front door, John called to Nathan.

"Remember my previous warning. I want my daughter given back to me whole and without blemish. That is your task and your responsibility."

"I haven't forgotten," said Nathan defiantly. "Her or your threats."

Daisy resisted the presence one last time. "John, you cannot scare us into submission. Jesus Christ is our rock and our salvation."

At her utterance of the name of Jesus, she felt no relief.

Had she already been damned?

"Miss Lawrence, as you well know, rocks break bones and tear human flesh. Be careful you don't lose more than a sister and a sorrowful mother. These times are most unpredictable, and I am a well-positioned man."

John's words would prove prophetic, and this evening would serve as a portent of things to come. A woman of darkness would soon emerge, an obscure combatant who would wreck what Daisy had worked to achieve.

Daisy understood this reality as completely as she knew details about his children. In her college years, she had reveled in the improper land of Paris. She was young enough to keep the past locked away in some unreachable place, never to be accessed, and to look to the future with awe and distance, caught in the moment's presence, enjoying life to the fullest. Now she was filled with the rust of a misshapen nail and the mystery of burning balls of sulphur and the prospect of eternal damnation. Her wild forest path crossed over a shining hill and descended into a land of gnarled trees and swift rivers of devilry, her layers of vice causing both interest and secrecy.

She almost collapsed as Nathan guided her along the lane, which led away from Vandeventer Place. She was thankful for his strength and his decency, which others failed to see but which was forever held within, for her to admire. Daisy's love for him grew deeper than she had previously thought possible, and she hoped his moral center would remain intact in the bitter face of temptation and persecution. Nathan would take the toughest road of life, the uphill climb toward the never ending role of Overcomer, and she would do her best to follow him on the journey, tired as she was and lost to sin. If she couldn't match him stride for stride, she would drop back and allow herself to fade into the patchwork of his background. Daisy owed him more than she could ever repay, as he restored her faith in men.

She clutched his arm and leaned close to his side.

Her walk with the Lord grew stronger with every step away from John Belmont's estate. The place was a pit of vipers, and she hoped never to return. She looked back, careful to remember the fate of Lot's wife.

NINETEEN

Psalm 19:3

They speak without a sound or word;
their voice is never heard.

August 1859

Nathan rested on a bale of hay and enjoyed the subtle breeze which wafted through the barn's front entrance. He had completed his chores early, which left enough time to relax before dinner and watch the twinkling stars as they presented themselves fully to him from the heavens. They adored him as they cherished all children, and he envied them because they were too old to be shocked by anything at all, especially the loudness of a father's drunken rage or the screams of a hysterical mother. They proceeded about the celestial without haste, their movements precise, their exultation soundless, and their insistence to inspire forever expressed.

Samuel arrived in his carriage and stumbled down the flimsy last step, falling into the dirt with a loud thud. Nathan stifled a gasp. He hoped to avoid his father's notice and the thrashing, which was sure to follow.

Samuel picked himself up and staggered to the front door, where he clumsily turned handle and fell inside. The blow knocked the breath out of him, and he laid in place quietly for half a minute before a groan gave an indication of life. He pulled himself up while he uttered a loud curse.

Nathan moved to an open window and squatted underneath.

"Let me guess," said June softly. "They wouldn't take you back."

Samuel's resentment came plainly through his slurred words. "You're right, darling, but then again, you're always right."

"It's only a few deadbeats, Samuel. You'll get new patients next week."

He located a flask and chugged its contents. "Hardly a day goes by that I don't relive my time in the war or that awful day from my youth. Why don't people see my suffering is as great as any man with a broken leg?"

June spoke in a lonely voice. "Let's not start this again, Samuel. It's getting late, and the boy hasn't eaten supper yet."

His temper flared like the summer heat. "Let him go without and sleep in the barn! All he cares about is that horse, anyway!"

Nathan's face flushed red.

Only a few years prior, his life had been peaceful and normal, but then alcohol fueled bitterness consumed his father and ripped the family apart.

Nathan sensed the fire building within Samuel.

"What I want to know is this. Why were you seen with Thomas Hannah riding the fence line last week, and why did I first hear about it today?"

"It was innocent, Samuel. I needed a chaperone out on the back forty, and he was kind enough to accompany me on the ride. Later, I explained the love of Jesus to him, and we were close to a breakthrough."

She turned away from her husband.

"Thomas seems interested."

"Oh, I'll bet he is."

Samuel paused.

"Interested in *you*."

She unfolded a piece of paper and spread it on the table. "I read Psalm 19 to him and explained what it means. It contains many twists and turns."

"Then explain it to me as if I'm your beloved Thomas Hannah." He took another swig. "Or do I not rate as highly?"

June plopped into the chair and spoke in a monotone voice while she read the first two verses. "The heavens proclaim the glory of God. The skies display his craftsmanship. Day after day, they continue to speak; night after night, they make him known."

Samuel slapped the table, startling Nathan. "So what does it mean?"

"In looking at works of creation, we learn truths that in no manner contradict what we discern through revelation."

"Similar to the truth which I discern from you."

"Samuel, *please*."

"You should call on your God to act as your vindicator. I'll bet He'll be more than happy to strike me down for my husbandly impertinence."

"May I continue?"

"By all means."

Nathan peeked through a pinhole in the wall. His mother shifted in her seat and sat up straight, clearing her throat. Nathan sensed pride growing within her. Something was about to happen. "How can I know all the sins lurking in my heart? Cleanse me from these hidden faults. Keep your servant from deliberate sins!" She shallowed her breath. "Don't let them control me. Then I will be free of guilt and innocent of great sin."

Samuel rubbed the table with his wedding ring, digging slightly into the surface, and the resulting noise scared Nathan. "Dear wife, even the most gentle of men who may wish no man nor woman harm, whenever he is provoked, this man may burst forth into a revengeful mood, especially when he sees the notion of justice overthrown within his own home."

Her breath quickened, and her nostrils flared. "You are a slovenly drunk who misquotes Calvin. The combination is obscene, Samuel."

Nathan entered the room. He attempted to play peacemaker.

June slapped his face and sent him to sleep with the horses.

He peeked at the stars in the heavens as he made his way to the barn.

They had seen it all, and there was no brutality which surprised them.

As Nathan bundled himself inside a mound of hay, hunger pangs echoed throughout his body. The night air grew chilly as the moon rose above the great ridge of St. Louis, which kindly glittered in the distance.

He would speak to his mother in the morning about her transgression.

Nathan spread the piece of paper flat on his bed and quietly read Psalm 19. Although he was smarter than most kids his age, he failed to understand the meaning of each verse. A cabinet door slammed shut, forcing his study to reach an abrupt conclusion. He'd only been vaguely engaged in the reading, but he vowed to return in the late afternoon for a full and careful perusal.

June called to him in a tired and annoyed voice.

"Nathan, are you ready to head to town?"

His head jerked, and his eyes faced the kitchen. "Yes, Mama."

He folded the paper and slipped it into his pocket.

Nathan rode with June in her wagon and took in the pastures of mixed grasses and clover. Cows grazed beside large clumps of manure as flies buzzed about their tops and fence posts reached for the gracious heavens. A dust plume rolled beyond a distant hill, tumbling toward a destination unknowable. The occasion seemed appropriate for deeper questions.

"Why was Pop angry with you last night?"

She patted his leg. "Just another argument between two people who've always struggled to get along. Nothing for you to worry about."

"Then why did you strike my face and send me to the barn?"

June turned toward the tall corn as the wagon passed by their fields. "Your father was depressed, and he had been drinking all afternoon. If I didn't hit you, he would've done much worse."

Nathan pondered her comment. "So you protected me?"

She nodded.

"In a strange way, yes."

She leaned over and hugged him. "I'm sorry for hitting you, honey."

"It's alright. I forgive you."

June smiled. "Good."

Her eyes misted. "Your forgiveness takes a big load from my shoulders. I hope you know how much we both love you."

"Pop doesn't love anyone."

"He does, in his own way, but he's got many unspeakable memories from the war and also from his youth. I think they wear on him something fierce. I know they keep him up most nights and interfere with his practice."

"Can we help him get better?"

"Only Jesus can help him at this point."

She considered.

"Lord knows I've tried my best."

"You read some Bible verses to him. I listened outside the window."

"Yes?"

"I found the piece of paper, but I couldn't understand the verses."

The sound of grass being ripped up and chewed met his ears.

She took a deep breath and exhaled. "Do you still have the paper?"

He retrieved it from his pocket. "Right here."

She chuckled. "It has become a well-traveled piece of paper."

Her words confused him. "I don't know what that means."

"Never mind." June took the paper from him and read through several lines before she paused. "Which part gives you the most trouble?"

He pointed at verses five and six. "Those two."

"Alright, we'll begin there. 'God has made a home in the heavens for the sun. It bursts forth like a radiant bridegroom after his wedding. It rejoices like a great athlete eager to run the race. The sun rises at one end of the heavens and follows its course to the other end. Nothing can hide from its heat.' Why are those difficult for you, Nathan?"

"What does it mean about the sun?"

"It rises from a night of silent repose as a man does in the morning and goes forth with optimism and eagerness to the employments of the day. Does this make sense?"

Nathan nodded his understanding. "I believe so."

"Alright, we'll continue. 'The instructions of the Lord are perfect, reviving the soul. The decrees of the Lord are trustworthy, making wise the simple. The commandments of the Lord are right, bringing joy to the heart. The commands of the Lord are clear, giving insight for living. Reverence for the Lord is pure, lasting forever.' Here, David is saying God's revealed truths are perfect, and they convert the soul. They make the simple wise and rejoice the heart." She hesitated and then gave a sign as if she felt an unusual and worrisome sensation. Nathan wanted to further discuss the previous night, but she was reticent, and her attention was engaged elsewhere.

A hot sound cracked through the air like nearby thunder.

Someone had fired a rifle at their wagon.

The awareness startled Nathan, and he jumped slightly in his seat.

June stopped the horses and got down to inspect the damaged wheel. She stood and looked to her right and then to her left. Nathan sensed nervousness welling within her. "We'll have to walk back home. This wheel is in no shape for travel." She tensed, clearly expecting an apparition.

Nathan folded the paper and stuck it in his pocket. He hopped down and considered the benefits of camping beside the corn. It might be fun to spend the night in front of a fire with his mother.

"We could stay here."

June gave him a weary smile and turned.

She scanned the rows of corn.

What could she be looking for?

"Your father will skin me alive if I don't have dinner ready when he's done with his patients. He expects me to be the consummate wife."

"I don't know what *consummate* means," said Nathan honestly.

A man appeared from the corn while holding a rifle against his shoulder. "That's my job, June." It was Thomas Hannah. "You thought you could get rid of me, but I knew you'd travel this direction. It was only a matter of time before the Cheshire cat found his pretty little mouse."

June squeezed Nathan's shoulder and nodded to the corn on the other side of the road. "Go play in there, Son. We'll only be a minute."

"Okay, Mama." Nathan did as he was told and ran fast into the corn. He dodged stalks as he zigzagged in a made-up game.

After a few steps, he stopped and listened to his mother's voice.

She sounded upset with the man.

He covered the ground quickly and drew closer, peeking through the rows. His mother and the man were smaller than he would have preferred, and he could barely hear their conversation, but something was off with the stranger, and Nathan knew better than to get too close.

"Thomas, there's nothing more to say. We've each made regrettable mistakes along the way and now we must end this affair like civil adults."

She paused.

"We cannot lose control of our faculties."

"You said you loved me, June. A man doesn't forget."

"I'm not willing to sacrifice my marriage for a drifter." She held up a palm to appease him. "I don't mean any disrespect. I only meant to say I've been having some trouble with my husband, and I was lonely."

"You aren't lonely anymore?"

"I am, but I've turned things over to God."

"That's what I like to hear. Let's say a big prayer and ask the bearded man in the sky what I ought to do with you. How about it, June?"

Her voice grew shaky. "Thomas, please. My son is with me. Let us pass, and we can forget this day." She turned toward the corn and scanned for Nathan. Her hand trembled, and her face went deathly as a ghost.

"Oh, I'll never forget what you did to me."

He leaned his rifle against the destroyed wheel and retrieved something shiny from a leather sheath on his belt. It was long and wide. The sun reflected off the metal surface, gleaming light into Nathan's eyes.

"What's that?" Her voice filled with terror.

"It's the knife I'll use to cut your throat."

"Run, Nathan! Did you hear me? Run away, Son! Do it right now!"

Adrenaline shot through Nathan's veins. He took off through the corn, first right, then left, zig zagging without clear direction.

After several minutes, he kneeled down and listened.

June Marsh called out in agony as Thomas Hannah raped her on the side of the road. Every so often, Hannah sliced her arm or her leg with the knife, and she screamed to God for help. Nathan grabbed handfuls of dirt at the base of a cornstalk, holding on for dear life. Should he continue running as his mother had instructed or should he barrel toward the wagon and attack Thomas Hannah with all his might? An image of the large knife flashed through Nathan's mind. He was scared to die, so he listened, hoping it was all a dream or a rotten joke. There were rough sounds like someone tossing tools into the wagon. His mother's voice no longer filled the air; a new stillness took its place. He laid down in the dirt and sobbed.

Minutes passed as Nathan waited for Thomas to come after him.

Delirium overwhelmed his mind, and he lost connection with reality.

A flurry of ants cheerfully marched about his face, carrying away bits of his shattered innocence. They took it to their homes in the underground, where it would be forever buried. They returned with a peace offering of eternal sorrow and said it was the best they could do on short notice.

After an hour, Nathan's break from reality ceased.

He stood and brushed off his clothes, as June would have expected. He walked toward the edge of the road where he found his mother's naked and blood-soaked body. Her mouth retained an ugly grimace, and her eyes were devoid of all expression. He rubbed the outside edge of his pocket and detected the folded paper. Nathan cried out to God and asked why He did not intervene on June's behalf. He waited for several minutes, half expecting a reply, but there was only silence, save the fierce rattle of cicadas from the trees and the dull roar of katydids from the fields. He studied the passing clouds and felt the gentle breeze touch his face and neck. What a confusing and horrible world he'd been born into, a place of beauty but also one of fury. It was no place for the decent, that much was certain. Men like Thomas Hannah made their own rules, and everyone in their path fled or were consumed like prey. Nathan left his mother's mangled body exposed on the side of the road. He took one last look before leaving and then continued.

He kicked at small piles of dirt as he walked and vowed to become a doctor like his father. Nathan would spend the rest of his life helping sick and injured people recover from life-threatening injuries. Someone had to play the role of God in this world. The job was clearly vacant.

<hr>

After the funeral, Nathan sat on the front porch of his father's farmhouse. The gate to June's garden swung lazily in the soft wind. Tilled rows of plants of various sizes arranged themselves between a mass of weeds, like railroad tracks amid a forested landscape. There was pulling to do, but Nathan would never get around to it. He would leave the garden as his mother had intended—carefully organized order which would succumb to chaos. She had written the story of the end of her life within the confines of her vegetable patch. Nathan was disgusted by the juxtaposition of her stated desire for tradition and her need for anarchy. There was no logic in her behavior, only lingering questions which would never be answered, and the ramifications of his own lousy existence troubled him immensely.

A whisper wafted across the breeze. It caught only his ear.

Lonely hunters seek rough hills of diamonds, hoping one will shine.

People arrived in fits and starts and congregated both inside and outside. Some threw horseshoes to pass the time while others ate unhealthy plates of food. Still others made a tiresome habit of patting Samuel on the back, offering condolences with a grim countenance and promises to help with the farm. They left muttering *what a shame* while lurking for another morsel.

John Belmont's carriage appeared around the bend and stopped in front of the house. He took a young girl's hand and escorted her across the green grass to the porch. They went inside to chat with the more social group.

After several minutes, the young girl came outside and sat beside Nathan on the bench. She looked perplexed. "What are you doing?"

"Leave me alone," he said. "I have nothing to say."

"I'm sorry your mother passed. Daddy said she was nice."

"She was."

"My mother is gone, too."

"Guess we're two peas in a pod."

She smiled. "Thought so."

"My mother was reading Bible verses to me before she died.

"Daddy said a man killed her on the road."

"Yes."

"Did she have a Bible in the wagon? It must get dusty."

Nathan shook his head. "The verses were written on a piece of paper."

Her eyebrows raised. "Do you still have it?"

Nathan rubbed his pocket. "Right here."

"Would you read the verses to me?"

Nathan scowled. "Never again."

"Could I read them? Daddy says I'm great at it for my age."

Nathan retrieved the paper and handed it to the young girl.

She studied the verses. "Did your mother finish reading all of them?"

He scanned the page and pointed to the last one June had read.

"I'll start where she left off then."

"Suit yourself."

"Reverence for the Lord is pure, lasting forever. The laws of the Lord are true; each one is fair. They are more desirable than gold, even the finest gold. They are sweeter than honey, even honey dripping from the comb. They are a warning to your servant, a great reward for those who obey them."

John Belmont exited the front door. He extended his hand to the young girl. "Catherine, it's time to go." He offered Nathan a sharp look.

"Yes, Daddy." She took his hand and arose.

John and Catherine walked across the grass to the carriage.

Before she climbed the step, the young girl looked back at Nathan.

He waved to her, but he wasn't sure why.

She smiled and waved to him.

Although she had read his mother's verses aloud, there was a darkness which floated about her. It followed their carriage down the lane and hid in their wake as they turned the corner to the right and disappeared.

He wondered if her oblivion might resemble his own.

TWENTY

Psalm 20:5

May the Lord answer all your prayers.

The airless Monday morning suffocated Nathan as Catherine talked with James. A smile carried in their voices as if they had known one another for decades and laughter was easy for them. James placed his hand on Catherine's arm, and her carefree lean into his space beat fierce against Nathan's brow, listing the keel of his sloop sideways in the flowing channel of his thoughts, changeable as they were, and stifling like the air in the main hall, tight and gray and inclement. He missed his lifelong friend and the mother of his three children. Although his resentment was hard to dismiss, they shared a kinship, a bond of mutual agony which traced to their early years, and it would stay at the forefront of his feeling for her, no matter how angry she might make him. They were forever linked by sharp and unruly misfortune, which cavorted recklessly throughout the fields of their lives, nestled into the impulse and yield of broken promises.

He looked about the main hall. Its fine high ceilings loomed down upon the patients who populated each line of beds. Thick sunlight entered through murky windows at the entrance and gas lamps rested stiffly on chandeliers, which ran from front to rear. Their light offered a facet of gleam which was once known but now forgotten, impatient footsteps through time, faded moments of nerves and vitality, now uninteresting and narrow of mind, caught without companionship, save what passed next to them in the hall. Like them, Nathan was unprosperous and vacant, reduced from gallantry to philosophy, the latter forced upon him by a new love.

His eyes fell on Belmont Hospital's resident psychologist, who worked tirelessly at John and Susanna Hutchinson's bedside, to small avail. Daisy possessed a rigid determination, which was born of a sympathetic nature and a ravenous desire for hope. Nathan's existence was made meaningful thanks to his newfound responsibilities, as poised and exploratory as they were to him, and it seemed natural to abandon his superficial cares once she entered his world. Her voice bore the strain in her eyes, and she sang a tender but fearful song of disgrace and downfall and a strictness which had formed within her over the course of her encumbrance upon this earth. He saw the flush of rules and order within her, demanding an audience with the waning number of reasons to live, hoping for a man to love her before it was too late, and the desires of this world won over her will. Her kind words of encouragement, sincerely delivered, increased his attraction to her. They were matched only by his perpetual scrutiny and his unbendable firmness and his tyrannical authority. He was a feverish brute intent on having his way, and she was a unique mentor in a land filled with hypocrites.

He turned toward Catherine and James once more.

They wiped tear marks from one another's cheeks and embraced. A simple decadence made itself clear in the warmth and safety of their hug, an authenticity which astonished Nathan and sent him longing for what he, too, had missed in his former marriage, the brilliance of a silent smile, the casual secret known only by two, the blind absorption into another.

Sheila arrived with food, interrupting his reflections. She made several trips out to his wagon and set each dish on an oak table to one side.

Daisy called Nathan over to sit with her, and he complied.

She went on about her theories and often grew excited about the tiniest bit of progress. He tried to calm her incessant enthusiasm, but his efforts made little impact. Catherine and Sheila observed their banter while serving breakfast, and occasionally they glanced at one another. He wondered how they might view Daisy. Was she a provincial product of the Missouri River, or was she a moral example who might lead them to their purpose?

Sheila served Heinrich Besseler a plate of eggs and ham, but he wanted nothing to do with a prostitute. He waved her off dismissively, and when she forced the food into his lap, he threw it to the floor, shattering the plate and spilling eggs on her shoes. She yelled obscenities at him in true Irish form, unwilling to take abuse from a man who whined about the past, as if no one else around him had ever experienced tragedy. Nathan wanted to step between them and promote her intrinsic worth, but decided against it.

Since their arrival, neither had displayed a hint of bravery.

Perhaps their argument was the first step toward healing.

Daisy retrieved her Bible and held it in her lap.

She ran her hand over his hair.

"You look tired," she said. "May I share a few verses with you?"

He stiffened and pushed her hand down. She frowned and tried to rub his arm, but he squeezed her hand and shook his head.

"You won't let me touch you?"

"Read your verses. I'm getting used to your recitations."

The pages made a crinkling sound as her fingers moved to Psalm 20.

"In times of trouble, may the Lord answer your cry. May the name of the God of Jacob keep you safe from all harm. May he send you help from his sanctuary and strengthen you from Jerusalem. May he remember all your gifts and look favorably on your burnt offerings."

Daisy picked up a pencil from the floor and placed it in her lap. She paused and gathered her wits about her before she continued. "I've thought about us, our working relationship, and whatever else we're doing."

"Alright," he said, half expecting the worst.

She raised her voice, as if the issue concerned her greatly. "I vehemently believe we're traveling down the wrong path. If we have any hope of helping these patients, we must return to the root of Western civilization."

Relieved at the unusual turn in her remark, he smiled. "You've spent too much time in college and not enough in the real world. Your intellectual ideas are great fodder for the classroom or the altar of a church, but they bring little to this hospital, where torment is a way of life."

"I disagree, Nathan."

"We're here to pursue science, not fairy tales."

She sighed. "What happened to your childhood faith?"

He fought the urge to be ashamed of her, although she vexed him. Her thoughtless exuberance sometimes made her say clumsy things.

"You know it was taken from me on the side of the road."

"Well, I pray your heart will once again open to the Most High, and when it does, He will work through you to transform this hospital into an unstoppable force for good. May I share the rest of the psalm with you?"

His eyes widened, and he turned away for a moment with clenched fists. He took a deep breath and exhaled loudly. She had claimed a visitation from Lucifer himself after they left Belmont's billiard room. Nathan carried her into the hospital and up the stairs to her cot and covered her with a blanket to ease her shivers. Her behavior caused him to question her sanity, but then again, it seemed the entire world was on the brink of madness, so who was he to say? He needed her to diagnose herself, a most arduous task when one had lost their connection to reality. For now, he sought to keep her scales balanced toward the cause of restoration, and so he spoke to her in a low voice while his eyes looked at the floor. "There is actual work to do, and I don't have time for lectures. We have many tasks and a looming deadline."

Daisy leaned forward and cupped her hand under his chin. She turned his face toward hers. "The spirits watch us, Nathan."

He lightly squeezed her arm and gave her a soft look. "Have you forgotten how I put you to bed that night? You had me plenty worried."

"The incident will never leave my memory. Now I must do everything possible to ensure you land safely in the hands of Jesus."

She paused.

"Time grows short."

His lips pressed into a fine line. "I'm right *here*, Daisy."

"Only a few more verses, Nathan. There are nine in total."

He looked past her at the flurry of activity in the main hall, knowing he must abidingly bear her stubborn nature if they were to wed.

Nathan felt a trifle dazed. "Please proceed."

Daisy held up the Bible as she read, clearly hoping the verses might resonate. "May he grant your heart's desires and make all your plans succeed. May we shout for joy when we hear of your victory and raise a victory banner in the name of our God. May the Lord answer all your prayers. Now I know that the Lord rescues his anointed king. He will answer him from his holy heaven and rescue him by his great power. Some nations boast of their chariots and horses, but we boast in the name of the Lord our God. Those nations will fall down and collapse, but we will rise up and stand firm. Give victory to our king, O Lord! Answer our cry for help."

When she finished, he gestured harshly, as Heinrich had done. "You've worked with the world's best minds and still you revert to superstition."

She placed her hand on his arm. "Good will happen only when you turn to Christ as your Savior. You must truly know Him and live the faith, and to do that, you must learn the pillars of Christianity and why they matter."

There was a starry aspect to her demeanor. She would not relent.

"Alright then, enlighten me. What have I missed?"

"You must understand this fundamental fact. God is the creator of our universe, and He makes the rules for us. We can never make them for Him, no matter how much we might want to or how hard we might try. It's up to us to learn His will for our lives and pursue it with every fiber of our being. Otherwise, we have little reason to be alive. Does this make sense to you?"

He crossed his arms and looked about the room.

Daisy gave him a stern look. "I'd like a reply, Nathan."

When none was offered, she left him in a huff and returned her Bible to the front of the main hall. She resumed work with her patients, and each avoided the other for a while. Sometimes neither understood why they were a couple, other than a decided physical attraction and a hesitant respect.

Sheila sat next to Heinrich, and the two talked naturally, like old friends. They even laughed at a shared joke, most likely at Nathan and Daisy's expense. Sheila smiled and brought Heinrich a full plate of eggs and bacon, which he proudly ate with a glint in his eyes and a grin on his face.

Only a few minutes earlier, they had argued like school children.

Nathan disliked the situation which unfolded before him.

He drifted to the front stoop of the hospital and watched people walk along the sidewalk. A man looked directly at Nathan and refused to turn when confronted by a return stare. Nathan shut the door and marched up the block, determined to force an encounter. The man spun around and hurried in the opposite direction and then ducked into an alley to his right.

When Nathan reached the entrance and proceeded to the end of the alley, the strange man was gone. Nathan leaned against the brick wall and gazed at the blue sky above, noting the path of the clouds as they moved from east to west. A hurt grew inside him, deep within his center, at the one place he allowed no access. The loss of Sheila proved more difficult than he predicted, her motherly embrace no longer available to him, and although he genuinely wanted her to find happiness in the arms of a worthy man, someone much greater and finer than himself, he longed for the comfort of her warm affections, the kind he had lost as a boy to the rough hands of a jilted murderer, and the type an erratic Daisy could never hope to replace.

Sheila refused to leave Heinrich's side and encouraged him to talk about the death of his family. It was a heart wrenching tale, and his recovery seemed like an impossibility. Ed shared the pain of losing his wife the previous year and then his son Ronnie. He explained his love of travel and of seeing the countryside by rail. Once he recovered from his somatic symptoms, he planned to sell his farm and return to his former life. Sheila perked up when she heard this and whispered something to Heinrich, who nodded.

Daisy tried to deny her jealousy as she watched the prostitute interact with the hysterics, but it was plainly obvious, even to her. She casually succeeded while Daisy's patients either worsened in her care or temporarily improved, later to regress into their previous somatic state. Nothing Daisy tried seemed to work, and the situation had grown tiresome. She wanted to plead and cry and blame others for her failures, but mostly she craved rest and isolation. Even Shirley came to life in Sheila's presence.

"I'll open a shop which specializes in blankets."

Shirley smiled as she shared her plans with Sheila and the others in the group. "A local factory takes pressed cotton and makes very nice exterior material, my favorite being blue. I'll get the cotton interior and then I'll use a smooth silk exterior to make the finest blankets in the state of Missouri."

"It's a fine idea," said Ed, beaming.

Samuel and Dora worked with Ida while Susanna danced about the room. Daisy admired Susanna's finely tuned movements and wondered if she might have been a dancer in her Pennsylvania youth. In a marked contrast with his wife, John laid on his bed and glared at the ceiling.

Daisy doubted any of the patients would return to normality, but she hoped talking through their pain might ease their struggle. She heard in her spirit to pray for them, but she discounted the message as her overactive creativity. She meditated on the reasons for her diminished faith, and why her daily walk with the Lord was now a withered memory. Daisy barely survived her encounter with Rosemarie, and it made her question her sanity and her ability to operate in civil society. Her conversation with Lucifer resurfaced those notions, and she now considered herself delusional and possibly deranged, ready to throw up her hands in genuine lunatic fashion. She still read her Bible, but the words no longer rang true, as her feelings for Nathan and the hysterics resonated more deeply than Jesus Christ or the idea of eternal life in a faraway realm. There were moments when she saw herself as a silly girl from the woods who knew nothing at all. She then remembered an angel with a flaming sword who had shined his effervescent light from within the forest which surrounded the rocks. Daisy closed her eyes and tried to forget her many torments, but it was no use; they piled atop her modest soul, and her will faded to near nonexistence.

Nathan repeatedly instructed her to abandon religion and immerse herself in the many wonders of science. If Daisy were to be honest with herself, she no longer knew what to think or what to believe. Confusion had watched from afar, discontent with its distance, and pledged to take hold of her mind perpetually. Perhaps Nathan was right, and she was a bitter fool.

Her attempt to hide behind a French woman's identity in New York had not improved her situation or her outlook. She eventually depleted her funds and then booked passage on a train to Chicago and took up residence with Frank Kaneski's family as an Austrian maid. It was a sorry excuse for an existence, but she learned a great deal about his past, and why he betrayed her in Europe. Her forced exit came when his mother announced Frank's impending arrival, happy as she was to have him home, expectant, but also sad, as if she blamed him for some unknown atrocity. Daisy asked the other servants what crime he might have committed, but each was reticent to speak of him as anything other than a philosopher of the utmost order.

She returned to Pierre's winery in haste, the prodigal daughter of distinction. He employed her in a minor capacity, aware of her despair and unwilling to risk his tough earned business with a woman of questionable character. Over months, she decided to end her life at the high ledge in the woods, but she could not get up the nerve to carry out her plan.

When she visited Tower Grove Park in St. Louis with her father, and the crazed assassin took a shot at his wife, Daisy viewed it as a sign. Her walk in the dark to Union Depot was filled with sadness as she strategized her demise. She would hide from Pierre all night, and in the morning, she would ride the early train west toward Kansas City. There was a trestle near Pollard which Daisy had walked many times during her girlhood, and a leap from the baggage car would be all too easy. The door to the car would slide open for her, and the morning air would be crisp, and the summer sun would smile as it chased the desperate chill from her cheeks. It would be a good way to die and a comfort to those she pained.

She could not break her curse, but she could release others from it.

Daisy had sat on a wooden bench under the gleam of electric lights and pondered her sister's fate. Whatever destiny might have befallen Rose would soon happen to her, and it was at this precise moment she met the man of her dreams. Each subsequent conversation with Nathan saved Daisy in every way a person can be saved in this fallen realm, at least in matters of the heart and free will and the certitude of death. Her family laid the blame for suicide at her feet over the years, seeing Daisy's presence in their lives as a ceaseless link to a cruel betrayal, one they would be pleased to erase. She did the same, departing for university in Paris at the first opportunity, an escape from her family's sordid history offering the only path to relief. Now, as in John

Belmont's billiard room, where Daisy's fragile mind conversed with the ancient face of evil, Rose spoke to her spirit and offered respite from the iniquity of this world. An eternal home of rest awaited, the one Rose had anticipated, while she peered over the side of Big Rock with crestfallen eyes.

It was a lush land of greenery without gray ash or specs of dust or scorching sun, painted in spasms of colors which drifted over the chalky tops of blue mountains. The soul could be happy there, unencumbered.

Join me, my dear. There are many delights which await your arrival.

A few hours later, Samuel sat Nathan's office and gave praise to his son for his provision of valuable care to those in need. When Nathan first accepted the role of hospital administrator, Samuel worried he might run away from the horrid blight of unwelcome responsibility and revisit more agreeable surroundings in Joanna Sinclair's brothel. He shook his head and dropped his eyes to the floor. The notion of his own time spent immersed in the bottle made him groan with regret. There was no stopping his recollections once they began, so he spoke of the future with a growing freshness, his mind affixed on what his son might yet accomplish in medicine. The old, dank convent of the past would finally give way to the hilled meadows of a life spent in meaningful achievement, and a perennial family would be Nathan's reward. Soon his head would turn toward marriage, and Samuel looked forward to another wedding, this one attended by decent folk, the kind who would give their shirts to a lost soul in need, stalwart spirits of God's grace and mercy who cared little for the Big Cinch's approval.

"Stop talking, Pop. Your meddling helps nothing."

Samuel leaned forward. "Daisy said she shared Psalm 20 with you, but after she finished, you were quite rude to her. Don't you realize she cares deeply for you and wants to see you saved before it's too late?"

"My soul is perfectly fine, and it needs no help from either of you."

Samuel's voice carried a tilt of excitement. "Your soul will only be perfectly fine when it is made so by the spilled blood of Jesus Christ."

Nathan felt his patience quickly flee. "This again? I receive enough preaching from Daisy so you can cease your ministerial duties."

"You've been confused lately," Samuel said. "Emotionally."

"I've been angry about our lack of progress with John and Susanna, and by missing the belligerent sarcoma in Ronnie's leg, not to mention the painful reappearance of my ex-wife and my being forced to deal with her presence for such a long duration and my captor being her homicidal father, the very bane of my existence for most of my life." He caught his breath and reconsidered. "I know you would like to claim the title, and a careful review is certainly warranted, but believe it or not, John was worse than you."

He paused.

"In short, life has rent me asunder."

"As for God, his way is perfect; the Word of the Lord is tried. He is a buckler to all of them that trust in him."

"Enough, Pop!"

Daisy opened the door and stuck her head inside the office.

"Everything alright in here, gentlemen?"

Nathan's mood grew hard. "We're *fine*. Get back to work."

She slammed the door. A loud thud reverberated throughout the room.

Samuel pointed at Nathan. "Neither of us is here to tell you what to do, but I encourage you to admit your jealousy over Catherine."

"I don't know what you're talking about."

"You know exactly what I mean," said Samuel, smirking. "Catherine became friendly with James, and you dislike seeing her with another man."

Nathan sat in silence as he stared at the far wall. How had his father discerned so easily? "I'll admit an awful jealousy burns within me. I don't enjoy seeing Catherine with James or Sheila with Heinrich."

Samuel arched his eyebrows. "Sheila, too?"

Nathan nodded.

"Well, that settles the matter. You must pursue a relationship with Daisy, something true and fine and with the potential to endure for a lifetime."

"Daisy Lawrence is like a brick house with no entrance or windows, nor any penetrating light." Nathan made direct eye contact and pointed at his father, hoping to end their dialogue. "I'm not a magician, Pop."

"You must be patient. She'll give you a sign."

"There's more."

Samuel stiffened. "This sounds ominous."

"When I'm around Daisy, I sense real danger."

"You have me confused. In what manner?"

"She could hurt me worse than anyone has before."

He paused.

"I cannot withstand another betrayal."

Samuel sat back in his chair. "I see."

Daisy stuck her head inside the office. "Nathan, you won't believe this."

"What?"

"Catherine is gone."

He stood quickly. "What do you mean?"

"She told a nurse she would travel by train."

"What on earth for?"

"She left to search for Martin."

"Her husband?"

Daisy nodded.

"What should we do?"

Samuel stood. "Nathan, your sign has appeared." He smiled at Daisy. "With that note of solace, I'll take my leave."

He pointed at Nathan once again. "Happy hunting."

At the street, Belmont passed them and wheeled.

"What's this I hear about my daughter?"

"She claimed to be an orphan and left the hospital."

Nathan and Daisy marched forward. There was no time to waste.

At Union Depot, Daisy pondered whether she should have accompanied Nathan. Although they were now more than allies, Catherine knew how to make people question their beliefs and their feelings. Could Nathan stay trustworthy, or would he acquiesce to her charms as Frank fell in Europe? There were moments when Catherine seemed like Rosemarie, and Daisy feared her descent into the black syrup of wickedness would accelerate unabated, while her entity probed Daisy for vulnerabilities and heralded its intention to reveal each loathsome aspect of her character.

Catherine represented every struggle Daisy had overcome in one mortal package, and her attempt to shrink from the world within the confines of Belmont Hospital didn't cover over her grotesque internal disposition. She hastily ran from their care to look for her husband, the same man who beat her senseless and left her for dead. What kind of woman prefers hot ashes to sunshine or the butt of a revolver to love? She once was a transcendent belle who possessed what the heart desires, but like June, she lost herself in the complex equations of life, seeing them as simpler than they were, blunting her spear against the crumble and the powder of primal lust.

The gray-eyed man at the ticket booth did not recognize a woman who fit Catherine's description. He stretched his arms and yawned.

They frantically searched the area, but the mass of people about the station obscured their vision. Nathan made his way toward the south end of the platform while Daisy went to the north. He spotted Catherine as she boarded a train three tracks over and called after Daisy to follow him. She pushed and shoved her way forward and descended the steps to the tracks and then made her way toward the westbound train, which ran to Kansas City and beyond to Omaha. She made it just as the train rolled.

Catherine found a seat at the rear of the car, facing the caboose.

Nathan and Daisy gingerly approached, careful not to upset her. They sat four rows ahead of her and waited. She did little for two hours.

Unable to delay any longer, Daisy moved to the rear of the car and sat beside Catherine, gently squeezing her arm. "Martin dumped you naked on the street in Dealey with a note for whoever might find you. On the paper, he called you a piece of trash and said he wanted nothing to do with you ever again. Honey, you've suffered enough of his abuse and now you must file for divorce. It's time to move on with your life."

Catherine's nostrils flared as if she had never heard such a made-up story. Her vagrant mind steadily played tricks on her, telling her the outlaw of her teenage dreams needed her and wished to reoccupy a space in her life. She contemplated the balminess and the tranquility of the morning and determined the woman who now sat beside her was of the lessor classes and could never be trusted with anything so fragile as the truth. Even if her words were correct, this urchin was in no position to dictate terms to a woman of first-rate breeding and a student of polite society.

The train lurched forward, jolting the passengers. Catherine took on a ragged appearance which made her seem of more advanced years, as if a bellow from across centuries had summoned her to creak open the great door of existence. She looked about with a brittle nervousness, and her youthful and magnetic countenance slipped into an inexplicable plainness.

After the train jolted them again, Catherine smiled in the same cold manner Daisy had witnessed at the cemetery. The entity was busy within her sorrowful heart, and she would soon affix her eyes to the celestial province.

Daisy looked over her shoulder at a worried Nathan.

When she faced her nemesis once more, Catherine had regained her fierce and solemn determination. She held little regard for happiness.

"You know there is something foul within me, Daisy, an indescribable evil which desires to inflict such damage on the world as to make it mostly unrecognizable. You've sensed it for some time, haven't you?"

"Yes, and also at your father's estate, while inside his billiard room."

"I'm told you conversed with several spirits there."

Daisy nodded.

"They gave me information and presented instructions."

"I am also receiving commands, and they must be followed if Nathan is to be protected. You defied his authority that night, which is not allowed."

"Nathan gave me no direction."

Catherine sneered. "He is not the one I speak of, and you know it."

Daisy sighed deeply. "I'll admit to being a very confused woman."

"As am I at the moment, but I know one thing for certain. Whatever lives inside me probed your mind for the dark memory of an aborted suicide attempt, and it planted the idea firmly in my own mind. It told me I should believe your words. Martin used me for access to my father's wealth, which is why we came home repeatedly over the last ten years, hands out, expecting a roll of money from my father. When he finally refused us, Martin was through with our marriage. He had never loved me, and he will murder me the next time our paths cross. Of course, I knew the truth of what you said, and I thought death at his hands would be the best choice."

"Your plans have since changed?"

"I will jump from your trestle and do what you could not."

"It would be a permanent mistake, Catherine, and you'll miss out on marriage to someone else, perhaps a man like James Clifton."

"He'll never accept me as anything but a wretch."

"You might be surprised," Daisy said. "He's been through a lot."

Catherine rubbed her bottom lip. Her breaths quickened.

A smile slowly formed, and her head tilted.

"You speak as someone with experience and knowledge. Where is your husband, Daisy? Why have you made no commitment to a man?"

Nathan pressed into the seat with Daisy, sitting on her far side.

She glanced at him and then looked back at Catherine.

"I was almost married once," she said defensively.

"In St. Louis?"

Daisy shook her head. "In Vienna."

"This man broke your heart." Catherine spoke matter-of-factly.

"Yes."

"Because of your heartbreak, you think we are sisters?"

"I had hoped for your friendship."

"I cannot be friends with a woman who sinfully toys with Nathan's affections, unwilling to pursue something real and lasting with him. If only he would look at me the way he looks at you, the way he used to look at me, many years ago, when I was younger and more beautiful."

She paused.

"Now it is you who has youth and beauty on her side."

Time had almost run out. "Catherine, please come back with us."

"No! You will not be honest with me!"

Catherine ran through the rear door.

"Where is she going?" asked Nathan. "There's no escape."

"She's looking for the trestle near Pollard."

His face lost all color. "Do you know it?"

"Yes. If she jumps, her life will end."

He craned his neck and looked out of the window.

He pointed. "We're almost there now."

Nathan rushed through the door. It slammed behind him.

It would be easier on everyone—especially Daisy—if Catherine gave into the pressure and jumped. Daisy imagined the body of a green-eyed woman landing on the rocks at the base of the trestle and told herself not to give into the pressure being applied by Catherine's unclean spirit.

The door opened again, and Nathan approached her seat.

"Get up now! We have to stop her!"

"I've recently thought of doing the same thing, Nathan. Only my spot is in the woods on my father's land. It's a tall ledge we call Big Rock."

He grabbed Daisy's hand. "We'll talk about *you* later."

They barely reached Catherine in time.

Nathan snatched her from an open doorway as she was about to leap to her death from the baggage car. He held her close to his chest, panting from exhaustion, gripping her in his arms. "You cannot do this!"

"Why?"

"Because I won't allow your death."

Daisy removed her Bible from her dress pocket and clutched it to her chest. She hoped God's Word would speak to her as much as to the poor woman standing in front of her. She reached forward and lightly squeezed Catherine's shoulder. "I'll share some of the New Testament. It might have a positive effect on your emotional state."

"I doubt it," Catherine said.

"This is from the book of James. Perhaps you'll think of your new beau as I read the verses. He will miss you greatly once you're gone."

"Daisy, stop." Nathan's face registered frustration.

Clearly, he was too tired to argue the point any further, so it was up to her to continue the heavenly battle. He would thank her later.

"What is causing the quarrels and fights among you? Don't they come from the evil desires at war within you? You want what you don't have, so you scheme and kill to get it. You are jealous of what others have, but you can't get it, so you fight and wage war to take it away from them. Yet you don't have what you want because you don't ask God for it. And even when you ask, you don't get it because your motives are all wrong—you want only what will give you pleasure."

Catherine interrupted. "What do the words mean?"

"God will protect those who trust in Him. If you'll stop running and turn your will over to the Lord, He will give you what you seek."

Catherine's eyes flashed restlessly about the car.

"Why won't you submit to Nathan?"

"Catherine, please." Nathan let her go but kept a close watch.

"I will not try to jump again, but I will receive an answer to my perfectly legitimate question." She glared at Daisy. "Why aren't you with this man?"

"I had a younger sister named Rose."

"So?"

"I failed to care for Rose in her time of need, and she lost her life. My mother died soon afterward. I've felt responsible for their deaths ever since, and it has affected my relationships with everyone I meet, most especially men." She hesitated. "I've tried to know the redeeming power of Christ and His agape love, but I often fail in my spiritual walk." She glanced at Nathan and wiped the tears from her eyes. "This man has helped me immensely, even to the point of rescuing me from certain death on several occasions. If you'll come back with us now, you can work at the hospital and help the hysteric patients. It's an opportunity to turn your trauma into a positive."

Daisy extended her hand and smiled warmly. "I would enjoy the pleasure of your company, and who knows, we might even become like sisters."

Catherine threw out her chin in a willful declaration of wisdom. Her voice dropped its bold edge and took on a tilt of sweetness. The worst would come next, a notion of blood and intimacy and a scolding confusion.

"I cursed myself by wedding Nathan while still married to Martin, and God took my children. Our Annie was the perfect daughter, and I doted on her even more than her father. Peter and Ely would have grown into extraordinary men who shaped the community into a better version of itself, but they all three died within one month. You cannot release me from my curse, so stop talking as if you can." She looked softly at Nathan. "I cannot function as a normal woman any longer. The pain is more than I can bear."

Catherine gave him a moment to process her words.

"*Please* let me go."

His eyes moistened. "Your father wants you home with him."

She stiffened. "It's where I belong."

Her words surprised Daisy. "You wish to leave the hospital?

Catherine shook her head. "My father's home is filled with demons of untold quantity, which is why I wanted to end my life, either through Martin or my volition, rather than venture to live with him. Instead, I will make my stand at Vandeventer Place, and the unclean spirits will devour my flesh like rabid dogs." Her chin quivered, and her shoulders curled over her chest. "I deserve their wrath, so it matters little what they do to me."

Daisy heard herself give into weakness, both in her soul and in her heart. "John will never allow you to stay with us."

Catherine smiled. "Neither will *you*, Daisy."

Daisy sighed. "You may be right."

"See, we're like sisters already. We each want the other dead."

<hr>

Friday afternoon, Nathan and Daisy helped Catherine pack her belongings to prepare for the awful task of going home. Catherine had chided Daisy all morning for the smallest infractions and took great pleasure at her expense, knowing full well Daisy wanted her gone, perhaps even from this sphere. Catherine also renewed her efforts to exasperate Nathan, and she giggled like a schoolgirl when she achieved success. She seemed to slip into the grasp of many unclean spirits, and Daisy hoped she might survive them.

Catherine sat on the bed and cried. "I don't want to leave."

Daisy read Matthew 28:19-20. "Therefore, go and make disciples of all the nations, baptizing them in the name of the Father and the Son and the Holy Spirit. Teach these new disciples to obey all the commands I have given you. And be sure of this: I am with you always, even to the end of the age."

"Is He really with us always?"

"The notion gives me strength during trying times."

Catherine's eyes fell to the floor. "Such as today."

Daisy tried to subdue her excitement. It wasn't right to want Catherine out of her life so badly, but she was human and flawed. It's what she told herself to justify her desires. An expedition into love awaited, and she would carry herself through the unfamiliar in hopes of her own survival. She long ago grew exhausted from the lonely journey through life. It was time to love someone and to be loved in return, to belong, to receive gratitude when it was deserved, to know proper security, and to trust a man to guide her and to stay with her forever. Daisy had suffered through many ordeals, and she would prove herself worthy of their lessons.

"We will miss you," she said. "Please know it in your heart."

Catherine's body jerked. She turned toward Daisy.

"You sweep me like dirt onto the street."

Daisy's eyes widened. "Not at all."

Catherine pulled away, retreating inside herself. "I was once beautiful, and people clamored for my attention, including young bookish girls like you." She laughed as she smoothed the wrinkles in her sleeves.

Daisy smiled gravely. "I'm sure."

Catherine's shoulders slumped, and her eyes fell to the floor.

"Am I now supposed to melt away and be afraid?"

Nathan looked at his timid ex-wife with soft eyes. "Honey, your father loves you, and he'll see to it you have everything you could need." He glanced about the room. "In a year's time, this hospital will be a distant memory. Your father will reintroduce you into society at the right moment, and you'll regale the Big Cinch with your compelling tales of woe." He smiled. "Your all-night balls will once again be the talk of St. Louis."

Catherine recoiled in disgust. "Is that what you expect of me, to become a parlor queen who wastes her life on trivialities?"

"I want you to be happy. That is all."

"You don't love me." She glared at Sheila, who sat nearby, talking to Heinrich. "Any more than you love that pathetic Irish waif."

Daisy glanced at Nathan and turned toward Catherine. "He's discussed the situation with her, and she understands the true nature of his feelings."

Sheila looked up, and Daisy smiled at her.

"I don't like that woman," said Catherine bitterly.

Daisy's eyes narrowed. She drew a quick breath.

"Sheila seeks the next stage of her life, which is what we wish for you."

Catherine put her face in her hands and wept.

"You want me *dead*." She looked up. "Why wouldn't you let me jump?"

John arrived and flew into a rage, sure Nathan had sabotaged his child's recovery. "If she doesn't leave with me today, I'll have you killed."

Nathan threw him a coarse look. "I've had enough of your threats."

John glanced at Sheila and then scowled at Nathan. "You couldn't resist bringing your soiled laundry to work. How inadequate you are."

Daisy's hand raised. "She has been most helpful lately."

He fell silent and looked intently at Sheila, as if trying to understand why Daisy would aid a courtesan from Joanna Sinclair's brothel.

He turned to her, annoyed. "Doing *what*, pray tell?"

"Sheila cleans his house and cooks delicious meals for the hospital. We interceded on her behalf, and she's glad to be free of her former profession."

John gave a snort of indifferent laughter. "You may take her out of the brothel, but you won't take the brothel out of her." His lips pressed together in a slight grimace. "However, I'll let it pass for now."

"Thank you." Daisy's bearing was light and confidential.

His arms folded across his chest. "We are *not* serving the Big Cinch yet, my dear, but when that day finally arrives, this gutter rat will evaporate like the morning mist. I believe I make myself clear."

"Perfectly." She forced a smile, and her palm pressed against her heart. "What will you do with Catherine once you get her home?"

John's focus drifted to his daughter across the room.

Catherine sat listlessly on her bed and clutched her stomach.

"We will reacquaint ourselves as father and daughter, repairing old family wounds as we go." His voice had lost some of its power.

"It's been a long time coming."

"It has, and I plan to make the most of her renewed health and vigor."

His restless eyes watched Catherine as she drifted inside and outside of herself, unsure which form she preferred. She was a figure on the edge.

He approached her and bent down. "I love you so much, darling." He stroked her hair. "Won't you come home with me today?"

She gave him a glazed look. "I'm not quite ready, Father."

"You look so lovely, my dear. We'll be fit as a fiddle in our cozy house. All the servants are filled with anticipation of your arrival. It will be like olden times, and we'll be the very best of sidekicks once again."

"I'm frightened by the memories of olden times."

"Nonsense, we are father and daughter." He stood and extended his hand to her. "Come, let me spoil you with the riches you deserve. I live to dote on you, my dear, and I won't be denied my fun."

Catherine touched her temple and closed her eyes.

She looked about the room uneasily and took a hard swallow.

Her eyes rose to meet Nathan. "If my excursion into the world fails, may I return to you? I need to know there is a place of refuge for me."

He exchanged glances with Belmont. "Sure, honey, but I don't think it will come to that. I may not agree with your father on many things, but I know he loves his only child. Let him guide you back to refinement."

She nodded.

"If you command me, I must go."

Nathan's cheeks flushed red. "*Catherine*."

"It's settled," said John, clapping his hands. "Let's leave this deplorable melee of sheepish imbeciles for greener pastures! Our arrival in Vandeventer Place will be met with a fanfare you cannot imagine."

Catherine rocked back and forth. She held her stomach as if pained.

"I can imagine quite a lot," she said absently.

"My daughter, you have suffered a gruesome ordeal. You deserve the world, and I'm just the man to provide what your heart desires."

She stared at Nathan and then at Daisy. "Not *everything*."

"Well, almost. Can it be enough?"

"I suppose it must be." Her face bent into a wounded smile.

After father and daughter left the hospital, Nathan and Daisy hastily withdrew to his office. They stared at one another, stuck between relief and shock. Dissatisfaction had finally given way to infatuation.

"It's nice to relax after a long and troublesome day." Nathan hesitated. "I sometimes wonder if I'll ever be able to balance work and family life." His eyebrows arched, and he grinned widely. "It's not my strong suit."

"I'm the same, fully committed or not at all."

"We seem more alike than different," he said lightly. "It's something I wouldn't have guessed the night we met."

"You were too inebriated to comprehend the intricacies of our potential pairing, but I calculated them for the both of us."

His eyes brightened. "You made it plain the next morning."

"Someone had to clean your house. And your life."

"Yes, it was a mess. I had floundered for ten years."

"Catherine can be quite damaging," Daisy said. "I'll pay her due credit."

"She seemed taken with your reading earlier. Perhaps you affected her, planted a seed, as you Christians like to say."

"The smallest seed may produce the largest tree."

Nathan gazed at Daisy as if the formality of their conversation with John had transformed into a sincere eagerness. "When you quoted the Bible on the train, Catherine interrupted you. I sensed there were more verses you wished to share in hopes of her restoration."

Daisy smiled. "You are perceptive."

"Would you like to continue?"

"Now?" She sat up straight in her chair and shook her head. "I won't bore you with the balance."

He waved his hand as if to say *please*.

"You wish to hear my preachy recital?"

He grinned. "I want to kiss you, but it would surely lead to a sinful act."

She blushed and fanned her face. "I feel the same."

"There are cots in the other offices," he said, shifting in his seat.

Daisy spoke with a nervous apprehension. "We are not married." She hesitated. "I'm no Catherine Belmont, but I'm also not a harlot."

"Point taken," he said innocently. "I desired to celebrate Catherine's departure, and my giddiness got the better of me." He settled into his chair and gestured impatiently. "Please complete the passage. Perhaps your words will extinguish my fire like a frigid waterfall."

Daisy smirked. "A bucket of water on your head might be exactly what you need." How would he react to her insolent comment? Her European co-workers had never appreciated her concrete sense of humor.

"It couldn't hurt." He gave her a warm smile.

The amorous tilt in his voice filled her with excitement.

She retrieved her Bible from her dress pocket and thrust it toward him in mock defiance, hoping he might take a risk and kiss her at the conclusion of her recitation. She found her place and snuck a last look at him. "Don't you realize that friendship with the world makes you an enemy of God? I say it again. If you want to be a friend of the world, you make yourself an enemy of God. Do you think the Scriptures have no meaning? They say that God is passionate, that the spirit he has placed within us should be faithful to him. And he gives grace generously. As the Scriptures say, 'God opposes the proud but gives grace to the humble.' So humble yourselves before God. Resist the devil, and he will flee from you. Come close to God, and God will come close to you. Wash your hands, you sinners; purify your hearts, for your loyalty is divided between God and the world. Let there be tears for what you have done. Let there be sorrow and deep grief. Let there be sadness instead of laughter, and gloom instead of joy. Humble yourselves before the Lord, and he will lift you up in honor." Daisy closed her Bible and placed it neatly in her lap. Her fingers rested on the cover, and her nails dug cautiously into the leather. She was unsure of what he might say.

"Am I an enemy of God?"

"Only you can answer that, Nathan."

He scrubbed a hand over his face and gave her an inquisitive look.

"What if my great deliverance depends on *you*?"

"Then you're in terrible trouble."

"Why is that?"

"I'm imprisoned by a dragon, and there is no escape from my maze."

TWENTY-ONE

Psalm 21:1

How the king rejoices in your strength, O Lord!
He shouts with joy because you give him victory.

The electric trolley traversed a portion of the financial district known as Olive Street Canyon. Nathan pointed at a mule-drawn wagon with stenciled letters on the side, which read Hammond Bread Company. On Washington Avenue, the trolley passed Rhodes's Bank and the Mercantile College and then reached the bizarre and tumultuous waterfront. They hopped to street level and took in the vastness of the Mississippi River. Water sparkled in some spots and muddied in others. Spiderwebs stretched between unused pilings, which gave way to the bustle of port activity. Eddies and whitecaps implied a general flow of the water's movement south to the lush greenery of the delta as rough men frothed and crashed against one another while they worked. Their bosses chattered and buzzed and threw mean looks at curious citizens who passed by them.

Samuel looked amused by Nathan as he stood next to him. He slapped his son on the back and spoke with feeling. "Are you ready for a pleasant riverboat tour? I hear they serve excellent meals in the saloon."

"I suppose." Nathan turned toward downtown. "Wouldn't you rather eat at a restaurant on Broadway? The Regency has been a staple for years."

Daisy gave him a pleading look. "Brenda showed the Grand National to me when I was a teenage girl. She will be most jealous of our extravagance, and it will take her weeks to recover her senses. I will gladly lord it over her."

Nathan was interested, but also a bit mystified.

"I thought you were the better person."

"I was," she said soothingly, "but I've decided to be more like *you*."

Samuel laughed. "Once again, she's got you pinned, Son."

Inside and underway, the saloon displayed an uninhibited romanticism, its elaborate carpet having been woven in England and reassembled aboard ship. Strong columns held up the twenty-foot ceiling, which spanned the length of the boat and curved downward to greet the floor. Mahogany tables covered with cotton cloths reposed underneath gilded plates, and people talked loudly in various spots about the room. Waiters delivered food to expectant guests at a nearby station who sat with hands folded neatly in their laps. They smiled and thanked the helpful server as they removed silverware from rolled cloth napkins. Soon, their conversation fell to an indistinct murmur, and the cascade of chuckles and splashes—sounds which emanated from the paddlewheel—once more flooded the room.

Nathan and Daisy discussed Catherine's restoration, along with Ida and Heinrich's recent progress. Both patients seemed ready for a return to everyday life, but each occasionally regressed into a state of hysteria.

"They've come so far, but it only takes a small push to send them over the edge into the abyss again," Nathan said. "It demoralizes me."

Samuel sighed. "Offer them a word of encouragement. You'd be surprised at how much comfort they might take from their physician."

The riverboat's horn blew its thunderous alarm.

Burr Waugh! Burr Waugh! Burr Waugh!

The haunting echo reverberated amongst the walls in the saloon.

A shaken busboy dropped a dish at the far end of the saloon.

Nathan jumped out of his seat and glared at the young man.

Samuel's hand raised. He gave Nathan a look of reassurance.

"Please sit down, Son. We're not in a war zone here."

"I know, Pop." He took a drink of water. "I've been on edge lately."

"Dora has as well, and I worry it will soon affect her work."

Daisy seized Nathan's elbow and pulled him down.

She smiled ruefully at Samuel. "What's at issue?"

Nathan muttered and fumbled about for his fork.

"She lost both her husband and son in the war," Samuel said. "I think I might have operated on one of them. We were in the same vicinity around the same time." His shoulders shrugged. "Who knows about such things?"

Samuel paused for a moment and returned Daisy's smile.

"You two seem to hold up nicely, and I believe you pair well."

They each blushed.

"We are exploring the matter," said Nathan pensively.

Samuel continued in a convinced way. "You need love in your lives. It's a reason to get out of bed each morning and greet the day with fervor."

Nathan took a sip of water. "Don't you love Jesus above all else?"

Samuel folded his napkin and nodded his amusement at Nathan's unfortunate try at mockery. "Unless we are to become celibate monks, He wants us to marry while we live in this fallen realm." Samuel hesitated for a heightened effect. "Might that be your new chosen profession?"

Daisy laughed. "I highly doubt it."

Nathan smirked at her and returned his focus to Samuel.

"Pop, I haven't seen you with a woman in thirty years."

"Your mother's death almost destroyed me." Samuel sighed heavily and rubbed his chest as if pained. "I suppose it is reason enough."

Nathan settled into his chair. He threw his arm over the back.

"I knew for years you needed a new companion, but I never broached the subject. You would have chewed off my head."

A mother walked her little girl to the water closet at the far end of the saloon. Nathan tried to stifle his memories of the cemetery's wrought-iron fence and the sun blanched stone angels, but they eddied through his mind like the mud and the sparkle of the river. He had cried at Annie's funeral and listened to people speak in low voices. The whisper of prayers and the rustle of flowers rang through his ears as if blared through a megaphone. Nearby, a yard worker swept an area clean to prepare for yet another departed soul. Nathan held Catherine close to his side, concerned at her lack of tears and her blank expression. All the while, he silently cursed God. The pious deity disavowed an entire city, leaving little in His wake but a beaten populace and the speed of a vindictive current, thick in its course, and bound for a gulf more irresistible to the spirit. Their last prayers concluded, Nathan's children had followed the carnivorous flow and were now content in their grand exploration of the wild and enormous forest of the celestial landscape, the one without a bearded man, the uncharted and expansive waters of the stars, where all roamed freely and the dust of our former lives blew in great strands of faith, rendering art in a vigil of hued frolic.

Nathan was madly in love with the past, and it would take more than a lucky chance to break himself free from the truth of its grace.

Samuel turned from his observation of the child.

He gave Nathan a communal wink, which acknowledged their shared knowledge of misery but which also lamented the vacant passage of years. "I missed your mother for a long time." His face grew troubled. "I still do, although I know I must move forward with my life."

"You've forgotten one important fact, Pop."

"Which is?"

Nathan watched the other patrons talk and laugh easily, as if they had never known sufferance. He would tell his father straight. There was little need for soft language in matters of the heart. "At your advanced age, you should be content with the rocking chair and the value of a worthy novel."

Samuel rubbed his chin and smiled, unconvinced.

"Has Dora mentioned me lately?"

"What's your sudden interest in her?"

"She's a fine-looking woman."

Nathan burst into laughter. "Cease your banter, Pop."

Daisy's hand reached for Nathan's, and he accepted her touch.

She spoke in a smooth and kind tone.

"I don't think your father is the *least bit* funny."

Samuel smiled at her. "Your observation sounds like a compliment, but it could also be perceived as an insult. I'll choose the former."

"I only meant you should pursue love, Samuel."

Nathan pulled his hand away from her. "At his age?"

"Yes, Nathan, at any age."

She leaned forward and addressed Samuel directly. "Dora is an outstanding worker, the best I've seen in any hospital setting. She seems to care about people, which was rare during my stay in Europe."

"I care," said Nathan quickly.

Daisy fanned her face. "About yourself."

Samuel burst into laughter. Although he loved Nathan, he took delight in the spoil and suppression of his son's hubris.

"You're both fired," said Nathan, scowling. "Daisy can clear out of my hospital." He rubbed the table with a guarded movement.

"Son, your mood needs improvement."

Unable to keep his anger, Nathan burst into laughter.

Daisy followed his lead, and they both giggled.

He took her hand and kissed her fingers. "I didn't mean it."

"Yes, I know." She grew more serious. "You would perish without me."

He dropped her hand. "I was doing just fine when we met."

"No, Nathan. You were merely days from death."

<hr>

Daisy worked with Ida for two hours on Tuesday morning. The girl was concealed inside a wrapper of anguish for only her to know, tucked away from the world without the love of family or the companionship of good friends. Her irreducible spirit had been diminished to the absurdity of her irrational fears, one moment afraid of her own pillow, the next of a passing fly, still the next a cheerful chirp of a robin outside the hospital walls. People who spoke loudly or laughed or merely tip toed beside her bed frightened her immensely, as if monsters lurked about the hall like ants at a picnic.

Ida was content to live out her days confined to an institution, whether it be Belmont Hospital or the asylum on Arsenal Road. She had ceded her stake in the mashed and crowded land of death, absorbed as it was with the shadowy comforts and unmoved by trivial matters of love. Daisy held enough interest for them both, and she kept the details of Ida's progress in a folder, turning to the notes for solace when her own faith fell from view. This feeble but intelligent young girl must be saved.

Samuel approached, wearing a confident grin.

Daisy's eyes rose from the floor. "Watch out. This child bites."

He sat and studied Ida. "Did your mother bite you?"

Ida glanced up at him and then resumed her role play with a primitive rag doll. The china head was made from porcelain, and the jet black hair was molded into fashionable curls. The cheeks were blazed red, as if fire had touched them. Part of the nose was gone, and the eyes were a crystal blue.

Daisy got up from the floor and sat in a rocking chair beside Samuel. "Ida never speaks. She hums a tune while playing with that doll. I've tried to get her to open up and talk about what happened, but it's no use."

Samuel nodded.

"Nathan explained the details to me." He leaned forward. "I made many mistakes with my son, and I'll bet your mother made a few with you."

Ida's eyes darted toward Samuel and back to her doll.

He considered as he rocked.

"Yes, it's what I knew to be true." He held his hat in his lap and leaned forward again. "Would you like to hear some of my story?"

Ida stared at her doll. She nodded her willingness to listen.

"When I was a boy about your age, there was a man who committed a crime, a robbery, or some such act. Anyway, his friend helped him escape from justice and was caught in his place. While two policemen walked him to the jail, the man asked about his fate." Samuel used an authoritative voice. "One policeman said, 'You'll most definitely hang', behaving as if it was a certainty. Well, the young man took his knife and cut the throat of the policeman. He slashed another man, which killed him as well."

Ida's eyes grew large. Her breaths quickened.

Daisy placed her hand over her heart.

"I don't think this is an appropriate story for a twelve-year-old girl."

Samuel held up his hand. "This one here has seen the worst thing a person can ever witness, and I want her to know I've seen it, too."

Ida looked at Samuel. Surprise was written on her face.

"How?"

"Folks from town captured the fugitive and strung him up." Samuel emulated men who pulled a rope downward to lift the murderer's feet off the ground. "Once they had him secured in such a manner, they stacked wood around his boots and lit the pile on fire." He looked down at the hat in his lap and then swiped tears from his eyes. "You may think the story is false, but I was there and saw the whole thing. The man burned to death right in front of me, and I couldn't do anything to stop it, being as young as you are now, but I wanted to help that man with every ounce of my strength. I don't care what crime a person has committed. No one should ever meet such a fate." He retrieved a handkerchief from his pocket and blew his nose. "It's the single worst event of my life, the one that has haunted me the most. Even the horrors of the war couldn't compare, and I saw my share on the battlefields and in the surgery tents." He bent down on a knee to meet Ida at eye level and squeezed her shoulders. "Now you know you're not alone in this world. Someone else has seen what you've seen."

Ida's eyes fell to the floor. "It was my mother."

"I know it was, and I'm sorry it happened to her."

Ida burst into tears. "It was my fault."

"How do you figure?"

"The kids picked on me at school for being smarter than them. Mother took me out and taught me at home, but we argued about it because I didn't think she could teach me anything. She had pushed me for weeks, and I was tired that day. I hated conjugating Latin verbs and wanted to go play outside. The birds chirped, and the sun was high in the sky. It was a perfect day for chasing butterflies and laying in the grass under a shade tree."

"Please, continue," Daisy said. "We want to know how it happened."

Ida breathed deeply. "Mother liked to wear crinoline petticoats, which was fine with me. I liked their fluffy appearance, and I had to agree. It made her waist appear quite small, especially with her shoulders exposed." Ida's eyebrows raised. "Mother could be scandalous when she wanted, but she only wore them around the house to feel young again. It's what she said, anyway." She looked at her doll for courage and then continued. "In the middle of our fight, she backed into the fireplace, and her dress exploded. It all happened so fast. One minute she was fine and then the next she was screaming. I didn't know what to do, so I froze in place." Ida clutched the doll to her chest. "Then she fell down, still burning, and the rug caught on fire. Men from next door rushed in and someone grabbed hold of me. They dragged me out while I kicked and screamed." She swiped at her tears. "Someone said I bit a man." She reflected for a moment. "I suppose I did."

Samuel and Daisy exchanged glances.

Daisy got on her knees beside Samuel. "Let me tell you one thing, Ida. It was *not* your fault. We've all had tragedies befall us, mostly in our youth. I don't know why we are tested in such a way, but we are tested. Sometimes God sees fit to purify our spirits through a crucible of fire."

Daisy cast a smile at Samuel. "Thank you for sharing with us today. It has relieved some of my burden, and it may help this young girl recover."

Samuel returned to his chair. "I hope so."

Dora approached. Her bearing was casual.

"Samuel, I congratulate you for your humility and your sincerity."

"Thank you, Nurse Pratt."

"Please, sir, call me Dora."

He smiled. "Yes, mam."

Daisy soaked in the moment, pleased they had progressed with Ida but also enthused about the potential bond between Dora and Samuel.

Ida stood between them as Dora stroked her hair.

Frank Kaneski entered the hospital. His green eyes were as piercing as Daisy had ever seen them. Alarmed, she rushed toward the stairs as Samuel and Dora called after her. Daisy would hide in Nathan's office and hope Frank would take the hint, but his playful enjoyment of the hunt and his sadistic consciousness of domination would overwhelm her paltry attempt at gamesmanship. If captured once again, her frail heart would crack wide open and generate more heat than a thousand suns. At Nathan's desk chair, Daisy heard the words she'd spoken to him on the Fourth of July.

The wages of sin are death, and the Lake of Fire burns eternally.

Daisy muttered unintelligible words and looked nervously at the office door. Nathan stared across the desk at her, hoping she might snap back to reality. After several minutes, he realized Frank Kaneski was in the hospital, most likely at Belmont's urging. Nathan must do something drastic or she would fall victim to hysteria. He closed his eyes and prayed quietly. *God, if you're up there, I hope you're on her side. I've seen her hands tremble when no one else cared enough to notice. She doesn't sleep well, and her stomach burns from an ulcer. She's weaker than you know, Lord, and at this point in her life, she won't survive another confrontation with a man who betrayed her so viciously.*

He listened for a word in his spirit, but heard only the tumult of activity from the main hall. Daisy stared blankly at the floor and hardly moved.

Frank called out from the top of the stairs. "Anyone home up here?"

Nathan opened his office door and spoke to Frank.

"Please wait in the main hall while I get my affairs in order."

"Alright, but be quick about it," he said. "I don't have all day."

Frank's leather shoes stomped down the stairs.

Nathan stuck his head into an empty office, which had been used recently for storage. An orderly named Jesse passed by the open doorway. Nathan grabbed him and shoved him against the far wall in the hallway. "We have little time before that man comes stomping up here to attack Daisy. Get some other orderlies to assist you." He pointed at the shadowy room across the hall. "I want you to make Daisy look like the busiest woman of all time, as if she hasn't picked up after herself in months."

Jesse's eyes opened wide. "Yes, sir!"

He ran to fetch another orderly named Stan and together they moved fast, scrambling and panting while they worked. In a flash, they appeared with a desk. A third orderly named Richard retrieved an empty file cabinet from a closet at the end of the hall and wheeled it into the makeshift office.

Jesse nudged Nathan and took a step backward to clear himself from the doctor's wrath. "We don't have any files for Miss Lawrence. What if someone peeks inside the cabinet and finds only air?"

Nathan considered and was a fair while about it.

He wished he could escape this encounter, but he was no coward.

"You make a good point," he said. "I'll have to create a distraction."

Samuel approached, followed by Dora and Ida. He gave Nathan a look of concern. "Is everything alright?"

A malice grew within Nathan. He retrieved a handkerchief and wiped sweat from his forehead. "I have things under control."

Dora smiled, easily convinced. She held Ida's hand.

Nathan sensed it gave the child comfort.

"Will you two look after her while I handle Daisy's situation? We don't want Ida to get lost in the shuffle after such progress has been achieved."

Samuel and Dora exchanged glances.

"We'd be happy to help."

Dora held up Ida's hand, swinging it playfully, and Samuel did likewise with the other one. "Let's go play a fun game in the hall."

"We don't know any games," said Ida sadly.

"Oh, honey, I'm an old woman who knows lots of fun games."

Nathan stuck his head inside the storage room. The men had hastened as instructed, and now the room actually resembled a working office.

Jesse and Stan wished Nathan luck and withdrew.

Nathan hoped it would be enough to free Daisy from her maze. If not, he would bring her inevitable encounter with Frank Kaneski to an abrupt conclusion. He was tired and irritated from a rough stretch of weeks and the last thing he wanted was another forced revisitation of the past, his or hers.

Nathan placed Daisy inside her new office. As she looked about the room, the sound of hurried and impatient steps from the hallway filled her with a ghastly dread. She heard Rose call faintly from her place of rest, asking Daisy to listen for the words she needed to regard, notions of a place more grand and lovely, a land where two sisters might be reunited with a dear mother and an artistic father. Daisy brushed off the spirit's call to adventure, as she did every night. She turned toward Nathan, and her eyes met his.

"What should I do when Frank enters? Pretend to work?"

He shook his head. "Study the Word."

Nathan opened a drawer and retrieved her Bible.

Daisy held it close to her cheek for a few moments. She placed it flat on the desk and flipped to the psalms, hoping David's wisdom might resonate.

She looked up from the text. "Please don't let me die, Nathan."

"I won't let anything bad happen to you."

"Will you give me your solemn promise?"

"I swear an oath."

She nodded her understanding. "Alright, then. You may collect him."

Daisy prayed Psalm 21 aloud as she sat alone. "You will capture all your enemies. Your strong right hand will seize all who hate you. You will throw them in a flaming furnace when you appear. The Lord will consume them in his anger; fire will devour them. You will wipe their children from the face of the earth; they will never have descendants."

Nathan opened the door and introduced Frank to Daisy. He spoke first and gave Daisy immense credit for Catherine Belmont's recovery.

She looked up from her Bible and spoke in a reasonable tone.

Frank waved her off with a dismissive hand.

"Your words are nonsensical, and here you are reading your book of myths. I trusted you had regained your senses, but I see now why you left Europe. America has always been the land that time forgot, a place where Puritans freely pray to their mysterious warlord in the clouds. Tell me, has a thief stolen your black steeple-crowned hat and your gray tunic?"

She blushed and closed her Bible. "Frank, please be civil."

"You've proven my theory as certitude."

Nathan sat in a chair opposite Daisy. "What theory?"

"A woman will never do the work of a man, even when she treats lunatics in an asylum, the lowest possible career position one might attain."

He paused.

"Other than prostitution."

Frank grinned as he pointed at Daisy.

"This woman is of ill repute, and I warn you, she cannot stay in one spot for a lengthy period. It's only a matter of months before she acts on her immoral impulses. Her kind of lewdness is usually reserved for back alleys."

Nathan held up a palm. "Now, hold on a minute."

Frank winked at him. "If I were you, I wouldn't get too attached."

Daisy had tried to stand firm but failed. She once again surrendered to Frank Kaneski, the lone man who had pierced her outer veil.

Please, Lord, don't let this man steal me away.

Nathan asked him to leave.

"You have no authority over me, sir. I will stay right here."

Nathan stood quickly and threw a hard punch at Frank, landing a blow on his nose. Frank recoiled and stepped backward as Nathan rushed forward and shoved him against the office wall. Daisy had never seen a man behave in such a forceful manner. It both surprised and shocked her.

Frank fell to his knees. "I believe you've broken my nose!"

Nathan whipped out a handkerchief and threw it at him.

"Here, take this. You can consider it a consolation prize."

Daisy realized a miracle had occurred.

When Frank had entered the office, he seemed as he was in Europe, powerful and commanding, a presence to behold, but he now seemed pallid and careworn, as if all the life was drained out of him. Her eyes moved to Nathan, who seemed larger and stronger than before their confrontation, as if some unknown force transferred every bit of Frank's vitality to him.

In an odd turn of events, she felt sorry for Frank. He was once so formidable, like the renowned city of Babylon with its famed walls and hanging gardens and a ziggurat which rose to the heavens, now a desolate territory of jackals and owls, forever to be uninhabited, its vainglory reduced to paw prints in the soil, its sanctuary to Marduk, king of the Babylonian gods, removed stone by stone, the temple's foundation sunken and filled with rainwater, the earth having swallowed up the golden throne.

He cried out to her as he held the handkerchief over his bloody face.

"You are supposed to leave with me today!"

She looked at him as a mother might gaze at a helpless child.

"Where would we go? What horrid fate did you have in mind for me?"

"You understand little, and it will lead to your downfall."

She gestured. "Alright, then. Please enlighten me."

"Rosemarie is dead." He looked up at her. Tears coursed down his cheeks. "I truly loved her, you know. She introduced me to a new world."

"One of foul wickedness," said Daisy softly. "You almost killed me."

"Rosemarie desired to murder you in Vienna, not me." He hesitated. "Our benefactors were angered by her vanity and her willingness to defy them." He wiped his face and sat on the floor as Nathan stood over him. "You must leave with me, Daisy. It is your destiny to leap from your high ledge with me by your side. I will escort you to the eternal, in keeping with Lucifer's wishes. He is a most expectant lover, and he awaits your death."

She needed more information. "How did Rosemarie die?"

"Does it matter?"

"I'd like to understand what happened."

He sighed. "We soiled your name in the press for over a year until our benefactors instructed us to cease our efforts. We wanted to marry, and she even entertained the idea of travel to meet my parents in Chicago." He slightly chuckled under his breath. "The notion of her in my mother's house was too frightful to contemplate. It would have been a war of the ages, of that I am sure. Of course, you would think Rosemarie obviously held the upper hand, but let me assure you, my mother is far more depraved."

"On this point, we agree. I worked in your mother's house for a year, posing as an Austrian maid. Iniquity abounded within her."

"Which is why I left for Europe at the first opportunity. I wanted to make my own way in the world and carve a place for myself."

"You certainly did that, Frank. Your words are repeated everywhere."

His eyes fell to the floor, and his voice lost all authority.

"After Rosemarie's death, everything changed for me. My ideas were stolen by our benefactors. What can be given can also be taken away, and it's exactly what happened to me. Credit for my efforts was given to another man, and my concepts were renamed under his banner." He took a deep breath and exhaled. "It was then I was told of my destiny, how it intertwined with your own. Rosemarie had tried to derail their efforts in a determined but inconsequential attempt at escape from the life she had been born into as a young girl so many centuries ago, as if her body would not suddenly turn to powder without their magic." He wiped another tear. "I suppose she loved me enough to try, and for that I will always be grateful."

"Your mother announced your homecoming. She seemed sad, as if you had committed an unpardonable sin. Now I know the origin of her angst."

He nodded his agreement. "She was most unhappy with our union."

Nathan sat in the chair opposite Daisy's desk.

"Why?" he asked sincerely.

Frank's eyes rose to meet his. "She was born into the cabal life just as Rosemarie had been born into it in Italy. There's no leaving the *family*."

Nathan pressed his back into the chair. "I see."

Daisy perked up. "Can you return to Chicago?"

"No, my mother will not allow it. I must fulfill my role."

"I'm not going anywhere with you. Today or any other day."

"You must not hold Nathan back, Daisy. It's not fair to him."

"Lucifer told you about Nathan?"

He nodded.

"After I found what was left of Rosemarie's body, I was given a vision of the future and his place in it. I was also told what I must do with you."

He looked at Nathan. "You are very important to him."

Nathan smiled. "I've gathered as much from your conversation."

Frank smirked and turned his focus to Daisy. "If you continue to deny Lucifer, you will meet the same fate as Rosemarie and worse, you will suffer for eternity at his hands. Why not come with me now and please him?"

"He said he would give me the entire world if I comply."

"Yet you mistakenly refused him." His eyebrows raised. "You have spent many sleepless nights since your betrayal in torment. Am I correct?"

She nodded.

He stood and extended his hand to her.

"Please come with me, Daisy." He glanced at Nathan and then turned back to her. "Leave him to the woman who must come next, his child of darkness. She alone can guide him like Circe to the underworld."

He paused.

"Nathan must be allowed to enter the next stage of his life."

"Catherine has already gone from this hospital. You are too late."

Frank cast a look of confusion. "John's daughter is only relevant to him." He had a revelation and gave Daisy a knowing smile. "You are unaware of the woman's identity. It's probably for the best."

"You mean it's not his wife?"

"Ex-wife," said Nathan politely. He seemed to enjoy their banter.

She smirked at him. "I stand corrected."

"Catherine matters little," Frank said. "She disrupted his past, deserting him in his time of need, souring him on the notion of love. Another woman was offered to him, a prostitute who would appease his need for a mother's encouragement and affection. You were brought into the equation as the ultimate destroyer. Once you are gone, he will never chance love again, and it will open him up to the larger world which awaits, the same world I was shown for an instant, the one which I must now leave." He extended his hand once more. "Please accept your fate."

Nathan stood. "It's time for you to leave."

Frank gave him an impatient look.

"She must come with me today, or all will be lost."

"The woman doesn't want to leave with you."

"Her wishes matter little. Lucifer demands her departure."

Nathan shoved Frank, and he took a step back. "Please, stop."

"Will you murder me if I don't?"

Frank wore a sheepish expression. "You know I cannot."

"Then get out of her office before I murder *you*."

A villainous smile formed across Frank's face. "Yes, that's it. Give into the feeling. Many innocent victims await the sharp edge of your knife."

"I'm giving you one minute to leave or you will die here today."

"It's not what I was told, Nathan. I must escort her home to Big Rock."

"Well, it's not happening today, pal." He shoved Frank hard.

Frank fell to the floor. Daisy gasped at his sudden weakness. He seemed to fade into a ghastly nothingness in front of their eyes, as Rosemarie must have done in Vienna. She momentarily rooted for Frank to rise to his feet and leave the hospital with a shred of dignity intact.

Nathan grabbed Frank and dragged him toward the door as he had done with Ida in the main hall. Daisy almost yelled for him to stop, but decided against it. Nathan jerked Frank to his feet and pushed him into the hallway.

Frank gave Daisy one last look. He seemed most infirm.

"I'm sorry for everything," he said. "I'm a complete failure."

"As am I," she said. "We share the trait."

He forced a smile. "And a similar outcome awaits us both."

He turned and walked down the hall. Daisy listened to the sounds of his shoes lightly stepping down the stairs. She was overcome with deep regret.

She placed her head in her hands and wept.

Nathan shoved a box out of the way and took a seat. "Well now, that was certainly entertaining." He took a deep breath and exhaled while he rubbed the knuckles on his right hand. He studied them for bruises.

Daisy gazed at the love of her life, astounded at his ability to defeat the notorious monster who took everything from her in Vienna, as if she was merely a temporary distraction. The notion of Rosemarie's entry into the afterlife lifted Daisy's despair and provided a sense of relief. She would never see Frank Kaneski again, nor would she be forced to look over her shoulder for a demon with dripping fangs. Daisy could not stop herself from smiling or from feeling chills up and down her spine. Finally, her misery had ended.

Thank you, Jesus, for bringing this man into my life.

She stared a hole through Nathan, which made him uncomfortable.

He shifted uneasily in his chair. "What are you doing?"

"I'm lost in admiration of your courage. You have a wagonload of bravery when you need it. I fold in a crisis, but you rise to the occasion."

"Frank and Rosemarie ruined your belief in yourself."

She nodded.

"They played a part, but others did equal harm."

"I'd like to hear more about it when you're ready to tell me."

"Another day," she said. "I'm exhausted."

"You should know I would have killed him."

"I believe you," said Daisy adoringly.

Nathan crossed his arms. "We're not all perfect Christians."

"I'm hardly the best role model. When Frank arrived, I shut down, believing his scrutiny would lead to my dismissal." She inhaled and exhaled. "For a moment, I feared for my life."

"Where was your faith?"

"Poof." She used her hand for effect. "Gone in an instant."

"You're right about one thing."

"Which is?"

"You're no role model."

She smiled. "Exactly."

Twenty-Two

My God, my God, why have you abandoned me?
Why are you so far away when I groan for help?
Every day I call to you, my God, but you do not answer.
Every night I lift my voice, but I find no relief.

April 1880

Daisy sat on the edge of a cliff, which overlooked a broad pile of rocks and beyond to a vast forested area. It was a suitable spot to contemplate her troubles and to discern how best to earn her father's affections. As the guardian of his daughter's trust, Pierre often refused to disperse his warmth, choosing to wander as a journeyman through the fields of wine and business, roaming restlessly up and down the hills and dales, apparently believing his absence might prove beneficial to his family, fatigued as he was from his perpetual cravings for somewhere else.

Rose begged to share in the beauty and recklessness of her older sister's everyday adventures, desperate to be included in her boldness and diligence.

Daisy avoided thoughts of Rose, caught up as she was in a scuttled and turbulent loneliness. She was incompatible with the values of most people she encountered, believing them either better or worse than her, the latter being most often the case. From an early age, she had been stranded on a solitary jetty which extended into the sea of intellectual vanity, and the barrenness of her isolation blinded her to the simple needs of others, abysmally gray and colorlessly out of vogue as they were in her estimation.

She leaned back on her elbows and recalled her father's comments from the previous evening. They had threatened to take her buoyancy.

"Your sister is destined for bookishness," said Pierre, as he sat at the kitchen table. "We made a mistake by giving you the name Daisy."

"Why, daddy?"

"We should have called you Wild Forest Rose."

"What would you have called my sister?"

"*Lina.* The name means delicate and pure."

"I'm not pure?"

He shook his head. "Far from it."

Daisy stared at the floor. His observation had hurt her feelings.

He squeezed her shoulder and gave her a smile. "Take heart. You are an *Adaline*, which means a noble and kind-hearted person."

"Then why did you call me Daisy?"

He sighed. "Your mother's friend, Henry, loved to paint landscapes." Pierre's eyes rested softly on her. "Patrice still has a particular fondness for daisies." He shrugged. "It was out of my hands from the beginning."

The transient memory fell into a mist and faded into the ether.

She pushed off her elbows and surveyed the trees, which began abruptly where the rocks ended. Daisy lost her temper as a fit of anger beset itself upon her. She embraced her fury as she gazed wistfully at the forest.

Daisy retrieved a piece of paper her mother had stuffed in her pocket and angled it with precision, allowing sunlight to highlight the words on the page. "I am scorned and despised by all! Everyone who sees me mocks me. They sneer and shake their heads, saying, 'Is this the one who relies on the Lord? Then let the Lord save him! If the Lord loves him so much, let the Lord rescue him!' Yet you brought me safely from my mother's womb and led me to trust you at my mother's breast. I was thrust into your arms at my birth. You have been my God from the moment I was born."

She wadded the paper and released it. She held her breath as it descended to the earth below her feet. Patrice had delivered an encoded message to her daughter, but Daisy did not understand its purpose.

Rose approached from behind a colossal oak. It provided shade on a hot afternoon, much like the tree at Mamre, which had covered Abraham's tent.

"I knew you were there the whole time," said Daisy over her shoulder.

"Why didn't you say anything?"

"I wanted to see how long you would hide."

"Can we go down to the rocks? I want to jump them with you."

"You're too young, Rose. It's not a game."

"We could have fun together, if you would allow it."

Daisy shielded her eyes and glanced at the yellow sun.

"Come sit beside me, and I'll read you this psalm."

"I don't like mother's Bible verses. They confuse me."

The hard surface beside her was cool and smooth. Daisy patted it.

Her sister watched fearfully and jealously from behind the oak.

"Rose, why are you angry at God?" She chuckled at the notion. "You haven't lived long enough to be mad at Him."

Rose sat beside Daisy and hung her feet over the edge. She picked up a small pebble and dropped it. The delayed ricochet made her smile.

"Tell me," said Daisy impatiently. "Otherwise, I'm going back home."

"Alright." Rose leaned backward and placed her weight on her hands. "I snuck out one day last year when you were in school."

"You walked alone in the woods like me?"

Rose nodded.

She gave Daisy a pensive look. "I had a good time until I saw mother and Henry in a meadow. They rolled around on a blanket with big smiles on their faces. When they saw me, she yelled, and I ran away."

The child must have made up a lie. "Mother never mentioned it."

Rose stood and wiped her hands clean on her dress. She rubbed her eyes and looked about the area. "The next day, she told me never to say anything, especially to daddy or I would be sent to a soldier's home."

"What?"

Rose wiped her moist forehead. "Mother got really mad at me."

Had their mother threatened Rose with reprisal?

Had she cheated on her husband with an itinerate painter?

Rose peered over the side. "I dream of those boulders at night in my bed, and I quietly ponder what it would be like to jump."

Dissatisfaction and contempt arose within Daisy.

Rose would soon ruin what was left of their decadent family.

"Do what you want," she said. "I'm not your keeper."

Rose threw up her head. "You don't mean it, Daisy."

"You know what? I think you are an accident."

"What does that mean?"

"It means you should never have been born."

Rose covered her face with her hands. "Take it back!"

"You're too young to understand, but there's a big difference in our ages. Pierre and Patrice had no plans for another child after I was born." A revelation overtook Daisy as she considered the age difference between her and Brenda. She drew back a little. "I'm also a mistake, so we're even."

Rose swiped a tear from her eye as she looked to the edge of the woods where the trailhead began. "I'm going down there. We can race."

"I'll stay up here." She was surprised by the abundance of Rose's tears. "It's too wet, and I have no intention of getting muddy this morning."

"Suit yourself." Rose moved with a weary step.

She grabbed a thin pine tree and descended several feet.

Daisy's harsh delivery had left her heavy-hearted. "It's clever to use the tree trunk for leverage." To keep her family intact, she must regain her sister's adoration, and she hoped Rose would accept her try at redress.

Rose stood silently. She peered down into the forest.

Daisy pushed further, unwilling to wait. "Henry has taught you well."

Rose frowned. "Don't mention his name. I hate that scoundrel."

Daisy grinned. "Yes, me, too."

Rose turned toward Daisy and swiped the tears from her cheeks.

She lost her footing and slid downward.

Daisy sat up straight. Her mind comprehended the unfathomable.

Rose landed on a boulder and bounced to the right. Her body laid still on the ground. It was contorted into an unfamiliar position.

Adrenaline shot through Daisy's veins. "Oh, my God!"

She recognized her error at once. "I'm sorry for taking your name in vain, Lord, but please don't take her. Our family will surely disintegrate."

An angel appeared at the edge of the woods. He stood seven feet tall.

He removed a glowing sword from his sheath and pointed it at Rose's body. The child's arm moved, and she groaned to life. Daisy ran down the hill without concern for her safety, hoping to thank the angel for being a messenger of God. When she reached her sister and gazed at the tree line, the angel's shimmering form had withdrawn into the woods.

Daisy chased the angel for a mile before she tired.

She stopped her pursuit and bent over to catch her breath.

A few moments later, she stood erect and listened for any sound.

There was only the song of the nightingale, its lovely melody out of place in the daylight hours. Daisy marched back to Rose, unsure what to make of the unusual appearance of a symbolic bird. As she reached her sister, the song ceased, and a sense of calm returned.

Rose turned back from the woods when Daisy helped her stand. She put her hands on her sister's shoulders for support, and her face wore an excited countenance, as if a miracle had occurred. "Did you hear the birdsong?"

"Yes." Daisy looked about the area. "It was peculiar."

"I dreamed of the nightingale just now."

Daisy wasn't sure what to say. "Alright."

"It talked to me peacefully, like a friend."

"I don't believe in such nonsense."

Rose looked at the top of the cliff. "You should."

"Why? Give me one good reason."

"They watch us from the trees. Someday they will come for you."

Daisy felt a chill run up and down her spine. "Who watches?"

Rose wore a half-crazed smile. "The good and the bad."

Daisy opened the front door. She was struck by the smell of the long grass seeded with wildflowers and the sight of butterflies and wrens which floated and darted above the swaying tips of the grass. Tall trees surrounded the meadow across from her house, and a trail between them led down to the banks of the Missouri. Daisy would reverently peruse her Bible under the canopy, and she would contemplate the elegance of the psalm. Amid the gurgle of the passing river and the chirps of squirrels high on their limbs, she would praise God for His mercy. He allowed Rose to live another day, which was a miracle worthy of veneration, but He also allowed Rose to fall.

Daisy wanted to know *why*, as fierce indignation mounted within her. It was accompanied by a grisly shame. She would give the Lord a liberal margin of forgiveness if He dared to speak the unmentionable truth.

Just before she reached the river trailhead, the front door of her house creaked open. Daisy turned toward the sound and shielded her eyes from the sun. Rose threw a vague accusation of a crime only she could calculate. Three weeks had passed since the fall, but Rose did not regain her eager outlook or her propensity to chat Daisy to exhaustion by the fireplace. Her soul seemed to have left her body to the ashes and the dust.

Daisy yelled across the meadow. "Do you need something, Rose?"

The door closed with a thud.

Daisy sighed and stepped onto the trail.

The door opened once more, this time quickly and with force. Daisy must choose her words carefully if she were to reach her ailing sister.

Patrice called out to her. "Where do you think you're going?"

Daisy exhaled loudly and then turned and marched toward her house.

She stood twenty paces from her mother, unwilling to budge.

"I'll read my Bible by the river."

"You were instructed to memorize the next two verses at the kitchen table." Patrice spoke in a panting voice. "It's important, child."

"Mother, I've already completed your assignment."

"You have not memorized the verses."

Daisy opened her Bible to Psalm 22. "Do not stay so far from me, for trouble is near, and no one else can help me."

"I know you can read." Patrice gestured strangely, as if frightened by an awful insight. "You don't understand the meaning behind the words."

"It's simple. David wants God to grant his wishes."

"What about the next verse?"

"I'm not sure about that one."

"Then you need to return to the table so we can discuss it."

Daisy closed the Bible and stared at her mother. Rose's glum demeanor had practically driven both Patrice and Daisy to madness, and it was merely a matter of time before one of them imploded. Pierre was no help. He spent his days drunk on wine in the cellar and his nights playing cards in town.

Daisy hoped the Lord would provide answers through His psalms.

"Why are you persecuting me? I did nothing wrong."

"You're no martyr, child, but you will follow our rules."

Daisy raised her fists and yelled at the sky.

Patrice gave her a faint smile. "Petulance is a fool's errand."

"Mother, she's so depressed. I cannot sit with her another afternoon." Daisy squeezed her Bible to her chest. "Please allow me some time to myself. I need to reflect on what happened so I can understand it."

Her mother's arms crossed. "You blame yourself."

"I should have been a better sister."

Patrice nodded her agreement. "Yes."

Daisy was called to defend her honor. She would not shrink from this necessary confrontation. "You should have been a better mother."

Patrice's eyebrows raised in alarm. "How so?"

"She was angry with you. It's why she slipped and fell."

"My child had no reason for distress. You've made it up."

Rose's accident had started a war of wills between a grieving mother and a forsaken daughter. Daisy prepared for the battle to come.

"I will take my leave, and there's nothing you can do to stop me."

"Please stay. I beg you, *ma chéri*."

"Don't call me your sweet darling. I know you blame me."

"I need you here, Daisy. I cannot handle this alone."

"Why should I? You know what you did."

She paused.

"You also know with whom you did it."

Patrice looked older now. "I was lonely."

"Aren't we all?"

Daisy turned her back on her mother.

"Please stay! We need you so very much!"

Daisy descended a thousand feet to the Missouri River and located her favorite wooden bench. She flipped open her Bible and read aloud, thankful for the time alone and hopeful for Rose's complete recovery, believing fully in the power of prayer and the holiness of the Lord. God would fix all which was wrong with the Lawrence family. He had the power to stop the clatter of bolts and chains and the sworn oaths of drunken fathers against mothers.

* * *

July 1880

Rose withdrew inside herself over the months which followed. Daisy often sat on her sister's bed and asked if she could help. Her offer was met with a stony expression. Something broke inside Rose when she fell, and even the doctor could not diagnose or treat the problem. Like everyone else, Daisy politely gave up on her sister. She stationed herself at the kitchen table and memorized verses in her Bible, obeying her mother's instructions to stay at home. It was a groping and indwelling season. She craved escape.

A gunshot rang in the trees. The sound reverberated off the walls.

"The Simpson family is hunting nearby." Patrice looked at the trees through the window. "It's not a good day to be outside."

Daisy gave her mother a curious look. "Are they on our land?"

Patrice stiffened. "Yes."

"Then Papa should tell them to clear out."

Patrice laughed bitterly and caught herself.

Daisy's lips pursed. "He won't do it, will he?"

Her mother sat at the table and ran her palm across the surface. "Tell me what you are reading, so I might feel better this morning."

Daisy flipped the pages in her Bible to Psalm 22. "I wanted to memorize the last three verses, but I'm having trouble."

"Read them to me."

"Let the rich of the earth feast and worship. Bow before him, all who are mortal, all whose lives will end as dust. Our children will also serve him. Future generations will hear about the wonders of the Lord. His righteous acts will be told to those not yet born. They will hear about everything he has done."

"It's a nice sentiment," said Patrice impatiently.

"What don't you like?"

"Daisy, I don't wish to argue today. Let me live in peace."

A gentle breeze wafted through the window and washed over Daisy. It offered relief from her mother's ramblings. "Doesn't God smile favorably on holy undertakings? Doesn't He hear and answer our prayers?"

Patrice stared at the table. "Not always."

Daisy's cheeks flushed red. "You don't pray enough."

Patrice stiffened again, but she spoke lightly. "I do. *Sometimes*."

She expected her mother to offer God the regard He required of her. The escapades with Henry in the woods must end. "You don't pray the right way, and it has cost this family a great deal, Mother."

"Daisy, you pray enough for us all."

The front door opened and closed.

Daisy jabbed her finger in Patrice's direction. "Mother, march down to the saloon and retrieve your husband."

Patrice pressed her back against the chair and faced the window.

She looked about the room for a few moments.

Her eyes flickered. "Did you hear something?"

"I hear a mother who will not accept responsibility."

Daisy paused.

"I'm not our matriarch, although you've forced me into the role more often than I'd care to admit." Daisy rubbed the tabletop, emulating Patrice. "I'm exhausted, Mother. You must return to the land of the living."

Patrice ran to the bedroom and searched frantically.

She rushed through the kitchen and opened the front door.

After a moment, Patrice turned toward Daisy and nodded.

"What, Mother?"

Patrice's eyes were filled with surprise and curiosity.

"She's *gone.*"

"What?"

"Rose has left us."

"I'll go after her."

"It will be too late."

Daisy trekked through the woods while she cursed her family. What had she done to deserve their arrogant neglect and their utter incompetence? When she caught up with Rose, Daisy would offer her sister a piece of her mind. It was time to settle all disputes once and for all.

At Big Rock, she gazed down from atop the cliff.

Rose's body laid bloody and deformed amid the pile of unforgiving rocks. Daisy sat and cried and leaned back on her hands as Rose had done the day she fell. She blamed herself for allowing her sister to run free in the forest, the same way Patrice allowed her to roam.

"She was too young to know any better!"

Daisy's eyes combed through the woods, searching for the angel.

She yelled louder. "Why did you do this to her?"

After a time, her tears ceased, and she resolved to help others. Mental illness was a scourge which plagued her family. With God's help, Daisy would become a doctor who studied the human brain. She would find a cure for the grievous malady and ensure no others shared her sister's fate.

Daisy started toward town at a brisk pace.

Pierre must leave the saloon and save his wife.

The nightingale sang a lovely tune from the trees as she walked.

Twenty-Three

Psalm 23:1

The Lord is my shepherd;
I have all that I need.

October 1893

Twelve days after Frank Kaneski left Belmont Hospital for good or for naught, Nathan and Daisy walked along Washington Avenue, taking in the Saturday afternoon sights. The news of Frank's death hit her harder than Nathan expected, and Daisy now carried a Bible most everywhere she went. Ten days earlier, the Globe-Democrat stated Frank's emaciated body was found hollow-eyed and bloodless in a hotel room, and the paper noted his previous connection to a wealthy family with properties in Chicago and in various European locales. The writer included no formal statement on Frank's released works, which were currently published under a different author's name. Daisy had kept the only extant original copy of *Consciousness of Domination*, his most popular title, as her organizational and editorial contributions demanded. Nathan hoped she might bear the weight of Frank's demise.

"What would you like to do next?" He glanced about the area.

"We should look for Sophie."

He stopped walking and frowned. "Back to work already?"

"It's who we are, Nathan."

"Well, the dog would not be this far downtown."

"How do you know?"

"James last saw her near Forest Park, which is miles from here."

A Quinby carriage buzzed in front of them on the avenue.

Her eyes followed it west. "I should have brought my Bible."

Nathan pulled her under an awning and hugged her close, caring little for the opinions of those who might judge them. A heartfelt passion almost overcame him, but he constrained his emotion, as their relationship was yet in an awkward and childish state, and boyish flattery might cause its spoil.

"We have all afternoon," he said. "The city is ours for the taking."

"Still, I think we should try."

Nathan held her close as he whispered reassurances into her ear. She leaned into his chest and wept. Her body shook exceedingly, but she made little sound, seemingly aware of their setting and the standard of propriety.

Her tears eventually ceased.

He handed her a clean handkerchief so she might dry her cheeks.

"I'm sorry for being upset, Nathan."

"I understand how you must feel," he said. "I've eternally grieved over the loss of my lifelong friend and the mother of my children in Catherine, not to mention how bothered I've been over losing my companion of ten years in Sheila. I feel a melancholy guilt for failing those who need me."

He led her up the street to a wooden bench, which the city had placed in front of Flanagan's Irish pub. He had not experienced such depth of feeling in his spirit since he watched Thomas Hannah hang and, as the murderer's feet danced and dangled, a nebulous vapor wrestled itself free from the flesh.

Nathan leaned in close so their mouths might touch in a wet and tender embrace, but Daisy drew her head sharply away from him. "It's traditional for ladies to receive a marriage proposal before the first kiss, not the other way around." Her cheeks had flushed bright crimson.

His body stiffened, impelled by a force so strong it threatened to sweep him along the avenue and into the fierce and unforgiving currents of the river. He must keep her trust in him or she would become frightened and throw up her hands. "You are no conventional lady, and we are no ordinary couple. I believe on those two points, we can agree."

She spoke in an elusive tone, as if she knew more than him.

"At first, I assumed you would be like Frank, and I would be a fool to repeat the mistake I had made with such a man." She ran her fingers along the smooth surface of the bench. "Over time, I realized you are much stronger than people know and much more capable than him, as Frank was given to vanity and greed. You are what some call a true believer, and once you commit to a plan you've visualized in your mind, there is no stopping you, as you feel compelled to bring the plan into reality. It's why both sides want you in their ranks, and it's why I must get through to you for before it's too late. What happens to me will matter little in the final analysis."

Music wafted from across the street, and his eyes rose to meet the marquee, which read Grand Opera House. "Alright, Miss Daisy Lawrence. If you won't kiss me, then you must follow my lead." He stood and dragged her behind him. They crossed the thoroughfare, dodging fast moving wagons and the electric trolley as it ambled east toward the cruel river.

"Come with me." Nathan pulled Daisy inside the empty lobby and then upstairs to the second tier, the exclusive level.

She leaned over the railing and peered at the floor below them.

"Won't we be asked to leave?"

"No one is here but the orchestra. Pop said they practice on Saturday afternoons for the week's major performance." He smiled at her. "You should learn to relax from time to time."

She looked faint. "I don't think we should be here."

Nathan took her hand and led her in a waltz, one he hadn't attempted since his last ball in 1882. "Frank and Rosemarie may have met tragic ends," he said as he kept a box step tempo, "but you must admit their deaths have lessened your burden. You may yet stake a claim at a Golden Age."

She bowed playfully. "Yes, my yoke is lighter now."

"I am also free of Catherine for the first time in my life."

She moved closer and hugged him. "How does it feel?"

He spoke with a suppressed eagerness. "Wonderful."

Daisy was drawn within of late, and her iron concourse had been complicated to traverse. Under the guise of the continuation of the search for Sophie, and after Nathan and the staff coaxed her for hours, she kindly accepted his invitation for a restful stroll through downtown. Their brief time together proved to be splendid, and he was glad to be in her presence.

He would keep their afternoon lively and filled with adventure.

The orchestra ceased playing, and the conductor smiled at them.

Nathan's hand cupped under Daisy's elbow, and his finger pressed lightly against her pinkish lips. His desire mounted as he gazed into her crystal blue eyes. Daisy's countenance grew soft, and her lips parted.

He gently ran his finger from side to side, wetting it with her saliva, and then retrieved it, chasing the urge to erase the distance between his mouth and hers. Her fingers grasped the back of his arms, pulling him ever closer.

His hand clutched the back of her hair, pulling her head into position for a lingering kiss. When their lips met, her posture slackened, and she let out an appreciative sigh. His pulse raced as they detoured into something completely new, a mad tumble into uncharted territory, a land engulfed by wildness and the cessation of worry, a place designed for investigation and experimentation, the most primal and basic of sensory experience, but also one built of fear and trembling, as it might become too good, too soon, and the perfection might overwhelm the mind's ability to cope.

He pulled slightly back from her and noted the prettiness of her face, the brilliance of her sidelong glance, and the intelligence of her smile. She carried a natural talent for wonder and romance, and he had never experienced a love like this in all his years, not even with Catherine. He threw caution to the haphazard wind and kissed her a second time.

Behind them, the Opera House manager clapped.

Startled, they quickly separated.

"I enjoy watching two lovers caught up in a warm embrace."

Nathan took Daisy's hand and pulled her along the aisle.

"We were just leaving."

The manager smiled. "It's probably a good idea."

On the street, Nathan gazed east and Daisy's eyes fell toward the west and Belmont Hospital. He knew she wished to return to her room.

She squeezed his hand. "I'm tired, Nathan. Can we go home?"

He shook his head. "I have a better idea."

He led her along the street toward D.W. Bell's department store.

Nathan tugged on her hand as he walked, practically dragging her behind him. With each alley, she peered into the darkness, finding nothing.

For the next twenty minutes, they relaxed around one another while they browsed through the store. Nathan discovered a camping section and plopped down on a surplus army cot. Daisy sat on an adjacent cot and recited the second and third verses of Psalm 23. "He lets me rest in green meadows; he leads me beside peaceful streams. He renews my strength. He guides me along right paths, bringing honor to his name."

"What does it mean?"

"David wrote it as a song of thanksgiving for the watchful care God had previously extended over him, and His assurance of future victories."

"Are there additional verses?"

She nodded and smiled.

"I must admit to liking this version of you, Nathan."

He smirked at her. "In that case, keep it to yourself."

She stiffened, having clearly received his message. "Even when I walk through the darkest valley, I will not be afraid, for you are close beside me. Your rod and your staff protect and comfort me."

She paused.

"Do you enjoy this? If not, I will stop."

"Somewhat." He looked about the section and then allowed his eyes to meet hers. "It's more interesting to me now than when we first met."

She nodded her understanding, and her face beamed.

"You prepare a feast for me in the presence of my enemies. You honor me by anointing my head with oil. My cup overflows with blessings."

As she spoke, a vision unfolded before Nathan's eyes. He stood alone in a wasteland which spanned across the great spine of the earth and the panting heart of the shoreless seas. Exhausted by the climb from the dense underworld of gloom, he searched for companionship and a path to redemption. Beyond the boundless space and the turning and twisting of fiery stairs, he saw the ghosts of shores long past. They rustled with heavy feet and groped in the eventide with the heaviness of clumsy hands, stealing the stars from the mutinous night as the unsettled sun drove toward an abrupt dawn. At first light, a green mountain arose from the ocean, lush with waterfalls and fruit trees, and on it stood John Belmont, alive with demands and coarse replies. He played his rash little games against his hired man, the mute and ignoble jester. With rage, he lit the green mountain afire and bathed in a pool of gold coins, their carnal worth fit for an Egyptian king. The face of God arose in the glassy distance with a violent laugh and a furious wind which beat furiously against the mountain's shores. He hurled a canary yellow fireball through a mass of darkened clouds, and molten sulfur consumed the green mountain and the waterfall and the trees.

Nathan next found himself in a desert of valleys filled with unruly jackals and howling wolves and wide-eyed owls. A group of people appeared beyond its boundary, with palms outstretched in a gesture of welcome. They presented him with a woman of truth and loyalty who had led them forth from the desert and into the autumnal oasis of their lives. Her sweet face now nursed its genuine desire, the kiss of a gentleman, pure of heart, tried and true, a man who might save her from herself.

Who was the almighty, great and terrible God, who created this strange assortment of green mountains and windswept deserts and unimaginable reckonings? What did the Most High want with a besotted relic from a forgotten era, a man perverse and wicked and evil, a soul unworthy of such a love as hers, the type which erased the sooty rags of bitterness and the tattered ends of hatred and the imprisoned flood of shameful tears?

He interrupted her recitation. "God isn't kind to his enemies, is He?"

"David's enemies."

"Aren't they one and the same?"

She considered his question.

"Good point. I hadn't thought of it that way."

She completed the psalm.

"Surely your goodness and unfailing love will pursue me all the days of my life, and I will live in the house of the Lord forever."

They sat in silence for several minutes until he could no longer bear the lack of communication. A subject change was in order, something to lighten the mood. "How are you enjoying your cot, madam?"

She ran her fingers along the rounded edge and across the surface.

"It's quite uncomfortable, sir. How about yours?"

He stretched out and faced the ceiling. "Oh, the canvas sags in all the right places. It's perfect for my back, which aches terribly."

They both laughed.

"I toss and turn most nights," she said.

He sat up straight and swung his legs over the side.

"We miss sleeping in our own beds."

"Do you ever get lonely?"

"I once used whiskey as a cure-all."

Daisy smirked. "And Sheila Byrne."

"Yes, her, too."

"Nathan, please don't invite her into your bed again."

"Yes, mam."

"I'm serious, Nathan."

"For your information, we slept in her room, never in my home. Sheila and Heinrich have grown quite close lately. I assumed you had noticed."

"Yes, but he was adamantly opposed to her at first. For a moment, I thought he was mimicking John Belmont."

Nathan smiled. "Well, he quickly got over her past once she listened to his sad tales of woe. It's quite ironic how a worthy companion makes all the difference to one's disposition."

"Do you think they have a future?"

He sighed. "Who knows about such things?"

"How do you feel about the prospect?"

"On the one hand, I'd be happy for them both."

"And the other?"

"I fight jealousy each time I see them together."

He paused.

"It's such a foolish emotion."

"She was all yours, in spirit and in her flesh. It's painful to give her up, even if she was never right for you. I felt the same about Frank."

Daisy noticed a cherry table with a Bible on top.

They each sat in a chair with the table arrayed between them and observed others as they browsed throughout the store. Daisy guessed at people's favorite pastimes from their observable habits. A woman who wore a contemptuous expression glared at them as she passed by their location; a man plodded dutifully behind her, his countenance bewildered and sullen.

"I'd like to have a dress like hers." Daisy's eyes glimmered at the notion.

"It looks expensive."

Daisy nodded her agreement. "Yes, it does."

When she snickered at the woman and then smiled at him, Nathan's pulse kicked up. He looked away to mask his impossible yearning.

"Someday soon, you should read the Bible," she said with firmness.

He picked up the book. "It's heavy."

"God's Word contains a great deal of knowledge and wisdom, which has been passed down from generation to generation and kept in perfect order."

He returned it to the tabletop. "Where would one begin?"

"There are many ways to go. Some say to peruse the Gospels in the New Testament first, study to the Old Testament second, and then return to the New Testament for a second reading."

"That process seems overly complicated."

"For you, yes." She picked up the dusty book and brushed off the leather cover. Her fingers wrapped around the cover in heady adoration as she clutched the Bible to her chest. "Since you are a scientist, I would start at the beginning and proceed methodically, but you should avoid moving forward until you've gained a full understanding of what you've read in each chapter and, more specifically, within each collection of verses." She dropped the Bible to her lap and flipped the pages to Genesis 1, the first chapter of the first book. "I'm not asking for a grand commitment. Just read a little."

"For you, I would do anything."

She grinned. "I'll believe *that* when I see it."

Nathan took the Bible from her and read. "In the beginning God created the heavens and the earth. The earth was formless and empty, and darkness covered the deep waters. And the Spirit of God was hovering over the surface of the waters. Then God said, 'Let there be light,' and there was light. And God saw that the light was good. Then he separated the light from the darkness. God called the light 'day' and the darkness 'night.' And evening passed and morning came, marking the first day."

He paused often to ask her questions about life and also about death.

With each answer, he returned to Genesis until he read the complete book. It felt good to learn about God's creative works and the formation of the nation of Israel, a topic his mother had loved to discuss around the kitchen table. June flattered the wrong outlaw and later suffered a grievous misfortune, a portion of which was delivered upon her son. The Word of God somehow connected Nathan to his mother across the vast chasm of time and space and death. He recalled the last conversation with her and the soft pat of her hand. A mother's touch was remembered even to adulthood.

"I'm ready to let go of June," he said in a factual tone.

Daisy's lip quivered. She looked toward the front entrance.

"Is it so easy to let go?"

"Only with you by my side," he said. "If you left me, I would be ruined."

Her eyes fell on him in amorous amazement, skipping his heart a beat.

"I feel the same," she said. "Fully committed or not at all."

Overcome by want, they ducked behind a corner for a third kiss. It was a most scandalous afternoon, an adventure for the record books.

A man approached and tapped Nathan hard on the shoulder.

"I saw you test every item in this section with no intention of buying a thing, and now you have the audacity to behave as if you just entered a brothel. Well, mister, you can get out of here this instant!"

Nathan burst into laughter. "Yes, sir!"

He saluted the man and then grabbed Daisy's hand. The couple giggled like schoolchildren as they exited the front of the store and stood on the sidewalk. They faced the glorious city of St. Louis, the future great capital of the world, and once more, Washington Avenue was theirs for the taking.

People brushed past them. Unclear in which direction was best, Nathan led Daisy east toward the waterfront. It seemed odd to have the afternoon for themselves, and he was determined to make the most of their time together. Perhaps they could take an electric trolley across the river to East St. Louis. There were fewer smokestacks and power lines over there, and it might prove an agreeable change of pace. They could sit at a riverside park.

They rounded a corner and heard a whimper from an alleyway.

Nathan peeked into the darkness and spotted a shadowy heap.

She drew close behind him. "What is it?"

"I believe Sophie had her puppies."

Daisy gasped. "Oh, no."

Nathan led her into the alley, and they continued to the middle portion, where they found her sickly body covered in muck. He bent down and ran his hand up her neck, down her spine, and along her ribs, feeling for breaks, bulges, anything out of the ordinary. Several puppies tried to suckle but failed; others climbed across them, hoping to reach the same goal.

Daisy clutched Nathan's arm. "Is she sick?"

"I'm afraid so, but I'm not sure what's wrong with her."

"We must help her, Nathan."

"I'm trying."

Daisy paced in the dimness. "We didn't do enough for her when we had the chance." She leaned against the brick wall. "I always make the same mistake, thinking of myself instead of others until it's too late."

"I've never seen you do *anything* for yourself," he said. "Stop wallowing in self-pity and help me lift her."

"You'll be filthy once you pick her up."

"I don't care," he said. "She needs our help."

Daisy bent down and gently shoved her hands under Sophie's head. Nathan tried to lift from her middle, and Sophie shrieked in pain.

He removed his hands. "It must be her spleen."

"Will she make it?"

He noted the blood on the ground. "I don't think so."

Daisy sat on the soiled bricks.

He pointed. "You'll ruin your dress."

"I don't care about it." She placed her face in her hands and wept.

Nathan stood and stared at Sophie for several moments.

There was only one thing to do, and he must get it done.

He faced Daisy. "Go back and tell two orderlies to fashion a cart with a box on top. We'll gather the puppies and bring them to the hospital."

"What will you do after I leave?"

"Sit here with Sophie until the end."

"Oh, Nathan."

"It's the least I can do."

"It's not your fault."

"Yes, it is. I never took James seriously."

She considered his words.

"Will you be alright? She looks so tired."

He nodded.

"She's lost too much blood. It won't be long now."

Daisy stood. Tears coursed down her cheeks.

"I love you, Nathan Marsh."

He sighed and felt so much older than his years might imply. "I don't love myself right now, and I'm not sure how anyone could ever love me."

"Well, I do."

He stared at Sophie and then the street.

He gestured toward the entrance. "You'd better go."

"You'll be alright?"

He nodded.

"I have to be."

TWENTY-FOUR

Psalm 24:1-2

The earth is the Lord's, and everything in it.
The world and all its people belong to him.
For he laid the earth's foundation on the seas
and built it on the ocean depths.

October 1867

Samuel arrived in late afternoon with a half-empty whiskey bottle and ambitions of finishing it by dinnertime. Through slurred words, he asked his son if there was anything to say, and the question confused Nathan, as he found it difficult to construct a worthy answer. He reverted to politeness, as was his custom when confronted by his father's drunkenness, a situation which had worsened of late. Nathan took on more responsibility at home and even helped his father make medicines, proving himself to be an eager helper and a candidate for medical school when he eventually came of age. Mistakes were occasionally made, usually by Samuel, but Nathan took the blame for each one and the back of his father's hand.

He hoped for something mildly pleasant to develop between father and son, perhaps a clear day amid many cloudy ones, but what he actually received dazed and horrified him, and he was unsure of where to go or who to see about his many problems. He knew only one thing for certain.

Nathan must search for a sanctuary before Samuel killed him.

He stood at Mr. Johnson's stoop with a hand over one eye.

The old man let him into the foyer. "What's wrong, Son?"

"Pop is drunk, and he hit me hard."

Mr. Johnson reached out, and Nathan instinctively flinched.

"I will not hit you, boy. Let me see."

Nathan revealed his darkened eye. His face had swelled.

"Any reason for his anger?"

Nathan spoke in a low voice. "He said I could have hurt someone."

"With bad medicine?"

Nathan nodded.

"Well, that'll do it every time."

He ushered Nathan into the study and sat in an upholstered rocker.

"I knew June to be a God-fearing woman," he said kindly.

"Yes, sir."

Mr. Johnson nodded while he rocked in his chair. "She was quite fond of the psalms and she told me she had you reading them, too. Is that correct?"

"Yes, sir."

"Can you recall any of them?"

"No, sir."

The old man rubbed his chin. "I find them to be a comfort, especially when my tomorrow seems wintry, and the path ahead seems unpleasant."

"Mom said they were a gateway to the Bible."

Mr. Johnson looked musingly at a desk near the window. "Never thought of them that way, but I suppose she was right. They certainly have a musical quality, and there's something mystical about them, too."

"I wouldn't know," said Nathan absently.

Mr. Johnson retrieved a Bible from his desk drawer and blew dust off the cover. "It's been a while," he said. "You and I are like two peas in a pod."

He placed the Bible in his lap and flipped the pages to the first psalm. He looked up. "Which one did she like best?"

"I don't know."

"Well, where did you leave off, if you don't mind me asking?"

"I don't mind."

Mr. Johnson gazed at Nathan with interested eyes, waiting for a response. Nathan's heart beat with a heavy, deliberate tread. He withheld an answer. The monotonous old man could figure it out for himself.

Mr. Johnson placed his elbow on the rocker's armrest. His face was sad and lonely. His eyes were tired, as if all of life's delights had already gone.

His eyes fell again on the book. "Alright then, we'll pick one."

"It was around twenty. That's all I remember."

Nathan knew the correct psalm as perfectly as he recalled his own name, but he would not offer such a special gift to a man he barely knew. June had wanted him to learn all fourteen verses, and he tried his best on the morning of her death to understand their meaning. In His infinite wisdom, the Lord took her, leaving behind a mixture of gritted teeth and lacerated flesh and bloody dirt. Before the change of seasons, while mother and son were still in the wagon, there was Psalm 19. Nathan would hold on to the memory of their last conversation and how her ephemeral hand patted the top of his.

"How about twenty-four?"

"Alright."

The old man flipped to Psalm 24 and blushed. "Oh, my."

"What's the problem?"

"It will be a long recitation, especially if you need me to decipher each verse, which is usually the case with young people." He looked at the clock and then spoke with feeling. "Do you have time for a proper study?"

"Only for part of it." Nathan had all the time in the world, but he hoped to get out of their impromptu Bible reading as soon as humanly possible.

Mr. Johnson chuckled under his breath.

"So here goes. 'Who may climb the mountain of the Lord? Who may stand in his holy place? Only those whose hands and hearts are pure, who do not worship idols and never tell lies. They will receive the Lord's blessing and have a right relationship with God their Savior. Such people may seek you and worship in your presence, O God of Jacob. Open up, ancient gates! Open up, ancient doors, and let the King of glory enter. Who is the King of glory? The Lord, strong and mighty; the Lord, invincible in battle. Open up, ancient gates! Open up, ancient doors, and let the King of glory enter. Who is the King of glory? The Lord of Heaven's Armies—he is the King of glory.' That gives you the sense of it. We can decipher each verse's meaning the next time you visit."

Mr. Johnson returned his Bible to the drawer and then confessed to Nathan with a sheepish countenance. "As you can probably tell, I haven't read those verses in a while. I'll need some time to uncover their meaning for myself." He leaned against the desk. "Do you think your father would attend a study group? We could apprehend the psalms together."

"May I wait outside?"

Mr. Johnson gave Nathan a disappointed look.

He gestured sharply toward the foyer. "Suit yourself."

After several hours on the front stoop, the sky fell to darkness, and the stars twinkled high in the heavens, offering Nathan a resolute message of surety. Every once in a while, Mr. Johnson peeked out of the window, but he did not join Nathan nor open the door to speak any words to him. Nathan appreciated the older man's sense of decency and his willingness to honor a younger man's wishes. Once Samuel had imbibed enough whiskey for one evening, he would pass out on the bed or the floor, whichever surface best suited his fancy. It would be safe to go home then, at least for the night.

My God, my God, why have you abandoned me?

The voice of Jesus echoed across the firmament.

The next day, Nathan stood at another stoop. He would have preferred to approach General Sinclair's house at night in hopes the lights would be out in every room, proving no one was home or everyone was fast asleep in their beds. What a terrible thing to knock on the door of a war hero in the middle of the friendless day! He told himself to be patient, as General Sinclair's daughter had made eyes at him with every delivery over the last two months, and she would gladly run interference on Nathan's behalf should the awkward situation become more unwieldy than he might bear.

As the door opened, he felt sick and wanted to run sulkily home.

Clouds overtook the sun, painting her face in shadow.

"What happened to your eye?"

"My pop is a drinking man. That is all."

Nathan felt a great and sinister burden on his shoulders.

"Well, alright then." She hesitated. "You don't say much, do you?"

"If I know a person, I talk a mile a minute."

The girl laughed and gave him a false curtsy.

"Would you like to come inside our fine home, sir?"

Nathan looked behind him and half-expected to find his father.

He tapped his chest. "Me?"

Her eyes flashed about her in a brazen way, rather like Samuel's, and she could barely contain her laughter. "I knew you were a shy one."

Her eyebrows arched. "I've watched you for months."

Warm blood rushed to Nathan's cheeks. "I *know*."

He looked about the private street and considered Aunt Joy.

The girl flung open her door and seized Nathan's arm.

"Please come inside and have something cool to drink."

Inside their parlor, the general shooed away his irresponsible daughter and scolded the boy profusely for corrupting Joanna's innocent soul.

"I'm no corruptor, sir."

"Do you take comfort in the Lord's many blessings?"

"I don't know what that means," said Nathan gravely. "My mother died some years ago, and I haven't continued my Bible studies since her passing."

"Yes, I know. It's why you're the wrong man for the job."

General Sinclair seemed gaunt, and his skin was rather pallid.

"What job, sir?"

"You wish to marry my daughter, Joanna. Isn't it why you're here?"

"No, sir." Nathan took a gulp before he uttered the next batch of words. "My father sent me to apologize for an error with your medicines."

"You mixed the wrong ingredients?"

"It's what my father says."

"Do you disagree?"

He paused.

"You'll probably say it was his fault all along."

Nathan nodded.

"Yes, if I were to be honest with you, sir."

The general glanced into a mirror and straightened his coat, as if preparing to leave for a rough journey and a faraway battle.

"I see." He sat in a parlor chair. "Fetch my Bible, Joanna."

She complied, and he flipped the pages to the middle.

His eyes rose to greet Nathan, and he snapped his fingers.

"Where did your last reading end? Come on, boy, I don't have all day."

Nathan jumped to attention and spoke quickly. "Our neighbor read Psalm 24 to me yesterday. I believe it contained ten verses."

The general eyed Nathan with suspicion.

"So you peruse the Bible more often than you would care to admit."

"My father had been drinking a large amount of whiskey, and I went to our neighbor, Mr. Johnson, for help. I think he took pity on us both."

"Possibly, or perhaps he saw potential in you, Nathan." General Sinclair closed his Bible and ran his wrinkled fingers across the leather cover. It was obvious the two had spent much time together. "David's words were expressed as a response to years of pious suffering. He endured many trials."

"I've also led a troubled life," Nathan said flatly.

"As have I."

"Then may I call on Joanna?"

The general spoke in a brisk tone. "You may *not*."

Early afternoon sunlight shifted its track, and the smell of rain filled the air. Just afterward, the sound of thunder ascended from the river and tumbled merrily into the Lucas Place parlor. It found Nathan's ear and gave him a ready excuse for the taking of his leave. Joanna would understand.

Perhaps they might stroll together another day.

"Father, please be reasonable," she said in a pleading tone. "We are both young and we must have an opportunity to explore a romance."

"This boy is the wrong man for the job."

"Give Nathan time to prove his worth. I have developed deep feelings for him since your illness began, and you must bless our pairing."

"I pray to get better, my darling, so you have nothing to fear."

"Please don't make me choose against you, Father. All is ask for is time."

General Sinclair wiped a tear from his eye. It was uncharacteristic for him. "My darling, *time* is a luxury I do not have to give."

Joanna turned away from her father and caught her breath.

"So it is true, then. You will soon pass?"

The general pointed at Nathan. "It's what his father says."

He forced himself to stand and coughed into a handkerchief.

As he pulled it from his mouth, bits of blood caught the sunlight.

The general showed the soiled cloth to Nathan.

"I must adjourn to my bedroom, Son. Tell Samuel it won't be long."

"Should I fetch him?"

The general stopped in the foyer. He shook his head and continued up the stairs. His boots stomped as they made contact with each oak step.

Nathan turned, and his eyes fell on her. "I'm sorry, Joanna."

"There's nothing for you to do," she said. "I must tend to his needs."

"Where will you go?"

She took a weighty breath and exhaled. "My father is a proud man whom I love dearly, but his health has been poor for some time, and it has led him to make unsound decisions in his business affairs. He has completely squandered his fortune and allowed his life to fade before my eyes."

Joanna sat in his favorite chair and rubbed the cherry armrests.

"I will move to a soldier's home if you cannot marry me." She gave Nathan a hopeful look. "Are you of sufficient means?"

"I am not," he said. "Each day I await my father's wrath."

Joanna answered with perfect cheerfulness.

"Perhaps we should move to a home together."

After the General's death and funeral, Nathan went to see Joanna Sinclair. Curiosity overtook him as they strolled about the sparse grounds which encompassed the soldier's home. From the outside, the house appeared tidy and unadorned. Paid for by Christian donations, it was inspected each week by deacons who saw it met the standard of cleanliness set by the church.

"My father said he knew Samuel in the war. Did you know about it?"

"He doesn't share much with me."

"Father sent many men to Samuel, and many were saved in the surgery tents." Joanna stopped and took in the surroundings. "I think he hoped your father might perform a similar miracle on his behalf."

Nathan bent over and picked up a handful of stones. He tossed them toward the back porch of the house. "He can't even save himself."

Joanna spoke casually, which concealed her genuine desire. "I won't be here for long," she said. "A woman in town who respected my father offered me a room and a stake. She runs a brothel with a saloon on the first floor and a lengthy row of bedrooms upstairs." Joanna grew loud and bright. "People say those women make a lot of money and live in fine style."

"They do?"

She nodded, beaming.

"By the time I'm twenty, I'll be rich."

"What will you do then?"

They walked in silence for several minutes while she calculated her best course. Joanna fell into a mournful train of thought, and it seemed an inner anger grew within her, the same as it had within Nathan after June's death.

Her voice fell low and gray. "When I've had my fill, I'll move somewhere wonderful and buy a house. Maybe you could live with me."

Across from them, an enclosed pasture of mixed grasses and sweet clover sheltered a grazing Quarter, a pawing Appaloosa, and a swishing Morgan mare. The threesome stood near a clump of scraggly trees that likely wouldn't know rain until November. A rabbit hopped past several ant hills which had sprung forth out of the dry earth. Poisonous monkshood added bluish spots of color to the rutted and dust covered landscape.

"Someday, I want a farm and my own horses," Nathan said.

"Anything you covet." Her eyes moistened. "You are the love of my life."

Nathan sat on a sun-warmed bench, still unsure of his feelings for her.

"Do you think your father went to heaven?"

Joanna sat beside him. "I don't know."

"Maybe he's with my mother."

She brushed bits of dirt and grass off her dress near her knees. "I think they're both dead, and that's all there is to it. We need to get the most out of life while we're here because nothing else matters."

The Morgan swished her tail, and a butterfly flittered atop the grass.

The house mother approached and stood before Joanna.

"I heard your conversation from an open window."

Joanna threw a defiant look at the woman. "So what?"

The woman slapped her hard across the face, sending her to the dirt.

Joanna rubbed her cheek and scowled.

"I will not tolerate back talk in my home," said the woman loudly.

"It's not your house," Joanna said. "The church pays the bills."

"Yes, and they hired me to run it for them so you can shut that wandering mouth." She pointed to the bench. "Get off the ground."

Joanna hastily complied.

Nathan noticed a hatch-type door which slanted into the hillside at the far end of the pasture, near a farmhouse. There would be shelves with crates of newly picked apples and jars of jam. Perhaps he could hide there.

"Now, listen, children. I know both of you are in pain. Nathan lost his mother as a boy and his father..." Her voice trailed, and she eyed the horses across from them. "Well, let's just say Samuel has his share of demons."

"You know nothing of our difficulties, living here on the church dole."

The woman huffed and placed her hands on her hips. "You are far too sure of yourself, young lady, and eventually it will cost you everything."

"Why should we listen to a spinster who's not even married?"

The woman sighed, as if holding on for dear life. "Because I was once just like the two of you. I lost my parents and suffered for a long time. It was only three years ago I recovered and worked my way into this position."

Her story intrigued Nathan. "What made the difference?"

"The Lord freed me from my servitude to sin."

Joanna bellowed a reply. "He took my father so He can go kick rocks."

"Child, you don't know what you're saying." There was a warm quality in the woman's voice. "But I understand your misery. I really do."

Joanna stood boldly and marched toward the house.

At the front porch, she waved goodbye and went inside.

The woman turned from Joanna. She sat beside Nathan and patted his knee. "I hope our shared experience comforts you," she said sincerely. "The Lord isn't done with you yet, Nathan. Sooner or later you'll return to Him."

His hands fidgeted for a moment. He tossed his last stone toward the root cellar in the distance, knowing it would never reach its destination.

Who was this woman to predict his future?

"I can feel it in my bones." She settled onto the bench.

"What about Joanna?

The woman gazed at the house and sighed.

"I'll do what I can, but I'm afraid her path is set."

Some years later, the orphan home closed. Joanna Sinclair had already moved to the riverfront brothel on Broadway Avenue. The Quarter and the Appaloosa and the Morgan mare avoided the monkshood, having a natural sense within that if they were to sicken and decay, they would be very sorry indeed, for grace was well worth having and could not be discarded without severe penitence. Joanna knew not to trust in God's righteousness.

Fear of the Lord is the foundation of wisdom.

Knowledge of the Holy One results in good judgment.

Even Nathan knew Proverbs 9:10 to be sensible advice.

TWENTY-FIVE

Psalm 25:12-13

Who are those who fear the Lord?
He will show them the path they should choose.
They will live in prosperity,
and their children will inherit the land.

Nathan descended the stairs and opened the door to the main hall. Daisy read her Bible in a rocker while Sophie's puppies played brightly at her feet. What a wonderful counter to his despair! She would shape them as she had molded Nathan over the past few months, and he was proud to know such a worthy person. Daisy was now his only redeeming trait—the harmony who subdued his battle—and the disregard of his duty to her made him feel like a deserter. She declared her love in the alleyway, but still he withheld a marriage proposal, as Sophie haunted his spirit, and whiskey tempted his flesh. He stood motionless, with hopeful eyes and parched lips, and wished his gaze on Daisy might last a lifetime.

Samuel arrived through the front entrance and sat in a rocker beside her.

He pointed at the puppies. "I see you're working on a Sunday."

She grinned. "Were we made for the Sabbath, or was it made for us?"

He held up his hat and returned her smile. "You have me there, madam." He surveyed the room. "Is Nathan in his office this afternoon?"

Daisy gestured toward the stairs. "He's content. Don't upset him."

Nathan approached and took a seat beside his father and the love of his life, the one woman who completely understood him, as she was the same.

"I could sit with you two a while," he said, "if you wouldn't mind."

"The more the merrier," said Samuel affectionately.

Dora led Ida to the puppies and asked her to keep them company.

"Yes, mam!"

Ida sat with the four females and one male—remaining survivors of an eight puppy litter—and played games of tumble and frolic. Dora sat beside them on the floor and read a children's book aloud. She was quite good at presenting the voice of each character as though they were a real person.

Ida looked up at Samuel and then at Dora. "Are you two married?"

Samuel glanced at Dora's reddening cheeks and smiled.

"Not yet," he said, "but we're the greatest of friends."

"Thought so," Ida said.

Dora closed the book. "Does our friendship make you happy or sad?"

Ida gently placed one of the female puppies on the floor and watched her flop onto her belly. She looked up, struggling to conceal her mounting enthusiasm. "I hope you have a huge wedding and the entire world attends."

Ida thought for a moment and then her eyes filled with delight.

"It would be the best thing that ever happened to me!"

"We'll have to do it then," Dora said lightly.

Ida smiled.

"My nomadic soul wants everyone to be joyful," said Samuel, tossing his hat onto the floor beside Ida and the puppies. "I haven't always succeeded."

"Me either," said Dora. "To be sure, I've rarely gotten anything right with relationships. Mine have always ended in disaster."

Samuel gave her a scoffing look. "You were married and had a son."

"Yes, but they were more pleased with one another than with me."

Samuel grew quiet, as if trying to retrieve himself from a blunder.

Nathan questioned if he should intervene.

After some consideration, Samuel leaned forward, unwilling to concede his sudden disadvantage. "You know what would surpass our wedding?" He rocked pensively, doing his best to seem nonchalant.

Ida perked up. "What?"

"If you came to live with us at my farm," Samuel picked up his hat and fumbled with it. "I mean to say, after we get married."

"In a big church?"

"The biggest around." Samuel pulled at one end of the hat. "The pastor might as well be family, and I bet he'd even let you attend the ceremony."

Dora gasped. "Do you speak in earnest, Samuel?"

He took her hand and gave her a warm smile.

"Why yes, my dear, I am perfectly sober and steadfast. I've put my dreams on hold for far too long, and it's high time I lived again."

He pulled Dora to her feet. "What do you say?"

"I don't know," she said. "You might change your mind."

He hugged her and then grabbed her by the shoulders. "Like my son, I'm learning to trust my instincts. Every cell of my being tells me you are the best woman in Missouri, and I would be a fool to wait another second."

He kissed her forehead. Tears coursed down her cheeks.

"Will you marry him?" asked Daisy.

Dora seemed bewildered for several moments, but then her countenance changed to one of certainty. "Yes, I believe I will."

"It's my turn to inquire," Samuel said. "Are you quite sure?"

Dora wiped her cheeks. "I'm an aging woman who knows her own mind. If you'll have me, you'll not find a more faithful companion."

"Then it's settled, and we must make plans for a wedding."

Daisy clapped her hands and exclaimed. "Please, everyone, listen!"

The room drew quiet.

"Samuel and Dora are getting married!"

Samuel and Dora kissed, and the room applauded.

Ida hugged the couple tightly. "Can I live at your farm?"

Samuel knelt and met her at eye level. "Only if you promise one thing."

Ida held her breath.

"To let us love you forever. Could you do that?"

"I sure could. Forever and ever!"

Ida embraced them both, and the room applauded again.

Nathan felt a tingling sensation along the avenue of his spine. He was lost in Daisy's blonde locks, her fixated concern for others, and her deep yearning to belong. She embodied everything he wanted in a pretty woman, and his love for her was good and honorable and immeasurable.

In his office, Nathan told Samuel he and Daisy had kissed.

"Well, that makes us two peas in a pod." Samuel seemed full of life. "Dora and I just did the same. Aren't we a pair?"

Nathan frowned. "You're too old for this sort of nonsense."

"You think June would disapprove?"

"Nothing like that, and I like Dora just fine."

He paused.

"She's been a big help around here."

"What then?"

Nathan spun his chair and faced the window. "I don't know, honestly."

Samuel was an uncommon man whose pain was magnified by his grim childhood and the war and the murder of his wayward wife. Perhaps he and Dora would buy cherry furniture and plant vegetables in June's desolate garden and restore the ramshackle barn to something which resembled health. Marriage was the most logical choice and the appropriate next step, and a union with Dora might defend them both from the tides of the rising sea, offering high ground and a firm roof and the comfort of a family farm.

Everyone deserved a second chance at happiness, even Samuel.

Nathan's eyes fell cautiously on his father.

"I suppose congratulations are in order."

"Thank you."

"Before you leave, something has been on my mind lately."

"This sounds ominous."

"Nothing too bad, but I'd like an answer."

Samuel shifted uneasily in his chair. "Alright."

Nathan gave him an emphatic look. "How can a scientist be a man of faith? Don't you wonder about the origin of the universe? Surely, its creation is not as simple as the particulars within the Bible make it seem."

Samuel considered his son's words for a while and then replied. "Son, I was lost after your mother died. I didn't want to hear from you or anyone else, not even my closest friends whom I'd known for decades."

"I remember all too well, Pop."

Samuel nodded his agreement. "I'm sure you do."

"Is that your best answer?"

"I'll say this, Son, and I hope you listen. You are finally asking the right questions. God doesn't mind them any more than He minds your anger."

"I'll need your help to understand it all."

Samuel shook his head. "You must take your own path to know God. I've walked mine, and now it's your turn." He stood and opened the door. "I wish you well as you begin your journey. Some answers won't be easy to accept. Trust me. I know from personal experience."

"Where are you going?"

Samuel answered without indecision. "I plan to kiss my fiancé again and then I'm going to purchase her a rather expensive wedding ring."

"Is that all?"

Samuel smiled wryly. "It's all for *now*."

Ida expressed the weight of losing her mother and the shame she felt about the accident. Daisy turned over the events from her own fiery past and the memories overwhelmed her emotions. She stifled the urge to cry, and her faltering breaths interrupted the story, causing her to get up and leave the area. Dora and Samuel called after Daisy and pleaded with her to return and fully share herself with them. Although she felt a connection with these new people, she was frightened by her newfound vulnerability.

Samuel followed her to the stairwell and took hold of Daisy's arm.

He spun her body, forcing her to face him and the adoring room. He would not allow her to leave without knowing how much she was loved and needed by them all. Samuel eyed Daisy with remorse and shared how he once drank whiskey to replace what had gone missing from his life.

Ida stood behind them. She asked Samuel if it had ever worked.

He wheeled, and his eyes fell on the young girl.

"No, dear. It only made things much worse. It took the love of Jesus to pull me out of the abyss, and I want you to know Him as we do."

"The fire wasn't His fault either?"

Dora smiled and rubbed Ida's head with affection.

She bent down and allowed her eyes to meet Ida's.

"He would never hurt us, but you know what?"

"What?"

Dora's eyes widened, and she spoke with passion. "He's there when we hurt, or we grieve, or we're sad, and He feels our pain as if it's happening to Him." Her eyes became strained. She looked at Samuel and wiped a tear.

"He does?"

Dora spoke in a convinced way. "If we'll pray regularly, Jesus will heal our wounds and bring good people into our lives."

"Like the two of you," Ida said.

Samuel and Dora glanced at one another and then smiled at Ida.

"Yes, dear, like us."

Dora paused.

"We'll tell you another fact."

"Alright."

"We love you, too."

Ida rushed toward them and hugged them in unison.

They tearfully hugged her in return.

Nathan and Daisy shared an awkward moment as they observed the emotional display. He swiped tears from his eyes, worried his weakness might scare her away. "Why didn't we have that kind of success with her?"

"We weren't praying properly," said Daisy politely.

Nathan sensed the twinge of embarrassment in her voice.

He invited her to spend Saturday with him on rounds.

"It's been a while, and I need to get out to see them."

She smiled and squeezed his hand. "It beats staying home alone."

"When you see where we're going, you may say otherwise."

"I will go where you lead, Nathan, as is my custom when in love."

———

Daisy had long wished for a second visit with Seymore Hagen, but she was confused about the revival of his health, believing his life to be nearing an abrupt end during their previous meeting. She hoped she could maintain her composure in his presence as Nathan had done. Today, as in all her other days, she would show strength when required and weakness when allowed, drawing her shawl over her head to withdraw from the rain and her tears.

Her meditations on the subject were soon interrupted by a shiny crow, which pranced and cawed from a gravestone to their right, startling her.

Nathan stopped his carriage. "We're here."

"Where, the cemetery?"

He stepped down and took her hand. "It's time."

"For what?"

"To pay our respects to Seymore."

As they walked, Daisy recalled Rose's funeral. "Pierre was a rock who tried to help my mother cope, but despite his best efforts, Patrice fell into a grim mourning, and her body quickly gave itself over to ill health. Rather than focus on what was gone and would never return, I tried to preserve what remained." She hesitated. "There wasn't much left to save."

They sat on a concrete bench and gazed at Seymore's marker. It was a curious and respectful staring, born of grief and shock and dread.

"I sometimes wonder what comes next." Nathan looked into Daisy's eyes, melting her. "I can thank you and Seymore for that problem."

"Your father, too," she said. "At least in recent years."

Nathan smiled. "Yes, he's also to blame."

"Have you forgiven Samuel for his transgressions?"

He frowned and looked toward the lane.

"Nathan, you are not a simple man to understand, and you give no inkling of what's really on your mind. I wish you would speak plainly."

"I'm an open book," he said. "What you see is what you get."

"My feelings for you are quickly changing. At first, you intrigued me, but it seemed clear you could not hold up your end of the bargain in a romantic relationship. I do not wish to be devastated again, Nathan."

"Me, either." He smiled. "How would you rate our potential?"

Daisy tensed. "You have severe anger issues which are caused by a deep sense of abandonment, but I see astonishing potential with you, Nathan, if you would only allow yourself to feel and to love and to move forward into the next stage of life." She caught her breath and thought of early mornings in the distant past, before the troubles began in her life, the sunny times of her childhood which were now cast across the great chasm of time, frosty like the wintery mist at twilight. "I hope I am present when you do."

"The notion of starting over torments me. I was comatose for a decade after losing Catherine and our children. I cannot bear it again."

She must dare to challenge him. His soul thirsted for a fight.

"If we will love, we will suffer grief."

"All of life comes at a cost," he said, nodding.

"I'm reminded of Psalm 25."

"In what manner?"

Thunderous drums of love stirred within Daisy, warming her. She would no longer throw her wild hands to the sky or run through life alone. He was the better element, and she was born to quarrel with his insatiable need to give himself over to darkness. God's indescribable glory encapsulated her, and she would boldly march to war on Nathan's behalf. "It refers to the Lord's patient nature and His bountiful provision," she said. "He never intentionally leaves us in a state of want." She hesitated. "Seymore said it was one of his favorites the day we visited his home. It must have comforted him as he ventured forth into the great unknown, as it would do for me."

"Please quote a portion."

"Now?"

"What better time or place?"

Daisy looked about the cemetery. "I suppose you're right."

"Seymore would enjoy your recitation."

"I hope so." She cleared her throat and began. "Remember, O Lord, your compassion and unfailing love, which you have shown from long ages past. Do not remember the rebellious sins of my youth. Remember me in the light of your unfailing love, for you are merciful, O Lord."

Daisy pointed at the sky, and the Lord's valor filled her.

"His love is steadfast, Nathan. Please commit those verses to memory."

"I've certainly been rebellious." His countenance fell to sadness.

Daisy sighed. "Yes, as have I."

"Sometimes I long for a restoration of my soul."

She quoted verse fourteen. "The Lord is a friend to those who fear him."

Nathan sighed. His gaze drifted westward, toward the horizon, and after some time, it fell on the three crows who sat on a nearby table. "I suppose that's correct," he said finally. The lowness of his voice prompted the crows to land in front of their bench. The quirky threesome ran madly into one another as they searched the grass for stray morsels of food.

"Try as I might, I cannot shake my fear, not of Him, but of this world and the brutality it offers," she said. "It's my most pathetic character trait."

"What might make the difference?"

Daisy leaned backward and felt the sun against her cheeks and her neck. "I'm not sure, but I must stop running. I know that much."

"Beyond that, what do you really want?"

"I'd like to belong to someone." She allowed him to consider her comment. "And also to a cause which is bigger than myself."

"For God," said Nathan, matter-of-factly.

"Yes." Daisy rubbed the edge of the bench and grabbed the side, doing her best to hide a rush of anxiety which threatened to overcome her.

She put the onus on Nathan. "What do you value most?"

"I used to trust my intuition, but I haven't done so for many years, at least until you entered my besieged existence and changed it for the better."

"Have you learned to trust yourself again?"

"I'm working on it," he said.

"Do you trust God?"

"I know He exists, or I think I know it."

Nathan paused.

"I haven't forgiven Him for stealing most of my life."

She patted his hand as June would have done.

"Maybe it's time you did, Nathan. He would like you to come home."

"What if I cannot? Will I be lost to eternity?"

Daisy took a heavy breath. Her eyes fell on Seymore's grave.

She pointed at the inscription. "Here lies a Godly man."

"Yes, he was," Nathan said. "I admired him for his faith."

"Someday your children will admire you in the same manner."

"That's not a fair thing to say, and you know it."

"This is love and war, Nathan, and all is fair."

Sunday afternoon, Nathan and Daisy sat with Samuel while he cast a line into the pond. On the far bank, lily pads and water lilies floated on top while reeds and long grasses poked through the surface, and weeds and wildflowers grew along a muddy strand, which was strewn with rocks and pebbles. Wind rustled oak and hickory leaves in the line of trees behind them, and as it passed over the water, tiny waves formed, pushing toward the other side, reserving all judgements, communicating the benefits of forward momentum and a curious nature. A smell of spearmint and sweet clover reflected from the rolling pasture, which stretched before them on its way to the barn and farmhouse. Clouds passed overhead, tranquil and aware, their motion reflecting off the cool wet face, rising the placid fish.

"I read something interesting recently," Samuel said.

Nathan took out his handkerchief. "What did you read, Pop?"

"A while back, the Committee on Public Health presented the Minnesota legislature with an Anti-Hoop-Skirt Bill, making it unlawful to manufacture or sell hoop-skirts within the state of Minnesota."

Nathan blew his nose. "Did it go anywhere?"

"Allergies?"

"I'll be alright," said Nathan, smirking.

"Anyway, someone floated a rumor that crinoline was soon to become a fashion once again, but the rumor was later determined to be mere gossip." He retrieved his line and cast it again. "Accordingly, the bill has been returned to the committee." He breathed deeply and then exhaled. "Do you think I should mention the development to Ida? She might like to know others see the dangers in those awful contraptions."

Nathan side armed a flat rock. It skipped it along the surface.

"Before the war, Aunt Joy took me to balls where those voluminous monstrosities were prevalent, all in the name of elegance and comfort, and even at a young age, I was shocked by the oblivious nature of the ladies who wore them, as there were a variety of dangers which might easily end their lives. There were fast moving carriages, heavy wagon wheels, careless feet, and, of course, roaring fireplaces which could send them screaming to a fervent end. Once the muslin dress caught fire, the steel would get white hot, and I can only imagine the horror Ida must have witnessed."

"A strong wind could upturn an unsuspecting victim," said Daisy, attaching herself to their conversation. "I'm glad those went out of fashion. Otherwise, I'd live even more against the grain than I do right now."

Samuel's eyes flashed from the pond to Daisy. "I saw a woman's dress flipped upward, near her head once, and as you mentioned, she landed squarely on her pelvic region. She and the crowd were most displeased."

All three laughed in unison at the mental portrait.

Daisy collected her thoughts and reined in her laughter.

"In such a moment, the lady must have felt completely alone."

Samuel pulled in his line and cast it away from Nathan's reach.

"She felt ostracized on many other days, the same as you." He stood and poked a y-shaped stick into the ground and laid his pole upon it. "She was considered a notable lady, as her family originated on the right side of a fabricated line, known to have *good taste* and all that assorted nonsense." He gazed across the water at the unseeable, his memories spanning the decades.

Samuel turned toward Nathan and placed his hand on his arm. "She was a fine woman, and if I had been a man of means, I would have married her."

"You would've missed out on Mom."

"Nathan, it's his keepsake," Daisy said. "Let him have it."

"Son, your mother and I were a lost cause from the start."

Nathan saw the need for a change of subject, as Samuel's mood had dimmed. He mentioned a minor breakthrough with Ed and Shirley.

Ed planned to resume his life on the road, and she dreamed of opening a boutique which specialized in monogrammed blankets. On Friday, she asked Ed to think of her and to write occasionally, and if he ever grew tired of the railroad, he should come home to St. Louis. She wanted a future together, if he was willing. If so, he should knock on her door.

Ed said it might happen since he was taken with her.

"Hot dog!" Samuel kicked over his pole as he clapped his hands. "Sounds like they are healing faster than you first thought."

Daisy perked up. "We must allow them time to work through their grief fully, before urging them to the next phase of life."

"Quite true, my dear," said Samuel kindly.

He set the pole on the y-shaped stick and looked toward the sky.

"This process has been both healing and frustrating," Nathan said. "Although we make steady improvement, they continually regress into their old form. I'm not sure there will ever be an answer, either from a medical or psychological perspective."

Daisy asked the men to share details about June's death and their own time in mourning, and each complied with her tough request.

"Nathan, why have you run from a life filled with hope and love?" She gave him an affectionate look and rubbed his arm. "Was it all you knew?"

"I felt safer on my own," he said. "Even when I slept under the trees."

"My father used to call me Wild Forest Rose for the same reason."

"We're two peas in a pod," he said.

She smirked at him. "We need a new phrase. That one is exhausted."

They both laughed.

Satisfied with Nathan's willingness to be open and honest with her, Daisy invited him to spend a few days at her father's winery in Pollard.

"About Psalm 23," said Nathan restlessly.

"Your mother's favorite. I haven't forgotten."

"It sounds better when you recite it to me, especially the part about lying down in green pastures."

"I could never replace her, Nathan."

"I don't need a mother."

"Then what do you need?"

"I need a wife."

TWENTY-SIX

Psalm 26:2

Put me on trial, Lord, and cross-examine me.
Test my motives and my heart.

Nathan sat with Pierre and Brenda as he waited for Daisy to serve the group supper. The question which lingered on everyone's mind wafted through the air and rested uncomfortably between them. It was only a matter of time before either father or sister accused Nathan of using Daisy for her talents and her perfect ability to see the good in others, even when the man caused her secret grief in the midnight hours, seeking her reluctant confidence with feigned affections, while finding it amusing to throw hostile accusations at her, ruining her ability to sleep or to become intimate in a highly vulnerable way or to reveal herself down to the core of her being. Daisy moved silently and awkwardly about the kitchen as the tension in the room rose to abnormal levels and threatened to explode the forced tranquility and pleasantness into a spasm of thrilling flames.

She served supper and asked if the food was at all edible.

"I love it," said Nathan between chews.

"It's a good thing you've learned these skills," said Brenda irreverently. "You'll need them when you and Nathan marry."

Daisy glanced at a smiling Nathan. She blushed.

"Brenda, now is not the time or the place."

"Why not?"

Pierre gave Brenda a reproachful look. "When you prod her with such vitriol, it makes her uncomfortable. Tonight, let's call a ceasefire."

"She's never been able to handle life's hard realities."

Daisy set the serving dish on the table. "Such as?"

"For starters, Rose was just like Henry," said Brenda with aggression. "Second, Patrice wouldn't allow her marriage to work from the start."

"I sense a third point."

"Our father did the best he could under difficult circumstances. We must stop blaming him for Henry and Patrice's failures."

"Don't forget Rose. She was no angel."

Brenda moved her plate and placed her elbows on the kitchen table.

"I wish things could have been different for us all. I really do."

She paused.

"Daisy, you must let your past go." She pointed at Nathan across the table. "Focus on what's right in front of you."

"You make it sound so easy, Brenda, but you missed the worst of it."

Brenda nodded her agreement. "Yes, I escaped the nightmare."

"So you have no right to counsel me."

Brenda went to Daisy and squeezed her hand. "You have emotional scars. Of that fact, I have no doubt." She took a deep breath, exhaled. "But your misguided attempts to ignore them have failed. You must make better choices." She looked musingly at Nathan and returned to her chair.

Daisy sat opposite her sister and glared. "What about you?"

"Alright, now I'm the one on trial," said Brenda with a sneer. "Fair enough. I'm an adult who can handle the truth, so let's have it."

Daisy gestured sharply at Nathan.

"Don't point at me," he said. "What did I do?"

"Nothing. Absolutely nothing."

"You want me to once again confess to my adoration of him?" Brenda pursed her lips and rubbed her forehead. "Haven't we covered this already?"

"Not well enough for me."

"It was so long ago, Daisy."

"Not so long that you kept it from me. You wished to marry him."

Brenda offered Nathan a sheepish grin. "You already know this, but I'll say it again. When I first saw you with Catherine years ago, I was smitten. I had dreamed of finding a man like you, and then suddenly you stood before me, gallant, strong, handsome, and Catherine was such a wondrous marvel of beauty, elegance, and prestige. It seemed like a fairy tale."

Nathan shifted in his seat. "I never knew, Brenda, but as I mentioned at Sarah Robinson's home, I remember seeing you at the Regency Arms. You were a splendid woman to behold."

Her cheeks flushed red, and she fanned her face. "Now you flatter me unnecessarily, but I appreciate your compliment, sir."

He pretended to tip his hat and smiled.

Brenda stiffened. Her countenance grew serious.

"I settled for my husband, Dan, which has made me very unhappy."

Daisy gasped. "Now is not the time for such revelations."

Brenda huffed loudly and waved off her sister. "I am tired of lies and half-truths. From this night forward, I intend to be honest to a fault."

"Please continue," Nathan said. "I find your candor refreshing."

Brenda nodded a thank you. "Recently in prayer, I heard from the Lord. Apparently, my husband is the right man for me after all, and as such, I will choose contentment over bitter regret." She took a sip of wine and forced a smile. "It will be better for the children if we stay together."

The group took several seconds to process what had been said.

Nathan looked at Daisy. "Do you have the perfect Bible verse for this occasion, perhaps something from the psalms?"

"You know me too well, but I believe Proverbs 16:9 better applies."

He gestured for her to proceed.

"We can make our plans, but the Lord determines our steps."

"Meaning we don't really know our own minds?"

"We may, but it benefits us to know the Lord agrees with our choices and decisions. Wouldn't you say that's a good policy?"

He gave her a playful smile. "I suppose."

Pierre kept quiet during the exchanges, watching and observing each verbal challenge and the immediate reaction. He turned to Nathan with eyes which had transformed from a gray dullness to a faint orange glow.

"So, what about you, the illustrious physician?"

Nathan tapped his chest. "Me?"

"When were you born?"

Daisy looked uneasy. "Father, is an interrogation really necessary?"

Pierre hushed Daisy's interruption. "Your date of birth, sir?"

"September 15, 1852."

"I heard talk of a murder." The air fell still as Pierre's boot rubbed along the wooden planks which ran underneath the table. They were covered in dust and grime. "Would you care to explain something about the event?"

Nathan took a deep breath and exchanged glances with Daisy.

As she had recited her last verse, Pierre's mind became wholly cognizant of an interloper in his midst, a strange man who would stay the night in his home with or without the intention of marrying his cheerless daughter, the one Pierre had never taken seriously in the same manner he took Brenda seriously. He intended to remedy the situation one way or another, and it might be at Nathan's expense. Seymore once advised to never disregard a cornered man, especially when his children were at stake. Nathan would keep his back to the wall and his hand firmly affixed to his knife.

Brenda set her wineglass on the table. "That is going too far, Papa."

"He's had enough time to get over the ordeal, and I'd like to better understand this man, where he originates, what makes him tick."

"My mother died when I was seven, a month before my birthday."

Pierre eyed Nathan. "Afterward, your father raised you?"

Nathan folded his napkin. "Pop enlisted as a Union surgeon in 1861, and he left me with my mother's sister. I knew her as Aunt Joy."

Daisy interjected as she refilled Nathan's water glass. "Samuel witnessed many atrocities during the war, but he keeps those stories to himself. The only one he shared came from his boyhood. A man was burned to death for murdering two policemen after helping a friend escape from custody."

Pierre mulled over her comments.

"Did Samuel share his war stories with you?"

Nathan shook his head. "Not really. After the war ended, he collected me from Aunt Joy's home and brought me back to our farm."

He paused.

"Pop mostly kept to himself."

"All the time?"

Nathan became annoyed. "He was a broken down drunk like you."

Daisy gasped. "There's no reason to lash out."

"He's pushing too hard." Nathan stood and kicked the chair backward. It bumped into the wall. "If you'll excuse me, I'll now take my leave."

Pierre held up both hands. "Please don't think me rude, sir. I merely want to understand your origins." He pointed to a claret of wine on the countertop. "Would you like a bit of our Merlot? It might help loosen the tongue and keep your disagreeable emotions at bay."

Nathan picked up his chair and sat. "A glass or two wouldn't hurt."

After twenty minutes and several glasses of wine, Nathan developed a pleasant countenance. "By the age of fifteen, life with Samuel was untenable. I sought help from Aunt Joy in August 1867. She hired a tutor in the fall and allowed a neighbor girl to study with me at the kitchen table."

"Catherine?"

Nathan smiled at Daisy. "Yes."

"Her life has been such a shameful waste," Brenda said in a grave voice. "Whatever became of your aunt?"

"She died on my birthday the following year." He raised a glass to toast. "I became a servant in the Belmont household the same day."

"Is that why you and John dislike one another?"

He nodded.

"By Christmas, I'd been excommunicated from the Church of Belmont, and I was forced to move back east with the tutor while I waited for school to begin. Professor Collins' wife wanted me to become part of their family, but I couldn't bear the weight of Colleen's expectations."

He took a long drink of wine and asked for another.

"I moved into a dormitory and focused on my medical studies."

"Remarkable," said Brenda admiringly.

His eyes looked past the group as he recalled the past. "After medical college, I apprenticed for Dr. Clanton Evans for two years and then returned to St. Louis with a letter of recommendation at twenty-two."

"Where you started your new practice," Brenda said.

"Yes, in 1875."

"What happened to Samuel during your time back east?" asked Pierre. "From all accounts, he has made a complete turnaround."

Nathan smiled. "Pop will soon marry a fine woman who works at our hospital as a nurse. He's come a long way, to be sure."

Daisy pressed her back into her chair. "Samuel became sober while Nathan attended medical college. Today, he's a new man at heart, and he's tried repeatedly to make amends with his son."

Pierre's eyebrows arched. "To what end?"

"At first, Nathan would have none of it." Daisy eyed her companion across the table. "I think he kept his father around as a means to begin his medical practice, leveraging Samuel's impressive client list."

"Catherine would have expected no less," Brenda said quickly.

Nathan flicked at the napkin. "You know her too well."

He redirected his energy toward Daisy.

"There's no way you will escape the wrath of this table tonight, young lady. The spotlight now shines directly upon you."

Everyone at the table laughed.

"Well, let's see." Pierre's eyes flashed restlessly about the table. "Our Daisy certainly has definable characteristics."

"Such as?"

"She must be of service to others."

"Daisy also loves history and traditions," Brenda said. "It's probably why she cannot let go of her past."

"She works long hours at the hospital and when she begins a task, it gets completed." Nathan hesitated. "Unless an earthquake strikes or there's a three-alarm fire." He grinned knowing, she could not deny his assertions.

Pierre laughed. "Our Daisy is no hedonist."

"Oh, no," Nathan said, chuckling. "Whenever Belmont establishes some ludicrous new protocol, she follows it to the letter. In her mind, it's the law and the gallows await those who violate his every dictate."

She bristled in her chair. "My need to help others led me into the field of experimental psychology, and of that, I am not ashamed."

"You have done a stellar job at our hospital," Nathan said. "I am more than satisfied with your performance."

Pierre drilled further. "Tell me about Catherine Belmont."

"Father, you are going too far. Give him an ounce of peace."

Nathan waved his hand. "It's alright, Daisy."

"Are you sure?"

He squeezed her hand. "Your father has a right to know about my past."

Nathan turned toward Pierre. "I'll summarize, if you don't mind."

Pierre crossed his arms. "By all means."

"Catherine rebelled against John by falling in love with a stable hand who drifted into town from nowhere. From what I was told, she had a death wish after my departure for college, wanting to die like my mother rather than be without my unyielding love." He rubbed the tabletop. "I don't know if I believe all of that or how much is hyperbole, but it's what others have said. Anyway, she eventually fell in love with the man's vicious nature, believing herself unworthy of a decent man." He winced at the mental portrait of her lying bloody and naked on the street in Dealey. "The more Martin became violent, the deeper her feelings ran for him."

Daisy dropped her eyes in a fond smile.

"I never realized she had a sadistic streak, but it explains a great deal."

Nathan nodded his agreement. "Martin could not sire children, and of course, he blamed Catherine. The man beat her senseless regularly."

Daisy offered a slight smile and a shrug of her shoulders. "Which led to her eventual development of Bell's paralysis and aphasia."

"Perhaps."

"The body can only take so much before it shuts down, Nathan."

"And the mind," Pierre said, rubbing his chin.

Nathan continued. "After several months, Martin dropped Catherine on John's front stoop with a note stating, 'I'm done with this trash.' Belmont nursed her back to health and papered over the unfortunate marriage. He filed an annulment in secret and allowed no one to see his daughter except a few trusted servants and maids. In private, he threatened their lives if any word leaked, and they believed his threats and his promise to pay them well for their trouble. Once she healed, Belmont approached me with a concocted story of her return from college and her suitability for marriage to such a fine specimen of a man." He offered the table a shy grin. "I was, after all, a newly minted physician with a sunny future."

"Your willingness to love her again must have aided her recovery," said Daisy sincerely. "It's certainly helped my own."

"I thought so," he said. "Belmont paid for the wedding and he even bought us a house in the Central West End."

Daisy faced Pierre. "Where Nathan lives today. He's not one to give up on people lightly or the home they once shared."

Brenda chimed in. "They quickly became social royalty."

Nathan felt more comfortable. He gladly confided every detail to them.

"Catherine made it her business to charm the Big Cinch."

"Did it work?" asked Pierre.

"Better than one could have hoped," Brenda said. "They were the talk of the town for several years."

"I hate to continue prodding, but I must ask." Pierre fumbled with his fork and spoon. He looked up at Nathan. "Did you have any children?"

"We had three, beginning with Annie in late August 1876. She died in July 1883. I'm usually bad with dates, but those are forever seared in my memory." He wiped tears which had quickly formed in his eyes. "My Annie was about to turn seven. Eli was four and Peter, two."

"This July marked the ten-year anniversary of their sudden passing and Catherine's desertion," Daisy said. "It's been difficult, to say the least."

"I'm sure," Pierre said. "How could such a thing happen?"

"Disease overtook the city faster than you can imagine," said Brenda confidently. "It was a terrifying and disgusting time to live there."

She mouthed, *I'm sorry* to Nathan.

"It's alright," he said.

Pierre sighed. "We can change the subject if you'd like."

"No need." Nathan stared at the table. "I was called away much of the day and night tending to sick families. Everyone in our household took ill, and all three of our children died within thirty days. Catherine survived the ordeal, but her grief overwhelmed her to the point of a mental breakdown. For three weeks, I tried to soothe her as best I could, but nothing worked. Eventually, she ran back to Martin, leaving me to grieve alone."

"During that time," Daisy said, "Samuel must have been your rock."

"He tried to help me, but like Catherine, I became lost."

Pierre breathed deeply before exhaling. "I know the feeling."

"Oh?"

"I met Patrice while in high school. She was lovely, but she enjoyed talking back to men, putting them in their place. She found me alluring in a strong, silent, and mysterious sort of way. There was something hidden inside me she wanted to dig out and keep all for herself."

"Sounds like love," Nathan said.

"It was not love."

"What then?"

"Convenience mostly."

He paused.

"We found a secret spot along the river. There was an old boat which remained sturdy enough for our purpose. Patrice was fast in those days, sure of herself, and determined to get what she wanted, but I was awkward and I lacked experience with women."

"Father, please," Daisy said, blushing. "Relent."

"No, he should hear about my past as I've heard about his. As your sister stated, we've had enough lies at this table."

"Alright, if you must."

"I clearly had failed to meet her expectations, and Patrice was not shy about sharing her disappointment, but for some reason, she adamantly pursued a relationship with me, and we married soon afterward."

"Did you love her?"

"Looking back, it's hard to say. I wanted to love her."

"Did she love you?"

"Not in the slightest."

Daisy gasped. "Are you serious?"

"Is she sitting here with us now?"

Daisy's face tightened. "No, she's certainly not here."

Pierre's eyes fell on Nathan. "Patrice took a lover, and his name was Henry Hayes. He was an itinerant painter, the kind who would convince a naïve but wealthy widow to give him money, a place to paint, and share her most intimate quarters. Scandal usually intervened, driving him to another city, another county, or another country. He toured around Europe for a time and then landed back in America."

"I never knew much about Henry," Brenda said. "Only that he stayed with us from time to time. Why did you allow it?"

"Like your mother, he was a tormented soul. I hoped she might get him out of her system, but it was a foolish idea, and I regret it."

"I knew more than I let on," Daisy said. "Henry was impatient and often refused to wait for Mother to slip away. On those days, Rose met him at their special spot."

Nathan sat up straight. "Why would he want *her* there?"

Pierre gave him a knowing look. "Because she was his daughter."

The group shared a guilty silence.

The words had never been uttered.

Tears coursed down Pierre's cheeks. "I tried to love as best I could, but Henry had such a hold over them."

Daisy walked to her father and hugged his shoulders. She wrapped her arms around his neck and chest. "Henry wanted Mother to divorce you and take Rose to live with them, but he had no security to offer, and Mother did not want to end up penniless and alone."

She paused.

"I find it strange what we pass to the next generation."

Daisy wiped her own tears and hugged Pierre tightly.

"Why not love?"

He patted her hand. "We've all been found wanting."

"Henry Hayes was a monster," Daisy said. "I'm glad he's gone."

"There's more, *ma chéri*."

"Which is?"

"You are also his daughter."

"I know."

She hugged Pierre and kissed his whiskered cheek.

"Somehow, I've always known."

After the meal, Pierre took Daisy's hand and led her outside to lean on a white pasture fence overlooking rows of grapes. It had rained earlier, and the air was moist. If it were not for the tension which still rested between them, she should have been happy. Daisy's sympathy for her father was pitted against her obsession with Nathan, and she treaded with care to save both.

"Will you recite a psalm for me?"

"Why?"

He gave her a fatherly smile, which was filled with friendship. "It brings me back to the days when you sat at the table and learned your Bible verses."

"It was a simpler and happier time."

"Yes."

She recited Psalm 26:9-10. "Don't let me suffer the fate of sinners. Don't condemn me along with murderers. Their hands are dirty with evil schemes, and they constantly take bribes."

Pierre swiped tears from his eyes. "Please stop."

"I thought you wanted to hear it."

"I did, but the pain is too much to bear."

"There's more to the psalm, papa."

Daisy paused.

"You'll find it uplifting. Please allow me to continue."

She took his silence as affirmation.

"But I am not like that; I live with integrity. So redeem me and show me mercy. Now I stand on solid ground, and I will publicly praise the Lord."

"I find it hard to keep my head up these days," he said.

"The King of Glory will help if you'll ask for it."

"You make it sound effortless."

She rubbed his arm. "It is, papa."

After they chatted about the winery and the farm operations and her work with the patients, Pierre warned Daisy about loving an older man.

"Nathan may attempt to recover his previous level of status."

Daisy sensed the contempt in his suggestion. There were moments when she wanted to weep and throw curses at her father. "You and I have agreed on little over the years, especially regarding my choice of men."

"I was right about Frank," he said.

"I opened myself to him. That is something, even though it cost me."

"We're delicate when we love," he said.

She clasped her hands and sighed. "You'd prefer me to be a noble and kind-hearted Adaline rather than a delicate and pure Lina."

"You will add more light to the world as an Adaline."

"Perhaps the sparkle of love will make the difference."

He smiled. "Now you're teasing me."

"Better you than Henry, I suppose."

Pierre apologized for his many mistakes, even if he wasn't her true father. "After your mother's death, I was a shell of a human being. I wish it was possible to do it all over again and right the wrongs of your childhood."

She tossed a pebble at the grapes, and it rustled through the leaves before landing on the thick, wet soil in silence. "It's the problem with time. You only experience this life one day after another. There's no going back."

He looked away. "I suppose not."

She was suddenly agitated. "Shouldn't we get back to the house?"

Tears filled his eyes, and he did not hide them from her.

"*Ma chéri*, I love you with all my heart as only a father could."

She shuddered and restrained her own tears. "I've never felt love from you, Papa, only anger at a world that took your beloved wife and at the two daughters who've held you back when you could have been a happy man."

He grabbed her and held her close and wept. "For decades, I have been a meandering fool. Please forgive a lonely old man."

She raised her arms and dropped them to her sides, and then clutched her dress with her fingers. Pierre's forceful embrace and his reluctance to let her go broke her heart. What a pathetic man he'd become.

Her mind shifted to Nathan. Could he stand strong until the end and never give into fear or guilt, never compensate or surrender? Could he be the right father for her children? Would he remain her valiant hero?

Daisy and Pierre returned nervously to the house while Brenda gave Nathan a tour of the inner workings of the winery. Daisy glanced over the kitchen and spotted the blood stains on the oak panels. She had worn white linen on the day of her death, and her blood had soaked them through, turning them into rags fit only for the cruel course of the muddy river.

There had been a conversation and then immediate action, the kind which lasts a split second but which lingers irreparably for a lifetime.

Nathan and Daisy stood at the entrance to Ead's Bridge just after the break of dawn as streaks of light ran across the gray wonderland of the overhead sky. A man who resembled Thomas Hannah appeared from the darkness and strolled past them. He smiled and politely tipped his hat. Adrenaline flooded Nathan's veins at the sight of the peculiar visage. He leaned against a railing for support as the apparition disappeared into the slow mist.

"Are you alright?"

"We're in mortal danger, and we must take our leave at once."

"From whom?"

It was strange to see his nemesis so near. "Thomas Hannah just walked past our position and vanished like Macbeth into nothingness."

Daisy squeezed Nathan's arm and placed her hand against his forehead. "Should we get you to the hospital for an examination? Thomas Hannah lies six feet under the grass. I doubt he'll bother us again."

Nathan regained his composure.

He brushed her hand away. "I'm fine. Leave me alone."

"Well, I'm glad no one else noticed your display."

"What if they had? Would you disown me?"

She smirked. "Don't be melodramatic. I'm merely looking out for your interests. You've gained considerable status of late, but your reputation has slogged through swampland for a decade, and we need firmer ground."

"For a Christian woman, you care too much for prestige."

"You may be correct. Europe has changed me for the worse."

"Does the Bible have anything to say about it?"

"Oh, yes. Vainglory permeates both the Old and New Testaments. Many times, Israel swelled with pride and turned its back on God."

"Let me guess. It didn't bode well for them."

She nodded her agreement. "They reaped the whirlwind."

"What about the New Testament?"

"The disciples asked Jesus to identify who would become the most important person in heaven. I can imagine there must have been a fierce internal dispute which led to their question."

"What was His answer?"

Daisy quoted from Matthew 18:1-4. "About that time the disciples came to Jesus and asked, 'Who is greatest in the Kingdom of Heaven?' Jesus called a little child to him and put the child among them. Then he said, 'I tell you the truth, unless you turn from your sins and become like little children, you will never get into the Kingdom of Heaven. So anyone who becomes as humble as this little child is the greatest in the Kingdom of Heaven.'"

She gave Nathan a moment to process the verses and then spoke. "I've always loved that passage because it says so much in so few words."

They stopped walking. He leaned against another railing.

"I feel like a stray dog sometimes."

"Who is scared?"

"Yes."

"Is it why you don't want to complicate your life?"

"Are you implying I fear failure?"

"Absolutely. As do I."

"I witnessed my mother's murder."

"I saw my sister's bloody and deformed body."

"Yes," he said. "We are two peas in a pod."

"No, two lost souls in need of Jesus."

They shared another awkward moment.

Should he kiss her? Should he ask her to marry him?

"Our cots are lonely." He took her hand in his.

She kissed his hand. "Each only supports one person."

"Pity," he said.

She smiled. "We must be patient. The Lord watches from above."

"He invented it, so He must approve."

"In marriage, Nathan, between two people in love."

"I love you, Daisy. That much is certain."

She gasped. "Do you mean what you say?"

"I do, without reservation."

"Then marry me, you fool."

"I will, *someday*."

"Not now?"

He shook his head. "There's too much left undone."

She took a deep breath and exhaled. "Fine, let's go."

As he had done during their downtown excursion, she took his hand and practically dragged him behind her. "Where are we going?" he asked.

"We have patients to save." She spun around and pulled him close to her. "I want children, Nathan, and you are going to give them to me."

Daisy marched forward.

He stopped and called after her.

"What if I'm not ready for more children?"

She wheeled and faced him with a cross look.

"You'll get yourself ready and you'll give them to me because that's what a man does when he's in love with the woman of his dreams, and I am that woman, Nathan, the one you always wanted, the one who will always love you, no matter how old you become, how rich, or how poor or how infirm in your old age. I'll be the woman by your side, for better or worse."

He gave her a smirk. "Well, alright then. When you put it that way, it doesn't sound so terrible." He passed her as he walked forward.

"Close your mouth, Daisy. It's wide open."

She followed him silently with a look of joy on her face.

TWENTY-SEVEN

Psalm 27:14

Wait patiently for the Lord.
Be brave and courageous.
Yes, wait patiently for the Lord.

Daisy read Nathan's book aloud and sounded out each word with clinical authority, defending herself from the dismal thoughts which broke sharply throughout the vestibules of her mind. Sympathy for the hysterics had become an obsession, and she spoke slowly to save them, the sentences contained within each page acting like morphine to her soul, inexplicably creating a want to get close to the wall and come down on the other side, sensible of impropriety, but unwilling to extinguish the last frail spark of her determination, at least not without Nathan's permission, as she was the ship under his watch, the gold pieces tossed into his treasure chest, resting firmly on a map to untold fortunes of love.

An October wind swirled against her window panes, rattling them.

Daisy squinted her eyes and spoke to the gaslit bedroom. "The skill of prescribing is uncommon among modern physicians. Many are they who struggle to compose a prescription in keeping with his general education. He who is blessed with this talent may draw on his medical knowledge with consummate judgement and proficiency, and all the corridors of medicine will serve at his pleasure." She had slipped into lucid nightmares every night for weeks without informing Nathan or anyone else at the hospital, and now she was drained and confused, and the text made little sense.

Daisy kneeled beside her bed and prayed silently to the Most High.

I lift my soul to you, Lord, and I am unashamed to place my trust in you. Show me your perfect ways and teach me to follow your loving guidance. I humbly accept your gift of salvation, and I eagerly await your return.

She fluffed her pillow and stretched flat on the bed. Would Nathan ever rediscover his faith? He seemed more interested in personal acclaim.

She prayed again. *Lord, you are tender and loving. Please forgive my youthful transgressions, for I lacked knowledge of your grace and your mercy. There was anger in me then, Lord, and I acted irresponsibly, but your glory and righteousness have convicted my wicked flesh and soothed my aching soul.*

The heavy book slipped from her hands. It landed on her chest and slammed shut. Annoyed, she quickly opened it again and flipped to a section titled, *The Combination of Medical Remedies*. "It's important to prescribe as few medicines as possible, and to use no vigorous remedy without clear knowledge of its intent. When usage becomes necessary, increasing doses should be employed until returning the body's systems to stasis. Further, strong drugs such as iron and arsenic should be administered independently to remove error and to allow for raising or lowering dosages one at a time."

Nathan trusted pharmacology over the Lord.

His writings made it clear to all who might see.

He had faced many obstacles throughout his tumultuous life. Was he ready for real and lasting relationship or would he run when presented with the next opportunity? When they first met, she worried about her place in the world and the many reasons why chancing love was a ghastly idea, but over time, his kindred spirit pried open her frightened and lonely heart.

Daisy put the book on the floor and considered.

Like her, Nathan possessed a transient essence. He had once desired to move out west and become an outlaw. In the same spirit, ambition drove her to Europe, where she worked with the best medical intellects in the world. Although she ultimately failed in her quest, the journey was taken in earnest. Nathan could not say the same. Would scuttling his prehistoric dream eat away at him over the years, and force a cold regret?

If they married, and he left her, there could be no recovery.

As she drifted, Daisy dreamed of a group of children who sat in front of Jesus and listened to His teachings in wide-eyed wonderment. They were the meek who shall inherit the earth. She inserted herself among them and sat.

Jesus extended His hand and called Daisy forward. She kneeled at His feet and shed tears of sorrow at her many betrayals. "Rise, daughter," Jesus said, as He patted her shoulder. "My return will not come until the last soul has been saved. Do not despair, for a remnant will form at the end, and your lineage will produce the last heir. Afterward, the clouds will part, and I will descend from heaven with a shout, with the voice of the archangel and with the trumpet of God, and the dead in Christ will rise first."

"I am nothing of consequence," she said through tears.

"My daughter, you are very important to my will."

She looked up at Jesus. "What about Nathan?"

"He is another matter. Soon a choice must be made by him."

"Will he choose wisely? I cannot bear to lose him to darkness."

"If he does, many will be saved."

"If he does not?"

Jesus gave her a look of warm compassion, filling her with peace.

"An untold number will be lost to the second death."

"Then we have much work to do," she said absently.

He gently squeezed her shoulders. At His touch, her eyes, which had been closed to the glorious realities of His kingdom, were suddenly opened. She saw the shining city with gates made of pearls and streets built of gold. It was surrounded by unbelievable colors and rolling landscape and majestic mountains which arose before flowing rivers of pure water which quenched more than a physical thirst. She followed Jesus through a colonnade which gave way to the inner portion of the city and then onward to the throne of

God, which towered above her and the river which stretched forth, creating a thin barrier to a grove of trees on the far side. Jesus led her into the water, and all the cares of a lifetime were lifted, replaced by a joy which could not be described in words, only felt in the spirit. Jesus pulled her by the hand, and they stood amid the trees. He handed her a piece of fruit.

"Do not eat this yet," he said.

She gave him a confused look. "May I ask what it is?"

Jesus extended His arm and gestured at a colossal tree.

"This is the Tree of Life."

Her eyes fell on the fruit. Her flesh tempted her to eat.

Jesus once again looked upon her with pure truth and grace.

"Do you trust in my righteousness?"

She took a deep breath and exhaled. "I try, Lord, but mostly I fail."

He held out His hand, as if asking for the fruit.

She gave it to Him, and her eyes fell low.

Jesus raised her chin with his fingers. "When your faith is sound, and you come to me in truth, hiding absolutely nothing from a loving God who already knows the number of hairs on your head and who knew what you would and would not do before heaven and earth were established, and when you trust my righteousness above all else, and when you accept the peace I offer you in full understanding, then you will be liberated from your servitude to sin." He tossed the fruit onto a bare spot of land, and a small tree shot up from the ground, offering new fruit. He gestured at the tree and smiled at her. "There is much work to be done, as you said, and much of it lies within the halls and corners of your own heart, Daisy. Your faith has been too easily stolen by the enemy, and you have hidden yourself from me."

"I am so ashamed," she said, trembling and harrowed. "No one could ever love me after what I did to my sister and after what my mother did to herself, which was also my fault, as everyone in my family knows."

"You will be tested soon, and how you react to the crucible of fire will determine your fate and the destination for many others around you. Lucifer makes many claims on your soul, and he is most persuasive. I was also tempted in such a manner, in the wilderness, all alone in the flesh."

"You were tempted by him?"

Jesus nodded.

"Oh, yes." His eyebrows arched. "I was human, just like you."

Her lips pursed. "You never sinned like me, which is the difference."

"I have taken on your sins, my daughter, and I often weep for you."

She buried her head in His chest and allowed herself to become completely open to Him, holding nothing back, trusting in Him fully and completely. Jesus held her tight against His bosom and kept her from falling to the ground in a ball of pitiful torment. She looked up at Him, and saw the tears course down His glorious cheeks, and she was further broken by the power of her own sin and what it did to others, most especially Him.

"May I hold on a little longer?" asked Daisy.

He pushed her away from His chest so He might look her directly in the eyes as He spoke softly to her. "That, my daughter, will be up to *you*."

* * *

Nathan read the single remaining copy of Frank Kaneski's book, *Consciousness of Domination*, and searched the text for a trace of an academic contribution which might be attributable to Daisy, but detected none. Nathan's life was more meaningful since her arrival. Why didn't she impact Frank in the same manner? Since childhood, Daisy had grown up in the church and around respectable people who observed a strict moral code. There were no unbelievers in her village, nor heretics to be burned at the stake. How did she go so far astray with a maniacal sociopath?

Frank's nihilistic ideas were barren of wisdom.

They were void of positivity, as nothing mattered.

War was inevitable, and any contribution to the advancement of society would eventually dissipate into fierce battle and the reddish mist of death. Humanity should either give up completely or attain the means necessary to control the fallen realm for its own ends. The determined pursuit of power would, over time, further mankind's ascension from mere mortality to the celestial realm. The concept of a *Gottheit*, or human deity, troubled Nathan the most. If Frank Kaneski did not believe in God, then why did he believe in the supernatural? Were there unexplored dimensions ripe for discovery?

Nathan discussed the origin of the universe with Samuel and argued against the existence of God, but after pondering the question further, he would categorize himself as an agnostic rather than an atheist. He had attended church as a child and listened to his Sunday school lessons, but life in a harsh desert terrain of two thousand years ago bore little resemblance to the ever-changing world of St. Louis. After his mother's death, he stopped caring altogether, believing God left him to the wolves of rank despair.

He closed the book and considered the definition of agnostic.

Nathan skimmed his bookshelf and found a quote from the biologist, Thomas Henry Huxley, who was known as Darwin's Bulldog due to his adherence to the theory of evolution and his condemnation of the Gospel accounts in the New Testament. "Thus it will be seen that I have a sort of patent right in 'Agnostic' (it is my trade mark); and I am entitled to say that I can state authentically what was originally meant by Agnosticism. What other people may understand by it, by this time, I do not know. If a General Council of the Church Agnostic were held, very likely I should be condemned as a heretic. But I speak only for myself in endeavoring to answer these questions. Agnosticism is of the essence of science, whether ancient or modern. It simply means that a man shall not say he knows or believes that which he has no scientific grounds for professing to know or believe." Did Nathan have any logical reason to believe in the Lord?

The answer was an unequivocal, no.

He had tried to be a good father to this three children, smothering them with affection and monitoring their activities in an effort to protect them. Catherine laughed at this unwillingness to give them or her any semblance of independence. Then they were each gone in an instant.

If Nathan had offered a kind word to God, perhaps even a mere bestowal of the season's merry greetings, frantic quarrels might have avoided him. It would be a blessing to hug his formidable daughter and to see his sons grow into fine young men and become fathers in their own right. It would be a tearful pleasure to walk Annie to the altar, and all would rejoice.

Samuel had presented three choices to Nathan. First, the universe had always existed, as most Western philosophers believed. Second, it was the product of the Greek *logos*, defined as the supreme imagination behind our collective entirety. Third, the universe was sourced from a sovereign God who, as the prophet Isaiah succinctly stated in verse 42:5, "created the heavens and stretched them out, created the earth and everything in it, and gives breath to everyone, life to everyone who walks the earth."

The first two options presented one with a fearful proposition. If true, the worship of nature and what feels good in the moment would ultimately fail to satisfy humankind's need for personal meaning and purpose. Despair would result, as it always did with nihilism. Nations would then be driven toward ideology and the accompanying lust for power and control, what Frank termed the *Consciousness of Domination*. Mass genocide would follow, unceasing, until millions were missing or dead. He closed his eyes and tried to shake the parade of human brutality which marched across his mind.

Then there was the concept of a holy and divine God.

Daisy had given Nathan a verse on a piece of paper along with a Bible.

He went to his desk and searched the top drawer and found the paper folded several times. Nathan placed it aside to be explored later.

He read John 1:1-5. "In the beginning the Word already existed. The Word was with God, and the Word was God. He existed in the beginning with God. God created everything through him, and nothing was created except through him. The Word gave life to everything that was created, and his life brought light to everyone. The light shines in the darkness, and the darkness can never extinguish it."

Might nature and all its beauty indicate God's presence?

Nathan scanned the page. Daisy had written a second verse below the first. He flipped to Psalm 19:1-4 in his Bible. "The heavens proclaim the glory of God. The skies display his craftsmanship. Day after day they continue to speak; night after night they make him known. They speak without a sound or word; their voice is never heard. Yet their message has gone throughout the earth, and their words to all the world."

The last line from verse four sang to his spirit.

"God has made a home in the heavens for the sun."

If the Lord had made provision for the ever-flowing sun, did He also plan for the return of a wayward son? The words were spelled differently and presented distinct and dissimilar meanings, but there was resonance.

Conviction gnawed at Nathan and pushed him toward something, anything else, but another day spent in nihilistic agony—hopeless, angry, afraid—like a roach who scurries from the penetrating power of the light.

He shut the Bible and stuffed it into a middle drawer.

Nathan trekked alone through city streets.

Harsh memories flashed about him. A conversation with his mother. The wagon and the fields and the splintered wheel. The approaching man and the frightful exchange of words. The horrors of human violence as blood spattered on hard pan soil. Footsteps as he ran. Corn leaves which slapped him in the forehead, the slivers cutting it slightly, his own blood trickling down his cheeks mixed with tears, both landing mercilessly on stalks and weeds and clay. He wasn't sure how far he'd run, but he'd collapsed at the end of it, ragged and braced against the inevitable.

He had pulled himself up and walked forward with an accelerating gait, the desire to outpace his mother's screams overwhelming any remaining sense of decency, her pleas to run away ringing loudly throughout.

Please, Nathan, run away!

Oh, God, please make him run!

Monday morning, Daisy rested in a rocker and watched Nathan move from bed to bed as he performed daily checkups. The first to arrive, she had worked for several hours, and now she took a moment to catch her breath.

She must avoid the temptation to fold under extreme pressure.

As Nathan smiled at her, the Holy Spirit prompted a silent prayer.

Dear Lord, please forgive my sins, for they are many, and please work on Nathan and guide him along the correct path. Ease his internal suffering so he might help others. He must learn to fear you, Lord, to gain wisdom and understanding. Allow him to know your glorious ways and your holy character and deliver him from harm. I cannot counsel him as he considers me weak and lacking in social graces. Release him from the center of Babylon and send him walking toward the city gate, so he might escape before judgement falls upon the wicked. It's coming, Lord. I feel it in my spirit and in my bones.

Please remove the scales from Nathan's eyes so he might also see. On this and all things, I lay my travails at the foot of the cross. In Jesus' name, Amen.

She opened her eyes and scanned the room for movement.

It had slowed down and become less oppressive.

The Holy Spirit prompted Daisy to share what transpired after her angelic encounter at Big Rock. She had followed the wooded trail a half mile, detecting no unearthly beings, and eventually gave up the search out of dejection and resentment. Did Daisy's prevailing bitterness lead to her sister's untimely demise? Rose was young and impressionable, and she looked up to her big sister in all things, simple and complicated, sensing her moods, emulating them. Did Daisy want her to end it all from atop the cliff?

She shuddered. The answer was a resounding *yes*.

Since they had become close, perhaps Nathan would believe her angelic story. More likely, he would fall back on his scientific training and strap her to a bed and then sedate her like a berserk pack-animal. She took a breath and exhaled. Either way, she must obey the prompting of the Holy Spirit.

She stood and called across the room.

"Nathan, we need to speak in your office."

"In a minute. I'm busy."

The prompting grew stronger. She must connect before it was too late. His faith had reached a crossroads, and he would soon choose unwisely.

Many lives weighed in the balance.

John Belmont thudded down the stairs and interrupted her thoughts. "You must come quickly," he said. "I have something to show you."

She pointed at her chest. "Me?"

John nodded toward Nathan and smirked. "Might as well collect him, too. He's supposed to be the administrator of this looney bin."

An hour later, they toured the St. Louis Forum.

"I've spared no expense for this lavish affair." John slowly waved his hand from right to left as a young woman entered and sat in the back row. "Once spellbound under your expert direction, our hysterics will perform a public exhibition on this stage, delighting our most prominent citizens and raising much needed funds for our hospital." John slapped Nathan's back. "Once this grand affair succeeds, our troupe will tour the nation."

Daisy argued for the humanity of the patients, but Nathan's attention was drawn to the woman with jet black hair who stared at the stage with attentive eyes. Daisy peered across the rising floor of the auditorium and noted the woman's beautiful features, her stylish clothing, and her perfect apportionment. She was eerily reminiscent of Rosemarie.

Nathan rapidly agreed to John's demands.

"That's splendid, my boy! I'm hosting a charity ball for the hospital Saturday evening." He cast a glance at Daisy. "My business manager said we might raise over ten thousand dollars if we play this right. The two of you will regale our Big Cinch with tales of triumph, and I want them every bit as mesmerized as our pathetic lot." His smile turned into a worried frown, and his voice fell in pitch. "My friends are men of taste, so tread softly."

His sentiment confused her. "How much Mammon is enough, John?"

Nathan grabbed Daisy's arm. "We'll be there."

John rushed toward the entrance.

Daisy tried to speak again, but Nathan instructed her to be quiet.

John wheeled and faced Nathan. "You remember what I said about showing success at my hospital?"

"Yes."

"The work is not finished, and I am displeased. You'll do well to delight me in all future endeavors."

"We're working diligently, sir."

"Use her European techniques to speed up the process. I want trained dogs who will bark on command, not recovered patients who expect to resume their normal lives. Together, we will make history."

"Yes, sir."

"A great deal of money is at stake."

John flung open the door and disappeared into the sunlight.

The door slammed shut, and the room fell dark.

TWENTY-EIGHT

Psalm 28:1

I pray to you, O Lord, my rock.
Do not turn a deaf ear to me.
For if you are silent,
I might as well give up and die.

September 1880

The overpowering night was interrupted by a light which began at the horizon as a line and grew brighter and reached farther until it encompassed the trees which grew along the Missouri River and highlighted the landscape ferns which splotched the forest floor with green and the desiccated cousins which spread gray and withered along the slender branches prayerful for rain so they might live again resurrected by the living water and the glory of Christ who sourced the heavenly light. Daisy reached out with her fingers and grabbed at the mystery and asked Him to dwell within her through faith. The light circled and penetrated and supported her, knowledgeable of her faults, filled with grace for her perilous truth.

Patrice shook Daisy awake from her dream. She had been sleeping in a corner near her bed with a blanked held firmly over her body and tucked under her chin. Daisy quietly climbed into her bed and under the covers.

Her mother's face showed many wrinkles and her hair was made of wide gray streaks. Daisy's hand trembled as she clutched the sheet.

"You look sad, Mama."

"It's not a nice thing to say, Daisy. Take it back."

It was the truth. "Alright, then. I take it back."

"Good, honey. Now go to sleep."

Twenty minutes passed, and Daisy could not drift.

Her feet paced the floor in the murkiness of her bedroom.

She tiptoed down the hall and heard a faint noise from the sewing room.

As she grew closer, her mother's sobs penetrated the flimsy wooden door, piercing Daisy's heart and troubling her fearful soul. She knocked and asked if there was anything she could do to help. Patrice fell silent for several moments and then begged her daughter to leave her alone.

In her bed, Daisy asked the angel to return.

She stared into the shadows for an hour and hoped for the slightest glimpse of movement, finding nothing but a featureless abyss.

Daisy sat at the table while she worked on her lessons. Her father entered the kitchen and stumbled toward the cabinet and once there he fumbled for a glass which he filled with water from a pitcher which lived beside the icebox. Daisy dropped her pencil and allowed it to roll across the paper and onto the surface of the table. It continued to the oak planks, which sturdily stretched themselves along the length of the kitchen, supporting its weight.

"I dreamed about Rose again last night."

Pierre sat at the table and rubbed his face.

"An all-powerful hand gripped her tightly, and she screamed for help. I reached out from a distance but could not get to her."

He stared at Patrice, who sat opposite him.

"Even if I had reached her, I could never defeat the hand of God."

He took a deep breath and slowly exhaled. "Rose dangled above the Lake of Fire. Her soul would be tossed into it within a few seconds. I searched to the right and to the left for assistance, but there was none to be found." He reached across the table and squeezed his wife's hand. "Our daughter begged me to know the Lord before it was too late."

"There's still time to save her," Patrice said. "I sense she's still alive, waiting for us to free her from such a horrible fate."

Pierre shook his head and released her hand.

"It was only a dream, but it felt all too real."

"It was real," she said determinedly. "I've had the same dream."

"Rose made me promise something. It was very important to her."

Patrice stiffened. "What did you promise?"

"Our names must be written in the Book of Life."

"What about *her* name?"

"It's too late for Rose. She has already died the second death."

Patrice shook her head in defiance of Pierre's defeat.

"The Bible says we rest in peace until the Lord's return." She searched her husband's face for any sign of a solution. "It hasn't happened yet."

"In our realm and our concept of time."

Pierre paused.

"For God, it's done."

"There must be another way." Patrice's gray-black hair swayed gently as she rocked back and forth. "I know there is."

"There is no other way, my love. Only to pray for our own salvation."

She grabbed a clump of her hair and tugged at the tangles.

"You saw Him cast her into the fire?"

Pierre shook his head. "I woke up before it happened."

Her body slumped slightly. "Then we can save her."

"Rose understood her fate all too well, even before she jumped."

Patrice gave him a half-crazed smile and spoke with a shaky voice.

"I can save her."

"No, it's out of your control."

Patrice became hysterical and cut herself with their sharpest knife.

Pierre rushed to her side and bandaged her wrists.

Daisy retrieved a mop and attempted to clean the blood from the floor.

"The planks soak it up, Papa."

"You must use more force! Are you weak and pathetic?"

Daisy rushed her words. "I'm stronger than *you*."

"Then show me." He wrapped Patrice's wrist with several strips of cloth.

Daisy dipped her brush into the water and pressed hard.

The relentless planks taunted her.

"I hate myself for being wicked," Patrice said. "I hate this fallen world."

Pierre tried to calm his wife's emotions.

He squeezed her close to his heart. "Please, think of all you will lose."

Her face contorted into a grimace. "You speak to me of Henry?"

"I speak of Daisy."

"She is a product of sin, and I will no longer mingle with iniquity."

"You don't mean it, Patrice." His eyes studied her, and his face took on a fearful countenance. "If you will calm down, I'll go for the doctor."

Patrice moved to the basin and furiously washed her hands.

Daisy worried her mother's bandages might slip, and the flow of blood might resume. It would prove much harder to stop a second time.

The harsh soap reddened Patrice's skin, but she continued.

Pierre wrapped his arms around her. "Please, stop," he said.

She pushed against him, freeing herself.

"Papa, please help Mama." It was all Daisy could think to say.

Patrice stared at the ceiling and raised her arms.

"I give thanks, Yahweh, for this bar of soap. My hands are wet with my child's blood, but I will wash myself clean on this very evening."

Pierre shot a glance at Daisy. "She's lost her sanity."

Daisy nodded her agreement. There were no more words.

"Lord, I will attend your church and kneel at your altar. Far and wide, I will present the voice of thanksgiving. Of your wondrous deeds, my mouth will speak." Patrice fell to the floor and sobbed into her dress.

Pierre knelt beside her. He carefully stroked her hair.

Daisy stood silent, watching in awe. She hoped for a safe resolution.

Pierre sat Patrice at the table and started for Doc Spirey.

Patrice smiled at her husband, and Daisy believed the worst had passed.

Pierre winked at Daisy and softly pulled the door closed.

"Lord, I cannot live one more hour in this fallen world."

Pierre's eyes registered confusion. "What did you say?"

He pushed the door open, and the creaky sound terrified Daisy.

Patrice lunged for the basin and retrieved the shiny knife. She sliced her throat, and her body crumpled to the floor before Pierre could reach her.

Thirsty planks soaked up the red tide, forever marking the day.

Patrice writhed and rolled to one side. Her pale form grew still.

Daisy asked the angel of the woods why she was born. Since her mother's death, she had pulled away from friends and family. If the angel of the woods refused to show himself, there would be no one left to love.

Crickets and katydids produced the only answer.

Her rage grew, and she cursed the angel. She threatened to chase him to the ends of the earth. When that didn't work, she dared him to fight her.

There was no sound, no resolution, no satisfaction.

Daisy walked among the green splotches which lined the forest floor and the mighty oaks which stretched wide and the tall hickories which arose to meet the celestial skyline. Resurrection ferns extended along the tree branches, their leaves curled and withered from a lack of rain. Sad and alone, Daisy said she was sorry and prayed for a sign from God.

Thunder roared in the distance.

She toyed with the notion of ending her life. It would be so easy to climb the hill and throw herself from the steep ledge. The bloodless rocks often called to her and tempted her to join them at the dark and lonely bottom. It would be painless, and she would find the end a pleasant relief.

A rainstorm approached. It boomed louder and grew darker.

Daisy looked for cover under the forest canopy.

Rain fell in sheets. The drops were plump and wet.

The rain opened the ferns and brought them back to life in only a few minutes. The event confused her. If God could resurrect ferns, why not people? Surely, her mother and sister were worth more than a plant.

TWENTY-NINE

Psalm 29:10

The Lord rules over the floodwaters.

As he sat in the gazebo at Forest Park, in what once seemed like the threadbare border of the frontier but now felt warmer and cozier and more centered than any place Nathan had previously encountered, he mulled the experiences and personal traits he and Daisy shared in common and weighed them against their profound differences. If the truth were to be told, she might be better off with someone more suited to her melancholic temperament, but the more he knew her, the closer they became. She was the most trustworthy woman he'd ever known. There were days when they were miles apart and others where their fascinations and dreams crossed paths, and dusty isolation gave way to the wild forests and tempestuous seas of their imagination. A magical world awaited, one without care for prettiness which fades or brokenness which cripples, a land filled with hope for children and a home and a hearth lit by a splendid flame.

Why wouldn't she accept his need to place science above religion?

A man who sold roses neared with a gleam in his eyes.

"I want nothing from you," said Nathan contemptuously.

The man's face fell sour. He made his way briskly to the gate and threw a sullen look at the gazebo before disappearing into the whirl of the city.

Daisy sat on the bench and patted Nathan's leg.

"No roses today?"

He smiled and sniffed the air for rain. "Why would I need them? You are here, and we are sitting together like two peas in a pod."

She turned from the street, and her eyes fell reproachfully on him. There was a burden within her which she needed to express, a stone which rested heavily on her back. "I suppose it depends on your mood. Are you controlled by reason or emotion this morning?"

"What is that supposed to mean?"

"During our last conversation with John, you caved to his absurd demands like a schoolboy. He's not your better, you know. Far from it."

"You skirted my question with a non-answer."

"Alright, how about this? You sometimes allow your emotions to get the better of you, and I must think logically for the both of us." She clenched her jaw before speaking again. "Your decisions now affect me, remember?"

Her words vexed him. "You are a tedious woman who wants her side dishes just so, her meat undercooked or overcooked, her water at just the right temperature. You need to learn to relax and enjoy life."

Daisy snorted. "Like you?"

"It wouldn't be so horrible."

"Well, let's see." Her voice carried a tilt of contempt. "Should I visit the brothel before or after I drink three bottles of whiskey?"

He took off his hat and ran his hand through his hair.

"Your manners have withered like a flower without water, and I find your lack of lady-like qualities to be most unbecoming." He looked past her at the busy street. "I never said you should give up all propriety, only that you should not take life so seriously that you routinely fall into despair."

"It's a thoughtful speech." She gestured curtly. "Are you quite finished?"

"I believe so, but you know I'm right."

"I know you won't fight for the patients in your hospital, the ones who desperately need your vigor if they are to have a bug's chance in this world." She swatted at the air. "We all need you, Nathan. I wish you could see it."

"I ask you to be reasonable, Daisy."

"You must return to morality, for my sake, if nothing else." She nodded tightly and carefully controlled her tone, as if holding back an insult. "I don't think it's too much to ask of a prospective husband."

"Let me remind you, I've been overwhelmed by a series of unwelcome responsibilities since I was a young boy. I've been forced to set my dreams and desires to the side, making my personal fulfillment an impossibility." His impatience got the better of him. "It's high time I won the prize."

"There's no reward other than helping those poor people get over their traumas. Wouldn't it be wonderful to see them integrate into the world again? Surely, you would value such an achievement."

"I am reluctant to help those in trouble. My survival comes first."

"If someone yelled for help in the water, what would you do, throw them a preserver and walk away? Would they cease to exist for you?"

He wanted to leave her alone, but forced himself to endure.

"Flailing arms may drag a man under water."

"Nathan, with Jesus as your Savior, all things are possible."

He threw up his hands, feigning defeat. "That's easy to say, but you don't bear the pressure of running a hospital. You heard Belmont. If I fail, he'll ensure my name is hauled through the mud for years."

"Approach him at the ball and make him listen. We cannot treat our patients like trained animals." She squeezed his arm. "You know I'm right."

He stood and studied the road outside the park entrance. Carriages passed the gate, but no one stopped or ventured inside. Daisy spoke with a heedless enthusiasm and without regard for tact or diplomacy.

He turned toward her. "I wish I shared your faith."

Daisy stood in front of him and put her head on his chest.

"Why is your faith so weak?"

Nathan scanned the other benches and found them empty.

He desperately wanted to kiss her in broad daylight. Did he dare?

"Although my father is alive," he said, "I feel like an orphan."

She drew away from him and gazed into his eyes.

"You believe God has abandoned you?"

"A long time ago."

"Did you call out for Him the day your mother died?"

"Not really."

Her eyes narrowed. "Or any other day, before or after?"

Nathan sat on the bench. She sat beside him and touched his leg with her own. They exchanged smiles. "Pop invited himself to the ball, and he even asked Dora to be his date. I don't know what's gotten into him lately."

"I think he's a good man who loves you and wants another chance at raising a child. He'll make an excellent father for Ida." She locked her hands together in a labored serenity and kept her countenance impassive. "He seeks atonement, Nathan. You should take note and do likewise."

"I was there for my children and for my wife."

"You've wanted to seek your fortune in the west since Catherine met you, and do not argue to the contrary. I think she knew your soul was not in the marriage, nor was it fully invested in parenthood. You are an adventurer at heart, and I must be a fool to have gotten myself mixed up with you."

"Don't hold back, madam. You should really let me have it."

Daisy's lips parted, and her eyes locked onto his.

Her fingers stroked her neck. "It's too late now, anyway."

"Why?"

She wrapped her arm around his waist and hugged him.

"I've fallen in love with you and there's no turning back."

He turned her head so their lips met and kissed her deeply.

Nathan pulled away from her and stroked her hair.

"I should help Dora locate a suitable dress," said Daisy, trembling.

"You'd better get one for yourself."

He kissed her neck several times and then whispered in her ear.

"Unless you want me to disown you."

She smiled. "We can't have that now, can we?"

Nathan and Daisy arrived separately to the ball on Saturday evening, and he sufficiently overcame his dread of the event, it having come so quickly after the Veiled Prophet ball which had occurred in early October. That one, he avoided like the plague, as Catherine was tapped to escort the latest queen, Florence Lucas, to the stage, and she would have been troubled by the theme, *Storied Holidays*, unable to bear the knowledge of the Christmases which had been stolen from her three children. She would have kept her emotions locked, never to be revealed to her father or Nathan or the new man in her life, whoever he might be, and she might even pretend to be bored with the artificial prestige of the annual gala event, but inside, she would die a slow and painful death, blighted by the loss of life itself.

Samuel looked about the room and then pointed at Dora. "I'm glad she's here. I couldn't face the Big Cinch without a good woman by my side. It would be like standing near a grizzly bear while holding a potbellied pig."

"Colorful as always." Nathan cast a frown at his father.

He leaned closer and whispered into Samuel's ear. "We must band together to stop Daisy from ruining this opportunity. I've run the race too far to see her destroy my chance of crossing the finish line."

"Keep your head up, my boy. God will provide a path."

"Forgive me if I don't trust Him."

Daisy arrived, looking radiant, and no one dared take their eye off her, including Nathan. She shined like a cut diamond in rich sunlight.

Samuel blinked rapidly as he openly gazed at Daisy. "Now there's your real prize, Son, and don't you forget it." His head shook in disbelief.

He nudged Dora, and they both smiled.

Nathan folded his arms across his chest. "What would you know about anything, Pop? It took you thirty years to ask a woman for a date."

"Yes, but now I'm getting married." Samuel offered a slight smile and a shrug. "Once I decide to do something, it happens."

"I'm not *you*."

Samuel chuckled. "On this, we agree."

Belmont appeared with a jaunty countenance. "Are you two characters going to bicker all evening, or might we have some fun?"

"Daisy and I were about to leave." Nathan tapped a foot as he spoke.

She lowered her eyes and clutched her diminutive purse.

Nathan hoped he could keep his hands off her at the hospital.

"Why on earth would you do such a thing?"

"To work with the patients."

"Nonsense," Belmont said. "This is a night for celebration."

He invited the couple into his billiard room for a money game.

From the crowd, another woman stepped forward, the one with jet black hair and emerald green eyes. She was the most sensual woman Nathan had seen in many years, even more so than Sheila, and his desire suddenly shifted toward her, no matter how energetically he might wish otherwise.

Daisy seemed flustered by the change in Nathan's focus.

The woman stood in front of him. "Do you approve of my dress?"

"It's very nice," he said. "Have we met?"

"She will benefit you honorably in the future, but we will not yet disclose her identity," Belmont said. "I invited her to join us this evening, so she might prove her worth. I assure you, she is a most proficient asset."

Daisy cozied up to John and patted his dinner jacket with a spurious admiration. "Please, sir, escort a lady into the privacy of your quarters. Whatever happens, we simply *must* have an audacious evening."

Belmont took Daisy's arm and beamed. "I like this one."

As they proceeded up the stairs, she turned and grinned at Nathan.

He surrendered to their lead and followed like a lost puppy.

Daisy sat in the corner as the seductive woman entered the room. The woman stared at her with vigilant eyes, which made her uncomfortable. Thankful the voices kept silent, Daisy said a silent prayer to Jesus.

Please, Lord, give me the correct words to convince this man.

John racked the billiard table and then slammed the pool cue into a stack of balls. The momentum sent several balls to the four corners of the table, startling Daisy. Her alarm made Belmont smile.

At this nod, the woman stood and acknowledged his authority.

"Thank you, John."

She turned toward Daisy. "John inserted spies at his hospital, Miss Lawrence, and they report to me each evening."

Daisy looked at the floor rugs and the wall tapestries.

She spoke absently. "Is that so?"

"Do you admire the architecture of this room?"

Daisy smiled at the notion. "I am waiting for the voices to prattle."

The woman glanced at John, and he gestured for her to speak.

"Our voices will be sufficient for this evening." She picked up a folder and opened it. "I'm told you've made meager progress with your precious hysterics. John and Susanna have been most troubling, wouldn't you say?"

"We have no spies," said Daisy defiantly. "Our staff cares too much."

"You'd be surprised." John held himself erect with the cue stick. "For example, did you know the Hutchinsons once dabbled in the occult?"

"I know nothing about them since they refuse to talk to us."

"Well, my sources have a lot to say. Apparently, they bought a Ouija board in Pittsburg and used it to conjure spirits of deceased relatives. Whether it was the original source of their madness isn't for me to speculate, but they fell into mania soon after the purchase. I'd say you have your hands full when dealing with those two." His eyebrows arched. "Doing battle with the underworld isn't for the faint of heart, Miss Lawrence. Are you sure your talking cure is up to the task?"

"To answer your question, yes, we've had difficult moments with them."

"With the other patients as well," said the woman violently. "Even the good ones, like Heinrich Besseler and James Clifton."

Daisy couldn't deny the validity of the woman's information.

"Yes."

"They've been reluctant to speak with you about their pasts." The woman glared at Daisy, expecting a prompt answer. "Is that correct?"

"Am I on trial?"

The woman laughed. "This is much more important, as more than one life weighs in the balance." She placed the folder on a table beside her. "I have information about their backgrounds, who they were, why they are with us. It should prove helpful in pushing through barriers."

"They must tell us in their own time," Daisy said. "When they're ready."

John slammed the cue stick on the table. It made Daisy jump.

"No! We will force the issue using your hypnosis techniques. This woman will deliver packets of background information to Nathan's office on Monday. Like a detective, you will confront each patient with their sordid histories until they break from exhaustion."

"You are an evil man," Daisy said, scowling, "and she is a vile serpent."

John's smile returned. "Exactly."

He picked up the cue stick and gestured for Nathan to join the game.

John's motivation remained unclear to Daisy.

"Why do you care what happens to them?"

"At first, I viewed them as a nuisance," he said. "They limited my ability to convince the good citizens of Vandeventer Place to trust my hospital."

"And now?"

"The hysterics are the ideal recruiting tool. If we can perform wonders with those loons, imagine what might be accomplished with normal people. We will tour the nation, drum up support, and I will make a fortune."

"You already have enough money," Nathan said.

John shot him a fierce look. "You keep out of this, boy."

"Mesmerism is merely one instrument from our tray," said Daisy with a convinced tone. "One which never results in a lasting cure." She swallowed hard in hopes of relieving the tension in her muscles. "We must consider their dignity. They come to us fractured, and we must endeavor to make them whole again." She glanced about uneasily and cast a glance at Nathan.

"I do not share your concern for nursery rhymes." John gazed doggedly at her. "I want results, and these modern techniques will provide them."

She paced for several moments and turned toward him.

"What happens if we refuse to comply?"

"I'll cast the hysterics back to Arsenal Road, where they belong. The asylum administrator has freed up space and eagerly awaits my transport. Once my hospital is cleared of these miscreants, I will start an advertising campaign geared only toward the Big Cinch." He sat on a stool and offered a grim smile. "There's one way to help your poor victims. Allow them to tour the nation in my show or see them become permanent wards of the city."

Daisy sat in a chair and pondered the ease of her defeat.

The woman's emerald eyes pulsated and sparkled, alive with a presence which wanted desperately to make itself known to the world, but which must wait for the opportune moment to be introduced. The devilish fiend must not stumble, weary beast it was, or risk losing advantage. Daisy knew these truths, as she knew details about Nathan's departed children.

Their photographs pleaded with her from the mantle.

Lead our father from the Lake of Fire. He is unreachable to all but you.

Daisy and Nathan stared at one another. She wanted him to go after John and talk sense to him, but it would do little good to suggest the logical course of action, as Nathan's body was affixed to his chair, and John was likely downstairs in the ballroom entertaining members of the Big Cinch.

The cue stick rolled off the rack and hit the floor.

Daisy flinched. "How did that happen?"

Nathan shrugged. "How should I know?"

"It's a sign from God."

"Daisy, don't start."

"John's unfair prejudices will ruin their lives."

Nathan drew out a clean handkerchief and wiped his brow. His posture inflated, steadying his voice. "Why don't you go home and cry about it? You'll feel better, and we can move toward a favorable resolution."

"My tears will not help us, Nathan."

"Why not?"

"They fix nothing."

He glared at her for what felt like an hour.

Daisy arose and abruptly left the room.

Nathan called for her, and she heard the curse over her shoulder as she descended the stairs. She stood at the edge of the ballroom floor and waited for John's approach. Nathan rushed up behind her and spun her toward him. Daisy pulled away from him and turned to meet John, who held up a hand and exclaimed, the sound carrying itself above the din of the gala.

"Leave it alone, Miss Lawrence! My decision is final!"

Nathan spun her by the shoulders, slightly pulling a muscle in her neck. "You are one stubborn woman!"

Daisy slapped his face. "You should fight for what you believe, not act like John's lackey." She instinctively recoiled, unsure of his response. When he stood firm, but only glared at her, she continued. "I read your book on making medicines. It's amazing, and you should publish it. I especially liked the introduction where you shared your thoughts on physician hygiene and medical morality. It's what every aspiring doctor must read before throwing themselves on the altar of greed and envy."

"No one would read it."

She drew back from him. "If they have a mind of their own, they will want to learn better methods and grow as a genuine healer, one whose mission is to restore human dignity along with physical health."

Nathan appeared injured, but he spoke without restraint. "That's just it, isn't it? We don't have minds of our own. We react on impulse and revert to what comes naturally. The flesh wants what it wants."

"You've read Frank's work, and his words have influenced you."

His eyes rolled. "I don't buy into his nihilism—the *Consciousness of Domination* or the *Gottheit*—if that's what you mean."

"Alright then, there's hope, but you're clearly a believer in the *supreme imagination*, which is where Frank's vile ideas originate."

She paused.

"If you believe in one, you will believe in the other."

"Meaning?"

"God defines our reality, not the other way around. When one considers the ordered systems found in nature, the sophistication of the human body, or the brain's willingness to manufacture somatic symptoms from suppressed emotion, it would be intellectually dishonest to argue such powerful and elaborate mechanisms evolved from rain which fell on rocks."

"I don't care about your rain or your rocks."

"They're not mine, Nathan."

The woman stepped near to him and whispered into his ear.

He gave her a languishing smile.

She turned toward Daisy. "Nathan's beliefs suit him."

Her eyes flickered. "I cannot say the same for your unsteady soul."

Daisy stepped closer to her nemesis. "What is your name?"

"It will be revealed in time, Miss Lawrence."

"Well, whatever your name is, you are like a thorny vine who intends to grow wild along Nathan's rough outer wall, but I'll have you know there are many layers underneath which you'll never access. Of that I'm certain."

"How so?" The woman appeared intrigued.

"It takes *love*, something I doubt you know anything about."

"Miss Lawrence, I can assure you, I have been prepared over many years. You do not know what I have witnessed or what I have weathered."

"The same holds true for me."

Several guests passed their position and continued along the hall to the drawing room, where drinks were served. The woman's eyes followed their movement. She turned to John, as if to ask for direction. He shook his head.

Daisy took Nathan's hand. "You have drifted so far from God, and I sometimes wonder if you'll ever find your way home to Him again."

She paused.

"May I share a verse with you?"

He snorted.

"Fine, go ahead. You'll do it no matter what I have to say on the matter."

Daisy spoke softly to the man of her dreams. "Galatians 6:7 tells us, 'Don't be misled—you cannot mock the justice of God. You will always harvest what you plant.' The apostle Paul continues in the next verse, 'Those who live only to satisfy their own sinful nature will harvest decay and death from that sinful nature. But those who live to please the Spirit will harvest everlasting life from the Spirit.' Please take in the words, Nathan. Really hear and understand them. Your future depends on it, and I don't want you to be eternally separated from Jesus, especially if there was something I could have done to help you know His true character."

"Nathan likes to sin," the woman said. "He likes to drink and fight and break down doors when the mood strikes. He doesn't enjoy turning his cheek, only to get slapped down again. It's in his blood."

"His father has been redeemed."

"I referred to his mother, June, not his father, Samuel."

Nathan grabbed the woman's arm and drew her near to him. "Who are you, and how do you know anything about my mother?"

"Your soul scours the earth in search of something you will never find."

Her voice carried the arrest of feminine seduction.

His anger persisted, as if she fueled his rage. "Which is?"

The woman squeezed his arm. "The mother you lost as a boy."

He withdrew from her touch.

"It's true, and you must finally accept it."

The woman gently pulled him near, unwilling to be outdone by Daisy's concern. "June is gone from this world, Nathan, and she's not coming home to you again." She hesitated. "Unlike Sheila or Catherine, or this feeble excuse for a woman who stands before us, I alone can take her place."

"Right now, I want nothing to do with either of you."

He left both women alone and marched to the front entrance. The door banged shut as he exited to the private lane and some unknown destination.

Daisy was unsure if she should follow him.

Let him go, child. Have faith in the Lord in all things and know you are loved. Act according to my will, and you will see light from a better day.

"You cannot win, you know, no matter how many silent prayers your offer to your God. In the last accounting, I will emerge victorious."

"You cannot defeat the Most High."

"Oh, no?"

Daisy shook her head, sure of herself after hearing from the Lord.

"Please follow me upstairs. There's something you should see."

"I must take my leave."

"It will be a brief presentation, but one you will find most interesting."

Daisy's lids felt heavy. She needed to rest.

"For now, I will assent." She hesitated. "Don't get used to it."

The woman ushered her into the cigar room and then left her alone.

Daisy sat nervously in a chair and felt the lines in her face deepen from the stress of the last few months. She detested the nefarious woman.

The door opened and Catherine entered the room. She seemed barely conscious. The woman sat her in a chair near Daisy and lightly stroked her fingers through Catherine's hair. She looked longingly at her and then turned toward Daisy. "Miss Lawrence, you can never succeed in your quest."

The woman moved briskly toward the door and exited the room.

Daisy leaned forward. "Are you alright?"

"You have nothing to fear." Catherine detached herself from their conversation and looked about the room. Her eyes followed an unseen object along the floor and the walls and the ceiling. She gave Daisy a distrustful glance. "Many spirits have taken residence inside me."

"I can get you out of here, Catherine, but we must hurry."

Catherine fell silent, and her eyes stared blankly.

Daisy stood and rubbed her shoulders.

"Please tell me you're well," she said. "I need you to be my sister."

Catherine looked up at her. "Sister?"

"Yes, I cannot go much further alone. I need you at my side."

"The spirits say you have no right to interfere in my life."

"I will, nonetheless. You deserve to be loved again."

Along the wall to their right, about halfway between the oak floor and the ceiling, something crackled. It moved higher, still crackling but without a visible form, and reached the ten-foot height of the ceiling. The sound moved across the room and came down again along the far wall to their left.

The crackle charged forth across the floor and bumped into a chair with a satin-lined back, knocking it over with a bang. Daisy startled at the motion and the smell of fire which now penetrated the air inside the room.

Catherine stood and looked at the chair with suspicion.

Her eyes fell on Daisy.

"I am cursed and soon I will be dead."

"Please leave with me, Catherine. I beg you to return to the hospital."

Catherine led Daisy to the door and opened it.

"There is no hope for me."

She stuck her head into the hallway, which was empty.

"You must leave before the spirits sink their teeth into your flesh."

She shoved Daisy into the hallway.

"Catherine, *please*."

A voice of authority, the one Daisy had heard during her earlier visit, spoke through Catherine. "Do as I say, or everyone you care about will be murdered within a week. Test me at your peril, for I mean what I say."

Daisy now understood the voice to be real.

She hurried down the stairs, catching the heel of her boot on several steps and nearly falling to her death. She reached the front door, and once there, she looked over her shoulder, terrified something awful would be fast on her heels. Where Catherine had stood, there was only space.

Daisy flung open the door and rushed outside.

The door slammed shut behind her. The air was thick and warm.

She had left her friend to die a second time.

THIRTY

Psalm 30:3

You brought me up from the grave, O Lord.
You kept me from falling into the pit of death.

Sunday morning, Nathan awakened in an unfamiliar bed, completely divorced from God, alone with no one but the sin which enslaved his flesh. He didn't remember how he got there, but he was fully dressed, a dull and minor blessing. Nathan stood and realized he was in Sheila's old room at the brothel. A ragged waif with matted hair and a missing front tooth now occupied the bed. Sympathetic to her plight, he placed money on the side table and disregarded her stifled *thanks*. He wandered down the crowded second-floor hallway. Men dodged him as they meandered into an out of rooms. Doors opened and closed, and women laughed blithely at the sight of a fresh customer with money in his pockets and wearing anticipation on his face. Nathan had been one of those men.

Joanna stared at him through an open door as he approached the stairs.

She moved to the door frame and offered her best smile. "Nathan, won't you come sit beside me on the bed? I'll make it worth the trouble."

There was a spark of attraction. His eyes washed over her body.

Joanna stepped near to him and straightened his collar. She kissed his neck in several places. "I finally have you all to myself."

Nathan looked down into her mirthful, ambitious eyes.

He studied her face. "I've thought about you over the years."

"Alice said you stumbled into her room last night and fell asleep. It's a pity, but I suppose she can't measure up to your darling Sheila."

Joanna grabbed his arms with surprising strength and yanked him into her bedroom. The door slammed shut behind him. "I'm here now." Her eyes became cat-like. "You so desperately need my help."

He removed her probing hands from his chest.

"I must go now. The hospital will not run itself."

"It will do exactly that once you find your calling."

"Dare I ask? What do you believe it to be, Joanna?"

"You will become like Jack the Ripper."

He laughed in her face. "Stop joking and get serious."

"I will show you how to murder. It is my specialty."

Nathan recalled Stonecipher's hanging. He lost his humor.

"I am a surgeon who already knows how to cut."

Joanna's chin jutted, and she crossed her arms.

"You know how to perform surgery within the secure confines of an operating room, but I will guide you to murder unsuspecting victims in the night, mostly street prostitutes who no one cares about, anyway." She continued over his refusals. "Jack the Ripper confounded London police for three years as he rampaged across the East End, gleefully cutting throats and mutilating abdomens. Our people trained him well, but his era has passed."

"You think I will do likewise in St. Louis?"

She grinned sadistically. "Our order values the spillage of blood, and I am a worthy teacher. I expect in the end, you will outperform Jack and gain notoriety for yourself in the Globe-Democrat and in the national papers."

His lips compressed into a frown. "Sarah Robinson will be proud."

"She had you pegged from the start, Nathan."

"I did not kill my mother," he said. "She was wrong in her assessment."

"Perhaps, but you will murder Sheila, the woman who reminds you of June's warm affections, the one who enabled your ten-year withdrawal."

"I would *never* hurt her. She is like a sister to me."

"She will be your very first kill, Nathan."

"You think you know me so well, Joanna, but I am no butcher."

"No matter, as I can bring you someone else. Once you have committed four or five slayings, your tastes will shift, and you will then be ready for a tour of St. Louis at night." This woman would do him in if he let her. "I will teach you to monitor people's habits, which ones wear clothing which makes it easier to overpower them, and which ones are vulnerable and let down their guard when we approach and offer money. People are easy to lure if one uses the proper bait." Joanna played with fire because she *was* fire.

She wrapped her arms around his neck. "I've missed you so much, my love, and our time has finally arrived. We will soon dispose of Sheila."

He ripped himself from her embrace. "Did you not hear me? I said she must be protected. Daisy and Catherine must also be unharmed."

"Each must meet their fate, Nathan. We do this for your benefit."

He drew his watch from his pocket. "How so?"

"Another woman has already appeared to you twice, and soon she will reveal herself fully to you. Your future will be interwoven with hers, and the two of you will become social royalty in St. Louis, and years from now in Washington, D.C. political circles, your name will be floated for the highest office in the land. Nathan, we must untether you from the women in your life who hold you back. Your continued association with them is pointless."

She turned from him and lowered her head.

"Please don't fear me. I will not hurt you today."

"What are you saying, Joanna? I don't understand."

He placed his hand on her shoulder, and she turned to him.

Her fangs dripped with saliva. He took a step back from her.

Joanna settled herself against his chest, and he allowed her to push him onto the bed. Her hot breath blew against his neck as she sniffed his skin.

"I could easily sever your jugular vein."

"You don't have the guts." He hoped his words were true.

Her head drew up from his neck, and she smiled.

"Wickedness abounds in us both, Nathan."

Her fangs retracted and what was left of her beauty returned.

"It's why we are so valuable to the cause."

"So what are you now, some kind of monster?"

She gave him an abashed look, and they sat with their feet touching the floor. "I have killed men, and I have taught men to kill." Joanna paused before she proceeded with her explanation. "For my service, Lucifer has granted me powers. I'm not a monster but of the *nachash*, a diviner, and I will be alive long after you and your special woman have perished from the face of the earth. I will watch the rise of the son of perdition in the century after next, and Lucifer will grant me a private audience with his excellency."

"So what do I have to do with any of this? I'm a nobody."

"Your lineage will produce Lucifer's heir, the man of the last days."

Nathan gave a low whistle. "You mean to say the fellow you expect to see way down the line in the century after next will come from my house?"

She nodded and smiled. "His name will be Jeremy Marsh."

Nathan took a heavy breath and exhaled. "Marsh?"

"It's a fine name, don't you think?"

"I think you're crazy, Joanna. That's exactly what I think."

She turned and tried to kiss him. He instinctively stood and went for the door. She gave him an amused look. "Don't be frightened of me."

"Keep your fangs to yourself. I've seen enough for one morning."

She laughed as if his quandary excited her.

"Oh, you will see so much more, my love. I will lead you through the murderous streets of St. Louis by night, and the mystery woman will guide your path through the political halls of polite society by day."

Her fangs appeared again, and her nose sniffed the air.

"Nathan, you will be surprised to fathom the depth of your iniquity."

He knew only one thing to say. "Get behind me, Satan!"

As he plodded down the steep steps, Joanna's laugh became a cackle.

It grew louder and more vicious, emanating from above and around him. It rang in his ears as he opened the door to the street.

He stopped and looked back, knowing it was a mistake.

Joanna stood at the top of the stairs with a sinister countenance.

Her eyes gleamed and her fangs extended.

She bounded down the stairs like a feral beast of the field, moving faster than humanly possible, and leaped over the railing to stand before him.

Joanna curled a finger, summoning him, and Nathan was pulled toward her with the sinful lust of a thousand generations. He shoved his hand into his pocket and grabbed his watch, holding onto anything recognizable.

"My love, it will be so easy."

"I must go, Joanna. Please relent."

She grabbed his arms and wrapped them around her waist.

"I will have my kiss, Nathan. It's been so long since we first met."

Her fangs dragged across his neck, tearing at his skin. He held his ground, aware any attempt to flee would end in death. Joanna's fangs retracted, and her soft lips kissed the laceration, extracting blood from it.

"You believe I owe you a kiss?"

Joanna gazed into his eyes. "You owe me much more, Nathan. I needed a husband after my father died, and you left me penniless in a soldier's home. I have since taken matters into my own hands."

"What will you do with me?"

"Teach you, if you are willing."

"If not?"

"You will meet the same fate as Miss Turner, who ran the home."

"Evelyn tried to help you, Joanna."

"She beat me with a belt and sent me to my room. I would hardly call that helping." Joanna gave him a sidewise glance. "Evelyn was *my* first kill."

"I must take my leave. Your malevolence has no limits."

Joanna bared her teeth. "The mystery woman will loosen the ropes which bind you, and together we will initiate you into our order."

Nathan willed himself out of the brothel and onto the sidewalk.

He marched toward the intersection, and there he saw the woman with jet black hair and emerald green eyes. She smiled at him, and then turned and walked to his right. He rounded the corner, and she was gone.

He searched for an hour, but she was nowhere to be found.

Inside the hospital, Nathan trudged up the stairs. He opened the door to Daisy's office and rushed to her side. He reached for her hand.

She jerked it away. "You are an abusive man, Nathan Marsh."

He sat and faced her across the desk.

"What did you do after I left yesterday?"

"Last night, I took a walk and counted the stars."

"They are almost as beautiful as your blue eyes."

She smirked at him. "They make me ashamed to know you. When I see them, I'm reminded of the number of women you've known and continue to know, even after you've fallen in love with me."

"I'll fight for your hand, Daisy, but you must realize I'm a shameful sinner at heart. I'll never change, not for you or for your God."

"Did she soothe your miserable soul?"

"Who?"

"You know exactly who I mean, Nathan. The woman you went to last night, the one who reminds you of your mother."

"Did you have me followed?"

She took in his appearance with unblinking eyes.

"It wasn't necessary. The Lord guides me in all things."

Daisy toyed with a pencil on her desk. "You are the love of my life."

He was relieved to know her feelings hadn't been tainted by his reckless behavior. "I'm sorry I hurt you, Daisy, and it was never my intention. I was foolish to retreat into a whiskey bottle and the arms of a woman who will never love me as you do. Sometimes, when I remember my past with Catherine and our children, especially my little Annie, I seek a stranger for company, someone who has suffered as I have, but also a person who expects nothing of substance from me. Can you understand?"

"You describe attachment issues," she said with a nod. "You've blamed your problems on Catherine Belmont, and she has surely been a troubled woman, but it's not *her* your heart seeks. It's your mother's womb."

"You know me better than most, Daisy."

"Sigmund said it best. We seek fulfillment of a prehistoric dream. Every child has at least one wish they must achieve as adults to be happy. Yours is a return to your mother's loving embrace, her soothing words of comfort, the pleasure you felt at her warm encouragement."

"Perhaps you're correct," he said. "If Freud is right in his assessment, then I must have June in my life to be happy."

"So, in your mind, you are doomed?"

"Yes, in a manner of speaking. My mother will never come back to me."

Daisy grabbed the pencil and pointed it at Nathan. "I wish your mother would come back to you, but not for the reasons you might imagine."

"Alright, I'll play along." He gestured for her to continue.

"No woman can compare with the portrait you've painted of June. You searched all those years for a goddess to replace your saintly, martyred mother. Well, Nathan, goddesses are not real, and no earthly woman of flesh and blood could over hope to satisfy you, not even *her*."

"Then I really am condemned, because I cannot change my prehistoric dream." His tone implied he did not deserve to fulfill his longing.

Daisy shook her head. "There's a larger truth, one missed by Sigmund."

"You mean to say your intrepid hero made a mistake?"

She sighed and gave him a remorseful look. "Like you, he is an atheist, an agnostic, or perhaps he is merely furious with the Lord and in rebellion, but he is a gifted thinker and a man ahead of his time in intellectual circles."

"Then what did he miss?"

"He focuses on childhood traumas which hamper the development of the human as he or she moves into adulthood, but Sigmund cannot realize there's more to the story. Children from proper Christian homes learn to look over the shoulders of their parents and to God as their heavenly Father. In contrast, those poor souls like you who suffer in early childhood cannot lose their psychological grip on one or both of their parents. They become furious with God because they missed out on what they believe is rightfully theirs—a contented home—and later, as children who inhabit the bodies of adults, they feel entitled to pleasure as a substitute, as you well know."

He nodded and settled into his chair.

"It's been my way for a decade. I don't know another avenue."

"You must release your grip on the trauma from your past."

Daisy pointed toward the ceiling, "Look to Jesus, and your mortal suffering will be replaced with a blessed hope from heaven."

In his tormented grief, Nathan watched three children play at his feet.

His eyes became moist with tears. He swiped at them.

"What if God takes both of your parents and then takes your wife and children? Do you have a magical answer for such a wretched outcome?"

"I'm sorry for your loss. It's all I know to say."

He knocked the chair down and flung open the door.

A staff member tried to ask a question and then fell silent as Nathan blew past him. Nathan slammed the door to his office and laid down on his couch for a much-needed rest. "If you're up there, Lord, I'm listening, but I must say to you in regard to the quality of your creation, Daisy Lawrence is one exhausting woman." He listened for a reply, but heard none.

Unsatisfied, Nathan rolled over and drifted to sleep.

Daisy felt his absence and, although she was still furious with him for his behavior the night before, she knew he was in pain. His suppressed emotions had bubbled to the surface, and he didn't know how to handle them. She knocked on his office door and hoped for an apology. When there was no answer, she cracked open the door. He was asleep on the couch.

She slipped inside the room and sat on a chair and stared at him while he slept. Was he still redeemable, or was he already lost? He awakened and became angry with her for making him uncomfortable. She decided a fight was worth it and prepared herself emotionally for the field of battle.

"People are inherently evil," she said politely.

Nathan sat up and allowed his blood pressure to settle.

"What a wonderful sentiment."

"Don't repeat the mistakes you made for ten years."

He took out a handkerchief and placed it against his brow.

"It's time we straightened out your misconception."

He folded the cloth and set it on the couch beside him.

A renewed interest shone in her eyes. "Which is?"

"Medicine is not a family affair," he said. "It's a transaction between willing parties. I give them treatment, and they give me money."

He grinned as he rubbed his thumb and forefinger together.

"Don't say such a thing."

"You don't get to tell me what I can and cannot say."

"Your patients love you, Nathan, and they are loyal."

"They will soon be dead, and I'll be left insolvent and alone."

He stood and paced the office floor.

"I must save my hide while there's still time."

"You care more than you let on."

"No one cares more than you, Daisy."

"What does *that* mean?"

"I read *Consciousness of Domination* and I didn't get a sense of your words anywhere in the text. If you had led Frank to Christ, you might have become the voice behind his ideas, but you failed in your task just as you have floundered with me, and now you hide from the world as you hid from him when he visited our hospital." Nathan gave her a scornful look. "You're a coward and a fool, and right now, I'm ashamed to know you."

She pondered his comment for a moment. "Is it why you went to be a different woman last night? You abandoned me for a prostitute in a brothel because you're ashamed to know a silly wretch like me? Did my fear and my guilt and my surrender drive you into the arms of another woman?"

Each paced the floor. They passed one another in frustration.

Nathan grabbed her shoulders and stopped her. "What are you saying? You sound like one of our hysteria patients. Are you losing your sanity?"

He spoke with a surprising suddenness. "I doubt you've ever been sane."

He plopped onto the couch and pressed his back against the leather and folded his arms across his chest, satisfied with his triumph.

"No man has ever taken me seriously, not even my father. I thought I could win approval in Europe but ended up shamed and shunned in the end. I'm not proud of seeking their validation or my relationship with Frank Kaneski, one of the worst men on earth while he was alive, but right now, Nathan, you are vying for first place with him, and I need you to restore my honor and my dignity in this relationship. You said you never wanted to hurt me, but it's precisely what you're doing. Please recant your view of my shoddy character and your presumption of my insanity."

She fought tears which might sweep her out of the office.

"I've suffered a great deal in my life, much the same as you, and I've striven every bit as hard to overcome the pain and to maintain my emotional and psychological health, but men like you threaten to shatter me into a thousand pieces." The flash of his mercurial eyes astonished her.

"I need your validation, and I will have it, Nathan."

He rubbed his chin and gave her a suspicious look. "I cannot respect a woman who says one thing but does another. You push me to become a better man, but what about you, Daisy? You've pitched a stake on the moral high ground, but what have you ever done? You ran away from your father's winery, from Charcot in Paris, from Kaneski and Freud in Vienna, even from God. When things become difficult, you look for the front door and run down the street, screaming and clawing your face, all the while placing judgement on me for failing to lead you out of your captivity. Do you expect me to be your Moses? Well, I don't have tablets of wisdom to share with you or any righteous knowledge gained from talking to a bush or a cloud or whatever form your old man might take in some ancient myth."

Daisy realized an important fact for the first time. She nodded her newfound understanding. "You'll never believe in God, will you? No matter what I say." She felt uneasy, as his confirmation was guaranteed.

"I'm not sure what you're going on about, but I am who I am, and it will have to be enough if we're to remain a couple."

The air between them grew thick.

"Nathan, I don't need you to be Frank Kaneski or anyone else but you."

He stood and put both hands on her shoulders and gave her a delighted smile. "That's good news because I have no intention of publishing a nihilistic treatise that is tailormade for a tyrant."

She continued, undeterred. "However, I need you to become a much better version of yourself than the man who stands before me now."

"Daisy, I spoke to the Lord just before my nap and I most thoroughly informed Him of His exquisite work in forming and shaping one of the most infuriating and exhausting creatures imaginable."

He paused.

"Does *that* make you happy?"

"Take back what you said earlier, Nathan."

"I won't do it."

She broke free from his grip. "Please, *for us*."

"You are insane, and your God is a figment of your imagination!"

She burst into tears and rushed away, leaving him alone.

As she marched toward the hospital exit, a portrait of Big Rock formed in her mind. Perhaps he was right, and it was time for the last leap.

Nathan was quick and fierce, a man to be reckoned with, and he had never loved her, at least not the way she thought he loved her. He hung around her with brass intentions and kept his true feelings bound within, wrapped in quietude, asking others to let him be. She believed she had dug for his buried treasure and found it, but the curtain which hung over the door to his parlor masked his secrets and his alarms and the true north of his character. He was an adventurer at heart, meant for no particular woman, only the notion of perfection unattainable which wafted on the wind. It was a promise of silver and gold and good weather on the high seas.

The truth was poverty and rage and a howling tempest.

Daisy would capture the depth of her love in a letter.

Then she would travel home to the Missouri River.

A wild forest awaited and her sister, Rose, beckoned from the rocks.

THIRTY-ONE

Psalm 31:10

I am dying from grief;
my years are shortened by sadness.
Sin has drained my strength;
I am wasting away from within.

November 1893

After a weeklong binge, Nathan awakened alone in his disordered house. A cool breeze infiltrated through open windows as he searched for a trace of Sheila's presence. Downstairs in the parlor, he picked up Catherine's photograph from his bookshelf and studied her extraordinary beauty—the sort found often in youth but lost to the ransack of time. The richness of fall filled the air and descended on him with a well-to-do prominence, but shadows cast by the flight of time proved more compatible with his current deportment, hardened and itinerant as it was at present. Instead of warmth and coziness, Nathan's home was not really a home, but an encampment against the grave, a halt on the march to death.

After he dressed, Nathan sat on his couch and stared through the bay window at the street which ran in front of his once happy residence. He might never recover from such a dastardly hangover, and he needed water. A dog barked in the distance, and Nathan's parched lips stuck together.

Belmont passed from right to left. He stopped with suddenness, and his eyes gazed at the upstairs windows as if lost in a forlorn remembrance.

Nathan opened his front door. He descended the concrete steps and grabbed a piece of wrought iron fencing someone had left near the house. If he struck Belmont down, the villain's spree of greed would decisively end, and Nathan might once again breathe tranquil air, at least until sentenced to hang for his crime. It would be worth a public execution to watch Belmont cower in terror. Like Catherine, the man deserved a just outcome.

"What do you intend to do with that spike?"

Belmont looked more annoyed than frightened.

With solemn hesitance, Nathan tossed the piece of metal to the concrete sidewalk behind him. It clanged, and the sound reverberated against every house along the street. Belmont tidied his jacket while he took inventory of Nathan's crabby appearance. He walked toward the intersection, but then turned around and gave Nathan a disgusted look. "You look atrocious."

Belmont wore a pained expression as he moved nearer.

"Thanks," Nathan said. "It's nice to see you, too."

Belmont faced the house. His eye moved quickly to the second floor.

"There were good times once," he said sadly.

Nathan's eyes followed John's to the upper windows. The breeze caused the curtains to billow and flutter about, as if lost in the throes of grief.

"They were few and far between, if we are to be honest."

"Yes, indeed." John wiped tears from his eyes. "Two verses from a favorite psalm come to mind. You'll find them most helpful in your present condition, that of a lowly drunkard without a foundation. 'When I refused to confess my sin, my body wasted away, and I groaned all day long. Day and night your hand of discipline was heavy on me. My strength evaporated like water in the summer heat.' Those are from Psalm 32."

Nathan glimpsed Belmont's hypocrisy, and he would call him on it.

"You, sir, are no Christian."

Belmont arched his eyebrows. "No?"

Nathan should have uttered words against his vile father-in-law years ago. It might have made a difference to Catherine. "In my estimation, it's counter to your nature to care what anyone thinks, the Lord or otherwise."

Belmont's eyes affixed themselves to the front door.

"I miss the sound of children at play."

Nathan gazed again at his upstairs windows. "As do I."

Unconvinced of the shared bond between them, Belmont's attention shifted back to the matter at hand. "There is work to be done, my boy."

"It will be there tomorrow, Belmont. For now, leave me be."

"Daisy invited me to examine the patients, and I will see it done."

"They need a few adjustments, John. It's a bit early for a field trial."

Belmont looked at Nathan incredulously. "Why?"

"No reason. We merely need to polish the edges."

"Miss Lawrence said they're ready, and I do not have all day."

He eyed his ex-son-in-law suspiciously. "Is something amiss?"

Nathan fixed his coat and pulled up his trousers.

Belmont approached and leaned in close. His nostrils sniffed.

He recoiled and stepped backward. "Daisy said you had taken some days off work, and now I see what you have been doing with your time. You look and smell horrible. Will you hold it together for much longer?"

"I'm not sure."

Belmont wheeled and marched toward the intersection.

He yelled over his shoulder while wagging a finger at the celestial.

"You'll impress me this afternoon, or you will be *finished*!"

Nathan mock saluted him. "Aye, aye, captain."

"I heard that!" Belmont disappeared around the corner.

Nathan gazed at his front entrance and recalled a cheerful portrait.

The door opened at Thanksgiving for grateful guests and then opened again the day before Christmas to receive the merriest tree in the county. A fast-aging Annie rushed off to school in the morning and returned home in the afternoon, filled with the joy of life. Eli and Peter played hopscotch in the street in front of their sturdy home, sensing the protection it provided, ignoring the smallest microbes which might pierce the grand gates of their flesh, ending their existence before it ever really began, sending them into the arms of a waiting God, the orchestrator of their demise, the one who took everything and left nothing for despondent parents but whiskey from a Broadway brothel and beatings from a vagabond gambler, bent on murder.

Nathan should return to bed and endure another nightmare.

It would be better than the travesty which awaited him at the hospital.

A dog in the distance offered a succession of rapid barks. The latter yelps were delivered at a higher decibel than the former. Nathan stood uneasily and briefly considered digging through his medical bag for a helpful lozenge. Surely, such a ruinous dog would appreciate relief from a sore throat, most especially when offered by an esteemed physician with many surgeries to his name, whatever that might mean to anyone in a hundred years.

He took a last look at his desolate windows and trudged toward the intersection. As he walked, his thoughts disembodied and swirled the space above him, taking in the sights up and down the lane, seeing all the way east to the river and west past the outskirts of the city. Nathan fought the urge to bump into hollow carriages and crammed wagons and to run his hand along the picket fences which stretched between houses. An outlaw way of life awaited, one of western eccentricity which carried a six shooter for sport and the madness of whiskey inevitably found in gutters. He would make hasty but determined arrangements, the evidence of his incompatibility with the field of medicine and experimental psychology soon to be on display at Belmont Hospital, and his separation from his duties as administrator would serve as a recompense for a life spent alone, swiveling back and forth between the pledge of love and commitment, and the verity of desertion.

Belmont showed the evidence of Daisy's recent success, and her progress astounded Nathan. It was as if she single-handedly built a road along a steep hillside with a shovel and a pickaxe, and he felt guilty for placing doubts on her skills or her resolute determination. From a remote vantage point, she had vigorously slapped his face, and her singular voice carried the day.

Nathan took in the dreary figures with full awareness of being bested.

As if on cue, James Clifton regressed into his old form, and the rest of the patients followed his lead, each declining before Nathan's eyes.

Belmont became annoyed with them. "Daisy's knowledge is interesting, but her obstinate desire to converse with them about their sordid histories inhibits her enthusiasm for mesmerism. I need you to continue her hypnosis work and make the breakthroughs she could not achieve."

Nathan gestured his readiness to comply.

Belmont pointed toward the stairs. "She gifted a letter to you. I left it on your desk." He smiled. "You'll be happy to know I didn't read it, but I'm hopeful the words contain some insight into her failures."

"I'm sure they will, John."

"Let all the godly pray while there is still time, so they may not drown in the floodwaters of my judgment."

"Another verse?"

Belmont nodded.

"Changed for my purpose."

"You do that often. Quote verses for your own ends."

"It's what they're for, my boy."

Nathan shook his head. "I'm not sure it works that way."

"It does for me."

Belmont slammed the door shut as he exited the hospital.

Nathan marched up the stairs, intent on taking a nap on his couch.

Daisy had left a sealed envelope on his desk with his name handwritten on the front side. He found a letter knife and tore open the envelope, hopeful for a declaration of love and a desire to rekindle their relationship.

He dropped two items onto the surface of his desk: a tiny note and a letter which had been folded in two places. The note directed him to his middle drawer and asked him to retrieve the Bible she had placed there. He must turn to Philippians 1:20 and read the verse aloud.

He sat in his chair and complied with her kind request.

"For I fully expect and hope that I will never be ashamed, but that I will continue to be bold for Christ, as I have been in the past. And I trust that my life will bring honor to Christ, whether I live or die."

He unfolded the letter and read from the top down.

Dearest Nathan,

You have hurt me beyond repair in this life, but not in the next. When Christ returns, I will be resurrected, and my name will be found in the Book of Life. Christ will lead me to the waters which flow from the Father's throne, and I will be filled with the Holy Spirit eternally. In that moment, my agony will be replaced with everlasting joy.

I hope someday you will worship the Triune God as I do, and we can meet on the banks of His life restoring river. Please know this: we will all feel ashamed if we do not give way to Jesus in all aspects of our lives, now and forever. You and I discussed Frank Kaneski's concept of a consciousness of domination, but there is another will, one not of late-night debate sessions or of breakfast table reasoning. It is an unconditional and immutable surrender of our own free will to the will of the Creator of the universe and everything which might be contained within it.

You will give the matter some consideration, which in the end will most likely result in your rejection of such a simple yet profound gift of forgiveness and salvation, one born of love, not power, of suffering, not comfort, or restoration, not anarchy. To that notion, I say, rubbish.

Jesus Christ knows full well what lies within your heart. You must shut out every other thought save this one: I will give everything to please Him and to cause the angels in heaven to rejoice. There's nothing finer in this realm than to know our meaningful works align with the perfect will of the Creator.

You must become obsessed daily with every ounce of

your mind, your body, and your soul to live for Him and Him alone. As was written in Psalm 1, you must meditate day and night on the law of the Lord. Like Saul on the road to Damascus, before you decide to follow the Lord, a crisis must take form in your life.

Nathan, your time is now.

He lowered the paper and wiped a tear from his eyes. He had never felt so alone in all his years. What was it about Daisy's absence that made him so lonely and starved for human contact? She was nothing like his mother or Catherine. Perhaps he would never learn the answer to such a complicated and perplexing riddle. He picked up the letter and read the rest of the lines.

Your crisis is one of total abandonment.

I know this pain because I feel it in my own heart. It's a bond we share, now and forever, but you must also realize God has nudged you throughout your life, and you were unresponsive or you debated Him, just as you argued with me during our many spirited conversations. Now the Lord has brought you to a crossroads, and He demands a choice. Are you for Him or are you against Him? You must recognize your vulnerable position before the enemy overtakes your lines. You must surrender your will to Jesus Christ entirely and permanently. I earnestly hope to see you on the banks of the river with an outstretched hand, asking for my own, leading me into the consecrating waters, our eyes bright as crystal as we honor the throne of God and of the Lamb.

Your eternal love,
Daisy Lawrence

Nathan set the letter aside. He gazed down at the street.

Sheila knocked on his door and stuck her head inside his office.

"May I enter?"

He rubbed his heavy eyes and turned toward her. "Of course."

She spoke deliberately. "I have a confession, something which has eaten away at my heart since you and Daisy rescued me from Joanna's brothel."

He rose and gestured for her to sit. "Let's hear it."

She took the chair opposite him. Her eyes dropped low.

"Please be aware, Sheila, you can say anything to me."

"Are we family?"

He smiled musingly at her. "After ten years, I would say so."

"You were the love of my life." She wiped a tear from her cheek.

"I feel a strong attachment to you, like a brother for a sister."

Her soft eyes filled with an inner glow. "I love you, too, Nathan."

"Can we make a family together, but without romance?"

She gave him an indulgent smile. "My feelings for Heinrich have grown steadily, which has come as a surprise to me after so many years spent with you and the knowledge you came to save me from Joanna's wrath." Sheila hesitated. "I know about her basement. All the girls hear faint screams at night, and we cower in the corners of our rooms when a man isn't there."

"If I had known your the depths of your desperation, I would have taken you out of there a long time ago." He moved near to her and knelt. "I was a drunkard and a selfish fool, and I'm sorry for my lack of interest."

"It's alright. I'm safe now." She looked away from him.

He cupped his hand under her chin. She must look him in the eyes.

Nathan spoke from the heart. He choked back his own tears.

"It's far from alright, and I will spend the rest of my life making it up to you." Shame overtook him. He took her hands in his and kissed them sweetly. His tears fell on her soft skin. "If you'll let me, I will be a loyal brother. I owe you a debt which can never be repaid, but I long to try."

"What debt?"

"You kept me alive during our time together. If not for your tender affections and your motherly touch, I would rest underneath the grass."

She raised her hands and caressed his bearded cheeks.

Her fingers traced the path of his tears.

"I must confess something terrible to you, Nathan."

She pulled her hands away and covered her mouth.

Her eyes expressed sadness and fear. "What is it? Please tell me."

Sheila clutched his arms and squeezed tightly.

"Joanna had a damnable hold on me and the other girls. I didn't realize it then, but I was possessed by a powerful demon. You stumbled in one night, depressed, angry, and drunk beyond repair. It seemed you'd been crying." Sheila took a long while to get out the next part, but then she continued. "You looked about for Joanna, but she was busy with another customer. She yelled through the door for me to entertain you for the evening. When I agreed, she instructed me to never let you go."

"You followed her orders for ten years."

Sheila's face grew troubled. "I'm sorry, Nathan, for my part in leading you astray. In your broken state, you would have slept with whomever you met. I took advantage of you because I needed a man to take care of me."

"So what's changed beyond escape from Joanna's basement?"

"Everything." Her face brightened. "I found this wonderful hospital and a stable job as a cook. Then I met Heinrich, who led me to the Lord."

"I'm pleased your life has taken a turn for the better." He returned to his chair and held the letter up to Sheila. "I wish I could say the same."

"May I read it?"

"I don't mind." He handed it over to her.

Her eyes scanned down the page, and her back stiffened. "I sense Daisy's pain." Sheila returned the letter to his desk. "Do you feel it, Nathan?"

"Of course."

"Be careful with her. She has been hurt too many times." Sheila arose with a warm smile, but her movement was guarded. "A woman knows another woman's heart, and Daisy cannot endure much more suffering."

Someone knocked on the door. Sheila turned and opened it.

"I almost forgot." She seemed nervous about taking liberties. "You look so haggard and you smell so rotten. I asked my assistants to cook for you."

A young man entered. Sheila pointed at Nathan's desk.

Her voice carried a tilt of laughter as she gestured at Daisy's letter.

"Please protect her heartfelt words, Nathan. They mean so much."

"Oh, yes." He folded the paper and stuffed it into his coat pocket.

She observed him as he ate. "Decide about her." Sheila's tone bore her sincere concern for Daisy. "She won't remain in St. Louis for much longer."

"I can always find her on the banks of the Missouri."

"Will she be alive by then?" Sheila's face grew hard. "When I decipher what lies beneath her words, I see Daisy slumped over her desk with tears of heartbreak coursing down her cheeks. She has recently contemplated the unthinkable, and Daisy is more than capable of carrying out her plans."

She pointed sharply. "You did this to her, and you must fix it."

"Don't take this too far, Sheila. I've never intentionally hurt anyone."

"That's just it, Nathan. You intend nothing with anyone, not even Catherine." Sheila stood quickly, as if to leave his office.

He looked through the blinds at the street and considered her comments. "I'm not beaten yet. I'll go to her, and we'll clear the air."

"It's a start."

"It's not enough to satisfy you?"

"Just be sure you know what clouded the air in the first place."

"I know this: I no longer hate James Clifton for loving my Catherine, and I genuinely wish the best for you and Heinrich. I am making forward progress, which is all anyone should ask of me. As you said about Joanna's demonic hold over you when you lived in her brothel, Daisy has completely seized my spirit. Try as I might, I cannot escape her piercing talons."

"There's a difference," Sheila said.

"Which is?"

"Her grasp originates from Jesus Christ, not from the pit of Hell."

"It's a place to start."

"The *only* place."

Thirty-Two

*Oh, what joy for those
whose disobedience is forgiven,
whose sin is put out of sight!*

Nathan took a mule-driven trolley to his house, changed clothes, and then walked several blocks to catch an electric trolley. His destination was the Laclede Hotel, and he prayed Daisy might be there. She had retrieved her things from her sleeping quarters at the hospital, and there was only one place left to check. As the hotel came into view, he looked about and absently checked his watch. His window of opportunity was growing shorter with each passing hour. Daisy would give him a contemptuous smile, express her patented tidings of death, and claim incompatibility with his temperament, an argument he couldn't easily refute under the circumstances of their separation. Nathan must establish their relationship on firmer ground, and he knew only one surefire method.

A hotel clerk delivered Nathan's message to Daisy, and a few minutes later, she appeared in the lobby. He directed her outside and around the corner to an alleyway, a location where they might speak in private.

She stood with her back against the street and peered into the depths of the gloomy realm. "I see your opinion of me has not changed."

Without asking permission, he spun her toward him and kissed her.

Daisy fell slack in his arms, and her lips betrayed her feelings.

He drew slightly from her. "Make love to me."

She feigned insult. "What? Here in this alley?"

"In your room." He leaned forward and kissed her neck.

"I cannot, Nathan. I am still a lady, even with my imperfect past."

His hand moved along her back as he kissed her deeply.

Her breathing quickened, and she pulled herself against his body.

Nathan whispered into her ear. "Intimate relations may improve our dispositions. It's helped matters in the past, with other women."

She broke free from his embrace and stood on the sidewalk. He moved nearer to her position and kept a watchful eye on the people who briskly passed by them on their way to somewhere else. Nathan nodded at a mustached man who gave them a careful look and offered his most jovial smile. The mustached man threw a look across the street and continued into the hotel. Nathan watched the doors, half expecting someone to burst through them with inflexible intentions, but the doors had fallen lifeless as a river mussel, so he turned once more to the problem at hand.

"We need a deeper bond, Daisy. That's all I'm saying."

She spoke as if his words offended her. "You want nothing more from me than you desired from Sheila or any of the other prostitutes at that wretched brothel on Broadway. Your unending scrutiny and your alignment with Frank's horrible theories have once again destroyed my chance at actual love." Daisy detected an ironic turn in her own remark and laughed bitterly.

"No decent man will ever find me worthy."

He stepped nearer to her, but she refused his affection.

"The Lord looks down from heaven and sees the whole human race."

She looked past him at the busy street and took in the city's clatter.

Nathan wanted so desperately to take her into his arms and love her.

"From His throne He observes all who live on the earth."

Nathan paced on the sidewalk and raked his hand through his hair several times. She was the most tiresome woman he had ever known.

She had grown more and more intolerant of his beliefs and his needs. "Why must you be so difficult? Other women made things easier for me."

"Other women have come and gone, Nathan, and I am not them."

"Alright, I'll change course. Walk with me to the bridge. Surely, *that* won't ruffle any feathers." He looked at the sky. "It's such a nice day."

A horse at the curb was harnessed to a small wagon. He looked Daisy in the eyes, confusing her, as she searched for a reason to decline the offer.

"I won't bite," said Nathan lightly. "I promise."

As they walked, he chatted about recent newspaper headlines, the weather, and increasing rail trade with the southwest. Eventually, he steered the conversation to a subject of actual consequence. "I read your letter."

"I hoped you'd wait until after my departure."

"It was too important, and you seemed distraught when last we spoke."

"You flatter yourself."

"Do you deny it?"

She stopped walking and gave him a coarse laugh. There was no humor in it. "You've shattered me like discarded serving ware, and I have no more interest in doing much of anything. Even serving the Lord seems pointless."

"What about your hysterics?"

Daisy kicked at a rock with the toe of her boot and looked up at him. "Someone will come along and take my place, just as they did in Europe."

"There will always be more," he said with a nod. "We live in dire times."

"Your statement has a ring of truth. I also know you'll recover your ambition for helping patients and, with it, their lot in life will improve. I'm no good for anyone in my current state of brokenness. Like my mother and my sister, I'm a square peg in a round hole."

"Will you work for Pierre at the winery?"

"Yes, for a while. He needs someone to sort his affairs."

"You don't even drink wine. What do you know about producing it?"

"It's a business like any other, Nathan."

She grinned at a small child who stood in a doorway.

"When his business has stabilized, I'll make other arrangements."

"Such as?"

Her countenance warmed, and she shrugged. "Who knows? Perhaps I'll hop a train for Arizona and become a desperado."

"That would be a sight to behold," he said, chuckling. "Daisy Lawrence, savage gunslinger at high noon, terrified hysteric by nightfall."

Daisy withheld a reply.

He hadn't meant to hurt her feelings. He must salvage the conversation. "You're much more eloquent in your writing. Is there nothing more to say?"

"Have you given yourself to the Lord?"

"I have not, although I'm no longer in the mood to debate you, Him, or anyone else. It has exhausted my every reserve."

She snorted. "More likely, it was the multitude of women and whiskey bottles you've consumed since our last encounter."

Nathan shook his head. "There have been no women."

"I understand you to mean you've steered clear of local brothels, but you've partaken of whiskey and you've fallen more than once into a drunken binge." She sighed and drew back from him, as if to prepare for an abrupt departure. "You should realize once and for all, Nathan, that your efforts to shield yourself from the past are no longer effective."

Daisy's firm bearing convicted him. "I suppose you're right once again."

She waved dismissively. "I further presume you will not alter your social manners or any aspect of your thinking toward the Lord?"

"No, madam, I'm afraid the man before you is a pitiful rogue, and I fear we may miss one another on the banks of your imaginary river."

"So be it." She nodded curtly, and her eyes grew cold as they bore through him. "It's time we end our relationship."

He snapped his fingers. "Just like *that*?"

"Tomorrow I will catch the morning train." Daisy gazed at the transient clouds. "We're passing ships who hailed but never heard."

She moved toward the hotel entrance. Nathan ran up behind her and spun her around to face him. "Please don't do this, Daisy."

"We no longer need one another. At least, I'm certain you don't need me." She gave him a look of defiance. "Truth be told, you never did."

An hour later, she awoke to an impatient knock at her hotel door. Daisy rubbed her weary eyes and whispered Psalm 32:3-4 before she answered. "When I refused to confess my sin, my body wasted away, and I groaned all day long. Day and night your hand of discipline was heavy on me. My strength evaporated like water in the summer heat."

A humble Nathan stood before her when she opened her door.

"They shouldn't have let you upstairs. How did you get past the desk?"

He looked nervously down the long hallway.

"Come downstairs with me. I must ask you a question."

"Alright, but only for a minute, and I will *not* sully myself for you."

"Understood."

Outside the hotel, Nathan asked if she would watch the patients perform at the Expo. He needed her there for support and encouragement.

"Nathan, you know I don't agree with John's plans for the hysterics."

"It will go smoothly, and then we can resume our work."

A man lurked up the street, near the intersection, watching her and Nathan converse. John must have sent the man to record her actions, and he would use the information against her, blackmail being his primary business specialty. She could inform the police, but men like John owned the judicial system, and there would be no justice in this life for pawns such as Daisy. She reminded herself to be strong and to place all her hope in Jesus.

Dear Lord, please watch over me, and keep me from certain death.

"The work you did with our patients was fantastic."

She stared at the man up the street. He turned his head and greeted a stranger who passed him at the intersection, tipping his hat with a smile.

"I barely scratched the surface to appease John, but our group must not become sideshow freaks," she said. "If I was given more time, I could have healed them. Sigmund's talking cure takes months, if not years."

Nathan promised to work with them on his own.

She thanked him, and they shared an awkward moment.

"I'll always love you, Nathan." She wiped tears from her eyes.

"After you left, I cried myself to sleep in my bed."

Daisy's laugh conveyed her sorrow. "I'm such a simple girl sometimes."

Nathan gave her his hand, and she took it. "I'm sorry for hurting you," he said. "I wish I could bring myself to become a better man."

"My proper home has always been with Pierre and the winery. My father desperately needs my help with his bookkeeping and many other tasks, which he cannot do consistently. I scold him, and he says he will do them, but they do not get done." She caught her breath and smiled ruefully at Nathan. "One day, when you've become the man you seek to be, we may meet again on the banks of the Missouri River. It won't resemble the hope of heaven, but you'll find it a beautiful location and a loving shelter."

Nathan put on his hat and tipped it toward her with a sly grin.

"Madam, I look forward to that day."

She squeezed his arm and tried to hold back her tears.

"Nathan, no matter what happens, please continue your work. Many lives, both now and in the future, depend upon it."

"I promise." His hand touched her cheek and then pulled to his side. "You've restored my ambition as a healer, and for that, I am in your debt."

After he left, she watched his form disappear around the corner.

She rushed to her bed, pulled up the covers, and cried herself to sleep.

THIRTY-THREE

Psalm 33:22

Let your unfailing love surround us, Lord,
for our hope is in you alone.

Nathan awakened on Sunday afternoon and pulled himself shakily out of bed. His feet knocked over an empty whiskey bottle, sending it *clink clink clink* across the oak, as lightning flashed outside his window and thunder boomed inside his head. He secured the glass panes as rain fell hard against the side of his house, and the raucous intensity of his hangover advanced with vigor, and his thirst grew into a rudimentary but critical dilemma which must be solved. He descended his stairs and scuttled past disordered furniture which had been strewn about the parlor in haste and stupor. The inside of his house grew dustier by the moment, and his need increased in equal measure. Through the backdoor with a pitcher, Nathan spied the hand pump. He stepped into the unkempt yard, now muddy, and looked about for any sign of his immutable Annie.

He was a lost cause. She had deserted him like all the rest.

While sheets of rain beat furiously upon his back, he retrieved water from the earth, which satiated his fleshly thirst but left intact the violence upon his spirit. He longed to nestle in the canopy of Daisy's love and to hasten with her into the blissful land of tomorrow, but there were too many clamorous voices, and memories sped toward him through the open doorway of his loneliness. They whisked into his consciousness, tumbling, falling, rising, each presenting a reminder of his ill-used life, which was now dented and broken, frayed and tattered, shameful of form and character. Yet beneath his base shabbiness there lurked a dim semblance of what he might have been and what he might still become—if only he still held Daisy's love.

Nathan perused the streets, lost in untroubled pastures, refuge found in his Aunt Joy, and a medical book which ferried him past youthful angst into the independence of adulthood. Ironclad memories of his children's deaths left their contained spaces in agitation, clapping him about the head, blending his tears with the torrent which fell reckless against his cheeks.

Up ahead, a form glimmered as it moved from right to left across the intersection. The figure took human shape and blocked his path, but seemed unaffected by the rain. Silvery eyes peered at Nathan, and an accusatory mouth threw words of challenge at him, piercing deep into his soul with a knowledge of harm done to others and many festive seasons missed.

The glow looked skyward. Raindrops ceased their incursion.

Now it was a sunny day with a slight breeze, neither too hot nor too cold. A comforting wind kissed Nathan's neck, and the sun thawed his face, delighting him in a world crafted and given by a featureless friend.

He turned to thank the form, but the intersection was vacant.

Nathan wandered to his mother's church and opened the creaky gate to the cemetery. He paused at the edge of the path, steeling himself for the battle which would surely follow. A small, still voice encouraged his faith.

He kneeled in front of his children's gravestones and wept.

Moist eyes reluctantly traced their names.

A-N-N-I-E

E-L-I

P-E-T-E-R

Each letter crushed his soul.

Before him stood a golden portrait of his darling Annie.

He spoke to her through a deluge of tears. "You were pure and innocent and filled with joy, while I've lived a life of debauchery and deceit."

Annie's twinkly portrait faded into the sun's feeble rays.

Nathan dropped to the soggy grass with a flop and a splash.

His bones ached. His heart grieved. His mind searched for answers.

The chilly rain returned. Nathan fell over to his back and let it soak him clean. He knew no ultimate destination, only torment. Daisy had lowered her gaze and deigned to take him under her wing, a rare occasion in the grimness of his experience. Her blue eyes, her coarse voice, the steadiness of her trust in the righteousness of the Lord—all were vestiges of a love once known but since vanished over the hill. He had thieved bits of her sweetness in their time together, and there would be a recompense for his piracy.

"Please forgive me, Annie." He turned toward her gravestone. "I tried to save you! I did everything possible to save all of you!"

He rested his head in the slop and gazed at his daughter's name, and then he grasped at Annie's unseen hand. "How could your mother leave me and run back to the monster who beat her? I was a better husband!"

The still voice spoke to him through the howl of the tempest.

Catherine is consumed by shame, which has shattered her existence. Remember your childhood bond and have compassion for her as she struggles against innumerable odds. She needs your love more than ever before, and only you can lead her to my guiding light. Your children rest in peace, and just as she will eternally be their mother, she will forever be your friend.

"You win, Lord. I'm too tired to resist you."

Nathan pulled himself up and wandered back to the main road.

He opened the front door to the hospital and hung his wet coat and hat on the stand. His shoes were drenched, so he removed them.

Dora hurried over with a wool blanket. "You must warm yourself or you'll catch your death in this foul weather. Is everything alright?"

He scowled at her and gestured sharply.

"I'm all by myself in this loathsome world, but yes, I'm alright."

She watched from afar as he climbed the stairs.

He closed the door and plopped down on his couch under the blanket.

Soon he dreamed of his children who slept under graves of green.

A decay of sanity inflamed Daisy's despair. Angelic songsters must herald the restoration of a scoundrel's faith, as the mists of his doubts departed and the peace of Christ perfumed upon their path. Her thoughts circled in the sky above her head with morose insistence until they caught something caustic which rendered them immobile. One by one, shreds of naivety floated breezily to the terrestrial firmament, where a cruel disaster laid in wait. Gullible ladies who meandered the fallen highway in search of a rakish love, desirous to reshape an adventurer into a virtuous man, knew only the gnaw of his toilsome burden and the ruinous glint of his wanton flesh.

Nathan had made a mess of her good judgement and reason.

Daisy angrily demanded Jesus answer her in prayer.

Why did you send this man to me, Lord? I am one way, and he's another, and neither of us will transform, so what is the point of our union?

The room kept quiet, save an occasional crunch from pine boards which settled themselves along the floor, curving and contracting with the daily change of temperature, striking blows to the balance of her dignity.

"Fine!" She climbed out of bed and spoke aloud. "If you want me on my face, then that's where I'll be, but I'm waiting on you, Lord, and the hour has grown late. I don't have many days left in this rotten world you've created. So you should move fast if you care about my fractious existence."

She recited The Lord's Prayer from Matthew 6:9-13. "Our Father in heaven, may your name be kept holy. May your Kingdom come soon. May your will be done on earth, as it is in heaven. Give us today the food we need, and forgive us our sins, as we have forgiven those who sin against us. And don't let us yield to temptation, but rescue us from the evil one."

Please Lord, send your mighty warrior angels to protect the hysterics. I renounce any authority evil spirits may hold over the people or the hospital building or the surrounding land. Please fill our patients with the Holy Spirit and remove any unclean spirits from within them and from around them.

Her emotions calmed, and she continued.

I leave all my problems and my struggles at the foot of the cross, Lord. Please save us from ourselves, for we know not what we do.

A voice spoke to her spirit.

When you met Nathan in July, your resilience was almost gone, and now you are stronger than you know. Be patient and allow me to work in his life.

"Will he ever find faith in you, Lord?"

When he is ready, Nathan will ask for my forgiveness.

"I'm frightened the waters will overtake him, and I cannot bear the thought of losing him to darkness. I barely hold on as it is."

The Lord prompted Daisy to read Psalm 33:20-21, and she complied.

"We put our hope in the Lord. He is our help and our shield. In him our hearts rejoice, for we trust in his holy name."

She slipped back into bed and pulled the covers over her head.

Daisy would hold on for one more day.

Nathan frowned as he awoke under the wool blanket on Monday morning. With Daisy in his life, he learned to sleep on a cot in another office, but in her absence it was taken up, and this thin, ragged couch proved an unworthy replacement. As he tried to move past the misery of her departure, he would need a suitable solution, as his home was now perilous to his health. The good days had long ago passed, leaving grayness and harrow in their wake.

He folded the blanket and tossed it on the end of the couch.

His feet were dry on the stairs, but more tired than yesterday.

He opened the door to the main hall, unsurprised to see Susanna dancing across the room, her mind miles from St. Louis, transported to the fiery rim of the sun or the smooth top of a distant mountain or the rocky deposits of a cool, shaded canyon. Her body was ready for today's twitch in the saddle, as was her best friend, a mythical Appaloosa, the crunch and bluster of a snow-covered peak Susanna's imagined destination.

Nathan watched her flitter and glide about the room.

As he gently rocked, he closed his eyes and fell into a curious dream.

His spirit lingered above his flesh, and soon it aligned with Susanna's as she graciously left the prison of her mind for faraway parts unknown. Her mare's feet clicked as she stepped against irregular rocks, and her tail swished as the kindred pair forded a babbling brook, the wintry weather of little concern for such an upright team of venturesome wanderers.

Nathan's eyes opened. He rubbed the heaviness from them.

Susanna's graceful movements ceased. She stood still, gazing at him.

Nathan threw her a concerned look and quickly left his chair.

"Is everything alright?"

She nodded politely and smiled. "Someone prayed for me as I danced just now, and the haze which clouded my thoughts lifted."

He led her over to the rockers, and they sat.

"Please continue," he said.

"For a long time, it felt as if I was encased in a block of ice, but recently, there was a change. Someone out there in the world has been praying special prayers for me. I don't know who or why, but I sensed the ice breaking, one sliver at a time, and then it fell apart in huge chunks until I was released."

She paused.

"Now I am free as a songbird."

John called out to her. "Susanna, you know who really loves you!"

Nathan glared at John. "Be quiet!"

He turned toward Susanna, hopeful for the right words. "Would you be willing to share your story with me? It might help ease your pain."

"Yes, I would."

Each surveyed the room as she spoke.

"I married John while living in Pittsburg in 1890. After he got into an altercation with his boss, he was fired, so we moved to the west through the St. Louis corridor. When we ran low on funds after we reached the city, we both took work as tenant farmers in the county. I became pregnant, so we stayed, and soon thereafter John fell into a strange depression which became schizophrenia. I tried to care for him during my pregnancy, but his illness finally drove me to hysteria just after our Beth was born. I was laid up in the bed, exhausted, and I couldn't feed the baby for several days."

"Susanna, cease talking with this man!"

Nathan glared at John, and he turned his head.

"When I finally checked on Beth, she was dead in the crib. I flew into a rage and beat on John, hoping he would arise and murder me. Instead, he cowered in the corner, and his weakness sent me into a dancing mania which I could not stop. Later, he gathered the baby into a blanket and ordered me to bring a shovel and a pickaxe. I followed him, dancing in circles as we walked to the middle of the field. Together, we buried our daughter in the dirt, and after it was done, I collapsed beside her grave as John walked back to the cabin with the tools. I wanted to die, but could not. Early the next day, the landowner found me lying there, unmoved, and he called the sheriff who arrested us for the murder. The court decided we were both unsound and delivered us to the city asylum. The building had no room, so we were sent here to this stark glacier of a hospital. Even when I danced about this hall, inside I was trapped in a block of ice with little chance of escape."

"I'm glad you've returned to us, Susanna. We've all missed you while you've been away, and it's my fervent hope you will stay with us."

Her arm gestured across the breadth of the enclosed space. "I've been here all along, Nathan, polishing the oak floor with my toes, but I couldn't rejoin the living while my baby was dead. The pain was unbearable."

Nathan grasped Susanna's hand. "What set you free?"

"Beth rests in peace, and she will spend eternity with Jesus Christ. When He returns with a shout, we will be happily reunited in the clouds."

"I hate to ask, but how do you know she's not simply gone forever?"

She let go of his hand, and her countenance grew serious.

"Last night, the Lord spoke to me in a dream. He said you have much work to do, and soon you'll receive an angelic visitor with a message."

Rather than heal, Susanna had slipped deeper into schizophrenia.

Nathan must convince her to reach out to her husband so the couple might seek wholeness together. He pointed to John.

"Do you think you think he might return to us?"

She regarded John with a defiant eye and then turned to Nathan.

"He killed my child, and I will never forgive him."

Nathan grew frustrated with her ponderous nature.

He paced the floor between the line of beds.

Samuel stood behind his son with a fixed intentness and his fists shoved way down in his pockets. "You're doing fine. Don't lose hope."

Nathan wheeled. "I cannot reach them, Pop. Not like she could."

"Daisy failed the same as you," Samuel said. "It bothered her greatly."

A sorrowful mist entered through the ceiling and drooped down on Nathan's head, seeping through the pores of his skin and running throughout his body with reckless abandon. He consumed the mist as much as it swallowed him, turning round and round within its reddish form. He gave out of breath as he took in the roomful of hysterics and schizophrenics, bent together in whispered gossip, imbued in the awareness of his inabilities.

"I can't live without her, and I certainly can't help *them*."

He gestured at the hysterics, whose faces had turned to confusion.

"They need a psychologist, not a besotted relic from another era."

Samuel grabbed Nathan's shoulders with clenched fists.

"This is your time, Son, not hers. I will see you make the most of it."

Nathan turned from his father and paced the line of beds again.

He reached the end and called over his shoulder. "Get your pistol ready, Pop." He wheeled and threw a sneer. "I think I'm finally ready to lie down."

"No! I will not allow it!"

Samuel rushed forward and twice slapped his son's face.

The strange fog clouded Nathan's mind in unpleasant conversation as voices prattled with one another, talking back and forth, each jockeying for prime position at the top of a hierarchy of power, one created of the debt of death upon our mortal flesh and our desire to avoid such a dreadful fate.

"Let it go," said Samuel decisively.

"Let what go?"

"You know exactly what I mean. *Everything*. Let it go."

"It's not so easy, Pop. There's been too much for one life."

"Lucifer will kill you if you let him." Samuel's eyes hovered restlessly about the room and then it seemed he might turn violent as his eyes affixed themselves on Nathan. "Call out to God and ask Him for deliverance."

Ghoulish memories were strewn like pebbles across his mind.

Susanna stood before him. "Do you distrust me, Nathan?"

"I don't know what to think anymore," he said.

"Well, the Lord told me something about you, a fact I didn't know."

Nathan glanced around with concealed annoyance. He understood she wanted him to ask for more detail. Reluctantly, he waved his hand.

She smiled. "Aunt Joy died on your sixteenth birthday."

Nathan turned to Samuel. "Why did you tell her about my business?"

Samuel glanced at Susanna and then stood with his back against her. "I hardly know this woman, and I did not tell her anything about you."

"No one else here would have known it, Pop, not even Daisy."

"Catherine knew," said Susanna kindly. "But she did not tell me."

"I'll bet she did, and you are just now recalling her woeful tale."

"The Lord told me something else, an even larger revelation."

Nathan sighed heavily. "Alright, out with it. I don't have all day."

"He said you spent time with a woman back east. She was beautiful and sensual, but much older than you and married to your newest benefactor."

Her words vexed him as recollections marched through his mind with a heavy and deliberate tread. He never spoke of Colleen to anyone, not even his father, upon his return from New York. Their paths, once separated, never reconnected and no letters from her were received in his household.

If Susanna knew her name, Nathan would surely take ill.

"Dare I ask for the woman's name?"

"Colleen Collins, and her husband was Roy Collins."

"There would be more names, known to no one here but me."

"Daughters."

"How many in the immediate family?"

"Three. Would you like me to recite their names?"

Samuel interrupted. "Son, is this really necessary?"

Nathan cast a troublesome look at his father.

"I must know what she knows, and then I must learn the source."

Samuel spoke in a guarded voice. "She was a participant in the occult."

Nathan turned to Samuel. "You surprise me. Is it actually possible?"

"More than possible. It's almost a certainty in my estimation."

Nathan nodded his understanding. "Do you consort with demons?"

Susanna shook her head in a convinced manner. "I do not."

"You did so at one time, correct?"

"Yes, but now I hear from the Lord."

"When in the past you heard from Lucifer?"

She nodded and smiled. "Like Daisy, I was enticed by him."

Nathan would allow himself one last glimmer of hope. She might have somehow discovered his affiliation with Colleen, but Susanna could never have learned the identities of her three children, as they were young and innocent and never spoken of by him to anyone outside their household.

"Please share their names with me."

"Rebecca, Elizabeth, and Laura."

"Who is the oldest and youngest?"

"Rebecca was the oldest and Laura, the youngest."

Nathan's face lost a portion of its color as his blood pressure fell.

The breath of a meddlesome spirit blew warm against his neck, and he drew back from Susanna, his feet catching one another and forcing a fall to the floor. Shapes moved about him as he hopped to his feet, careful to avoid a complete breakdown or a kidnapping of his faculties, whichever might first come to pass in this macabre house of horrors some called a hospital.

The hysterics sprang from their beds and formed a circle around Nathan. They stood as witness to his personal sacrifice and encouraged him to release his bottled trauma. He resisted, unsure if he might trust their mortal intentions and unable to accept the pressure of the situation and the immense vulnerability it presented to him. The group moved closer and several embraced him. The staff saw what was happening and joined the patients, as did Sheila, who had prepared breakfast in the kitchen and came to the front to better understand the source of the commotion.

Overtaken by the power of the moment, Nathan relived every memory and experienced every debilitating emotion of his tragic life. He fell to the floor and writhed in agony. Sheila got on her knees and soothed him.

"You are *not* alone," she said kindly. "We are with you."

Sheila turned to Heinrich. "Please hold him in place."

Heinrich readily complied.

"No, stop! What are you doing to me?"

The shapes and the voices continued in a maddening rush and whirl.

You have no right to live! Too many people have been hurt by you!

Nathan pushed against Heinrich, kicking and screaming, but the vigorous German man held him tighter and tighter and called for the others to help him, which they gladly did, until Nathan stopped fighting them and relaxed. He wept and moaned and cried out to Jesus Christ. "Please send your mighty warrior angels to protect me, Lord. I need your intercession."

The reddish mist which had become an impenetrable wall disappeared.

An angel who stood seven feet in height stepped forward and clapped a gleaming hand on Nathan's shoulder. His voice was clear and crisp as he recited Psalm 33:6-9. "The Lord merely spoke, and the heavens were created. He breathed the Word, and all the stars were born. He assigned the sea its boundaries and locked the oceans in vast reservoirs. Let the whole world fear the Lord, and let everyone stand in awe of him. For when he spoke, the world began! It appeared at his command."

The angel pointed to Nathan. "Jesus now rests on your shoulder."

Several people exchanged glances, including Nathan, who looked at his shoulder and imagined a miniature version of Jesus who sat there and waved good tidings. The enormity of his tension was relieved.

He chuckled loudly, and so did the other patients.

The angel turned to Susanna, and his shimmer brought out the beauty in her face, long buried underneath lines and wrinkles created by tragedy.

"Can you forgive your husband? If so, the gates of heaven will open to you." The angel towered above the group in humility.

Susanna gazed in awe and wonder. Her mouth grew tender.

"It's so hard," she said sadly, "and my pain is so great."

The angel quoted Psalm 33:18-19. "But the Lord watches over those who fear him, those who rely on his unfailing love. He rescues them from death and keeps them alive in times of famine."

She turned to John and gave him her earnest attention.

"Will he ever repent?"

"Let's ask him." The angel walked over to John and stood in front of him, calibrating his sentiment and his willingness to receive the Lord's gift of salvation. "You have a last chance at repentance, John Hutchinson. I am an emissary of the Most High. If you repent of your sins and accept Jesus as your Savior, your burdens will be lifted. You made mistakes in your youth, which led to your descent into madness. Now allow Jesus to set you free."

John burst into tears and fell to his knees.

The angel bent down and helped him return to his feet.

"You do not worship me but our Lord, Jesus Christ."

John stared wide-eyed at the angel, astonished at his presence.

"Will you decide today to accept Jesus Christ as your Savior?"

John nodded as tears coursed down his cheeks. "If He will have me."

The angel called Nathan to stand beside him.

"You are a man of healing, correct?"

"Yes, I try to heal people in whatever manner possible."

"Good. Then would you like to become a healer of souls?"

"I don't know *how*."

"Gather your friends and place hands on this man. Ask God to fill John with the Holy Spirit and to work His will in this man's life. Call the unclean spirits out of him in the name of Jesus Christ, and John will be delivered."

Nathan did as requested, and John's deportment changed. He was tinted by a crimson glow as blood entered his formerly pallid face, and his sleepy eyes stirred to life. Nathan was dazzled by the impossibility of this moment as his hand returned to his side. "Are you alright?"

"I'm better than alright." John presented a grin and a manifest desire for the Lord. "I am now washed clean by the blood of Jesus."

The angel directed Susanna to stand beside her husband.

"Because of your ties to the supernatural, each of you will be given the burden of prophecy. As a couple, you will travel the world and announce the imminent return of Jesus Christ. Some will think you've gone mad, and others will pay no attention, but a select few will heed your call and repent. Your lineage and the lineage of those you lead to Christ will help form the remnant. In the last days, only a few will survive the Tribulation, and many will be martyred for their faith, but those who remain alive when Christ returns will behold a glorious sight. The Millennial Kingdom awaits them."

John hugged his wife, and they wept as a unified couple in Christ.

He wiped tears of happiness from his cheeks as he turned to the angel.

"The Lord has spoken through you," he said, beaming. "We will carry out His perfect will. We have a reason to live because of Him. Hallelujah!"

The group rejoiced in the blessed hope of heaven. When they at last stopped hugging and crying tears of joy, they looked about for the angel.

Where he had previously stood, there was empty space.

Heinrich helped Nathan to his feet. "You will no longer travel the broad highway as a solitary man. You are like us, and we are a group of survivors who have endured great and terrible afflictions. Always know you are loved."

Sheila patted Nathan's back. "Please listen to him."

Nathan shook Heinrich's hand and offered a faint smile.

"Thank you," he said to the German. "I heard what you said."

He turned to Sheila. "Will you give them breakfast?"

"It would be my pleasure," she said. "What will you do now?"

"I'm going upstairs to contemplate what just happened here."

"What about *your* breakfast?"

"There's no way I could eat. This encounter has drained me."

"Please take care of yourself, Nathan. We cannot lose you."

He withheld a reply as he headed for the door to the stairwell.

James called to him. "We'll fight anyone for your honor! You are a kind and decent man at heart, and we love you."

Nathan ascended the stairs and flung open the door to his office.

At his desk, he pushed his hands together and prayed aloud.

"Lord, I have never been a religious man, but I repent of my sins and ask you to work your will in my life, no matter if it may mean life or death."

He waited a few moments for an answer and then flipped through several sections of the Bible, unsure where to start or when to stop.

He closed the book and rubbed his temples.

My son, I have been with you all along.

Nathan sat upright in his chair. "Lord, is it you?"

Yes, I am with you now as I have been with you all your life, and when you suffered, I ached along with you, not only on the cross during my crucifixion, but by your side as your mother bore an unspeakable agony. I was there when you roamed the countryside after your parents fought so viciously with one another. I was there when Aunt Joy took you into her home and also when she died. I was with you when Annie, Eli, and Peter passed one by one and when Catherine abandoned you for a man doomed to his own destruction. I have never forsaken you, my son, for I have loved you since before creation, counting the hairs on your head before your birth, and I have patiently waited for this day when you would finally come to know my nature as a loving God.

Nathan's anger mounted, and his cheeks flushed red.

"Why didn't you help me, Lord, when I needed you most?"

In all your years, you never called on my name. You do not have because you do not ask, and I will not interfere without an invitation. You did not pray to me, nor did your parents. If you had reached out to me in humility and sincerity as you do now, I would have stepped in and removed you from such a destructive situation, but as you did not pray for my intercession, I endured the torment along with you. Each time others hurt you, they also hurt me, and I would appreciate your asking for my help daily as I would like to be released from your oppression as much as you would wish for a waiver.

"My mother was a God fearing woman, and you allowed her murder."

She read my word often and attended a grand church, which was well regarded in the St. Louis community, as was its pastor, but she did not strive to maintain a relationship with me on a daily basis. June asked for my help only on the day of her death, which by then was too late, as I barely knew her.

Nathan pondered the loss of his sanity.

There was a genuine possibility he had broken with reality.

He took a deep breath and exhaled.

"I've been very upset with you, Jesus, and for that, I'm truly sorry."

Because I seek an eternal relationship with you, I long for your love, but I will also tolerate your hatred if it comes from a place of sincerity and a yearning to gain wisdom. The Lord paused so Nathan might understand the meaning behind His words. *What I cannot bear is your apathy.*

Nathan took his Bible and kneeled on the floor.

"Lord, I beg you to forgive me. I thank you for remaining at my side through so many years of strife. Both now and forever, I surrender to your will and I humbly ask you to work your perfect will through me."

You must reform and live a godly life. I have big plans for you, Nathan, but I will not work through an unclean vessel. Once you fully return to me, I will work through you to accomplish my will. We must hurry, as there is little time before the harvest. There are many souls to save before I return!

That night, Nathan read Daisy's theories about aphasia, hysteria, and hypnosis. She had done a stellar job of cataloguing their case histories.

He stretched himself on the bed amid a battle of thoughts which raged and brawled inside his mind. How could he have been oblivious to the misery in the world, not only in himself and Daisy, but everywhere else?

Nathan offered a spoken prayer to Jesus.

"Lord, there are many orphan children living in soldier's homes, working as servants, or roaming the streets with barely any food to eat, and many of them will end up in our hospital because of starvation or brain injury or psychological desolation. I ask you to work through me, Lord Jesus, no matter the personal cost to my flesh or my reputation. I care nothing for status or material gain in this fallen realm. Every child in St. Louis who hurts must be saved, and I will dedicate my life to each of them."

Daisy slumped on a bench and hid her eyes from the glare of the brutal sunshine, thankful for the approach of a noteworthy cloud which floated face down, imposing its mantle over the hilly street. Peculiar strangers dragged themselves along the sidewalk and cast superior looks as they passed behind her location. A trolley-driver with a pompous chest considered her attentively and then mistreated his mule, who was confused about which way to go. Daisy wished harm on the driver for his foul wickedness.

Indian summer heat oppressed her spirit and sapped her strength. God's heavy hand was upon her as she searched the gilded sky for answers.

She spoke aloud, no longer caring what others thought of her.

"I've acknowledged my sin to you, Lord. It's no longer hidden, but out in the open. I am the only living link to Henry Hayes, the destroyer of my family. There is no place for me anywhere in this world, as there was no longer a place for Henry, my mother, or my sister." She looked up and squinted. "You know how hard I've tried to fit in, Lord, but it's no use."

She paused.

"The only question is whether to take poison like Henry, or to fling myself from atop Big Rock like Rose, or to slice my jugular like Patrice."

Daisy's eyes met the sky. "What say you, Lord?"

A fight broke out on top of the building across the street.

Two men, most likely drunkards, had left the bar on the first floor and were now throwing punches at one another. She sat up straight, fearing the worst. They were dangerously close to the edge and could fall any second.

Daisy's mouth fell open in disbelief.

One combatant was the same man who fired a pistol in her direction on the Fourth of July and accosted her and Nathan on their way to John's frightful estate at Vandeventer Place. She put her hand over her mouth as she realized the other man had tackled his lunatic brother in the park.

Could both men be insane?

It would appear so by their behavior.

The lunatic ceased fighting and glared at Daisy.

He called down to her. "You are the enemy of this world!"

The lunatic sneered and then resumed the fight.

"What in the world is going on here?" she asked herself.

People heard the shout and stopped in the middle of the street. The mule driver called up to them. "Hey, you two up there! Stop making fools of yourselves and come down here this instant. The police have been called!"

The driver's words distracted the lunatic. His foot slipped off the edge, and he fell four stories, landing on the mule driver and killing them both in the blink of an eye. Daisy slammed her back onto the bench and gasped.

Did she create the very portrait she had painted in her mind?

She stared at the sky. "You are a cruel God. I never meant for such a thing to happen. Those madmen could have been redeemed if you had tried harder." She listened for the Lord's reply but heard only shouts and cries.

A siren sounded from the distance. She looked about the area for the nightingale. The noise grew louder and nearer as the police wagon arrived.

The lone man at the top of the building called down to Daisy.

"You'll die the same death!" He sneered and waved and hooked his thumbs into his pockets, performing a haughty dance, circling close to the edge like his former opponent. "You just wait and see, Miss Lawrence!"

She rushed through the intersection and turned the corner, thankful to be leaving such a vile snake pit, where more men were infested with demons than not, and decent men of God had become a prized rarity.

Daisy packed her room quickly and fought the urge to weep on her knees. She'd had quite enough of life away from her small town on the Missouri River. She knelt beside her bed with her hands clasped together and said a prayer for the two dead men and any family they might have left behind. Daisy also prayed for Nathan and Catherine, two nomadic lovers who were forever connected by parenthood and loss. Perhaps they should throw off the cloak of indifference and reunite in flawless matrimony.

As the prodigal daughter, Daisy would make other plans.

Until you hear otherwise, my daughter, remain in St. Louis.

"But why, Lord? I cannot stay in this den of vipers!"

The clip clop of hooves outside her window gave a meager reply.

"I will stay in St. Louis at your discretion, Lord, but it will be done in protest. I sometimes lose my faith because I do not understand your will."

A hotel guest wheezed as he passed her door with a stomping manner, his voice low and thick as he spoke to another guest in spiteful dispute, each of their temper's flaring amid a ruddy fog of curses and sworn oaths of murder. Daisy would readily leave this wretched city tomorrow if the Lord would agree to her departure. It was a place fit only for the grave.

THIRTY-FOUR

Psalm 34:17

The Lord hears his people when they call to him for help.
He rescues them from all their troubles.

Nathan descended the stairs and entered the main hall. Sheila called to him from the far end, where she sat with the group at a long table. She pulled out a chair at a spot selected just for him, and his mind fell inert as he sat and chatted with the patients, the same dreary souls he formerly despised. They were now prominent figures to him, a poem of love to his newly saved heart, and he wanted to collect the ghastly remembrances of their histories, the cheer of their renewed interests, and the hopeful dreams of their futures. He would hold his friends near to his heart and keep them everlastingly safe from the depredation which the world so longed to bring upon their brow, their poor health and low spirits taking longer to restore than he might have predicted when the angel appeared.

Sheila set a plate before him, and the food smelled delicious.

Heinrich waved his hand at Nathan. "Please wait for a blessing."

Nathan dropped a cloth napkin into his lap.

"Almost forgot." He looked around the table. "Still new to this life."

"You'll get there faster than we did." Sheila sat at her place.

She pushed her hands together in the shape of a steeple.

"Dear Lord, we pray in the name of Jesus, and we thank you for your many blessings and for the wonderful food you've provided for us." Sheila opened her eyes and glanced at Nathan. He was already peeking at her, and he smiled. She closed her eyes quickly and continued. "We honor your holy name and we thank you for your many blessings in our lives. Amen."

The table said, "Amen."

Nathan cut his steak and took a bite. "This is terrific, Sheila."

"As always, my dear," said Heinrich happily.

He turned and gave her a kiss on the cheek. She accepted it with grace.

Nathan held up his knife. "I'm glad the two of you are together."

Sheila turned to Heinrich. "Nathan and I had a conversation a few days ago about our past relationship and how we might proceed as brother and sister." She refilled Heinrich's cup from a pitcher and handed it to him.

He threw Nathan a confused look. "Is it what you want?"

Nathan nodded his approval. "More than anything."

"You are not angry with me for falling in love with your Sheila?"

Nathan pressed his back against the chair and considered his words. He must choose them carefully to convey the genuine nature of his feelings.

"I was annoyed with you at first, Heinrich, when you would not stop crying over the deaths of your wife and children." Nathan's lips pulled together in a slight grimace. "I know the devastation of terrible loss, so please don't misunderstand." He looked thoughtfully at Sheila and then back at her new beau. "I've since come to know each of you on a much deeper level, and my estimation of your character has grown tremendously." He tried to give them both a hearty smile, but wavered. "If Daisy and I were to be honest, we did not know what we were doing, and we were surely just as broken as each one of you. We were merely better at hiding our grief and at numbing our pain through constant work, which helped in that regard."

"You've suffered along with each of us," said Sheila comfortingly.

"Our anguish has become your own, Nathan, and sometimes I fear for your health. You must be careful not to lock yourself inside our prison."

"You have been in no prison, at least not like these hysterics."

Her eyebrows arched. "Oh, no?"

He looked about the table, confused. "They've experienced debilitating grief after losing a loved one or some other trauma, which led to somatic physical symptoms like paralysis or the inability to speak."

She took a deep breath and exhaled. "You think so little of me."

Nathan went over to Sheila and took her hands.

"I would like to understand more about your past."

Sheila blushed and glanced around the table. "It's no more or less than anyone else here." She raised her chin in soft defiance, and her eyes grew heavy with despair. "When I consider what occurred, I grow so tired."

"Will you tell us about it?" asked Nathan. "Heinrich should know everything about the woman he loves. I think you owe it to him."

Nathan kissed her hand and returned to his seat.

She turned to Heinrich. "Do you feel the same?"

"I do," he said. "Allow yourself to fall into brokenness with me, my sweet darling." He looked gravely into her eyes and smiled from the heart. "I would never turn my back on you for any transgression from your youth."

Sheila glowed with warmth as her eyes met the others at the table.

"I've never felt such love in my twenty-seven years on this earth."

"You have become like a mother to us," said Nathan with a euphoric satisfaction. "The one we all forgot we needed."

"Mothers serve their family. They don't whine about the past."

"You will do wonders when you have children of your own," Heinrich said. "Before that can happen, my dear, you must reveal yourself fully."

"If you insist." She held out her hands and weighed them in the air.

Heinrich took them and kissed her fingers. "I do."

Sheila glanced at Nathan, who nodded to her for encouragement.

"Alright, here goes." She hesitated. "My grandparents died in the Great Famine of '47, when the potatoes took ill with blight, and many people starved to death. My father never got over it. He blamed the British crown and the Irish politicians for their apathetic response, and he vowed never to need help from anyone. My mother died of cholera when I was a young girl, and I took her place as my father's helper around the farm. When the famine came around again in '79, my father had fallen deep into debt, and he could no longer secure additional funds for our farm operations."

Nathan stirred in his seat. "Why not, if you don't mind me asking?"

She sighed, and her face looked older than her years.

"He had a reputation for telling people what he thought of them, thinking he could always remain a self-sufficient man."

"He found out otherwise," said Heinrich, nodding.

She gave him a faint, melancholy smile. "Yes."

There was something solitary and lenient in her bearing, something which spoke of an ancient distress, mended and tempered and irreparable.

"I was thirteen when the famine began and fourteen when my father took his own life. He sent me to beg our neighbors for enough food to keep us going another few days and I found his body upon my return. They were so nice to us when I offered a meager plea for sustenance. I carried a box which they had filled with vegetables and even a bit of meat."

Sheila took up her napkin and stretched it with her fingers. Heinrich stroked her back, and she turned to him. He drew her near, and she wept against his chest; her body shook with violence, and she clutched his shirt. Nathan gestured to the others, and they gathered around her chair, kneeling and leaning and offering kind words of love and support. He kept his seat and gazed at her with admiration as he brushed the tears from his eyes.

"Please continue," he said. "You are in a house of love."

Sheila sat up straight and wiped her face with the napkin.

She looked at everyone and smiled. "I know it. You are all so wonderful to me, and I do not deserve such affection after all I have done."

"We don't care about your mistakes," James said. "We love you."

Shirley handed Sheila her blue blanket, which Sheila held in her lap.

"Thank you," she said, squeezing Shirley's arm.

"We won't leave your side until you share the rest with us."

Sheila wiped a tear and ran her hand up and down Shirley's arm.

"The U.S.S. *Constellation* and another ship, the *Exalted*, arrived in port, bringing aid to our region. Since I had no way to sustain myself after my father's funeral, I made my way to America, specifically to New York, where my uncle had moved some years prior to the famine. I assumed I could easily find him, which was stupid and naïve of me, but I was a young girl with no real knowledge of the world. I hopped aboard the *Exalted* and asked the young sailors for transport. They were in training, as the ship was old and no longer fit for military use. I thought, since they were near to my age, they might want to help me get to a safe harbor, but I was wrong."

"I can guess what happened," Nathan said soberly.

Her lip quivered, and she looked away. "It's too dark and painful."

Heinrich stroked her hair. "Please, my darling. I need your honesty."

Her breaths quickened, and she gave him a frightened look. "Will you help me through the hellish forest? I feel as if I'm melting inside."

Heinrich gripped her. "I will do anything for you, even suffer death."

She wept in his vigorous arms. "Please don't let me go, Heinrich."

He whispered soothingly to her. "I will always keep you safe."

The others stroked her hair and spoke kind words to her, and after a few minutes of sobs which emanated from cavernous recesses, she recovered.

"They gave me passage, but I was forced into prostitution aboard ship. Even the captain got involved after a while, and by the time we reached New York, I was a hardened veteran of the high seas. There was nothing they didn't have me do under threat of death. I was lucky to have made it at all."

"Did you find your uncle?" Nathan was amazed at her courage.

"I wish it was so, but he was nowhere to be found. Someone said he left for St. Louis and had made a new life here, so I found my way across the United States, by hook or by crook, mostly through turning tricks in some random town, saving my money, and then moving to the next whistle stop."

Nathan's cheeks reddened at the injustice of Sheila's life. She never chose such a line of work, but it was carelessly forced on her at such a young and delicate age. He'd always detected a profound gravity about her, and a curious embarrassment, unusual for women who worked at Joanna's brothel. He thought of her out near the distant horizon of the sea, fighting for her survival among men of the lowest character, their kind multiplying since the war innumerably. Something lifted the day Nathan met her, as she led him from the depth of the grave into the light of living, and he owed her a debt more grand than all the treasures in Solomon's mines.

"I take it you went to work for Joanna upon your arrival in St. Louis?"

"Yes, and that's when I met you, the man who saved my life."

"If anyone's life was saved, it was mine," said Nathan abruptly. "You are an angel of mercy, and if you ever feel low about yourself, you should know I will always feel exactly the opposite. It is my honor to know you."

"Thank you, Nathan. Your love means more than you'll ever know."

She turned to Heinrich. "What about you?"

He stiffened. "I've told you everything already."

"You kept the worst locked inside, hidden from me."

He disregarded her question. "Please, let's move to a more peaceful conversation. I cannot bear all of this gloomy and bitter talk."

"I must know the depths of your pain, as I know my own."

"If I spoke my thoughts aloud, you would find them uninteresting."

"I would love them," she said, a bit damped by his reticence.

Nathan looked at Samuel, who nodded. He turned to Heinrich.

"Please, for her sake, share more about your family."

"I told her they died in a fire which destroyed a city block."

"Yes, but you spoke fast and changed the subject."

The weight of his past sat heavily on Heinrich's chest.

He dropped his eyes and spoke with an intensity of feeling which surprised everyone at the table, as he was usually a reserved and stoic man when not consumed by a flood of tears. "My Margareta kept the children while I worked at a mill several blocks from our room in a Boston boarding house. While she prepared my lunch, as she did each day for me and our two daughters, Britta and Lucy, she set a fire somehow and tried to put it out, but she was badly burned on the hands and face." He turned to Sheila. "The neighbors said she called to them from the floor of our little apartment, but they could not get the door open, and the fire had spread so very quickly."

His body shook, and he wrapped his arms around himself.

Sheila rubbed his back and spoke lovely words of hope in his ear.

He wiped his eyes with a napkin and continued.

"Britta and Lucy would not have known what to do or how to help their mother get out of the room. People said it happened so fast they couldn't believe it. The wood in the drafty building was ancient, and the timbers went up in seconds. The fire was made worse by the rugs on each floor and the heavy blankets Margareta had placed over the windows to keep in the heat. She and our daughters were caught in the smoke and died."

Heinrich examined the food on his plate.

"I heard the news and rushed home to the reek of smoke and cinders."

He stabbed the meat with his fork.

"That's all there is to say on the matter."

Ida tugged on his sleeve. "Here you go, Mr. Heinrich."

He turned to her, and she handed him her singed china doll. It had only one good eye, which looked at him with a disparaging glint.

Heinrich burst into tears. Ida hugged him and then sat in her chair.

"It's good to let it out constructively," said Nathan with a warm smile of encouragement. "In the past, you cried without sharing the most painful details which surround your grief, and it did nothing to ease your suffering."

"It's how we became hysterics," said James after a moment of thought.

"Yes, that's correct. It has been Daisy's assertion since the beginning."

"Jesus has cleansed our souls to His satisfaction, and that will make all the difference," Susanna said. "We will never return to our former state."

John squeezed his wife's hand and kissed her fingers.

"No fallen soul can be saved without knowing the love of Jesus."

She leaned against him with her shoulder and smiled.

"I thank you all for remaining here for a while longer, so we can ensure your mental and physical health remains stable, and so we might appease Belmont." Nathan gestured to the group. "It is most appreciated by me."

"You're most welcome," said Shirley with a smile. "Ed will soon return as well, and I will take up residence with him at his farm once we wed."

"No more work as a section hand on the Arizona line?"

"It will be my first and only attempt at making a family. For him, it is his second, and he has vowed to do everything possible to see us happy."

"Well, that is wonderful news," said Nathan kindly. "Let's toast."

The group clinked their water glasses together and wished Shirley well.

Dora, who sat at the far end of the table, dignified and solemn, coughed behind her hand. "We must finish our meal and clean up, for the hour is growing late, and we must get the young one to bed. We all need our rest."

Samuel chuckled beside her. "You'd best comply, everyone."

"I am no taskmaster," she said, feigning offense.

"Oh, no?" asked Samuel with a grin. "Where has my fiancé gone?"

"You're not funny, Samuel, and you know it, too."

Nathan settled into his chair and thought of Daisy.

"When I've finished with the cleanup," said Sheila affectionately and in her best Irish brogue, "you might sit with me and Heinrich in the rockers. It would do you some good to get your mind off the wee blond one for a bit of time." She stood behind him and clutched the back of his chair. "If you keep moping around this hospital, I might soon have to give your head a smart wallop." Sheila's hand whacked his head, and then she smoothed his hair.

Heinrich laughed from his belly, and it showed in his eyes.

She quickly rounded the corner of the table and winked at Nathan.

He raised his chin and gave her a permissive smile. "I have the intention of saying coarse words to you, Miss Sheila Byrne from western Ireland, but to keep my friends and you as my newfound sister, I will refrain."

She laughed. "Good, then you'll sit with us?"

"I will," he said. "Some coffee would be nice."

Sheila pointed toward the kitchen at the back of the hospital.

"It's in the cupboard three over from the basin. Go make some."

"Yes, Mother."

She popped him with a cloth napkin as he walked beside her.

"I'll mother you the way it should have been done," she said.

He caught the napkin and snapped it at her playfully.

"Oh, it was done this way, alright. I had many slapped cheeks."

Sheila stood and placed her hands on her hips.

"It's why I'm sad about Daisy," she said. "The woman might have been a thorn in my side from time to time, but she knew how to smack those bearded cheeks of yours without leaving a permanent mark, and I miss her."

"More than I ever thought possible," said Nathan helplessly.

Sheila wrapped her arms around his waist and squeezed.

"I know, honey." She drew back from him. "Will a sister do for now?"

"Yes, but only if you go with me to my mother's church."

She cast a ponderous look. "I don't think so."

"Why not? You love the Lord as we all do."

Nathan gestured toward the group.

She snorted her displeasure at such a ridiculous idea.

"They wouldn't want the likes of me in their grand church."

"Oh, yes they would," said Samuel in a convinced voice.

He stepped near her and Heinrich. "If not, they will deal with me."

Nathan smiled at his father and turned to her. "Me, too."

She smirked at him. "You don't go to church."

He leaned forward with conscientious enthusiasm.

"I do now, and I want all my friends to attend with me."

"Even a lowly prostitute from the bowels of hell?"

The group gasped in unison. Nathan took her shoulders and clutched them tightly with his fists. She instinctively pulled away, as he was likely causing her some bit of sore distress, but he would not let her go, for if he did, she would leave this collection of miscreants forever and make her way to the western frontier in Arizona or California or perhaps south to Mexico. He saw the self hatred in her eyes and he knew it better than she did, having borne the millstone of shame around his neck since childhood, but she was to be saved by the blood of Jesus Christ and not lost to the fires of perdition.

"Let me go, Nathan. I'm an unworthy cause, even to you."

He pulled her tightly against him. "I'll never let you go, Sheila."

She wept as her body fell slack in his arms. "You already did."

He whispered into her ear. "Now you have a much better man."

She nodded.

"Yes. Sorry to say it to you, but he is, Nathan."

"Then allow him to make you happy, for my sake, and accept Christ in your heart once and for all. We are a lowdown bunch, but we are yours, lock, stock and barrel, if you'll pardon the expression." He pushed her slightly away and wiped her eyes. "Will you marry Heinrich and make a home?"

She looked at Heinrich, who stood nearby. His eyes were moist.

"Will you still have me, even after my silly display of love for *him*?"

"I would be honored to know you as my wife and to make children."

She sighed and squeezed Nathan's arms with her fingers.

"Then it's settled."

Nathan let her go, and she turned to Heinrich. "I cannot remain in St. Louis. There are too many memories which would ruin any chance for us."

"Must you leave?" asked Nathan sincerely. "We can still be a family."

Her voice regained some of its strength. "I will always love you, first as the man who saved me from the certitude of death, and second as my youthful love, the one every person struggles to lose, but I cannot make a home with this man if we stay here, where you live with another woman, most especially the one who grates on my every nerve as if my head were suddenly thrust into a mechanical vise. Someone would die a slow death."

At this, Nathan chuckled out loud, knowing it was the truth.

"Where will you go? Please do not say the southwest."

"I have a brother who sailed to Pennsylvania," Heinrich said. "While in Boston, I traded several letters with him, and he has done well for himself there. His last correspondence mentioned available land north of a great city where many Moravians have congregated in free worship of the Lord."

Nathan thought of his mother. "Philadelphia?"

Heinrich nodded.

"Yes, and the town is called Waldenburg."

<hr>

Nathan helped Sheila and Dora clean the dishes in the kitchen, and Sheila taught him how to make a fine pot of coffee, which he drank with pleasure at the front of the main hall. He sat on the end near the door with Sheila to his right. Heinrich took position on her other side, and James asked if he might join in the fourth rocker. Nathan gestured cheerfully for him to sit.

Sheila rubbed Nathan's hand. "I worry so about you."

"I'll be alright, once this business at the Expo is settled."

"Do you believe John will reverse course?" she asked.

"No, he is fully intent on using everyone here for his ends."

Heinrich clapped his hand down upon his knee.

"Whatever you choose, we will support your decision."

Nathan gave him a smirk. "Yes, until the two of you leave me alone."

"You'll have the others for company," said Sheila reverently.

He looked about the room and gestured at the beds.

"I'm concerned the group of misfits will lose connection with one another, each falling back into their own pursuits and concerns."

Sheila patted his hand. "It's up to you, Nathan, to keep them together."

"As a remnant?"

"Yes, until the Lord appears in the sky with a shout, we must maintain fellowship with like-minded Christians, the genuine kind who love Jesus and wish to take up their own cross as He did." She smiled at Heinrich. "Once we settle in Waldenburg, we will seek those who truly follow Christ."

"Will you mind leaving the Catholic church?"

"My father rarely attended mass, so I know little of the Catholic ways, other than to hear of the ceaseless flow of money though our diocese."

James, who had been quiet, cleared his throat and interjected.

"My mother was a former Catholic, and I can attest to such a claim."

Nathan leaned forward in his rocker and addressed James.

"Do you miss Catherine? It would be understandable, given the close bond the two of you formed while placed here in this hospital."

James swallowed. "Yes, very much. She considers me an outlaw."

Sheila smiled at him. "I would wager she sees more than a shallow role you might have once played while exuding the folly of youth."

"I would hope for more with her, as you have with Heinrich."

"Will you call on her at Belmont's estate?" asked Nathan.

James rolled his eyes at the notion. "He would never entertain a scoundrel like me in his fancy home, nor would the servants let me into the foyer, much less his drawing room for brandy and private conversation."

The group chuckled all at once.

"Yes, it would be a fine sight," Nathan said. "It's better you don't, to be quite honest. She has returned for all the wrong reasons, and I fear she has given herself over to the side of darkness, her greed and envy now aligned with her father's." He sighed. "It was my worst fear while we were married."

"We might pray for her deliverance," James said. "Jesus heals all."

Nathan considered.

"Perhaps if we isolated her from him during the Expo, we might convince her to renounce her affiliation with the Big Cinch and the demons in her midst." Another thought occurred to him, one which proved more troubling than the rest. "She may have trouble leaving Belmont's fortune behind, once and for all, as she has depended on his money since birth."

"Her type usually does." Sheila rocked with pursed lips.

"I didn't give up on Sophie," said James with devotion, "and I won't give up on Catherine." He sat thoughtfully for a moment. "I might even reconcile with my parents on her behalf, as they would like her immensely."

"Reconciliation with parents is a lengthy road," Nathan said.

James nodded.

"Mine has been a long time in the making, and I'm now ready."

He looked at Nathan. "Samuel said the puppies are doing well at his farm and growing into spectacular young dogs. I thank you for saving them from the alley and for attempting to save Sophie. I sensed sweetness in her."

Nathan felt the overwhelming urge to cry. He spoke with a cracked voice. "I so desperately wanted to save her life, and it gutted me to fail."

He paused.

"I look back to what had become a glorious afternoon spent in embrace and adoration, and it seems my relationship with Daisy rolled down a steep embankment from the moment of Sophie's death, and I haven't been able to resuscitate whatever it was which brought us together at Union Depot."

The woman with jet black hair and emerald green eyes entered through the front door and asked Nathan to speak with her in his office.

Nathan moved quickly to his feet. "Yes, by all means."

He turned to Sheila, who regarded the woman with narrowed eyes.

Her eyes met his. "Please, I beg you, Nathan. Be careful of this one."

Nathan bent over and whispered into her ear. "You're safe."

Sheila gently shoved him. "I can take care of myself, but I am concerned this woman will change you into someone we no longer know."

"Why would you say such a thing? We're only going to talk upstairs."

"This one is of the devil, Nathan, and you must mark my words. She's worse than Joanna." Sheila leapt to her feet and pushed toward the woman, forcing Nathan to stop her. She pointed at her newly realized nemesis.

"I know your order wants me dead, but you won't get me."

"When we want you, it will be all too easy," said the woman sharply.

"Perhaps, but you cannot have Nathan. He now belongs to Jesus."

The woman retrieved a handful of envelopes from her purse and held them up for all to see. "Once he discovers who he really is and who actually owns his future, your time with him will reach an abrupt and unsentimental conclusion. Nathan will make many discoveries as he is mentored by me and others, and in the last accounting, he will emerge as a new man, one you will find monstrous and unrecognizable." Her eyebrows arched as she cast a subtle smile. "Rest assured, his fury will soon find its way to *you*."

"You are a vile snake!" Sheila raised her hand to strike.

Heinrich grabbed her arm from behind and pulled her near to him.

"I have her now, Nathan. You may converse with this woman in peace."

Nathan nodded to Heinrich. "Thanks for your help."

He walked with the woman to the stairs and opened the door. His hand gestured for her to ascend to the second floor, and she complied.

Nathan turned toward Heinrich.

"Please take care of Sheila. We both know she's far too valuable to lose."

Heinrich nodded his commitment. "I will. You have my word."

He directed his future wife to the kitchen against her refusals.

Nathan trudged upstairs and took a seat at his desk.

He looked out the window, gauging the blackness of the night, and then swiveled toward the woman. "What could be so important?"

"We have many things to discuss, Nathan. Time grows short."

His eyes took in her sensual beauty and her animalistic nature. It was as if she had been created by man rather than born of God's Handiwork. "Alright, fine, but why did you act as if you know me or control my life?"

He checked his watch. "It's a bit late for riddles, so speak plainly."

She placed the bundle of envelopes on his desk.

"Not many chairs, are there?" she smiled. "Why do you work in a dour setting like this? It's not proper for a man of your stature."

She sat opposite him.

He pointed at the envelopes. "I will not open these without your name."

Her eyes fell to the floor. "It's not yet time."

"When?"

The woman gave him a flirtatious look. "Soon, my love."

He shifted in his chair. "Your games exhaust my patience."

"There are things you do not know, Nathan, about your mother."

He leaned forward. "What?"

"June was raised in a prominent Philadelphia family, which she left behind to marry your father, who was a penniless medical student. After his graduation and many arguments with her father, she and Samuel moved to St. Louis, where they purchased a farm and he began a practice."

"I know those facts."

"Here's what you don't know. June's parents were immersed in a cabal which operates behind the scenes in our society, pulling business levers and pushing government buttons. I was born into a similar family in New York, but my parents were murdered for their attempt to leave the Consortium."

"Consortium?"

"Yes, it's a name they use for themselves."

"Are you a member?"

She nodded graciously. "I am."

He picked up a pencil and wrote a few notes. It occurred to him he seemed a bit like Kincaid interviewing a suspect at the police station.

"Why were your parents murdered?"

"You'll want to know my name first."

He gestured for her to continue.

"Laura Collins."

She smiled at him, but her countenance seemed unhappy.

"Colleen's daughter?"

"One of three."

He recalled her sister's names. "Rebecca and Elizabeth."

The light from the gas lamp flickered slightly.

Laura and Nathan both eyed the lamp and then stared at one another.

"Rebecca and Elizabeth were my two sisters."

"You used the past tense," he said. "Are they well?"

She shook her head. "They are dead, along with Roy and Colleen."

His breath was taken from him. Nathan gasped for air.

He stood and marched toward his door and then stopped and turned toward her. He went over to her and grabbed her by the shoulders and shook them, knowing she would push him to the edge. "It cannot be."

Laura gave him a soft look. "Would you like to hear about it?"

He took a deep breath and exhaled. "I'm not sure."

She waved her hand to her right and pointed at his chair.

"Please sit like a gentleman, so I may begin."

He complied.

Laura took off her leather gloves and clutched the arms of her chair.

"This will be most painful to hear."

"I'm ready," he said.

"When you met them, they had left the cabal, and Colleen hoped to avoid their fate by turning you to the dark side. She thought it possible to appease Lucifer if she brought out the murder and the fornication which abound within you, but she failed in her quest, as you know."

"How did she die?"

Laura's hands quivered. She clenched her fists and opened them.

"Please continue," he said. "I know it's difficult, but you are safe here."

"Am I?" She clutched the arms again.

"With me, you are, but I cannot speak for your people."

She gave him a coy smile. "There is no spot on this green earth which lies untouched by the Consortium. You have no idea of their capabilities."

"If you cannot speak about it, I will take you to my home for the night. You may sleep in my room, and I will return to my cot here in the hospital."

Laura straightened her posture. "Just before I turned fifteen, I was kidnapped by rough men. They took me to a home for a ritual ceremony. I was stripped naked and forced to my knees in front of an altar. I believed the robed people would murder me, but I did not know what was about to take place. My mother and father were brought into the room. They were also naked, and their hands were bound behind their backs. A man stepped forward and shoved a long knife into my father's chest, and he fell to the floor, dead. Blood gushed from the wound as my mother looked at his still body in horror. I wanted to scream but could not make a sound. My mother kept her silence, but her face was lifeless as a ghost. Her eyes fell on me, and she mouthed the words, *I'm sorry.* The man stepped forward and cut her throat, and her twitching body fell to the floor beside my father's corpse."

Laura had spoken lightly and confidentially, but now her voice fell low.

"Other men collected as much blood as possible and poured it into a gold container. They placed the vessel in front of me near the altar."

She stopped and hastily wiped a tear.

"I'm sorry that happened to them and to you, Laura."

"Thank you, but I am not finished with the story."

He pressed his back into the chair. "There's *more*?"

"Yes."

"Alright." He gestured for her to continue.

"I didn't know this because I was innocent, but my two sisters and I were pitted against one another for selection as your wife. I was chosen over them for reasons which remain unknown to me, but it's irrelevant as they are no longer alive on this earth." She hesitated. "They were brought in next and made to fall to their knees in front of me. Rough men spread the blood over their skin and on my flesh and then they cut Rebecca and Elizabeth's throats as they kneeled three feet in front of me, spilling their blood on the floor between us. Their blood was smeared across most every inch of my flesh. I was told not to make a sound or I would be executed. As I mentioned, I was in mortal shock, and it would have been nearly impossible for me to verbalize a word or even to scream at the top of my lungs."

Nathan put his head on the desk and wept.

Laura spoke to him in a wintry tone. "Our training must soon begin."

He raised himself and wiped the tears from his cheeks.

"I don't know how to respond to such gruesome savagery."

She nodded her agreement and thrust herself forward in the chair. "Now you understand, Nathan. These are people who have no sense of humor and who play no games. They will murder me if I fail in my task."

"Which is?"

"To lead you to Lucifer as your wife."

He paced the floor in his office. His mind painted a portrait of her youthful naivety shattered in minutes. Her entire family was murdered in front of her eyes, with only her sensual flesh left behind and given over to evil. Laura's words rang true, although they were nightmarish.

He stopped. "What about my mother?"

Laura gave him a curious look. "What about her?"

"Was she murdered for leaving her family?"

Laura's eyebrows arched. "It's certainly possible. They train killers for certain tasks, and her murderer may have been sent to her on a particular mission." She hesitated. "I have not been provided with that level of detail, but I can get it if you'd like."

He looked about with restless eyes. "That won't be necessary."

"You already know the answer, don't you?"

"I believe I do."

Laura stood and drew near. "Will you make love to me?"

Her question astonished him. "Tonight?"

She nodded.

He pointed at his thin, ragged couch. "Here and now?"

Her eyes drifted toward the office door. "At your home."

He pushed her back a step and opened the door.

"I will take you to my house, where you may sleep for the night."

"Yes, my love." She drew against him, unwilling to allow any distance between their bodies, and touched his arm. "I am now your servant."

Nathan must avoid more carelessness. "Please don't misunderstand. Once I know you are securely tucked away, I will return to the hospital. There is work to do here, and I am quite comfortable on my pitiful couch."

Her moist lips parted. "Where you lead me, I will follow."

He smirked at her. "I was afraid you'd say that."

Nathan pointed toward the hall, and they left his office.

At Nathan's home, he left Laura on the couch in the parlor while he went upstairs with the lantern to make his bed. After a few minutes, she appeared in the bedroom doorway, naked, and ready to give herself over to him.

Her body moved closer. He asked her to stop.

"What's the matter? Do I make you nervous?"

"Of course."

"Then we must remedy the situation. I was bred to become your wife, Nathan, and after the death of my family, you are all that is left. The cabal trained me for the last ten years, and you do not know how many men and women I've watched die or the number of times I have bathed in human blood. Once you learn to kill, we will both wallow in your spoils of war."

She spread her palms flat and rubbed his chest.

"Do you like this?"

Nathan gave her a scornful look.

"I don't wish to hurt you, but I will if you don't cease."

Her emerald eyes looked up at him. "I long ago accepted the risks to my personal safety, and I am prepared to die tonight."

She rubbed his back as she spoke to him. "Nathan, I need you to ask me a question which I will now recite to you. Can you do that for me?"

Her amorous presence weakened his resolve. "I suppose."

She ran her fingers through his hair and kissed his neck as he had kissed Daisy's neck in the park. An urge welled within him to ravage her.

"Do you want to be taken, or do you want to be murdered?"

She would kindle his wolfish appetite and make him prone to yield. He was upset by her intrusion into his life and her attempt to derail his walk with Christ, but there was contentment to be found in her hedonism.

He withheld a response.

Laura took his arm. "Please ask me, Nathan."

"I would never ask a woman such a question."

"Oh, yes, you will. There's a bloodlust within you which has lain dormant for many years. Joanna will help you express it, and I will help you enjoy your carnal lusts. There is murder and lasciviousness in you, Nathan, and I am here, along with Joanna, to bring your inner beast into the open."

Nathan considered her words. He thought of the long and narrow road to Christ, the many temptations and persecutions which must be overcome.

"I knew Joanna years ago, when we were adolescents. I understood her to be defiant and unruly, but not one given over to insane violence."

Laura smiled mischievously and took the lantern from his dresser.

She held it near her flesh, further inflaming his passion.

He grabbed the lantern and held it away from her.

"You don't want me?" Her lips pouted and then she kissed his neck and whispered. "Oh, but you *do* want me, so awfully it makes you tremble."

He shoved her away from him and gathered himself.

"Joanna mentioned a mystery woman who would soon visit me."

Laura nodded.

"Joanna and I are united in our efforts to shape you, Nathan."

"I must admit, she scared me when I last saw her. Her father was a highly decorated general in the war, and he wanted his daughter to find security."

"Like Rosemarie, who was a child of the medieval nobility, Joanna has been granted exceptional powers as a diviner. You and I will complete our earthly tasks for Lucifer and then we will pass away, but she will live on until the son of perdition arises who will lead mankind to the highest plane of evolution." Laura stepped forward. "We will become spirit beings, and Lucifer will see to our every need. Comfort and pleasure are his specialties."

She was charming, but she mocked his newfound faith. "I have been saved by the blood of Jesus. I have no wish to take part in your darkness."

She placed her cheek against his chest and wrapped her arms around him. "Those who have been saved may fall into the pool of sin from time to time." Her head tipped back, and her eyes met his. "Isn't that so, Nathan?"

He broke free of her grip. "For others, but I am committed."

A storm brewed within him. He found it hard to contain himself.

"Yes, that's why you are so valuable to our cause."

Laura pointed toward the shadowy corner.

"Please look over there." She drew near and gripped his arms. "Some items were placed behind your bedroom door before you arrived, and I think you'll find them most delightful for our evening together."

Nathan took the lamp and shut the bedroom door, revealing three objects: a whip, a leather strap, and a steel knife. "What would you have me do with these, go on a rampage throughout the city?"

Her eyes burned like sulfur. "It's your choice."

He took the weapons and placed them on his dresser.

The ends of the whip hung over each side.

"I'm serious." He scowled at her. "Why did you put these in my house?"

"I completely surrender myself to you, Nathan, right here and right now. You may cut me to death with your knife or you may beat me severely across my fleshly body with your whip, or you may bend me over your bed and spank me with your leather strap." Her eyebrows arched. "I would prefer the latter choice, but it's your decision to make."

"I thought you said Joanna would elicit my bloodlust."

"So our training has begun, as I predicted. Please ask me the question."

A shadow descended on him, and his mood fell to furious anger.

A reddish mist floated into the room from the hallway.

The walls pulsated in cadence with her emerald eyes.

"Laura, you must stop this lunacy. Release me this instant."

"Please, Nathan."

She bent forward and rubbed his bearded cheek. "Do as I say."

"Alright, do you want to be taken, or do you want to be murdered?"

Laura took up the leather strap and clutched it tightly. "I seek to be taken by you, Nathan, as I am your property, and I offer you my absolute and endless submission." She placed the strap in his hand. "You must use your superior strength to guide me about the room and onto the bed and beat my bottom with this strap. In this manner, you will you take ownership of my flesh and my mind. Once bonded in dominance and submission, we will be one, and only then may we offer our intertwined spirits to Lucifer."

He sat on the bed, and his eyes fell to the floor. Who was this woman to tempt him so fiercely? She located the core of his masculinity and massaged it with the essence of her femininity, coercing it to awaken with little regard for brutality. All women were sociopaths who desired to manipulate, and all men were psychopaths who desired to murder and pillage, and thus, could intellectuals explain human nature in a nutshell. Pagans embraced these primal cravings, hoping to harness them for their own ends, but Christians knew a greater wisdom. A sincere and humble faith in Jesus Christ led the fallen to approach Him in truth—without lies or machinations—and to receive His grace, which was delivered freely as an act of love. The redeemed could then learn to trust in His righteousness and gain the peace which often lacks understanding. The last step was liberty from a servitude to sin.

Nathan squeezed the strap in his hand.

He wanted to use it on her so badly it terrified him, for he knew if he acquiesced to her charms and used the strap, he would next use the whip, and his destiny would forever be sealed, as the knife must inevitably follow.

Had Laura come here to die at his hand?

Would her sensuality restrain his yearning to drain her fleshly blood onto the floor? Could he control himself once the shadow and the mist unleashed the beast within him? It had been many years since he spoke to Colleen about such things, and she had almost sent him down a ferocious path toward madness, but his force of will had prevailed over hers.

He turned to Laura. "The presence of the knife confuses me."

"You think it to be Joanna's purview?"

He nodded.

"She will take you through the city streets and show you how to kill. You will be reticent at first, which is to be understood, so she will bring unwary victims to you in a basement underneath her brothel. The workers who provoke her are taken there, where they are disposed of at the amusement of local businessmen or politicians or church leaders. You would be most surprised to learn what has transpired in Joanna's ornamented basement along with the identities of those who have taken part in such activities."

After a silence, he spoke resolutely to her. "I don't want to kill anyone, Laura, not even you right now, although I find you to be wicked."

She read his mannerisms and the difficulties his mood presented. "As are you, Nathan, but you suppress the iniquity which abounds within you."

"No, I have given myself to Jesus Christ, who has washed away my sins."

"The cross will not save you from *yourself*, Nathan." She sat beside him on the bed. "We have someone special in mind for your first murder, a mark of low status who will not be missed. From what I've gathered from Joanna, there were many instances over the last ten years when Sheila was close to her fate in the secret basement, but your voice intervened on her behalf."

Laura kept her eyes on him. "Once you have given yourself over to the dark arts, you will be gratified to dispose of such a burdensome annoyance."

She patted his hand. "Don't worry, Nathan. I will be there in the room while the ceremony unfolds, and we will both adorn ourselves in her blood."

Nathan arose from the bed and paced. Laura's words washed over him like fire, and they ignited a flame deep inside he thought was extinguished.

"I will assist your ascension as you win over the card rooms of the Big Cinch and I will guide you through the political corridors of power."

"As a simple surgeon who barely holds onto his position?"

She smiled. "No one will care at first about the death of a few street prostitutes or tramps who sleep off their booze in back alleys, but once enough are eliminated, the citizens will take notice and an outcry will commence for justice. The current political administrations at the city and state level will not comply with our demands, so we will remove them, one by one, and replace them with men such as yourself who do our bidding."

"I am supposed to kill all those people?"

"Yes, and you will begin with your lovely Sheila, who enabled your weak and feeble withdrawal and who will now propel your career to new heights."

"She is the sweetest person I know, and I would never hurt her."

He paused.

"You have the wrong man, and it's time for you to leave my home."

"We have selected you for a meteoric rise to prominence."

He smirked. "As long as Lucifer controls my every move."

"Your every *thought*, Nathan. He will have no less from you."

How could this happen after being saved?

Laura picked up the leather strap and kneeled.

Her palms held it up to him. "I am yours to do with as you please."

Nathan took the strap and placed it on the dresser with the whip and the knife. He turned toward her, and she kissed his hand and pushed her cheek against it. He could no longer stop himself from taking her fleshly body. His desire had grown too powerful, and her feminine charms were too intense. "Please stop," he said. "I beg you to cease this at once."

Laura's attentive green eyes gazed at him. "I cannot."

He fell to his knees in front of her and dropped his face to the floor.

"Please, Lord Jesus, come to my aid in my time of distress. I am a weak and immoral man, and I cannot hold out another moment amid such dire temptation." She ran her fingers through his hair as he prayed. "Lord, I humbly ask for your intervention. I am completely lost to my sin."

Recite the Lord's Prayer, as I instructed my disciples.

"Yes, Lord, I will do as you command." He hesitated. "Our Father in heaven, may your name be kept holy. May your Kingdom come soon. May your will be done on earth, as it is in heaven. Give us today the food we need, and forgive us our sins, as we have forgiven those who sin against us. And don't let us yield to temptation, but rescue us from the evil one."

A brilliant white light from the heavens shone through the bedroom window and burst open the double panes. A fierce wind blew through the room and separated Laura from Nathan as if she was caught in floodwaters. The wind pinned her to the bed, terror-stricken and vainglorious, as she could not move, other than to squirm and fight helplessly against it.

Sit in a chair and observe her, Nathan.

"Are you sure, Lord? My hunger for her remains fervent."

There is a lesson to be taught, and you must obey my command.

Nathan complied.

A scalpel appeared in his hand. He gripped it with a practiced ease.

Look past the outer layer of her body. See what lies inside.

Nathan clutched the scalpel and peered at her chest. Her heart beat within it, and a foul energy circled around it and flowed through it.

You were born to become a healer, Nathan, and the time has come for you to remove the wickedness which abounds within the human heart.

"Should I cut it out of her with this scalpel?"

If it is the only method you know.

"Is there another way, Lord? Please help me discern."

As you look past her sensuality and overcome your desire for her flesh, you will view her as a surgery to be performed, and, because of Daisy's influence, you will also see this woman as a psychological case to be thoroughly examined, but she is much more than those things. Like you, Laura is a lost soul in need of redemption. She needs spiritual healing, and this is the path I have in store for you, Nathan. You must lay hands on Laura and heal the inner person, her spirit, which can then constrain the flesh through a newly discovered faith and a firm willingness to trust in the righteousness in Christ, and in turn, she will help others to discover their own faith in Christ and the truthful grace which follows. It will prove her purpose for living, and the enemy will hate her for it.

The demon inside Laura spoke in a guttural voice.

"I will leave her body if you will assure my freedom."

Demon, be muzzled!

The demon complied.

Her emerald eyes flickered as she struggled to break herself from the Lord's invisible restraints, the weight of the moment written across the strain of her face. She threw a harsh look at Nathan. "I'm not ready for repentance, and I do not seek your help. I am bound to Lucifer for life."

This demon has a stronghold in her heart.

Pay careful attention to what happens next.

"Yes, Lord."

I will remove my restraining influence, allowing the demon free will.

Laura got on her knees and curled her finger, beckoning Nathan to join her in the bed. "If you will lie with me tonight, I will become pregnant with your son, and our lineage will spawn the man who will arise in the last days."

"What is his name?"

"It's a name you've heard before today."

"Demon, I would like to hear it again."

"You test me at your peril, Nathan."

"Give me the name or I will call on the Lord to compel you."

"Jeremy Marsh."

Nathan pressed his back into the chair and raised his eyes.

"Are her words accurate, Lord?"

Yes.

"Is there a way I might stop this terror from happening?"

It is time for you to make a choice. Will you serve Christ even unto martyrdom, or will you serve Lucifer and gain untold power and riches in the material world? I caution against the latter, as Lucifer's time grows short.

Nathan put his face against the floor. "I repent, in the name of Jesus Christ. Please forgive my sins, Lord, as I ask Jesus to be my Savior, now and eternally. I lay my cares at the foot of the cross and surrender my will."

Laura was once again pressed flat on the bed.

"Please stop, Nathan! I beg you to stop praying to your God!"

"Lord, please work your will in Laura's life, whatever it might be now and over the course of her years. I know your will to be perfect, Lord Jesus, and I will not question it, but I also ask you to direct her back to you, Lord, as she's never really had a chance, much like myself, and I think it's time she felt your guiding hand, if you don't me saying so in prayer."

Demon, leave this woman and reside in the abyss.

The demon lifted, writhing and screaming in agony. It sailed upward to the ceiling and continued through the wall. Laura's sultry body became pale and gaunt. She burst into tears and pulled the cover over herself.

"Thank you, Lord, for removing the demon from her."

He considered for a few moments.

"Does this mean she's saved?"

I know the end from the beginning, whose heart is pure at its center, and no matter what sins they have committed or how far they have drifted from me, I know those who will come back to me in the end. She has not yet repented, but that day will soon unfold, and I will accept her pleas for forgiveness.

"What will happen in the meantime? Will her spirit remain free?"

This was a demonstration for your benefit, as you must learn how little power unclean spirits actually carry, and how they fear the name of Jesus.

"Yes, Lord. They flee in your presence."

Laura refused to repent today so another demon will enter her and bring additional demons with him, causing her flesh and her mind much misery. It will be up to you and Daisy to lead her permanently into the light.

"Do you have plans for Laura, as you do for me?"

Like you and Daisy, she is very important to my will. There is another lineage, separate from yours, which must be protected. Lives depend on it.

The light from heaven faded to darkness, leaving only the lantern to illuminate the room. Nathan stretched out on the floor, exhausted.

"Thank you for helping me, Nathan." She sat up and held the sheet against her chest. "I will not give myself over to the Lord, even with all I have seen and heard here today. I hope you can forgive my transgressions."

"Why, Laura? I cannot possibly understand."

"No one leaves the Consortium. My parents were the exception, as they lived for years in freedom, although I distinctly remember their ongoing fear of being captured and killed. It kept my mother up most nights."

"Colleen claimed to be a Christian," he said, "but she did not live the faith. She was a misguided woman who never left Lucifer's side."

"I've been bred for my role, Nathan. I was in the womb when you met my mother, and I was trained for ten years after her death. There is no other path for me, as I have bathed continually in human blood, and I am trapped by my iniquity." She reached for his hand, and he gave it to her.

She kissed his fingers with moist lips. He pulled his hand away.

"Please join me, my love. We could be happy."

"You will burn in the Lake of Fire. You know that, right?"

"Lucifer promises ascension to the spirit realm once we achieve victory. Your childlike vision of hellfire is merely a tool used to scare the gullible masses into submission. There is a spiritual battle which wages above us and about us. Our side will either succeed or die. There is no middle ground."

She looked tired and uncertain, although she claimed surety.

He wished more than anything for Daisy's presence. She knew the Bible better than anyone, even Samuel, and she would have the right words.

He missed Daisy so much it hurt. "I need you to leave my home."

"Please, Nathan, be reasonable."

"I want to help you, Laura, but you are far too wicked."

As she disappeared into the night, Nathan thought about Thomas Hannah. Perhaps he should have helped him seek God while he awaited execution. It might have made the difference in his eternity. Nathan wondered where Laura would spend hers, with Jesus or with Lucifer.

He hoped it might be the former.

The front door slammed as she exited.

Nathan descended the stairs and peered into the darkness, searching for her. A Quinby carriage had positioned itself at the end of the street. Laura rushed toward the carriage with her bundle of clothes in both arms.

The door flew open, and she climbed inside.

The carriage vanished into the night.

Catherine returned to the hospital in a listless and inanimate condition. Her father claimed she could no longer live outside the confines of the hospital, and she was now Nathan's ward to do with as he pleased. Although she possessed a singular talent for charming the drawing rooms of the Big Cinch, her unwillingness to remain in the diplomatic role for long had been a problem all her life, and now, with Belmont's plans in full motion, he could afford no weak links or faulty cogs in his business machinery.

"I stayed up late last night in debate about the proper course of action, and I've ended our relationship." He hesitated. "My daughter has always acted like an orphan, so now is her chance to become one."

"You can't mean it, John. She's your little girl."

Belmont gazed with sad eyes at Catherine on the bed. "She once was a beautiful portrait who men desired, but now she's an expressionless frame."

"How will you cope without her in your life?"

"Same as I've always done. I will endeavor to make this hospital shine like a new penny." He surveyed the length and the breadth of the main hall. "Yes, this is my new offspring, and it will become the premier destination for the world's elite, starting with the Big Cinch." He gestured at the line of beds. "Right now, our facility is small and only holds a few patients at once, but soon, these walls will tumble like the walls of Jericho, and I will rush up the ramp of bricks, ready to lay siege to all who get in my path." His voice lowered an octave. "I will burn the barrels of wheat as I consume all."

"There you go again, John, twisting God's Word to support your sin."

Belmont eyed Nathan. "It's a pity your encounter with Laura Collins did not go as planned. You should know she suffered for her failure."

"You admit to membership in her order?"

Belmont smiled as he nodded. "I am a high priest, my boy."

Nathan could no longer contain his disgust. "I knew you to be a greedy and envious man, but not one given over to evil." He looked at Catherine on her bed. Her face was blank as she stared at the floor in front of her. "She will be much safer outside of your den of vipers, where she was no doubt plagued by demons." His eyes grew moist as he realized his part in sending her into such a ghastly environment. It was done out of spite and a desire to be free of his feelings for her, so he might pursue something fine with Daisy.

Belmont gave his ex-son-in-law a look of contempt.

"Think what you will of us. It makes no difference to our plans."

His boots spun on their heels. He marched toward the door.

Nathan called to him. "I will endeavor to save your little girl once again."

Belmont wheeled. "At one time, I might have cared for such a project, but now you have bigger fish to catch." He looked at the others. "I want this group shipshape and ready to perform on command. There will be a large audience at the auditorium, and I want them dazzled by the glory of your performance. Nothing less will suffice, and failure will not end well for you."

"Is that a threat to my life?"

"Call it what you will, but our order only allows so many chances."

He threw a sadistic grin at Nathan. "Laura has now failed us once, and the pain she received was commensurate with our level of disappointment."

"As your frustration grows?"

"Her level of regret will follow. Do I make myself clear?"

"Crystal."

"Good." Belmont flung open the door and abruptly exited.

Once more given over to exhaustion, Nathan adjourned to his office, where he prayed for forgiveness and guidance. He called out to God and asked Him to work in Catherine's life. After he received no reply, he descended the stairs and approached Catherine, who seemed catatonic.

Nathan sat beside her on the bed and patted her leg. "Honey, I know you are in there somewhere, waiting for deliverance from the demons who inhabit your flesh and control your behavior. If you'll call out to Jesus in repentance as I have done, He will heal your pain, and the demons will flee."

Her pupils were black as midnight. "I cannot see you, Nathan, as my sight has been taken from me by one of my spirits, but I have gained a greater perspective on your future in our order, and I long for the day when you have murdered Sheila, because next you will turn to *my* death, as your spree inches ever nearer to your beloved Daisy, who will leap at your command from the high ledge in the woods. Each of us will leave this realm at your behest and you will be crowned prince of the St. Louis order, taking my father's place as high priest." She placed her hand over Nathan's and smiled. "His torment will be prolonged and unspeakable."

"We were once in love, honey. Please come back to me."

Catherine squeezed his flesh. "I loved you more than my own life, even as a young, naive girl. After the death of your mother, I knew you needed a worthy replacement, and I strove to become *her* for you, Nathan."

"I know you did, and I am grateful for it."

She removed her hand. "No one can replace June."

"I didn't understand that for many years, but now I do."

"Even while you lived with Aunt Joy, there was a part of you which judged me unacceptable. I felt it then and I feel it now." Her voice cracked as she fought the urge to cry. "I hoped we might venture out west, far away from the confines of St. Louis and the many restrictions it placed on our love, but it was not to be, and you left me for college back east."

Nathan rubbed her back, aware the demons would not enjoy his touch. She stiffened, and her head swiveled quickly as she pushed near to his face.

"Do *not* do that again, Nathan, or you will be torn to shreds."

He instinctively sprang from the bed and paced in front of her.

The leader of her demon pack had addressed him.

Could Nathan chance a physical encounter? Unclean spirits were known to provide strength above normal human levels, and Nathan might not survive a head wound, the type which she had suffered at Martin's hand.

He must bypass the spirits and reach his best friend.

"I never intended to hurt you, Catherine."

She turned to him, and her sinister eyes softened. "Do you recall our stroll along Aunt Joy's lane? I asked you never to leave me alone."

"Which I did." He took a heavy breath and exhaled. "I'm so sorry."

Tears coursed down her cheeks, and she swiped at them.

"I hated myself and wanted to die. A gambler visited my father on some business, which was unknown to me. He called on me without my father's permission, which I allowed because I was so distraught in your absence." She clutched the sheets. "Your love made me whole, and your abandonment destroyed my will to live, which I have never fully regained, even while we were married and we had three children. I knew eventually you would realize my lack of worth and decide to leave us for western canyons and open skies."

"Then we lost Annie and our boys," he said sadly.

"There was no reason for you to stay with me. All was lost."

He leaned over and wrapped his arms around her. "I would have stayed with you, and in fact, when you fell into a debilitating stupor of depression, I sought the help of every neurologist in the state and even reached out to Daisy's mentor, Charcot, in Paris. I would have done anything for you."

Her eyes had been shut in gentle remembrance.

They opened and grew red hot.

"You would control my spirits then, as you would control them now!"

She broke free from his embrace and stood. Her fists grabbed him with surprising strength, and she threw him down to the oak floor. His body tumbled and rolled as if made of cloth and cotton, and his head turned just before impact, saving his face from serious damage. He quickly stood.

Catherine circled him like a wolf after prey, her inflamed eyes on him.

He held out a palm. "I have loved you since the first moment we met at my mother's funeral. You are the best friend I've ever had, and my first love. As Sheila mentioned earlier, those are hard to get over, and we've known great hardships together, so it's even more problematic to express how much we mean to one another, but I love you, honey, and I always will."

"Don't mention that harlot's name to me, Nathan, or I will rip the flesh from your bones." The reddish mist entered the hall, violently impelled by a strong wind which swept it along the floor so it surrounded Nathan's body. "You love the imbecile, Daisy Lawrence, so do not speak to me of past love which was lost to the hands of time, or other poetic nonsense."

Once again, Nathan was tested, and once more he dropped to his knees in supplication to the Lord and prayed for deliverance from the Most High.

"Dear Jesus, I cannot defeat the legion of demons which inhabit this woman, no matter how much I might wish to save her, the mother of my children and my best friend since childhood. Please help me!"

Your faith is weak, Nathan, and that is why you fail.

"I want to believe you, Lord, but I have not seen enough."

Recall what happened at your home.

"I am too weak and ineffective to defeat such a colossus."

Catherine drew next to him in the mist.

"You dare to call your first love a monster?"

The voice of God rang through the rafters, and the building quaked.

"I tell you the truth, if you had faith even as small as a mustard seed, you could say to this mountain, 'Move from here to there,' and it would move. Nothing would be impossible." Jesus allowed His words a moment to register in Nathan's mind. "This is the wisdom I shared with my apostles."

Catherine's body crumpled to the floor, and the mist dissipated.

She panted with unmerciful force. Nathan feared for her heart.

"What is your name, demon?" asked Jesus from the rafters.

Catherine's eyes raised. "Legion, for we are many."

"You will leave this woman at my command."

"Please, Lord Jesus, do not send us to the abyss."

"Where would you have me send you?"

Catherine searched the room. "These hysterics are like pigs."

Nathan looked to the ceiling. "Please, Lord. Save them."

"You believe no one cares about these people, but Nathan cares a great deal for them, and he is your chosen one, the man you have picked to lead your army of doom into the next century. You have surely miscalculated in your arrogance and incompetence. Your plans will be pushed further into the future when my restraining influence has been removed due to apathy."

"Until then?"

"Leave Catherine Belmont and reside in the abyss."

The spirits writhed and screamed and sailed through the wall on the left side of the building, leaving Catherine's meek form in a ball at Nathan's feet.

He kneeled and laid hands on her in prayer and supplication to the Lord. "This is my former wife and the mother of our three children. I ask you to forgive her sins, dear Lord, in the name of Jesus Christ, who shed His blood on the cross for our sins, so we might be free. Your yoke is light, Lord, and we sing praises to your holy name day and night, as you are worthy, worthy, worthy, and we long to know the glory of your presence eternally."

Her body shook, and she cried out to God as she rose to her knees.

"I repent of my sins in the name of Jesus, and I accept the free gift of salvation. Please forgive my sins, Lord, and work your perfect will in my life. If you wish me to die right here and now, then there will be good in it."

Nathan gently rubbed her back. "Honey, he wants you to *live*, not die."

She burst into tears and fell into Nathan's arms.

He gathered the patients to hold her as she experienced a lifetime of suppressed emotions fully and without restraint. The pain left her body, and she received a word from the Lord, which prompted her to recite Psalm 34:10-18. Sheila opened her Bible to the correct page and handed it to Catherine, who read aloud. "Even strong young lions sometimes go hungry, but those who trust in the Lord will lack no good thing. Come, my children, and listen to me, and I will teach you to fear the Lord. Does anyone want to live a life that is long and prosperous? Then keep your tongue from speaking evil and your lips from telling lies! Turn away from evil and do good. Search for peace, and work to maintain it. The eyes of the Lord watch over those who do right; his ears are open to their cries for help. But the Lord turns his face against those who do evil; he will erase their memory from the earth. The Lord hears his people when they call to him for help. He rescues them from all their troubles. The Lord is close to the brokenhearted; he rescues those whose spirits are crushed." Catherine handed the Bible to Sheila.

Sheila smiled. "Jesus Christ makes all things possible."

She shed tears of joy and then recited verses 19-22.

"The righteous person faces many troubles, but the Lord comes to the rescue each time. For the Lord protects the bones of the righteous; not one of them is broken! Calamity will surely destroy the wicked, and those who hate the righteous will be punished. But the Lord will redeem those who serve him. No one who takes refuge in him will be condemned."

They held hands and moved around the room in a circular motion.

The group sang *Hallelujah! Hallelujah! Hallelujah!*

They stood still and offered a solemn prayer of thanksgiving.

Nathan was gladdened to provide care for his friends in need. He gave thanks to God for giving him such noble responsibilities. He prayed for strength, which was sure to be needed in the following days and weeks.

Dear Lord, Catherine's earthly father may consider her an orphan, but her heavenly Father will never forsake her in this life or the next. For this and your many other blessings, dear Jesus, we are most grateful. Amen.

In the days which followed her deliverance, Catherine took over some of Daisy's administrative duties, and Nathan watched her from a distance, pleased with her efficiency in carrying out her duties. Like Daisy, she'd found her calling in helping at the hospital and working with damaged people.

James said she needed a gesture of encouragement, and Nathan agreed it might help solidify her feelings of belonging to God and to the makeshift family which had formed within the hospital walls, a place once cold as ice.

He ushered her into Daisy's office and offered the space to her.

Catherine smiled at him. "This room belongs to Daisy in her pursuit of God's will. It is not my place to take it from her, nor is it yours."

"I've already coordinated the removal of Daisy's office furniture and have instructed the staff to put several boxes in the corner."

She placed her hand on his shoulder and shook her head.

"I heard from the Most High last night in a dream. He told me to dissuade you from this course of action. This is not meant to be a storage room, but a place where the Lord's work is undertaken."

Nathan stopped the men. "Perhaps you're right."

"Go to her, Nathan. I've known you since childhood and I've never seen you so taken with another human being. You two are passionately in love."

"I will think about what you said." He sat on a box and looked at her. The thing that stuck in his mind lately was her growing relationship with the Lord. She had always moved too fast for others to keep up, but her prayer life and her Bible study had already outclassed his own. "I do love her, Catherine. I'm sorry I never showed you a proper love, the kind you deserved. I was a man in search of an identity, unknown to myself, unaware of my place in the world, and unwilling to become vulnerable to you."

She squeezed his hand. "I know your painful search all too well because I shared it. When we were younger, I said we had only known pain and death, as if we were cursed, but now you've found the answer to your lonely riddle in Daisy Lawrence, and I suspect you are her answer as well. Do whatever it takes to win back her trust. It's all I ask of you."

He nodded, and she hugged him tightly.

"Go and make the world a better place." She pulled away, smiling, still holding onto his arms. "Don't forget to pray for Samuel, who took so much from you as a boy. If you continue to curse him, even when you are alone and you think no one can see your behavior, you'll only curse yourself. As Jesus instructed, we must pray for those who have hurt us. They need prayers much more than we do and usually have no one praying for them."

He placed his hands on his knees and sighed. "You're a good woman, Catherine, deep inside your heart where it counts the most, and you'll soon make a husband very happy. The Lord will not see you alone for long."

She contemplated his statement. "It's up to the Most High to decide my fate. He is the best matchmaker, and His will is perfect."

"In all things," Nathan said.

She gently shoved him. "Go and perform His will today."

Daisy browsed through a department store, hoping to find something for Pierre. She wanted to make amends once she went home.

Two women walked by who gossiped about their husbands.

Their conversation shifted to the event at the Expo. The women planned to leave their husbands behind and watch the show without them.

It would be quite adventurous, but they mustn't get caught.

Daisy raised her eyebrows as she scanned a rack of men's suits. She chuckled at what masqueraded as a scandal among some people. If those women knew what actually occurred, the beat of their hearts would cease.

A glass vase fell from a careless grip and broke into pieces on the floor.

Eager to please the store owner, a young clerk approached and told the woman to pay for the item. She became loud and argued in her defense. The aisles were too narrow to traverse without difficulty, and the table holding the vase was uneven and unstable, much like the clerk's position if he didn't learn his place. The woman with jet black hair and emerald green eyes slid past the outraged woman and stood before Daisy with crossed arms.

Daisy found a flight of stairs and followed it to the basement.

She stood in the dark and tried to keep hyperventilation at bay.

Daisy fell to her knees as a choking sensation overwhelmed her and a reddish mist filled the room. She silently prayed to God for help.

The room filled with light, and the mist vanished.

A mighty angel appeared to her and spoke softly and kindly.

"You will remain in St. Louis until instructed otherwise by the Lord."

Her breaths normalized. "I have my free will."

The angel nodded his agreement. "Yes, and you will use it."

"Then why must I stay here?"

"Information awaits, which will influence your decision."

"To what end?"

"Whether to stay or leave this realm. Once done, Daisy, it cannot be undone. Keep it in mind, the next time you consider flinging your helpless body from atop Big Rock. Your sister does not lie in wait at the bottom."

The basement fell dark again.

Daisy made her way upstairs and out of the store.

Ahead of her, near the intersection, men shoved the seductive woman into a black Quinby carriage. Daisy turned to her right as the carriage sped away and eyed three fliers for the show at the Expo. She took one and studied it and considered it heavenly confirmation. She would see Nathan one last time, if for no other reason than to watch his presentation and pray for a brief mention of her work. Afterward, her family would share a Thanksgiving meal at her father's hotel. Then she would accompany Pierre home to Pollard, where a final choice would be made at her spot along the Missouri River. She would make a list of reasons to stay and also reasons to leave. This fallen realm had placed a stony weight upon her shoulders since childhood, and it was high time she removed it. The world was hard and lovely and altogether terrible. *To be or not to be* was asked by the most famous playwright in history. It was an unserious line about a serious question.

Is this life worth seeing through to the end?

She looked about the intersection, expecting a cadre of supercilious glances and mirthful sneers, but surprisingly found only strangers with little regard for her antics or her problems. Daisy marched forward in a slight huff, knowing one thing for certain: she had read far too much Shakespeare in college, and her mind fell to melodrama at every opportunity.

THIRTY-FIVE

Daisy arrived at Pierre's hotel with little right to be dismal, as Thanksgiving was around the corner and next would come Christmas, the most jolly season of them all. Her mind fell into a fog as she searched about for a chair amid a melee of cheerful guests and slap happy visitors. Brenda appeared in the doorway, a gentlewoman born and a bestower of snide tidings, her cheeks aglow with a joyful merriment at Daisy's loveless expense, and her eyes sparkling with a severity of gladness. She took off her coat and led Daisy to satin backed settees which had arranged themselves nicely about a mahogany table. She removed her white leather gloves, kept pristine for libertine occasions apart from Dan and the children. The wind was in her trees, and her birds chirped with lofty delight.

"I believe our princely father will be late," said Brenda with a grin.

"I told Nathan the night we met, they were both disasters."

Brenda folded her gloves in her lap. "Pity you let him go."

"Father?" Daisy smirked at her sister.

"Don't be a daft fool. You know exactly of whom I refer."

Pierre descended the steps. He appeared cranky and hungover.

Brenda arose. "It's about time, Father. We've been here for hours."

Daisy snorted and thumbed at Brenda. "She arrived minutes ago."

"Figures," said Pierre with a frown. "Always the dramatist."

"I learned my art from the two of you," said Brenda haughtily.

Pierre plopped into the chair opposite them. "It's a wonder Daisy made it here at all," he said. "I've never seen a more lost child in all my days."

Daisy took a deep breath and asked Jesus for help.

"I will have you know the Lord guides my every step."

"Did he tell you to run off your last chance at marriage?"

She sat on the edge of the chair, her posture straight. "You two treat me like a child, and I will tell you in no uncertain terms what I think of your behavior." Daisy caught her breath. "What happened to Rose and Patrice was *not* my fault, and I will no longer accept the blame or your criticisms."

"I merely looked out for you as a proxy for our mother," said Brenda defensively. "Patrice was difficult at best, and I took the full brunt of her depression and her rages before you came of age."

Pierre held up his hand as a peace offering. "Henry Hayes was nothing but an itinerant painter, and I should have chased him from our door from the start. Instead, I allowed him to destroy the rest of our lives."

"Well, Father, perhaps it's time to cease your consumption of alcohol, which clouds your painful memories and numbs your emotions."

Daisy paused.

"Let's face it. Patrice wasn't worth your love."

He looked about for a waiter and then snapped his fingers.

She quickly kneeled in front of him and gazed softly into his eyes.

"Brenda and I are worth it, Father, and we have always loved you. I'm sorry you lost your favorite little girl, your Wild Forest Rose, but we are standing here right now as your living children. Will you *please* love us?"

His arms fell to his sides in surrender, and his eyes grew misty.

"For once, she has made a bit of sense," said Brenda, kneeling beside Daisy. "We love you and we always will. Won't you give us a chance?"

"Oh, *ma chéri*," he said to Daisy, "it is you who are the wild one. Yes, I loved Rose with all my heart, and it broke me to lose her, but you are the one who gave me the most hope. As much as I wanted you to stay along the banks of the Missouri, I knew you must be set free in your Paris university."

He looked at Brenda apologetically and placed his palm against her cheek. "I love you too, my dear, so don't you worry. However, I always knew you would marry a nice but dull man and you would live a nice life in a private place as a woman of means and privilege."

"I have certainly done so."

"Yes, and you've made this old man proud."

His tender eyes fell on Daisy. "This one filled me with aspirations for a better world. She is the daughter most like me, as she has the intelligence and the empathy to make great things happen." He stroked her hair. "I lacked the courage of conviction and the determination to succeed, which you have in droves, and that makes you my wild one, even more so than Rose, who threw away her life at a young and tender age."

Daisy wrapped her arms around Pierre and spoke softly to him. "Thank you, Father, for releasing the pain I've kept inside since their deaths."

"You're welcome, *ma chéri*."

He pulled Brenda into their circle and hugged them both tightly.

"I love each of you with all my heart and soul.

With that, he gently shoved them aside and beamed.

"Now, let's go to the Expo. I need a glass of champagne."

Daisy and Brenda exchanged glances and then laughed in unison.

Pierre strode through the hotel's entrance and to the street.

They called after their grumpy and disheveled father.

"Don't leave us behind!"

When they arrived at the Expo, Brenda and Pierre continued to their seats in the auditorium. Daisy looked about for Nathan in the lobby, but saw only patrons with the glitter of expectation in their eyes. She turned toward an usher who smiled and extended his hand. He offered her a program.

"She is with us."

Daisy wheeled, and her eyes fell on the woman with jet black hair and emerald eyes. "You have no right to be here," said Daisy defiantly.

"It's time we were formally introduced. I am Laura Collins."

Another woman stood beside Laura in a dress which fit poorly and appeared to be of lessor quality than most. Laura whispered into the other woman's ear and pointed to a door to their right. Her flickering green eyes watched the woman leave, and then she smiled at Daisy with a surety which startled her. "That is Joanna Sinclair, an old friend of Nathan's."

"The one who cut Sheila," said Daisy decisively.

"I know nothing of the sort," Laura said. "What I do know is you must come with us to the balcony, where we will watch the performance together in our private box. It will be a most comfortable place for you to fail."

Daisy gasped. "In what manner shall I fail tonight?"

"Nathan came ever so close to joining our order while we conversed in his bedroom. He was most tempted, even more so than our leadership predicted, and when he gives himself over to greed tonight, I will take him from you with the ease of a feather against a chin." Her voice fell low and guttural. "I will have my way, as I am a most expectant lover."

Daisy took a step backward, as she recognized the voice of Lucifer who spoke through Laura. "You have given yourself to the dark side, and you will pay dearly for your rebellion. What happens to me doesn't much matter, but sometime far in the future, you will regret what you do here tonight."

"I will celebrate your demise as your blood flows to the floor."

A shadow descended over Daisy, and a reddish mist surrounded her, claiming her will for its own. Laura held out her hand, and Daisy took it, unable to stop herself. "We will take our leave for the balcony now, where Joanna awaits with bated breath. After the performance, I will go to Nathan, and we will make love in his home, which will soon become *my* home, and will never become *your* home, and Joanna will finish the job left by our departed Rosemarie. Her fangs will sink into your neck, and your blood will taste sweet, and your pallid body will be thrown over your ledge."

Daisy wanted to pray, but the words would not form in her mind.

She had succumbed to Lucifer's charms in John's billiard room.

Was she forever claimed by the dark side that night?

Laura led her upstairs to a private box and placed her snugly in between herself and Joanna, who leaned over and whispered unkind things into her ear. Joanna's lips gave bitter curses and made vile threats of a cruel death.

The music began, but the lights remained bright. Perhaps there was still an opportunity to escape. Daisy spotted her father and sister below in the audience. They looked about for her with concerned faces.

Laura gestured toward the floor and gave her a victorious sneer.

"If you get away from us, we will murder them tonight."

Daisy clenched her jaw and flared her nostrils.

"You are possessed with demons. Does it make you feel powerful?"

Laura's eyebrows arched as she pondered the question.

"How curious you might ask such a thing, but yes, it quite does."

Daisy recalled Frank Kaneski and the wicked Rosemarie Bello in Vienna. She thought about Jean-Martin's reaction to the rumors spread about her, how quickly he shunned her from La Salpêtrière, even though he loved her. Daisy recalled her depression while she traversed the ocean, how in her room she alternated between bouts of seasickness and mournful weeping.

She thought of her despair at returning to work at Pierre's winery.

Daisy smiled at the portrait of Nathan at Union Depot and how he seemed larger than life. Although he was gallingly inebriated, she sensed a unique quality about him. He was different from other men, kinder, more insightful, and his intuition was sharp as a tack. If they were to marry, he would make her the happiest woman alive. Daisy placed her hand over her mouth and held back the tears. She stared at the exit and wanted to run.

Her life had taken so many wrong turns.

How did she end up in this wretched situation?

Samuel arrived with Nurse Pratt, and they sat behind Pierre and Brenda.

They looked about for her as the lights dimmed and the music gained momentum. Daisy surrendered to the reality of imminent death.

"Will you attempt to run?" asked Laura.

Daisy shook her head. "No."

Joanna patted her leg. "I will enjoy ripping you to shreds."

"I'm sure you will." Daisy grew frustrated by the wait.

She turned to Joanna. "Why don't you simply get on with it?"

"You seem ready to die."

Daisy nodded.

"I have been for some time, so do it *now*."

Joanna gauged the size of the audience.

"There are far too many people for such a vulgar display."

Daisy pressed her back into her chair. "Then you are weak."

Joanna's fangs appeared. She leaned over to Daisy and sniffed her neck, aware of her ability to murder her right *there* and right *now*, and the depth of the temptation almost drove her to act, but Laura whispered to Joanna, reminding her to keep her composure, as this was Laura's affair, and she would decide who must die and at what juncture it would occur.

Joanna settled into her chair. "As you wish."

The curtain rose to reveal Nathan on the stage with Heinrich Besseler, who cried about his deceased family. Nathan followed the German man and asked him harsh questions and used Daisy's railroad tuning fork to mesmerize him. Heinrich moved close to the edge of the stage, and Daisy sat up straight. She calculated the distance to the floor below.

How could Sheila allow such a horrendous display?

Nathan next introduced James Clifton to the audience as a paranoid and delusional patient who displayed somatic symptoms such as paralysis. He placed James in front of a window frame, which was used as a prop, and asked the audience to observe and note each nuance and subtlety of the patient's hysteria. Then Nathan brought Shirley to the stage on a bed and explained her somatic experience of suffocation. Shirley gurgled as if someone stood over her and squeezed her neck with both hands. Her eyes bulged like a madwoman, and she periodically called out for her blanket.

Nathan rolled Shirley's bed off the stage.

Ida Barnes was instructed to sit on a stool, which she did, but only for a few seconds, and then she roamed about and moved from object to object.

When asked to speak, Ida displayed such a high level of anxiety, many audience members squirmed and asked Nathan to send her away.

Ed Wilson wept for his son and then crumpled onto the floor in a convulsive heap. Nurses and orderlies rushed to his aid while the audience looked on in fascination. Susanna Hutchinson danced about the stage like a ballerina while her husband, John, spoke in a bizarre language.

The patients drank wine and fell about like drunkards.

"I hope you die a ghastly death," Daisy said. "This is a grim spectacle."

"Ah, not such a Christian woman, after all. Where are your manners, Daisy?" Laura grinned. "Oh, that's right, you were raised without them."

Joanna pointed at Pierre. "Your father enjoys their tomfoolery."

Laura nodded her agreement. "It's not everyday someone else is laughed at for being a lush, and it must be refreshing to witness balance restored."

Nathan told the audience he could make the patients do anything he chose, as long as their bodies could withstand it. He asked for requests, and people shouted for the patients to dance or to hop or to crumple themselves into a ball. Someone brought a bicycle onto the stage, and the audience shouted for Heinrich to ride it, which he did while sobbing to the audience.

Had Daisy ever known Nathan at all?

Each of their lives had finally hit rock bottom. She felt like a fool for embracing her fears over their love, and for leaving him to his strong vices.

At least Nathan took risks. Daisy could not say the same.

She peeked at Laura and measured her attentiveness.

Laura's skin had grown anaemic, and her hands quavered.

Joanna sniffed the air. "Something has changed."

At intermission, ample wreaths of cigar smoke filtered to the stage as Nathan took a breath and looked upon the fevered crowd who half fawned, half sneered, and half applauded. The curtain fell, smothering the grandeur of the moment, and Nathan quickly changed clothes backstage. His door remained open to smiling faces and the tempered fullness of time.

Special Agent Fremont Lacy wafted past as a prairie cloud of dust.

Nathan stuck his head into the hallway like a cat afraid of a meaner and more powerful mouse. Agent Lacy threw Nathan a sharp wink and then rounded the corner. Nathan inquired about the attendance of the president.

When no issue reached his ears, he considered the innumerable changes since his first glimpse of Daisy. The night he met her, he was a drunken recluse, and another week in such a condition would have ended his days.

Nathan sat in a wooden chair and stared blankly at the hallway.

People rushed past his dressing room on their way to unknown but seemingly important destinations, their heads filled with fiery ambition, their feet bound to better their condition, no matter the personal cost.

A portrait of the unrepentant Thomas Hannah, who dangled and tugged at the end of a rope, once more haunted him. He should have led the murderer to God, but instead Nathan watched his existence end in defiance, with the full knowledge his name would go missing from the Book of Life.

It was one more mistake in a lifetime filled with them.

"Penny for your thoughts?"

Laura's eyes fell over Nathan like a wintry twilight as she struggled to stand tall before him. Her skin was ashen, and her form was fragile.

He offered her his seat, which she took.

"Thank you." She fanned her face. "A pall has come over me."

"Where were you just now?"

"In a private box with Daisy and Joanna. I was stalwart for my task and reasonably vigorous, which has been a problem of late, but then the air about me shifted, and I became afflicted by the most peculiar infirmity. "

She confused him. "I thought Daisy went home to Pollard."

Laura shook her head. "We will not allow her departure."

Nathan grabbed Laura's shoulders. "What will you do with her?"

"Joanna intends to finish what Rosemarie began in Vienna."

He raised his hand to strike hard against Laura's face, and she turned in terror and trembling, as if the force of his blow might kill her.

His hands fell to his sides. Her imperfections grew like a cancer.

"What's happened to you?" He leaned against the counter.

"I work for the order." She seemed shaken by the question.

He looked up at her as he put on his shoes, right, then left.

"No, ever since God called the demon out of your body, you've seemed pale and bony and defective, like you've contracted a rare disease. Is there something I should know about the condition of your health?"

She boldly threw up her chin.

"Your question tells me you comprehend nothing."

"Tell me."

"They beat me with a whip, one very similar to yours, in fact, after I returned to John Belmont's estate. As I mentioned, the leather strap is preferable to gashes across my flesh as I gaze at the glint of a knife."

"There was a threat of murder?"

She nodded.

"I've failed twice, and now I am here to try a third time. If I cannot turn you this evening, then I will be allowed no more opportunities."

Nathan half-turned and then hesitated. "We haven't spoken since you rushed out of my house. How did you fail a second time?"

"I followed Daisy to a department store."

"Bell's?"

"Yes, that's the one. There was a commotion after a spoiled woman dropped an expensive vase, or what passes for one in this part of America."

"Did you speak to Daisy?"

"I confronted her in silence with the intention of dissuading her from staying in your life or St. Louis for that matter, but I never got the chance to have a word with her in such a melee of activity, and then she ran downstairs into the basement, where yet another light from your god shined on her."

"You saw the light?"

"Under the door, which she had slammed in my face."

"Good for her," said Nathan with a proud smile.

"It was a most unfortunate turn, as my handlers beat me severely."

He considered for several moments.

"Would you like me to examine your wounds?"

Her eyes moistened, and she swiped tears from her eyes.

"You are most kind, but no, I have been treated by excellent staff."

He took a sober breath and exhaled. The Consortium would have the best available physicians on the payroll. He ran through a list of names.

He gave up his inquiry with a sympathetic shrug.

"I have something special planned for the second half of the show, which might interest you. I will take the hysterics to a different place."

She slipped from the chair and kneeled in front of him.

"Please, Nathan, give yourself over to evil so we might be one."

"With Lucifer?"

She kissed his fingers and leaned against him. "Yes."

"I will not forget my love of Christ or of Daisy Lawrence."

He paused.

"Kill us both if you must, but we will not recant our faith."

"You will die for your god?"

He stroked her hair. "I will."

She looked about the room with restless eyes. There was conflict within her, a rage which emanated from a lifetime spent in torment, but also a yearning for the quietude of peace and the joyful contentment of love and the possibility of trust in the righteousness of Christ. She squeezed his hand and leaned into him and tugged him downward to the floor to sit beside her one last time. He complied with the simplicity of her need. She was a baby in the womb when he met Colleen, and he was merely a fifteen-year-old boy, and neither had any real understanding of the brutality which this fallen realm presented, the delusion most often found in the day rooms of an asylum where test subjects were poked and prodded, but just as clearly detected in the broader world where no one spoke of its lunacy, the rush to pride and its accompanying sins scaling the eyes of the blind masses.

As Nathan sat beside Laura and held her tightly, he hoped the push of the blade would be fast and clinical shock might obstruct her tribulation.

He wiped her cheeks and kissed her forehead.

There was a glimmer of sweetness which somehow remained locked within a shadowy recess, a pocket left only for her, and a survival mechanism Nathan knew all too well. Her body shook gently as she wept against his neck and his hand cradled her head. She clutched his shirt and moaned in agony, and he kicked the door closed with a *thud*. This moment was meant only for them, two lost and broken souls who had traveled similar paths.

He was blessed by the love of Christ, while Laura would be executed.

At the end of the Millennial Reign, she would know the second death.

Her sobs calmed. "You'll never turn?"

"I'm eternally committed to Jesus Christ."

Laura tilted her head backward and revealed herself fully to him. "I was thrown into an unspeakable ordeal as a young girl, which I thought I could not withstand. Every week, men and women were paraded in front of me, and I bathed in the freshness of their blood. This went on for the entire year, and there were at least four hundred in that time, possibly four thousand, over the course of my ten-year training regiment." Her voice cracked. "I struggled to hang on each day as the order said horrific things to me and taught me to think like a murderer or an object of sexual lust." She glanced at him, and he smiled at her for encouragement. "I was desperate to endure, and the Consortium gave me the best opportunity for longevity, so I absorbed their plans and made them my own." She took a sad breath and exhaled. "Now I no longer think or feel like a human woman."

Laura clutched his arms. "Nathan, I think I have lost my mind, and I'll die a disagreeable death." She buried her head in his chest. "I *see* the knife."

"If you're open to it now," he said in a whisper, "there's a path to safety in the arms of Jesus Christ, who died on the cross for your sins."

"I'll never know security again," she said. "Once I fail them tonight, there will be no more chances, and at that point, my fate will be sealed."

"The Lord will cover you with His grace if you work His will."

"I've seen too much, Nathan. I've *done* too much."

Her story was beyond reason or any sense of acceptability. Nathan was a new Christian with a limited understanding. He looked about the room, aware for the first time how small it was and how tightly they held one another in the confined space. There was a strange bond which had formed between them since her arrival, one not of love, but primeval pain, the knowledge of the irrecoverable disembowelment of youth, the replacement of optimism and hope and the desire for agape love with greed and wrath.

He would try to help her, but he was one man, and they were feral.

Her moist eyes met his, and she wiped the tears from his cheeks.

Laura softly kissed his lips. "I so badly wanted you to love me."

He stroked her hair. "You desperately need love, and you will have it, but first you must give yourself over to Christ and know *His* love. Only then will you know genuine healing and, once restored, God will lead the right man into your life, and you will marry him and you will raise a family together."

She stiffened.

He hadn't meant to hurt her. "What's wrong?"

She sat up straight and swiped the tears from her eyes.

"I must go."

Laura stood. She seemed stronger, but disoriented.

He grabbed her elbow. "Please repent. I beg you."

Her eyes closed, and her hand steadied herself against him.

"Please don't leave. I *do* love you, Laura, but as a younger sister."

Laura steeled herself and gave him a determined look.

"Once Daisy has been eliminated, perhaps your mind will change."

She pushed past him and left the room.

He stuck his head through the doorway, but she was gone.

After intermission, Nathan asked the audience if they had enjoyed the parlor tricks. The audience clapped and hollered and issued demands for more.

"The second half of the show will differ from the first."

Someone yelled from the audience. "Don't change what works!"

Nathan sat on a stool and spoke loudly, his voice reaching the back of the room. "I've been unhappy for a very long time."

He had loved his three wonderful children, and the pain of his wife's departure after the suddenness of their deaths almost destroyed him.

Catherine resurfaced after ten years, beaten almost to death.

Her father, John Belmont, asked Nathan to restore her health and the hysteric patients to a functional state. After Catherine healed, she left the hospital for a triumphant return to the social circuit, and Belmont turned his attention to the hysterics, demanding Nathan teach them tricks through mesmerism. He would take them to various cities so the public could witness the power of hypnosis and the competency of Belmont Hospital.

To keep his position, Nathan had agreed to the wicked plan.

Daisy grew incensed. She shifted heavily in her seat.

Nathan had omitted her groundbreaking methods and glossed over her participation as the resident psychologist at Belmont Hospital.

"The work was difficult, and I was often exhausted, but I reminded himself not to expect earthly rewards for my tireless efforts."

Daisy called out from her seat. "Tireless efforts?"

Joanna's head whipped around, and her body stiffened.

"Do not make a scene in hopes of escape."

Her voice carried a tilt of desperation.

Nathan ceased his talk. His eyes squinted in her direction.

"Do you have something to offer, Miss Lawrence?"

She glanced at Laura, who slumped feebly into her chair since her discourse with Nathan. Few words had been said upon her return.

Daisy stood and pointed sharply at the stage. "What about the many late nights I spent with the patients while you couldn't be bothered?"

Joanna looked about nervously, as if she expected someone in authority to step into the scene and deliver an outcome. She sneered at Laura.

"This is *your* project. I am merely along for support."

"I am aware." Laura struggled to sit up straight.

Her words were slow and her voice irregular.

"What is wrong with you? Have you no desire for Lucifer?"

Daisy's chin was on one shoulder and then the other as she watched the two women glare at one another and waited for someone from behind her to step forward with a weapon and make dire threats. When no one appeared, she wheeled and descended the stairs as speedily as her feet would carry her and made her way through the double doors into the lower level of the grand auditorium. She marched up the aisle, feeling bitter and hurt.

Her feet stopped. She gave him a resigned look.

"You think me a monster, Miss Lawrence?"

The audience murmured at the peculiar turn of events.

She turned and gestured at Joanna and Laura in the box.

"I marvel at how stricken Laura suddenly appears. It's as if she now suffers from an undiagnosed malady. I am further surprised at how unsure of herself Joanna seems, as if she is unaware of her beastly capabilities or perhaps she questions if she might dare use them in such a public setting."

She threw a harsh look at him. "Have you become their leader?"

Nathan smiled. "Let's find out, shall we?"

He ushered James onto the stage and asked him to sit on a stool.

"Nathan, please stop your abuse of these patients."

He nodded.

"One moment, madam."

Nathan addressed the audience. "You will now see something different."

He turned toward James, who came alive on stage and behaved normally. "You fine folks might wonder why my demeanor has suddenly changed for the better. Well, there's only one reason, and it's the two people who stand before us, along with the love and grace of Jesus Christ."

James paused.

"I grew up in a wealthy family on Fifth Avenue in New York, but because I would not follow in my father's footsteps as a railroad speculator, he wanted me out of his home. I left his fortune behind and ventured out west for adventure. I worked on the Central railroad line for a time and eventually ended up in St. Louis, where I took a job at John Belmont's cotton press by the river. Over time, I saved enough money to buy a wagon and supplies for a journey to Oklahoma, where I intended to race for land."

He gave the crowd a faint smile.

"I would show my father what noble success looked like."

"As is often the case in youth, my enthusiasm got the better of me, most likely because I was used to wealth and privilege and knew little about how the world operates. Well, I started the race early, and a soldier with an eye for justice shot me right off the back of my horse." He squared his shoulders as his body shifted on the stool. "You might think the rifle bullet would have killed me, but it turns out the fall off my horse and the brain injury I suffered as I hit a rock on the ground was the worst offender. I recovered and gained enough strength to travel southwest."

He took a breath and calmed himself.

"Would you like a glass of water?" asked Nathan kindly.

James shook his head. "I can continue."

He turned to the audience, who sat on the edge of their seats.

"I ended up dead broke and in the company of killers who masqueraded as traveling gamblers. I'd only been with them a week when I realized the serious nature of my mistake. After several farmers were killed for little reason other than their intention to live off the land and one by one our group was caught and thrown into the local jailhouse, myself and another man, Thomas Hannah, were sent to prison in Huntsville, Texas."

Catherine and Shirley sat on a stool on each side of him.

James smiled at them and squeezed their hands.

"After the Austin state capitol building burned in 1882, Thomas and I were farmed out to haul stone for a new building. Thomas found a means of escape while I continued my sentence, suffering in the process, as we were cell mates, and the warden blamed me for letting my friend go free. After my sentence expired, I moved to San Francisco where I worked odd jobs, including maintenance for a large hotel, until it burned to the ground. Tired of the west, I made my way back to St. Louis, and found a job working in a factory. Somehow, Thomas found me and made threats about my death, which caused me to fear for my life. All remained calm for a time, and it appeared Thomas had moved on, but on Thursday, June 22nd, I walked to work a few steps behind a coworker from the factory who sits to my right, Miss Shirley Fletcher. I left my boarding house unaware of his intentions, but soon Thomas stepped forward and strangled Shirley in front of me. He sneered and told me I was next, which paralyzed me with fear, as you might imagine. Another man saw the crime as it unfolded and rushed to Shirley's aid, and Thomas disappeared into a nearby alley. Well, afterward, I couldn't go back to the factory because of my shame and fear."

Shirley spoke softly. "Overcome with hysteria, I ended up in Belmont Hospital." Someone yelled for her to talk louder, which she did.

"All the time, I felt as if someone strangled me! It was dreadful!"

James patted her back, and she beamed at him.

"I could not stay in my boarding house or resume my job at the factory, and somehow I fought off my hysteria and found employment at a bakery, where I worked for a nice man named Chester Langley. He gave me a cot in the back and three meals a day. A week passed without incident, and I believed the worst had passed."

James paused.

"The night of July 3rd, which was a Monday, several men got into a saloon brawl over politics, and Thomas hurled a beer glass at Chester, who then went home. When Thomas and the other two men passed his bakery, Chester floored them all with a club while I lurked afraid in the background, once again unsure what to do. Thomas got to his feet and stabbed Chester nine times as I watched in horror. The other two men ran down the street and disappeared into the night. Thomas dropped the bloody knife and said, 'You cannot escape me, James,' and as men approached from a next-door restaurant, Thomas ran into an alley which separated the two buildings. The men chased him to the end and cornered him until the police arrived."

The crowd murmured their excitement and looked about the room.

"A detective questioned me about Chester's murder, and I told him about my time in prison with Thomas. I was sad about Chester's murder, as he was a decent man who didn't deserve to die. I failed to mention Shirley Fletcher or June Marsh, but I said Thomas had bragged about murdering other people. The judge held Thomas while the detective tried to convince me to testify in open court, but I fell into a state of shock and hysteria."

Nathan interjected, giving James time to calm his emotions.

"Detective Kincaid took James to the city asylum for evaluation, and the administrator forwarded him to our hospital for treatment. When James saw Shirley, his hysteria deepened, which was a major setback to the case, but because of the possibility of uncovering evidence of additional murders, the judge kept Thomas until James could be restored to health. He advised Kincaid to heal James quickly, as Thomas could not be held indefinitely."

"Later, the memory of Thomas bragging about the June Marsh murder from thirty years ago rushed to the surface, and I knew Thomas could easily kill me whenever he took a notion. I was frightened out of my wits."

Nathan patted his shoulder. "When his memories returned during his treatment, James told us the story, and the rest is history."

"What the doctor hasn't told you is he testified in *my* place."

He wiped tears from his eyes. "I am most grateful to you, Nathan."

"I should have stood against Thomas as a boy, but I lacked the courage."

"Well, as a grown man, you are brave beyond measure."

Nathan smiled at James and then gave the floor to Catherine.

She scowled at her father. "I know you are an evil man, but how could you turn James into a sideshow freak after all he's been through?"

John threw her a grave look. "I do what needs to be done, which is a reality you've never understood. Life is not your version of a fairy tale."

"You expected me to join your order and take part in your iniquity, and when I would not, you cast me aside, just as you did to my mother."

"She was a troublemaker like you," John said.

Nathan gently took Catherine's arm and shook his head.

He raised his hands to the ceiling. "Dear Lord, we open our hearts to you in prayer and repentance. Please protect Catherine and the patients from the demonic realm and the cabal who might wish to harm them."

Nathan turned to the audience. "Before Thomas hanged, we chatted briefly, and he gave me more information about his background."

He paused.

"An orphan Thomas was raised as a servant in Philadelphia. He had anger issues and often lashed out in fury at those in his vicinity. He was fired from his position and traveled west to Alabama, where he got a job on a steamboat that delivered cotton up the Mississippi River to St. Louis. He planned to save money and make his way to California and then onward to Alaska, seeking the last frontier, but after he was pressed into a stall by a horse while he worked at a livery, Thomas saw Dr. Samuel Marsh, who needed extra help on his farm. My father hired Thomas to break and train his horses, which went well for a few months until Thomas and my mother grew too friendly and fell into a relationship, which forced my father to fire him. After he murdered my mother for revenge, Thomas went to Texas."

Nathan lamented his hatred of Thomas and his reluctance to pray for the man who killed his mother. If he prayed as a young boy, many of the calamities which followed would not have occurred, and if his family had prayed together during his boyhood, his mother and father would not have quarreled, she would still be alive, and Thomas Hannah might have been saved. No one knows a man's soul but the Father. He would like to have given Thomas a chance at repentance through prayer.

Nathan vowed to reach many for Christ before it was too late.

He asked the audience to repent, as the clock ticked, and God's return drew nigh. "Tomorrow is not guaranteed, and judgement awaits us all."

After a moment of silent prayer so people might repent, Nathan and Catherine gave the credit for restoration to Daisy. She showed them the power of love and led them to Christ, which had made all the difference.

Nathan called Daisy forward to take a well-deserved bow.

Daisy pointed to her chest. "Me?"

He smiled broadly and waved her toward the stage. "Yes, you!"

She climbed the steps, turned to the crowd, and took a breath.

"In 1876, they called St. Louis the Future Great City of the World."

Daisy let each person consider what the title might mean to them.

"Well, if we are to become the next great metropolis, our citizens must treat people as human beings." She hesitated. "Sigmund Freud was a mentor of mine in Vienna, Austria, and he coined a concept called the prehistoric wish. Now, as you sit here tonight, each of you might ask what this term means and how it applies to all of us. As a child, I had three great wishes. My mother had a form of hysteria, and she eventually committed suicide. My father was a traumatized man and a severe alcoholic. Throughout the term of my childhood, I longed to help people recover from crippling emotional problems, and although I went to Europe and worked in Paris and Vienna, I never felt I enhanced anyone's lives." She pointed at Nathan. "Because of this man, I achieved my childhood dream, as I have been able to help these patients who stand before you on the stage tonight." She wiped her eyes. "I had wanted to live in the great city of St. Louis since I was a girl, and I got to do that, too, which fulfilled my second wish."

A newspaper reporter asked for her third wish.

She smiled at him. "It's an excellent question, sir."

Daisy looked about the auditorium. "My third and final wish was to have a family and a home to tend, which was all my own."

"Has it come true?" asked the young reporter.

"I'm working on it." Daisy blushed as she glanced at Nathan.

The audience clapped and cheered.

Daisy closed her eyes and said a silent prayer of thanksgiving.

My dearest daughter, recite Psalm 35:1-8.

Let them know my will for them comes from trustworthy righteousness, and I will grant them grace if they will come to me in humble truth.

"Yes, Jesus."

Her eyes opened, and she spoke reverentially. "The Lord prompted me to pray aloud to you from the psalms. Please remain seated."

A voice called out from a private box near the back of the room.

"You will *not* pray the psalms in my presence! Nathan's pitiful prayer to his god is worthless and weak, but Daisy Lawrence, you will surely die if you recite your god's verses." Joanna sprang forth, elongated, fanged, and muscled beyond that of a beastly man. Her abominable feet gripped the top railing, which rested thirty feet above the floor, and she snarled at the stage.

The audience craned their necks.

Joanna screamed obscenities at the Lord and praised Lucifer.

Daisy stood her ground, as did Nathan and the others on the stage.

Joanna turned to her cohort and gave her a disgusted look.

Laura's deep-set eyes seemed heavy and her body lethargic. The glare of her paleness hurt to see, even from a great distance. Streaks of gray ran through her once seductive hair, now matted. Laura struggled to lean forward and fell against the top rail. She gripped the brass with her fingers.

Joanna threw a sneer at Daisy and Nathan. She raised her knuckled hands and her hairy arms to the sky and called on the name of Lucifer.

The reddish mist which had flooded Nathan's bedroom and the Expo lobby entered through the doors and deluged the rows and aisles. A shadow descended, first on box members and then the rest of the riveted audience, enervating Joanna and Laura, who now resembled her former self, as her skin was colorful and her musculature fine and the allure of her wickedness irresistible. Laura stood next to Joanna. Her hair was jet black, and her eyes were an attentive emerald green. She was perfectly shaped for her purpose.

She curled her finger at Nathan and beckoned him forth.

"You want me *now*. I can feel the energy of your longing."

Her words were spoken softly, but they wafted to the stage with perfect clarity, and throughout the auditorium, men gazed at the mystery harlot.

Joanna pointed to Daisy. "I will murder you where you stand!"

She stood on the rail and summoned Lucifer's wrath.

His spirits appeared. They swirled haughtily about the ceiling and dipped downward to dazzle audience members, who gazed open-mouthed in awe and admiration, paralyzed by the temptation to take what was given.

Some were beautiful and mesmerizing, while others were hideous and bloodcurdling. Each danced and bobbed and seduced a most willing crowd.

Frozen in fear, Daisy once more called upon the Most High.

"Dear Jesus, we repent in your name and we ask you to forgive our many sins. Please fill us with your Holy Spirit and remove any demons from within us and these spirits who would tempt and persecute us from outside our bodies. There is a war, Lord, and we are your noble Christian soldiers."

Recite the Lord's Prayer, as I instructed my disciples.

Daisy smiled as she remembered Vienna. "Our Father in heaven, may your name be kept holy. May your Kingdom come soon. May your will be done on earth, as it is in heaven. Give us today the food we need, and forgive us our sins, as we have forgiven those who sin against us. And don't let us yield to temptation, but rescue us from the evil one."

A heavenly white light shone down from the rafters, and a mighty wind swept in from the street and the side exits as the doors flew open. The spirits cowered in terror as the light encompassed and swallowed them.

Joanna remained defiant, even in the face of the Lord's presence.

"I will kill you, Daisy Lawrence! Your blood will taste sweet!"

She leapt from the balcony with superhuman strength, more than a match for gravity and the floor, which enticed her from thirty feet below.

A beam of light penetrated her ghastly form, and her momentum ceased. Joanna was caught for a moment in mid-air where she squirmed and struggled and simpered. The light intensified, and she was transformed into a delicate waif. She seemed astonished and fearful and apologetic as she crashed to the aisle, where her bones shattered like glass and blood flowed about her like a river of reckless tears. Hers was a soul lost to the maelstrom.

A man leaned over her and turned toward the stage.

"This woman is dead."

Nathan approached Daisy with a Bible. He flipped the pages to Psalm 35 and held it open for her while he stood near to her side.

"O Lord, oppose those who oppose me. Fight those who fight against me. Put on your armor, and take up your shield. Prepare for battle, and come to my aid. Lift up your spear and javelin against those who pursue me. Let me hear you say, 'I will give you victory!' Bring shame and disgrace on those trying to kill me; turn them back and humiliate those who want to harm me. Blow them away like chaff in the wind—a wind sent by the angel of the Lord. Make their path dark and slippery, with the angel of the Lord pursuing them. I did them no wrong, but they laid a trap for me. I did them no wrong, but they dug a pit to catch me. So let sudden ruin come upon them! Let them be caught in the trap they set for me! Let them be destroyed in the pit they dug for me."

Daisy looked at the audience and studied the faces nearest to her, hoping the Lord's message reached clear hearts and newly opened eyes.

"I will read further in the Word."

A man called out from the back of the room. "Praise, Jesus!"

He moved forward to the area below the stage and knelt, weeping, and asked for the Lord's forgiveness in all things. Others joined him.

The hysteric patients descended the stairs and knelt beside those who had come forward, each praising Jesus and offering their souls in repentance.

They asked Him to become their Savior, both now and for eternity.

Daisy wiped tears of joy from her cheeks and read verses 9 and 10.

"Then I will rejoice in the Lord. I will be glad because he rescues me. With every bone in my body I will praise him: 'Lord, who can compare with you? Who else rescues the helpless from the strong? Who else protects the helpless and poor from those who rob them?'"

John Belmont became furious at Nathan.

"You, sir, have sacrificed your position at my hospital!"

His cheeks fell beet red as he pointed a finger at Nathan's chest. "I will install my agent as the replacement administrator."

Agent Lacy tapped John on the shoulder and addressed Nathan.

"President Cleveland would like you and Miss Lawrence to accompany me back to the Oval Office for a conversation. He has taken a keen interest in your affairs over the last several months."

Nathan grinned at John.

"We'll see what the president has to say about *your* hospital."

John smiled, unconvinced. "It is mine to do with as I please. I funded Cleveland's campaign and I can install a new leader anytime I choose."

He addressed the audience.

"The show is over, folks, and it's time to leave the auditorium."

A frail woman, half bent over, approached the foot of the stage. Daisy instantly recognized her as Laura, her former nemesis, who had once again become whole and healthy when Lucifer's spirits arrived, but who fell into mortal disrepair at their hasty departure. Now, she was sullen and decrepit and misshapen. She groped for Daisy and fell to the floor at her feet, unable to take another step. She pulled herself nearer and placed her cheek against Daisy's boots. Tears coursed down her cheeks as she wept.

Nathan quickly descended the stairs and kneeled over her.

"Laura, please repent before your body loses its will to fight."

He ran a finger along a streak of her gray hair, once sensual, and looked into her formerly attentive eyes. She grabbed his hand and squeezed lightly.

Daisy sat beside Laura amid the muck and the grime.

She stroked Laura's hair in tandem with Nathan.

His eyes fell on Daisy. "You'll ruin your dress."

"I don't care about it," she said with a faint smile.

"Like Sophie?"

She quickly swiped tears from her eyes. "Yes, like Sophie."

Daisy must be strong for this waif on the verge of death before them. No knife would be required as Laura's mind and her body and her spirit had decided to lie down in the dirt which reposed under the green grass.

Daisy scooted beside Laura and placed the woman's head in her lap.

Laura clutched the material of Daisy's dress with her fingers.

Her eyes raised.

"I came here tonight with the intention of stealing your man away from you and from your god, but it seems in the end you have prevailed."

Daisy placed a strand of hair behind Laura's ear. "Joanna came her to sink her fangs into my jugular, and later to teach Nathan to murder."

Laura's eyes fell to the floor. She clutched Daisy's dress harder.

"It won't be long now."

"Please repent," Daisy said.

"It's no use. I am too far gone."

"You may avoid the second death. Please ask Jesus to forgive you."

Laura sobbed, and her frail body shook.

"You don't know what I've done, Daisy. The Lord would never forgive a wretched pagan like me, a woman who knows only sex and murder."

"Repent, and your demon will lose his stronghold."

Nathan put his hand on Daisy's shoulder. "You're pushing her too hard." He turned and smiled at Sheila and Catherine, who hovered nearby.

"Please repent," said Sheila comfortingly. "It's time you let go."

"I cannot. They trained the godly life out of me."

"You are in this condition because of me. My prayers backstage have laid waste to your plans and also to the health of your body and mind."

"You prayed for my demise," said Laura, nodding. "It is fitting."

"No, I prayed for your eternal *life*."

Sheila kneeled and bent over Laura. She waved for Catherine to do the same. "We must lay hands on her, Nathan. The angel said you have the power to heal, but we must lay hands on her and call out to Jesus."

"I am a surgeon who knows how to cut. I know nothing of this."

Sheila popped his head. "Then you must *try* right now!"

"Alright!" He scowled at her and rubbed his head.

They placed hands on her flesh and prayed the Lord's Prayer.

Laura's body stiffened and vibrated under their touch.

"Why do you help me, Sheila? I wanted you dead."

Sheila smiled down at her. "I know, honey. We all make mistakes."

"You weren't exactly kind to me either," said Catherine with contempt.

Laura's eyes flickered. "Many demons entered at your father's behest."

Catherine removed her hands and fell backward.

Nathan grabbed her and pulled her back to her knees.

"Cease your thoughts about him and help this woman!"

She flashed an innocent look. "Alright, Nathan. Don't get mad."

They placed their hands on Laura with a whole commitment, unwilling to let her suffer the fires of perdition. She writhed underneath their touch and fought them while each begged Jesus to remove her unclean spirits.

When they paused, Laura begged them to stop.

"Let me go, please."

"No," Nathan said. "I won't allow it."

Daisy smiled. "Neither will I."

"I've seen too much. I've *done* too much."

"We know. You said the same thing backstage."

"Nathan, I bathed in human blood for ten years."

She turned away from them, lost to her shame.

Daisy grabbed her chin and turned her face.

"Now it's time, Laura, for you to be washed clean by the blood of Jesus. He spilled it on the cross for all of mankind, which includes *you*, no matter how bad you think you are, or how egregious your sins." She pointed to Nathan and then to herself. "Do you think we are saints?"

"More than me. I watched people die."

"So did I, and so did Nathan, and so did others. We are each a product of our sin, and we all sin, no matter how much we might wish otherwise."

Laura's eyes fell across her torso and her arms and her legs.

"I was covered from head to toe. Does God want a bloody mess?"

Daisy burst into tearful laughter and rubbed Laura's cheek.

"Jesus shed His own blood so you might live."

"I want to believe you!" Laura moaned faintly.

"Please repent, Laura. It's time to let go of the past."

"Daisy, you cannot love me after I wanted to eliminate you."

"I love Jesus Christ, and He is enough. He has brought good people into my life, including the man I love with all my heart and soul, Nathan Marsh."

"Could you ever forgive me?"

"I forgive you, as Jesus has forgiven me. I tempted my sister Rose to leap to her death, and I pushed my mentally ill mother to commit suicide."

Daisy paused.

"I talked my way into a Paris asylum and worked with patients without a bit of actual knowledge or experience, and I called it ambition and success."

"You helped people," Nathan said.

"No, I abandoned them for Frank Kaneski, and I deserved every ounce of Rosemarie's wrath she had to give me. It's a blessed miracle I survived."

She gestured at Sheila and at Catherine and then at Nathan.

"We've all sinned and we've all fallen short of the glory of God."

"Will you lead me in prayer, Daisy?"

Daisy's heart jumped, and tears of relief burst forth.

"Oh, yes, my dear, it would be my honor to lead you to Jesus."

Laura squeezed her hand. "I think I could be ready if you'll love me."

"He loves you, honey, and it's all that matters, but I *do* love you."

"Me, too." Nathan placed his hand on Laura's brow.

"Dear Jesus, please loosen this woman from the demon of infirmity, as you did in the synagogue on the Sabbath. As we lay hands on her, Lord, please make her straight again, so she might glorify your name."

Nathan encouraged Laura to offer a prayer of repentance.

"Lord Jesus, I repent of my horrible sins. I come to you in truth, for you know the worst of my faults and the pain I have caused others. Please forgive me today as I pass into the valley of death and allow me to Rest In Peace."

The light returned, and a voice boomed from the rafters.

"Nathan, you have done well, and she has returned to me."

"Yes, Lord."

"I have plans for Laura as I have plans for you and Daisy. A lineage will spawn from her, which will save many souls, including a very important one at the dawn of the Last Days." He allowed them to process His words. "Sheila, you also have a lineage, which will be revealed to you in due course. For now, you are to marry Heinrich and make a new home in Waldenburg."

Sheila nodded her willing compliance. "Yes, Lord."

"As for you, Laura Collins, arise and walk a sinless life."

Color filled her face as the Lord restored her health and vigor.

She sat up, immersed in the baptism of faith, unclothed in the stark reality of her truth and honored by the forgiveness of His grace, full in her trust in the righteousness of Jesus Christ, made joyful and contented by a peace which defies understanding, and liberated from her servitude to sin.

The impromptu altar call took place below the stage and continued for an hour. Everyone who attended the event at the Expo was saved except for one man—John Belmont. He used his free will differently and would for all time until he took his last breath of life. It was his decision to make, and the Lord did not interfere, free will his ultimate gift, and ours alone to use for good or for ill, eternal bliss or fiery consequences our ultimate destination.

THIRTY-SIX

Psalm 36:12

Look! Those who do evil have fallen!
They are thrown down, never to rise again.

December 1893

Nathan and Daisy exited Washington Depot and hailed a cab. The street was covered with snow, which blew in thick clouds and covered the sidewalks with a downy white texture. The irreducible minimum of Daisy's luggage had almost consumed Nathan's energy as he lugged three bags through the station, and he was thankful the cabbie loaded them onto the back of his carriage. They would drop the bags at their hotel and then go to the White House for an appointment in the Oval Office with the president of the United States. They hoped to leave the consultation without an angry word, but apologies for their display at the Expo would not be forthcoming, nor would they bestow season's greetings on John Belmont, benefactor to Cleveland's campaign for reelection in '96.

The cab stopped in front of the prestigious Raleigh Hotel.

Daisy looked up at the seven-story structure in wonder, and she held her hat as her head tilted backward. "Nathan, this is too expensive."

She turned to him. "We can stay somewhere else."

He smiled. "Only the best for my girl."

The cabbie unloaded their bags and left them on the sidewalk. He started for the carriage and turned. "You two make a friendly couple."

He tipped his hat and climbed aboard the cab. "Try to keep it sweet."

"We will." Daisy waved at the man as the cab surged.

"You say that like it's always been easy for us."

Her countenance grew playful.

She squeezed Nathan's arm and hugged him.

"Perhaps, but our future is bright."

A porter approached and asked to take their bags.

"Why, yes, by all means."

Nathan hooked Daisy's arm. "Madam, shall we enter our abode?"

She laughed. "Yes, sir. Where you lead, I will follow."

The lobby was grand, as it was renovated earlier in the year from the Palais Royal department store which had operated inside the Shepherd Centennial Building, the upper floors a temporary home to the Pension Office until the government agency moved to its permanent residence.

A dotted marble floor led them to a granite counter desk, and along their path, luxurious couches of leather and cotton reposed between Corinthian columns, and green plants of assorted varieties interspersed with merry Poinsettias, and at the far end of the lobby, to their left, elegant and timeless tunes played on a mahogany upright piano. The recessed ceiling above them offered delightful patterns amid three layers of crown molding.

Daisy tapped Nathan's shoulder as he spoke to the clerk.

"I could get used to this," she said with a cheerful face.

He brought her to his side. "Someday, we'll travel in fine style."

"Do you promise?"

"I do." He half-turned and then stopped. "It may not happen soon."

"Maybe when we're older." Daisy shrugged.

"It would be nice to travel without care for our safety or our funds."

She nodded and bit her lower lip.

"First, you must expand your medical practice."

His lips pinched. "Now *that* may take a while."

"Don't sell yourself short. I recall saying the same the night we met."

Nathan sighed and then smiled. "I remember all too well."

He handed their room key to the porter, who guided them to the narrow elevator. At their floor, the young man led them down a ceaseless hallway, where mustached and bearded men sat in rockers and peered at the happy couple as they traversed the vast interior landscape.

Finally, the porter reached their room and inserted the key.

As he swung open the weighty door, he gauged their reaction.

The size and elegance of the space made it fit for royalty.

Daisy gazed through the double-paned windows which overlooked the city street seven stories below their room. Her hands shielded the morning sun from her tired eyes. She threw a look of frustration at Nathan.

"Did you have to pick the top floor? You know I'm afraid of heights."

He laughed out loud as he handed the porter a tip.

"Your ledge along the Missouri would beg to differ, madam."

She put her hands on her hips and then dropped them to her sides.

Nathan had bested her, and she knew it. He could get used to *this*.

The porter smiled. "Thank you, sir, and I hope you have a very nice honeymoon." He gripped the handle and backed himself out of the room.

"Why would he think we were married?" asked Daisy faintly.

Nathan grabbed her shoulders and kissed her lips and her neck.

He drew back slightly. "It's because you look so radiant, my dear."

"We picked one room instead of two to save money." She pushed him away with a gentle shove and sat in a chair. "Please don't kiss my neck."

"You dislike it?"

She gave him an indulgent smile. "The opposite, so please cease."

"An unsullied woman sits before me," he said politely.

Daisy laughed. "I wish it were true, for *your* sake, but I am trying."

"You are the most wonderful woman I've ever met, Daisy, and I am so pleased our paths crossed on such a night as the Fourth of July, an occasion meant to celebrate the independence of our great nation, but one I will always remember for another, more lovely reason, one of the mended heart."

"I love you, Nathan Marsh, and I will until the day I die."

"Don't stop there, Daisy Lawrence, for my love is eternal."

She drew near to him and wrapped her arms around his waist.

"Forever will our souls be intertwined with one another and with Jesus."

Their lips met in a tender embrace. He kissed her neck and her mouth and rubbed her back until neither could stand another second without an unchaste action which would violate their sacred vow to the Lord.

Nathan went to the door and flung it open.

"Shall we take our leave?"

"I believe we must, kind sir, or the walls of Jericho will fall."

At the entrance to the White House, Nathan knocked.

The door creaked open. "A tour will begin at the top of the hour."

"We have an invitation to meet with the president."

The man read the letter carefully. "I see."

He handed the paper to Nathan. "Please wait one moment."

The door closed and then opened a few minutes later.

"Please remove your hat and follow me."

Soon they stood in the East Room near a group of tourists who sat about in chairs or on upholstered couches. Some stood with hat in hand and stared blankly as they waited for an arbitrary clock strike, which might allow their visitation to commence. As in the Raleigh Hotel, ceilings ascended to euphoric heights, and doorways adorned themselves in wreathed columns, and flourishing plants in ornamented vases articulated the colossal nature of the chandelier which descended like a winged Medusa. Above heavy wooden doors, recessed Roman arches, encased in glass, saluted reverent visitors with the stunning architectural brilliance of the building and of Washington, D.C. itself, purposed to impress and intimidate foreign leaders upon their arrival. The doors opened, revealing the president of the United States.

"Hello, Doctor Marsh and Miss Daisy Lawrence."

Cleveland extended his hand. "Please join me."

The tourists peered at Cleveland, who nodded and smiled at them before he wheeled and led the baffled couple into his private domain.

Inside the Oval Office, they glanced about the room with concealed awe.

President Cleveland watched them as he leaned against his desk.

Nathan gestured to his right. "I like your little Christmas tree."

"Do you think the tree is why I brought you here?"

Nathan frowned. "No."

"The reason is simple and straightforward, so let me get right to the point. I read your book from cover to cover, and I enjoyed your ingenious methods of creating medicines and I especially appreciated your guidance to physicians, instructing them in proper medical hygiene. I also read Daisy's theories on the treatment of psychiatric patients and the importance of showing them respect as human beings who matter to God."

Cleveland paused.

"I feel guilt for my role in your ordeals over the last several months, but I am happy to have learned about your character in such time."

Nathan gestured sharply. "So why are we here?"

"I formally offer you a new and different position."

Nathan exchanged a glance with Daisy.

"What kind? Do I have to wrangle crocodiles in Australia?"

Cleveland chuckled and crossed his arms.

"I wouldn't ask you to leave this continent, and in fact, I quite hope you remain in Missouri indefinitely. Your departure would put me in a bind."

"Alright, I'll bite. What's the job?"

"I need you to run a medical college in St. Louis." He hesitated. "You may know the location, as it will be housed on Gratiot Street."

"The old relic from before the war?"

"That's the one. My people have restored it to sound health."

He paused, as if prompting them without a hint of rebuke.

"You'll run day-to-day operations for the college while Daisy will teach psychology electives. Neurology may prove a middle ground."

"Is this a joke?"

Daisy blushed. "Nathan, this isn't the time or the place."

Nathan brushed her off and turned to Cleveland.

"He knows what I mean."

"I'm afraid I don't, sir."

Nathan eyed Cleveland's desk and glimpsed a letter, which most likely outlined their activities. "You've had men follow us for months. They stood outside the hospital entrance and watched us at all hours."

"Along with your house."

Nathan nodded his agreement. "Yes, there, too."

He considered.

"Were they at Joanna's brothel?"

"My men are quite thorough. They leave no unturned stones."

Daisy gasped. "Surely, you didn't infiltrate our staff."

"As I mentioned, my men are good at their jobs."

Cleveland gestured at the two couches. "Shall we sit?"

"I suppose." Nathan settled onto the soft fabric and felt along the surface of the cushion with his palm. His eyebrows arched. "This is nice."

"I'm afraid leisurely activities will become a fond memory once you undertake the responsibilities required by this mission," the president said gravely. "You will often feel overwhelmed and desirous of relief."

"We'll be fine."

"It will mean even longer hours than you previously worked at your hospital and a schedule which bursts at the seams." The president turned to Daisy and softly touched her shoulder. "You two should discuss what the increased workload might do to your relationship."

They exchanged glances and laughed.

Cleveland gave each of them a confused look.

"I see little humor in my statement."

Nathan rose quickly with a spring in his step and went to the window and looked out at the snow covered lawn. "Without work to occupy us, we want to strangle one another. Let's just say we aren't the layabout types."

Cleveland smiled. "My wife and I are much the same. We believe our care and diligence for others must preside over our own interests."

"Then we are in agreement," said Nathan decidedly.

His eyes fell on Daisy, and his hand patted her leg.

"If you feel we should decline, I will abide by your judgement. Without doubt the medical college will place demands on our lives. We both know you dream of having children, and there may be little space for romance."

"You don't want them?"

"Oh, I do, with *you* most definitely, but my calling comes first."

"Thank you."

"For what, exactly?"

"For thinking of my wishes and for considering my fears."

"The president has piqued your interest. Am I correct?"

Her face grew determined. "I am intrigued by the many possibilities this situation presents to us." She clutched Nathan's arm. "We could send men into the world with a penchant for prescribing only the best medicines and only when they are absolutely necessary. What's more, we could instruct them in psychology so no one will ever be left behind again. When I imagine the plethora of physicians and psychologists who might flow from our college, the potential for positive impact on the world astounds me."

"Should we take residence in the building?"

"Yes," she said. "We must never let it out of our sight."

Nathan pondered her comment, and he savored how far they had come since their fateful encounter under the gleam of the Union Depot lights.

He grinned at Cleveland and slapped his knee.

"Mr. President, we formally accept your offer."

Unconvinced, the president turned to Daisy.

"Do you feel the same, madam?"

She beamed at the president of the United States.

"I do, sir, I *honestly* do."

Nathan kneeled in front of the president's desk, and Daisy worried about his knees, as the English rug would do little to protect them from the thickness of the oak floor panels. He held up a ring which seemed dense and heedless of the direction of the light, as it shined incandescently and brought out sudden tears which had been stored inside for a very long time. On either hand were the accoutrements of the Oval Office, but before her was the formerly low and rambling outlaw of renown, who spent ten years in blunder and desolation, and with enough whiskey to become a tavern.

A fearful aide barged in and interrupted her blissful proposal.

"Excuse me for one moment. I'm sorry for the intrusion."

The president turned to his aide. "Yes?"

He nodded several times as the staffer whispered into his ear, and then his face broke into a smile. "I am so glad they made it."

The aide shuttled through the door and closed it.

President Cleveland's eyes fell lightly on Daisy and Nathan.

"You should stand. There is someone here to meet you."

Nathan sighed quizzically as he rose from the plush couch.

"What now?"

The door opened to reveal several people, most likely tourists who followed a hap-hazard course from the front door and got lost on the way to the East Room, their dusty trail having led them to the Oval Office, where they would now carelessly interrupt the best moment of Daisy's life, the one she had waited for since Rose's death in the woods. She sighed heavily in anticipation of another broken heart as she gazed through the curtainless window at the snow covered lawn. The streets near the hotel would be alive with activity, and Washington Depot would provide her with transport home. She could leave this wretched place and be just as careless with her ultimate destination as these unruly intruders, their steps guided into the lovely land of her wedded fantasy, the curious exactitude of their timing most unpleasant and destructive to Daisy's mood, now quite unlike one predisposed to marital harmony, which was all she wished for since girlhood.

James and Catherine entered with buoyant faces and stood next to the tourists. "We have a surprise," James said. "It's one we think you'll like."

An older gentleman stepped forward. "I am his father, and it seems I have you to thank for my son's restoration." He gripped Nathan's shoulders and pushed them together. "My wife, Mary, and I are most grateful."

President Cleveland interjected.

"I apologize for the unexpected nature of this interruption, but I wanted you to meet your new patrons. These are the Cliftons, and they will be most beneficial to my campaign in '96." His voice fell low. "Don't worry, Son, these are good Christian folk who detest the machinations of Lucifer."

"Will they help you seek out the doers of iniquity?"

The president smiled. "Yes, they will, and from all aspects of society."

"James asked me to marry him, and I have accepted." Catherine drew near to Nathan and kissed him. "I've loved you since our youth, and I will always love you as the father of our children—Annie, Eli, and Peter—may their souls Rest In Peace, but I have reached a crossroads in my life."

Nathan nodded and wiped the tears from her eyes.

"I know, honey. It's time."

He looked up. "James is a fine man, and he'll do well by you."

She hugged Nathan. "I know he will, and he'll do right by you, too."

"How's that?"

The older man extended his hand. "I should formally introduce myself. My name is Walter Clifton." He turned to his son. "James tells me he described my occupation as railroad speculator. Well, that might have been true years ago, when James was much younger, but now I am very wealthy."

"What do you want from me?" asked Nathan with a smirk.

"From *us*," said Daisy, correcting him.

"Alright, from us. What's your angle?"

"We are ashamed to say it, but we decided James was an incurable outlaw, a man who likely had a deficiency of a sort which disabled him."

"What changed your mind?"

Walter turned to James and then Catherine. "For one, the deep and enduring love they so obviously share, but moreover, it was his resolve to make a fresh start, and the gratitude he has shown all of us since he returned to our home. He's a new man who is ready for greatness."

"I'm still not cut out for running a railroad as my father might wish, nor for living life along the many twists and corners of Fifth Avenue."

Nathan seemed confused. "What then?"

"I will administrate your college, and Catherine will ensure its worthy acceptance in the community. Although she no longer has her father's support, she still holds sway among many in the Big Cinch. Our efforts will free your schedule to teach classes and to oversee other professors."

Nathan's face showed tension as his eyes fell on Daisy.

She turned to James. "Are there any other stipulations?"

He smiled. "You must keep the position for life."

Walter stood beside James. He placed his hand on Nathan's shoulder.

"The stakes are too high to accept your resignation in a year."

They gladly accepted the generous offer.

"That's wonderful." Walter happily hugged Daisy and shook Nathan's hand. "James and Catherine will accompany you on the train tomorrow, and James will have our attorney in St. Louis draw up the papers."

Afterward, silence overtook the room.

President Cleveland sensed the awkwardness of the moment.

He blurted to Nathan, "What are you waiting for, man?"

"You don't mind, sir?"

The president blushed. "We rarely receive good news in here."

He slapped Nathan's back. "As I said, get on with your business, doctor. You must be quick about your words and sincere in how you say them."

The president grinned at Daisy with tears in his eyes.

His voice fell low. "This one is a clever sort who'll accept no less."

Nathan kneeled and took Daisy's hand and popped the question.

"Yes, by all means, *yes!*"

The Cliftons joyfully clapped, and the president cheered loudly.

He recovered and gestured at the door.

"You must now leave me to important affairs of state."

As they left the room, he called out to Nathan.

"Take care of her, Dr. Marsh. Daisy is the real thing."

Nathan tipped his hat. "Yes, Mr. President."

The president smiled and closed the door.

In the hallway, they studied the Gilbert Stuart portrait of George Washington, which was saved from British hands by Dolly Madison in 1814. The painting stood seven and one-half feet tall and almost five feet wide, and it distinctly captured the steadfastness and the decency of the Republic's first president, the former soldier who grasped a sheathed sword in his left hand, but who wore the apparel of a civilian, symbolizing unity of power.

Daisy reached out and ran her fingers along the frame.

"You'll get us thrown out of here if you aren't careful," Nathan said.

She cupped her hand underneath her chin. "As I stand here and look at this stunning portrait of George Washington, and I think about what he endured and what he achieved for our nation, I'm reminded of Psalm 36."

"Recite it to me," Nathan said.

"It has twelve verses, so I'll need to read from the text."

"Alright then," he said, "we'll need a spot to relax."

He led her to a nearby bench, where they sat.

She retrieved her Bible from a pocket and ran her finger from verse one to verse twelve. "Would you recite it for me?"

He smiled. "Did my abrupt proposal distress you?"

Daisy laughed. "Not at all, although it was a surprise which thrilled me, especially since you proposed in the Oval Office, of all places." Her hand rubbed along his arm. "I enjoy listening as you speak the Lord's Word."

"Well then, I must oblige your kind request." He cleared his throat and began his recitation. "Sin whispers to the wicked, deep within their hearts. They have no fear of God at all. In their blind conceit, they cannot see how wicked they really are. Everything they say is crooked and deceitful. They refuse to act wisely or do good. They lie awake at night, hatching sinful plots. Their actions are never good. They make no attempt to turn from evil. Your unfailing love, O Lord, is as vast as the heavens; your faithfulness reaches beyond the clouds. Your righteousness is like the mighty mountains, your justice like the ocean depths. You care for people and animals alike, O Lord. How precious is your unfailing love, O God! All humanity finds shelter in the shadow of your wings. You feed them from the abundance of your own house, letting them drink from your river of delights. For you are the fountain of life, the light by which we see. Pour out your unfailing love on those who love you; give justice to those with honest hearts. Don't let the proud trample me or the wicked push me around. Look! Those who do evil have fallen! They are thrown down, never to rise again."

A guard asked them to move on with their business.

Daisy and Nathan snickered as they exited through the front doors.

"Do you think Catherine's heart may wander?"

Nathan shook his head.

"She loves James, so she'll stay put. However, I sense stress in her heart."

"In my estimation, Catherine worries James will be so focused on his work that he won't take her daily struggles into account." Daisy smiled wanly. "One thing is certain. She couldn't bear his eventual abandonment."

"It won't ever happen." Nathan's eyes brightened.

"How can you be sure?"

"Like us, Catherine and James are tired of turning away from God." He paused.

"They've learned the value of prayer, and its effect on their stability."

"I hope you feel the same," said Daisy thoughtfully.

"Oh yes." Nathan's tone grew firm. "For many years, I neglected to pray, but I can now say with certainty that prayer works."

They wiped a snowy bench and sat. Carriages passed on the street.

"Are you happy for Catherine? Please say yes."

Nathan drew Daisy's body nearer to him.

"I couldn't be more thrilled for Catherine. She's finally found faith, hope, and love, the greatest of which is love." He looked about the area and then glanced at the front door. "What's taking them so long?"

Daisy put on her fawn leather gloves. "Catherine is protective of James. She's probably got him wrapped in cotton candy and stuffed in a box."

Nathan laughed. "You may be right."

"That's usually the case." Daisy gave him a coy smile.

She pulled him close and gentled her voice. "You said Catherine found faith, hope, and love, with the greatest being love?"

His eyes grew restless. "What about it?"

"We also found love." Daisy wiped a joyous tear with her gloved hand.

She lightly kissed his lips. "I'm the luckiest woman on earth."

He smiled and enthusiastically returned her kiss.

Nathan and Daisy watched the White House front entrance and waited for Catherine and James to exit. They were orphans no more.

***

The four passengers stood in line, waiting to board the train for St. Louis.

A porter shouted, "All aboard!"

Each couple took their place in the Pullman car.

Catherine's eyes fell on Daisy. "We'll spend time with the Cliftons for Christmas, since I cannot stand to be in my father's home ever again."

"What about John? Will you forgive him?"

"I am trying, but my heart continually fills with rage."

James took her hand. "You must forgive him as Jesus forgives us."

She gazed silently at the countryside, her countenance indifferent.

"You will give the demons a new stronghold to use against you."

"I know," she said. "You're right, and I'm wrong, but I cannot help my emotion. Perhaps in time I will bring myself to forgive my father."

"As Nathan has mentioned, prayer is the best remedy."

"Yes, but what if my father never repents? We have free will, you know."

Daisy gave Nathan a concerned look.

"Is something wrong? You seem tense."

He glanced at Catherine and then turned to Daisy with a troubled look. "I want children again, but I'm concerned I will make many mistakes."

"Everyone makes them," Daisy said. "You will be fine."

He shook his head. "I cannot gamble with what I cannot afford to lose."

Catherine kneeled in front of him. "My dearest Nathan, you were a wonderful father to our children. There were never any doubts about your kindness or your devotion. They knew your love as I did."

"I failed to save them, honey, and it's the biggest mistake of my life."

She sighed deeply. "Your biggest mistake was a refusal to pray."

Catherine returned to her seat and then gestured at Daisy and James. "Just look at what happened when you reached out to Jesus. If I'm upset with you for any past sin, it's taking so long to lead us to the Word."

She paused.

"Each of us desperately needed Jesus."

Nathan gave her a warm look. "I am so happy for you."

"If you and Daisy had failed to intervene, I would have surely died."

Daisy wiped a tear from her cheek. "I was about to commit a contemptible act. I'm ashamed to say it now, but it's true, nonetheless."

"It would have been a permanent end," Nathan said. "For all of us."

James expressed his gratitude for all they had done.

At one time, he was an authentic outlaw who roamed the west with the likes of Thomas Hannah. He was glad Nathan intervened in his life.

"You must join us for Christmas," Catherine said.

"We have other plans."

Nathan beamed. "I formally invite you to attend our gala event."

James straightened his posture. "What do you have in mind?"

Nathan smiled. "You'll see."

Their rickety locomotive passed farms and boroughs as it meandered over the shine of bright hills and down into the haze of snow covered valleys. The two couples slept soundly that night, as they were no longer affected by the ice-capped mountains of their present or fearful of their mysterious futures, which extended before them in esoteric and pensive suspension.

As for the past, it held no sway over them and never would again.

———

At the conclusion of their Saturday wedding, Nathan kissed his beautiful bride, and Daisy raised her foot behind her, lost in the moment's joy and tipsy with happiness. Her cares had been flattened down, as both Jesus and Nathan loved her, and she would never understate her value again.

Daisy held her husband's hand and radiated effervescent jubilation as she turned toward the crowd and spoke Psalm 23. "The Lord is my shepherd; I have all that I need. He lets me rest in green meadows; he leads me beside peaceful streams. He renews my strength. He guides me along right paths, bringing honor to his name. Even when I walk through the darkest valley, I will not be afraid, for you are close beside me. Your rod and your staff protect and comfort me. You prepare a feast for me in the presence of my enemies. You honor me by anointing my head with oil. My cup overflows with blessings. Surely your goodness and unfailing love will pursue me all the days of my life, and I will live in the house of the Lord forever."

A Clifton family member called out from the right side.

"Praise Jesus!"

Another yelled from the left side. "Amen!"

Catherine and James beamed as they applauded.

Everyone in the small church surrendered to their happy ending.

The couple held up their hands and faced the adoring crowd.

"Jesus be praised. Lord, you are welcome in this house of worship and in all our lives. Please work your perfect will in our hearts and minds."

Daisy's angel appeared at the back of the congregation.

Her eyes fell on Nathan. He also saw the angel.

"I saw him before my sister died," she said. "He brought Rose back to life so I could try to save her." Daisy dropped her head. "I failed."

Nathan lifted her chin and gazed into her eyes, seeing into her soul.

"Rose used her free will. She made her choice to live or to die."

"Yes, but..."

"You saved *me*, and I will forever be grateful."

Nathan and Daisy exited the church, bound for a downtown hotel, the same room where Daisy had contemplated the unthinkable.

This time, happiness would prevail over sorrow.

The angel beamed with delight as Daisy passed him on the sidewalk.

"You were always destined to choose wisely," he said. "It was merely a function of time and gaining an understanding of God's will for you."

Nathan stood directly in front of the angel. "All I know to say in this moment is Hallelujah!" He squeezed Daisy tightly and lifted her.

The angel laughed. "Be assured, Nathan and Daisy, you've pleased the Lord today. There is much rejoicing in heaven as we speak."

Daisy climbed into the carriage, dropped her head, and said a silent prayer of thanksgiving. *"Thank you, Lord, for everything, even the adversity."*

My daughter, you have made me a proud Father.

You were NEVER a mistake.

EPILOGUE

Psalm 37:25

Once I was young, and now I am old.
Yet I have never seen the godly abandoned
or their children begging for bread.

June 1894

Daisy Marsh reached the end of her chalkboard as she addressed her engrossed classroom, which was filled with respect for her prominence as a national figure in the field of experimental psychology, and her unlimited excellence in weaving Christian topics into her scientific tutelage. The last class before the summer break occurred the day before, on Friday, but she called the students back on Saturday morning for a discussion of Psalm 37 and David's general principle regarding the prosperity of the wicked, which will soon fade into the fervent heat of the Lord's return. The faithful hearts of Overcomers should stay contented in God's will and avoid flashes of envy—even when afflicted—for if the wicked flourish today like hemlock in the pasture, tomorrow they will smolder.

Laura Collins handed a printed copy of the psalm to each student.

She returned to the front and stood near the professor, inspecting her, as Daisy was five months pregnant, and the baby often fluttered in her belly.

Nathan opened the door and eased into the classroom. He retrieved his watch from a coat pocket, and his eyebrows arched in annoyance.

"We mustn't be late for our appointment."

Daisy smiled, thankful she could count on him, as she frequently ran long in her presentation, the topics absorbing her and her pupils alike. She wished the class a good weekend and reminded everyone to be careful.

As each student collected their belongings and trickled into the hallway, they hugged her neck and offered an earnest prayer for a healthy baby.

A young man, Aldrich Whitlow, from an illustrious Chicago family, surpassed expectations in his first year of medical study. He filed past Laura, and she blushed as he gave her a flirtatious smile, which disturbed her thoughts like a gust before the approach of storm. Laura could not forbear another moment and glanced about the room in search of something, anything else to cease the whispering accusations of guilt and shame, bending and kicking against any possibility of joy she might someday know.

Daisy gave her an encouraging look, but Laura kept silent.

Aldrich's face reddened from lack of attention, and he left the room.

"I couldn't speak when he looked at me," Laura said.

Nathan shut the door after the last student was gone.

"It will be alright. You merely need more time to recover."

She looked up at him. "My senses or my sanity?"

He smiled. "A bit of both."

Mr. and Mrs. Marsh changed clothes in their upstairs apartment.

Daisy noticed the clock and hurriedly put on her dress. If the Marsh family expected to arrive at the Clifton wedding before it ended, they would have to make better time. She chided Nathan for not interrupting her earlier, as he knew she could not stop talking about her obsessions.

They rushed along the corridor and bickered the whole way.

"Please stop," said Laura as they exited to the front steps.

She threw a fearful look at Daisy. "You'll hurt the baby."

Daisy eyed Laura for several moments, her jet black hair streaked gray.

She took a deep breath and exhaled. "You're right, my dear."

Daisy's eyes rose to the celestial, where Nathan's city pure had once been lost to the insatiable misery of death but was now restored to brilliance.

"There are no clouds, and the sun shines warmly from the heavens."

Nathan hooked his arm under Daisy's. "Shall we see them married?"

She grinned. "We shall."

The three took a shortcut across the thick lawn to meet the trolley at the intersection. Laura rushed forward and took Daisy's free hand.

"I must steady you. There are gopher holes everywhere."

Daisy drew back. "I grew up on a farm."

Nathan chuckled. "She was nervous about the animal tracks in my attic during our second meeting, and don't let her convince you otherwise."

Laura's weakened body stumbled and fell.

A Frenchman who performed maintenance duties for the medical college ran over and helped her rise. He forcefully brushed clippings and grime from her dress, and his hand moved along her legs to her backside.

She pushed on his arm. "That will be enough, sir!"

"My apologies, *madame*. I meant no offense."

Nathan turned to the man. "We haven't been formally introduced."

The two shook hands. "I am Nathan Marsh."

"Yes, sir. Everyone around here knows your name."

"And yours?"

"My name is Paul Barreau."

"Who hired you, if you don't mind me asking?"

"I inquired last week, and Mr. Clifton gave me the job."

Nathan considered.

"Have I done something wrong, sir?"

"Not at all, but I wasn't consulted on the matter." Nathan gave up his questioning with a shrug. "James has been busy lately, with his wedding plans and his other assorted tasks. Although he and my ex-wife will be married in a small church, you would think this to be the year's best ball."

Paul chuckled. "It's the same in my village of Marchand, which lies near the emerald shoreline. There are many land owners who pride themselves on the size of their weddings and the esteem their Thoroughbreds provide."

"I take your meaning," said Nathan in a guarded voice. He turned to Daisy, who smiled at Laura. The younger woman's once attentive eyes fled to the far corner of the lawn. Nathan understood her reticence and her pain.

He shook the Frenchman's hand again. "Thank you, Paul."

"I hope the wedding goes smoothly, sir."

Nathan leaned close to Paul's ear and spoke confidentially.

"Me, too, but with my ex-wife, anything is possible."

Paul looked confused, but he smiled as if he inferred.

"We'll take our leave then." Nathan tipped his hat.

"Yes, sir."

Laura looked back at Paul as she boarded the trolley.

He smiled warmly at her, and her head turned abruptly from his gaze.

Daisy patted Laura's knee. "Within fifteen minutes, you attracted two men, and with your humorless deportment, it's a miracle from heaven."

"Nightmares anguish me and interrupt my sleep."

"Do you pray for deliverance in those gloomy hours?"

Laura nodded.

"Yes, but I feel like Eve in the garden after she had eaten the forbidden fruit of the Knowledge of Good and Evil and was ashamed of her nakedness and was clothed in the skin of her favorite animal, a blameless lamb."

"God made those clothes for Adam and Eve and it was the first sermon, preached in holy action rather than with simple words. The only path toward redemption lies through the shed blood of a living sacrifice."

"Yes, and I have cursed my life, so it must be given to Him."

"Perhaps, but we laid hands on you at the Expo and your demons were cast out in the name of Jesus, and you repented for your misguided deeds."

Laura closed her eyes and put her head on Daisy's shoulder.

"When I weep over my sins, the demons taunt me."

Daisy longed to escape this tormented soul, but she had abandoned her sister Rose in such a predicament and she failed to save Sophie in the alley. She would see Laura lifted from the depths of her ruinous gulch, the trunks of her elms bent, and their branches tossed wildly about, brambles and thorns tugging at her dress and scratching her arms and legs and ashen face.

Daisy was obliged to brood over Laura and to rekindle her warmth.

"They feed on your negative emotions." She softly stroked Laura's hair and took another deep breath. "Honey, you must forgive yourself."

"It wasn't so easy for *you*." Nathan gently bumped Daisy's shoulder.

Daisy pushed back against him. "I know, but Laura has seen the power of Christ, and she must learn to pray continually. We cannot do it for her."

Nathan gazed at the teeming street. "I lament Sheila's departure."

"Don't change the subject."

"I'm not. It's just I know Sheila has the same difficulties as Laura, an unwillingness to forget her past and forgive herself for her transgressions."

"She'll do well with Heinrich. He wants several children."

"A sizable farm operation in Waldenburg will demand sturdy backs."

The trolley hit a bump in the road. Daisy shifted uneasily in her seat.

"Are you alright?" Laura gave her a worried look as she sat up.

"Yes, my dear. I'm the same since you last asked me."

Laura frowned and dropped her head. "You think me foolish."

Daisy cupped her hand under Laura's chin. "We love you, honey, and what's more, Jesus Christ loves you." She dropped her hand. "He knew your path before He created the universe, and He has taken on your sins as His own. Please don't further our Creator's suffering on your behalf."

Tears coursed down Laura's cheeks. "I deserve death, not happiness."

Daisy's eyes stared straight ahead, and she spoke in a matter-of-fact tone. "We all deserve death."

She turned to Nathan. "What was your comment about it?"

"All the trees in the forest must fall, no matter how mighty."

"Yes, but Jesus has risen, and He grants us eternal life."

She gauged Laura's mood and changed her tack.

"I think you should pursue marriage and raise a family."

Nathan leaned forward.

"Yes, it's a fine idea, and it would take you out of our dusty college."

Laura gave them both a hurt look. "You no longer seek my help?"

Nathan reached across Daisy's lap and rubbed Laura's knee.

"It's nothing like that, honey, but we wish to see you move forward."

Laura still looked uneasy. She withdrew into herself.

Daisy put her hands tenderly on the younger woman.

"Catherine has done so, and Sheila. You must do likewise."

Laura's palm covered her mouth. She moaned, and her body shook with the overwhelming power of her regret. Other passengers took brief notice, and their eyes fell contemptuously on her trembling form. They quickly turned away, unconcerned with the travails of strangers on a trolley. Only Nathan and Daisy held any hope for Laura's restoration, meager and bleak as the lowly waif was at present and had been since her near brush with death at the Expo the previous November, when repentance saved her from certain doom, and Joanna met her eternal fate in the Lake of Fire.

Cold weather had passed, and it was now time for a rejuvenation of life and spirit and the outlook on one's future, most especially when two worthy men regarded her as a potential for marriage, made obvious by their bearing.

Laura interrupted Daisy's musings. "You misunderstand me."

"Your plight or your intentions?"

Laura considered the question. "Both, I think."

Daisy smiled and placed a strand of hair behind Laura's ear. "Help me better know what goes on inside that head of yours. Right now, I am concerned you wish to take my place as the most forlorn soul in Missouri."

"Men interest themselves with a woman's beauty, but I have lost all concern for my appearance and at night when the demons return, and I remember what I have done, my body falls to the floor in a whimpering heap, and my disgrace and my complicity and my sadness become more than my heart can withstand." She wiped tears from her eyes and her cheeks and smiled at Daisy. "I know Jesus has saved me by His shed blood, and for such an awful sacrifice, I give Him thanks, but it does little good when I feel the blood of thousands on my skin, and when the probing fingers of the demons massage my muscles, promising the world if I might only relent and accept their gift of matchless sensuality, and offer me the world on a platter."

"We asked you to attend church with us, but you declined," Daisy said. "It seems most obvious to me you require baptism, which you have also spurned, no matter how many times we have begged and pleaded with you."

"You are frustrated with me." Laura's statement seemed a question.

"Yes, I will admit it. God wants to restore you to full health, but you refuse to trust in His righteousness and to find peace in His will."

"I bathed in human blood. Was that according to His will?"

"Of course not, but He allowed it because you did not turn to Him, and He knew there was a better path for you over the course of time, once you were outside of the order's influence and could learn of His agape love."

"I won't step foot into a church because I know many of the pastors are part of the Consortium and have participated in the order's rituals, including my own, which took place each week in secret as a test of loyalty among the elite. How can I trust them or God when such happens?"

"It's a brutal world because it is fallen. We are unwise to be shocked by its nature and we are unclean if we live according to its measure of success."

Laura nodded her agreement. "This is why I will work outside of the influence of any church or organization. The demons call me names, and they never let me forget my past, but they also foretell my destiny, and it has become most clear to me, there is but a thin window to achieve my goals for Christ if I wish to atone for my misbehavior." She squeezed Daisy's arm. "I see horrible portraits in my nightly visions. There will be wars in the next century and a great turning away from the will of the Father. Before this begins in earnest, I must lead a tiny but influential contingent of souls away from Babylon. They must be recruited into Christ's kingdom at all costs."

Daisy was confounded by Laura's words and a bit vexed by her.

"You are twenty-six years old. Marriage should come first."

Laura turned to the passing street. Her voice fell low.

"I have visions of a ghastly fate, which is what I deserve."

"And you think you must give up all hopes for happiness?"

Laura smiled ruefully at Daisy.

"Yes, in this life, which I renounced by doing Lucifer's work."

Daisy pressed into her seat. "Then we must disagree."

At the church entrance, Nathan embraced Daisy on the front steps.

"My loving wife, you must stop talking to Laura and kiss me."

He motioned for Laura to go inside.

"Yes, sir." She tugged on the handle.

"I think it's stuck." Laura let go. "I am still so lethargic."

"Use what vigor you have to get it done."

He gestured to her. "I have faith in your regenerative abilities."

She pulled harder and the weighty door opened. The interior crowd stared at the couple who arrived late for the wedding and who now kissed so brazenly on the steps, their cares tossed to the violent flurry of time.

Laura shut the door. She smiled at Nathan and Daisy.

"See, my dear?" asked Nathan cheerfully. "Everything will be fine."

Daisy straightened his lapels. His fingers ran through her hair.

"By the way, the Lord gave me our baby's name."

Nathan cast a quizzical look. "Isn't it a bit early to select one?"

She shook her head and smiled. "Not for us, because he's a boy."

Daisy drew near to him as he pondered her statement.

"There's only one name which befits our child."

He sighed. "The suspense will end my days."

She chuckled. "His name will be David, the worthy King of Israel."

Nathan reflected for a moment. "God spoke to you?"

"Yes, through the Holy Spirt."

"Well, it's good enough for me. David will be our son's name."

Laura gasped. "Just like *that*?"

Nathan snapped his fingers. "With Christ, all things are possible."

Daisy laughed as she recalled her former lack of faith.

Nathan turned to the front door and then smirked at his wife.

"Must they host their wedding in June?"

Daisy smiled and hooked her arm under his.

"Your mother would have it no other way."

Laura found her courage and opened the burdensome door. It would make all the difference in the years ahead, as her life separated from her protectors, and the many twists and bends unfolded along the undiscovered earth. She must learn the value of her name and her actions, bound as they would be to the will of the Lord. Wild beasts who called themselves men would send her crawling in the blackness of eventide, where her struggles would accumulate. She must put her trust in the righteousness of God, who cast Himself as a martyr on the cross made of wood and allowed His body to be nailed against its gnarled density. Like Nathan and Daisy Marsh, Laura Collins was no longer a member of this world, but the next, and she would fight her way across the desert sun and the howling plough of torrential rain.

Afterword

Jesus suffered alongside you and he cried when you shed tears.

He loves you eternally and longs to know you in a personal relationship, one of grace and truth and a restored righteousness, so you might know a peace which defies understanding and so you might gain a blessed liberty.

Please allow the scriptural references found throughout *Wild Forest Rose* to point you to the Lord's Holy Bible, as faith comes by hearing and hearing by the Word of God. There's a supernatural power in the text, but we should excavate the truth from its pages and assemble the assorted puzzle pieces into a coherent chronology and theology.

It's a journey which must begin somewhere, so why not today?

He reaches out His hand and asks you to step onto the path.

Jesus is the light of the world.

He will guide you on your way.

Acknowledgments

A special thanks to all those who helped make this novel a reality.

Your helpful assistance in navigating the many revisions, the never ending edits, and the painstaking proofreading process was invaluable.

Any remaining mistakes are most certainly mine.

About the Author

Ken Fulmer has worked for a number of years in the computer field as a network engineer. Since college, he has dreamed of becoming a writer.

A father of one daughter and many pets, he lives with his wife in the rolling hills of North Carolina.

Wild Forest Rose is his first Christian romance novel.

Visit www.kenfulmer.com.

Author Q&A

How would you describe your writing style?

Great romances carry a sense of adventure and the two main characters seem like our best friends, people we can't wait to spend time with day after day.

My novels promise the discovery of Christian romance, which develops slowly over many chapters and the restoration of broken family bonds which have caused deep emotional wounds and now seem insurmountable.

Along the way, characters will overcome their pasts and learn the Lord's purpose for their lives as they help those more vulnerable than them.

How does place influence your writing?

My favorite stories offer unique settings, and fascinating characters populate their pages. Many of my novels will take place in Gilded Age locations within the United States, such as St. Louis in 1893, but others will drift across expanses of sea to Europe, South America, and other faraway lands.

Our family loves life in the rolling hills of the North Carolina Piedmont, but we also enjoy the flatlands of the Sandhills, the sand swept houses of the Outer Banks, and the panoramic views of the Blue Ridge mountains.

I will set many stories within the confines of this wonderful and varied state.

It's more than our home; it's our great love.

Is this Nathan Marsh's story?

Toward the beginning of the novel, the story tilts a bit in his direction, but as the plot progresses past the midpoint, Daisy Lawrence takes center stage.

As the exciting conclusion nears, their fates become fully intertwined.

Who is your favorite character in this novel and why?

The characters came alive during my writing process and today I am equally partial to both Nathan and Daisy. I also appreciate Catherine and Sheila a great deal, not to mention Samuel, Laura, and the hysteric patients.

Will these characters appear in another series?

Sheila and Laura do not get enough closure, which I hope to rectify.

Do your story ideas come from real life or from your imagination?

For me, life is mystical and baffling and genuine all at once, so an idea might originate from personal experience or from an article or a documentary. Sometimes the narrative unfolds quickly in my head, while at other times, it's a methodical process of developing a simple concept into a complex tale, filled with interesting characters and places and events.

Each story is a journey for the reader, but also for the author.

Do you write to a schedule or only when inspiration arrives?

Early morning is my best time, as then my creative urge peaks.

I admire those who write in an ad hoc fashion and do it well, but as an obsessive-compulsive person, planning is in my blood, which translates to the creation of several reference documents at the start of my process.

What is your most passionate life pursuit?

I find writing for the Lord to be my most meaningful calling.

During my elementary school years, I used action figures to create story after story, and as I look back now, the process seems to align with what Freud termed our *Prehistoric Wish* (i.e., what we most loved to do as a child).

I diverted from the land of imagination while working in the business world, and the opportunities afforded by my career have been a blessing.

With that said, it's been a sincere thrill to explore a creative vision once more and I hope to fulfill the Lord's calling for my life by introducing others to the Most High through the psalms, which are a special gateway to the Bible.

I also enjoy quality time with my family and our pets.

What is your next project as a writer?

In my contemporary novel, *Love So Lovely Born*, characters grapple with heavenly grace and revealed truth as they search for love and restoration.

Reading Group Questions

1. Why did Nathan hide for ten years prior to meeting Daisy?
2. Why did Leland wish to know about Catherine Belmont?
3. Who was the woman who smiled at Nathan on the train?
4. Would Special Agent Lacy have followed through on his threat?
5. Why did Daisy study the photograph at Union Depot?
6. Was her account of the Tower Grove Park event accurate?
7. What did Nathan ponder as he left Daisy with her father?
8. Why was Thomas Hannah so important to Nathan?
9. Did Nathan have an obligation to restore Catherine to health?
10. How did Aunt Joy and Nathan help one another?
11. Was Nathan right to hit the other boy?
12. Why did Catherine tell Nathan never to leave her alone?
13. What impact did the Civil War have on moral society?
14. What made Daisy upset as she visited with Heinrich?
15. What kind of monster was Rosemarie?
16. Who or what gave her special powers?
17. Why did Daisy fall for a vicious man like Frank?
18. Was Nathan good to those patients on his roster?
19. Was Roy a decent man at heart?

20. Was Colleen a moral woman in the end?
21. Did Nathan succeed or fail with Ronnie Wilson?
22. What was the entity Daisy detected within Catherine?
23. Why did Daisy suspect Nathan was the wrong man for her?
24. What caused the hysteric patients to suffer somatic symptoms?
25. What happened to the horse Nathan and Daisy rescued?
26. Why wouldn't Frank marry Daisy in Vienna?
27. Why did Daisy clean Nathan's house?
28. Why did Daisy wish to save Sheila from the brothel?
29. Who tormented Daisy at Belmont's estate?
30. Why did Thomas Hannah murder June Marsh?
31. Was Samuel ultimately to blame for her death?
32. Was Nathan close to his mother?
33. Why did Catherine leave the hospital?
34. Why did Daisy wish to rescue her?
35. How did Nathan so easily dispatch Frank on his second visit?
36. Why did Rose make her fateful decision?
37. At what moment did Nathan and Daisy genuinely bond in love?
38. Why was Joanna so angry and rebellious as an adolescent?
39. What dark secrets were revealed during the winery visit?
40. Why did Belmont wish to use the hysterics as pawns?
41. Why did Patrice take drastic action?
42. Why was Laura so committed to her wicked cause?
43. Why did Joanna become a monster like Rosemarie?
44. What caused Nathan's sinister regression?
45. What led Nathan and Daisy to break up?
46. What caused Nathan's Christian conversion?
47. How did Nathan finally reach the hysterics?
48. Did the hysteric patients become like family?
49. What ultimately became of Laura Collins?
50. What became of Sheila Byrne and Heinrich Besseler's union?

www.ingramcontent.com/pod-product-compliance
Lightning Source LLC
Chambersburg PA
CBHW040213170726
48295CB00014B/651